THE
EXPERT

THE
EXPERT

LEE GRUENFELD

A DUTTON BOOK

DUTTON
Published by the Penguin Group
Penguin Putnam Inc., 375 Hudson Street, New York, New York 10014, U.S.A.
Penguin Books Ltd, 27 Wrights Lane, London W8 5TZ, England
Penguin Books Australia Ltd, Ringwood, Victoria, Australia
Penguin Books Canada Ltd, 10 Alcorn Avenue, Toronto, Ontario, Canada M4V 3B2
Penguin Books (N.Z.) Ltd, 182–190 Wairau Road, Auckland 10, New Zealand

Penguin Books Ltd, Registered Offices:
Harmondsworth, Middlesex, England

First published by Dutton, an imprint of Dutton NAL, a member of Penguin Putnam Inc.

First Printing, April, 1998
10 9 8 7 6 5 4 3 2 1

REGISTERED TRADEMARK—MARCA REGISTRADA

Library of Congress Cataloging-in-Publication Data

Gruenfeld, Lee.
    The expert / Lee Gruenfeld.
      p.   cm.
    ISBN: 0-525-94406-0
    I. Title.
PS3557.R8E96   1998
813'.54.—dc21   97-38284
                                                                          CIP

Printed in the United States of America
Set in Sabon
Designed by Leonard Telesca

For Pop
- FUS (SIC)

This world is run by people who know how to do things. They know how things work. They are *equipped.* Up there, there's a layer of people who run everything. But we—we're just peasants. We don't understand what's going on, and we can't do anything.

—Doris Lessing
Dorothy, in *The Good Terrorist*

We have not overthrown the divine right of kings to fall down for the divine right of experts.

—Harold Macmillan
Speech, August 16, 1950,
Strasbourg, France

P r o l o g u e

Wednesday, January 21

His mind knew that the walls of the narrow tunnel weren't really closing in on him, weren't really threatening to squeeze him so tightly as to slowly and agonizingly suffocate the life right out of him. The same mind that had convinced him to come down here in the first place, and which had promised fervently to keep reminding him that it would only be his claustrophobic panic that was contracting the otherwise perfectly stable walls, that mind was losing the battle with his bowels, which were churning so forcefully he was certain the others must be hearing it.

Love of country or family wouldn't have had a chance of luring him into this Fallopian escapade, nor would honor or altruism, not even a direct order from old Zedong himself. It was money that had landed him in the enclosing darkness, and it was money on which he concentrated in order to drive out the overwhelming delusion that the encroaching walls were only seconds away from pinning him into choking immobility and entombing him beneath the surface forever. He focused so fiercely he barely heard the dull *clang* the pipe he was carrying made as it struck something unseen jutting from the wall to his left.

"Quiet!" Li Xiaoxiang hissed into the darkness.

As the echoes of metal banging on stone disappeared back down the tunnel, Xiaoxiang turned to cast a punishing glance at Zho Yung, the light from his miner's helmet illuminating the terrified man's wide-eyed face. Yung was by far the biggest and strongest of them, but it was quite clear who was in control of this operation. Xiaoxiang took a moment to look at the three others in turn, making known in advance his likely impatience with any further displays of incompetence or inattention. He made a downward pumping motion with his hand, urging them to silence, and they nodded rapidly, realizing with relief that their leader's anger was now spent. Ling Naijing stepped backward to assist Yung with the long metal pipe, ensuring that it wouldn't hit the stone wall again as they moved forward.

Xiaoxiang turned away from them and pressed ahead, twisting his head left and right to shine light on the walls. The only sounds were their feet shuffling atop loose stones. Each man was weighed down by the heavy knapsack he carried. Before long, Xiaoxiang stopped and held up his hand, bringing the others to a halt. He pointed upward wordlessly, and they followed his gaze to a plate of dull steel embedded in the stone ceiling. He motioned for them to set their packs down—*quietly!*—and as they began to do so, he removed several tools from his belt, including a tape measure.

When he was satisfied that his men were coordinated and busy, Xiaoxiang reached upward and laid the butt of the tape measure against a small slot in the metal plate. He measured off exactly twenty-four inches, which brought him to a flat spot in the surrounding stone to which he pressed a finger. With his free hand he removed an awl from his belt and wordlessly began to chip away at the spot he had marked. The rock was hard at first, but once the top layer was gone, it gave way to crumbling cement, which came away easily. By this time the men had finished unpacking and they watched him work.

Soon the cement layer ended, and Xiaoxiang replaced the awl with a small screwdriver, taking much smaller pieces this time and slowing his pace down. After a few more minutes, two thin wires were exposed, one red, the other green. He allowed himself a smile of reassurance toward his men, and they exhaled with satisfaction.

Xiaoxiang unclipped two wires from his belt, each about two feet long, alligator clips at both ends. He took one of the wires and clamped both clips to the green wire above his head, the ends two inches apart. Then he reached up with a diagonal cutter, positioned it around the green wire, and paused. Closing his eyes, he squeezed the handles of the cutter. The tool made a loud *click* as it bit through the wire.

They listened for the sound of an alarm from somewhere overhead, but heard nothing. Patiently, Xiaoxiang performed the same operation on the red wire. Then he waved Yung upward. The big man hefted a crowbar and placed its split tip in the slot of the metal panel. After a nod from Xiaoxiang, he pulled the bar in a direction away from that of the red and green wires.

The panel didn't budge.

Yung looked anxiously at Xiaoxiang, who said reassuringly in

Mandarin: "Old. Rusted. Probably not moved since the bank was built. Try again, Zho. Put your back into it!"

Yung closed his eyes and pulled on the crowbar once again, grunting with the effort. As he strained, Naijing reached up and pulled with him. There was a scraping sound and a trickle of dust from above their heads.

"Ah!" Xiaoxiang exclaimed, his prior admonition for silence now forgotten. "Again!"

The two men leaned into their task, and the panel groaned back another inch. Xiaoxiang looked over at the dangling wires. The two feet of jumper wires he had attached ensured that the electrical circuit was still complete. Without them, the red and green wires would have snapped apart as the panel opened, breaking the circuit and triggering an alarm.

Yung and Naijing continued to struggle with the panel, and after twenty minutes, it was open wide enough for a man to slip through. The jumper cables had almost pulled taut, and Xiaoxiang signaled for them to halt.

Yung made a stirrup of his hands, and one by one the others clambered upward through the panel. As Yung began handing up their equipment, Xiaoxiang looked around.

They were in the currency exchange room of the People's Bank of Beijing. Along one wall, Xiaoxiang saw row after row of small metal drawers, some three hundred in all. It would have been nice to break into the bank's central vault, but he knew that the walls and floors there were three feet thick and riddled with more modern sensors and alarms than this old room. That vault held all the on-the-record instruments, including negotiable securities such as bearer bonds, difficult to unload in China anyway.

But this room was different. It held hard cash, mostly the kind that was illegal in China and for which accurate recordkeeping was a liability rather than an asset. The money was the private, personal stash of the bank's richest traders, kept close at hand, in drawers marked with each customer's name. The amounts were modest, usually less than twenty thousand U.S. dollars per customer, just enough to quickly complete small, private transactions without the need for annoying paperwork. The money was simply handed over to couriers. Each transaction was small enough not to attract the interest of various bureaucrats charged with keeping an eye on the private funds of the country's nouveau capitalists. But multiplied by the three hundred or so drawers lining the walls? It was a staggering sum to the four ragged peasants staring at the riches that awaited them. And the room lacked the sophisticated security of the central vault: it was a risk the bank took to avoid attracting nosy bureaucrats.

Xiaoxiang waved Yung and Liu Ming over toward the wall. Ming hefted a thick canvas bag as Yung opened the first drawer and pulled out a thick wad of paper. He held it up for their leader to see.

Xiaoxiang aimed his helmet light at the stack of bills in Yung's hand and grinned. "Marks!" he said. "German. Very good!"

Yung threw them into the bag and opened the next drawer. British pounds this time, and in two more drawers as well. Then there were French francs, Italian lira, pesetas, kronen, rand, yen . . .

Naijing started at the other end, filling a bag himself as Xiaoxiang looked on in satisfaction.

Yung paused as he peered into the first drawer in a new row. His hand moved forward tentatively, and slowly closed around a large wad of paper. As he eased it up out of the drawer, the distinctive green color made itself evident even in the dim light of their lamps.

"Are these dollars?" Yung breathed. "American dollars?"

Xiaoxiang nodded. Hundred-dollar bills, at least a hundred of them. When sold on the black market, that handful of currency alone would make this operation worthwhile.

Yung grinned and carefully placed them in the bag, then went happily back to his task.

When he was satisfied that things were well in hand, Xiaoxiang pretended to wander aimlessly toward the door at the far end of the room. With one glance back at his preoccupied colleagues, he opened the door and slipped through.

He walked quickly down a narrow corridor, counting the doors on his right. When he got to the fourth one, he stopped and reached for his belt hammer, holding it above the doorknob set into a combination lock. Fearful that the noise of the blow might alert someone on one of the floors above, he winced in preparation for smashing the knob, then decided to take a look at the lock.

It was a rudimentary push-button type consisting of five black buttons. Punching three of them in the right order would open the lock. Using his flashlight to peer closely at the buttons, he noticed that three of them were shinier than the others, the paint worn off from years of use. Three buttons. Only six possible combinations.

On his fourth try, he was rewarded with a green light above the panel and a soft click. He turned the knob and entered the room.

In the center of the room stood an Amdahl 470 mainframe computer illuminated only by its own glowing panel lights. Receding from the machine and into the surrounding darkness were rows of tape drives, disk units, console monitors and printers. It was an old machine, the hum from its water cooling units throbbing through Xiaoxiang's feet.

Wasting no time, he turned to shine his helmet light along the walls until he spotted a bundle of thick wires emerging from the back of an otherwise featureless metal enclosure about six feet tall, and disappearing through a hole in the wall. He stepped closer and peered at the cables to verify that they were phone wires. He took off his helmet, ran a hand through his hair, and sat down at the lone console attached to the box.

He pressed a button on the keyboard, and the sleeping plasma display sprang to life, its distinctive orange glow shining painfully into his eyes until he got used to it. He pressed another button and the display changed: a series of characters indicated that a remote transaction was taking place. He forced himself to remain calm until it finished. Interrupting it in the middle might cause someone at the other end to phone in and demand that an operator attend to the problem.

It was a full three minutes before the display cleared and only "Waiting . . ." appeared in the upper left corner. Xiaoxiang quickly hit the Escape key, got the command prompt, and typed in "Disable," followed by a press of the Return key.

He prayed silently as the screen offered no response, then exhaled as the cursor dropped down three lines and prompted, "Outgoing message?" This was the message that would be returned to any remote user trying to phone in while the lines were disabled.

"Reloading software," Xiaoxiang entered. "Estimated reactivation 1115 GMT." That would give them forty-five minutes. He didn't dare risk a longer period because no bank of this stature would permit its primary funds transfer trunks to be down that long while half the rest of the world was awake and doing business.

He heard several clicks from the machines around him, and then the words "Trunks disabled" appeared on the screen.

Without any hesitation, he put his helmet back on, stood up, and went around to the back of the tall metal enclosure, turned the two protruding thumbscrews counterclockwise, and lifted the back panel off.

His helmet light revealed a hopeless confusion of multicolored wires, circuit boards, and bus lines. He ran his eyes across the swirling profusion of parts until he spotted a red metal box no larger than a pack of cigarettes. At either end of the box were silvery heat sinks, flat fins of metal designed to carry away heat and prevent damage to the delicate apparatus within. Six wires ran through the topmost sink into the box, and four protruded from the other end. The extra two at the top were the power supply.

Xiaoxiang used a screwdriver to carefully unbolt the box. When it hung free, he clipped all the wires, power first, let the box drop into his hand, and then put it in his pocket. That's when he heard the sound.

He quickly switched off his helmet lamp and squeezed himself back behind the enclosure. He didn't have a view of the door but saw a glint of light bouncing off the front panel of the main computer. As the reflection of the light moved away from him, he realized that whoever was out there was coming his way.

A familiar feeling began to work its way up his spine, at once paralyzing and calming. The adrenaline rush made the back of his head hot, and his hand automatically went inside his jacket and found his push knife, a terribly lethal and effective weapon shaped like a T. One crossbar fit in his palm. A razor-sharp blade shaped like an elongated arrowhead protruded from between his third and fourth fingers. The shape would allow him to plunge the knife with a pushing motion backed by all the force he could muster, with no danger of slipping.

The door creaked as it opened slowly. Xiaoxiang managed to turn slightly in the small space so he could put one foot in front of the other, getting most of his weight on his back leg. It was easy to tell by the intruder's light how close he was. At the right moment Xiaoxiang would leap forward from behind the man and drive the knife deep into one of his kidneys. It was a cruel method of execution, but the awful pain would make it impossible for the man to cry out and alert other guards. Assuming he was alone, Xiaoxiang could get back to the currency trading room and get the others through the floor and down the tunnel before anyone else would realize what was going on. Of course, that would mean that the operation was a failure, but his men would have no way of knowing that. As long as they got some of the money they'd come for, they'd be happy.

He could hear the man's breathing now, and he held his own breath, his mind shrieking with impatience as his years of training kicked in and forced his body to relax. His grip on the knife tightened and he leaned still farther back, poised to leap.

"Xiaoxiang?" the shape whispered.

It took him a moment to re-orient himself. He quickly repocketed the knife and stepped from behind the enclosure, causing Liu Ming to stumble backward in surprise.

"What the hell . . . !"

Xiaoxiang put a finger to his lips, then said excitedly, "Bring the others!"

"But why?" Ming asked, his brows knitted in confusion.

Xiaoxiang smiled and gave him a small shove backward. "Bring them! Trust me!"

Ming blinked and then hurried out of the room, returning moments later with the others. Yung was still clutching his bag, now half full, afraid to release it from his grasp. Naijing looked around at the machinery and the blinking lights.

"Computers!" Xiaoxiang said.

Naijing nodded in understanding. "Are they working?"

"Yes. Completely operational, as far as I can tell."

Naijing grinned. "The parts are worth millions!" he said, and now Yung and Ming understood as well.

"We don't have much time," Xiaoxiang said, then waved them to the back of the metal enclosure housing the transmission equipment. "Watch."

He reached toward a rack-mounted circuit board and flipped back the two light blue plastic pins holding it in place. Drawing out the board, he stopped as one bundle of the attached yellow wires grew taut, then squeezed the black plastic connector and pulled until the bundle sprang free. Two more bundles and the board came away from the rack completely.

Xiaoxiang held it up for the others to see. "They have to come off clean, nothing broken, or they're worthless. Got it?" He waited for answering nods, then pointed to the transmission enclosure. "This one first. It has the most expensive boards. Then, as much as we can grab in"—he glanced at his watch—"thirty minutes, no more."

Working feverishly, they managed to clean out a good number

of the devices holding circuit boards. Xiaoxiang then directed the men to go back to the currency room and start hauling out the bags and equipment through the floor panel. When they were out of sight, he reached into the transmission enclosure, grabbed handfuls of wire and began yanking them out. Then he put his weight behind his hands and started bending the rack guides, doing as much damage as he could. He put his foot on one end of the back panel lying on the floor, then pulled the other end up, twisting the panel in half.

He went around to the other enclosures the men had ransacked, and tried to do as much damage to them as he could as well. In the time remaining, he used his large screwdriver to smash in plasma displays, then opened disk drives, removed the data packs and threw them forcefully to the floor, making sure the delicate surfaces cracked apart. On his way back across the computer room, he tore a few reels of tape from their spindles and spun them across the room. The rest he destroyed by running a powerful alnico magnet he had brought with him across the hundreds of reels hanging from their mounts. Finally, at the door, seconds remaining and with no more fear of noise, he smashed the knob and lock with his belt hammer until they fell away in pieces.

In less than thirty-five minutes, he and his gang had trashed a six-million-dollar computer installation beyond any hope of repair.

On his way back to the currency trading room, Xiaoxiang patted the metal box in his pocket to reassure himself it was still there. Naijing, his head sticking up from the panel in the floor, was beckoning him wildly. With one last look around, Xiaoxiang dropped through the floor. He reached up to replace the panel while his companions scurried back through the tunnel.

When he caught up with the others, Ming said, "I figure two, three weeks to unload it all. Then we meet at Naijing's place to divide it up. Okay by you?"

"Sure," Xiaoxiang said with as much enthusiasm as he could fake, clapping Ming on the shoulder.

He would never see any of them again.

PART I

OPENING

C h a p t e r 1

Monday, May 18

Rebecca Verona stared out the window and tried to ignore the spasm somewhere near her pelvis so the others in the room wouldn't notice. She kept her arms folded across her chest in an attitude of deep contemplation, pretending to be lost in some important thought, when all she could think about once the cramp subsided was the ache in her breasts, the heaviness across her back and how awful her face must look from the bloating that seemed to fill her body from the toes up.

She clamped her jaws together and tapped a finger against her upper arm, another indication to the onlookers that she was reaching momentous decisions instead of fighting down the urge to spin around and tell them all to fuck off so she could go home and lie down. The acid gurgling around in the nether reaches of her esophagus made her regret the last two cups of coffee, even though the diuretic effect of caffeine might eventually help to relieve the pressure of all the water trapped beneath her skin. On the other hand, she could feel that same caffeine pushing her irritability index somewhere into the ionosphere. *Zero to bitch in sixty seconds,* as Arno Steinholz once half joked. Whole goddamned office probably had her menstrual cycle mapped out in their freaking Daytimers, calibrating their calculations based on the days she wore entirely too much makeup. God help any unsuspecting opposing counsel who tried to approach her about a settlement on a maxi-pad day; poor bastard would wind up wishing he'd gone into forestry instead of law.

"Guy's here, Becky." Justin's voice, using the diminutive of her name, a privilege reserved for a rare few.

Justin. What the hell was it with parents and these names, anyway? What was the matter with John, Mary, Susan? Or Rebecca, for that matter?

She caught herself just before she hauled off and slugged Justin Ehrenright for what his parents did twenty-eight years ago. Closing her eyes and taking a steadying breath, Rebecca nodded and dropped her arms, picked up her chin and turned around, ready to enter the fray.

As bad as she felt and knew she looked, she still got subtly appreciative glances from Steinholz and Ehrenright from the other side of the conference table. What they mistook for some barely perceptible increases in her curvature were just breasts so swollen they felt black and blue, but that was her own business, as were her aching feet and back. Her dark brown eyes, which she was certain were now sunken back into wadded-up hot dog rolls of watery skin, looked to them only more exotic than usual, slightly narrower and more mysterious. When she pulled herself up to her full five-foot-nine height, angular face framed by cherrywood brown hair drawn into a ponytail that lay across one shoulder, her physical presence commanded the room, as it had since she was a teenager.

It commanded a courtroom as well, and Rebecca learned early on that there was little downside to lightly exploiting her looks to a good end. If it gave her an edge in a job interview or a cross-examination or a presentation to a prospective client, where was the harm? She'd gotten to enjoy her effect on men—and women—although she still couldn't convince herself that she didn't look like Jabba the Hut for a few days every month.

"Best get started then," she said with a nod to Ehrenright, his cue to go get "the guy." Ehrenright turned quickly and went out toward the reception area, while Steinholz began pulling papers out of his leather attaché and arranging them on the table in front of him. Janine Osterreich, one of the firm's internal shorthand reporters, flipped open her dictation pad.

"Dirksen," Rebecca said idly, referring to their imminent visitor. "How dependent are we on him?"

Steinholz pursed his lips and tilted his head without looking up. "Pretty damn." With his light brown hair worn long, wire-rimmed glasses over large, soulful eyes, generous lips and an overall softness of manner, he fit perfectly the image of the deeply introspective right-brainer, given to instant intimacy with strangers and long conversations laced with keenly perceptive insights into the human condition. In truth, he was a tech-snoid of the first water, a physicist at heart and a master logician who came late to the law because it hadn't occurred to him earlier how the vagaries of legal cockfighting presented puzzles more satisfying in their solution than those of atoms and energy.

"He okay?"

"Seems to be. Hasn't done much of this. Being an expert witness, I mean."

They both knew that could be good and bad. Good, because he wouldn't look to the jury like a hired gun, someone with a Ph.D. who ran around renting himself out to the highest bidder. Bad, because he was an amateur at this. At least the hired guns knew the ropes, knew how to work a jury and not get caught in traps during cross-exam. For professional experts, their performance at each trial was like a tennis player's at each tournament: you needed to score enough wins, put on an impressive enough show, to stay on the circuit and keep getting invited back. Didn't matter if you were honest, if you were smart as hell or preserved your professional dignity. What mattered was if your side won the case.

Rebecca sat down heavily, or so it seemed to her, waited until Steinholz was looking away and gently massaged the bottom of her left breast, lifting it to relieve some of the pressure on the poorly designed ligament trying gamely to hold it up; she feared Cooper's droop worse than cancer. When Steinholz turned back again, she put her forearms on the table and rested her chest against them. It helped a little, and it brought her eyes to the case file arrayed before her. *Universal Data Systems* v. *Tamarack Ltd.* Another case of a computer vendor at war with a dissatisfied customer, each alleging satanic behavior on the part of the other, all because they had been too anxious to close a deal to bother worrying about the fine details. Now, backed up by phalanxes of well-paid lawyers, they were ripping each other's throats out, long past caring that the cost of pursuing the case would likely exceed the amount of any recovery. It wasn't business anymore; both sides were after justice. Rebecca hated when that happened, but she made a good living at it, because once the antagonists crossed that threshold, any notion of civility, compromise, sound business judgment or common decency evaporated in the icy vapor of their blind intrasigency. And whenever businessmen begin fighting with their balls instead of their brains, lawyers start phoning their decorators, auto dealers, and stockbrokers.

UDS had pitched Tamarack hard on their completely integrated order entry and accounting system. They were state-of-the-art—who wasn't?—they had a list of references a mile long, and they were going to make Tamarack their showcase installation; say, when we're all done, would it be all right if we brought prospective customers over so we can show off what a good job we did for you? They warbled rapturous arias about *solutions* rather than computer programs, and promised a system so advanced that Tamarack's productivity would triple inside of a year while their competitors opened veins in frustration at being left in the dust.

Tamarack, a sporting goods manufacturer, lapped it all up, dreaming of the tours they would give their customers, the ads they would run with photographs of employees happily ensconced before computer terminals, shipping out product so fast they'd probably have to buy their own fleet of trucks.

But along the way they got a little sloppy explaining to the UDS analysts how their business ran, even forgetting to mention a satellite operation in Wisconsin that needed to be hooked into the main system.

And nobody remembered to factor in how much support would be required and which side would pay for it, and what would happen when changes were required or transient power failures blew the databases out or how partial shipments would be handled and a thousand other seemingly small details that nevertheless had a profound effect on the architecture of the new system. Nobody even thought about how to prepare current employees for the changes that would occur in their jobs.

The problem-riddled computer system almost wrecked Tamarack while UDS nearly went under trying to fix all the problems. Someone at Tamarack with half a brain left finally pulled the plug on the whole mess and got the company back on its original Stone Age but functional systems before it was too late.

Rebecca sighed as she thumbed through only one of several huge stacks of paper on the conference table. She knew that, within a small margin of error, both sides were equally at fault. UDS had oversold its capabilities, and Tamarack had failed to exercise due diligence in determining the suitability of the system for its needs. Both sides were grossly negligent in failing to clearly specify everybody's rights and obligations in the written agreement. It was bad contracts, not bad faith, that was the real cause of the custom computer industry's deservedly rotten reputation.

Rebecca's firm was representing Tamarack, not because they believed in that company's version of events but because Ray Tamarack had called them first. Welch, Tobias & Wysocki would have been glad to take either side of the case; it made little difference, because the outcome would have nothing whatsoever to do with who was right. Everybody other than the warring executives already knew that it wasn't really anybody's fault or, more correctly, it was everybody's fault, which was essentially the same thing.

Rebecca stifled a groan as a new pain arose behind her eyes. Her tongue felt gummy and thick and she had a sudden craving for a glass of ice water, but at that moment the door opened and Ehrenright walked back into the conference room. Behind him, his steps tentative, walked Jules Dirksen. The expert.

Rebecca didn't like the tentative steps. This was the point in the case in which their expert was supposed to bounce jauntily into the meeting and tell the assembled attorneys that his analysis was complete and he was ready to single-handedly win their case for them. At two hundred bucks an hour of unsupervised invoice inflation, it wasn't too much to ask, but no such barely restrained enthusiasm issued forth from Mr. Jules Dirksen, CDP, CCP and CMC, not to mention CSP.

"Jules," Rebecca said, extending her hand. "Nice to see you."

Dirksen took her hand, perhaps a little too earnestly, as though eager to establish some human contact so she wouldn't hate him after he hit her with the bad news. "You as well, Rebecca. You look great."

She smiled at him, thinking, *That what you say to your male clients? You look great? Nice suit?* "Thanks, Jules. Nice of you to notice."

He beamed back, delighted that his Dale Carnegie–furnished charm was working its magic on her, softening her up.

"This is Janine," Rebecca said, indicating the woman sitting with her pad at the ready. "She's going to be taking some notes for us."

Dirksen nodded at Janine perfunctorily, then said to Rebecca, "You know, I never put the names together—Verona—but wasn't Wendy Verona your sister?"

Unbeknownst to Dirksen, the air in the room abruptly dropped several degrees. Steinholz stirred uncomfortably while Ehrenright winced openly. Of the two associate attorneys, Ehrenright was the one who actually looked like a prototypical nerd. He kept his curly hair short, so much so that the thick legs of his nondescript black glasses stuck out behind his ears. He wasn't careless about his appearance, but wasn't fastidious in his choice of clothing either, his tastes in suits and shirts running more to the expedient than the fashionable. Virtually any shirt in his wardrobe could go with just about any suit, and the same was true of all his ties. Yet his image also belied his persona: it was Ehrenright who, between the two, depended more on his insight into the human psyche than he did upon the kind of encyclopedic knowledge Arno Steinholz was able to call upon.

"Yes, and she still is," Rebecca answered evenly. *Was.* That was how everybody phrased it, like Wendy didn't exist anymore since her bright star winked out of the heavens.

"What a tragedy. A real tragedy. Where is she now?"

"New York."

"Some coffee, Jules?" Steinholz offered, smoothly detouring the conversation, and when he saw no immediate reaction, "Water, tea . . . ?"

"Ah, tea. Perfect."

Effete prick, Rebecca thought, pushing her sister out of her mind. Dirksen didn't have a Ph.D. so he went out of his way to affect an academic air, maybe impress jurors with it, not experienced enough to know that jurors suspected academics almost as much as they suspected lawyers.

Rebecca mentally pulled herself up short; what the hell was she doing? The guy hadn't been in the room for two minutes and she was ready to yank his heart out through his throat. *Settle down!*

She pointed to a seat and Dirksen sat down immediately, nervously fiddling with his overstuffed schoolbag attaché. Rebecca let him go on for a bit, highlighting the contrast between the computer specialist's obvious anxiety and her own, equally obvious, cool. "Been working hard?" she asked casually.

"Oh, yes," he said, nodding vigorously, making sure she was appreciative of his Herculean labors on the client's behalf. "Takes an awfully long time to go through all this stuff, eh?" He patted the nearest stack of paper affectionately, as though he and the thousand sheets had become close friends during their many long hours together.

Rebecca flashed him back a knowing smile. "Don't I know it though. But we sure do appreciate your efforts, Jules. I want you to know that." She dripped sincerity, and it caught Dirksen off guard. *Sincerity is everything,* Allen Wysocki liked to say. *Once you can fake that, the rest is easy.*

"Ah. Yes, well, only too glad to be of help, hm?"

Just the reaction she was fishing for. Now he was helping them, and admitting it. A few seconds ago he had been an expert, a hired genius sitting lonely and friendless in the cold tower of his purported objectivity, fully prepared to cast down judgments that might commit them to eternal damnation if need be, even though they were the ones who were paying him, heroic in his determination not to be swayed by the ugly exigencies of commerce and advocacy.

Now he was glad to be of help. *Jules, my man, do you really think we fork over that kind of dough for you to do a book report?* Rebecca spotted Ehrenright through the open door and timed her question carefully. "So. What've you got for us?"

Just as Dirksen was about to answer, Ehrenright came in carrying a cup of hot tea in an elegant china cup, a wedge of lemon perched on the saucer, a linen napkin underneath. Dirksen accepted it gratefully, and was now in their debt as he framed his answer. He fumbled with the lemon and tried to speak at the same time. "Actually, Rebecca, I'm afraid you may not like all that I have to say on the matter." He glanced at her out of the corner of his eye, expecting anger and surprise, quite prepared to deal with both, having rehearsed for this conversation for most of the past two days while pressing the firm's accounting department to get his invoice current before this meeting. Rebecca could see that he was determined not to be pushed around.

"I doubt that, Jules. I just want to get the opinion of someone I trust, to get a handle on what really happened." She saw him stop squeezing the lemon. "Whatever you have to tell me, it can only help."

The lemon slipped from between his fingers and landed on the bare tabletop. Dirksen grabbed the napkin from underneath the saucer, spilling some tea in the process, and dabbed as casually as he could at the moisture threatening to stain the rosewood surface. "Oh, okay. Good. Well"—he cleared his throat—"it's not entirely clear to me that Universal failed to adequately design all the features Tamarack required. Not clear at all."

Rebecca nodded, creasing her eyebrows in thought, taking notes on her legal pad. "Okay. Well, that's too bad. What else?"

Dirksen paused in his dabbing, not believing that she was so easily dismissing a key portion of her case strategy. He blinked several times, not quite knowing what to do next, since he had planned a good hour of explanation about how he had come to this devastating conclusion. He forgot the tea and the lemon and scrambled for his notes.

Rebecca couldn't hide a grimace: hadn't Steinholz told him not to write anything down? Once Dirksen was declared an expert, the other side had the right to subpoena anything he committed to paper, not just his working notes but even his appointment book or his grocery lists.

That's why Janine Osterreich was with them, taking notes. It was a sneaky trick Rebecca had invented to circumvent the rules of discovery. Janine was taking notes for the attorneys, and whatever she wrote down was privileged and unavailable to the opposition. This way they could have a written record of the expert's often convoluted thought processes for him to refer back to without requiring them to reveal anything to the other side.

Rebecca shot Steinholz a withering look, but he only shrugged and nodded helplessly. *I did* tell *him; what was I supposed to do, hook a camera to his tie?*

"Here we are. Oh, yes. Testing. Tricky subject." *And more billable hours to unravel the Gordian knot, no doubt.* "You see, you're saying that Tamarack's testing of the software failed. But—and here's the tricky part—if we're saying in the first place that the system wasn't designed properly, then how could it be expected to pass any tests?"

Rebecca only stared at him, so Ehrenright said, "I don't get it," despite having gotten it perfectly, as had Rebecca.

Dirksen bit readily, his hands flapping excitedly. "Follow me on this. We're saying that the system wasn't designed correctly, right?" He waited for answering nods. "Well, if that's the case, then how could it be expected to pass any tests? Don't you get it? It's like a double whammy. If you didn't design it right in the first place, well of course it isn't going to pass any tests! It was the wrong stuff from the beginning, so if you hit UDS for screwing that up, it's hardly fair to then go after them for failing acceptance tests!" He spread his hands and sat back in triumph.

Rebecca wanted to bash his smug face in, wanted to say, *Listen, you flaming asshole: you don't decide what's fair. You just answer the questions we ask you and don't go off writing the other side's closing statement to the jury!* Instead, she nodded, admiration written all over her face. "Now I get it. Very clever, Jules. Good piece of reasoning." She looked to Ehrenright and Steinholz for confirmation and got the expected looks of agreement.

Buoyed by the approbation of the attorneys, Dirksen continued on, happily decimating every piece of their intended strategy, fully expecting that at any moment they would throw up their hands, laughing, ready to go and tell their client to drop the case because he, Jules Dirksen, had proven beyond all question that it was hopeless.

He finished, then sat back, beaming. "Questions?"

Rebecca threw up her hands and let them drop back onto the table. "Goddamn, Jules, you are a piece of work. All of that in just a few weeks." Assenting murmurs from her colleagues. "Hey, I gotta say it: I am truly impressed. Worth twice your billing rate." She leaned forward and poked him in the arm, whispering conspiratorially, "But don't tell the client I said that, okay?"

Dirksen laughed, his eyes crinkling in self-satisfied mirth. He picked imaginary lint off his pant leg. "Well, you been in the business as long as I have . . ." He looked around, the sentence requiring no completion.

"You the man, Jules," Steinholz said.

"So. Where do we go from here?" Dirksen asked nobody in particular.

"Right." Rebecca unbuttoned one sleeve of her blouse, then the other, looking down at her notes as she rolled each cuff back one turn. She sensed Ehrenright and Steinholz staring at her expectantly, felt like she was poised on the starting blocks of an Olympic swimming pool, thought she could literally feel endorphins squirting out of her brain and soaking her cells like a powerful narcotic. She felt the cramps subsiding, her headache receding and the ache in her back starting to relax.

"Mind if we go through all of this a step at a time, Jules?" She flashed him a brilliant smile.

"Absolutely not!" he shot back in delight, standing to take off his jacket and loosen his tie.

"Okay then," Rebecca said in a let's-get-to-work tone. "Now, you say that you don't necessarily believe that Universal failed to adequately design all the features Tamarack required, right?"

"That's correct. Design of a system is a two-way street, you see, a, um, a collaboration. Yes, that's it. A collaboration. Equal responsibility on both sides."

"Explain that, Jules," Ehrenright prompted him. The Verona technique: *Keep 'em yapping away until they give you the opening.*

Dirksen turned eagerly to Ehrenright, happy at the opportunity to expound on his craft. "There are two sides to every system. The first is, what is the thing supposed to do, and second, how do you program the computer to do it. Now, the what is it supposed to do, that's the customer's responsibility. See, they know how their business runs: what paper moves around, what reports do I need, how do I build an order. They have to tell the computer guys that so they have enough information to go off and program the system."

"And you're telling us that Tamarack didn't do a good job of teaching UDS about their needs?" Rebecca asked.

Dirksen held up his hands defensively. "Not necessarily. I'm only saying that, given the documents I've looked at, it's not entirely clear. And if Tamarack didn't do a good job, then how could UDS be expected to program a good system?"

Rebecca threw down her pencil and leaned her head way back. *I declare these Games open.*

"Jules, lemme ask you something, make sure I understand," she said as casually as she could, staring at the ceiling. "These UDS guys, they're supposed to be the experts, am I right? The ones with three hundred combined years of building systems?" She was quoting directly from their marketing literature.

"That's how they represented themselves, true."

"Okay." She looked back down, elbows on the table, chin resting on top of her hands, as though working through some logic in her mind and thinking out loud. "Okay. Now refresh me here, because I don't really remember. How much experience did Tamarack have in putting together computer systems?"

Dirksen smiled amiably, indicating that he saw the trap and wasn't falling for it. "You know that already, Rebecca. They're not in the computer business, how could they be expected to—"

"No, no, no." She waved her hand in front of her face. "What I mean, did they have any experience working with a vendor to design a computer system before?"

Dirksen thumbed some papers in front of him without looking at them. "None that I know of. They were using some off-the-shelf stuff from years back."

"Yeah, I thought it was something like that. So these guys had never worked with anybody before to design a system."

Dirksen had to admit that was true.

"And another thing—and I'm trying to remember back to UDS's proposal to Tamarack—UDS said they were world-class experts in order entry and accounting systems for medium-size businesses, didn't they?"

She didn't wait for an answer. "So let's work through this," she continued. "I don't want to put words in your mouth, believe me, but is there a case to be made that the responsibility for getting Tamarack to fully describe its custom requirements really rested on UDS's shoulders?"

She saw Dirksen mulling it over, and pushed forward. "It's like, suppose I go to an auto repair shop, I got something screwed up in my car, right? I say to the guy, 'It's making this weirdo grinding noise, and every time I switch this thingamabob over here, black stuff comes out of the exhaust and I hear a loud pop.' Now, I don't tell him that the carburetor is dirty, or that the manifold rings are shot, or I got blowback in the exhaust. That's *his* job. Else why do I pay him?"

Dirksen tapped his lip and began to nod slightly, considering but not necessarily agreeing just yet.

"Don't get me wrong, Jules," Rebecca said. "I'm not trying to say that there was no fault on Tamarack's part. Hell, we're all smart enough to know that there's a lot of blame to pass around. All I'm asking, can you as a professional reasonably say that the UDS people, who are supposed to be the experts at this stuff, did they have a responsibility to pull what they needed out of Tamarack employees, and to know if what they were getting was good stuff? Based on that mile-long list of other projects UDS presented in their proposal?"

Dirksen rocked his head back and forth. "It's an interesting point," he mused out loud.

More scholarly bullshit. "Yeah. You don't have to opine as to whose fault anything is, Jules. But can you say that UDS had the primary responsibility to ensure that the system matched the customer's needs?"

"Probably," Dirksen admitted. "Probably. I see what you're driving at."

"Here's a possibility," Steinholz chimed in. "They fix-priced the contract, if I remember correctly. Wasn't that the case? So, Jules, isn't it possible that UDS, in its zeal to win the business, underestimated the amount of work it would take and did everything they could to force their existing system on Tamarack?"

Way too harsh! "Not purposely, Jules," Rebecca said. "But doesn't it make sense that here and there they figured, well, it would be easier for Tamarack to change some procedures rather than to reprogram the whole darned system?"

Dirksen stayed silent. Thinking it over.

"Lemme put it another way," Rebecca pressed. "In your experience, which is considerable, is this a common occurrence in the business?"

"No question about it. No question. But my problem here, I look through all these papers and I don't necessarily find hard evidence of it."

Again with the legal analysis. "Something you gotta understand here, Jules." Rebecca leaned forward and got serious. "You're an expert. That means something real specific in the law. It means you're allowed to express opinions based on your experience, without mathematical proofs. You say to the jury, look, the last eighty times I was in a situation like this, such-and-such happened. And if you get hammered on cross, you can say, 'Well, I'm an expert and that's my opinion!' That's allowed."

As Rebecca leaned back to let that sink in, Ehrenright said, "The only requirement is that you believe it, Jules. That you feel comfortable in your professional capacity. It's all up to you as an expert."

The subtle flattery was working. They could see Dirksen, the center of attention, the man holding all the cards, struggling to help them out, to tailor his opinion-making mechanism without compromising his integrity. His eyebrows creased as he asked, "Why wouldn't Tamarack tell UDS that they had a whole other operation in Wisconsin?"

Steinholz shot back, "Why on earth wouldn't UDS ask Tamarack if they only had the one location?"

"Seems about the most obvious gosh-darned question in the world, Jules," Ehrenright piped in. "Wouldn't you have asked that in this situation?"

"Certainly," Dirksen had no choice but to answer.

"So again," Rebecca picked up, "with you feeling perfectly comfortable, isn't it reasonable for you to testify that UDS, the computer professionals in this transaction, that they had the primary responsibility for ensuring that the specs for the system got together properly?"

Dirksen's response should have been quicker in coming, so Ehrenright prompted him. "Isn't that the responsibility *you* assume when *you* do these kinds of projects?"

"Yes," Dirksen said finally, slapping his hand down on his thigh. "I sure do."

"Shouldn't other experts?"

"Definitely. Irresponsible not to!"

"I think I understand where you're coming from on this one, Jules," Rebecca said, making it sound like a request for clarification on his thinking, like she was still working it out in her mind.

"What you're saying," Steinholz offered, "is that, even if Tamarack employees weren't the sharpest in the world, UDS should have been smart enough to know if they were heading toward a good spec. Right?"

"Right," Dirksen answered, fully on board now. "Any good computer professional has that responsibility."

"So you have no problem saying that in your testimony. I mean, you believe it, speaking as a professional."

"I most certainly do."

Ehrenright grinned widely and clapped his hands together. "Terrific! Well done, Jules." Rebecca and Steinholz nodded in agreement, and Dirksen beamed in the halo of their approval.

Rebecca raised her eyebrows toward Janine, who nodded back that, yes, she'd gotten it all down on paper. Rebecca would use it as a reminder for Dirksen when the actual testimony preparation began.

"So let's move on." *When you've made the sale, stop selling.* "Now, on your point about this testing business—"

There were two sharp knocks on the conference room door, which opened immediately thereafter. A face appeared, looking at Rebecca without even acknowledging that anybody else was present. "Verona, got a minute?" said Allen Wysocki, managing partner of the firm.

Rebecca wondered if the other people in the room could sense the instant tension she felt, the same autonomic discomfort that welled up whenever she was in the same room with Wysocki. It took an effort of will even to be civil toward him.

She flipped her hand palm up on the table: *Is this really necessary?*

Wysocki sniffled and pressed his lips together: *Yup.*

"Guys, why don't we take a break?" she said. "Couple minutes, max. We're doing real well, here, Jules, and I don't want to break the momentum." She patted his arm, then rose to follow Wysocki out the door and down to his office. Strict rules of the firm forbade hallway or elevator conversations on sensitive matters, and when

Wysocki didn't say a word on the way, Rebecca followed suit and stayed silent until they were seated in his expansive corner office with the door closed.

"This important, Allen?" She jerked a thumb back over her shoulder. "This geek is doing the ethics tango, and I'm busting my chops turning him around."

"Surprised you got Janine Osterreich in there," Wysocki said. "Thought you didn't like her."

"I don't. Spends half her time at the dentist—"

"So she's got bad teeth—"

"—and when she does decide to come in, she's a pain in the ass."

Wysocki gave her a *So are you* look but let it go. "Then how come—"

"Because she was the only one available. You pull me out of that meeting to discuss personnel problems?"

Wysocki seemed not to hear. "Can you settle this, Becky?"

She blinked. "That supposed to be a serious question?"

They both knew that nearly all of these kinds of cases settled out of court before the commencement of trial. Even hyped-up, vengeful executives weren't crazy enough to trust a jury of ordinary citizens with a complex technical case. Who'd bet their company on that kind of crapshoot? First you took everybody's depositions, including the experts from both sides, and made a careful analysis of who was telling the better story. Then you sent all the involved parties back to their offices so the attorneys could do some real negotiating, and when you thought you had a workable deal, the lawyers went back and tried to sell it to their clients, using threats and intimidation if necessary to browbeat them into it. Once in a while you actually started the trial, and settled a few days into it after one side or the other got scared. On even rarer occasions, you actually finished the trial, turning the case over to a jury. But if you had to do that, it was generally because the opposing parties had really lost their minds and were so consumed with rage that they wouldn't listen to their own lawyers, which made you wonder why they'd hired you in the first place. That wasn't going to happen in this case. That's why Rebecca wasn't too concerned about shamelessly manipulating Dirksen, and possibly confusing him: he may get deposed, but he'd never wind up testifying at trial.

"What I mean is," Wysocki said calmly, "can you settle it now?"

Rebecca, Ehrenright and Steinholz had been billing nearly ninety hours a week on this case, around $17,000. It could easily continue at that rate for another two months, and Wysocki was not normally so sanguine about giving up that kind of cash flow.

"What is it, Allen?" She fidgeted uncomfortably in her seat, anxious to get back to the conference room. Even more anxious to get out of Wysocki's office, out of his presence. She could feel her dysmennorheal surliness begin to reassert itself.

"Something's come up."

"No shit. What?"

"Computer thing."

Gee whiz.

"Department of Justice."

That got her attention. "Somebody's suing in federal court?"

Wysocki shook his head. "It's a criminal case, Becky. Felony violation of national security."

"Sounds juicy. Who're the guilty bastards?"

Wysocki uncharacteristically toyed absently with his tie and watched his fingers work as he answered without looking at her.

"Tera-Tech Integrated."

Rebecca looked vacantly straight ahead, then winced as a fresh cramp hit her full force.

Chapter 2

Allen Wysocki was a true legend, an eagle among the hawks of tort litigation. His star began to shine in the early eighties, when a dozen law firms and sixteen expert witnesses, led mostly by Wysocki, took on the U.S. light airplane industry. They brought suit on behalf of the estates and families of people killed in tragic—and, as the lawyers attempted to prove, avoidable—crashes of Pipers and Cessnas. It became something of a holy war, the crusaders gaining strength with every victory, the

manufacturers retreating into ever larger settlements to avoid protracted litigation.

That exhilarating experience taught Wysocki that there were no
practical limits to what you could accomplish within the boundaries of the law if you had the energy, the right resources and committed clients. You needed only a few early victories to fill the
reservoirs enough to sustain the remaining battles.

But that had been just the start. The real apotheosis came in
1994, when Wysocki engineered the largest class-action settlement
in history. He and his colleagues forced a handful of manufacturers
to allocate $4.5 billion to pay off claims of breast implant–related
illnesses, achieving not only justice and compensation for the victims but the kind of heady notoriety for himself that brought renewed hope and tears of joy to other practitioners of tort litigation
as well. And there was nothing wrong with getting famous fighting
for just causes.

"Doesn't make any sense, Allen," Rebecca said when she was
able to refocus. She had no idea how much time had passed, but realized that, however long it had been, Wysocki had stayed quiet
and given her the time. "You know I hate Perrein," she continued.
"So what's the point of this?"

Tera-Tech president and founder James Perrein. Wysocki may
have known the gist but he couldn't know the substance, so he had
no idea of the pain the mere mention of Perrein's name caused her.
Although she'd never be able to forget, she had become somewhat
adept at suppressing the thoughts for increasingly longer intervals
of time. "Also seems a bit of a coincidence."

"He asked for you specifically."

Whatever puzzlement she might have entertained turned immediately to suspicion: James Perrein did nothing without calculation.
"Why." An accusation more than a question.

"Simple. Way he figures it, you'll fight twice as hard for a man
you don't like if you believe he's innocent."

"But I don't believe he's innocent."

Wysocki looked her in the eye for the first time since they sat
down in his office. "You don't be— You don't even know anything
about the case!"

"I don't give a shit. Whatever it is, he did it. And I'm changing
my stance on capital punishment."

Wysocki smiled at that. At least now they could settle down into
a serious conversation. But Rebecca wasn't smiling back and

Wysocki's face turned dour again. "This is unprofessional, Verona. Give the man a fair hearing."

"No." This was not a street-smart way to handle the managing partner of the law firm into whose little bag you'd tossed all your career marbles, but Rebecca sensed that she had some kind of an upper hand here.

Wysocki frowned and glanced out the window. Turning back to her, he jerked a thumb over his shoulder. "That still America out there? They repeal due process while I wasn't looking?"

Well, this was rich, Allen Wysocki preaching legal virtue. She didn't bother to help him understand that hearing him wax lofty on due process was about as compelling as Joe McCarthy on the first amendment. It wasn't working anyway, so Wysocki abandoned the founding principles and got down to the stuff that really counted.

He leaned forward and lowered his voice, whether to intimate some sort of confidentiality or to underscore the deep importance of his words, she couldn't tell. "Case like this, you handle it well, who knows: could jump you onto the fast track for partnership in this firm. Win it, we'll have the decorators in your new office ten minutes after the jury comes back."

Probably not a good time for Rebecca to remind him that he'd been telling her for two years she was already on the fast track. Especially since he pretty much just told her this case could make it happen. Good time for her to be less snippy.

"Look," Wysocki implored her, "meet with the guy, what harm could it do? Perrein's a big-shot celebrity since he started this whole campaign, this encryption export shit. Very important stuff."

"I hear about it all the time. Don't understand any of it."

Wysocki sat up straight. "You serious?"

She nodded.

Wysocki shook his head. "Me neither. Not a word." He seemed pleased when she smiled back. "C'mon, just take a meeting with the client. We'll do it over lunch. No commitments here; we'll discuss what you want to do about it afterwards."

"*Prospective* client. That's what you meant, right?"

"Sure. Whatever." He waved a hand in the air as he bent forward to push his chair back from the desk.

Rebecca made no move to stand up. Wysocki paused, seeing Rebecca hadn't taken the hint that the matter was now resolved. He sat back in the chair, and the pleasant expression still on his face made his next words all the more sinister.

"Exactly how much more negotiating do you think the managing partner of this firm plans to conduct with an attorney in his employ," he said quietly, with no upward inflection at the end to indicate it should be taken as a question. And thus did he disabuse her of any notions that there was actually an alternative for her regarding a preliminary meeting, or regarding anything.

To salvage some small scrap of dignity, Rebecca, rudely jarred out of the fantasy that she actually possessed some modicum of autonomy, made a meaningless demand to which she knew Wysocki would acquiesce. "Lunch is out. An office meeting, around a conference table. Ehrenright and Steinholz sit in."

Wysocki played along with the charade of her power to make demands. "Done. I'll be there as well."

Now that Wysocki had made their relative positions plain, Rebecca thought it wise to reestablish some sort of civility, fraudulent though it would be. "So when did I get to be such a technology expert anyway?"

"Since you won your patent infringement case for the Taiwanese. Every cyber-slug wants you on his side, Becky. Don't fight it: you're in demand. You think that source of business is gonna die out?"

She didn't hear any of his last sentences. The Taiwanese case was the beginning of the whole sorry business with James Perrein in the first place, although she hadn't realized it until it was too late. Amazing how even some of your best work can swing around later to bite you in the ass.

"I don't get it."

That was the thing about Arno Steinholz. He didn't waste a lot of time pretending to have caught on to something and then have to sit around hoping it would become clearer as the conversation wore on.

But this wasn't terribly complicated. Rebecca looked at Justin Ehrenright, who held a hand above the table, palm down, and rocked it back and forth as he said, "You're telling us, if the jury somehow gets wind of the fact that there was bad blood between a defendant and his lawyer, but she's willing to defend him anyway, therefore he must be innocent?"

Rebecca held her hands up, then let them drop. "So what's not to understand?"

"Why does that mean he's innocent?" Steinholz asked.

"Because, why would she defend someone she doesn't like if she thinks he's guilty?"

"Because he's paying her a ton of money?" Steinholz offered.

"Or it's a big, visible, career-making case?" Ehrenright threw in.

"Or things are slow at the firm, and partner candidates need to show they can bring in business, and she may be mad at him but she isn't stupid or self-destructive?"

"Or—"

"Okay!" Rebecca shouted, then lowered her voice. "Okay. But that assumes that you let the jury sit around and guess. What if we assume nothing, and somehow tell the jury what we want them to hear?"

"You serious about this, Becky?" Steinholz asked.

"Perrein and Wysocki are."

"It's got a few problems," Ehrenright said.

"You're paid to anticipate problems." Rebecca looked from one to the other. "What, you're all of a sudden gun-shy because you think it's personal?" She could tell from their discomfort that this was exactly the case, and she shook her head and harrumphed noisily. "Pair a' wimps, I got here. Knew I shoulda hired women."

Steinholz smirked, then put his hands behind his neck and leaned back in his chair, looking skyward. "First problem you got, ABA Rule three-point-four."

"Ah, yes: Rule three-point-four." Rebecca nodded her head vigorously. "Should've thought of that."

Steinholz nodded, still looking upward. "You don't have the slightest goddamned—"

"—notion of what Rule three-point-freaking-four is, right. So why don't you tell me?"

The walking legal encyclopedia disguised as Arno Steinholz sat forward and folded his hands on the table. "Paragraph E, to be specific." He waited for the expected contemptuous snort from Rebecca and got it immediately. "Paragraph E provides that a lawyer at trial may not state a personal opinion as to the guilt or innocence of the accused."

"Who says I'm gonna state an opinion?"

"Ah, then I misunderstood." Steinholz looked apologetic. "See, for a second there, I thought the idea was for you to tell the jury you believed fervently in your client."

Ehrenright figured he might as well pile on, too. "Yeah, you sure had me fooled, Becky. Because I thought, you hating Perrein and

all, that if you believed in him, the jury would think he was innocent. But now . . ." He threw his hands up in resignation. "Now,
what with you not stating any opinions, well . . . !"

He shrugged and held a hand out toward Steinholz, who said,
"Now, no problem with Rule three-point-freaking-four." He
dropped back against the chair, reached forward and flipped his
writing tablet closed. "Of course, now you don't have a reason in the
world why Perrein would want you for his lawyer anymore, so . . ."

Rebecca looked from one to the other and back again. "Swear
to God, one day soon I'm gonna toss both your sorry butts out that
window there."

"Swear to God, one day I'm gonna jump," Steinholz threw back.

"What the hell's the difference?" Rebecca answered. "It's a
case, isn't it? And you both know damned well there's plenty of
ways for a lawyer to vouch for the client without coming out and
saying so. Like speaking to the press, say, or how passionate you
act in front of the jury."

"In that case," Steinholz said, flipping open the pad again, "you
coming over all Sarah Bernhardt in court, there's nothing we can
do to help you plan it. So you want to talk some real strategy or
should we hold hands and sing 'Kumbaya'?"

"Nothing to plan," Rebecca said. "I haven't even agreed to take
the case, only to have a meeting."

"Then why are we having *this* meeting?" Ehrenright asked.

"Because I want both you smart-ass Supreme Court candidates
there with me. Got a feeling this is going to be about more than just
looking up cases. We need to press this guy, try to get a feel for
what's going on here."

Ehrenright was looking at her and blinking, as though he hadn't
heard a word she'd just said. "You haven't agreed to take the
case?" he said with exaggerated enunciation.

"No." Rebecca looked at him and frowned. "S'matter with
you?"

Ehrenright stared a moment longer, broke into a wide grin, then
reached behind him into his back pocket. Steinholz stood up immediately and followed suit. Ehrenright was quicker and had a twenty
out and down on the table first, but Steinholz's bill came out immediately thereafter.

"Before that meeting ends," Ehrenright said, and Steinholz nodded his agreement.

Rebecca looked at the twenties for only a few seconds before reaching into her purse and pulling out two of her own, depositing them on top of the originals. "Nobody pushes *me* around," she said defiantly.

"Never doubted it for a second," Ehrenright said as he scooped up the money and handed it to Steinholz for safekeeping.

Chapter 3

Wednesday, May 20

The preliminaries seemed to have more informal chitchat than was usually called for in such gatherings. It might have had to do with the six different perceptions held by the six meeting participants as to the significance of Rebecca Verona and James Perrein being in the same room. They may have differed in their knowledge of history, but every one of them knew that that history made it perfectly appropriate to be awkward and uncomfortable right now.

As reluctant as any of the others to dive into the heart of matters, Rebecca knew that there had been enough foreplay: time to get to the main act. She smiled politely. "So what are we looking at here, Phil?"

Philip Mastilir, Tera-Tech Integrated's chief corporate counsel, nodded his agreement that it was time to get to work. He took a moment to organize his thoughts, then said, "Department of Justice brought an indictment against Jim a couple of days ago. They say he sold some computer chips to the mainland Chinese—their intelligence ministry, specifically—and that these types of chips are on a list of items that are forbidden to be exported." He stopped to make sure the general overview statement had registered. It had, but he was getting back looks of skepticism.

Steinholz cocked his head. "They were defense related, weren't they. The chips."

The question seemed out of left field, but Mastilir answered, "Technically," causing Wysocki and Ehrenright to look over at

Steinholz with a mix of admiration and puzzlement. Perrein didn't look at him at all, and Rebecca suspected it had something to do with her associate's long hair and John Lennon glasses. She wondered if Perrein could see the small hole left over from the earring Steinholz used to wear.

"*Technically.* What does that mean?" Steinholz asked. "They for use in weapon systems?"

"No, no, no," Mastilir said forcefully. "Nothing like that at all. There's all kinds of crap on the forbidden list haven't gotten squat to do with weapons. The chips are encryption devices." Seeing the blank stares around the table, he added, "You use them to put messages into code. Like those old Captain Marvel secret rings, only a little more sophisticated than that."

"That's it?" Rebecca asked, breaking into the protracted silence that had followed Mastilir's explanation. When the corporate attorney merely shrugged, Rebecca said to Perrein, "*That's* why you got indicted?" She looked around to see if she was the only one surprised, then addressed herself to Mastilir. "Not exactly serial murder we're talking here, Phil."

"Might's well be, the way they're coming after Jim and his company." Mastilir sat up straight and pushed his papers off to one side, then stood up and began removing his jacket. "Look, lemme back up a tad." He shrugged off the remaining sleeve and draped the jacket over the back of his chair. " 'Cuz this is a damned sight more serious than I just made it sound."

He sat down and pulled the chair in closer to the table. "How much you all know about encryption?" Steinholz started to gesture with his pencil, but before he could speak, Mastilir said, "Not you, Einstein; I'm talking to the normal people."

Steinholz reddened as the others laughed, but smiled along with them as he caught Mastilir's guileless smirk. "I was gonna say, not much," Steinholz said with feigned petulance, "but now I'm not gonna help you at all."

"Oh boy, I'm on my own," Mastilir said. "I was gonna let Jim give the lecture, but that'd be like the president talking about Medicare: we'd be here all goddamned day and you wouldn't understand a word of it."

Mastilir pulled a yellow legal pad toward him and took out his pen, laying it atop the sheets of paper. He had no need of diagrams, but, like most attorneys, he felt more comfortable just having pen and paper handy. "What we're talking about is really simple. You got stuff you want to send to somebody, like a private message, some confidential information, sensitive data—what you want to do, you want to put it into code. That way, only the guy who has the key can read it." He spread his hands and looked around, getting only *So what?* looks back.

He nodded once—*See? I told you it was going to be easy*—and went on. "Problem is, ever since the Enigma project in the big war, the science of *breaking* codes has moved a lot faster than the art of *making* them. 'Bout ten years ago, a couple Israeli guys invented a new method, said it was unbreakable. Billion computers running a billion years couldn't do it, or something like that. The world goes nuts, or at least those kinds of people who care about stuff like that, everybody figures the problem is solved . . ." He paused for effect.

"And somebody figured out how to break it," Rebecca ventured.

Mastilir pointed at her. "Same two guys who invented it. Trying to prove it couldn't be cracked . . . ?" He opened his hand and slammed it down on the table. "They cracked it!" He grinned widely and looked around, his infectious good humor almost irresistible. "So it's everybody back to the drawing board, tearing their hair out, it can't be done, ohmigod what're we gonna do . . ." He had grabbed his head and was rocking it back and forth, pleased at the smiles his one-man show was generating.

He took his hands away from his head and held them up. "And then, whaddaya know?" He pointed at Perrein. "Jim here hires a guy, Whitman Helfie, if you can believe that handle, and sonofagun if the guy doesn't invent an unbreakable code."

He expected skeptical looks and got them. "Except this time, it's for real. I'm not going to get into the technicals, because I don't understand a single word of them, but this code simply cannot be broken."

"How do you know?" asked Ehrenright.

"Because it can be proven," Steinholz said, startling Mastilir, who waved for him to go on.

"With the Israeli technique," Steinholz said, "everybody *thought* it was unbreakable because it looked hard. The way they were going about it, it was easy to show that the 'billion computers for a billion years' estimate was reasonable. Problem was, they weren't going about it the right way. Turned out there were some shortcuts."

He looked at Perrein. "With the Tera-Tech method, it can be

proven mathematically that there are no shortcuts. When very large Mersenne primes are utilized, even the standard sieve protocols—"

"Ah-ah-ah!" Mastilir said loudly, banging his fist on the table. "Y'see? Whud I tell you!"

Steinholz covered his face with his hands and absorbed the laughter at his expense.

Rebecca used the brief intermission to consider how personable and charming Perrein's in-house lawyer was, and wondered how much of his genial theatrics sprang from Wysocki's undoubtedly having told him that she hadn't yet consented to handling this case. Mastilir was generating waves of camaraderie and Gemütlichkeit, but Rebecca had no way of knowing if this was his normal mode of operation or a special, command performance designed to win her over.

"Forget all o' that," Mastilir was saying. "Point is, Tera-Tech came up with something so secure it could change the world. It's called the 'enhanced key encryption system,' and you might want to write that down 'cause you'll be hearing a lot about it."

Ehrenright looked admiringly at Perrein, who ought to have been drinking up the spotlight but seemed not to care very much. Only Rebecca knew that his seeming insouciance was really just arrogance: James Perrein only perked up when people he considered to be important were paying him homage. This lot in here? Big deal.

"Market must be enormous," Ehrenright said to Perrein. "You stand to make—"

"Market's nonexistent," Perrein said gruffly, and then went quiet, not bothering to explain his comment despite the puzzlement on Ehrenright's face inviting him to do so. Rebecca thought that Perrein might have taken to the associate attorney, who probably looked a great deal like the kind of pallid lab rats upon whose technical abilities and manic work ethic his company depended, but no sign of approval had been evident thus far.

The young associate looked around the room to see if he was the only one not getting it, but his colleagues looked equally confused.

Rebecca figured she was the one the script called for to ask the obvious question, something like, *Golly gee, Jim, whatever do you mean?* So she kept silent and sat calmly, refusing to be sucked into his game.

"Okay, we're getting way ahead of ourselves here," Mastilir intervened smoothly. "In order to make this secret coding thing work, you can't use pencil and paper to get it done, you gotta use a computer. And in order for you to do that, you gotta put this whole coding technique inside a little piece of a computer's brain."

Mastilir reached for his pen and pulled the yellow pad in closer. He drew a simple rectangle but didn't bother showing it to anybody: it was just to help him think. "What we're talking about is something called an encryption chip. What it does, it automatically puts information into code, so outsiders can't read it while it's going from one place to another. Good example is an ATM machine. You stick your card in"—he mimed the action in the air—"then the machine has to call up your bank and find out if there's money in your account. To do that, the ATM has to send your card number to the bank, and the bank has to send back your account balance. That's not the kind of information you want an eavesdropper to be able to get by tapping into the telephone line."

He flapped his hands around rapidly. "So the ATM scrambles your card number into code before sending it. The bank's computer knows how to unscramble it. And the bank scrambles your account information into code before it sends it back. Simple. But that's part of the problem: those codes are very simple, and easy to crack."

"So why don't we hear about this?" Rebecca asked. "Sounds like eavesdropping doesn't happen very much."

Mastilir agreed. "That's because, usually, the small amounts involved don't make it worth the time and trouble. But now suppose you're Chase Manhattan, trading information with Citibank. We're talking billions now. Hundreds of billions. Account numbers and passwords could be worth a fortune to anybody who could crack those codes. Same thing with a bank communicating with Switzerland, or Germany, or Tokyo."

"But again, we hardly ever hear about it."

"That's because they'd rather lose a few million here or there then let their customers know how vulnerable they are," Mastilir responded. "Banks get whacked a hell of a lot more often than anybody thinks, and they tend to take the hit without involving law enforcement, just to keep it in the family."

"Or say a defense contractor wants to transmit the blueprints for its latest fighter plane to the Pentagon," Steinholz added. "Turns out they can't do that. They use human couriers. Because nobody trusts current encryption technology enough yet."

"So where does Tera-Tech fit in?" Ehrenright asked.

Now Perrein spoke up. "If you had a coding system that was

impossible to crack, it opens up a whole world of possibilities for people to protect their information. It would save businesses and governments huge sums of money every year, and ensure the kinds of privacy we don't have now." It was a well-rehearsed and professionally delivered sound bite.

The next part wasn't. "And, speaking for my own self-interest, it would enhance America's competitiveness in the encryption field. That means a fortune to the companies that could give the world that kind of capability. The market is in the billions."

"And Tera-Tech is working on that?" Wysocki asked.

"Sort of." Mastilir sighed deeply and drummed his fingers on the yellow pad. "Like I said, Tera-Tech has already solved the basic encryption problem. We got a method that can't be cracked. Period." He stopped.

Ehrenright frowned, his impatience with the dramatic procrastination clearly in evidence, if still lighthearted. He simply wanted to get to the good part. "Phillip," he said commandingly, leaning forward to compel the attorney's full focus. "What. Is. The. *Problem!*" He spat the last word through clenched teeth, a ferocious look on his face as he bore in on Mastilir, who laughed, getting the message that he'd stretched the tension far enough.

"The problem," he replied, "is that it's against U.S. law to export that technology to a foreign country."

In his surprise, Ehrenright's face lapsed back into its former geniality. "How come?"

"Because the code can't be cracked."

"Wait a minute," Rebecca said. "The government won't allow you to sell this method overseas because it works as advertised?"

"Exactly. They've been trying to weaken the security ever since the technology was invented. Not just for our method but for other systems as well."

"But why would they want to do that?" Wysocki asked. He was rarely surprised by myopic intransigence on the part of government bureaucrats, but there was usually some rationale, however labored, and he could see none in this posture.

"For the same reason they imposed the export ban," Mastilir replied. "Net net, the government doesn't want any system around that they can't crack." He added, with unmistakable, sneering sarcasm, "They say it's necessary for law enforcement purposes."

Perrein explained further. "They're afraid bad guys will use encryption systems to scramble messages. That means the spooks can't listen in. And they don't like it when they can't eavesdrop on people." His voice was heavy with contempt for this blatantly Big Brother-ish policy.

"So what's the solution?" Rebecca asked.

Mastilir answered, "The government wants a way to break in if they need to."

"That's it?"

"That's a lot," Perrein shot back.

"It'd be kind of like a wiretap, right?" Ehrenright wasn't challenging anything—yet. He was just pressing to try to understand better. "Tapping a computer instead of a phone?"

"Yeah . . ." Mastilir agreed.

"Doesn't sound unreasonable," Ehrenright concluded.

"Oh, no?" Perrein said. "*You* try selling an encryption chip to some company in France or Russia, then tell them, Oh, by the way, did I mention? The CIA can tap into your private data any time they damned well please!" He looked around at the others. At first, to Rebecca at least, it looked like he was soliciting approval for ridiculing Ehrenright's innocently offered straw-man argument. Then she realized he was demanding agreement with his point of view, assuming he would get it from these lawyers who wanted his business.

"Good point." Wysocki, ever the diplomat. But he had substantive questions of his own. "Even so, isn't there still a big U.S. market?"

"Hell, no." Perrein, never the diplomat. "It's a global economy. Any company of even modest size is going to be doing business overseas. And what's the point of having a coding system if none of your foreign customers can use it to communicate with you?" He shook his head. "If we can't export the method, it's dead in the water."

Rebecca tried to stay focused on the fact that their job here was not to commiserate with the client but to get the salient facts out on the table in preparation for winning a case, even though he was still a *potential* client and they hadn't taken the case yet. "Okay, so the government wants a key for itself. Anything else?"

"Yes." Mastilir appreciated the businesslike approach and switched into it easily. "A limitation on how long the customer's key can be. It's measured in bits. The more bits, the harder it is to break the code. The limit is now fifty-six bits, and that's not enough."

"Because . . . ?"

"Because a nine-year-old with a Nintendo machine could crack it," Perrein said impatiently, as though they all should have realized this for themselves.

"But if the government has its own key," Steinholz said, "what do they care how strong the code is?"

Perrein looked uncomfortable for the first time. "Well, it's because nobody knows how to *give* them a second key just yet. So what they're saying is, okay, go ahead and sell these things overseas, but you can't use more than fifty-six bits until you give us our own keys."

"Fifty-six because . . . ?"

"Because they know how to break a fifty-six-bit code without a key. So we can't go over the limit until we figure out how to give them one."

Rebecca nodded in understanding. "Okay, but like it or not, that's the law, right?"

"Yes," Mastilir agreed. "But." He leaned back on his chair and jerked a thumb to his left. "Jim here's been on a very public crusade for the past two years to get the ban lifted, because it's going to kill American business in the global market. To put it mildly, he's not well liked in federal law enforcement circles." He started patting his hips and chest, searching for something, then reached into his shirt pocket and pulled out a red-and-white metal disk about the size of a fifty-cent piece. He put it on the table and slid it over to Rebecca.

Rebecca picked it up; it was a lapel button, reading, "When privacy is outlawed, only outlaws will have privacy." She smiled and tossed it to Steinholz, then took up her pencil and tapped the eraser end on the table. "So, Phillip, let's cut to the chase: what are they charging your client with?"

"The government claims that it discovered a microchip somewhere in mainland China that contains Tera-Tech's enhanced key system. Not programmed in, like you'd write a computer program on your PC. The method is built right into the hardware, during the manufacturing process, a highly sophisticated piece of engineering. What it means is, and this is just what they're claiming so it's probably complete horsepucky, it means the Chinese now have the ability to encode data in a way that U.S. intelligence can't possibly decipher. They're charging Jim with manufacturing the chip and selling it to the Chinese." It didn't sound all that terrible, so he added, "And according to laws you guys probably never even heard of, it's kind of right up there with treason."

Silence followed in the wake of this news. Then Perrein started to speak, but Rebecca held up her hand immediately. "Stop right there!" Perrein halted in mid-word. "I don't want you to tell us what you did or didn't do!"

"No," Perrein insisted. "That's a trick you pull if you think a client is guilty. I'm telling you my company didn't do this."

Rebecca slumped back in her chair, fearful that Perrein might have irrevocably damaged her ability to represent him. Knowing that his position was one of never having committed the offenses charged, strict ethical guidelines of the profession could eventually make it impossible for her to put Perrein on the stand should facts come to her attention that contradicted his assertion.

But having heard him blurt it out already, there was little harm in hearing him out.

"I admit that Tera-Tech is on the cutting edge of this kind of technology, no great secret since I've personally lobbied for revisions to those idiotic laws, but I'm telling you, flat out, that not only did we never sell chips like that to the Chinese, we never even *made* devices like that!" He was looking only at Rebecca now. "Tell you the God's honest truth, I don't even believe they exist."

"Why?"

Perrein turned to Wysocki. "This is a privileged conversation, right?"

"Certainly."

"What I mean, nothing I tell—"

"Jim," Rebecca interrupted. "The only two kinds of people in this room are attorneys and a client. You can do whatever you want, but none of us can ever breathe a word of anything said in this room. Okay? Now: tell us why you don't believe those chips exist."

Perrein took a deep breath, clearly about to reveal something important and uncomfortable. "Because there's one major problem with the enhanced key system:" He looked at Mastilir, asking one more time if he could really say this, and got a nod of approval to continue. "It's too slow," he said when he'd turned back to Rebecca. "It really does work, it can't be cracked, but it takes for-goddamn-ever to put a simple message into code, even with a massive computer, because it's so complicated." The tone of his voice hinted at some displeasure at this predicament or, more precisely, that there was blame to be apportioned for it. Rebecca wondered what hapless scientist back at Tera-Tech was still licking wounds he'd received at Perrein's hands.

"So you can use it for short messages," Mastilir explained, "but if you tried to encode big chunks of data, it would be faster to load it onto a rickshaw and carry it to wherever it was going."

"So what good is it?" Ehrenright asked, mindful of the impolitic nature of the blunt question only when it was too late.

Perrein seemed to take no offense. "Right now, very limited. But if we can find ways to shortcut the encoding, or build specialized, superfast computers dedicated to this one process, we could make it practical. But that's years away."

"Which is why," Mastilir opined, "it's got to be a very circumstantial case the DoJ has against Jim. If the government can't put an actual, physical chip into evidence—which they can't—then how the hell do they plan to claim Tera-Tech built it?"

"How do you know they don't have it?" Steinholz asked.

"I told you," Perrein said with mild annoyance. "It can't exist, because *nobody* could have built it. Tera-Tech is the world leader in the field, and we're years away from doing it ourselves."

Steinholz was immune to intimidation on matters of logic. If Perrein couldn't stand up to *him*, his potential lawyer, they couldn't dare put him on the stand and subject him to cross-examination from a hostile prosecutor. "So your position is that the government is lying? They made the whole thing up? And you're willing to bet this case on that?"

Perrein had obviously never heard it put so succinctly before. "Something like that."

"Why would they do that?" Steinholz was very good at this, and Rebecca made no attempt to interfere.

Mastilir answered on behalf of his client. "To put Jim behind bars for the rest of his life and serve notice to anybody else who might be thinking about violating national security laws."

Rebecca made a skeptical face, and Perrein caught it immediately.

"Listen, what reason could I possibly have for wanting to do something like that? Just think about it for a second." He waited a few moments to give them time to postulate some motivating scenarios, then began to lay them out on his own. "Even if the Chinese paid a few million for those chips, that's chump change, and I sure as hell don't need the money, and neither does my company."

"Maybe now," Steinholz conceded. "But what about two years ago?"

"Check the books, son." It was evident from Perrein's crisp delivery that he was confident in his handling of these challenges. "We were up to our asses in cash. I may own the company outright but that doesn't mean I wasn't making deals and grabbing investor dough wherever I could find it." He turned back to include everyone else in this part of the conversation. "Doing something like illegally selling chips to a foreign power is an enormous risk—"

"And you're a legendary risk taker," Ehrenright threw at him.

"But not for the sake of risk alone," Perrein countered easily. "I take chances when there's a big return possible. And in a deal like that one, it's all risk and no reward. I mean, come on, you couldn't even *tell* anybody that the Chinese had those chips, so they were useless for transmissions back to the United States and there's no other practical value!"

"There's sure as hell a practical value to Chinese intelligence," Steinholz challenged.

"But what would *I* get out of it?" Perrein was into the game now, even enjoying it, having realized that this kind of mock cross-examination was eliciting relevant information at a much faster rate than a tedious interview could. "What am I gonna do, send coded basketball scores to Beijing? Even assuming for a second that I didn't give a damn about my own country, that all I cared about was my own self-interest, there's no rational reason in the world why I would do something like this!"

The conviction in his voice was impressive, and Steinholz, for one, needed no further details for now. "So what is it?"

"I told you: I embarrassed the feds, and now they want me."

"You think it's simple revenge?" Ehrenright asked.

"No." Perrein calmed down a little. "They're not that stupid, and neither am I. Fact is, I was winning the debate. My opinion made more sense than theirs, and a lot more people were on my side."

"What they're essentially doing," Mastilir theorized, "is crafting an *ad hominem*: if you can't attack the argument, attack the arguer. By branding Jim a traitor to his country and a high-tech criminal, it'll cast aspersions on every point he was trying to make, no matter how valid it might have been. And that will end the debate, because anybody who supports Jim's side of the controversy will look like a Perrein supporter, and who wants to support a traitor?" He folded his arms across his chest, as though it were so obvious on the face of it, nothing further need be said.

"Sounds a little far-fetched," Rebecca observed skeptically.

Perrein flicked his eyes toward her without moving his head. "And you sound a little naive."

Naive? Flares started going off in Rebecca's gut, and she looked at Perrein like she was about to spring over the table and go for his throat.

Mastilir saw it. "Everybody hang on a minute. The point is, they've handed down a formal indictment. That means they're going to prosecute Jim and he needs good representation. Now I'm no litigator, so I have no problem with Welch, Tobias & Wysocki taking over the case. I handled the arraignment, and that's about the extent of my criminal expertise right there."

"Speaking of which," Steinholz jumped in, having seen what Mastilir saw and wishing to defuse whatever interpersonal situation might be brewing, "why didn't you object to the venue, since Tera-Tech's up north and the complaint was filed in Los Angeles? Why's the case down here?"

"I did object. The prosecutor maintained that the sale of the chips was made in Los Angeles, so they could file here."

"*I* stopped Phil from pressing the point," Perrein said. "A lot of the judges up there, I know them personally. Which means they'd have to beg off the case, on account of conflicts and whatnot. Besides, and this is the part that really counts, I want this tried on the facts, not technicalities. I didn't do anything and I want my name cleared. All those committees I serve on, all that community crap I do so the good citizens with too much leisure time won't spend it hassling our asses off?" He shook his head and sat back. "I start off with a lot of bullshit tactics and delaying maneuvers, it isn't going to make me look very good, win or lose."

Rebecca wondered how Mastilir came to let his client win that argument. Then again, a control freak like Perrein probably didn't give him any option. "Not likely that you'll be able to base your defense solely on the argument that the government failed to prove its case," she said, making certain to talk about *your* rather than *our* defense at this point. She stole a glance at Ehrenright, who had his hand up to his mouth, and thought she detected a smile he was trying to hide: *Before that meeting ends* had been his prediction on how long it would take her to accept the case. One wrong phrase out of Rebecca and he and Steinholz would win her forty bucks.

She turned away from them to face Mastilir full on and not risk breaking out into the giggles if one of them made a face. Mastilir looked puzzled at her comment, wondering why she felt they wouldn't simply be able to assert that the government failed to prove its case, and not put on a defense of their own, so she explained. "You may be right, Phil: it'll probably be very circumstantial against Tera-Tech, but those federal prosecutors aren't stupid. My guess, we won't be able to just throw it to the jury after the government presents its case, we'll have to mount an affirmative defense that proves Tera-Tech didn't do it."

As Mastilir rubbed the side of his nose thinking about this, Rebecca said to Perrein, "And even if their case is so shitty it looks like we don't need to put on a defense, we still need to clear your name. If we rest on the basis that they didn't prove anything, and leave it like that, the public is going to wonder. That won't do your reputation much good, even if you're acquitted."

Wysocki, despite being an egotist who liked holding center stage, was also savvy enough to know when to sit back and be quiet, as he had been doing for the past half hour. He could see that Rebecca and her two associates were handling things perfectly, increasing the client's confidence with their probing questions and perceptive insights. He also knew when enough preliminary groundwork had been laid and it was time to go for the close.

"I gotta go along with my colleague on this one, fellas," he said, reluctantly, as though it ran so counter to his instinct that his mere willingness to entertain the notion completely validated it. "Getting you acquitted in a court of law is one thing, Jim; an acquittal in the court of public opinion is quite another."

"But you're saying something more than that, aren't you, Rebecca?" Mastilir asked, even as he nodded his agreement with Wysocki. "You're saying, you don't believe the DoJ would move this case to trial unless they had something more than just a boatload of insinuations."

"Count on it. Case this visible, better not to go to trial at all than risk losing it. And looking incompetent in the process."

"Which means," Wysocki said, still going for the close, "that we need to get discovery underway ASAP and find out what they really have." Getting vigorous nods of assent from Mastilir and Perrein, he turned to his colleagues and began barking orders. "Rebecca, what you gotta do right away, you gotta get out and sew up the best damned experts you can, before the government gets its hands on them. Let Justin and Arno read through the complaint and start the background work. Way I see it—"

Without thinking it through, Rebecca glared at Wysocki and said, "I haven't agreed to anything yet," which stopped the conversation, as well as a few hearts, cold.

It's generally not a good idea to corner your boss in front of subordinates and potential clients, but Rebecca knew she was sitting in the catbird seat. What she also now knew, and resented, was that Wysocki had never told Perrein or Mastilir that she was only considering taking the case and hadn't committed to anything beyond this meeting, as she and Wysocki had agreed. Had she not shut down his stream of detailed marching orders, her option to decline would have evaporated as the conversation progressed and solidified her role. Wysocki, of course, not only was aware of this but had deliberately engineered it, and that transparent attempt at manipulation angered her, so Rebecca felt compelled to sabotage it. But rather than diplomatically try to cover for her managing partner and save him some embarrassment, she'd gone right for his jugular and left him bleeding out on the ice.

Mastilir caught it immediately. "Understood," he said agreeably. "Just got caught up in the excitement, is all," making it seem as though it were his fault rather than Wysocki's. "Your call, Rebecca: What's the next move."

Angry as she was with Wysocki, she found herself drawn to Mastilir and his straight-up, friendly attitude. His willingness earlier to own up to his professional limitations was affecting, and she knew she'd have to waste little time massaging his ego were they to work together. She had no desire to entangle him, even very peripherally, in the intricate web of her negativity toward her managing partner.

She looked at him, all traces of her earlier ire gone. "I think we've gotten some key issues aired, although you and I both know a lot more are gonna bubble up later."

He looked heavenward. "Probably an understatement."

Rebecca smiled. "Right. But listen, how about you let me and Jim have our own discussion for a couple minutes, okay?"

Before she could come up with a rationale for doing that, Mastilir rapped a knuckle on the table and stood up. "You stay here. Boys, let's go drink some of that godawful coffee Wysocki keeps around for his cheap clients."

Wysocki, Ehrenright and Steinholz got up immediately and

headed for the door, knowing that Mastilir had made the right call in clearing them out without asking any questions.

When they were alone, Rebecca looked directly at Perrein in order to preclude any idea that she was somehow disconcerted by the prospect of confronting him. He returned her look, clearly untroubled himself, but she would have expected nothing less: hard to be troubled when you have no conscience.

"So now tell me why you want me to handle this case."

He acted as though the question had surprised him. "You're one of the best computer litigators in the business. Least the Taiwanese sure as hell think so."

Rebecca tried to hide her astonishment. How was it possible that he could bring that up to her so casually! And if he felt any unease at having done so, it didn't show on his face. *Was he even human?*

"And there's another reason," he went on. "You hate me." He said it using the same tone and manner as though he were asking a salesclerk for toothpaste. "If I can get you to believe in my case, you'll fight twice as hard. And if we can somehow bring out in court how much you detest me, that'd make it even stronger."

Rebecca had to consciously fight back her shock at how impassively he was saying these things, how callously he was treating the disaster that had been their prior relationship, considering nothing but its usefulness to him as a tool in his present predicament. "How do we bring it out?" she forced herself to say, trying to sound as unemotional and detached as Perrein. "There's an ABA rule against a lawyer's vouching for her client's innocence."

"Nobody has to come out and state anything—we just imply it. I don't know how, you're the expert. Maybe we'll get lucky and the prosecutor will bring it up. Maybe you bait him into claiming there's a conflict, your working for me." He seemed to like that idea. "Yeah: he opens the door, then we get to bring it all up, and your deciding to defend me anyway, and use it to our advantage."

His emotionless calculating over how to exploit a traumatic experience finally pushed Rebecca over the edge. She had nothing left to prop up her effort to suppress her emotions and remain purely analytical.

She slumped back in her seat. "You're the most cold-hearted bastard I've ever met, Jim." She kept her voice flat and even, so it was a simple statement of fact and not an emotional outburst.

He seemed genuinely surprised, and said nothing as Rebecca

went on, hoping her matter-of-fact delivery would underscore the objectivity of her conclusions. "Nothing would make me happier than if you went to prison for fifty years. The balls, even approaching me with your little problem after using me like a toilet . . ." She laughed, looking down and shaking her head in amused disbelief. "It's incomprehensible. Really."

"You know, I really did care for you, and—"

That was it. "Fuck you, Perrein!" Rebecca slammed her arms down and rose halfway out of her chair in one fluid, lightning-fast motion that made Perrein draw back reflexively. "*Fuck you!* I wouldn't hesitate to slice your dick off and shove it down the disposal, so don't bullshit me any more than you already have!" She waited a few more seconds to make sure he understood that any further smarmy protestations of innocence on his part would be similarly received, then sat down and kept staring at him.

Perrein may have been a bit shaken, but he recomposed himself quickly and judiciously decided to forgo that particular mode of entreaty. "Okay, look. We're both professionals, this is a pure business deal, with great benefit to both of us." He waited a moment to see if she was going to pounce again. "I've got to have my innocence proven, and my company's as well. You want to make a name for yourself, maybe make partner in the firm. Aren't you enough of a pro to put aside personal feelings and take a businesslike approach to the matter?"

"Like you put aside your personal feelings and took a businesslike approach to me two years ago?" She regretted it immediately, knowing that someone like Perrein would quickly find such self-pitying pronouncements tedious. *And how the hell come you know so damned much about my status in this firm!*

But Perrein clearly had too much at stake to risk voicing his annoyance. "Okay, I deserved that, Becky—" The look that came over her face stopped him in his tracks.

"Don't fuck with me, Jim." She delivered the warning in slow and measured tones that accentuated the venom beneath. "*Don't you dare fuck with me,* coming over so repentant all of a sudden! You don't think you *deserve* anything"—she rose up once again, slowly this time, and hovered over him, making a tight fist and holding it in front of his face—"so keep your bullshit charm in your pants! And if you call me Becky one more time . . ." She cocked the fist, which was reddening from the pressure of holding it, in the air behind her ear. "Swear to God I'll smash your face in and quit the case. You got it?"

"Jesus, Be—Rebecca: What're you getting so . . ."

She kicked her chair back abruptly, knocking it over with a loud bang, and leaned even further in toward him, face turning red and eyes blazing with naked menace. "Have you *got it*!" she spat, slamming her trembling fist onto the table.

"I got it!" Perrein, his face betraying his fear, held up his hands. "I got it."

Rebecca wondered for an instant why he was being so contrite, and then realized that it was because he believed she had tacitly agreed to take on the case. But she was having trouble fathoming why this was so important to him, to the point where he was willing to impassively absorb this kind of abuse rather than risk having her change her mind and withdraw.

She got control of her breathing, then said, "I'll be right back." She whirled around without waiting for any acknowledgment and quickly left the room.

Relieved that none of the others were milling about right outside the door, she made her way to the women's room and locked the door behind her. Flicking on only the right-hand tap, she leaned down, filled her hands and pushed her face into the icy water, waiting until most of it had spilled out and then rubbing her face vigorously with what was left. Good thing she didn't normally wear much makeup.

She rested her hands on the sides of the sink and looked up at herself in the mirror, water dripping from her nose and chin, and then began laughing as she reached for a paper towel. Gently dabbing at her face, she waited for the laughter to subside before turning back to the mirror and pushing aside stray wisps of hair. She turned her head from side to side, mopping up what drops of water still remained.

She got hold of herself and regarded her reflection one last time. "Jesus," she said out loud, "that felt good." Then she forced the smile away, opened the door and stepped back into the hall.

She motioned to the others as she strode past the coffee room without stopping, and they dutifully followed her back to the conference room. She was all business now, and took over from Wysocki as they discussed various strategic options. She enjoyed the bit of disorientation she detected in Perrein, but otherwise pointedly ignored him as she managed the discussion of his case as though he weren't even in the room.

But Ehrenright eventually drew him in, asking about potential experts. Before he could answer, though, Steinholz said, "That's an easy one: Radovan Terescu, at Cal Tech." He looked at Perrein for verification. "Guy probably knows more about this stuff than any ten others you could find."

"Forget it." Perrein pressed his lips together and shook his head. "Bit of bad blood between me and him. He wouldn't do it."

Rebecca looked meaningfully at Mastilir: *Anybody around he doesn't* have trouble with? Mastilir answered with a shrug he hoped only Rebecca could see.

"Besides," Perrein was saying, "he's going through a nasty divorce and he's in no frame of mind to be useful." Rebecca marveled at his clinical assessment of another man's troubles only in terms of their utility to him.

"You got some other possibilities for us to look at?" Ehrenright asked him.

"No problem. Plenty of smart people in the field. My human resources department keeps track of all of them, so they'll be able to help you."

Rebecca, stiffening, thought that Perrein was watching her in order to see whether she would betray any emotion at his last statement: Tera-Tech's head of human resources was Perrein's wife, Allison. Or at least she had been last time Rebecca had cause to notice.

"Manny Singh is head of the department," Perrein said finally. "Been there about a year."

Wysocki looked around the room. Things were going well. "So, Verona," he said confidently to Rebecca. "What do you think?" With his unerring eye for such things, Wysocki had picked the perfect moment to nail down everyone's commitment to the cause.

Which occasioned in him no small bit of anxiety when Rebecca answered, "Let me think about it," as she savored the look of surprise on Perrein's face.

She was equally pleased at the inward groans that only she could hear emanating from Ehrenright and Steinholz as they saw their twenty bucks each land in her pocket.

Chapter 4

Rebecca sat alone in the front row of the Forum. Technically it was now the Great Western Forum, the new appellation stemming from a precedent-setting deal in which the bank of the same name paid the Forum's owner a million dollars for the right to rename it and slap its logo all over the building. The concept soon grew to the point where pro sports teams sold corporations the rights to sponsor time-outs, instant replays, plays of the day, players of the game, and, perhaps before too much longer, individual urinals down in the rest rooms.

A Kings reserve forward blazed his way down the ice toward her, rooster tails of shavings spraying up behind his flashing skates, his stick moving so fast back and forth that it seemed to encase the clattering black puck in a cage. He slewed sideways as he approached the end of the rink, drew the stick back high into the air behind him and whipped it forward in a blur. The puck rose up off the ice and rocketed into the goal, drawing the restraining net behind it like a comet's tail before rebounding and dribbling out of the small enclosure.

The forward raised his arms in triumph and slammed into the barrier in front of Rebecca with a thud, his head and arms falling over the other side nearly into her lap. He looked up at her. "Yo."

"Yo yourself, Jack."

"It's Jacques. Told you a million times. *Jacques.*" Panting, he picked up his head to look at her, sweat pouring off his brow. "What, you go to law school to get stupid?"

Rebecca lifted an elbow toward the goal. "Nice shot. Is it harder with a goalie in the way?"

" 'Pends on the goalie. You wanna skate?"

"No, I wanna go bowling. What've I got?"

Jacques Kliesem glanced up at the digital clock high overhead on the massive scoreboard. "Twenty, thirty minutes till the Zamboni comes."

"You through?" she asked as she bent over to tighten the laces on the skates already on her feet.

Kliesem hung his head back down and exhaled a long breath. "Am I ever."

"Gimme a lift."

Kliesem dropped his stick on the ice and held out his arms. Rebecca turned and leaned back, falling into his hands, feeling the impossible strength as he lifted her straight into the air. He deposited her gently onto the ice and held on until he was sure she had her skates stabilized.

"You gettin' fat or what?"

"You losing muscle or what?"

He smirked at her, then leaned over the barrier to retrieve her shoes and set them up where she could easily reach them later.

"How you been keeping, Jack?" she asked as she picked her arms up overhead and leaned first to one side, then the other.

"Good." He pursed his lips and rocked his head back and forth, then bent over to pick up his stick. "I'm good. I get the urge, I just hit the ice a couple of hours, it goes away."

She nodded in understanding.

The urge for a heroin fix never went away; you just did your best to hold it in abeyance until you regripped. She had defended him on a simple possession charge as a favor to his girlfriend, an old classmate of Rebecca's from their undergraduate days. He had been a star amateur hockey player in Minnesota, come to the big city and gotten seduced by the life, spirited away by the easy promises of recreational pharmaceuticals and other seductions.

The plea bargain was one of those rarities in law when all the complex forces of rule, procedure and personnel coalesced into a single moment of sweet righteousness. It was clear to everyone that Kliesem wasn't cut out to be a chronic recidivist or troublemaker. The judge was a season ticket holder for the Los Angeles Kings and a personal friend of the coach, who gave Kliesem a day-to-day contract at the league minimum. If he could make the team and stay clean for six months, the judge would clear his record of any mention of the unpleasantness.

It was doubtful that Kliesem would see much ice time during the season because he really didn't have the stuff at that level, but the coach was so taken with his relentless determination and tireless work ethic that he kept him on, mostly as an inspiration to some of his other players who were slipping headlong into prima donna-ism. ("More we pay 'em, less they work. Go figure.")

Rebecca had handled the case *pro bono*, but the unexpected payback was worth more than money: on game days, the coach let her use the ice between the time practice ended and the Zamboni machine came to condition the surface for the evening's event.

She bent her knees slightly and put pressure on the blades of her skates, causing her to begin a slow slide away from him. "Get lost," she said, checking over her shoulder to see where the rough spots lay.

"Don't want me to watch?"

"Hell, no."

"Don't hurt yourself," he said as he moved off toward the long part of the rink to let himself out through the home team box.

Rebecca continued to skate backward, faster now, circling the rink and checking the stands to see who might be watching. Three or four of the cleanup crew, bored into near somnambulance, couldn't care less if the Rockettes were down there doing kicks buck naked.

She turned, skating forward, and raised a leg straight out behind her, dropping her head so her hands almost touched the ice. The friction between blade and ice melted the surface infinitesimally, creating a microthin layer of water over which the smooth metal rode like a hydroplane. The silky slip of the blade over the ice was a delicious feeling, like flying, with only occasional turbulence as the blade hit a gouge in the surface and sent a ripple through her legs.

She straightened up and twisted backward again, skate over skate, to pick up more speed, whipping around the opposite end of the rink in preparation for a final burst of acceleration down the straightaway. As she came out of the turn, a deep rut in the ice caught the outside edge of her left skate, stopped her foot from completing its pushoff and sent her tumbling toward the wall.

Instinctively, she flattened herself out so she hit the wall full length, distributing the force of the impact across as much of her body as possible. It didn't hurt much, and she rolled as she hit the ice and slid along the wall, letting the momentum dissipate without trying to fight it.

She slid to a stop just in front of the visitors' penalty box, on her back, staring up at the massive suspension struts that upheld the roof without the need for girders rising from the floor. Flying without support. She wondered: if the roof suddenly realized nothing was holding it up, would it collapse?

She closed her eyes and let the comforting coldness of the hard surface seep slowly through her sweater. In her mind, the distant roar of an appreciative crowd wafted her way, intermingled with the complex clanging of twin bars of nickel-plated steel beneath the feet of a figure skater as she leaped and whirled over pristine white porcelain. She could see the young girl's face clearly, the features tiny, rhinestone dots at the corner of prematurely hard eyes so they would glint into the cameras as she sped by. The smile so practiced and plastered that Rebecca couldn't believe the fans actually fell for it. Shouldn't have been too much of a surprise, though: they believed what the media told them to believe, and the media didn't make money by exposing the turbulent eddies below but by broadcasting only the sparkling surface, presenting it as all that is good and pure and noble. At least until the athlete stepped over some vaguely defined and largely arbitrary line, and then they gleefully ripped her to shreds.

Rebecca watched the graceful leaps, the sweeping arm motions.

Wendy. As she looked at fourteen years of age. Rebecca hadn't thought of her sister in weeks, and felt guilty for it. Despite herself, she could never resist the recurring urge to open the cardboard box she kept in a closet, to pull out the newspaper clippings, to pretend for a few seconds that things turned out differently than they actually had. Wendy won the world championships at the age of fourteen. Less than twelve weeks later, she and Uncle Charlie flew first class to Lake Placid—Rebecca and Mommy followed a few days later in a Dodge minivan—to compete in the Winter Olympic games, a two-week extravaganza whose sole purpose was to answer a single question: which new fairy princess would win the women's figure skating gold medal? The competition was fierce, the worldwide interest frenzied, and Wendy wiped up the floor with the other would-be Cinderellas, signing eighty million bucks' worth of endorsements before she even made it to the medal stand, Uncle Charlie as her manager lined up for twelve million in commissions, the family happy forever.

That had been the plan. It wasn't how things worked out. Too bad, since Wendy and Charles had spent hours rehearsing a special piece prepared by the choreographer. It started with Wendy sitting, eyes tightly shut, hands clasped beneath her chin, muttering something the crowd couldn't hear but they knew consisted of fervent praying. As soon as she heard the roar rise up from the stands, Wendy would open her eyes and her mouth in total shock, grab the sides of her head and look around in confusion, as though for confirmation. Her eyes would drift to the scoreboard and then she could begin squealing in earnest, and after the initial shock began to dissipate, she would leap up from the bench and sprint for the sidelines to give her uncle a hug.

No danger of her coach stealing the spotlight, either. Charlie'd had it written into his contract that the victory hug went to himself alone. Any deviation and the coach forfeited the bonus money for winning the Olympic gold.

Snapping herself back to the here and now, Rebecca rose to a sitting position, her back resting against the boards that circled the rink. Allen Wysocki had made it fairly clear that taking on *United States v. Tera-Tech Integrated, et al.,* was the career move of a lifetime. All she had to do was devote the next year of her life to publicly defending a man she'd rather be emasculating with pinking shears.

On the other hand, Wysocki had also made it pretty clear that refusing to take the case would likely spell the end of her career at the firm. She knew it would not come overnight, not with a forthright sacking, but over time, as she was assigned crap clients pressing crap cases that should have been flipped to green associates still studying for the bar.

She slapped her head, trying to clear it: what the hell was the big deal here, why all this *agita*? It was a simple business decision, that's all it was. She was a lawyer. James Perrein was a client, a rich and famous one at that. And there would be a hotshot federal prosecutor looking to make a name for himself by taking on a highly visible case. Wasn't she enough of a professional to put aside her inconsequential personal feelings and simply do the job she'd been trained for?

She draped her arms over her knees and dropped her head, rubbing her forehead back and forth until it hurt. Who was she kidding? Trapped in a courtroom for how many months next to a man with whom she had collided catastrophically and who likely hadn't the slightest idea of what he'd done to her life?

But maybe it wouldn't ever get to trial. She brightened momentarily and picked up her head. Maybe she could place the case out, without having to spend much time in the same airspace with

Perrein. Sure, that was a possibility. And, hey, maybe she could sprout wings and shit hundred-dollar bills while she was at it. . . .

She dropped her head back down onto her forearms. It was possible that, if she took the case, it could turn out disastrously. It was possible that her scrambled emotions would interfere with her effectiveness, possible that she would make a fool of herself, *possible* that she might even end up accused of malfeasance owing to her failure to clearly judge each strategy and tactic in the cold light of judicial propriety. All those things were *possible.*

But for damned sure, if she didn't give it a try, Wysocki would see to it that she ended up writing wills for nursing home residents in San Bernardino.

She was beyond trying to decide which was the best alternative to lean toward. It was only a question of which would be worse to avoid.

She had until morning.

C h a p t e r   5

Tuesday, May 26

It seemed to Rebecca that she was spending an awful lot of time lately trying to hide her discomfort from people. Maybe that was a symptom of lawyerly immaturity. Maybe the sign that you had graduated into the big leagues was when the effort to distinguish between truth and dissembling became so minimal it was natural, like breathing.

Rebecca was uncomfortable at this moment because she didn't know if she had been misleading this client all along or had just started a few minutes ago.

"But we're right, Rebecca," protested Robert Khoulek, president of Tamarack Ltd. "We're right and those bastards are wrong!"

Those bastards were Universal Data Systems, against whom Rebecca and her team had been vigorously supporting Tamarack's case. Heretofore, Rebecca had supported, even encouraged Khoulek's anger against the supplier of his company's new computer system. She had her expert witness, Jules Dirksen, exactly where she wanted him in terms of staking his entire reputation that UDS had badly wronged Tamarack.

"Bob," she replied soothingly, "let me ask you something." She looked deep into his eyes, as though challenging him to think hard, using only cold business logic. "You want justice, or you want the check?"

It was a loaded question, to which there could be only one answer. As phrased, it presupposed that the two options were mutually exclusive, and that to opt for justice was to place his personal desire for vengeance above the interests of his company. It intimated that the true titans of industry cared little for anything but the bottom line, and were willing to suffer humiliation and perceived defeat so long as the business benefited.

But she had underestimated Robert Khoulek's resistance to intimidation of that ilk. "Why one or the other? You're a good lawyer, we're in the right . . . why not see it through?"

A perfectly rational question. "Look, you assume that you're right and UDS is wrong, like that was some kind of basic truth just waiting to be discovered, and if I do my job right and the jury's paying attention, they'll discover that truth and simply announce it."

Khoulek nodded, because that was a pretty good description of how he saw things, despite Rebecca's faintly sarcastic tone and the intimation that he was mistaken.

"But the fact is," she continued, "as we sit here, Tamarack is neither right nor wrong. That determination doesn't exist out there somewhere, waiting to be discovered and revealed. All we have is a set of facts, and the two sides don't even agree on those."

She leaned forward and put a hand on his arm. "What I'm trying to tell you, Bob, is that the only thing that determines who's right in this case is the jury's verdict. And the very fact that this case has gone this far means that the jury's verdict is at least fifty-one percent crapshoot. If it were any more certain than that, UDS would have surrendered a long time ago."

She could tell from his expression that she'd gotten to him, and it was only a matter of closing the deal. "I'd love to keep taking your money, Bob. Believe me, it doesn't hurt my reputation around the office to make some steady rain." She sat back and let her hand drop onto her lap. "But I'm your lawyer, and I have an obligation to make sure you understand all the ramifications, the risks as well as the potential rewards."

"So why am I hearing this now, and not before?"

Another good question, and she was ready. "I sat with Dirksen during his deposition. He handled it well, but not that well."

"Maybe he's the wrong guy."

Rebecca shook her head. "He's good, but so is their guy; I could tell from the questions they were asking Dirksen, questions their expert armed their lawyer with. It's not just a matter of who's better, Bob: fact is, you've got some holes in your case. And we've discussed those. Deposing the experts is our best way of getting a handle on where they're going, and I'm telling you, this ain't no slam-dunk for us."

"So you're saying we should settle."

"If you can get a reasonable deal. That doesn't mean you walk away happy; that's not gonna happen. But a reasonable compromise, and—this is important now—one that doesn't depend on who's right and who's wrong. You gotta come into the negotiating assuming you're both equally at fault. That's the hardest part. Because compromise doesn't mean that they abandon their position in favor of ours."

Khoulek thought about it for a long time without speaking. Rebecca had gotten to know him well over the past few months, and sympathized with his feelings of outrage at the treatment his company had received from UDS. She wanted to beat them at trial as much as he did.

She also knew that he was a good businessman. "Won't we look weak," he asked, "approaching them about a settlement?"

It was over. "Not at all," Rebecca replied, keeping her voice calm and not displaying too much enthusiasm. The decision was supposed to be his; her job was just to lay it all out for him. "There's a mandatory settlement conference anyway, and we have to report to the judge that both sides made an honest, good faith effort to try to come to some agreement without requiring a trial."

Khoulek nodded as he considered this potentially face-saving procedure. "Unless I miss my bet," Rebecca said, "their attorney's having the same conversation with them. What I suggest, you and UDS's guy stay out of it at first. Let me sit down with their lawyer and work something out—we're both used to it and our egos won't get in the way."

Khoulek smiled at that last dig, as she knew he would. "What are you thinking?"

"A walkaway deal. Tamarack doesn't pay any of its outstanding bills, you keep all the hardware, and the crappy software if you want it, and hold UDS harmless from further liability."

"But then we throw away all the money we've already spent!"

"Yeah, you do. And UDS doesn't get full payment for all the hardware they sold you, or for all the man-hours they put in."

"They didn't put in those man-hours!" Khoulek retorted angrily.

"Of course not! That's why you're not going to walk away happy. And UDS will still lose a great deal of money and that's why *they* won't be happy!"

Rebecca stood up and began pacing. "Everybody's gonna be miserable," she admitted. "But both companies can lick their wounds and get back to business. You can use the money still left in the original budget to get somebody else in who can do the job."

"You mean like Dirksen?"

"No. Too much appearance of conflict. Dirksen won't want it to look like he supported you against UDS just so he could steal the business from them." *Dirksen probably wouldn't give a shit but, personally, I wouldn't let him program my VCR.* "Besides, I can find you much better guys to do this job."

She knew he wanted to leap at the deal, but that it was killing him to consider admitting defeat. And, might as well face it, worse yet to do so in front of a woman.

So she had to make defeat look like anything but. "I think the thing you have to consider is, what's the very best thing to do from a business point of view? If you put your hurt feelings aside"—*you wimp*—"and take a cold, hard look at this from a strictly bottom-line perspective"—*you manly, corporate stud, you*—"what's the most stand-up thing to do? What do you report back to your board of directors, that they got justice they didn't care about in the first place? Or that you stood up, took the hit and got the whole sorry mess behind them and got their business back on track. Which one you think they're gonna want?"

Right on the edge . . . time to push him over.

"Bob, you want to tell them the problem is over or that it's still a problem?"

Wednesday, June 3

Rebecca looked at her watch: ten minutes early. She got out of her car carrying only her leather-bound writing pad and a purse and walked across the parking lot, stepping onto the cobbled pathway between the Beckman Auditorium and a biological research building whose main walk was inlaid with a mosaic depicting stylized strands of DNA.

The California Institute of Technology's main campus in Pasadena usually escaped the thick marine layer that often blanketed the rest of the Los Angeles basin in June. It was at least ten degrees warmer here, away from the ocean, than on the West Side. The morning sun shone brightly, casting dramatic shadows across the southern slope of mile-high Mt. Wilson, and the observatory buildings standing out in sharp relief at the top seemed to be just across the street.

The sweet, heavy scents rising off the broad lawns and shrubbery added to the atmosphere of serenity that lay over the campus, masking the intellectual turbulence usually raging within its buildings. It could be argued that, at any given moment, there was more raw cerebral horsepower concentrated within these few acres than in any other place on the planet. Certainly there was no greater abundance of Nobel-canonized faculty members.

Rebecca had taken Wysocki's advice and left Ehrenright and Steinholz to read the full complaint and begin the preliminary work while she hunted for a suitable expert witness. Perrein's personnel department had put together a list of candidates based on their wide-ranging knowledge of who was who in the industry. While they were able to provide great precision in evaluating likely strengths and weaknesses and grouping the names according to desirability, what they couldn't do was assess the subject's willingness to participate in a criminal proceeding.

Rebecca's search was not going well. She had been turned down flat on the phone by the first three people on the list before she'd even had a chance to get into the details of her pitch. She was beginning to wonder if there wasn't some less volatile euphemism available to replace "expert witness," a phrase that seemed to be as repellent to many scientists as *pro bono* was to many attorneys.

Jessica Muller, the first woman on the list and a full professor on Cal Tech's electrical engineering faculty, had the same initial reaction. But Rebecca, falling back in desperation on an implied sisterhood-among-professionals theme, persuaded Muller to at least speak to her, if only to help her get a little more insight into why all the scientists in the A group were turning her down.

That was a bit of a ruse; Muller had been highly praised by Tera-Tech's human resources director, who had replaced Perrein's wife in that position a year earlier. Rather than immediately launch into a recruiting speech, as she had done with the other three, Rebecca planned to take this one slowly, establishing some kind of personal connection with Muller before moving into the hard sell.

It wouldn't be easy, considering that Muller had candidly warned her in the clearest possible terms that she would be wasting her time coming all the way to Pasadena.

She continued to wander the pathways connecting the old, ivy-covered structures, gradually making her way full circle until she came to the entrance of the electrical engineering building, a more modern edifice somewhat out of character with its immediate neighbors.

It surprised her that there were no guards in the lobby. She was so used to seeing security people in nearly all the buildings in which she did any kind of business that she had to remind herself that this was a university. She followed Muller's detailed and predictably overengineered instructions, emerging on the third floor, which consisted of a long hallway flanked by identical office doors. As she walked toward the fifth door on the right, she paused to read the obligatory academic humor taped to intervening doors: radioactivity warning labels, a "Gone Fission" sign, a music-loving professor's apology for his absence: "Out to lunch. Usually Bach by one. Offenbach sooner."

There was a cartoon on Muller's partially opened door as well: A confused-looking man in the witness box, dressed in overalls and a John Deere hat, was being cross-examined by an angry lawyer, who says, "So you admit it! *You* planted the corn used by the distillery to make the whiskey sold to the bar that served my client, causing him to have an accident while driving home drunk!"

Rebecca considered just turning around and leaving before she wasted any more time, when she heard a barely concealed giggle from behind the door. She pushed it farther open and found Professor Jessica Muller, eyes crinkling above the hand that was covering her mouth, watching her.

Muller, still laughing, dropped her hand on the doorknob and said, "Oh, God, don't tell me you don't have a sense of humor!"

Rebecca stared at her blankly, then looked at the cartoon and back at her again. She shrugged her shoulders and said, "But I don't get it."

Muller's smile disappeared and she stared at Rebecca, doing a poor job of hiding her disbelief.

"I mean," Rebecca said, looking at the cartoon again, "did the guy grow the corn or didn't he?"

Muller could only blink, not knowing what to do next.

Rebecca let it go on for another few seconds, then said, "*Now* who doesn't have a sense of humor."

Muller's jaw dropped as her eyes widened, and then she slapped Rebecca's forearm. "You had me going there!" She smiled broadly in appreciation for having been one-upped.

"Makes two of us," Rebecca replied as she followed Muller into the office. She stuck her hand out as she closed the door behind her. "Rebecca Verona."

"Jessica Muller." She shook Rebecca's hand, but without the kind of bone-crushing force often thought mandatory for a professional woman in a man's game. "Well, shit, if that didn't scare you away, might as well have a seat and get comfortable." She dropped down onto a well-worn chair at the side of her desk, and motioned for Rebecca to do likewise on a newer model opposite. "Your dime."

Rebecca set down her pad and purse and folded her hands in her lap. She wanted this to be as informal as possible, to reinforce the idea that she wasn't here to try to change Muller's mind.

"What I'm trying to understand," Rebecca began, then started over. "I don't have any problem with somebody who doesn't like my client or thinks he's slimy or whatever, and decides not to help us out." She waited for some response from Muller, who turned up her mouth and shrugged: *Sounds reasonable.* "But what I don't get," Rebecca continued, "is why people, you included, are telling me to go stick it in my ear before I even get a chance to tell you what the case is about."

Muller waited to make sure that Rebecca had finished framing her question, then looked up at the ceiling and scratched her neck. Rebecca figured her for about fifty years old, based mostly on the lines around her eyes she obviously made no attempt to hide. Her skin showed some minor sun damage, and Rebecca guessed her sport was tennis, and only on weekends. She was trim but not athletic, maybe five foot seven, her hair graying at the temples, again with no effort at concealment.

"You deal much with scientists?" Muller asked, still looking at the ceiling.

"Of course, all the time. Every case I—"

"Nah." Muller dropped her head back to level. "I'm not talking about guys searching for the next big bug spray or better suntan lotion." She narrowed her eyes and peered at Rebecca. "My guess is that you're used to dealing mostly with business scientists. Corporate guys. Researching product improvements for Procter & Gamble."

"As opposed to . . . ?"

"The kind who do basic research not knowing what they're going to find. Or if it's going to pay."

"Is there a difference?"

"Yeah, there's a difference." To Muller, it was such an obvious distinction she wasn't quite sure how to explain it. "One's an inventor, the other's an explorer."

"Very poetic. I don't get it. Is there, like, a moral here somewhere?"

Muller nodded, smiling, appreciating the barbed attempt to puncture her deliberate obfuscation. "Sort of. One searches for truth, the other tries to create it."

"Dr. Muller . . ."

"Jessica, listen. You know anything about the scientific method?"

"A little."

Muller sniffed. "Whatever you knew, you forgot. Part of your training required you to unlearn it. The scientific method is about verifiable truth. What you can't prove, you can't say. What you can't verify, you can't claim. There's no such thing as 'reasonable doubt.' The burden of proof is on everybody, not just one side. The only rule is reproducibility, and you don't convince with emotion or guile, you convince with experiment and hard results."

"And what does this have to do with being an expert witness in a lawsuit?"

"Working for one side, that's what. And being required to make statements that are simple and definitive when the world is complex and ambiguous. Answering *yes* or *no* when *probably* or *doubtfully* are the right answers." She stopped to draw a breath. "Devising premises to support a conclusion, when the opposite is more appropriate."

Rebecca started grinning somewhere in the middle of Muller's diatribe. "Hey, it took me four years of law school to learn all that!"

"And you learned it well, from what I'm told."

"You checked me out?"

"You checked *me* out . . ."

True. "But aside from all that abstract philosophy, what's your problem?"

Muller ran her hands up and down her face a few times, then rubbed her eyes. "Rebecca, you remember a case a few years ago, some poor guy driving along and he hits a horse?"

"Sure." It was a particular favorite of tort reformers everywhere.

"Way I remember it," Muller said, taking her hands from her eyes, "the horse damned near totaled the car. Guy's wife died. Well, the farmer who owned the horse, he didn't have a pot to piss in, especially seeing as how his only horse just died, so the driver sued the carmaker. Now"—she put one hand on the armrest of her chair and leaned on it, tilting her body in the other direction—"suing is one thing. But he won! And the carmaker had to pony up money, no pun intended, like they're the ones who stuck this horse in the middle of the road!"

"And that bothers you."

"Bothers me? What're you, kidding? Where's the logic in it! I not only do science, I teach it. I'm trying to get students to believe in the scientific method and then they go out and read about stuff like that. . . . How do I explain that there's still a role for reason in the world?"

Rebecca nodded thoughtfully, as though seeing Muller's point. "Okay, that's one example. Any others?"

"Hundreds of 'em. Some palm reader in Chicago. Somebody in the hospital leaves an X-ray machine on for too long and she claims she lost her psychic abilities. Couple hundred thousand dollars, I think that one was worth."

Rebecca listened respectfully. "That about it?"

"For starters." Muller was curious as to how Rebecca could possibly deflect these notorious examples of the law subverting science.

"Lemme ask you something," Rebecca said, unfolding her hands. "You say you're a scientist: how'd you hear about those cases?"

The question took Muller aback. She waved a hand idly. "I don't know. Read about them somewhere."

"Did you read the actual cases? Court transcripts? Legal summaries?"

Muller shook her head.

"But you assume they happened the way you read them."

"Didn't they?" Muller drew back slightly. "Why do I get the feeling I'm about to get my head handed to me?"

"Because you have good instincts. Let's take the car case. You're right, a guy driving his car along a back country road slams into this horse. The horse flies up into the air, lands on the roof, crushes it and kills the guy's wife." Rebecca spread her hands, seeking agreement on the basic facts.

"Okay." Muller spread her own hands, amiably mocking the nonargument Rebecca was making thus far.

"So the guy's lawyer is looking over the facts of the case, and something about the weight of the horse and how high it flew up over the car bothers him. So he gets hold of the federal safety standards for auto construction, then goes out and buys some used cars, exact same make, model and year, and he starts dropping horse carcasses on the roofs from various heights, and you know what?" Rebecca paused and leaned forward. "He finds out that this particular model doesn't meet the standard. By a long shot. And he also figures out that, if they had *been* in compliance, there's no way that horse could have crushed the roof."

She enjoyed having Muller's full attention. "And so the simple fact, Professor, is that if the manufacturer had built that car the way they were supposed to"—she sat back, keeping her eyes on Muller—"that guy's wife would be alive today."

Muller, hanging on Rebecca's words, stayed quiet for few seconds, then said, "Didn't know that." She snapped herself back into focus and said, "Okay, so that's one. What about the psychic? And no, I didn't read that case either."

"I did. She was in the hospital for some diagnostic X rays. Some half-assed technician not only turned the juice up way too high, he left the thing on for about ten times longer than he was supposed to."

"So she lost her psychic powers," Muller sneered.

"She claimed she did," Rebecca said, ignoring the sarcasm. "The jury threw that claim out."

Once again, Muller grew serious. "They did?"

Rebecca nodded slowly. "They did. But the X rays really did fry her brain. She had terrible migraines, severe memory loss, problems with motor skills . . . and that's why she was awarded damages. Headlines the next day? 'Woman who claims X rays destroyed her psychic abilities gets a million bucks.' Technically true, but deliberately misleading."

Rebecca watched Muller carefully. The scientist was considering this new information, processing it, running it up against her well-entrenched prejudices and weighing the impact. What Rebecca had told her was the truth, unvarnished by the overweening self-interest of paid lobbyists.

Rebecca had her now.

Muller looked toward the one window in her office, idly rubbed the spot beneath her nose, then looked back at Rebecca as she said, casually, "Fine. So now let's talk about breast implants."

Rebecca tried, for about half a second, to feign puzzlement at this strange non sequitur, but there was no sense in trying to fool Muller. Rebecca closed her eyes, but did manage to suppress the groan that threatened at the back of her throat.

"And one Allen Wysocki," Muller went on. "I believe you know him?" She smiled in glee at Rebecca's distress. "And don't bother to argue with me on this one, Ms. Verona, because I *know* that case." She stood up, turned, and reached toward a shelf about a foot above her head. "I *have* read the transcript." She grabbed a very thick, wide, loose-leaf binder and tugged at it until it dropped into her hands. "And I know *exactly* what happened."

She dropped the heavy binder on the edge of her desk right next to where Rebecca, with no attempt to conceal her embarrassment, was hanging her head. The loud thud startled her upright.

"And by the way," Muller concluded with exaggerated finality as she sat back down, "I use to fly little airplanes for fun." She tapped Rebecca on the knee to get her attention. "Notice I said, *used to.*"

"I noticed." Rebecca sighed. "Christ, you play rough!"

Muller bowed her head slightly in sportsmanlike acknowledgment of the compliment. "But I do provide tea for the wounded." She stood up again and set to the task of brewing up a pot.

Muller knew from the attorney's reaction that she didn't need to fill Rebecca in on why she no longer flew little airplanes for fun. It was because Allen Wysocki led a cabal that effectively destroyed the entire U.S. light airplane industry. In one case a pilot had pulled the front seat out of his Super Cub in order to mount a large cinema camera in front of where he was sitting, then insisted on taking off even after the airport operator, who pleaded with him not to, placed a van at the end of the runway to try to stop him. The pilot went ahead anyway, crashing into the van, and Wysocki went to work. He didn't sue the airport operator; he sued Piper, and won $2.5 million.

Wysocki sued on behalf of the estates of pilots who had cracked up their planes while stone drunk or whacked out on cocaine or who had simply run out of fuel. He sued manufacturers when their equipment hadn't even been on the plane. Even when Wysocki's gang lost, the manufacturers spent millions defending themselves. By the time his tiny hit team of a handful of law firms and expert witnesses was in full swing, the cost of an airplane had skyrocketed by fifty percent in order to cover the manufacturers' liability insurance premiums. Finally, both Cessna and Piper, grand and historic pioneers in the production of affordable airplanes, gave up and simply ceased production of light planes altogether.

That exhilarating experience taught Wysocki that there were no practical limits to what you could pull off within the boundaries of the law. But that was just the start. Wysocki didn't make real history until 1994.

"Four and a half billion dollars."

Muller looked down at the transcript and shook her head, then looked back up at Rebecca. "Not a shred of hard evidence that those implants caused any disease at all, and Wysocki and his street gang got the manufacturers to cough up four and a half billion dollars. And let's not forget a nice even billion for the attorneys."

She dipped a silver ball into a pot of hot water and waited for a defense from Rebecca, but none was forthcoming. She pulled the tea ball out of the pot and shook it up and down a few times, then laid it down on a saucer with a *clang*. "Take anything in it?"

"Yeah: double shot of strychnine."

When science failed Wysocki's case, he paraded the ill women themselves in front of the jury, and they defiantly proclaimed, "We *are* the evidence!" Then he and his pals completely redefined the role of the expert witness. No longer did experts have to cite evidence from the peer-reviewed literature to back up their opinions: it was now legitimate for them to stand up and say, "I'm an expert,

and I say so!" Their opinions *were* the evidence, and it was patheti-
cally easy to sway juries with emotion-laden displays and arguments that made science and logic not only irrelevant but downright
distracting.

Muller poured the strong tea into two cups and handed one to
Rebecca, who took it gratefully. "Those experts," Muller said, between puffs of breath on her tea. "You think anybody in that field
still respects them?"

"But they were professional, and well credentialed." Rebecca
took a small swallow from her cup and grimaced slightly as the hot
liquid touched her tongue. "Why don't you trust other professionals in your field?"

"Because any whore scientist can manufacture evidence out
of thin air." Scowling, Muller set her cup down on its saucer so
she could gesture with a free hand. "Hell, the tobacco companies
do it all the time. And then you get a bunch of jurors who never
made it past the fifth grade and can't tell DNA from DOA, and
you ask them to make billion-dollar decisions based on complex
epidemiology?" She shook her head and reached for the cup again.
"C'mon, some of them can't even stay awake during the testimony.
Plaintiffs' attorneys love those kind of juries: they can confuse the
living hell out of them and get them to vote based on who wears
the nicest suits in court!"

Rebecca was not about to argue, and also wasn't about to add
that the educational level of the juror was irrelevant: every magi-
cian knew that—the smarter the audience, the easier they were to
fool. All you had to do was convince them that the "right" verdict
was a resounding validation of their intelligence and a vindication
for the hapless plaintiffs who, while clearly victims of *something*,
were not necessarily victims of the defendant.

"I understand what you're saying, Jessica, but you have to
understand, those were all civil cases. Mine is a criminal case.
They're different."

Rebecca moved toward the window and sat down on the sill.
"In a civil matter, you're basically being asked to testify as to who's
the bad guy, based mostly on a lot of gray areas, most of which are
in your head. But you don't really know. Nobody does, because—
and don't quote me on this—hardly anybody ever really is or isn't."

Muller shook her head once, sharply, and opened her eyes wide.
"Now you lost me."

"It's all a matter of interpretation. Sure, everybody'd like to think that someone either did it or didn't, but he's only guilty or innocent when a jury *declares* him to be guilty or innocent. Up until then, who the hell really knows?"

Muller stayed silent as she considered it, so Rebecca kept pressing. "As an expert witness in a criminal case you don't get as caught up in shading your opinions, because the central question is very black or white, a matter of facts and not opinions."

Rebecca got up off the windowsill and returned to her chair. "Jessica, I'm not asking you to testify as to whether my client's a good citizen or a traitor or a criminal. All I'm asking is, come and help figure out if he made the chips. It's all science, no bullshit."

"You're very persuasive." Muller exhaled slowly. "But it still doesn't wash with me. I watched a lot of good experts get trashed in the Simpson case, and that was supposed to be science, too."

The instant Rebecca heard those words, she knew it was all over. Muller leaned back, watching the disappointment Rebecca failed to hide, and then thought it only fair not to let the impassioned attorney feel that her arguments had fallen on unsympathetic ears. "I've got to tell you one more thing, as long as we're here."

Rebecca looked up, not really interested in the substance of anything else Muller had to say at this point, but finding herself liking the scientist despite her refusal to consider joining the defense.

"Rebecca, there is no way in hell I'd ever perform any service for a firm run by Allen Wysocki. Then I'd be just another whore working for the biggest pimp of all."

It took Rebecca a moment to get past her surprise at this harshly delivered observation and consider one of its implications. "Which is what you're saying I am?"

"I didn't mean that at all."

Rebecca believed her, but didn't have the stomach to refute her assessment of Wysocki. Bottom line, Rebecca was fairly sure she'd feel the same way if their roles were reversed.

Fact was, Rebecca detested Wysocki and everything he stood for, which she considered to be the dark underbelly of the law that gave attorneys such a bad name. But to tell Muller of the acrid bile that rose in her throat at each new display of Wysocki's titanic conceit would mean that she would also have to tell her why she continued to work for him, which was basically because it was rare for an up-and-coming associate to leave a partnership track in a prestigious firm for something as petty as principles. Besides, nothing obligated her to practice law the way Wysocki did, and she was getting an entire career's worth of experience just being around the firm and working with its near-mythical elder statesman, whose bell jar of despicability she would leave one day when the timing was right.

It was just as well that Muller wasn't going to join the case anyway. Rebecca could see that the scientist was extremely intelligent, fiercely independent, possessed of a well-developed sense of right and wrong, concerned about justice, the scientific method, and professional integrity . . . in short, everything you didn't want in an expert witness.

Rebecca liked her experts malleable. Not liars—not exactly—but people not so single-minded that they couldn't accommodate subtle shades of difference and nuance, who grasped the impact of slight shifts in mood, tone and choice of words. People who wouldn't stare at the courtroom ceiling and ponder philosophy, murmuring damaging inanities like, "Yes, well, I rather suppose that might be a possibility," but instead could say, "No, it's *not* possible, period," and could stick to it even under withering cross-examination that would crush weaker mortals. Witnesses who would do things her way, and grasped from the outset what her way was without needing to be told explicitly, who understood the nature of the complex, unspoken agreement that when they took the client's money, there were services to be rendered for that money, a compact that didn't brook a lot of high-minded, conceptual rumination on the finer points of the basic thesis required to go to bat for her client. Essentially, the lawyer had a right to the testimony her client had paid for.

Which didn't mean you could be careless. You didn't want some smart-ass prosecutor coming up to your witness during cross and thundering, "Excuse me, Professor: In your testimony during *Darryll* v. *Darrell* twenty years ago, didn't you come to exactly the *opposite* conclusion?"

No. Rebecca liked Jessica Muller, Ph.D., but she would never do. She was what attorneys called *the dark expert of the soul.*

So that was that. "Well, I tried." Rebecca sighed as she slapped her thighs and stood up, behaving with as much good grace as she could summon up over her disappointment. "It was nice of you to give me the time, anyway, and I appreciate it."

She held out her hand. Muller stood quickly and grasped it with both of her own. "I enjoyed it. Debating with you, I mean. You should've been a scientist."

"You should've been a lawyer."

Rebecca let go and bent to pick up the writing pad she'd left on the floor. Muller opened the door in preparation for escorting her down the hall, but Rebecca stopped her and pointed to the cartoon still on the door.

"Mind if I have this? There's this guy, I swear he really won't get it."

"It's yours." Muller reached under the piece of tape and detached the cartoon, handing it to Rebecca.

"One thing occurs to me," Muller said as they began walking down the corridor together. "I were you, I wouldn't be all that worried. Without an actual chip in hand, the whole case is, what do you call it, circumstantial? Moot? How does anybody expect to prove who made a chip without even seeing the damned thing?"

"It's a good point," Rebecca answered, her admiration for Muller rising another notch. "But the real point is that the government thinks it has a case. They brought an indictment, and those guys ain't dummies, believe me."

"I suppose not." They arrived at the elevator and Muller said, "Listen, the guy you really want to go after is Radovan Terescu." If Rebecca's face betrayed anything at the mention of that name, Muller didn't seem to catch it. "There's nobody in the world knows more about this stuff than Rado."

"I've heard the name."

"He's working on something called an *ovalauricle wire*. My guess, it's going to revolutionize the microchip and probably win him a Nobel prize. I could give him a call . . . ?"

"Let me think about it. Thanks again, Jessica," she added quickly before Muller had time to consider why she had declined the offer to introduce her to Terescu.

Exiting the building onto Cal Tech's lush campus, Rebecca inhaled deeply but took no pleasure in the mixed scents of newly cut grass, honeysuckle and the freshly baked pretzels being sold just outside the Beckman Auditorium.

All in all, she'd accomplished only one solid thing in the time spent with Muller. She'd made sure to tell the scientist just enough confidential information about the case to create a potential conflict that would prevent the prosecution from ever soliciting Muller's assistance for their side.

Then she realized that Muller would never consider it anyway. So she really had wasted her time.

Chapter 6

Tuesday, June 9

Despite the half dozen unresolved major issues swarming around in her head, Rebecca did her best to try to keep this meeting with Arno Steinholz and Justin Ehrenright on track and orderly. The issue of the moment was whether they could count on the prosecution's case being largely circumstantial owing to the fact that they didn't have an actual microchip in hand.

"Do we know that for sure?" Steinholz asked.

"How could they possibly have one?" Ehrenright, with a talent for seeing to the heart of things and moving on, often chided Steinholz for his tendency to add layers of often irrelevant nuance that only complicated their analyses. "Whud they do, steal it right out from under the Chinese?"

"Well, what if they have one that was never sent overseas?" Steinholz insisted. *His* talent lay in quickly identifying ramifications and intricacies that needed to be considered in case the other side was also considering them. He felt that it was his job to balance out Ehrenright's unfortunate proclivity for oversimplification and inattention to potentially critical subtlety. "Suppose they got one before it left the country, maybe even bought it undercover, pretending to be agents of another country or something?"

Rebecca relied on the dynamic but collegial tension between them, encouraging the spirited debates from whose chaos truth and order inevitably emerged. "How would that tie Tera-Tech to the Chinese specifically?" she asked Steinholz.

"Maybe they think they can show that Tera-Tech made it, and therefore Tera-Tech was the one that sold it to the Chinese."

Ehrenright shook his head. "Showing that Tera-Tech made it

still doesn't prove they sold it to the Chinese. Doesn't even prove that it's the same one the Chinese have."

"If the Chinese even have one. How do we know that?"

"We don't. But it's in our discovery request." The discovery process was the mechanism by which each side fulfilled its legal obligation to provide certain information to its opponent. Unless stymied by successful objections, discovery requests were tantamount to court orders compelling the production of evidence and its transfer to the adversary. Which didn't mean that the other side couldn't play a wide variety of games to try to avoid compliance.

Rebecca let the discussion go on until she felt that they had pretty much exhausted the topic, and then redirected them toward worrying about her failure thus far to secure a suitable expert witness.

"It's interesting," she observed, "that the prosecution hasn't yet approached any of the people I've been speaking with. I mean, considering how much time they've had to do that before they even handed down the indictment."

"Not all that surprising in a federal case, actually." Steinholz stretched his arms high above his head and moved them from side to side, trying to relieve some of the stiffness in his shoulders. "Zuckerman's probably just gonna use a government witness, maybe someone from the FBI or the NSA. They've got a boatload of technical wizards who— Becky?"

Steinholz stopped moving his arms and looked at Rebecca, who was staring back at him, openmouthed and apparently not listening to a word he was saying. He waved a palm up and down. "Hello? Earth to Verona . . ."

"Who?" she said softly.

Steinholz frowned. "Who what?"

"The prosecutor." She cleared her throat to get rid of the gravel in her voice. "The one you said was going to use government experts."

"You mean Zuckerman?" Steinholz heard Ehrenright ineffectively stifle a small giggle, and was about to do the same when he saw that Rebecca wasn't laughing. Or smiling. Not even a little.

Steinholz dropped his arms and surreptitiously waved a hand at Ehrenright to get him to quiet down. "Didn't you know?" His tone had gone from casual to deferential, even solicitous.

Rebecca could only shake her head, as though in a trance.

Steinholz looked at the papers in front of him. "I mean, that's some coincidence."

Ehrenright grunted. "What's so surprising? Zuckerman's the government's number one technology guy in this district."

Rebecca knew that they were aware that there used to be some kind of a thing between Zuckerman and her. They thought it was no big deal, and besides, it was fairly common for attorneys too busy to cultivate relationships outside their own professions to find themselves defaulting to other lawyers.

But that's all they knew.

"Jeez, Verona," Steinholz said, holding up the thick sheaf of papers. "Didn't you read this thing?"

She shook her head slowly, appearing to her colleagues' relief to come out of the trance a little. "Wysocki wanted me to go out hunting experts while you two read—"

Wysocki . . .

Secretaries, associate attorneys and a few clients quickly stepped aside to avoid the small sonic boom Rebecca was leaving in her wake as she careened through the suite in the direction of the managing partner's office. Torpedoing her way past the laughably ineffectual protestations of his secretary, she tore open the door and stormed in.

There were two men sitting in the chairs in front of Wysocki's desk. The managing partner stayed cool. "Rebecca . . . ?"

Clamping her jaw together so tightly it hurt, she said to the two visitors, "Would you gentlemen be so kind as to excuse us for a moment? Bit of an emergency."

The two wasted no time clearing out, much as would a seaside population before an impending force five storm.

Wysocki crossed his arms but didn't say anything, waiting.

Rebecca hadn't given any thought to the words she would use once she actually got here. "David Zuckerman's the prosecutor on the Tera-Tech case," was all she managed initially, but she felt the magma building up somewhere down below.

Wysocki blinked, pointed toward the door and recrossed his arms. "Those were potential clients I was meeting with."

"You told me not to read the indictment," she said, ignoring his comment and trying to ignore the pressure in her chest that made it difficult for her to speak coherently. "You told me to get started tracking down experts."

Wysocki, unmoving, waited for her to continue, but when she didn't, he said, "*This* is the emergency?"

Wysocki's glib sarcasm finally tore open the thin crust holding back the seething lava. "You bastard!" Rebecca spat at him as she advanced toward his desk. "You stopped me from reading that thing so I wouldn't find out Zuckerman was prosecuting!" She came up behind one of the visitor's chairs and gripped the back of it, the feral look in her eyes causing Wysocki to subconsciously lean back away from her. "Did you and that sonofabitch Perrein dream this up together?"

"No," he answered as calmly as he could, his voice conveying the impression that he was under no obligation to respond to the accusation, and was doing so only out of courtesy despite her wholly inappropriate outburst. "I didn't even know about Zuckerman."

When Rebecca straightened up slightly, loosening her grip on the back of the chair as she considered his reply, Wysocki relaxed a little. "You getting paranoid, Rebecca? Seeing conspiracies in everything James Perrein does?"

"I doubt it."

"After all, he admitted freely that he wants you on this case because you hate him. He was straight about that, wasn't he?"

"Are you fucking kidding me?" The malevolence that had begun to dissipate reestablished itself with full vigor at his preposterous and self-serving naïveté. "The only reason Perrein wants me on this case is because my old boyfriend is the prosecutor! Why the hell do you think Perrein stopped his corporate lawyer from objecting to the venue in Los Angeles?" She didn't bother to wait for a response, but banged her hand on the chair and said, "It's because Zuckerman's name was on the indictment!"

This was obviously news to Wysocki. He put his palms together, prayerlike, and touched the tips of his fingers to his lips as he contemplated this new state of affairs.

Rebecca stayed quiet, knowing that Wysocki was smart enough to grasp all the implications, and started to regret her intemperate and apparently misdirected outburst.

"Boy!" Wysocki said suddenly, chuckling as he broke into a wide grin. "You really gotta hand it to that guy!" He shook his head in admiration and wonder as he let his hands come apart and drop onto his legs with a loud slap. "He's one smart cookie, all right!"

Rebecca, reverting once again to pit bull mode, thought, *Yeah, a sonofabitch piranha like you would think that was cute!* But, honoring a faint self-preservation signal emanating from somewhere deep within her brain, she kept it to herself. "I want you to tear up the engagement letter naming me lead counsel on the case."

"Too late," he said, smile fading. "Already been accepted and signed."

Rebecca was at a loss and Wysocki, with as much solemnity and compassion as he could muster, said gently, "I didn't think Zuckerman's presence on the case would make any difference, Rebecca."

A cascade of synapses clicked in Rebecca's brain, and she jerked her head back toward him, eyes widening. "I thought you said you didn't know about Zuckerman."

Gotcha!

Bad move. "Hey!" Wysocki's eyes suddenly grew cold and hard and he stood up, hands on his desktop, leaning forward. Any trace of deference or tolerance he might have been showing her evaporated as he lifted one hand to point at her threateningly. "Don't give me any more mouth, miss!"

He waited until he saw some sign of surprise in her eyes, maybe a little fear, then straightened up and ran his hand over his tie. He brought his voice under control to underscore his authority, the kind that required no shouting to make sure the other person was listening. "I cut you a lot of slack, but don't you *ever* forget who's running things around here!"

He paused, making sure that there was no more defiance coming his way, then tugged at the bottom of his vest and sat down. "Now you're either on this case or you're out of the firm, so go cool off somewhere until you can stop thinking with your crotch!"

"Allen—"

"We're through, Verona." Wysocki depressed a switch on his intercom. "Kathy?" he said in a tone so calm and mellow it contained not a hint that anything unpleasant had just transpired. "Would you ask Kenny and Vic to come back in, please? Thanks."

He looked back up at Rebecca, and waited for her to leave. The door opened behind her, and she forced herself to be professional, acting pleasant to Wysocki's two visitors, apologizing charmingly for the interruption. "But, once again, Allen's taken care of it as he always manages to do somehow."

They never caught the sarcasm, and were profuse in their insistence that she think nothing of the little interruption, looking leeringly from her chest to her face and back again. Kenny obviously considered the interruption a small price to pay for that brief introduction to her right breast, and Vic felt the same way about the left. She sized up the soft skin puffing around their necks and the uncoordinated slouch of their limbs, and was fairly certain she could render them both unconscious before they even realized what hit them, but desisted.

She was too upset to pay much attention to the locker room giggles coming from behind Wysocki's closed door as she walked away and tried to visualize what it would be like defending a former lover whom she hated from a prosecutor she'd never quite gotten over.

Chapter 7

Tuesday, June 16

It wasn't getting off to a great start.

Not because of her brawl with Wysocki; she'd pretty much gotten over that, having unleashed her frustration on Steinholz. That conversation made her feel better, not because she'd managed to do anything about the situation, but because she'd stymied Steinholz into seeing it her way. "Damn, Rebecca," he'd said. "Couldn't you have gone in there calm and businesslike and discussed it like two professionals?" And she'd replied, "You have polite discussions if you have a reasonable difference of opinion. How do you have a polite discussion with someone who deliberately misled you and tricked you? What do you say, 'Gosh, Allen, can I have a few minutes to discuss what a lying sack of shit you are?'" Having actually rendered Arno Steinholz mute by force of logic was very satisfying, as long as she didn't take into account the propriety of bashing the managing partner in front of an associate.

Rebecca, not exactly a gold medalist in the keeping-one's-temper event, nevertheless prided herself on the pains she took not to let any private animosities interfere with the business of winning cases. That determination was likely to be sorely tested in *United*

States v. *Tera-Tech Integrated* given the heady mix of personal interests she had in the case's primary participants. And her own assessment of how well she was keeping the lid on was often at variance with the less subjective opinions of colleagues she trusted.

It wasn't going to be easy, and that's why she wished things had gotten off to a better start, because the beginning of the trial was only four months off and she still didn't have an expert witness in whom she had great confidence.

It wasn't for lack of trying, or for lack of qualified people: Tera-Tech's personnel department had done an excellent job of drawing up its list, as Rebecca was discovering as each top-drawer candidate turned her down. Their objections, although often couched in stereotypically inflated academic prose, were beginning to reveal a pattern of several basic categories.

Some were fearful of angering the lawyers, and thereby not being paid, if they felt unable to put the desired spin on their findings. Some felt that if the other side won, even if they deserved to win, it was too easy for everyone to blame the expert for having done a bad job. Others didn't want the loftier-principled of their colleagues to think they were whores, betraying the purity of their avocation to the Mammon of more economically motivated pursuits. And some, but surprisingly few, simply didn't have the time, unwilling as they were to shortchange their research in favor of a diversion that did nothing to advance either human knowledge or their own careers, not necessarily in that order.

Rebecca's frustration peaked during a conversation with Professor Beresford Tipton of Berkeley, during which she listened to him prattle on for a half hour of seemingly interminable philosophical discourse on the flaws inherent in American jurisprudence, most of them relating to the indefensibility of illogical rules governing the introduction of evidence. He was just transitioning to the pestilent influence of free market imperialism on the structure of the court system when Rebecca, worn out and losing patience not just with him but with all of them, interrupted to blurt out, "Don't you even care anything about justice?"

Tipton, startled out of autopilot lecture mode, thought carefully about her challenge before responding. "Justice?" he repeated. "Okay, I'll tell you what: I'll serve as your expert if you agree to put me on the stand no matter what I find, and let me tell it in my own words. Can't get more just than that, so what do you say?"

Rebecca's dogged efforts were especially exasperating because another theme that ran through all her interviews was that the man she really wanted was Professor Radovan Terescu. Reluctant as the scientists were to acknowledge it, they grudgingly admitted that he probably knew more about chip fabrication than anybody on the planet, and had even been mentioned as a Nobel prize candidate for his dazzling creation of something called X-ray laser etching, which they hadn't bothered to describe and Rebecca studiously avoided asking about. Two of them also mentioned the ovalauricle wire, just as Jessica Muller had. Rebecca had a tough time squirming out of explaining why Terescu wasn't being considered.

Nevertheless, she did manage to get several reasonably good candidates in the pipeline. They each had the requisite credentials, at least on paper. Ph.D.'s from top schools, respected articles in major professional journals, countless speaking engagements around the world.

But none of them seemed to have done any notable work in recent years, which rendered suspicious the currency of their technological knowledge. While one or two managed to scrounge incomes off the speaking circuit as their grant money dried up, the others seemed to be living primarily off the expert witness tour. They had their patter nailed down as though they were auditioning for lead roles in a Shakespeare festival. Gradually, Rebecca came to realize that their dearth of recent publications had less to do with lack of time than with fear of going on the record with things that could later be used against them in court. Better to keep one's opinions private than print them for any opposing counsel in the country to dig up and use in cross-examination.

Now that she had a workable though far from exemplary stable from which to choose, Rebecca decided to have a go at Terescu anyway. He would be the ideal choice, even better than Jessica Muller, despite Perrein's warning that Terescu would never agree to help them. What could be better than a witness who hated the client nevertheless acting on his behalf, except maybe a *lawyer* who hated him doing the same thing, which they already had? The love of justice triumphing over personal animus would be very powerful in court.

She picked up the phone and dialed the private number she had gotten from Jessica Muller, so she wasn't surprised when he answered himself.

"Doctor Terescu, my name is Rebecca Verona. Does that ring a bell?"

"Ah . . . afraid not, Miss Verona." His voice was pleasant and friendly, betraying no annoyance that a stranger had obtained and used his private office number. "Are we acquainted or are you famous?"

Rebecca laughed. "Neither. I'm an attorney." Silence at the other end. "For Tera-Tech Integrated." Even heavier silence, and she could swear that the temperature of the phone she was holding dropped ten degrees, so she hurried on. "Please, Professor: just give me a few seconds."

"I'm listening." It sounded like a cross between a threat and a dare.

"Tera-Tech and its president have been accused of some wrong-doing by the U.S. government. We believe that the charges are completely false. And we need an expert in microelectronics, someone of your ability and stature, to look at the evidence and help us figure out what's really what."

The flattery bought her nothing. "You're a defense attorney; you're paid to believe the charges are false."

"That's true. But in this case I think we'll be able to prove it. Now look, I know there's some bad blood between you and James Perrein—"

"Bad blood?" Despite hearing only two syllables, it was easy for Rebecca to detect that some strong emotions underlay his words. "He stole my best graduate student right out of my lab. A student who was privy to one of my key discoveries, who took everything I taught him to Tera-Tech's research division. Is that sufficiently compelling to warrant some bad blood?"

She had to think fast to try to save this. "I understand. Look, I'm going to be candid with you: I don't like him much myself. We had a run-in of our own in the past. But I'm trying not to let that get in the way of doing what's—"

"Ms. Verona." She stopped immediately. "Your attitude is admirable. I doubt it would be so had your little 'run-in' been of more consequence . . ."

Rebecca felt an urge to zing him a good one for that baseless assumption, but restrained herself, trying to keep the objective in mind.

". . . but I assure you, my sense of justice does not extend to helping provide it to Mr. Perrein. Guilty or not, I'll celebrate the day he's convicted."

"Wait a minute, Professor—"

"Ms. Verona, please don't force me to be rude and hang up in the middle of your sentence. There's nothing to discuss."

She waited a moment, and when he didn't hang up, said, "Thanks for your time, sir."

"You're welcome," he replied, and clicked off.

Monday, June 30

Rebecca made her way down the corridor toward the conference room that her team had expropriated for the duration of the case. It had a lock on the door, to be used without fail whenever the room was not occupied. Only Rebecca, Ehrenright and Steinholz had keys. When the case was concluded the locks, as per firm policy, would be changed prior to the next case.

Steinholz had summoned her to the conference room over the intercom. Only nine-thirty Monday morning and she could tell from his voice that there was already bad news. That wasn't surprising: you rarely got good news in the middle of a case. Most of it consisted of setbacks that you tried to view as a natural part of the process.

"So," she said as she entered and took a seat. "Our client molest a goat or something?"

"Wish he had," Steinholz said. "Could say it was consensual."

"We got our first batch of discovery replies from Zuckerman," Ehrenright said, tapping a pile of folders in front of him. "Usual bullshit objections and refusals. Except this." One folder lay separate from the stack. Ehrenright picked it up and let it drop.

"Which is . . . ?" Rebecca prompted him.

"They have one of the chips."

Rebecca could only stare at him at first. "Where'd they get it?" she managed finally.

"They don't say."

"They *have* to say!"

"And they will," Steinholz put in. "As soon as we sign federal secrecy agreements."

Rebecca had stiffened as they were speaking, as if poised to spring into action and handle the situation, show the guys that she was prepared for anything and thrown by nothing.

"Shit," she said softly, then slumped back in her chair and sighed. There was no putting a brave face on this one.

"They got it out of China," she said, mostly to herself.

Chapter 8

It was like abandoning the old case and starting a completely new, completely different one. All of the contingent strategies they had been developing were effectively rendered useless, having been based on the expectation of a circumstantial prosecution case consisting largely of indirect evidence.

But now the government had revealed that they had physical possession of one of the microchips in question. Justin Ehrenright's first reaction had been to file a motion for sanctions, considering that the prosecution had deliberately misled them into thinking they didn't have the chip. Clearly, they must have had it for months, and Ehrenright ranted on about their callous disregard for procedure, their duplicity in perpetrating a fraud upon the defense, and several other equally egregious and potentially felonious violations of the time-honored canons of due process.

Of course, as Rebecca and Steinholz well knew, the prosecution had played strictly by the book in seeing to it that her team wasted most of its valuable preparation time. No paper filed by the government, beginning with the indictment itself and on down through the latest batch of discovery replies, hinted even remotely that they didn't have a chip. It didn't say they *did* have one, either, but there was nothing in the filing of the charges that required them to reveal evidence beyond that necessary to convince the grand jury to hand down the indictment in the first place, and Zuckerman could have met that standard without writing more than would fit on his business card.

Then the government had stalled, quite legally, in providing the required discovery information requested by Rebecca's team, filing objections that they knew would be overruled but would waste time. Rebecca could try to protest those, but then Zuckerman would come after her for having pulled the same stunts in stonewalling the prosecution, so it was a zero-sum game and both sides let it go.

Which didn't alleviate Rebecca's new set of worries based on her revised perception of the strength of the government's case, which had risen from questionable to seriously troublesome. Following a sudden impulse before she could stop to figure out its origin, she called Jessica Muller.

"Rebecca. Good to hear from you! You miss the sound of my voice?"

"That's exactly it," Rebecca replied, glad that Muller seemed pleased to hear from her. "I love the sound of people telling me to go jump in a lake and nobody's done it in a while . . ."

". . . so you figured you'd called me. Okay: go jump in a lake. Since this is undoubtedly about you trying to recruit me again, might as well get it out of the way early."

"Very considerate. But there's a new twist."

"Rebecca—"

"They have an actual chip. The government, I mean. They've got one."

Muller stayed quiet for a few seconds. "Really?"

"So they say."

"Huh." Rebecca could practically hear her synapses firing. "Certainly presents a problem for your client."

"And one hell of an opportunity for any engineer in a position to get *her* hands on one."

"I caught the *her*. Boy oh boy . . ."

"We'll have to open it up, you know."

Rebecca heard Muller catch her breath. "They gonna let you do that?"

"They won't have a choice."

More silence, then Muller sighed. "Doesn't change anything, Rebecca. All my objections still apply."

But I got you close, didn't I! "Will you at least think about it a little? For the sisterhood," she threw in playfully.

Muller made a gagging sound. "Listen: I'm the only sister *in* this locker room. Yeah, I'll think about it, but only to maybe throw some ideas at you."

"You really wouldn't even consider—"

"Not if wild crows were pecking out my eyes. But if I get any useful thoughts, I'll give you a call. Maybe we can do lunch someday soon."

"I'd like that, you with your huge budgets and all."

Meeting several minutes later with Steinholz and Ehrenright, Rebecca declined to tell them that she had tried once again with Muller. It was now their immediate task to sift through the backgrounds of the four experts on their short list and choose one. That choice would be further contingent on a series of interviews to make sure that the finalist could not only handle himself in front of a jury but would have the requisite compliability to fervently support their case.

Feeling down, and not wanting to infect her colleagues with her potentially contagious melancholy, she left them alone to start the process without her. She figured that the best favor she could do them would be to knock off for an hour or two and clear her head.

She stopped at a salad-by-the-pound shop and put together a lunch, then headed for Santa Monica, finding a bench along the bluffs that overlooked the Pacific. She ate while watching in-line skaters rolling up and down the strand, wondering how it was possible that so many people in southern California could have that much leisure time on a weekday. Flexible jobs she could understand, but what was this barely pubescent, darkly tanned future blond bombshell coming her way doing out of school?

The young girl, lean, fit and flexible, did a perfect pirouette without discernibly slowing her forward motion. As she drew closer, Rebecca could see that her eyes were half closed, seeing only enough to avoid a collision, as she moved through a world of her own. Her movements were fluid and graceful, without a hint of either effort or concern that she might flub a maneuver and fall. To her they weren't even maneuvers, Rebecca realized, not a formalized series of carefully prescribed steps. She was just doing whatever she felt like, and doing it very well.

It sent a reminiscent shiver through her, a pang echoing faintly from the distant past. She looked down at the salad in her lap, her former hunger now forgotten. She was up for some serious self-flagellation, so she thought about the time Uncle Charles Malacore had one of his little chats with Wendy while a physical therapist worked on her younger sister's knee. Young Rebecca, cramping badly from some spoiled mystery meat dredged up from the ice rink's culinary archives, watched from the doorway and waited for a break in the strictly one-way conversation as Charles tried to help Wendy understand her problem, which was a combination of ingratitude, lack of discipline, insufficient drive, too much whining and slacking off, and no competitive fire. An interesting set of deficiencies for an athlete considered by most experts to be on the verge of winning the world championship.

And Wendy certainly had no appreciation for just how big this deal with the Coca-Cola people could be, even though Charles made her swill down gallons of the stuff every time she left the house, despite the carbonation making her stomach hurt during practice. There were Coca-Cola bumper stickers all over the car, logos all over her schoolbooks . . .

Well, it doesn't pay dime one unless you win the Worlds, Charles hammered at her. *That's the bottom line right there, miss. No gold, no sponsorship. It's simple. Even you can understand that, can't you? Or maybe you just don't care. Is that it? You don't care? Don't care what we've sacrificed? You're not willing to work hard because you don't appreciate our sacrifice?*

Rebecca always wondered whether she had been the only one in the room who could see the tiny tear trickling down her sister's cheek, the balled fists pressed against her thighs. When Charles momentarily ran out of breath and words, Rebecca hazarded an interruption. "Uncle Charlie . . . ?"

It was a serious mistake. After Charlie threw her out of the room, the rest was a blur, walls and corners strobing past her stinging eyes until, on the ground and sobbing uncontrollably, Rebecca looked up to find her mother standing above her, watching, making no move to help her.

Rebecca got control of her crying and looked up at her mother, hoping for everything, expecting nothing.

"Did you interfere again, Rebecca?"

Steel doors began shutting down in the little girl's soul.

"Didn't Uncle Charles tell you a million times—"

He was still Uncle Charles back then. Only later in life would he metamorphose in his niece's mind from Uncle Charles into the Pumpkin King.

As the lanky collection of the skater's loose limbs continued to flow toward her like a thread of mercury, Rebecca tried to recall the exquisite feeling of defying a hard, unyielding surface, motivated by nothing other than the pure joy of it. It occurred to her that the last time she'd felt that way was on a crisp winter's afternoon on a frozen pond in Brooklyn's Prospect Park, her left hand comfortable and warm somewhere inside her father's large, callused, soothing mitt. After that—after Vincenzo Verona died—it was all business. All nightmare. After that, she couldn't recall a single instance of simple gladness unadulterated by the substrate of guilt fashioned from Uncle Charlie's sadistic notions of a work ethic that brooked no unproductive pleasure.

The California cutie spun backward and jumped into a smooth toe loop as she passed, casting a sly glance at Rebecca as she landed: *You don't need to tell me I'm cool; I know it,* the look said, with all the joyous, forgivable egotism of youth. Rebecca tried to guess how old she was. Probably fourteen, going on thirty-five, subconsciously drinking in all the gladness she could before the dark shroud of real life descended on her.

Fourteen. Rebecca and Wendy had both failed to begin menstruating on time. As with many young female athletes and dancers, all that intense physical activity had suppressed the production of leptin, a hormone that triggers puberty, although only Wendy got stuck with a voice that sounded like she breathed helium all day. When they both stopped skating, Wendy's periods eased in gradually and were fairly normal, maybe because she was still only fourteen. Rebecca, on the other hand, had worked out strenuously until she was nearly eighteen; when it was time for her body to get itself synchronized with the real world and the moon, it was as though the gods of Menses had hurled thunderbolts down at her to make up for those lost years. The resultant bouts of anemia left her too weak to cope with the steel-belted cramps, and the combination almost drove her into clinical depression until a smart ob-gyn figured out the right mix of chemicals to balance things out a little better. Better, but still not good.

Every month she cursed her uncle, keeping her resentment of him alive. Which was basically unfair, because he never pressed her to pursue skating. In fact, he never pressed her to do much of anything except stay the hell out of his and her sister's way. But skating was the only means by which she felt she had even an outside shot at participating in the "family's" central pursuit. Somehow, the lesson that ought to have been learned from the fact that she had to work twice as hard as Wendy to accomplish half as much was lost on her. Only later in life did she berate herself for wasting so much time and effort on a useless struggle that exploited her weaknesses rather than capitalized on her strengths.

She polished off the rest of the salad as the breeze from the ocean behind her began dying down prior to changing directions. Then she swigged the last of the grapefruit juice and inhaled a Snicker's bar, leaving a barely visible speck for the seagulls so she wouldn't have to admit to herself that she'd eaten it all.

She took the rest of the afternoon off, resting up for the grind that would start tomorrow.

Tuesday, June 30

Arriving before seven, Rebecca was surprised to run into Arno Steinholz making the day's first pot of coffee.

He was apparently surprised as well, nearly dropping the bag of French roast decaf he favored as she came up behind him.

"Didn't mean to startle you there, son," she said.

"Startle me? Where the hell have you been?"

Rebecca looked at her watch. "What, do you live here or something? What am I supposed—"

But Steinholz was shaking his head, frowning. "Quiet down, f'Chrissakes. I'm talking about yesterday." He waved the bag and a measuring spoon as he spoke, having forgotten he had been holding them. Rebecca smiled in amusement as grains of coffee bounced out of the top of the bag.

"You got a call from Muller yesterday," he said.

"Jessica Muller? What about?"

"She wouldn't say." Steinholz rediscovered his hands at that moment, and set the bag and spoon down so he could wipe the stray coffee that had sprinkled onto his pants. "But she said it was important. I left the messages on your machine. . . ."

"Didn't pick them up. What time's she get in?"

Steinholz shot her an unmistakable so-where-were-*you*-last-night leer, wiggling his eyebrows up and down. As Rebecca pulled a fist back in preparation for decking him, he said quickly, "No idea. But she's got voice mail. Leave her a message, where you're gonna be, and she'll get hold of you."

He watched her as she nodded thoughtfully, then said, "You been speaking to her about changing her mind?"

Rebecca smiled. "Persuasive negotiator that I am."

Steinholz shook his head as he turned back to his coffee preparation, muttering, "Amazing . . ." to himself just loud enough for her to hear, then held his cup under the brew spout for a few seconds and left.

She poured a cup and was about to head for her office when she spotted Janine Osterreich coming into the room. Rebecca was in no mood for the inevitable awkwardness should they meet with no one else around; Rebecca didn't like her and knew Janine knew it. She ducked back behind the L-shaped counter and into a small supplies room, watching through the partially opened door so she would know when Osterreich was gone.

The secretary–shorthand reporter eyed a large box of doughnuts as she prepared to make a pot of coffee, apparently not noticing that a fresh one had just been made and was still dripping into the carafe. Her eyes kept darting back to the doughnut box.

Finally, walking to the door and peeking out into the corridor first, she hurried back in and opened the box. She reached inside for a particularly gooey chocolate eclair, broke off a large piece, and stuffed it into her mouth, eyes closing as she ate it.

Rebecca stared in openmouthed disbelief. She could practically see the woman's teeth corroding before her eyes, then watched as Osterreich picked up the carafe that Steinholz had prepared and poured herself a cup. She'd known all along that the pot she was making was superfluous; it was just an excuse to stick around and snarf down half a fat pill.

Osterreich took her cup and walked to the entryway. Rebecca put her hand on the knob of the supply room and prepared to push it open, then saw Osterreich pause and turn around, bite her lip, then walk back in. She was looking at the doughnut box again, a pained look on her face. Some kind of struggle was going on, and then was lost as she opened the box and pulled out the other half of the eclair.

Rebecca watched in revulsion as Osterreich ate it, wiped her lips with a paper towel and left quickly.

Shaking her head, no doubt in her mind that Osterreich would be making many such trips to the coffee room that day, Rebecca went back to her office and left a message for Muller. Her phone rang less than five minutes later.

Rebecca made sure not to sound gloating or presumptuous. "So, what is it: you miss the sound of my voice?"

"Don't be a smart-ass. I'm sending you a bill."

"Izzatso. For what, exactly?"

"One obscenely expensive lunch, that's for what."

"Seems to have slipped my mind. Did I enjoy it?"

"No, but Radovan Terescu did." She waited for Rebecca to react.

"Terescu? And I'm paying because . . . ?"

"Man's a sucker for good food. Fancies himself an epicurean, but he's no drinker. Took less than half a bottle of an ill-bred but amusing Bordeaux to get him to agree to at least listen to what you have to say."

There was no playing this one cool. "Get outta town! You serious?"

"Calm yourself, lady. He's probably already sobered up and sorry he made the commitment, and even you aren't likely to actually sign him up."

"Sure, I know that." *Stand back and watch me, Professor.* "But maybe he can be useful in helping us locate someone who could do the job better than the candidates we've got lined up."

"Maybe. Anyway, I did my part, God only knows why. Rest is up to you."

Chapter 9

IBM, at least in the good old days, had a strict policy handed down by Tom Watson himself from Mt. Armonk: no drinking with a prospective customer until after the deal was signed and he was no longer prospective. In that era, captains of industry had few compunctions regarding the imposition of their personal moral codes on all those in their employ.

Allen Wysocki had an office drinking policy, too: no alcohol until there was a client it could be charged to. Arno Steinholz, the firm *maven*, went home to fetch a '79 Château Margaux from his personal stash, with a promise from Rebecca that he could replace it after the stores opened that day and charge it to client 32-2153, Tera-Tech Integrated.

Steinholz had hovered outside Rebecca's office earlier as she spoke on the phone with Muller. As soon as he heard the receiver being replaced, he walked in, saying, "She gonna do it?"

He was crestfallen as Rebecca explained that, no Muller still wasn't interested, but had arranged for them to meet with Radovan Terescu. She got the same reaction from Ehrenright when he came in a few minutes later.

Both voiced their deep concern that using Terescu was a tremendous risk. Yes, he was a well-respected expert, and if he does believe that Perrein didn't make the chip, it would be a powerful weapon for the defense. Nevertheless, they both felt that it wasn't worth the risk that his personal feelings might get the better of him and ruin their case.

She let them have their say, then made a command decision and overrode them. It was understood that, from here on in, there would be no second-guessing; everybody would be full-bore committed to the course of action Rebecca had laid out.

So while Steinholz was off getting the wine, Ehrenright called Laurent Gounod at home, catching him just as he was leaving. While studying for the bar, Ehrenright had represented Gounod, who owned the restaurant La Vie en Rose, in a small matter involving a fraudulent worker's compensation claim by an employee whose primary source of income turned out to be a series of similar claims from other counties in the state. Ehrenright had accepted no fee, but had thrilled his girlfriend with a private dinner in the kitchen of La Vie en Rose specially prepared for just the two of them by one of L.A.'s fastest-rising culinary celebrities. Since that time, although the restaurant normally required twenty-four hours' notice for catered lunches delivered to the customer's premises and served by a staff waiter, Ehrenright was exempt from that requirement.

By twelve-fifteen, a small table in a spare conference room had been laid out for four with a white tablecloth, elegant linen napkins, cut-crystal glassware, and sterling silver cutlery. A single tapered candle burned in the center, and the Margaux was happily breathing away off to the side as a tuxedoed waiter surveyed his handiwork approvingly.

Professor Radovan Terescu arrived at the appointed hour of twelve-thirty. Steinholz went out to greet him and escort him back to the conference room, where the scientist drew back in surprise and delight at the layout.

"You have lunch like this every day?" he asked, smiling as the others laughed.

"Of course. Why?" Rebecca stepped forward and held out her hand. "I'm Rebecca Verona."

Terescu took her hand. "Radovan Terescu. Rado, to my friends, which is anybody who provides a meal like this in the middle of a workday."

He was about five foot ten, barely an inch taller than Rebecca, and somewhere in his mid-forties. Terescu's Slavic features were deeply etched, and Rebecca's first thought was that he would photograph well. There were no blurry edges on his face, everything well defined, even his hair, which was slicked back and locked in place. His frame was compact and solid looking, despite a slight paunch, and he wore his custom-tailored, close-fitting suit easily. This was a man who dressed well every day, not just for special occasions.

As the rest of the introductions were made, Rebecca noticed that his English wasn't that much different than had he been born speaking it, with the exception of the standard Eastern European difficulty with the *th* sound and some slight shifts in vowel intonation that seemed to lend him an air of urbane mystery. She guessed that he had emigrated from his native Romania at a very young age.

He spotted the bottle of wine and patted it appreciatively. "I'm starting to get a little worried about what other of my secrets Jessica divulged. I hope your client"—there was no mistaking the contempt with which he said *client*—"is paying for this."

Rebecca assured him that this was the case, and they sat down. The waiter took his job seriously, and managed to serve and clear efficiently while making himself nearly invisible. While he was still in the room, they stayed on topics that would not compromise case confidentiality. Although savoring each sip of the superb wine, Terescu actually drank very little. Rebecca at first assumed that Jessica Muller had been exaggerating about the half bottle he had consumed at lunch the day before, but then thought that he might be purposely avoiding any deleterious effects to his faculties prior to their turning to the real substance of this meeting.

He was affable, inquisitive and disarmingly modest, preferring to focus on the others rather than himself. He asked penetrating questions, and seemed instinctively to zero in on Steinholz as a kindred intellectual spirit, especially when it came to the physical sciences.

The waiter finished brewing up a fresh pot of fragrant coffee, served dessert, waited for a lull in the conversation and then said, "I'm going to leave you folks to some privacy." He told Ehrenright to call the restaurant whenever they wanted everything picked up, and then left.

"Well, Radovan . . ." Rebecca said with a smile.

He smiled back, nodding, took the napkin off his knee and set it on the table. "This is where I sing for my supper, yes?" He reached for his wineglass and twirled it in his hand, then took a sip.

"What I'm interested in first," Rebecca said, "is the story behind why you and James Perrein, uh, aren't exactly bosom buddies."

Terescu sniffed, swirled the wine around in his mouth and then swallowed. He seemed to be structuring his thoughts prior to responding.

"I had a graduate student in my lab. Brilliant boy, really a first-class mind, and not at all afraid of hard work. A Vietnamese refugee, so that's not unusual."

"How'd you find him?"

Terescu grinned. "He was working for a reverse engineering company in Saigon, disassembling U.S. chips in order to steal their secrets for Southeast Asian companies. He was very skilled at it, word got around . . . I sponsored him into the country myself, gave him a nice position . . ."

His voice trailed off as some memory moved behind his eyes, and he looked down at the table as he spoke. "He worked on one of my most difficult projects, very important, a way to make high-speed computer chips programmable without slowing them down." He caught himself and looked around the table, noticing some bewilderment in Rebecca's and Ehrenright's faces. "You must stop me if I say something obscure, eh?"

"Why don't you explain that, Professor," Steinholz suggested.

"Very simply, there are two ways to make a microchip. One is to build in all the functions, and once they're inside, you can never change them. Like, say, the chip inside your VCR or a digital watch. Those are special-purpose chips that do one job. The other way is to allow the chip's programming to be changed. This is what you have inside a personal computer."

"But why would you ever lock them in place?" Ehrenright

asked. "Why not make them all programmable? Then you have so much flexibility."

Terescu raised his eyebrows and nodded vigorously at Ehrenright. "An excellent question! The reason is, the chip is faster when its functions are fixed and unalterable. It doesn't have to consult with a program every time it does something. Once you introduce programming, the speed drops dramatically."

"But who cares how fast the chip in your VCR is?" Ehrenright asked.

"Nobody. It was just an example. But for some chips, like the ones that process television pictures, you must have tremendous speed so the picture on the screen keeps up with the signal coming in through the antenna. In fact, the chips we are talking about are called signal processors for just that reason: they take signals coming in, which represent enormous amounts of data, and must process them at very high speeds."

"And almost all of those are special-purpose chips," Steinholz added. "Once you burn in a function, that's all they can do."

"Exactly," Terescu said. "If you try to make them programmable, they get too slow. My ambition was—is—to leapfrog two generations ahead of current technology and create blazingly fast chips that can be used for a variety of purposes. The work on programmability was crucial to that undertaking."

"And then you lost your grad student," Rebecca prompted, trying to keep the conversation on track.

A cloud crossed Terescu's face. "Your client stole him from me. Not like a man, he didn't come to me and say, Professor, I'm giving you fair warning that I'm going to try to recruit this boy, which is done all the time."

Terescu squeezed his lips together and set the wineglass down, as though fearful of inadvertently crushing it. "He seduced him with money, with fantasies of owning a piece of the prize one day if he were successful. The worst part, the student was less than a year away from earning his Ph.D., and he left the program to work for Tera-Tech."

The lawyers were all sympathetic, even encouraging, and they let Terescu continue to vent his smoldering anger without trying to convince him that Perrein was anything other than what Terescu already thought he was. When it looked like he had pretty much finished, none of them professed any love for Perrein; Rebecca even confided that she couldn't stand him, either.

"So why are you taking on his case?" Terescu asked her.

"Couple reasons, Rado." She hoped he was sensitive to the collegial candor she was trying to communicate. "First of all, it's good business for the firm and, to be honest, for me and these two guys."

Terescu dipped his head slightly in acknowledgment of her candor.

"Second, Perrein is entitled to be defended. If he's guilty, let the government prove it and send him away, but I don't want them being able to do that just because they're big and powerful and have unlimited resources."

"His right to be defended doesn't obligate you to be the defender," Terescu said.

"True. But here's the last part: I think he's innocent."

"Why?"

"Can't tell you that without violating client confidentiality."

"Ah, yes. Sorry."

"No problem. But if I thought he was guilty, I wouldn't have taken on the case." *And so much for being straight with the good professor.* "James Perrein may be a shithead"—Terescu looked up in surprise—"but he's an innocent shithead and doesn't deserve to go down for something he didn't do."

"Tell you the truth, it wouldn't bother me if he did."

Rebecca found Terescu's lack of guile enchanting, and decided to return it. She leaned forward and said in a soft voice, "Tell *you* the truth, me neither!"

Terescu laughed, some of the tension leaving his face.

"Regardless of what you may think about lawyers," Ehrenright offered, "some of us care about doing what's right. It isn't required that we like a client to believe in him."

Terescu took a deep breath and reached for his glass again, laying his fingers over the base and moving it around on the tablecloth so the wine swirled and left ruby red curtains in its path.

"Fact is," he said offhandedly, "Tera-Tech *couldn't* have made those chips."

He picked up the glass and brought it to his lips, unaware that the three attorneys had, as though a single organism, suddenly gone rigid. Steinholz flicked his eyes toward Rebecca just as she was doing the same to him, and then Ehrenright. Both associates knew to keep quiet, that the next move was hers.

She picked up a water glass and took a small sip. "Really?" she asked as casually as she could. "How come?"

"There's really only one method that even has a chance of producing a chip anywhere near that powerful. It's called X-ray laser etching—"

"You invented that!" Steinholz blurted out.

"Did I?" Terescu looked at Steinholz in feigned surprise, then at the others. "What do you know about that!"

The three of them laughed, including the red-faced Steinholz, and then Rebecca asked him what it was.

"The details aren't important, but it's a way of making nearly submicroscopic transistors on microchips."

"How does it work?" Steinholz asked without thinking, and tried to ignore the glare it earned him from Rebecca.

"The theory is actually very simple," Terescu replied, and Rebecca was dismayed to see him warming up to the technical topic in preparation for giving a lecture, but it was too late to do anything about it. Besides, it was a good way to assess how adept he'd be at explaining arcane technology to a lay audience.

"The challenge in making these computer chips is to get them to work as fast as possible. Now, a chip is about the size of your thumbnail, but it contains many transistors. Thousands, and sometimes millions. One way to make the chip faster is to make each transistor smaller and closer to its neighbors. That also allows you to put more transistors on the chip without making it any bigger."

He leaned back and shook his head slightly, taking a deep breath at the same time. Rebecca sensed his frustration, not at any inability to explain the matter, but at what a difficult problem he had just described.

"When you have a forest with a lot of trees, you say that it is *dense*. Same thing with these chips: the more transistors and other stuff you try to squeeze onto them, the more dense they become. We call it component density, and that's what all of us are working on: how to get as much component density as possible."

Terescu held his hands out, palms up, his eyebrows raised. Ehrenright nodded his grasp of the problem—Steinholz was apparently already aware of it—and Rebecca found herself curious to see where this tale was going.

"Most chips are made using a simple technique." Terescu sketched in the air with his hands as he spoke. "You make a slide photo of the pattern you want to put on the chip. That pattern shows where all of these components—the transistors and other things—where all of the components go. Then you shine a bright light through the slide and onto the chip surface. This prints the pattern on the chip. It's just like spraying paint through a stencil, see? Or projecting a slide onto a screen, except the image is smaller than the slide instead of larger.

"Next thing you do is dip the chip in acid. This washes away the surface, except where the pattern was printed. When you take it out of the acid, the pattern of all the transistors and wires is etched right into the chip. You repeat the process for each layer of the chip, and you're done."

"Like developing a photograph," Ehrenright ventured. "Or making a lithograph."

"Very much the same, which is why it's called photolithography." Terescu smiled, folded his hands in his lap and leaned back. "Simple." The attorneys smiled back, knowing that it wasn't that simple, that there was more, but the basics of this chip-making stuff was easy to understand, at least the way Terescu was explaining it. "But"—he held his hands up again, a rueful smile on his face—"there are one or two little problems." His hands fell to his lap and the others laughed. "The smaller these things get, the harder they are to make. Why? Well, you may not believe this, but light itself is too big to use as a tool."

He kept smiling as Rebecca sat back in disbelief, just as he had intended. "It's true. I'll explain." He shifted in his seat, getting comfortable.

"Suppose you wanted to paint a picture of a nice tree, hmm?" Answering nods. "You take a thick paintbrush and start with the trunk—nice, broad strokes. Then you take a smaller brush and paint the biggest limbs and branches, then a smaller brush for the little branches and the leaves, and an even smaller brush for the twigs and an even smaller brush for the little buds . . ."

He sat up straight and put his hands out. "But then you try to paint the patterns on the leaves themselves, and what happens?" He slapped his hands down on his thighs. "You don't have a brush small enough! You can't do it."

He adopted a sad look as he sat back in his chair. "And that is as much detail as you can provide in your painting."

He brightened. "But then someone comes along and hands you a new, special brush. The tip is barely the width of a single hair, and now you can paint the pattern on the leaves. Now you get ambitious, and you want to add a spiderweb, but, again, you don't have a fine enough tool, and even if you did, the paint you're using isn't thin enough to accommodate it and still stick to the canvas . . . and that's it. Brushes and paints have reached their limits, and your traditional tools won't do the job."

Rebecca asked, "How does this relate to making chips photographically?"

"In this case," Terescu answered, turning to her, "light is our paintbrush. Light rays are very narrow, especially ultraviolet rays, and we can use them to make extremely tiny transistors. But at some point"—he turned to Ehrenright again—"believe it or not, the light itself is too 'thick' to make things as small as we like. It simply cannot be focused any finer because we're down to a single wavelength of the light and it can't be further divided. And so light is no longer useful below a certain size."

He pointed to Steinholz's wrist. "It would be like trying to engrave an inscription on your watch using a sledgehammer and a chisel. But fortunately, there are certain kinds of rays that are finer than light. Like ion beams. These are made up of electrons rather than photons, and can use them to make even smaller transistors. It's called ion-beam lithography. But wouldn't you know it?"

Ehrenright nodded vigorously, knowing what was coming. "Right," Terescu said. "Even ion beams reached a limit, and we needed something smaller."

"And what was that?" Rebecca asked.

"X rays," he answered. "Extremely fine, but very difficult to work with. They're used the same way as light—you shine X rays through a slide onto the chip and then wash away the unexposed parts."

"And that's what you invented?" Ehrenright asked.

"No. My work began where even X-ray lithography could no longer do the job."

"How?"

"My method doesn't use a slide, and it doesn't use a photosensitive surface on the chip." He paused, trying to find the words to simplify a dauntingly complex process. "What we do is use an X-ray laser. The beam is aimed directly at the surface of the chip. As a computer steers the beam around, it burns away the surface, carving transistors and other things directly into the chip. It's terribly slow, but it can make components so small they cannot be seen even with a standard electron microscope."

Rebecca realized that Terescu's explanation was perfectly tailored to a nonscientific audience, and she felt herself absorbed as he described his process. Somewhere in the middle, it occurred to her that this scientist could hold a jury equally rapt. She tried to visualize how he would appear on the stand going through their rehearsed direct examination.

Terescu sat back. "And that's X-ray laser etching."

Steinholz, utterly rapt, asked, "How small are we talking here?"

"We've gotten down well below a micron, but further refinements are inevitable."

"What's a micron?" Rebecca asked.

"A millionth of a meter." Terescu could see it meant nothing to her. He looked around for a moment, then reached across the table, grabbed a stray hair and yanked.

"Youch!"

"It's all for science," Terescu said, reaching for Ehrenright's pad and flipping to a clean page. He laid the hair down on it and said, "A human hair is close to the limit of how fine a line the human eye can see."

As the others peered down at it, Terescu said, "It's about a hundred microns wide."

Steinholz ran the calculation in his head and looked up, eyebrows raised in amazement.

Terescu nodded. "So the kind of transistors I'm talking about? Three thousand of them laid end to end would be no wider than this hair."

"Good God," Rebecca breathed, transfixed on the single strand barely visible on the yellow paper.

"And you're saying that's how the chip was probably built?" Ehrenright asked.

"No, no, no!" Terescu shook his head forcefully. "Impossible! Look, everybody knows Tera-Tech is researching in the field, but this technique is so new, so difficult. . . . If what you told me about this chip is true, the required component density would be five years ahead of where I am, and your client is nowhere near that."

"How do you know?" Ehrenright asked.

"Because *nobody* could be!"

"Are you sure?" Rebecca pressed him.

Terescu exhaled loudly. "It would be like somebody announcing tomorrow that they've got an electric car that gets five hundred miles on a single charge. There are severe problems that haven't yet been solved. May never get solved."

"Hang on a minute," Rebecca said. "Jessica Muller said something about, uh, what was it . . . oracular wires . . . vehicular, something like that . . . ?"

Terescu threw his head back and laughed. "Oracular wires! I like that!"

Rebecca laughed along with him as Steinholz said, "I think that was *ovalauricle*, Becky."

"Yeah, whatever. That's different from laser etching?"

"You're a perfect straight man, Ms. Verona," Terescu said. "The fact is, X-ray laser etching is old news already. Plenty of labs are working on it now and I'm no longer interested, except as a tool for my real work."

Terescu grew serious. Rebecca assumed it was because he was still in the process of wrestling some knotty problems with these wires; the X-ray laser process, by contrast, was well into the development phase.

"Making the components very tiny is one thing," Terescu was saying. "Frankly, it's relatively easy. But hooking them up to each other is quite another." He sat back on his chair and grew thoughtful. "We were very surprised to find that connecting them is much, much harder than making them. As a matter of fact, without a good solution to the interconnect problem, we might as well stop the work on making components smaller altogether. It would be like, uh . . ." He hunted around for an appropriate analogy. "Imagine creating a train that can go three hundred miles per hour, except that there's no track that could take the strain. Developing the track now becomes more important than speeding up the locomotive."

"What's so hard about connecting them up?" Steinholz asked, his own knowledge of the field apparently having run out at this level of sophistication. "Can't laser etching make small wires, too?"

Terescu thought about it for a second. "Yes, but that's not the point. What counts is whether a wire that small will actually work. . . ."

Rebecca found her attention drifting as Terescu explained what the problem was, and what he proposed to do about it. She was now satisfied that there was no expert in the world who combined this professor's knowledge, hands-on expertise and ability to make difficult concepts accessible. She turned her thoughts to the more immediate challenge.

They had to have him.

She could tell from Steinholz's frowning expression and Ehrenright's thoughtful nods that Terescu was impressing them with the immense difficulty of whatever the hell the problem was. She heard him start talking about the ovalauricle wire, and watched as Steinholz's eyebrows slowly rose in wonderment. Ehrenright was having more trouble grasping the concepts, and Terescu slowed down to make sure he understood. Rebecca waited politely until he had finished and the two attorneys had peppered him with a barrage of questions.

She nodded, as though tracking right along with them, and then said to her colleagues, before they could ask any more questions, "Why don't you guys give us a few minutes, okay?"

That seemed to startle them, until they remembered what the point of the meeting was. "Just don't finish all the wine," Steinholz said as he reluctantly got up.

As they made their way around the table toward the door, Rebecca reminded Terescu that anything said between the two of them was strictly confidential.

Terescu smiled wryly and said, "You don't really think you can twist my arm into joining your defense, do you?"

Rebecca's face and voice grew serious, all traces of earlier amiability gone. "I have no intention of doing that."

She waited until the door clicked shut. "First of all, it's not clear how much we really need you: when I attack the prosecution for failing to adequately demonstrate where the chip came from, we're probably going to get the charges dismissed anyway."

"How do you know they won't be able to show where it came from?"

"Because to do so would put too many intelligence assets in jeopardy. These guys, they'd rather lose a nuke than blow their cover." Then she conceded it anyway. "But that's always a risk, and not to be properly prepared would be a serious breach of the client's trust. So we have to cover all the bases."

She looked down at the table, then back again. "Doc, I'm not going to try to put anything over on you. From what they tell me, you may be the smartest person I've ever sat face-to-face with. No, don't wave it off. I said I'm not going to try to put anything over on you, so do the same with me, okay? That's why I asked the others to leave the room. I may never get a chance to speak with you again, so let me just lay it all out in the open, then we'll shake hands, you can leave, and that'll be the end of it, okay?"

Rebecca picked up her wineglass, stood up and came around the table, stopping behind Ehrenright's chair, which was next to Terescu's. She set the glass down and used both hands to swivel the chair around to face him. He did the same with his own chair, showing her that he had no fear of being swayed by a direct, personal assault. Rebecca sat down, crossed her legs, and leaned back.

"Radovan, let's talk. About things that really matter, just the two of us, and it never leaves this room, all right?" His face remained impassive as he slightly lifted and dropped one shoulder, and she didn't wait for any further cues to continue.

"I'm not going to kid you: if the government puts on a decent case, without you, I may have some problems. That's why I need for you to sign on." Simple, declarative sentences, clear and unambiguous. Like mathematical equations, things that Terescu was used to and behind which he would suspect no subterfuge.

"Now, that's *my* problem," Rebecca went on, "not yours. I know that. I haven't yet given you a reason why it's in your interest. You hardly know me, so you have no cause to want to help me out." She shrugged nonchalantly before he could mount any form of polite protest. "I understand perfectly, and I'd feel the same in your shoes. What I want to show you is why it may be in *your* interest. I'm not doing that because I'm a good human being. I don't know you either. We're not friends. This is a business deal. If it doesn't make sense for both of us, equally, there's no reason to continue, right? But if we both stand to gain, then we ought to be able to put aside our differences with the client and do *ourselves* some good."

She casually flipped a hand up and let it flop back down on her arm. "Listen, I hate the sonofabitch as much as you do." The slight startle response in Terescu's features was just what she had hoped for. She knew it was prompted not by her unexpected second use of a mild profanity, but by the admission that her feelings toward Perrein were more than just casual disregard. That needed to be cemented in.

"You're surprised? You shouldn't be. He's a conniving, underhanded bastard, and normally I wouldn't cross the street to save his life."

Terescu smiled, and Rebecca returned it. They were now fellow conspirators in the I-Hate-James-Perrein underground. "But here's the thing, see . . ." She uncrossed her arms and tapped a finger on the armrest. "If we can use *his* predicament to *our* own advantage, what difference does it make if he benefits in the process? I'm being real straight with you here, Radovan. You think lawyers are concerned with justice? Well, they are. A lot of the time. But we're also concerned with our careers, and our egos, and our bank accounts. This is a big, visible case for me. I win it, I'm flying up the ladder like a rocket. I want that. And the way I look at it, if I can do it off James Perrein's back, well, to me, that's like a double goodie, see? Because even if I save his sorry ass, I come out better than he does. All that happens to him, he spends a ton of dough just to put himself back to where he was when he started. There's no net benefit. In fact, the whole thing will tarnish his reputation a little even if he wins."

Terescu was beginning to show some interest, and she kept the momentum going. "But me? *I'm* in the catbird seat. I'm the hottest lawyer in town, and the firm has a few million of Perrein's precious dollars in its pockets to boot. That's why I don't have a problem with this case. Way I look at it, I'm the one using Perrein, not the other way around."

She never took her eyes off Terescu, studying his expression. She thought she sensed surprise mixed with a hint of distaste.

Perfect. "Now let's talk about you, Radovan. And if I'm out of line here, hey: you let me know and I'll quit, okay?" She held his eyes, conveying no discomfort. "I'm guessing this divorce business has occupied your whole life the last two years. It's okay, I don't know any details. But I've got friends in similar situations, seen cases in court, I know how it can tear your very soul out. I'm betting you haven't gotten done half the work you should have in the last two years. I'm betting that, eight times a day, your concentration gets broken because your mind can't help drifting back to your wife, the marriage you used to have, and what it's become. How many papers have you published recently, how many lectures have you given to your colleagues at major conferences? A lot less than you used to, would be my guess." It wasn't a guess at all; she'd discussed his recent behavior at length with Jessica Muller.

She held a hand up in the air and pointed two fingers at him, confident that her words were hitting home and that she could extend her presumption. "You need a diversion. You've got to get yourself into something that'll occupy your mind, that'll challenge

you in a way you haven't been challenged in a long time. Because
the kind of challenge you think you get in the lab?" She waved a
dismissive hand at him. "Nobody pushes back at you. You don't
get to *win*!"

She leaned forward very slightly and dropped her voice a quarter octave so that it took on a throaty quality. "You need a fight,
Rado. You need an adversary who'll fight back, push you right to
the wall. You need an opponent so fierce he'll fill your mind day
and night, pushing all the irrelevant nonsense to the side. You think
I'm insensitive, telling you your divorce is irrelevant? Well, lemme
tell you something else, Professor, and in a few weeks' time you tell
me if you don't agree."

She leaned forward a little more now, letting her posture reflect
the excitement in her words. She could feel her eyes glistening,
sensed that the tension in her voice was mingling with the heady,
intoxicating scent of her perfume as it drifted, driven by the heat
of her skin, off her neck. "There is nothing on God's green earth
comes *close* to doing battle in the courtroom. Not war, not sex,
nothing can make your blood race around at ninety miles an hour
like staring down the cross-examining beast and sending him back
whimpering to his cave. A few weeks in that arena and I swear to
God, the whole goddamned rest of your *life* will seem irrelevant!"

Rebecca watched, staying silent, as a tiny flicker of her conta-
gion sparked and caught hold somewhere deep inside Terescu,
speeding up his breathing by a slight but clearly perceptible margin.
She needed to fan that tenuous flame, but not by drawing out this
particular line any further, and she waited until the precisely correct moment to break the spell she had just woven and move on.

"And the best news for you, it doesn't end when the case is
over." Her tone hardened, not a great deal, just enough to smooth
out the raspiness and go from inspiring to irrefutably logical,
businesslike, even a touch derogatory. "Listen, you damned near
won a Nobel prize, but let me tell you something you already
know: nobody out there beyond a tiny circle of computer nerds
knows you even exist. You're the best in the world. I've talked to
them all, and everybody says the same thing. Don't you deserve a
moment in the sun? The stuff you're doing, Christ, it'll change the
world! You want to end up like Philo Farnsworth, nobody even
knows you were alive?"

She hurried on before he could say anything dismissive. "You
don't have to be modest with me, Rado. Modesty is for people who

have nothing to brag about, you and I both know that. I was straight with you; I want my name out there, and you need to admit to yourself that you wouldn't mind that so much either. All those countless hours in that lab, laboring in isolation, talking only to that inbred bunch of scientists who only talk to each other . . . ? Come on, there's gotta be more than that!"

She dropped her voice again, this time to a near whisper, leaned forward and put her hand on his arm, squeezing it firmly. "This case can give it to you, Rado! Give it to you big, and all of a sudden! You got an overgrown, egomaniacal Goliath of a justice department seeking revenge on a single citizen just because he dared to stand up to them and tell them they were full of shit. And *you* can be the white knight, the principled scientist who breaks his own rules and risks unwanted publicity because he believes in a man's innocence. You're the guy who stands up and tells all those government experts that *they're* the ones who're full of it, and that you can damned well prove it, too. And the beast goes slinking off and it's you left standing out in the sunlight, Rado. *You.* Because you stood up and did the right thing, painful as it was for you personally, and from that day on you're no longer an obscure academic creating stuff nobody understands or gives a rat's ass about. The world knows who you are, Rado, and from then on, it's your call. As much or as little as you want, it's *your call!*"

Rebecca waited a moment, then drew her hand away from his arm, a subtle indication that she was stepping back outside of the space they had been sharing for the last several minutes, never to share it again unless he stepped back into it himself.

She knew that there were no longer any forbidden subjects because she'd correctly divined his soul and it was now safe to go in for the kill. She tapped the toe of her shoe against his and reset her voice back into normal conversational mode. "And isn't some little somebody out there gonna be damned sorry she's no longer married to Professor Radovan Terescu."

She sat back and stayed quiet for a long time, letting it all sink in, letting him play out all the fantasies, seeing in his face that she'd gotten to him.

Now, the most important step of all: closing the deal in a way that didn't make it look like he'd blindly fallen for all the tales she'd been spinning. It had to end with Terescu feeling he was in control, making the correct decision not out of any self-interest but because it was the only noble course of action.

"It's the right thing to do, Professor. The man is innocent and we both know it. You said so yourself. So how about standing up for him and helping me out on this one?"

Terescu seemed to shake himself out of some other realm, nodding his head slightly as if still weighing the pros and cons, even though that decision process had ended minutes ago.

He took his time, tapping his finger on his thigh, then looked up at Rebecca and asked, "What's the going rate for an expert witness like me?" They were the first words he'd uttered in many minutes.

"Figure, two hundred an hour."

"Good. I want four hundred."

Rebecca sat up straight with a comical expression on her face, both at his presumption and her own relief. "What!"

Terescu smiled back mischievously, obviously glad to have come to a decision, to be a member of the team, and to be about to win Rebecca's approval. "I got to stick it to him a little, don't I? Preserve my self-respect?"

Rebecca stared at him a moment longer. Shaking her head and leaning forward back into the bell jar of the intimacy she'd been carefully cultivating, she said, in her best Bogart, "Louie, sounds like the beginning of a beautiful friendship."

Rebecca was tempted to get Steinholz and Ehrenright back in the room for a bit of celebration, but it was too soon to risk Terescu getting the impression that he had lost some battle the rest of them had known all along was going to take place. Instead, she summoned Janine Osterreich over the intercom, and instructed her to take notes as she and her new expert discussed specifics in preparation for drafting a formal letter of engagement.

After Osterreich left, Terescu asked what he should be doing to prepare.

"Take a few days to clear the decks back at the lab," Rebecca advised. "This is going to be a little consuming in the beginning. Then you'll get a bit of a break, and start up again to prepare for your testimony at trial. If it comes to that," she added.

"Is there a chance it won't?"

Rebecca looked up at the ceiling and thought hard about the possibility of a plea bargain or dismissal. She started thinking about the specifics of the charges, the evidence, the nature of the government's discovery replies . . . then she thought about David Zuckerman.

"No," she said, bringing her gaze back down. "This one's going to trial."

Terescu thought about that, then said, "Well, should we get your two friends back in here?"

Rebecca turned to the intercom again, and a few minutes later Steinholz and Ehrenright returned. Before Rebecca could say anything, Terescu said, "Looks like I've been shanghaied."

Steinholz stuck his hand out, and tried not to sound like some kind of victory had been wrought. "I'm glad, Rado. I think you might actually enjoy it."

Ehrenright nodded his agreement and offered his hand as well. "Arno here is already salivating at the thought of having a real scientist all to himself. Be careful."

Terescu smiled appreciatively as he shook hands. "It would be a relief spending time with people other than . . . what was it you called them, Rebecca? *Computer nerds?*"

Steinholz rolled his eyes in contempt. "Two years she's had a VCR, it's still blinking midnight." He looked at the remaining wine, then his watch. "What the hell," he said, reaching for the bottle. "Day's shot anyway." He began pouring it into their glasses.

Terescu picked his up and said, "You know, now that I think about it, there's something really appealing about James Perrein sitting in court, biting his tongue and his nails both, having to depend on *me* to keep him out of jail."

He looked down at nothing for a moment, then put the glass back on the table and rubbed his hands together. "Well, gotta get back, start making arrangements," he said.

They shook hands all around again, and Ehrenright said, "I'll see you out."

"Not necessary." Terescu started for the door, then stopped and turned around. "You know," he said, something having just occurred to him. "Perrein may be an amoral and self-centered sonofabitch, but I don't think he'd sell out his country."

The other three nodded encouragingly, and then he was gone.

Rebecca and Ehrenright happily nursed their wine, but Steinholz looked troubled. "Funny," he said, looking at the door, "what Terescu just said."

"How so?" Ehrenright asked, unconcerned.

Steinholz idly fingered a napkin, still looking at the door. "It's just that, well, Perrein wouldn't consider the sale of the chips to be selling out his country at all." He turned toward Rebecca. "He's been lobbying for the deregulation of those kinds of exports, so if he thought he could get away with it, he sure as hell wouldn't think it was harmful to the U.S. I mean, China even has most-favored-nation trading status with the U.S."

Rebecca tilted her head forward and stared Steinholz down. "What say we don't share that little insight with our expert witness, okay, Arno?"

"Course not." Steinholz shook it off and took a sip of wine, then added, "But it wouldn't be the first time Perrein wormed his way around some law or regulation he didn't like."

Rebecca winced—did Steinholz know how close he'd gotten to the mark with respect to her old affair with Perrein? "Speaking of Perrein, guess I'd better go call him."

Alone in her office, Rebecca dialed Perrein's number and was put through immediately. She thought fleetingly of the time she couldn't get him at all, then pushed it aside. Bracing herself, she told him the news about their new expert, then listened politely as he ranted about what a dumb idea it was.

"You never vetoed it, Jim."

"I never thought you'd bother to go after him, much less actually sign him on!"

"I don't think we have much of an option. He's the best there is. Besides"—she'd saved her best shot for last—"you're the one who came up with this strategy of hiring people who hate your guts. Well, he fits the bill."

If he took offense at that, he didn't show it. He grumbled a bit more, then said, "One thing, and we're not going to negotiate about it: Terescu doesn't come anywhere near the company."

"Are you nuts?" Rebecca practically yelled into the phone. "How the hell's he supposed to get prepared to defend you if you won't even—"

"Listen, you hired him, it's your problem."

"It's *our* problem, dammit! I'm not the one under indictment!"

"I don't give a damn. I'm not going to let him use defending me as an excuse to get his grubby fingers on my company's technical secrets."

Rebecca tried to explain how detrimental this could be to their case, but he was resolute and she knew it was useless to try to change his mind.

"Aren't we being a little paranoid, Jim?"

"Yeah? *You* try running a high-tech company someday. Far as I'm concerned, a paranoiac is just someone who knows all the facts."

She sat in stunned silence after they'd rung off, and considered the situation she'd just engineered so cleverly. Two-thirds of her defense team, along with the client, thought she was off her rocker for hiring an expert who hated the defendant. And even though the basic concept had been created by the client himself, she knew for certain that if it backfired, all the blame would fall on her, the attorney whose job it was to provide that client with sound advice.

She didn't doubt that Steinholz and Ehrenright would stand up for her if things went south. She also didn't have any doubt that James Perrein would throw her to the dogs to save his own skin.

C h a p t e r   1 0

Monday, July 6

It was so convoluted that Rebecca decided not even to try unraveling it.

Lines of tension shot out all over the room, found their marks, then rebounded to score fresh hits. It seemed to her that, were she to sprinkle talcum powder in the air, laserlike beams would be rendered visible, flashing connections that shifted with each turned eye, averted glance or awkward greeting.

Despite the anxiety attendant to even considering the idea, Rebecca had bitten the bullet and gathered the principal participants of the defense case in one room. Jim Perrein was off in a corner speaking with Justin Ehrenright, not by choice but by default, because he was the only attorney left, considering that Arno Steinholz was busy buttonholing Radovan Terescu, who in turn was only too happy to be engaged in that conversation because it allowed him to avoid Perrein, who was not only trying to avoid him right back but was also staying away from Rebecca, who wasn't talking to anybody.

As far as she was concerned, it could go on like that for the rest of the day, everybody having naturally come to rest at their own levels of least discomfort. But now that they were all here, there was no excuse for not getting started.

"Why don't we all sit down?" she said as she stood to shut the door to the conference room. It was only then that the matter of seating occurred to her, and she thought she now had an inkling of how Kissinger and Duc Tho must have felt in Paris negotiating to end the Vietnam War.

Fortunately, the roundtable in this particular room had nine chairs for the five attendees, and the intervening seats gave the impression that the separations between antagonists were several times their actual physically measurable widths. Rebecca wondered, fleetingly, if she should give some smarmy, political convention speech about the necessity of their all getting along for the common cause, but sobered up quickly in favor of letting sleeping pit bulls lie. The deciding factor for her was the likelihood that she would be the first to violate her own admonition by permanently disfiguring her client should he piss her off.

They sat around and stirred coffee, arranged papers, shredded napkins and scratched themselves while waiting for Rebecca to get things rolling. As far as she was able to observe, Terescu and Perrein hadn't once even looked at each other since they arrived. She had no illusions about their eventually going fishing and getting drunk together, but it was necessary that some mode of communication be wired up, regardless of how stiff and precarious it might be. First order of business was to establish that the main purpose of these kinds of meetings was the dissemination of information.

"Got us a judge assigned," Rebecca announced. "Catherine Goldin. Arno's been up before her, twice, was it?"

"Once at trial, once at a hearing. They call her the Watutsi."

"I've heard that," Ehrenright said. "Black, six feet tall . . . looks like she could do an Ironman on a moment's notice."

They discussed the judge for a few more minutes, comparing Steinholz's personal experience with her to the general courthouse scuttlebutt Rebecca and Ehrenright had heard. Catherine Goldin's notorious glare was a likely throwback to warrior ancestors who only had to stare at their enemies to intimidate them into retreating. Many an unsuspecting young attorney had crumbled under that withering mien, not realizing that, while she had little tolerance for the incompetent or unprepared, Goldin relished learned debate and was fully prepared to change her mind, and her rulings, if sufficiently powerful arguments could be mounted. She was particularly creative in formulating ways to deal with tricky situations for which other judges might declare mistrials, and her overriding criteria for those solutions were adherence to the law and fairness to the parties involved. She was almost pathological in her abhorrence of nonmaterial technicalities that subverted justice, and she had faith in her own judgment, so banking on any concern she might have about being overturned on appeal was a futile investment.

"The good news for us," Rebecca said, addressing herself to Perrein, "is that we can count on her to do the right thing, to listen to properly constructed arguments. Valuable trait in a judge, predictability."

"She's also a baseball freak," Steinholz added. "Easily the most feared first baseman in the Thursday night league."

Rebecca kept things limited to uncontroversial topics for the first half hour, just getting everybody used to talking to each other. While Terescu and Perrein both threw in the occasional question or observation, they thus far hadn't said anything to each other, or responded to any of each other's comments. Terescu's ban from the Tera-Tech premises had not been mentioned. It was simply too laden with emotional land mines and, since it couldn't possibly result in any productive discourse, Rebecca wasn't about to allow it to come up.

But they had to open up a link. "Rado," she said, "you said you wanted a list of the equipment in Tera-Tech's factory . . . ?"

"I got that," Perrein said, flipping open his glove leather attaché and withdrawing a manila folder. He shoved it across the table toward Terescu.

"Ah, good. Thank you." Terescu reeled it in and opened it, running his eye down the first sheet of paper. Neither of them had looked directly at the other.

They all stayed quiet as Terescu reviewed the list. "One or two things here I don't recognize."

"Such as?" Perrein prompted.

"This here," Terescu said, pointing to something about halfway down the page. "A Therm-a-Tech B50?"

"That's a wave solderer."

"Oh. What do you need it for?" Terescu looked at Perrein at last, peering at him over the tops of his reading glasses.

Perrein looked back at him. "We put together our own test rigs.

Turns out our customers got wind of them and wanted some, so we sell them now."

"What's a wave solderer?" Steinholz asked.

Terescu and Perrein both started to answer at once, and laughed nervously. Perrein held out his hand and said, "Please . . ."

"No, no." Terescu shook his head. "I'll keep reading."

Perrein turned toward Steinholz. "Damned clever piece of equipment. When you have a couple hundred devices on a circuit board, you've gotta solder a few thousand little connectors underneath the board."

"Some job," Ehrenright commented. This was all completely irrelevant, but Rebecca decided to let it go on; it was the first time since the meeting began that anybody actually seemed to be interested in anything.

"Yeah," Perrein continued. "Used to be, you'd have to hire a whole South American village to sit there with soldering guns, and they'd screw up half of them anyway. Then we got robots—perfect job on each connection, do about a hundred a minute . . . and paid for themselves in about a hundred years."

Steinholz and Ehrenright laughed, but Rebecca noticed that Terescu hadn't, even though she was sure he was listening.

"Now this wave solderer, this is really something. You have this basin filled with molten solder. Heavy stuff, it lays there like smooth glass. You lower this circuit board over it until the connectors are sitting barely a hair above the solder. Then you shoot a burst of sound into the basin at one end, and it starts a wave on the surface of the solder. As the crest of the wave passes underneath the board, the molten solder is lifted up, and it touches every single connector on the board on its way across the basin."

Steinholz was enthralled. "So it doesn't make any difference if you have a hundred or a thousand connections to solder . . ." he began.

"Exactly," Perrein said. "They all get done in less than a second. Each one perfect, each one damned near cost free."

Steinholz was shaking his head. "I gotta see that thing work."

"Anytime," Perrein answered without thinking. His face betrayed no recognition of the secondary insult he'd just heaped on the banned Terescu, but Steinholz pressed his lips together in quiet acknowledgment of his gaffe.

Terescu seemed not to notice. "Couple other things here as well. I'd like to get the technical details on them."

"Manufacturers' published specs all right?"

"Not a problem. But tell me, has Tera-Tech modified any of them?"

"A few."

"Then I'll need details of the modifications as well."

"I'll get them to you. We keep paper trails of everything we've done."

"Very good. Do you have any outside contractors who do some work for you?"

"None. It's all in-house. Like it says in our ads."

"And outside research?" If he meant that sarcastically, referring to the graduate student he believed Perrein stole from him, it didn't show. He was behaving like a professional.

"None."

Terescu nodded. "Good." From Terescu's point of view as an expert, Tera-Tech's all-in-the-family approach made his job easier in terms of eliminating any avenues the prosecution might seize upon as enabling the company to have made the chips.

But Rebecca realized what an important question Terescu had just asked from an overall defense perspective: if there were no outside contractors, there would also be no way to shift the blame should the evidence begin stacking up against Tera-Tech.

Terescu was on the third page when he laid the papers down and took off his glasses. "You've got two pretty large ion-beam lithography devices here. The bigger one: is it the highest-resolution beam you've got?"

Rebecca hadn't been paying close attention, but thought she detected some hesitancy before Perrein nodded and said, "Number one top dog on the production floor."

"You sure?" she asked.

"Positive." There was no trace of his earlier, probably nonexistent indecision. "I know every machine on that floor. Besides, anything more powerful than that would still be considered experimental and there's no way we'd put it on the line. It would be slow, too. No sense bogging down production when we don't need that kind of power."

"And these haven't been modified?" Terescu pressed.

"Just the belts that transport the wafers once they're inside. My guys thought they were too rough, so they smoothed them out. I can get you the details."

"But no tinkering with the beams themselves?"

"Uh-uh," Perrein said firmly. "No reason to."

It went on like that for a while, straightforward Q&A about technical matters. It was easy to see where Terescu's questions probed for potentially incriminating information, but that was what they were paying him to do: better he should uncover it here, before trial, than have the lawyers learn of it from the prosecution later. Perrein apparently understood the concept as well, taking no offense as Terescu machine-gunned questions at him.

When he had exhausted all the points he could come up with off the top of his head, Terescu closed the folder. "All I can think of for now. Although I'm sure to have more once I really get under way."

Rebecca thought it a very impressive performance. Terescu'd had only had a few minutes to look at the list, but easily grasped the potential problems implied by nothing more than that simple inventory of Tera-Tech's physical machinery. If Perrein felt the same, he didn't show it; his face was completely neutral.

"Am I needed?" Terescu was asking. "I've got an awful lot of analysis to do . . ."

Assured that he was free to go, Terescu stood up, electing to wave good-bye to the table as a whole rather than shake individual hands. It might have been her imagination, but Rebecca thought she detected a glimmer of hurt feelings in his manner, and why not? He probably felt that he had risen to a difficult ethical obligation, and the least Perrein could have done is treat him with a bit more appreciation, thanked him for his involvement, whatever. But he had received nothing in the way of gratitude, no subtle indication that Perrein even welcomed his participation. Rebecca would have to take pains to make sure he didn't regret his decision.

"How's our strategy progressing?" Perrein asked, intruding on her thoughts.

"Good," she replied reflexively. "But I think we got a little sidetracked in our first meeting."

"How?" Perrein asked warily.

"You spent some time showing us that you really had no motivation to do what you're accused of—"

"Which is true."

"—but the fact is," she continued, ignoring his irrelevant comment, "the prosecution doesn't really have to show much in the way of motivation. If they make a solid case for you having sold the chips to the Chinese, they can make up a few half-baked rationales and that's all they need."

"On the other hand," Steinholz said, having rehearsed this with Rebecca, "if what they have is wildly circumstantial, very indirect stuff, then the only way they're gonna be able to back it up is by showing some heavy-duty motivations on your part."

"Not sure I follow."

"Let's say you were accused of murder," Steinholz explained. "If they have a gun with your prints, powder burns all over your hands, six eyewitnesses and a videotape of you shooting the victim, nobody's going to much care what your reason was."

He waited for some indication that Perrein was following, even just a nod of the head, and tried not to be put off by the shrug and sarcastic lip curl that asked, *Just how stupid do you think I am?*

"Okay. But now let's suppose the gun was wiped clean, there are no witnesses, no burns, no tape, and all they have is that the gun was registered in your name." This time he didn't pause to see if Perrein was tracking. "Now they've got a tougher case, but if they can demonstrate that you had strong motivation to knock the victim off, like maybe you had just taken out a million-dollar policy on his life, or you blamed him for your dog running away . . ." He let his voice trail off and spread his hands. "And if they can't, the jury will acquit."

"So what's wrong with that?" Perrein asked.

Steinholz was starting to get a little irritated, and Rebecca didn't blame him, but it needed to be kept in check. "Nothing," she said. "Except that it isn't going to happen like that because they've thought it through. We already know their case is largely circumstantial. And that means the government"—she still couldn't bring herself to say *Zuckerman* in front of Perrein—"is going to have to explain *why* you would have made and sold those chips. They're going to have to come up with some reasons the jury will buy, so they can get a conviction. You follow?" *Sneer at* me, *bigshot.*

"They're going to invent motivations for me to have done what they're charging me with?"

"Exactly." *Assuming they're inventions.* "Now, what do you suppose those might be?"

Perrein looked away distractedly and swiped at some nonexistent lint on his sleeve. "How the hell should *I* know?"

"I think you do." She said it accusingly, just to get his attention. He turned to look at her but didn't say anything. "You know this business inside and out. You've been debating the issue for three years. You gotta have *some* notion of what they could come up with to explain why you would have been tempted to export those chips."

"But I didn't export them, and never considered it, so I haven't spent time thinking about why I should!"

A bell went off somewhere in Rebecca's head, followed by her own voice speaking to her: *Tell me again why I'm being so polite to this douche bag? I'm stuck with his case, but it's not like I'm trying to keep a client happy so he doesn't take his business elsewhere. And I'm sure as hell not interested in any follow-on work. . . .*

A sudden feeling of lightness suffused her. "Okay." Rebecca nodded several times, then began picking up the papers in front of her and stuffing them back into folders. "But here's the thing: We've got pretrials coming up in four weeks, and if you don't arm me with some possibilities so I can anticipate them and plan out how to deal with them, you're gonna hamstring your own case."

"I told you, it would have made no sense for me to do it. Now you're asking me to come up with reasons that *do* make sense?"

"That's precisely what I'm asking." She stopped shuffling papers around and drilled him with her eyes, enjoying her newfound freedom to be as much of a cynical bitch as she felt like. "Unless you think that David Zuckerman is so goddamned stupid that he'd go to trial with shitty evidence and no way to explain to the jury why the defendant would commit the crime."

Steinholz and Ehrenright, flustered and self-conscious, elected to keep still as Rebecca and Perrein stared each other down.

Perrein broke first. "So what do you want me to do?"

"I want you to go and give this some thought, and then I want you to come back and tell us exactly what Zuckerman is going to claim were your reasons for selling those chips to the Chinese."

She held up a hand before he had a chance to repeat his misguided objections. "The better a job *you* do, the better the job *we're* gonna do. It's your ass, so it's your call." She went back to gathering up her notes.

Perrein scowled and drummed his fingers on the table, unaware of the heightened tension in the room. "Do I have to be there?" he asked after another minute.

Rebecca stopped packing and regarded him suspiciously. "Be where?"

"At the trial."

Rebecca remained motionless as Ehrenright looked from Perrein to her and back again. He was about to supply a stock answer but decided to let Rebecca handle this one.

"What are you talking about, Jim?"

"I'm talking about I got a company to run. We're still open for business, in case you forgot, and if I let these DoJ jerks tie me up so bad it all goes down the shitter, they win even if they lose."

Rebecca set some papers on the table and rested her hands on them, leaning forward toward Perrein. "In case *you* forgot, you're looking at prison time here, Jim. How do you plan to run your company from a cage in Allentown?"

Perrein pointed a finger at her and said angrily, "Usually when I hire lawyers, they go and handle things so I don't have to! What am I paying you for, if I have to spend all this time anyway!"

The question was so revealing of his ivory-towered cultural isolation that it didn't merit a reasoned response. Perrein was having trouble grasping the difference between a criminal and a civil case, and seemed unable to get over the notion that there actually existed a problem he couldn't buy his way out of.

"Technically," Rebecca said, "you can waive your constitutional rights to be present at the confrontation of your accusers and the cross-examination of their witnesses against you."

She sat down and folded her hands atop the papers. "But this case is going to be decided by a jury. These aren't law professors or learned scholars, they're just ordinary folks, okay, the kind of people who spend years planning an overseas trip, then stay in Holiday Inns and eat McDonald's so they can feel more at home. And if it comes down to which side they choose to believe based on nothing more than how everybody behaved in court while doing nothing, there's not a hell of a lot we can do about it."

She read nothing in his face as he stared down at the tabletop, although he did seem to be considering her words, so she went on. "They have to see you sitting there day after day, hurt, indignant, outraged, but stoic in the belief that the truth will out and your innocence will be affirmed."

Still nothing to indicate his reaction. "Otherwise, you're not a man seeking justice. To them you're just some corporate puke too contemptuous of the whole process to even bother to participate in his own defense."

That got his attention, and he looked up at her sharply just as she shrugged and stood up again. "But like I told you before," she said as she resumed putting papers and file folders back in her attaché, "it's your call. We'll let you know when procedure requires your presence, and the rest is up to you."

Seeing that she was almost packed up, Steinholz and Ehrenright grabbed at their own papers, neither wanting to be left in the room with Perrein once Rebecca was gone.

Chapter 11

Tuesday, August 25

When the Empire State Building in New York was completed in 1931, it set a new standard not only for monumental architecture but for more modest structures with monumental pretensions. The seventeen-story United States Courthouse at the corner of Spring and Temple in downtown Los Angeles looked from the outside like it had been built only the week before, but in fact had been constructed during the Roosevelt administration in 1937, six years after the completion of its 110-story stylistic predecessor in New York, with which it shared several motifs. These included a series of setbacks on the lower floors topped by clean lines rising straight up without further interruption. But unlike the graceful, light and soaring Empire State Building that drew one's eyes skyward, the squat and imposing courthouse was anchored firmly to the ground, solemnly conveying the gravity of its purpose despite the light pink color of its stone and the maroon trim outlining each of its windows.

California's Central District was second only to New York's Southern District in size, requiring its trisection into another layer of subdivisions. This courthouse served the Western Division.

Rebecca spotted Zuckerman walking toward the Main Street entrance, the less imposing back side that sported no plaza or lawns but did have a set of wide steps leading up to three bronze doors topped by stone columns. It was the first time she'd seen him since the case began, more surprising than it sounds since, unbeknownst to James Perrein, Zuckerman and Rebecca had lapsed into a surprisingly amiable, albeit entirely platonic, friendship in the aftermath of the disaster that Perrein had precipitated between them. They'd never spoken of that final chapter in their original relationship, sticking largely to professional or other emotionally innocuous matters. With Perrein's reappearance they had, by unspoken mutual assent, not so much consciously avoided each other as just not sought each other out. Rebecca suspected that Zuckerman's rationale would be similar to her own, and just as flaccid, that their legally mandated antagonism implied a conflict were they not to suspend their friendship.

From the vantage point of that enforced separation, Rebecca regarded Zuckerman as he approached the steps. He looked, as always, contemplative and brooding, that apparent state of mind comporting well with his slightly melancholy Mediterranean face. His skin was of just a deep enough shade to distinguish it from a good tan, and his dark hair, eyebrows and eyes completed the impression of pensive introspection. Tall, and lean, he might have been labeled wiry were he carrying less well-muscled bulk somewhat on the order of a professional tennis player's.

Rebecca hesitated, suddenly and inexplicably at a loss, considering that they were reasonably good friends. Seeing him like this sent her back to the first time they'd met, when his physical presence had caused her to stammer uncharacteristically despite his congenial and friendly manner. She was tempted to turn around before he spotted her, but that was pointless; she was going to be spending an awful lot of time with him over the next few months—they both knew that was not a conflict but a necessity—so she quickly gathered herself and resumed her normal pace, determined to behave normally, hoping he hadn't caught the falter.

"Hey," she called to him. "Heard the good news and the bad news?"

He turned, one hand on the railing, and replied without missing a beat. "What's the good news?"

"They found Hitler alive," she said as she walked up and mounted the first step. "He didn't die in that bunker."

"And the bad news?"

"They're gonna try him in L.A."

"Har de har har." He resumed his climb, Rebecca in his wake. "The hell're you so chipper about, anyway? Don't you know what a licking you got coming?"

"That a promise or a—"

"Yeah, yeah. See what happens to your sense of humor when I take you apart at trial."

She caught up to him at the top of the stairs. "Usual bet?"

"Candy from a baby."

They passed by the engraved plastic sign Rebecca always found so anomalous in a judicial setting—"No placards or demonstrations on U.S. Courthouse property, 18 USC S-1507"—and entered the building in front of a row of metal detectors. She had remembered not to wear a belt with a metal buckle lest she be forced to choose between getting half undressed or undergoing a faintly discomfiting phallic wanding.

She paused, as always, before the strange but arresting statue of Abraham Lincoln as a young man, shirtless, a thumb hooked into the waistband of his pants, carrying a book. The oversized head, hands and feet were reminiscent of Michelangelo's David, but on Phen-Fen.

"Still think that crazy statue's sexy?"

She nodded. *Looks like you, David.* "Half-naked president. Y'gotta love it."

They passed underneath a high arch separating the entry lobby from the inner building. The president and his veep smiled down from incongruously colorful and artless photographs mounted high overhead. Bypassing the elevators, they walked up using the wide stairwell reminiscent of an old elementary school. Emerging on the second floor, they were immediately shunted off to the first unlocked room by a marshal walking shotgun as two of his compatriots escorted a group of manacled prisoners through the hall. This was an oft-repeated ritual since, unlike more modern structures, the courthouse had no back corridors designated for the transport of potentially violent miscreants.

A minute later, they were buzzed into the hall leading to Judge Catherine Goldin's chambers. Eschewing formal airs, she met them herself in her assistant's anteroom and said hello to Zuckerman, then introduced herself to Rebecca as she ushered them in.

It was a beautifully decorated room, cozy despite its eight-hundred-square-foot size. At the far end, expensively leathered Chesterfield couches flanked a marble coffee table and two antique wing chairs. The other end accommodated a pair of round conference tables. A broad desk dominated the center, and the room was almost completely surrounded by floor-to-ceiling bookshelves done in rich woods and illuminated with recessed incandescent lamps.

On the only shelf not completely filled with books, there was a picture of Goldin shaking hands with President Gerald Ford, who'd appointed her, and a plethora of baseball memorabilia, including team photos of players wearing "Hang 'em High" T-shirts sporting Lady Justice holding not a set of scales but a noose. In each picture, Goldin was the player holding a trophy.

When they were seated, Rebecca and Zuckerman occupying the facing couches and Goldin on a chair, Rebecca asked the judge how familiar she was with the facts of the case at this early stage. She responded enigmatically, "Why don't we get started and find out."

But she had a few preliminary matters on her mind before they got into the specifics of the case. "Mr. Zuckerman's been in my court before, but you haven't," she said to Rebecca. "So let me just explain a few procedures in order to preclude any misunderstandings."

"I'd appreciate that."

"The Central District of this court goes all the way up to the Monterey County line, so we get jurors from as far away as Oxnard and Santa Barbara. They can stay overnight on jury days, but they often elect to commute, so we justices go out of our way to try to be accommodating. Even though the court day usually ends at one-thirty, if the jury wants to, we'll start at eight in the morning and go through to three or later, and they still get out in time to beat the traffic home."

Goldin folded her hands in her lap and got to the point of all this seemingly trivial information. "I look at my job as making sure that the jury is inside the courtroom as much as possible, not cooling their heels in the jury room while we haggle over technicalities. So there will be no sidebars unless it's an emergency."

Rebecca couldn't hide her surprise. "Then how do I explain an objection? Or justify a question?"

"You bring it up beforehand, in chambers. Think of every line of questioning you propose to pursue and any possible objections the prosecution might raise. We'll solve them all before we bring the jury in. And if something unexpected comes up that we can't get past, I'll excuse the witness, we'll move on to another area, and then I'll recall him the next day after we've had a chance to talk in chambers."

Goldin's assistant knocked softly on the doorjamb and stuck her head in. "Sorry, Your Honor. Judge Bardwick on the line?"

"Excuse me," Goldin said. "Only be a minute."

Rebecca had never had an uninterrupted chambers conversation with a judge in her entire career, so this was no surprise. She looked down at her notes but Zuckerman was speaking to her.

"Becky," he said. "Don't waste time bringing the judge up to speed. Trust me, she's already read every scrap of paper associated with the case."

Rebecca heard Goldin returning, too late for her to acknowledge Zuckerman's tip, and they took up the matter of the tutorial portion of the trial, the piece in which the prosecution tries to acquaint the jury with the technical underpinnings of the testimony they're going to be hearing about.

"I want to use Ivars Petorsky," Zuckerman said, "to explain the basic issues as neutrally as possible, try to save some time."

Rebecca nodded, trying to look as agreeable and reasonable as possible in front of the judge. "I don't have a problem with that, long as I can review the questions and answers in advance."

Goldin asked that the initial tutorial be kept simple, not sprinkled with excessive technical detail the jury wouldn't be able to relate to without some context. Later, during the more substantive testimony, they could hear additional detail as it became relevant. "For example, teach them what encoding and decoding are, but leave out any discussion of trapdoor algorithms at this point. If it becomes necessary later, I'll allow it. Same thing for public key encryption."

Rebecca tried to keep her features even; this judge knew more about the topic than she did herself.

"What about escrow keys?" Zuckerman was saying.

"LEAF, yeah," Goldin said, as Rebecca, lost, struggled not to panic. "Not clear to me it's even relevant. Ms. Verona, is it your intention to challenge the validity of the ITARs?"

Rebecca lost the struggle. *What in the flaming hell is an ITAR!*

Zuckerman, perceiving her distress, came to the rescue. "Your honor, I doubt this trial is the proper venue to challenge the regulations concerning the export of encryption devices."

Goldin looked at him in surprise, not realizing that Zuckerman was only throwing a lifeline to Rebecca. "Now why would that be? It seems the perfect place to—"

"Your Honor, it's a moot point anyway," Rebecca interrupted, catching on quickly. "I have no intention of challenging the ITARs, much as I'd like to. I'd only do that if my client violated them, but he didn't break any laws and that will be our sole defense."

Goldin had begun nodding halfway through Rebecca's explanation. "Suits me. What else?"

Zuckerman announced his intention to call a witness who was an expert in the international marketing of high technology. Goldin stayed quiet, since there was no need for her to respond to a proposed action on the part of an attorney unless the other objected, which Rebecca did, questioning the relevance of such a witness.

"We need to establish a motivation for Perrein to have sold those chips," Zuckerman explained. "It's obvious that he didn't do it for the money—it would only be a couple million and he hardly needs it." Just as Perrein had told the defense team. "For all I know he *gave* the chips to the Chinese. We think there were two other reasons. One is that he needed to test the chip technology under live conditions, using real-world data that his designers might not have correctly anticipated. He couldn't do that in this country without revealing what Tera-Tech was working on.

"Secondly, he may have been setting up the marketplace. Clearly, Perrein believes that the export ban will be lifted one day. If he got himself in tight with the Chinese early on, he'd have a head start into the largest market in the world." He could tell that Goldin understood exactly what he was talking about. "I have a witness who will testify as to the plausibility of these motivations."

Rebecca also saw the judge swallowing Zuckerman's argument. "Your Honor, I move *in limine* to completely exclude any such testimony. It's pure speculation not backed up by a single shred of evidence." As she had promised herself she would, she kept her voice calm, reasonable and moderately paced. Because her mind usually moved so much faster than her words, she could plan ahead and not stumble; the net effect was a delivery so smooth it might have been scripted. "If the government is allowed to invent a motive out of thin air and demonstrate that it's *plausible* without showing that it's *applicable*, it makes a total mockery not only of the rules of evidence but the concepts of prosecutorial burden of proof and reasonable doubt. Is counsel seriously suggesting that my client is a criminal because it was *possible* that he had a motive?"

"My goodness, you always that literary when you're angry?" Goldin exclaimed. "I'll grant your motion. However, I'm not going to specifically prohibit the government from asking questions along those lines of other witnesses, as long as they're relevant in context. You can raise objections at those times and I'll rule on them individually. Next?"

Rebecca, buoyed by this significant victory, jumped right into the big one. "The defense demands to be allowed to examine the chip being held in evidence by the Department of Justice. Examine it internally as well."

Zuckerman shook his head forcefully, and Goldin crossed her legs and rested her chin on her hand, knowing that this wasn't going to be dispatched easily. Signaling to Zuckerman that Rebecca's request was reasonable and proper, and therefore the onus was on him to try to counter it, she nodded for him to make his argument.

"We're adamant on this one, Judge," he said, sitting up on the edge of the couch. "If that chip gets damaged or destroyed, not only will our case be threatened, but the national security ramifications will be very serious. Furthermore—"

"That's not our—" Rebecca began, but Goldin held up her hand and gave her a stern look.

"Let's let him finish, okay? I promise I won't rule until both of you have had all your say."

"Right now the chip is in perfect working order," Zuckerman continued. "We can demonstrate the chip's functionality because we can hook it up and actually run it. If the defense *accidentally* loses or destroys the chip, our case is out the window."

The implication of his emphasis on the word *accidentally* was not lost on Rebecca, but she held her tongue as instructed.

"More importantly . . ." Here Zuckerman paused, wondering if it was wise to remind Rebecca and Goldin of their security obligations, then thought better of it; the point would be self-evident. "If we ever do confront the Chinese in the open, we need to be able to show them a working chip as proof of our charges. Should it be mishandled and rendered inoperative, the Chinese can just laugh at us and continue to deny everything.

"Now the thing is, Your Honor, and I don't know if counsel is aware of this, but opening up a microchip chip to look inside is a destructive process. It can't be done without ruining the chip. So there are two separate issues here. One is whether the defense gets physical possession of the chip at all. And if they do, can they open it up, and the government strongly objects on both counts. Now"—Zuckerman looked at Rebecca—"I think I can anticipate counsel's counterargument, so let me add that we're willing to concede that the prosecution will only present evidence against Tera-Tech based on the surface features of the chip and the results of our performance testing." He looked back at the judge. "In other words, Your Honor, the government won't be able to look inside the chip, either."

First waiting a few seconds to make sure that he was finished, Rebecca asked him, "What kind of case is that?"

"We're willing to let it go to the jury on that basis, and take our chances."

"Then we'll take the position that there's no evidence the chip came from Tera-Tech, that this is a frame-up, and there's no independent corroboration of your tests."

"Fine," Zuckerman responded, and Rebecca realized too late that she'd stepped into a trap. She had essentially offered a condition for acceding to Zuckerman's position, and when he accepted it, it cut off her ability to keep arguing. Replaying it quickly in her head, she further realized that she'd gotten nothing out of the exchange. All she'd done was threaten to adopt a particular defense posture, over which Zuckerman had no say anyway.

Zuckerman was smart enough not to gloat over it, but moved on immediately, anticipating another objection and dealing with it. "In the interests of fairness, the government will run any reasonable tests requested by the defense, and report the results back promptly."

"What's reasonable?" Rebecca asked, sensing that there might be a possibility of resurrecting her argument after all.

"It can't involve destructive testing. The chip stays in operating condition at all times."

"We strenuously object to the use of chip data supplied by the government," Rebecca said to Goldin. "We have absolutely no way to independently verify that the results are accurate . . ." A couple of new ideas made themselves evident to her even as she was speaking. ". . . or if they really hooked it up and ran it, or that the chip even really works, for that matter, or if there's even anything inside it at all!"

As Terescu urged her to, Rebecca pressed as hard as she could, because a proper examination could not be performed unless they took the chip apart. But Zuckerman was right, that taking it apart would destroy it. He stood firm in his basic objective of not releasing the chip to the defense, and Goldin had little choice but to agree with him.

"However," she reminded him, "your case is largely circumstantial already and will be weaker without a detailed examination.

The defense is going to be free to hammer that point all they want."

Zuckerman didn't try to dispute that. "For reasons of national security, we'll have to take that chance."

Recognizing that Goldin was leaning toward his side, Rebecca asked, "How can the defense be sure we got all the testing results?"

"What's the difference?" Zuckerman replied. "We can't use anything we haven't disclosed to you anyway. . . ."

"The difference is, how do we know you haven't found something that might benefit my client, and you're sitting on it?"

Zuckerman was stymied as to how to respond to that conundrum, and Goldin jumped in to ask her what she wanted.

"I want an affidavit that the defense has received every scrap of paper that was generated, and I also want the right to subpoena everyone involved in the tests."

Zuckerman, surprised but relieved at such an easy out, readily agreed to the affidavit and said he would supply a list of names of those involved in the testing. He added that he'd be calling most of those people himself anyway, and so the defense would have an opportunity to cross-examine without issuing subpoenas.

Having failed in her primary mission of getting her hands on the chip itself, Rebecca participated only halfheartedly in the largely minor remainder of the pretrial matters, returning to her office in dejection.

"Don't see how you could've won no matter what you did, Becky," Steinholz said consolingly after she'd reported on the meeting. "This is really starting to smell like a scam on the government's part."

"Just proves my point," Terescu agreed. "The chip is a sham. That's why they're afraid to let us see it for ourselves. So what do we do?"

"Take our lumps for now and move on," Rebecca said. "No choice but to move ahead with your analysis, using their data."

"The good news," Ehrenright observed, "is that we have some pretty good grounds for appeal if it comes to that."

As they were breaking up, Rebecca took Steinholz aside and asked, "What the hell is a trapdoor algorithm?"

He raised his eyebrows in surprise. "Well, when you put a message into code, you use a key. Usually, the person receiving the message uses the same key to decode it. But there's a problem with that."

"And that is . . . ?"

"Once I have your key, I could use it to read all of your other messages, too. But let's say there's one key to put messages into code, and a *different* key to decode them. Now I can't read any of your stuff, even though I can still send you coded messages. You could even publish the encoding key in *The New York Times* so people could send you coded messages, but nobody would be able to use it to read your other information. So putting a message into code is like dropping it through a one-way trapdoor: you can put it into code, but you can't go the other way. It's called a public key system, because you can make your encoding key public without harm."

"Is that relevant for us?"

"It's the whole point of Tera-Tech's system." He asked her where she'd heard the expression.

"From Judge Goldin," she replied. Steinholz was impressed.

Rebecca sighed and leaned against the doorjamb. "I can't put it off any longer," she said wearily. "I gotta get up to speed on all this stuff. Shit, I didn't even know what the ITARs were."

"Oh, gee, nothing important; just the laws under which the DoJ indicted our client."

Rebecca started to bite her lip when Steinholz added, "But cheer up. You really don't need to be familiar with those, except the very basics."

"How come?"

"Do we plan on challenging the ITARs?"

"Course not. We're taking the position that our client didn't violate them, just like I told the judge."

"So then why worry the details? All we have to do is show that he never committed the acts alleged. If he didn't do anything, then he didn't break the law, so what difference do the details make? Forget about 'em."

The thought cheered her, but then Steinholz said, "Concentrate on the technology, Becky. I'll handle most of it, but you gotta be ready to pounce if stuff comes up in cross we weren't expecting."

She sighed again and nodded.

Chapter 12

Thursday, September 17

She was used to it by now, that shuf-
fling gait, the tiny steps, as though the visitors were making a last-
ditch effort to avoid ever entering the conference room. Something
in their minds tried to deny that the distance from the reception
area to whatever room Rebecca was in was finite; maybe if they
slowed their walk, they'd never reach her.

She had special receptors to detect the aura of a challenge brewing, some delicious one-on-one work to be done, a heavyweight
matchup in which the expert's superior intellect and experience
made her the underdog, and therefore her victories much sweeter.
The last time those detectors started twitching was when Jules
Dirksen, the expert witness in *Universal Data Systems* v. *Tamarack
Ltd.*, came through the door. But at this moment they were lighting
up the switchboard as Radovan Terescu made his halting way
toward her den.

He shook hands perfunctorily but didn't look Rebecca in the eye
as he busied himself taking off his jacket, setting down his attaché
case, fumbling with the locks and a symphony of other minor
movements to delay introduction of the main theme. Rebecca easily
maintained the outward calm that appeared whenever her blood
began to speed up its trip through her arteries. It was an instinctual, preternatural adaptation response, heightening the anxiety,
and therefore the susceptibility, in the adversary. The equally
poised and untroubled Steinholz and Ehrenright did nothing to alleviate Terescu's mounting apprehension, and even Janine Osterreich's complete indifference contributed to his unshakable sense
that everyone else was in harmony and he was the only one who
was going to introduce sour notes.

"Been working hard, Doc?" Rebecca asked casually.

"Yes!" Terescu fairly shouted before catching himself and
lowering his voice. "Yes. It's, uh, it's not been as smooth as I'd
anticipated."

"Howzzat?" Ehrenright asked as he took a seat.

"Well . . ." Terescu forced himself to stop his busywork and keep his hands still. "I request tests, yes? And then I wait for the results. Only when I see those do I know what further tests are required, and I have to submit new requests. Then there's a day or two of absurd questions from the government people, 'to clarify,' they tell me; 'We want to be absolutely certain we comply with your wishes, Professor.' "

Rebecca pointed toward the chair and Terescu dropped down onto it. "But in the time they take to 'clarify,' they could have run the tests ten times."

"So they're just delaying things," Rebecca suggested.

"So it would seem. And needlessly adding to your expenses."

"Not a problem. You need more time, I'll file an affidavit and get you whatever's required."

Terescu shook his head. "Shouldn't be necessary."

Rebecca looked over to make sure Osterreich was transcribing the conversation. Anything their expert committed to paper was discoverable by the prosecution, but not privileged discussions such as this one. This method of keeping things out of the opposition's hands while still allowing the expert to record his thoughts was Rebecca's personal contribution to the time-honored tradition of using the law to circumvent itself.

"Okay." Rebecca flipped open her legal pad and slapped her pen down on the blank sheet. "Bottom-line it for us before we dive into the detail."

Terescu nodded and prepared to start shuffling things around again, then thought better of it and folded his hands. "I wish I had the smoking gun, the one item that would end this case today," he began, bravely looking at each of the three of them in turn. He bit his lip. "But I don't. My news is not pleasant." He looked at Rebecca. "It doesn't look so good for your client." He stopped, jaw muscles tight as he waited for the inevitable looks of devastation in his small audience.

Rebecca stared at him for a few seconds, expressionless, then smiled. "What're you looking so damned glum for, Rado?"

Terescu blinked rapidly several times, his lips parting slightly. "Why am I—" He turned his head sharply to look at Steinholz, then Ehrenright, getting back only untroubled expressions, and he frowned in confusion.

Ehrenright slouched back on his chair and shrugged his shoulder. "Truth is truth, Doc," he said almost apathetically. "Our job isn't to make stuff up, or hope things are what they aren't. It's to play the cards we're dealt, make the most of 'em." He sat forward and pulled a pen out of his breast pocket. "Whatever you came up with, we'll deal with it."

Rebecca knew that Terescu had been dreading this moment for weeks, the tension in him mounting by the hour. Now that they'd decompressed him so rapidly, the sudden cessation of that strain left him almost weak with relief. With gratitude. And, most important of all, vulnerability.

"So watcha got, Rado?" Rebecca uncapped her pen and sat forward. "Conclusions first, then how you got there."

"Certainly." As Terescu pulled papers out of folders, Rebecca was pleased to see that they all seemed to consist of test reports from the prosecution investigators. It appeared as though, as instructed, Terescu had made few notes of his own.

He laid two sets of papers side by side. "First, there is no doubt that the chip in question uses the exact encryption methodology as that developed by Tera-Tech's scientists." He looked around the table to make sure everyone understood, then explained that he had submitted to the government a large chunk of complex data and asked them to run it through the chip and give him back the results. Meanwhile, he ran the same data through a Cray supercomputer at Cal Tech using Tera-Tech's method. The results of the two encryptions were identical.

"Can't say that's too surprising," Steinholz commented. "If that weren't true, they'd have no case whatsoever."

Terescu agreed that this should not have come as a major shock. "However," he added, "you should all know that it took our Cray over six minutes to perform the encoding." He looked around meaningfully. "The prosecution reported that it took the chip less than a second."

That meant nothing to Rebecca, but she heard Steinholz draw in a sharp breath. "The Cray is fast?" she asked.

"Most powerful computer in the world," Steinholz responded. "About the size of this room, cooled with liquid helium . . ."

"I don't ever remember being more shocked in my life," Terescu threw in for emphasis. "Of course, the chip is a specialized computer with a single task, and the Cray is general purpose, but still . . ." He knit his brows in concentration as he tried to think of a way to communicate the significance to Rebecca. "A three-year-old breaking the sound barrier on his tricycle would have surprised me less."

"Amazing," Rebecca said to herself as she scribbled a few notes. Were Terescu able to decipher her nearly illegible scrawl, he would have read, *Pick up orange juice on way home.* "Okay, the encryption method built into the chip is Tera-Tech's. What else?"

"The matter of how fast the chip is." Terescu had loosened up, any lingering trepidation having been fully dissipated by the amiable tone in the room. "It has to have at least 256 million transistors, and—"

"Hold it a minute," Rebecca interrupted. "Two hundred and fifty-six? Seems awfully precise for an estimate."

Terescu and Steinholz exchanged smiles. "Actually, it's a round number, Becky," Steinholz explained. "Computer scientists do everything in powers of two. Next lower number would be 128, next higher 512."

Terescu nodded his concurrence. "Trust me, this is a ballpark figure. The important point is, there are only a few places known to be working on things even close to that advanced, Tera-Tech being one of them. They may not have announced anything yet, but they have people on staff who have devoted their whole lives to such things, and they're all in the Fabrication Research Group. If this chip really does what the government says it is doing, well . . ."

"You said *close*," Rebecca reminded him. "And only at a few places. How close do we know other outfits have gotten?"

"Not even half that," Terescu said.

"So two-fifty-six is . . . ?"

Terescu shook his head. "Beyond unbelievable."

"But there it is."

"So they say."

Rebecca folded her arms across her chest and sat back. "I understand. What else?"

"I studied the list, the one Perrein gave me, the list of all of Tera-Tech's equipment, and I don't see anything on it that would even approach being able to provide the capabilities of making this chip in quantity."

However . . . Rebecca said to herself.

"However, that doesn't mean that they don't have some highly sophisticated lab techniques that might have allowed them to build each chip individually, since they are working very hard on fabrication research. One could assume that they have developed some capabilities in the lab to . . ."

Rebecca shifted mental gears as Terescu continued on, mumbling something about the amount of heat the device generated. She didn't need to listen to the arcane technical details; as far as she was concerned, they were not only irrelevant but distracting. She reserved a small portion of her attention to detecting vocal patterns that called for her to nod her head or grunt acknowledgment of a key point, and used the time to get herself organized.

A few minutes later he began finishing up, the three attorneys listening in rapt attention, Janine Osterreich filling page after page with indecipherable shorthand transcription she would later decode and type up.

"I guess that's pretty much the heart of it," Terescu said, folding his hands again and looking around.

"Very thorough, Rado." Rebecca looked down and quickly scanned her notes: a grocery list; a reminder to change the oil in her car; some thoughts on the final draft of the *Universal Data Systems v. Tamarack Ltd.* settlement agreement. "Nice job!" She looked at her colleagues to solicit their concurrence.

"Wish it could have been better news," Terescu sighed, stretching his arms out in front of him to relieve some imaginary kinks.

"Like Justin said," Rebecca reassured him, "it is what it is. Can we go back through some of it, see what we have in terms of your testimony at trial?"

"Oh, certainly," Terescu said eagerly, assuming he'd be lecturing while everyone else took notes.

Rebecca flipped to a clean sheet. They'd been talking for nearly an hour, but as far as she was concerned, there were really only three, easily memorized problems to be handled.

"Let's talk about the encryption method used in the chip. It's the same as Tera-Tech's, right?"

"Exactly the same," Terescu answered. "To the last bit."

"Got it. Now, do I understand correctly that Tera-Tech published the results of their encryption research before the government clamped down?"

"They did," Ehrenright said, pulling a pamphlet-sized document out of a folder lying in front of him and sliding it across the table to Rebecca. "In a journal."

"Gave lectures on it, too," Steinholz added.

Rebecca opened the folder as she nodded at Steinholz's comment, then looked back at Terescu. "So lots of people could have had access to it and duplicated it."

"Yes," Terescu agreed. "But they couldn't have built it into a chip."

"Wait a minute," Rebecca said, smiling genially. "Gotta take this one step at a time or else dummies like me are gonna get lost!"

As Terescu returned her smile, Ehrenright said, "And you gotta remember, Professor: all testimony is for the jury's benefit, and it's a pretty good bet a bunch of them never even made it through high school."

"All I'm trying to understand at this point," Rebecca said, "is that the simple fact that Tera-Tech's method showed up somewhere doesn't necessarily prove that Tera-Tech had anything to do with it. Is that a reasonable assumption?"

Terescu, perceiving that a gentle remonstrance had just taken place, agreed readily, nodding his head as he spoke. "Definitely. Doesn't prove a thing."

"Ah." Rebecca glanced at Osterreich, who nodded back at her: *Got it.* "So let's move on to the next point, all those transistors crammed onto this chip." She tapped her pen on the legal pad. "First of all, why is such miniaturization important? I've always wondered about that anyway. What's the point of making these things so tiny?"

The question struck Terescu as an irrelevant aside, but he answered it anyway. "You must bear in mind that it takes time for electrical signals to travel from one place to another on a chip."

"But isn't that incredibly fast?" Rebecca asked in surprise. "I mean, like the speed of light or something?"

"It's very fast, but not the speed of light," Terescu answered. "Not when they're traveling through wires. And in a chip that is executing millions of instructions each second—the time it takes for the signals to get from one transistor to another? Those delays start to add up."

"Okay, I'm following."

"You want to try to reduce the amount of time the signals take to get from one component to another, and one way to do that is to put the components closer together. And therefore you have to make them smaller. The smaller you can make them, the faster the chip. Roughly speaking, make the chip half as big, and it runs twice as fast."

"I understand," Rebecca said. "And more speed means more computing power?"

"Exactly."

"And making their chips as powerful as possible is pretty important to everybody involved in this field, right?"

"Certainly. That's what the research is all about. And, of course, getting the individual components to work faster as well. No sense moving the signals around quickly if each component handles them too slowly."

"So Tera-Tech isn't the only outfit in the world working on, uh, what do you call it, cramming in as many transistors as possible . . . ?"

"Component density."

"And doing things to make each component work faster? I take it lots of people are working on both these areas?"

"Of course."

"And haven't other companies recently announced some major breakthroughs? And aren't there universities doing research like that, schools that are afraid to publish scholarly papers for fear of being beaten out of lucrative technology transfer contracts?" At this point in the conversation, these were essentially rhetorical questions, to which Terescu had no choice but to nod in agreement.

"Hell," Rebecca continued, "most of those professors—no disrespect intended—they start new companies of their own to commercially exploit their research. Even you, Radovan: can't your, uh, watchamacallit, your X-ray laser and those gold wires, can't they be used to achieve densities like that?"

"Yes, and in fact I have, on an extremely small scale, but it won't be seen in real working chips for many years. It's still in the pure research stage."

"Well, let's not bring *that* up unless you're asked, but the point is, lots of people are doing stuff like this and not talking about it, so how does it prove that Tera-Tech made this chip?" She stopped and waited for an answer.

"It doesn't, necessarily, but when you add up all of the other—"

"Don't add it up!" Rebecca nearly yelled, then caught herself and lowered her voice, but not her emphasis. "*Don't add it up!* We're just building reasonable doubt about each individual piece. If you express a professional opinion that each of these pieces could have been done elsewhere, that'll give us all the doubt we need. Let's not do the prosecution's job for them, okay?"

Rebecca smiled, making light of a tactic that was blatantly deceitful but perfectly legal, standard operating procedure for the defense.

"Okay . . ." Terescu agreed hesitantly.

That's all Rebecca wanted, and there was no reason for her to belabor the point and risk his backsliding. "And as to Tera-Tech hiring people into the fabrication group, well, that's pretty vague. I hired a Guatemalan lady with a master's in history. What does she do, teach my kids history? No. She cleans my house!"

Terescu laughed along with Steinholz and Ehrenright, nodding sheepishly, as though it had been his own failing not to have recognized such simple logic in the first place.

"You don't know exactly what they're doing there, so why speculate?" Rebecca finished, sealing the point and making it seem perfectly reasonable. "Now, this possibility that the wizards in Research might have knocked out a few experimental chips in the lab instead of the production line . . ."

Terescu picked up the thread. "You have to assume that they were doing intense research on component density and therefore—"

"Why do you have to assume that?"

Terescu looked around at Steinholz and Ehrenright, seeking some support for what he thought was simple common sense, but he found only expressions mirroring Rebecca's own look of perfect innocence.

She was used to this reaction from scientists. They felt as though they'd fallen through a looking glass into some bizarre netherworld where two plus two had a negotiable result and they were the only inhabitants who didn't seem to know exactly what was going on.

"Well," Terescu chanced, sensing that it was probably futile, "how could they possibly be working on fabrication research unless they—"

"Hold it a second." Rebecca picked up a copy of Tera-Tech's equipment list and handed it to him. "Do you see anything on that list that would be able to produce these kinds of densities?"

"No . . ."

Rebecca held her hands out. "Okay, then why assume anything?"

Terescu still wasn't willing to abandon common sense completely. "Well, the prosecution is going to assume—"

"Never mind what they're going to assume! You got a list, that list won't do it, and therefore you can express the opinion that you don't believe they had the capability."

"But I don't know that for sure. I only know what's on this list!"

"My whole point!" Rebecca said, grinning and patting Terescu's arm, as though he had come to some kind of brilliant understanding on his own and just hadn't realized it. "You don't know for sure, and *they* don't know for sure. That's reasonable doubt right there, and that's all we need."

Terescu tried to think about it in terms of legal reasonable doubt rather than the kinds of probability he was used to dealing with, and in that context it actually made some sense. "I suppose it's fair for me to say that others are as likely as Tera-Tech to have made great strides in this field of research."

"Exactly!" Rebecca said, underscoring his conclusion. But it wasn't enough. "And you said, when we first met, that you didn't believe Tera-Tech could have made it. That there's no evidence that they have the capability. Isn't that still true?" She put a note of hopefulness in her voice, intimating not that he might disappoint her by expressing a harmful opinion, but by reversing an earlier statement upon which she had come to rely.

He wasn't about to do that. "Well, more so even than that: I don't know of *anybody* who has the capability."

That was too much. *Gently now; don't make a big deal out of it.* "Well, let's not bring that up in court."

"Why not? It's true."

"I know. But when you get right down to it, it's very speculative. And the prosecutor can ask you if you have personal knowledge of every laboratory in the whole world. That will make you look weak." Although she meant *weak* in terms of the case, she wanted Terescu to take it personally.

"I understand. Just stick to the facts."

"That's it. You can never get into trouble if you stay with what you know."

Steinholz and Ehrenright could tell that Rebecca had another reason for suppressing this bit of insight regarding who else might have the capability, but they had no idea what that might be.

Having gotten Terescu exactly where she wanted him, Rebecca quickly wound things down and got him out of there. The more time that passed, and the closer to trial it got, the more difficult it would be for him to come back to them with further doubts.

* * *

"Big thing now," Rebecca said to her colleagues, "is to get down to the task of laying out the direct examination of Terescu and Perrein, and we also need to plan for every possible cross-examination angle we can think of to go after the prosecution's witnesses."

But Steinholz was still puzzled by her last instruction to Terescu. "Why not let him get up there and state that he doesn't believe any of it, that the chip is complete bullshit? Isn't that pretty powerful?"

"Yeah," Ehrenright agreed. "How does it get better than that?"

Rebecca hesitated before answering. "What if the chip does exactly what the government says it does?"

After a long pause, Ehrenright responded first. "You think that's possible?"

"Possible? I've been trying to tell you guys: quit assuming the prosecution has its head up its ass. Suppose Terescu gets up there and says this chip can't exist. Then suppose they get up there and demonstrate it right in front of everybody." She looked at them to make sure they grasped the implications.

"Terescu looks like a complete schmuck," Steinholz concluded. "All his credibility right out the window."

"And he's our only expert."

"Do you believe the chip is real?" Ehrenright asked.

"I have no way of knowing. But I'll admit I have a funny feeling about it." *Because I know David Zuckerman all too well.* "And we can't take that chance."

PART II

ARGUMENT

Few spectacles can be more absurd than that of a jury composed of twelve persons who, without any scientific knowledge or training, are suddenly called upon to adjudicate in controversies in which the most eminent scientific men flatly contradict each other. How can ordinary tradesmen and farmers be expected to weigh evidence, the delivery of which occupies many days, and which bear upon subjects which can only be described in language altogether new and foreign to their understandings?

—*On Trial by Jury and the Evidence of Experts*
(Author unknown, 1899)

Chapter 13

Thursday, October 29

"All rise!"

The door behind and to the left of the bench opened and Judge Goldin walked in. The change in the atmosphere of the room had less to do with the automatic respect accorded a federal judge than with the judge herself, six feet of smoothly rolling gait that would dominate any closed space she chose to enter. She didn't bother to look around the room, but concentrated strictly on the decreasing space between her and the bench, as though this little walk were more important than anything that might be going on in the rest of the courtroom. She didn't do it deliberately, or even consciously, and was quite unaware of the effect. As most people who plied the federal court knew, four years ago she had fallen over a sound cable taped to the floor. She wasn't hurt, or even very embarrassed, at least at first, until the court turned into a European soccer stadium as half the assembled trial participants scrambled madly to demonstrate their concern.

She took her seat and began arranging some papers in front of her, then lifted her gavel and rapped it twice to bring the court to order and announce the official beginning of the session. The clerk read the name and number of the case, along with a brief summary of the charges. Goldin folded her hands and finally looked up for the first time. She quickly ascertained that both defense counsel and prosecutor were present, along with the defendant, and asked, "Both sides ready?"

Rebecca and Zuckerman rose up halfway out of their chairs, responding in the affirmative, and sat back down.

"Good. First order of business, I'm ordering some limitations on coverage. None of the direct participants will speak of this case to anyone not also directly involved. This applies to all the attorneys, the defendant, the jurors and court personnel. And there will be no cameras of any kind allowed in the courtroom."

She waited for the expected hubbub, but declined to use her gavel. She swept the room with her disapproving gaze, and the murmuring died quickly. "There is no reason for the lawyers to speak to the press. Reporters can see for themselves what's going on in here, so the attorneys don't know any more than the press does. And if you do know more, you shouldn't be telling them anyway."

"Your Honor . . ."

"Mr. Zuckerman."

"One of the purposes of having a public trial," Zuckerman said as he rose, "is so that potential wrongdoers can see the consequences of breaking the law. If this defendant is convicted, the people ought to be aware of that, and the process that got him there."

"I'm sure the newspapers will do an adequate job of reporting it to them."

"But they should see for themselves."

"Then let them come here and sit in court with the rest of us. Ms. Verona?"

"Your Honor, as far as the government is concerned, my client is a traitor to his country, and his reputation has already suffered. Even if he's acquitted, it will be difficult for him to salvage that reputation unless the people see the process firsthand."

Goldin smiled ever so slightly, knowing what both attorneys knew as well regarding Rebecca's motivation, that she could use the government's reticence to expose matters of national security to her advantage. That didn't seem to bother Zuckerman, though, since he'd also argued for a televised trial, apparently confident of a conviction without such exposure.

But Goldin also knew that Rebecca's tactic wasn't dependent on there being a camera in the courtroom. "You can tell them all about it afterward."

"May we approach?" Zuckerman asked, adding, "Thirty seconds, tops." He felt comfortable requesting a forbidden sidebar because Goldin hadn't informed them in advance of her gag order.

"Bottom-line this for us, Judge," he began when both he and Rebecca were standing before her. "Are there any conditions at all under which you'd let cameras into this courtroom?"

"Off the record?"

Both attorneys nodded their agreement.

Goldin leaned forward and kept her voice low. "Never happen. I'm not going to have this trial OJ'd, the three of us trying to win Emmys instead of seeking justice. This one gets tried in the courtroom, not the press, and I don't want to sequester this jury."

Rebecca jerked a thumb over her shoulder without looking back. "You've still got to wrestle with Johannsen over there."

"Shaking in my boots. Step back." She held out a hand and the clerk put a piece of paper in it, but she didn't have to read it. "Okay, I'll hear from the media representative now."

"Thank you, Your Honor." The voice came from a stocky, well-dressed young woman walking forward from the audience section, through the low swinging door, past the attorneys' tables and up to the podium. Her movements were polished, as though she had been born and raised in this room, and she skipped the usual microphone fiddling and instead spoke out in a strong but carefully modulated voice.

"I'm Barbara Johannsen, representing various media companies in their wish to—"

"Hang on a second," Goldin said, disrupting a performance that clearly had been carefully rehearsed, but for which no contingencies had been worked out in the event of an interruption. "Whom do you represent?"

Johannsen recovered well. "Networks, newspapers—"

"All of them?"

Johannsen hesitated, not sure what was behind the question, and therefore not sure what spin to put on her answer. Maybe the judge was questioning whether she had the mandate to speak for all media . . . ?

That had to be it. "Most of the majors, I believe."

"Good. For the record, you're the only media rep I'm going to hear. My ruling will be binding on all of them."

"I think that'll be all right."

"I'm so glad. You may proceed."

"Your Honor, we're objecting to the blanket gag order the court has placed on the participants in this trial. We don't believe it's fair or proper. We're moving to allow a camera in the courtroom, a single pool camera providing a feed to the various networks and local stations. We further move that seats be set aside for the exclusive use of reporters, and also that the participants in this case be allowed unfettered conversations with the press." The opening statement was a good one, clearly laying out the purpose of her presence.

Then Johannsen lapsed into the tired, self-servingly patriotic phraseology of the fourth estate. "This case is a matter of national importance . . . the people have a right to know . . . gagging the attorneys is a violation of First Amendment principles . . ." Thankfully, she managed to work in the obligatory and hopelessly hackneyed "chilling effect" only twice, and "slippery slope" only once.

Goldin listened with practiced patience until Johannsen ran out of platitudes. "Here's a problem I have, Ms. Johannsen: You've sat in on trials, right?"

"Of course, many times."

"So you know that there are certain things the jury is not supposed to hear. Like if the lawyers argue about some questions they'd like to ask a witness, or some piece of evidence that's been introduced, things like that, right?"

"Yes, but—"

"And you also know that lawyers are not supposed to vouch the evidence. That means they're not allowed to tell the jury what they personally believe, or their opinions about the merits of the case, right?"

"True. However—"

"They have to follow a strict set of guidelines designed to protect the rights of both sides. Now, what do lawyers do when they talk to the media?"

"They provide information and insight that isn't—"

"I'll tell you what they do." Goldin folded her arms and leaned forward, gazing intently at the hapless lawyer. "They try to convince everybody out in the world that their side of the case is correct, and the other side is psychotic for even attempting to put forth an opposite position. And they're not bound by any rules of evidence and procedure when they do so." Goldin tilted her head to her left and then back again. "Now this is an unsequestered jury. They're inevitably going to hear and see media coverage of this case. So if the lawyers engage in sidewalk harangues with your clients, then they get to tell the jury all of the things they can't tell them legally."

Johannsen wisely decided to stay quiet.

"And here's another thing: Let's say for the sake of argument that a defense attorney doesn't believe in his own client's innocence. He's still legally obligated to fight for that client. But the law does *not* require him to go out and do so for the newspapers, which is going to make it look to the world, and the jury, like he knows it's a losing cause, or ought to be."

Goldin stopped. Johannsen waited a few seconds just to make sure. "But isn't it up to the lawyers themselves to exercise restraint in that regard? Shouldn't they be the ones responsible for not revealing information or opinions that might influence the jury?"

"Good point. And therefore, they shouldn't be saying anything they didn't say in court, which means you don't get any additional insight and information beyond what happened in this room, which you are welcome to sit and observe. So I've got only two options in trying to protect the interests of the parties, as well as of justice: one is to sequester the jury, the other is to gag the attorneys and the defendant. I'm not going to sequester this jury, so we'll set aside four seats for the press, but your motion for a pool camera is denied and the gag order stands."

Johannsen, flustered at having her motion denied so quickly, and right in front of her media clients, gamely tried to carry on. "But the public has a *right* to know!"

Goldin sat upright and started spreading papers out on her bench. "So tell them. It'll be a matter of public record anyway, transcript available to anybody in the country for the cost of photocopying it. How many copies get requested will give us a good indication as to just what the people are interested in."

"But they have a right to see it as it happens!"

Goldin stopped shuffling papers and looked up. "Says who?"

"The Constitution."

"Really." Goldin rifled through some documents off to her side, pulled out a pamphlet and held it up. "C'mere." Johannsen looked around to see if it appeared to anybody else like she was supposed to approach the bench. "Come on, Ms. Johannsen. I'm not having you arrested."

As a ripple of laughter ran around the room, Johannsen stepped forward, and took the pamphlet from Goldin's outstretched hand. "Show me where," Goldin said, and leaned back.

Johannsen made a show of not having to open the book. "Article Six. The accused's right to a public trial."

Goldin shook her head. "If it's a right of the defendant, he can waive that right. Where's the public's right to have it on television?"

"It's a generally accepted principle."

"So's astrology. Want me to rule on that, too?" She waited for the laughter to die down again. "So which is it, Ms. Johannsen: a constitutional right or a generally accepted principle?"

"I can produce expert witnesses," the red-faced lawyer declared assertively.

"On what? The law?"

"Yes, as it applies to First Amendment rights."

"Ma'am. I *am* an expert, remember? It's what they pay me for. And I have no interests except the court's, so I'll keep my own counsel on that topic."

"Uh, um, Your Honor, we're going to file an appeal," Johannsen said gamely.

Goldin shrugged her shoulders. "Be my guest."

"But we need time to prepare an appeal!"

"Take all the time you need."

"Will you postpone these proceedings until we've filed?"

"Nope."

"But that's not fair!" Johannsen was practically whining now, her former composure visibly evaporating.

"Then appeal *that*."

Even though Zuckerman and Rebecca sympathized with the beleaguered media attorney, they had to work at stifling giggles at the conundrum the judge had just presented to her.

Goldin looked out over the courtroom. "Anybody talks to the press or leaks anything not presented in open court, they go to jail and the jury goes to a hotel. Questions?"

Goldin looked back to Johannsen. "Don't take it personally, Counselor: you did a nice job and your clients should appreciate your efforts." Translation: *There's your gift, but my decision is final.*

Rebecca exchanged pained smiles with Ehrenright and Steinholz as Johannsen hesitated at the podium, adding as many milliseconds as she could to the interval before she had to suffer the wrath of her clients out in the hallway. Rebecca would like to have told her that she hadn't had a chance in the first place, that Goldin had her mind made up before the argument was presented, but that would have violated the sanctity of the judge's off-the-record remarks, so Johannsen would just have to take whatever was coming.

"Everybody having enough fun?"

The smiles vanished beneath the weight of Perrein's icy tone. Steinholz looked nervously away and pretended to occupy himself with some papers.

"I'm really happy you're all so amused, but when do we get down to worrying about *my* ass instead of NBC's?"

"Mr. Zuckerman," Judge Goldin's voice intruded fortuitously, "do you wish to make an opening statement?"

"Thank you, Your Honor."

Going first was never easy. Once the atmosphere in the room had switched over to real trial mode, with lawyers and witnesses jousting zestfully, there was nothing discordant about standing up and making speeches, firing questions or behaving with the studied theatricality that made litigation so rewarding. But the initial transition from the feeling that a random crowd had gathered in one room to the opening of the formalities was a strange one, as it must be to the first actor onstage who speaks his lines while the audience is still murmuring about how hard it was to find a parking space.

Prosecutors were used to it, though. They always went first.

Zuckerman subconsciously straightened his perfectly straight tie as he walked to the podium. In a county court, he would be free to roam in front of the jury box, pausing here and there for effect, pounding on the railing or looking individual jurors in the eye at close range. In the much more formal federal environment, he would remain at the podium for the duration of his opening statement, and wouldn't even greet the jurors with a perfunctory *good morning*.

"My name is David Zuckerman, and I am prosecuting the defendant on behalf of the government of the United States of America. We have what might appear to you all to be a complicated case. It involves some pretty tricky technology, and I'm not exaggerating when I tell you that even professional scientists don't quite understand it all."

He could sense the jury's growing discomfort, which he'd deliberately provoked. "But don't worry," he said, smiling. "That's the bad news; the good news is that most of it really doesn't matter all that much, and we're going to take the time to explain to you the parts that really count."

Most of the jurors relaxed visibly, relieved that they weren't going to be called upon to pretend that they understood arcane science. They were acutely aware of the pounding the Simpson jurors had taken because of their obvious inability to grasp complex principles of biology. The defense had deliberately exploited that lack of knowledge by hopelessly confusing them whenever it appeared that something damning to their client was starting to sink it, predicting correctly that what the jurors couldn't understand, they could be made to doubt or simply ignore. Zuckerman was telling this jury that this was not going to happen in this trial.

"The defendant has been charged with making a special kind of computer chip that makes it possible for people to send secret messages to other people. Now, this is done all the time in the United States. Your bank uses chips like these to send your account information to other banks. The reason is so that nobody can eavesdrop on the line and get that information, which would make it easier for them to steal your money. Sounds like a pretty good idea, doesn't it?"

Zuckerman was careful to pace himself so that he got nods of understanding. If there were any signs of confusion, he would stop and go over it again. "But there's a problem: it turns out that organized criminals and terrorists can use the same kind of chip to hide their activities. And that also goes for foreign countries, some of whom have the potential to do harm to the United States."

He had them paying close attention now, and he glanced meaningfully at James Perrein, sitting quietly and staring straight back at him, as Rebecca had instructed him. Turning back to the jurors, Zuckerman said, "And that's why there are laws to prevent those chips from falling into the wrong hands. Now that man sitting before you, the defendant"—he pointed to Perrein without turning around, as though the accused were something less than human— "that man made some of those chips and sold them to Red Chinese spies." He used the old moniker for mainland China to capitalize on any lingering anti-Communist sentiments, along with the still weighty "spies" that conjured up images of the nastier aspects of the Cold War, now dormant but still capable of evoking strong negative feelings.

"Understand that there is no dispute in this trial that selling these devices to the Chinese is against the law. That's a simple fact. The only question is whether the defendant or his company did it. If they did, he's guilty of very, very serious crimes. So your only job in this trial is to decide whether the defendant committed the acts with which he's charged. My job is to prove to you that he did."

Zuckerman paused and seemed to gather his thoughts, but he was only giving the jury a chance to digest what he'd told them so far. "We don't have a videotape of him doing it," he said, smiling again. "We don't have an eyewitness who can swear that he was there when it happened. This is real life, not the movies, and things aren't always simple." Several of the jurors nodded knowingly, indicating that they weren't so naive as to believe that television and the movies depicted the real world.

"What we have is known as circumstantial evidence. I bet a lot of you believe that circumstantial evidence means that we don't really know anything and our proof is going to be weak. But that's television talking, not real life. It's Perry Mason telling the prosecutor, 'You haven't got a prayer: all you've got is a circumstantial case!' "

The jury smiled appreciatively. "*Circumstantial* doesn't mean that there's no evidence," he went on. "All it means is that nobody saw the defendant commit the crime. It means that the proof lies in evidence of the circumstances surrounding the commission of the crime. And we can show you that the defendant is guilty because there is plenty of evidence to prove it. We will show you that his company had the technical ability to make those chips."

Zuckerman put his hands on top of the podium and leaned forward. "We will show you that James Perrein had plenty of good reasons to want to do it. We will show you strong evidence that the chips were manufactured by his company, Tera-Tech Integrated, because that company invented the method that is built into them. We will show you an actual Tera-Tech chip that had been running inside a Chinese computer."

He paused, taking his hands off the podium and straightening up. He looked from Perrein to the jury again, then said in a softer voice, "And when we're through presenting our case, there isn't going to be a shred of doubt in your minds that James Perrein broke the law."

He let his gaze linger on them for a few moments longer, then addressed the judge. "Thank you, Your Honor."

"Ms. Verona?"

Rebecca rose and faced the jury, not leaving her place. "Ladies and gentlemen, my name is Rebecca Verona, and I'm defending Mr. Perrein against the government's charges." She turned back to Goldin. "Your Honor, we'll reserve our opening statement."

"Very well. Mr. Zuckerman, please call your first witness."

"Government calls Mr. Ivars Petorsky."

The Defense Intelligence Agency cryptography expert rose from his seat in the audience and stepped briskly toward the front of the courtroom. It was difficult to tell if he was just affecting the air of an absentminded professor or if he really was partial to brown suits, bow ties and a generally disheveled appearance.

Zuckerman wasted little time establishing Petorsky's credentials. Since this was basically an educational seminar for the jurors and the judge, there was little to be gained by boosting the credibility of a witness on whom nobody would be relying for anything. Instead, Zuckerman moved quickly to the substance of the tutorial testimony.

"Mr. Petorsky, can you tell us in simple terms what cryptography is?"

"Certainly. The concept is very simple. It only gets hard when you actually try to do it."

Petorsky turned to the jury. "What cryptography is, it's a fancy way of talking about sending someone a message only he can read. You do that by putting the message into code. Those of you who are at least my age might remember Captain Marvel secret encoding rings when you were kids. Same thing. You take a message and put it into secret code, and that way nobody else can read it unless he knows the code."

"And how is that done, Mr. Petorsky?"

"You need two things: a method and a key. When we were kids, we used a simple substitution method: the letter A really meant B, B really meant C, and so on. Which letters you use to stand for other letters is called the key. All you had to do at the other end was substitute the right letters for the coded letters using the key, and you could read the message.

"To use some fancy words, the original message is called plaintext, because it's text that you can read plainly. Using the key to put the message into code is called encryption, or encoding. Unscrambling it at the other end is called decryption, or decoding. And that's all there is to it."

Zuckerman nodded in approval. "Thank you, Mr. Petorsky. Are there methods other than simple substitution?"

Petorsky turned back to face Zuckerman. "Many others. Each has its own advantages and disadvantages."

"How about an example."

"Okay. The problem with simple substitution is that it's a very easy code to break."

"Hold it a second. What does that mean, to break a code?"

"It means to look at a secret message and figure out what it says, without knowing the code beforehand."

Zuckerman stole a glance at the jury, saw the surprise on their faces. "Is that really possible?"

"Oh, sure. It's done all the time. As long as you have enough secret messages to work with, there are lots of ways to break the code and read them."

"I don't get it." Zuckerman hoped that his skeptical expression was mirroring the jurors' own feelings. "A secret message looks like gibberish. How can you possibly read it unless you know what the code is?"

Petorsky turned to the jury again. "Let's take the simple substitution code as an example. One of the things you can do is look at how frequently a particular letter appears in the coded messages, and match it with letters in English that appear with about the same frequency. Suppose you see the letter *X* being used more than any other in the secret messages. It's probably an *I* or an *E*, because those are the most common letters in English. But which one is it? Well, if you see it a lot at the ends of words, it's more likely an *E* than an *I*. And there are hundreds of tricks like that one."

Zuckerman looked to see if the jury was getting it, then said, "I see now. You said, the more messages you send, the easier it is for someone to break the code. So how do you protect your data if you have a lot of messages to send?"

"One thing you might do is use a different key every time you send a message. Of course, the problem is that you have to make sure the person receiving your messages has the key for each one. Sending around hundreds of keys carries its own set of risks."

"Doesn't sound like substitution is a very good method."

"Oh, it's terrible, and rarely used for sensitive messages. You can pretty much forget about substitution codes altogether for serious work."

Zuckerman looked at the jury again. It was plain that they were following every word, Petorsky doing an excellent job of making the topic sound so simple anyone could follow it. The jurors seemed very pleased that such a forbidding subject could be so easy to understand, and were concentrating hard to make sure they kept tracking along. Zuckerman's job now was to cover some more difficult concepts without losing them. "So what other methods are there?"

"Many of them. Usually, they involve doing the same thing to each letter instead of a different thing, like you do in substitution."

Several jurors were blinking, sitting back, on the verge of being upset because they didn't grasp Petorsky's last statement, and they had been doing so well.

"Afraid you lost me there." Zuckerman frowned, and looked at the jury as though he were seeking their help. Relieved that the lawyer didn't get it either, some of them frowned back at him: *Ask him some more questions and let's figure this out together.* Pleased at the rapport he was building, Zuckerman said to the witness, "Can you explain a little further?"

Petorsky smiled. "I don't think I phrased it very well, Mr. Zuckerman. It's really much simpler than it sounds. What you usually have instead of a substitute for each letter is a single key that looks like a number, let's say 12345. This number is used to scramble the original message, using a computer, in a way that's very, very difficult to crack."

"So all you have to do is give that number, the key, to the other guy, and he can use a computer to get the original message back?"

"Exactly."

It appeared to Zuckerman that the jury was still catching it all. "Does the size of the key make any difference?"

"Big difference. The more numbers in the key, the harder it is to break the code. I gave the example of 12345, but a key with thirty or forty digits is much more secure. Except that we use computer terms to talk about the key, so we say 'bits' instead of 'digits.' The more bits, the better the code."

"New methods are being invented all the time, aren't they?"

"All the time. Although, frankly, I don't think there's going to be much more of that going on."

"Really? And why is that?"

"Because once you find a method that nobody can crack, you don't need to do a lot more work."

"And does such a method exist yet?"

"We think so. It's called enhanced public key encryption."

"Can you explain to the jury what that is?"

"Not easily. It's based on the fact that the key the sender uses to put the message into code is different from the one the receiver uses to decode it at the other end. But what's important is that, as far as we know, this code cannot be cracked if the number of bits in the key is long enough."

"Where did this method come from?"

Petorsky pointed to Perrein. "The defendant's company invented it."

"Mr. Petorsky, why is all of this so important? Does anybody really care besides spies and secret agents?"

"It's extremely important, Mr. Zuckerman." Petorsky twisted his head toward the jury without shifting the rest of his body this time. "More and more business transactions are being done by computers. Trillions of dollars are transferred electronically around the world each day. If these messages aren't put into code, somebody tapping the lines could discover account numbers and passwords and steal billions."

"Does that actually happen?"

"Yes. It's a constant battle, and companies are spending an awful lot of money on expensive and complex ways to get around the problem. Many of them are too afraid to even do business electronically, which puts them at a big competitive disadvantage. Defense contractors are still using human couriers to send blueprints and other sensitive documents around, which wastes time and costs money, and is also risky."

"So it's important to business."

"Yes, but to individuals also." Petorsky turned to the jury again. "Sometime in the next few years, all of you may be carrying something called a smart-card. It'll be about the size of a credit card, and you can carry it in your wallet. It will contain an amazing number of things about you, like your bank balances, your complete medical history . . . if you're in an accident or have some kind of medical emergency, doctors and paramedics can find out instantly if you have any allergies or other conditions they need to know about so they can save your life.

"But these are things you want to keep private. Without a good method of encrypting all this information so unauthorized people can't read it, nobody in his right mind would want one, no matter how useful it might be. The smart-card will have a little computer built right into it that keeps all this information in coded form."

Rebecca glanced at Steinholz: *Exactly the way Perrein had explained it.*

Zuckerman frowned, crossed his arms over his chest and rubbed his chin. Out of the corner of his eye, he could see that the jury was surprised by his expression. It was all so easy to follow, what was his problem? He let it go on for a moment longer.

"Mr. Petorsky, I'm confused about something." Zuckerman paused, waiting until the jurors' full attention was on him, then tilted his head up and tapped his chin. "Why is there all this computer crime going on when we now have the enhanced key system available? I thought you said it was unbreakable."

The jurors now understood what had been bothering him. They, too, were now confused: Didn't the new method solve all the problems because it couldn't be cracked?

"It *is* unbreakable, for all practical purposes. Problem is, it isn't in widespread use."

"Why not?"

"Couple of reasons. First of all, it's so complicated that it eats up a lot of expensive computer time. That may not be a big deal if you want to send a simple message, like somebody's account number and balance.

"But suppose you're a bank in New York that needs to update account balances in Chicago, which means you have to transmit information for a million accounts. Using the enhanced key system, you simply wouldn't be able to get all those accounts coded fast enough, even using very powerful computers. That's partly because banks like to use a key that's about 256 bits long. The longer the key, the better the security, but it also takes more computer time to do the encoding."

"Is 256 bits really necessary?"

"Objection!" Rebecca's intrusion was a dissonant note in the heretofore smooth repartee between Zuckerman and Petorsky, and it rudely reminded everybody that this was a trial and not a college lecture. But Rebecca knew that Zuckerman was getting close to the issue of the law limiting the number of bits allowed, and she didn't want Petorsky, who had clearly won over the jury, expressing the opinion that 256, which Tera-Tech's system required, really wasn't necessary. "This is supposed to be a tutorial, and opinions such as counsel is soliciting aren't part of the deal."

"What's the objection, Ms. Verona?"

"Outside the witness's area of expertise."

Goldin nodded. Rebecca was right, because very little expertise at all had been established for Petorsky prior to his testimony. His job was simply to educate the jury on some fundamentals so they could follow the more substantive testimony to come later on from other witnesses. He wasn't entitled to express expert opinions on behalf of the government.

However, Goldin wanted to know if it was important enough to worry about. "Is there controversy about the necessary number of bits for secure encoding?" she asked Rebecca.

"Goes to the very heart of the case, Your Honor."

"Actually," Zuckerman said, "it really doesn't. The law is the law, and we're not here to argue its merits."

"Then it's irrelevant, isn't it," Rebecca fired back.

" 'Fraid she's got you there, Counselor," Goldin said. "Objection is sustained."

Zuckerman clenched his jaw and took in a deep breath. "Mr. Petorsky, are there any other reasons why the system isn't in widespread use in this country?"

"Yes. The most important one is that it is against U.S. law to export it to other countries. And in order for it to work, both sides have to have it. Otherwise, you'd have to use one system for inside the U.S., and a different one for data going outside our borders. Much too unwieldy."

"I don't get it. It seems like this system would be a good idea for everybody, so why can't we export it?"

Rebecca sat silently. Steinholtz nudged her arm with his elbow. "Aren't you going to object?" he whispered. "Why let him explain the government's rationale?"

Rebecca leaned into him. "Why not? It's such transparent bullshit, let him do our job for us. You think the jury is gonna be sympathetic to a government that insists on being able to eavesdrop on damned near anything it wants?"

Petorsky, who had been amiable and kept up a light tone in order not to intimidate the jury, grew thoughtful. He folded his hands on top of the wooden bar in front of the witness box. "I'd be speaking for the law enforcement community rather than myself, but I believe I can fairly represent their thinking."

Zuckerman looked toward Rebecca and raised his eyebrows. She flipped a hand palm up and let it drop back down on the table, signaling provisional acquiescence, but not on the record. Zuckerman turned back toward the witness. "Go ahead, sir."

"We've spoken a lot today about the benefits of strong encryption. But there is another side to the story."

Rebecca leaned back in her chair, almost slouching, a slight and expectant smile on her lips. She hoped the jury was reading it as *This is going to be good* or *Let's see him handle this puppy without damaging the prosecution.*

"Law enforcement people are very afraid that these kinds of powerful encoding systems could also be used by criminals and terrorists to hide their information and communications, posing a threat to public safety. This view is shared by a lot of other countries as well."

"Could you explain what they're afraid of?"

"I think so. One of the best sources the government has for discovering the activities of terrorists and sophisticated criminals is through the use of wiretaps that are authorized by court order. The results of these taps, as well as such things as seized computer files, are also used in criminal prosecutions to get convictions. If the FBI or the intelligence community or local police suddenly found themselves unable to interpret these sources, the effect on public safety could be devastating."

Rebecca sat up straight and looked over at Perrein, who hadn't explained it quite that way during their first case meeting and was now nervously tapping his fingers on the side of his seat. He didn't look back at her.

"Isn't this a little paranoid?" Zuckerman asked, playing straight man.

"Well, it kind of sounds like it. But it's happened already, and that's just with ordinary encryption, not the enhanced key system."

"Well." Zuckerman exhaled loudly, forcing himself to smile in self-deprecation in order to show he was a good sport. "Sounds like some kind of dilemma, trying to protect privacy and public safety at the same time. A seemingly impossible—"

Steinholz nudged Rebecca again and she blinked, startled, then rose up out of her seat. "Objection. He's editorializing again."

"I'll withdraw it. Mr. Petorsky, is there some middle ground between complete access to strong cryptography and the needs of law enforcement?"

"Objection. Witness is not an expert, and soliciting his opinion would be improper."

"I'll rephrase: Sir, is there a *proposed* middle ground between complete access to strong cryptography and the needs of law enforcement?"

"Yes, there is. Without getting too technical, the idea is basically to give commercial users a very strong encryption system, but at the same time doing it in a way that allows law enforcement people to tap into the data if they need to and if they get proper authorization."

"Doesn't sound easy. How do you do that?"

"Couple of ways. One is to limit the number of bits in the key. The limit used to be forty, because government experts can crack a forty-bit code without too much trouble.

"Another way is to design a system that can use *two different* decoding keys instead of just one. The second, extra key is for law enforcement to use if it has to. It's called an 'escrow key,' because you put it into escrow somewhere and the government can get it only when authorized by court order. It's also called a LEAF, which stands for Law Enforcement Access Field."

"Sounds like a good idea. Any problems with it?"

Petorsky smiled, indicating that it was a touchy subject. "Well, that kind of depends on your point of view. The government thinks it's fine. Business users are less sure. For one thing, they don't like the idea of an extra key floating around that is available to the government. It makes foreign customers a little nervous, too, especially since many of them believe the CIA is involved in industrial espionage."

"But it wouldn't be any different from law enforcement's current ability to eavesdrop on phone lines, would it?"

"Not really."

"Is the government actively involved in trying to work this through, trying to reach an acceptable compromise?"

"Definitely. In fact, the administration just made a major concession, signing into law a significant change to the export laws."

"And that was . . . ?"

"You can now export encryption systems using keys up to fifty-six bits long instead of forty. But the other side of the deal was that the encryption industry promised to have a key escrow system in place within two years. Once that second key is available to law enforcement, everybody is free to go ahead and use as many bits as they want."

"So why would anyone want to fight such a reasonable compromise?"

Rebecca was concentrating so hard on Petorsky's words that she didn't feel Steinholz poking her again until he threatened to leave a major contusion on her forearm. "Object!" he hissed loudly, but Rebecca looked at him uncomprehendingly, so he stood up himself.

"This is completely irrelevant, Your Honor. The question has no value whatsoever in deciding this case, and is intended only to inflame the jury against the defendant."

Goldin waved both lawyers up to the bench. "How do you figure that?" she asked Steinholz.

"Two reasons: first, it's going to come up that our client fought against this law because it isn't 'reasonable' at all, it's absurd. So I don't want this witness—*or* the prosecutor—telling the jury that anybody who doesn't like the compromise is an idiot."

"How do you know what he was going to answer?" Zuckerman asked Steinholz.

"Because he's a prosecution witness, that's why, and because you even asked the question, and how you phrased it. You wouldn't have bothered if you didn't know in advance he was going to defend the law." He turned back to Judge Goldin. "Frankly, I don't care what he was going to answer. It's an improper question for a tutorial witness we allowed in without challenge."

"What's the other reason?" Goldin asked without commenting on what Steinholz had said so far.

"The export laws speak for themselves, Your Honor, and we don't need a lecture on how they got there or if they're good or bad or how anyone feels about them. As the prosecutor himself put it earlier, the law is the law, and we're not here to argue its merits. Unless," he added, looking at Zuckerman, "we plan on asking this jury to determine if they like the law or not when they decide our client's fate."

Zuckerman said calmly, "Just wanted to impress the jury with the importance of the matter."

"We're conducting a criminal trial in federal court," Goldin responded. "How much more impressed you want them to be? Objection is sustained."

"Mr. Petorsky," Zuckerman said after they had returned from the sidebar, "didn't you say earlier that these strong encryption systems are still a problem because they take up too much computer time to be really useful?"

"That's true. All of the legal wrangling aside, they still have to come up with a practical way to get it to work under real conditions."

"Would one way be to come up with a superfast microchip that could do all the encoding and decoding at high speed?"

"That would pretty much do it, yes."

"And the value of that chip to its inventor would be . . . ?"

"Astronomical."

"Thank you, sir. No further questions."

"Ms. Verona," Goldin said. "Would you like to cross-examine? Please bear in mind that this is a tutorial witness, so your cross should be limited to correcting factual errors."

"Thank you, Your Honor," Rebecca said as she rose. "Just a few quick questions."

Rebecca made her way to the podium, carrying no notes, and got down to it immediately. "Mr. Petorsky, about this great compromise of the present administration's: it allows a fifty-six-bit code, right?"

"Correct. For the next two years until the second key becomes available."

"So what does law enforcement do if it needs to break into some data, since you also said they could only crack a forty-bit code?"

Petorsky hesitated before answering. "Actually, they can now crack a fifty-six-bit code."

"I see. But nobody else can, right, like some company's competitor?"

"I didn't say that."

"You mean somebody else besides government experts could also tap a company's private data?"

"It wouldn't be easy."

"Of course not. It would be just as hard for them as it would be for the government experts, right?"

Petorsky's discomfort was not lost on the jury: had he tried to pull something over on them? "I suppose that's true."

"When you get right down to it, these bit limits on secret codes really have only one purpose, don't they? To make the encoding weaker. Less secure. Correct?"

"Yes."

"Which really doesn't solve the original problem."

"But it's only for two years, until the escrow key is developed." Petorsky was now clearly defending, rather than simply explaining, the government's side of the issue.

"And in those two years, how many foreign companies do you figure are going to let their data be sent to and from the United States when they know the U.S. government, or God knows who else, for that matter, could read all of it anytime they wanted to?"

"Objection!" Zuckerman said. "Outside his area of expertise."

"I'll withdraw it," Rebecca said, knowing that the point had been made. "Mr. Petorsky, you said that the biggest problem with the key escrow scheme is that it might make businesses nervous, knowing that the government has a way to tap their data whenever it wants to."

"That's correct."

"Didn't you leave a little something out?"

"Don't know what you mean, ma'am."

"You said that my client's enhanced key system is the most powerful, most unbreakable coding method known."

"Yes, I did." His reply was hesitant, Rebecca's deliberate non sequitur throwing him off.

"In fact, it's the only one known to be essentially unbreakable, isn't it."

"Yes."

"Which means that all the others are potentially vulnerable to being tapped, right?"

"It would be very difficult."

"But not impossible."

"Theoretically, it is possible to break the others."

"Okay. Now that *major concession* the administration made, that *significant change* in the export laws in exchange for developing a second key?" Petorsky nodded. "Sir, where would my client's enhanced key system fit under that proposed key escrow law?"

Petorsky ignored her sarcastic emphases but wrapped his fingers around the sides of the witness chair and stayed silent.

"Sir?"

"It wouldn't," he finally said.

Rebecca drew back in bewilderment. "What do you mean?"

"The enhanced key system couldn't be used under the proposed plan."

"Couldn't be used? But why not?" She looked at the jury, her expression one of surprise and distress. "It's the only truly secure system in the world!"

Petorsky took a breath before responding, eyes looking downward, and gave his answer as though he were in front of the principal confessing to having pulled somebody's hair. "Because there's no way to create an escrow key in Tera-Tech's system."

Rebecca appeared stunned, and kept that expression on her face as she looked at the jurors, several of whom had raised their eyebrows, or sat up straight, or otherwise indicated their surprise at this little nugget that the prosecution hadn't brought up.

Rebecca appeared to recover from her shock so she could ask her next question, which she did very slowly and deliberately. "Are you telling us that, under this brilliant compromise, *nobody* would be able to use the only unbreakable coding scheme known to exist?"

Petorsky looked deflated, all traces of his earlier spark and enthusiasm gone, giving the impression that he had been caught in some giant, carefully rehearsed lie. "Basically, that's correct."

"Well." Rebecca folded her arms across her chest. "Some major concession *that* was."

Zuckerman jumped up. "Your Honor, I object to—"

"No further questions," Rebecca interrupted dismissively as she turned to go back to her seat, stealing a glance at Zuckerman that the jury could see, and shaking her head in disgust.

It had been a start. A grand start, in fact. Philip Mastilir greeted her just outside the courtroom on her way out.

"You shot par today, Rebecca," he said, smiling.

Rebecca bowed her head slightly and flashed him a half smile of her own, hoping it looked appropriately modest.

"Problem with pars," Mastilir continued, just as Rebecca noticed that his smile didn't reach his eyes, "only thing they're good for is keeping you in the game until you get enough birdies to win."

Rebecca felt the good feelings start to leach out of her system. "You want to speak a little English now, Phil?"

He inclined his head toward a nearby alcove that looked as though it once might have held a statue, and they walked to it together.

"Petorsky's *schvanz* is now two inches shorter," Mastilir said, "I'll give you that." He frowned and lifted his shoulders. "But what was the point?"

Rebecca regarded him neutrally, so he understood that she was deciding whether she even wanted to have this conversation at all. It would be a privilege she would grant rather than a right he thought he already had.

She set her attaché case down on the marble floor. "Zuckerman had him saying the government had offered a reasonable compromise regarding data security. I showed the jury that it not only wasn't reasonable at all, it cut Tera-Tech completely out of the picture."

Mastilir nodded thoughtfully. "So what?"

"What do you mean, so what?" Rebecca was getting irritated with his cryptic jabbing, and she let it show. "We damaged his credibility!"

"But why?"

"Dammit, Phil! I haven't got time to play—"

"The guy was a tutorial witness, Becky. His only job was to get the jury comfortable with the technical issues. What I'm asking, why make him look like a jerk?"

Rebecca crossed her arms and squeezed them tightly before answering. "He was trying to tell the jury that there was no justification for Perrein's criticizing government export policy. He tried to snooker them by not mentioning that Tera-Tech's system would be dead in the water under that policy. He failed to mention that, if the government could break a fifty-six-bit code, then so could anybody else with the same expertise so their compromise policy was total bullshit."

Mastilir had been nodding in seeming agreement as she ticked down these points. When she was finished, he said, "I ask you again: so what?"

Before she could get violent, Mastilir held up his hands and said quickly, "What's any of that got to do with whether Jim sold computer chips to China?"

Rebecca held still, not answering immediately. Finally she said, "It didn't directly address that issue. It wasn't supposed to. Petorsky didn't either."

"Then what good was it?"

"Think of it as talking about character in a murder trial. Just because a guy loved his kids or was good to his mother doesn't mean he didn't do it. But it does make it look less likely. That kind of thing can sway a jury if they're on the edge."

"Okay." Mastilir nodded agreeably. "I can see that. Except, if Jim had justification for thinking that the government's policy was bullshit, and you demonstrated that it really *was* bullshit, then wouldn't that make him more likely to have violated it, not less?"

"You missed the point."

"And that was . . . ?"

"I was trying to show bias on the government's part," Rebecca answered, growing more confident in the rationale she had just invented. "The government knew that Perrein was right, and they were in his face because of it. What we showed by exposing their supposedly neutral witness was that they have it in for him. That maybe the reason he got indicted was because he was making too much trouble, poking holes in all their self-serving crap about weak security systems being just fine."

Mastilir considered it, rocking his head back and forth a few times. "So that was the point of you grinding Petorsky into hamburger, was it? To show that the government's prosecution of Jim is malicious?"

"That was the point," Rebecca replied, uncrossing her arms and picking up her attaché, but remaining politely in place.

Mastilir turned his head slightly but kept his eyes on her. "You figure I'm a pretty smart guy, Becky?"

She couldn't hide her surprise at his question that came out of nowhere. "I'd say you sure are."

"Damnedest thing, then, me missing the point."

She shrugged. "Happens."

"How smart you figure that jury is?"

She didn't answer.

"Smart as me?" he pressed.

When she still didn't answer, he said, "You figure *they* got the point?"

She read his look as he started to walk away as smug, condescending, self-satisfied and superior. "Mastilir," she called when he was a few steps away.

He turned as she walked up to him, his head back, briefcase in both hands hanging in front of him, as if he were expecting some acknowledgment, however grudging, of the sense he had been making.

She kept her voice low. "I got enough critics in this case," she said evenly. "Next time you want to lecture me, take a fucking number."

Chapter 14

Friday, October 30

"United States calls Dr. Melanie Fuster."

An encryption specialist from the National Security Agency, Dr. Fuster seemed painfully aware of her weight problem as she made her way to the witness box. Above average in height, and giving off an overall impression of bigness in all dimensions, she was wearing a smocklike affair chosen to disguise rather than reveal the contours of her body. Rebecca felt sorry for Fuster, but the litigator in her knew that people harboring a lifetime's worth of self-doubt made easy targets in cross-examination: they often went too far out on dangerous limbs to try to enhance their prestige.

Once Fuster was seated, Zuckerman started off the rehearsed repartee by having her establish that Tera-Tech's encryption system, using a 256-bit key, was completely impossible to crack. He then asked her if it was likely anybody would ever figure out how to break the code.

"Highly doubtful, unless somebody invents a new kind of math we've never heard of. But even if they do, nobody will ever crack it the way it's implemented in this chip."

"Why?"

Fuster rearranged herself slightly. "Took us a while to figure this out, because the chip wasn't behaving the way we expected it to. Then we discovered the reason why: after the chip encodes the incoming message, it sends it right back through the encoding system for a second time."

"You mean it takes the secret message and encodes it *again*?"

"Yes. It's called double-crypting."

"And what's the significance?"

"Well, if the original pass was impossible to crack, double-crypting makes it four thousand times more impossible."

Zuckerman smiled and looked at the jury, hoping they would catch the clever turn of phrase. Two of them seemed to. Four others appeared as though they were smiling because they thought they were supposed to. As for the rest . . . "And how impossible is that?"

Fuster thought about it for a second, then replied: "God couldn't crack this code."

"Does this relate to the speed of the chip in any way?"

"Thing is, we were all pretty blown away by how fast the chip operated when we thought it was only making one pass through the encoder. When we realized there were two passes . . ." She looked down and shook her head, groping for words to convey the amazement she and her colleagues had felt. "We were all stunned. I mean speechless. It meant the chip was twice as fast as we originally thought. There wasn't a person on that team thought they would see anything like it for at least—"

"Objection!" Rebecca said, standing up. "This witness was not qualified as an expert in chip design or processing speeds or anything else to do with computer hardware. And she's testifying as to what was in other people's minds."

"Sustained."

Fuster went on to confirm that the encryption performed by the chip was exactly the same, down to the last bit, as that described in Tera-Tech's published papers.

Zuckerman nodded slowly, conveying that this was important and expected. "So there is no doubt in your mind that the technique inside that chip is the enhanced key system developed by Tera-Tech?"

"None whatsoever."

"And have you ever seen that technique built into a single chip before?"

"Nothing even close."

Zuckerman walked slowly back to the podium, hands clasped behind him, acting as though he were formulating a new question based on the startling revelations he'd just heard. He turned to face the witness. "Doctor, our tutorial witness stated that the current legal limit on the number of bits allowed in an encryption device to be exported to a foreign country is fifty-six; do you recall that?"

"Yes, that's the limit for at least another year or so."

"And you said Tera-Tech's enhanced key system uses how many bits?"

"Two hundred and fifty-six. Way over the legal limit."

"Objection," Rebecca said, feigning boredom. "Calls for a legal conclusion."

"No, it doesn't, Your Honor," Zuckerman countered. "All it calls for is reading the law. It's just a simple fact."

"Then why ask this particular witness?" Rebecca said, making sure she looked at Judge Goldin and not Zuckerman.

"I'll overrule the objection, but only because it's harmless," Goldin said. "Let's stay *en pointe* with the witness's expertise from here on in."

"Thank you," Zuckerman said, then turned his attention back to Fuster. "Over the legal limit, okay." Rebecca rolled her eyes but let it go: the cat was out of the bag anyway, so why look childish to the jury by making useless objections? "And do you also recall the previous witness testifying that the export regulations require a second, escrow key for use by U.S. government law enforcement?"

"The LEAF key. Yes."

"And does the Tera-Tech system allow for such a second key?"

"No."

"Will it ever?"

"No. It's technically impossible."

"Thank you. Nothing further."

Rebecca wondered if Zuckerman would have brought this last point up had she not already done so with Petorsky. Could there possibly be some way that the enhanced key system's inability to use a second key was actually *good* for the prosecution's case? Or was he just beating her to the punch so she couldn't make it look like he'd been trying to hide it from the jury? Sometimes the best way to handle a strong opposition point was to bring it up yourself and dismiss it lightly.

"I think I know where he's going with all of this," Steinholz said at that moment as he put a hand up in front of his mouth and leaned in toward Rebecca so Perrein couldn't hear. "He thinks maybe we're going to try to show that Tera-Tech's system could have been in compliance with the law when Perrein allegedly sold it to the Chinese. Like we're going to say it only uses forty bits and it *does* have an escrow key."

"But we're saying he never sold it to the Chinese in the first place."

"What if we change our minds?"

"Okay. So how did he hurt us?"

Steinholz lowered his voice even further. "He just proved that Tera-Tech's system *had* to have been illegal when it was sold: it could never have used less than 256 bits, and it could never have had an escrow key."

Judge Goldin waited for Zuckerman to resume his seat. "Do you wish to cross-examine, Ms. Verona?"

No, I'll just go out for a burger and some fries. "If it please the court."

As she made her way to the podium, Rebecca tried to integrate Steinholz's insight into her planned cross-examination. She shuffled some papers to buy more time, then began as she made her way to the podium. "Doctor, how was your computer able to duplicate Tera-Tech's technique?"

In the short time it had taken Zuckerman to sit down and Rebecca to stand up, Fuster's entire demeanor had shifted from amiable cooperation to recalcitrant hostility. Not only was her new interrogator on the wrong side of the case, she was pretty and looked as though she could wear head-to-toe Spandex with perfect ease. "We have a program running on our computer that incorporates the enhanced key system."

Rebecca reached the podium, set her papers on top and began arranging them. "And where did you get it?"

"I wrote it."

Rebecca stopped shuffling the papers and looked up at Fuster, her hands poised in mid-motion. "You wrote it!" She frowned, rested her elbows on the podium and rubbed the side of her face, appearing lost in confusion and surprise. "But in order to do that," she began slowly, looking down at the floor, "didn't you have to know how the technique works?"

"Of course."

"A general idea, or did you need specifics?"

"I needed every last specific, down to the tiniest detail."

Rebecca stayed hunched over the podium, her posture conveying nonchalance. "So whadja do, steal it?"

"Objection!" Zuckerman said loudly. "Argumentative, leading . . . and insulting!"

Rebecca made a what're-you-getting-so-excited-about face and waved a hand in the air. "I'll withdraw it. Dr. Fuster, how did you get all the details?"

"From a scholarly paper. In a journal."

"A secret journal?"

"Of course not. Anybody can get a copy."

"Who wrote the article?"

"Dr. Whitman Helfie."

"You know him personally?"

"I met him once or twice."

"Where did you meet him?"

"At technical conferences."

"Whom were you representing?"

"My employer. The NSA."

"And who was Doctor Helfie representing?"

"Objection, relevance." Zuckerman stood up, looking annoyed. "Where is all of this going?"

"I believe we're about to find out, Your Honor," Rebecca said, her voice serious and portentous now, in marked contrast to her earlier nonchalance.

"Overruled."

"Who was Helfie representing, Dr. Fuster?"

"He was representing Tera-Tech Integrated."

"Tera-Tech?" Rebecca stood up straight and whirled around to look at Perrein, then back at Fuster. "He was representing the *defendant*?"

"I believe so."

"He worked for Tera-Tech?"

"Yes."

Rebecca's mouth was open in surprise. She'd practiced it in the ladies' room just before court, and Sarah Bernhardt couldn't have done it better. "Are you telling this court," she said slowly, dragging every word out, "that the Tera-Tech scientist who invented the enhanced key system published every detail of it *in a journal*?"

"I guess so."

"So anybody who picked up a copy of this journal would know exactly how to program a computer to use the technique?"

"Objection. Calls for speculation."

"She's an expert," Rebecca said, knowing that Zuckerman knew it as well and was only trying to disrupt her momentum. "She can speculate."

"Overruled. Witness may answer."

"Yes, anyone could program the technique into a computer."

"Would he have to be an expert in cryptology?"

"No."

"Would he even have to understand the technique?"

"Not really."

"So any reasonably competent programmer could get this technique into a computer, is that right?"

"I suppose so."

"Or even into a single chip."

"Oh, no. Not into a chip. That takes a special kind of expertise."

"But anybody who could build a chip would certainly have no problem programming the enhanced key system into it, isn't that right?"

"Not at those speeds."

"I'm sorry . . ." Rebecca picked up some random sheets of paper, the closest ones at hand, and quickly riffled through them. "I'm looking at my notes concerning your expertise. You're a cryptologist, aren't you?"

"Yes."

"I don't see anything on here about computer hardware expertise, digital methods of computation . . . are you claiming to be an expert on those topics as well?"

"No. But I do have some familiarity."

"So what? So do I."

"Objection," Zuckerman said in a disdainful voice.

"Withdrawn." Rebecca turned toward Judge Goldin, and said as pleasantly as she could, "Your Honor, if counsel wishes to qualify this witness as an expert in computing machinery, the defense will have no objection to their doing so at this time."

"Mr. Zuckerman?"

"No, Your Honor. We don't wish to present such qualifications."

"You may proceed, Ms. Verona."

"Dr. Fuster, I didn't ask you about processing speeds. Let me repeat the question: Anybody who could build a chip, regardless of whatever else the chip could do, would have no problem programming the enhanced key system into it, isn't that right?"

"Yes, that's right."

"And therefore, the fact that the chip in evidence incorporates Tera-Tech's method doesn't prove that Tera-Tech built it, right?"

Zuckerman, who'd been hanging on every word waiting for an opportunity to pounce, did so now. "Objection, outside the witness's area of expertise, calls for a legal conclusion."

"It's not a legal conclusion, Your Honor," Rebecca said. "It's common sense."

Goldin said, "Then it more properly belongs in your closing statement, Counselor. But the witness may answer."

"It doesn't prove that Tera-Tech built the chip," Fuster said between clenched teeth. "But taken together with everything else—"

"Everything else?" Rebecca interrupted. "*What* everything else? You're the first substantive witness!"

"Well, you know . . . all the other stuff . . ."

"You mean everything else the prosecution is going to present that the jury hasn't heard yet but you already know all about?"

"Objection," Zuckerman rose half out of his seat, then started back down as he finished speaking. "This isn't proper inquiry."

"Just following up on the witness's own answer, Your Honor."

"That's true, but I'm instructing the jury to disregard the witness's superfluous remark, the one starting with 'Taken together with everything else,' and I'm also instructing the witness to restrict her answers to the questions asked."

"Just one more question." Rebecca set her papers down and folded her arms across her chest, a defensive gesture in anticipation of Zuckerman's objection. "What is your position on whether the enhanced public key encryption system ought to be exported out of this country?"

"Objection!" Right on cue. "Irrelevant and outside this witness's area of expertise!"

"Goes to bias, Your Honor," Rebecca said calmly, with singsong inflections to underscore the obviousness of her point.

"I'll allow it."

Fuster clasped her hands together tightly, choosing her words carefully. Rebecca could see her mental gears spinning, thinking, *What does this lawyer know!* "I don't feel that it is in the best interests of national security to allow its export."

"Feel strongly about it, do you?"

"It's an opinion, no more, no less."

Rebecca rocked her head back and forth, giving the appearance that she was weighing Fuster's answer, and was coming down in favor of believing it and letting the matter go. "Your Honor," she said slowly. Still considering . . . "May we have this document placed before the witness?"

Goldin waved the clerk over to the podium, where she took the sheets of paper Rebecca was holding aloft. As Rebecca walked a few steps to hand a copy to Zuckerman, Goldin said, "Marking it defense exhibit one. The clerk will place the document before the witness."

Zuckerman spent less than a second examining the paper, reading only the heading at the top. "We object to the introduction of this document, Your Honor. Defense counsel never provided us with one in advance."

"With all respect to counsel," Rebecca said to the judge, never looking in Zuckerman's direction, "the defense didn't feel it necessary to provide the government with articles written by its own witnesses. In fact, we're contemplating filing a complaint against the prosecution for failing to provide *us* with this in advance."

"Objection is overruled. You may proceed, Ms. Verona."

"Dr. Fuster, do you recognize this document?"

"Yes. It's an article I wrote for a journal some time ago."

"When?"

"Don't remember exactly."

"I don't need it exactly. Was it before or after you programmed your own computer with this encryption method?"

"After, I think."

"You think?"

"Yes. I mean, yes, it was after." Fuster took a deep breath and let it out slowly.

Rebecca took a half step back from the podium. "Would you kindly read the sentence I've circled, please, out loud to the court?"

" 'This technique is so powerful—' "

"A bit louder, if you wouldn't mind? Jury needs to hear you."

Fuster glared at Rebecca, then twisted in her seat to face the jury, but without looking any of them in the eye. " 'This technique is so powerful that it simply cannot be broken. Not now, not ever. Anyone who puts it in the hands of a potential enemy to this country is a traitor who should be hung from the highest yardarm.' "

Fuster tried to hold her chin up high as she put the paper back down with an audible slap.

Rebecca remained calm and unruffled by the petty display of defiance. "And the second sentence I've circled, please." A command, this time, not a polite request.

Fuster glanced at Zuckerman, which Rebecca ignored, then picked the paper up and took her time locating the relevant passage. " 'And, as far as I'm concerned, every country in the world is a potential enemy.' "

"Thank you," Rebecca said, all politeness once again. "Are those in fact the words you wrote?"

"Far as I remember."

"So it's fair to say you felt pretty strongly about it, isn't that true?"

"Well, sort of, but it's fairly common to exaggerate a little for some dramatic effect when you're trying to put across an opinion."

"I understand completely," Rebecca said. "So can the jury assume you were exaggerating a few minutes ago when you said the method in the chip matched the one published by Tera-Tech?"

"No!"

Rebecca shot the jury a meaningful glance. "No more questions for this witness."

Perrein was grinning as Rebecca returned. He made a fist and pumped it sideways as she took her seat. "Showed the bitch, didn't we!" When Rebecca didn't respond, he poked Steinholz in the ribs with his elbow, settling for a perfunctory lip curl from the embarrassed attorney.

Judge Goldin turned her attention to the prosecution table. "Redirect?"

"What's he gonna do?" Perrein whispered to Rebecca.

What am I, a fucking psychic? "We'll know in a few seconds." *I know already.*

Zuckerman stood up but didn't move to the podium, communicating to the jury that this was a simple matter that could be disposed of without a lot of time or formality. "Doctor, is there any opinion involved in the analysis you did? Any room for interpretation?"

"None whatsoever."

"So the question is totally yes or no: the encryption in the chip matched the Tera-Tech method or it didn't, right?"

"Correct."

"And it matched perfectly, did it not?"

"One hundred percent."

"Thank you. Dr. Fuster, have you ever seen this technique programmed into a single chip before?"

"Never."

"Any idea why?"

Fuster was back on track, eager to grab hold of a question that would restore her credibility. "The program requires so many calculations that it eats up tremendous amounts of computer time. We have a Cray supercomputer, one of the most powerful in the world, and it took that machine, running nothing else at the same time, nearly six minutes to encode a relatively small message. That makes the technique useless in a conventional computer. It would take forever to get the job done."

"Unless you had a computer much more powerful than a Cray?"

"*Much* more powerful." She flashed Rebecca a sneer. "More powerful than anything in existence."

"Objection," Rebecca sneered back. "Outside the witness's area of expertise."

"Withdrawn." Zuckerman sat down slowly, a look of satisfaction on his face. "Thank you, Doctor. No further questions."

Zuckerman's next witness was the head of the team that ran all the tests on the chip, including those requested by Radovan Terescu. He swore under oath that everything reported by him or any member of the team was exactly as it really happened. It was short and to the point, and Rebecca declined to cross-examine him.

After the lunch break, Zuckerman summoned Anthony Frazier, Ph.D., executive director of the Association of Semiconductor Manufacturers, the premier trade organization for Silicon Valley heavyweights. Frazier testified that Tera-Tech was well known to be one of the leaders in the development of very advanced, high-speed microprocessors. Frazier himself had visited the facilities on one occasion. Knowledgeable speculation was that they were making tremendous strides, and being very secretive about it.

"Is that unusual?" Zuckerman asked.

"Well, think about it," Frazier answered eagerly, having a good time authoritatively speaking his scripted lines under Zuckerman's patient guidance. "You've got an industry that moves so fast, products are obsolete almost as soon as they hit the market. When Intel's Pentium chip was first made commercially available, all the talk was already about their next generation of processors. So it isn't at all unusual for companies to play things pretty close to the vest."

"But isn't there a lot of empty hype?" Zuckerman the fair-minded prosecutor, asking questions that might undercut his own case, purely in the interests of justice.

But not to worry. "The thing about the computer technology industry," Frazier said, lowering his voice, seriousness oozing out of him, "is that it's probably more immune to charges of hucksterism and deceit than almost any other consumer business you can think of, because virtually all of its customers are experts who can't be fooled, at least not for long. Its product reviewers are the harshest critics, its distributors the hardest-driving deal makers, and its competitors are rabid, fanged mongrels ready and able to rip their rivals to shreds when the slightest weakness appears. You don't find a lot of exaggeration because you can only pull that once before everybody sees through you."

"And progress has been extraordinary, hasn't it?"

Frazier snorted in a way that communicated that this was, if anything, an understatement. "Mr. Zuckerman, if the automobile industry had proceeded at the same rate as the semiconductor industry over the past three decades, a Rolls-Royce would get twelve million miles a gallon and cost about twenty bucks."

The jurors were unable to contain their amazement at this comparison, and their gasps were clearly audible throughout the courtroom.

"And the smart money had it that Tera-Tech was on to something . . ."

"Something big, yes."

"And they had to get it right first time out of the chute."

Frazier closed his eyes and nodded, an unmistakable high grade for his star pupil, the prosecutor. "Exactly right, Mr. Zuckerman."

These were all highly speculative questions and answers that had no foundation and were totally improper. Zuckerman was completely baffled as to why Rebecca wasn't raising any objections, which he had been expecting and was prepared for.

"Thank you, sir. No further questions."

But there were much more effective ways of tearing apart a witness's testimony than simply to object and abruptly end the improper questioning. Which is why any litigator worth his—or her—salt felt that cross-examination was better than sex.

Zuckerman turned back to his table slowly, as if reluctant to break contact with his clicked-in mentor who was only too willing to unselfishly share whatever modest insights he might have to offer. At least that's what the jury was thinking. Rebecca knew that her lack of objections had scared him.

Rebecca rose, smiling in approval of the display of male bonding between Zuckerman and Frazier and how good it seemed to have made them both feel. Frazier smiled back, relishing the coming rhubarb and the number he was going to do on this unsuspecting innocent who was dabbling well outside her zone of competence.

Rebecca took her time, and looked up at the ceiling as though she were formulating her first question in her head even as she stood there. "Dr. Frazier." She brought her head down and looked at him. Gently and kindly. "You said that it wasn't unusual for high-tech companies to be secretive about their research, isn't that correct?"

"Most definitely."

"Can you give us an example?"

Frazier laughed easily. "Well, that would be illogical, wouldn't it? I mean, if a company is being secretive, how would I know what they were trying to hide, right?" His snide look of superiority was meant to underscore the contrast between his quick-wittedness and the defense attorney's comparative stupidity in failing to perceive her gaffe.

"Ah. Good point." Rebecca smiled and took the rebuke with good humor, then, still smiling, said, "So then how come you know they're hiding something?"

Frazier's condescending grin stayed on his lips but began to fade from his eyes. "Sorry?"

"You said that they routinely keep their research secret, but you can't cite examples because there's no way to know, since they're hiding it. So how do you know that they're hiding anything in the first place?"

Frazier could only stare at her. Zuckerman jumped in to try to rescue his witness. "Objection. Vague, and she's trying to confuse him."

"I think your point is made, Ms. Verona," Goldin said, but not without a hint of amusement. "Let's move on."

"Certainly. Dr. Frazier, in your personal opinion, what is the biggest recent advance in the field of high-speed chip fabrication?"

"Well, let's see." Back on safe ground, Frazier tried his best to relax again. "I'd have to say it was Dallas Digital's announcement of their BaseLine device."

"Which was?"

"They claimed to have built a chip containing 125 million transistors."

"I see. That a lot?" Of course it was. Rebecca was just throwing him a softball to get him off guard, and Frazier chuckled as it floated over the plate.

"Is it ever," he said.

"*Sounds* like a lot. Tell me, was the chip already in production at the time of the announcement?"

"I don't believe so," Frazier answered easily.

"In fact, they barely managed to even build it before they announced it, isn't that so?"

Frazier faltered slightly and grew wary. "I think that might be true. Although I must tell you, there is a great deal of skepticism in the industry concerning whether DD really managed the feat. A great deal of skepticism."

"Oh." She looked dejected. "So there's a possibility they didn't really do it?"

Frazier leaped on it. "Oh, absolutely. For all anybody knows, they could be years away."

"And so there's a good possibility they chose to release the news of their latest breakthrough well before it actually saw the light of day?"

"So it would seem."

"Well, gee, hardly sounds like playing it close to the vest, does it, Doctor?"

Zuckerman, who had been trying to catch Frazier's eye and warn him, jumped up. "Objection, argumentative!"

"Withdrawn. Dr. Frazier, you said you visited Tera-Tech's campus at one point."

"Yes, I did," he answered, somewhat confused by the lawyerly byplay, but knowing that things weren't going quite right.

"Can you tell the jury what occasioned this visit?"

"Well, I'm afraid I can't talk about that."

"Because?"

"I signed a confidentiality agreement with Tera-Tech before I was allowed on the premises."

"I see. Your Honor, I have a document that I would like the witness to examine."

Goldin gestured to her assistant. "The clerk will place defense exhibit two before the witness."

Rebecca handed one to Zuckerman, who said without looking at it, "Your Honor, this is the first the prosecution has heard of this."

Rebecca responded immediately. "This is the first the defense has heard that the witness was planning to withhold testimony based on a private agreement."

"Take a moment to read the document, Mr. Zuckerman," Judge Goldin directed.

Zuckerman read it quickly, then let out a sigh and looked up at the judge.

Rebecca waited for a nod from Goldin, then said, "Mr. Frazier, have you seen this document before?"

"Yes."

"Can you tell us what it is?"

"It's a copy of the confidentiality agreement I signed with Tera-Tech."

"And this is why you feel it is inappropriate to disclose information you learned during your interviews?"

"Yes. Exactly."

"Would you kindly read subparagraph one of paragraph thirteen?"

"Okay."

"Out loud, please?"

"Oh. Sorry." Frazier reddened slightly at the snickering from the gallery, which ended instantly at a glare from Goldin. He cleared his throat. " 'You agree not to divulge any of the above-referenced types of information unless ordered to do so by a court of competent jurisdiction.' "

Rebecca started to say, "Your Honor, defense respectfully requests that the court—"

Goldin held up a hand and Rebecca came to a halt. "Mr. Perrein," the judge said, "are you still president of Tera-Tech Integrated?"

Steinholz nudged Perrein and he stood up. "Yes, ma'am."

"You want to waive the confidentiality provisions of this agreement?"

Rebecca nodded at him and Perrein said, "Yes, I do."

"Fine. Mr. Frazier, you may answer the question. And this court of competent jurisdiction orders you to answer any questions put to you by the attorneys in this case until the court instructs you to do otherwise." She waved Perrein back down onto his seat.

"Why did you visit Tera-Tech?" Rebecca asked again.

"They wanted to hire me."

"As what?"

"Part of a team working on advanced chip fabrication."

"I see. And what did Tera-Tech tell you about the state of their research? You don't have to be specific."

"They said they were on the brink of radical breakthroughs that would completely revolutionize the industry."

"Ah. And what were some of those breakthroughs?"

"They weren't too specific."

"Are you saying that because of the agreement?"

"Actually, um, no. They didn't give me any specifics."

"That's all right. What were some of the general areas?"

Frazier cleared his throat. Then he cleared it again. "They, uh, they didn't really say."

"They didn't really say, or they didn't say at all?"

"I guess they didn't say at all."

"Okay, no problem. What kinds of things did you see them working on in the labs?"

"Didn't visit the labs," he answered tightly.

"All right, so what did you learn from talking to the researchers?"

"I never spoke with any of those people."

"None of them?"

"No."

"Well, whom did you speak to, then?"

"The vice president of human resources."

"You mean the head of personnel."

"I suppose she might be called that."

"So bottom-line this for us, Doctor." Rebecca put her hands on her hips and looked up at the ceiling. "Are you telling the jury that everything you know about Tera-Tech's being 'on the verge of radical new breakthroughs' came from a recruiting speech delivered by someone from the administration department who was doing her best to hire you?"

"Objection, argumentative!" Rebecca could tell from Zuckerman's tone of voice that he knew he hadn't a prayer of being sustained.

"Overruled," Goldin said. "Witness may answer."

"No, not really. I mean, it's kind of common knowledge in the industry."

"Oh, common knowledge!" Rebecca repeated, dragging the words out slowly as though they explained everything with perfect clarity. "Common knowledge, sure. Isn't it also common knowledge that the earth has been visited by aliens who are taking over the bodies of citizens in preparation for colonizing our planet?"

"Objection!"

"Withdrawn." Rebecca placed both hands on the podium and

stared intently at Frazier. "Is it true that a lot of rumors race around your industry?"

"Sure."

"How do you tell the difference between rumors and common knowledge?"

"Uh, well, by the source. If the source is reliable—"

"Did any of your sources about Tera-Tech have firsthand knowledge of the company?"

"Firsthand?"

"Yes. Like were they employees, did they have consulting contracts there . . . in other words, were any of these sources you're relying upon ever actually inside the company?"

"I don't think so."

"Okay, let me make sure I understand. Tera-Tech was trying desperately to hire you, invited you onto the campus, but they wouldn't tell you a single thing about what they were working on, isn't that right?"

"I suppose that's right."

"And yet you think that some of your sources, people who never even set foot on the premises like you did, people with even looser connections to the company than yours, you think that these people have some kind of reliable inside knowledge of Tera-Tech?"

"Objection," Zuckerman said, anxiety evident in his voice. "Counsel is badgering the witness."

"Overruled."

"Doctor?"

"Well, you just tend to put more credibility in some people than others."

"I see." Rebecca never took her eyes off him. "By any chance, was your choice of whom to believe in any way influenced by who the prosecutor told you might be credible?"

"Objection!" Zuckerman looked quickly from the judge to Rebecca and back again.

"Overruled. Witness may answer."

"Not at all!"

"Just a few more questions, sir. What direct evidence do you personally have regarding the status of Tera-Tech's research into high-speed chip fabrication, not including what you've been told by people who have no connection with your company?"

"Well, very little, really."

"You mean none." She waited for an objection from Zuckerman but had a feeling it might not come.

It didn't. "It would appear that way," Frazier said weakly.

"Have you read any papers published by Tera-Tech scientists?"

"They don't publish anymore."

"So your answer is no. You've read no papers coming out of Tera-Tech."

"That's true."

"As an authority in this field, am I correct in assuming that you're familiar with the status of patents filed by companies as they make research advances?"

"Keeping track of the latest patents is one of the things I pride myself on, yes." Frazier's voice strengthened slightly.

"Good. So how many patents has Tera-Tech filed on super-high-speed, super-high-density encryption chips? Just a rough idea, doesn't have to be exact."

"I don't know of any."

"None? They've filed for no patents?"

"No. But that's not unusual."

"Please explain."

Frazier knew from Rebecca's lack of surprise that she had known the answer in advance, that this was a trap, but he couldn't imagine what it was. "When you file for a patent, you have to disclose the complete details of the invention. Lots of companies don't want to reveal to the competition what they're up to in the labs."

"Now, I may be wrong here, but isn't the whole point of a patent precisely to protect those inventions?"

Frazier risked another patronizing smile. "Yes, well, things don't always work out that way. People can read the patent and try to get away with slight variations and claim them as inventions of their own. Some foreign countries don't even recognize U.S. patents."

"Oh, I get it now." She waited until relief came over Frazier's face. "So how about an example?"

"Um, well, I can't think of any right off the top of my head."

"Is that possibly because high-tech companies file, quite literally, hundreds of patent applications every week? That the Patent Office is so backlogged they can't even process them all?"

Zuckerman again sought to rescue his witness. "Objection. Beyond this witness's expertise."

"Can you answer the question, Mr. Frazier?" Goldin asked.

Rebecca casually picked up a copy of a semiconductor industry trade publication. Frazier's picture was on the cover over a story title, "Patent Avalanche—How to make sure yours is protected."

Frazier, watching her every movement, swallowed and said, "I do believe she's correct."

Rebecca put the magazine back on the podium, facedown. "So you're telling this court that it wouldn't be unusual for a company that really had this chip—it wouldn't be unusual for them to risk a multibillion-dollar market for it by trusting such a technology to something as weak, unclear and risky as plain old trade secret protection? Is that what you're saying?"

Zuckerman objected again. "Way beyond this witness's area of expertise."

Rebecca turned to face him. "Way beyond the expertise of the president of the most important semiconductor trade association in the world?" She turned back to Goldin. "I'm only doing exactly what the prosecution did, asking him about what's ordinary and customary in a business he knows intimately."

"You offered him up, Mr. Zuckerman," Goldin said. "Objection is overruled, witness may answer."

"It's possible to rely only on trade secret protection."

"Possible. Your Honor, might I request that the witness be directed to take a day or two and come up with examples of high-tech companies declining to patent their key breakthroughs?"

Goldin looked at the witness box over the tops of her reading glasses. "Can you do that, Mr. Frazier?"

Frazier fidgeted and tugged at his collar. "It would be difficult. After all, if a company declined to file a patent so as not to reveal a secret, well then, how would I know about it?"

"He testified that it's common practice," Rebecca intervened.

"Because I've heard about it. I don't necessarily know the specific details of a specific case."

"I see." Rebecca paused to see if Goldin would object to her resuming her examination. When no such objection seemed forthcoming, she turned back to Frazier and said in a strong voice, "In other words, it's *common knowledge*, right?"

"Objection!" Zuckerman shouted, jumping out of his chair. "Argumentative!"

"Withdrawn." Rebecca picked up her papers, jogged them together and threw one last look of contempt at Frazier before turning away. "No further questions, Your Honor."

Wednesday, November 4

Zuckerman spent the next day calling more witnesses, and Rebecca dispatched them easily. However, she and her team began to get an uneasy feeling that Zuckerman was building a strong case anyway, because even though each one of his points was individually refutable, taken all together they constituted what might appear to be a string of highly unlikely coincidences.

Rebecca was also growing concerned that, thus far, the prosecution hadn't introduced a single bit of evidence to back up its contention that the chip came out of China. If they didn't do that, there was a strong likelihood that the judge would direct a dismissal of the entire matter before the defense even put on its case. To deflect Zuckerman away from this detail, Rebecca tried to keep making a big deal out of getting physical possession of the chip. But she knew Zuckerman wasn't that careless, and so she shifted back to wondering *how* this was going to be handled, rather than *if*. Mastilir had been right: pars weren't going to do it in this game.

She had sent Steinholz and Ehrenright back to the firm's offices at the lunch break so they could work on revamping their planned questions for the defense portion of the case, and these thoughts ran through her mind as she made her way back there after the end of the day's chamber meeting with Judge Goldin. Sharing her concerns with them in the case conference room a short time later, she said, trying to put a positive spin on things, "Look at the bright side. Even if they make it look like Tera-Tech manufactured the chip, there's no way Zuckerman can get in any evidence that it came from China, not without compromising intelligence sources."

"Actually, there is," Ehrenright said, pointing toward Steinholz, who took a sheaf of papers bound in a red vinyl cover and shoved them across the table to Rebecca.

She looked at them and frowned. "The hell is this?"

"It's trouble," Steinholz replied. "Something they don't teach us about in law school, because it's hardly ever used."

Rebecca turned the binder over, then back again, and opened it up to the cover page. "*This* is how he's going to get it in?"

"Gotta be."

"Then how come he hasn't brought it up in pretrial yet!"

"Because he's being crafty; wants to bring it up mid-trial so it can be a nice surprise for us, ignorance of the law being no excuse for our not having seen it coming. He's banking on the fact that we won't be prepared to argue."

"Maybe we won't have to," Ehrenright said hopefully. "Maybe it won't come up."

Rebecca looked at the red-bound papers, as though the details hidden within might make themselves known to her if she stared at them long enough. Only one thing did: "Tomorrow," she said, half to herself.

"Tomorrow what?"

"He's going to bring it up tomorrow. They're almost at the end of their case. Only one witness left." She nodded with certainty. "He's going to bring it up tomorrow." Rebecca shook the papers in her hand. "How the hell am I supposed to get prepared to argue this thing tomorrow? I never even heard of it!"

"Don't worry about it," Steinholz responded. "You won't have to."

Before she had a chance to try to find out what he meant, Ehrenright said, "Our client wanted to know if he needed to be in court tomorrow."

Rebecca bit her lip. "Knew that was going to come up soon. What is he, bored?"

"Apparently he's not as enamored of your Oscar-contending performances as we are, and he feels he's neglecting his business."

"What'd you tell him?"

"I told him that nobody could force him to be here but that he'd be hurting his case."

"And he said, you're all doing a fine job and I don't see that I'm adding anything."

Ehrenright shrugged by way of affirmation.

"Dammit!" Rebecca folded her arms and squeezed tightly. "If we lose it, fine. If that sonofabitch loses it for us . . ." She shook her head, unable to complete the sentence.

Chapter 15

Thursday, November 5

"United States calls Mr. Lawrence Krazny."

A man in his early fifties rose from the audience section. Medium height, close-cropped thinning hair combed straight back, a slight paunch perfectly complementing his short-sleeved white shirt and the nondescript brown tie ending somewhere above his belt. Lawrence Krazny, carrying an old-fashioned, grade school–type notebook with black-and-white marbling on the cover, walked with unconcerned self-confidence, the been here, done this, routine.

Zuckerman, already at the podium, watched with satisfaction. Not watching Krazny but Rebecca, slouched back on her chair, head resting against her hand, scribbling idly on the yellow legal pad in front of her. Such displays of casual disdain and boredom were a sure sign that a lawyer was worried about a witness and wanted to make sure the jury didn't see it. Probably just as well her client decided to play hooky today.

Krazny was sworn in, and Zuckerman leaned against the podium. "Mr. Krazny, who is your employer?"

"I work for the FBI, in the crime lab." Pride in his voice. Rebecca had him all figured out already. He'd been a geek in high school, a member of the "audiovisual squad" that set up slide projectors and overheads. At home he built ham radios, but only because the personal computer hadn't been invented yet. He worked the scoreboard while Biff and Bobby Ray ran the football up and down the field. Now all those guys worked at Jiffy Lube and he, Larry "Four-Eyes" Krazny, worked for the FBI.

Way cool.

"And what do you do in the crime lab?"

"I analyze chemicals. Mostly residues from crime scenes."

"Any particular specialties?"

"Well, I guess I'm considered somewhat of a, uh . . ."

"No need to be modest, sir."

"Inks. I'm an expert in inks."

"Inks. How does that come into play?"

"We can often demonstrate that the ink used in, say, a ransom note is the same ink that a suspect may have used in some prior writing. Things like that. It often proves the key in cracking a tough case."

Cracking a case, Rebecca thought to herself. *Beats cracking open a can of motor oil any day.*

"I understand. Were you asked to take a sample of the ink that was used to label the microchip in evidence in this case and analyze it?"

"Yes, I was."

Zuckerman walked to the prosecution table and picked up a plastic bag. "Government's exhibit three, Your Honor," he said, holding it aloft. From the corner of his eye, he was able to see most of the jurors straining to get a glimpse of the little gray rectangle that had stirred up such a ruckus.

"So entered."

When the clerk had taken the bag and placed it in front of Krazny, Zuckerman asked, "And was this the chip you examined?"

"Yes. You can see right here where I scraped some off."

"And what did you find?"

"Objection." Rebecca stayed slouched as she spoke. "Vague and open-ended."

"I'll rephrase," Zuckerman said. "Mr. Krazny, did you find anything unusual when you analyzed the ink?"

"Sort of. It has some magnetic components, so it can be read by a machine."

"Objection. Calls for speculation, assumes facts not in evidence." Rebecca sat up straight in her chair before the judge had a chance to rule or Zuckerman to rephrase. "Wait, I retract my objection." She was delighted at the surprise and indecision on both the judge's and Zuckerman's faces. "Your Honor, might we inquire of counsel if it is his intent to show that the ink used in marking the chip is of the same type my client uses in normal operations?"

"Mr. Zuckerman?" Goldin asked.

Zuckerman, startled, answered tentatively, "Yes, that's my intention." An upward inflection on the last syllable made it more of a question than an answer: *What about it?*

"In that case," Rebecca said, resuming her former slouch, "the defense will stipulate to it."

Zuckerman and Judge Goldin both stared at her. "Are you certain?" Goldin asked skeptically.

"Yes."

Goldin shrugged. "Mr. Zuckerman, did you intend to elicit any other evidence from this witness?"

Zuckerman looked down at his papers, as though hoping they might hold some clue as to why Rebecca would so blithely offer such an enormous concession. "I, uh . . . I guess not."

He sounded unsure, so Goldin waited until Zuckerman looked up at her and nodded. Then she turned to address the jury: "The defense has made a stipulation on this point. What that means in plain English is that you are to regard this point as conclusively proven. You are to assume that the ink that was used in marking the chip in evidence is the same type of ink as that used in the defendant's company for marking its own chips. Clear?"

All the jurors nodded, and then Goldin addressed Krazny. "Thank you, sir. You may step down."

"Excuse me, Your Honor!" Rebecca stood up abruptly, and Krazny paused halfway out of his chair just as Zuckerman stopped halfway down on his. "I haven't cross-examined yet!"

Goldin frowned. "Didn't you just stipulate to his testimony?"

"Yes, but the point I stipulated to is not the basis of my cross-examination, and I didn't intend to waive my right to question this witness."

Goldin thought about it for a second. "Okay. I have no idea where this is going but you may proceed with your cross-examination, Ms. Verona."

"Thank you, Judge." It was one of the rare times Rebecca actually wished James Perrein was close at hand; let him see how she was about to earn the fees he was paying, see if he complained this time. She clasped her hands behind her back, reluctant to begin because then it would have to end, and she wanted this to go on forever, like delaying a climax because the longer you held off, the better it was.

A surprising number of people entered the profession because of the opportunity for gut-level victories otherwise not available to them. When Rebecca first encountered David Zuckerman, her initial assumption about him was that he had gone into the law for the same reason many smart but *nebbish*-y boys did, for a sort of revenge against humiliations suffered at the hands of schoolyard bullies. Physically unprepossessing, from backgrounds that valued mental agility over athletic prowess, these kids found in the law a level playing field in which those with stronger fists could no longer capriciously impose their will on them. A Jewish only child with a long ancestry of scholars and intellectuals, Zuckerman seemed a likely candidate to have emerged from such a background.

But then she'd seen him on the basketball court, during the annual prosecutors vs. defense attorneys "Pros and Cons" game sponsored by the state bar association. Fluid and instinctual movements betrayed a lifetime of competitive physicality. He'd even been recruited by some second-tier colleges offering basketball scholarships, but he'd chosen instead to carry on the family tradition of intellectual achievement by enrolling at Princeton, and then Yale Law.

No, David Zuckerman was not the put-upon punching bag sublimating some childhood desire for revenge.

Rebecca was. And here she stood again, before a crowd, taking her turn on the ice after Wendy's performance, feeling the disregard streaming down from her mother and uncle and from the crowd, the few people bothering to look at her only feeling sorry for her predicament.

But now it was different. Now it was delicious. And the sorrier for her they felt, the better this was going to be. She'd watched him under direct, this arrogant, cocksure nerd of a goddamned government flunky testifying not on behalf of the truth but for pitiful self-aggrandizement, and doing so at her client's expense.

At hers.

Fuck you, Lawrence Krazny . . .

Rebecca smiled at him prettily. "Let me make sure I understand your testimony first, Mr. Krazny. What you're telling us is that the ink used to print some numbers on the chip in evidence is the same ink that Tera-Tech uses in printing on its own chips, is that right?"

"Definitely."

"I understand. And you can tell this because the ink has some unique characteristics . . . ?"

"Exactly. The ink is ferrous, so it can be read automatically by magnetic character readers."

"I see. Same ink on both the chip in evidence and Tera-Tech chips."

"Right."

"So what does this suggest to you?"

"Sorry?"

Rebecca looked around her: *This is a tough question?* "What conclusion did you draw?"

"Objection. Calls for a legal conclusion." Zuckerman couldn't hide his anxiety, nor the fact that, in the absence of any notion where Rebecca was headed, he was throwing punches in the blind. "Witness wasn't asked to draw any conclusions, just tell us if the ink was the same."

"I'll withdraw it," Rebecca said easily. "Mr. Krazny, do you know why you were asked to examine the ink?"

"Objection! Irrelevant."

"*Irrelevant?*" She turned to Zuckerman in theatrical disbelief, then addressed the judge. "The man's an expert witness, Your Honor. Does counsel expect us to believe he had no idea why he was dong this analysis?"

"Counsel's beliefs are immaterial, Ms. Verona. What *is* the relevance?"

"I'm entitled to explore his bias."

"Objection is overruled. You may proceed."

"Mr. Krazny, why were you asked to examine the inks?"

"Um, it would be evidence that the Chinese chip was made by Tera-Tech."

"The Chinese chip. Why do you call it that?"

"Well, that's where it came from, didn't it?"

"How do you know that?"

"Everybody knows that!"

"Is that so?" Rebecca jabbed her forefinger at him and said emphatically, "How do *you* know it, sir?"

"They told me."

"Who's 'they'?"

"Well, Mr. Zuckerman, some CIA guys . . ."

Zuckerman began sweating. "Your Honor, where is this going?" he asked, now knowing perfectly well where it was going.

"A little leeway, please, Your Honor," Rebecca said, annoyance creeping into her voice. "I'm almost done."

"All right, but get to some point, Ms. Verona."

"Okay, Mr. Krazny. So you were told the chip came from the Chinese, and you determined that it had the same ink as Tera-Tech chips, and from this you conclude what?"

Zuckerman stood up again. "Same objection, Your Honor. Calls for a legal conclusion."

Rebecca gripped the sides of the podium. "No, it doesn't. Nothing legal about it, just simple logic, especially since the witness already knew a good deal about the case."

"Objection is overruled. Please proceed, Ms. Verona, but you're running out of rope."

Don't need much more. "Mr. Krazny?"

"Well, obviously, the chip was made by Tera-Tech."

"I see." Rebecca felt currents of warmth begin to flow down her back. "And were you rewarded for coming to this conclusion?"

"What do you mean?"

"I mean, did you get a pat on the back? An attaboy from your boss? Did they throw a party to celebrate the results of your analysis?"

"I guess they were pleased."

"Because your job was to help them nail Tera-Tech, is that right?"

"Objection!" Zuckerman was nearly shouting now.

"Goes to bias, Your Honor," Rebecca said, her calm voice contrasting sharply with Zuckerman's, saying to the jury, *Which one of us is in trouble here?*

"Overruled."

"Mr. Krazny?"

"They were pretty happy, I guess."

"Was your assignment to get some dirt on Tera-Tech?"

"No. My job was to analyze inks."

"But you knew perfectly well what they were after, didn't you?"

"I knew what their objective was, yes. But it didn't color my analysis. All the proof's in here." He tapped his notebook. "Anybody else can verify my findings."

"Which were that Tera-Tech made the chip, right?"

"You bet!" It was a confident, proud pronouncement, daring Rebecca to work her way out of *this* one. But the fingers on his right hand tapped nervously on the notebook still lying unopened in front of him.

The warm currents grew stronger, reaching her legs and threatening to weaken her knees. "But didn't you just tell us that your findings were limited to establishing only that the same inks were used? Did I misunderstand, or are you now telling us that your findings are that Tera-Tech is guilty as hell, just as your employers, the ones who pay your salary, just as they believe?"

"No. I mean, uh . . . Well, you know what I mean." He nodded at her, encouraging her to do the same, to just let it go.

She complied. "Sure do, Mr. Krazny." Then she looked at the

jury, inviting them to tag along for the show, and stepped to the side of the podium, hands behind her back again, feet slightly apart. "Who manufactured the inks?"

"Manufactured them? I—I don't know."

"You don't know?" She made it sound like it was the most incredible thing she'd heard so far today.

"No."

"Didn't you even bother to find out?"

"No."

"Why not?" Her questions were machine gun bullets streaming across the room.

"I wasn't asked to do that. I told you, I was only supposed to determine—"

"I know. If the inks were identical."

"Which they were!" he said defiantly.

"I believe you. I truly do. We stipulated to it, remember?" She paused, waiting for him to stop fidgeting. "Mr. Krazny, would it surprise you if I were to tell you that the same company that supplies Tera-Tech with its ink also sells it to Panasonic, GE and Sony for printing serial numbers on videocameras?"

Krazny blinked but didn't answer. Rebecca stepped to the defense table, reached into her satchel and pulled out a brown, medium-sized grocery bag, set it down heavily on the table with some metallic rattling sounds, then looked back at Krazny and waited for his answer.

Krazny stared at the paper bag like he thought it was getting ready to explode. "I guess that wouldn't surprise me, no."

"Okay. Would it surprise you if I were to tell you that Disney uses it on Mickey Mouse watches, Hewlett-Packard on calculators, RCA on portable radios . . . ?"

Krazny hesitated again, and Rebecca put her hand on the bag. Krazny licked his lips and looked anxiously over at Zuckerman, who had been waiting for an opportunity, however tenuous, to put a stop to this.

Rebecca never took her eyes off Krazny. "Are you getting secret signals from the prosecutor, Mr. Krazny?"

Zuckerman leaped. "I object! There's no basis for such an insinuation!"

"I'll withdraw it." Rebecca stepped into the line of sight between the witness and the prosecutor. Krazny looked as though she'd just stepped on his oxygen hose. His lips flapped soundlessly as Rebecca said, "Well?"

"I, um, no. No. Wouldn't surprise me. I guess."

"So here's a last one." She went back to the podium. "Would you be surprised if I told you that three quarters of the semiconductor manufacturers in the entire Silicon Valley use the same ink!"

Krazny ran his hand through his hair. "I have no way of knowing that," he said weakly.

"Of course not! You never bothered to check once you got the answer the prosecutor was looking for!"

"Objection!" Zuckerman said angrily. "She's badgering the witness and putting words in his mouth!"

"Have you a proper objection to make, Mr. Zuckerman?"

"Leading and argumentative!"

"I'll withdraw it." Rebecca turned away from Krazny and shook her head. "No more questions for this"—she twisted slightly and looked back at Krazny with undisguised contempt—"this *expert*," she spat with disdain.

She sat down, and hoped the glow wasn't too noticeable, likely not an issue since courtroom spectators were more focused on the excited murmuring coming from the jury box.

"Goddamned *dazzling*!" Steinholz whispered, nudging her knee with his own. Rebecca turned to see Ehrenright in the first row of the spectator gallery fluttering his eyelids rapidly, his mouth hanging open, and she turned back quickly, trying not to laugh.

To stop herself, she only had to look down at the prosecution's witness list in front of her. Of the sixty-five people on the list, Rebecca had been fairly certain Zuckerman was going to call only nine, all of whom had already testified. Therefore, if she was right, his witness pool was exhausted, and it was time for him to handle the issue of where the chip was found.

It was eleven o'clock. An hour to go until the lunch break. Zuckerman rose and said, "Your Honor, may I suggest we break early for lunch? We've only one item left, and it might be better if we went through it with no interruptions."

And there it was. But why the request for an early lunch?

Ehrenright leaned forward and grabbed Rebecca's shoulder. "A moment please, Your Honor?" she said, then turned to huddle with her two associates.

"You see what he's doing?" Ehrenright whispered. "He assumes we're not prepared to argue against his next motion because we don't know what he's going to spring on us."

"What's that got to do with lunch?" Steinholz asked.

"Simple. He wants to make damned sure that—"

"—that we don't use the break to run off and do some quick research after he shows us his hand," Rebecca finished for him.

Steinholz smiled. "Excellent!"

"Sorry, Your Honor," Rebecca said, facing forward again. "Just needed to clarify something. What was that again, an early lunch break?"

"Yes. Any objection?"

"Course not; no problem here."

They watched in satisfaction as Zuckerman grinned and whispered something to his co-counsels, who smiled back and stole knowing glances at the defense attorneys doing their best to look worried before going off to eat sushi and talk about the Lakers.

"Mr. Zuckerman, is your next witness ready?" Judge Goldin asked as soon as court resumed.

"Your Honor, we have no more witnesses. However, there is one small matter before the jury is brought back in." He handed a stapled sheaf of papers to one of his colleagues, who rose, walked it over to the defense table and handed it to Rebecca. "The government would like to introduce a sworn statement from the Department of State asserting that the chip in evidence, government's exhibit three, was recovered from a computer in the People's Republic of China."

Rebecca stood up. "A question for the prosecution, Your Honor?"

"Go ahead, but address it to the court, please."

"Certainly. Counsel said they have no more witnesses, so at what point will we be able to cross-examine whoever made the statement?"

At a cue from the judge, Zuckerman responded, "It was not the government's intention to introduce another witness."

"In that case," Rebecca said calmly as she remained standing, "defense objects, Your Honor. Lack of foundation, improper procedure, no prior opportunity to examine."

"Are you both ready for argument?" Goldin inquired, knowing that this wasn't going to be a quick one.

The objection was expected, of course, and Zuckerman was prepared. "Ready, Your Honor."

"Co-counsel will argue this issue for the defense," Rebecca announced. Arno Steinholz, much to Zuckerman's surprise, stood up, holding a three-ring binder with colored tabs sticking out of the neatly organized pages within.

"Very well. Please explain the basis for your objection."

"Thank you, Your Honor. I believe we can dispense with this quickly." Steinholz displayed none of the throat-clearing fumbling of a novice litigator, but spoke clearly and confidently, addressing the judge and not the opposition. "We don't actually have a problem with the statement itself, and we'll withdraw our objection if allowed to cross-examine whoever is making the statement. Even though there are no more witnesses on counsel's list, we won't object if he wants to add whoever made that statement."

"The statement constitutes a deposition," Zuckerman replied, "which is admissible."

"Not so," Steinholz countered. "Not according to Rule Fifteen of the Federal Rules of Criminal Procedure. There is no 'exceptional circumstance' as described in the rule. But maybe we haven't heard all the circumstances. Is this State Department employee likely to become unavailable because of a lack of memory? Is he in the witness protection program? Is he likely to die from a grave illness if he appears in court?" He was quoting directly from the Rules.

Steinholz looked at Zuckerman, as though expecting a response, then turned back to Goldin. "If not, our client has a constitutional right to cross-examine his accusers and he wishes to cross-examine this one."

"The Department of State isn't *accusing* anybody of anything," Zuckerman argued. "It is only a percipient witness as to the origin of a piece of evidence."

Steinholz was already shaking his head as Zuckerman finished. "Any piece of evidence whose verification would implicate the defendant is by its very nature accusatory."

Zuckerman paused, pretending to think about that last point, then smiled slyly at his two co-counsels before turning his attention back to the judge. "Well, Your Honor, as it turns out, Rule Fifteen is not the controlling statute here." He cast a smug smile at the defense table. "The Classified Information Procedures Act is." One of his colleagues handed Zuckerman a legal pad. "May I explain?"

"Briefly, please."

"Certainly." Zuckerman laid the pad on the podium facedown, demonstrating that he needed no notes. "Basically, the purpose of this Act is to prevent a defendant from leaking any classified information the government might have to disclose. The way this is done, we introduce a statement containing facts that the classified information would tend to prove. So the secret stuff stays secret, and only the facts relevant to the case are disclosed."

"Seems pretty straightforward." Goldin was already aware of the provisions of the Classification Act, but it was up to the attorneys to present her with the portions they considered relevant and argue about them. "Counselor?"

Steinholz looked at Zuckerman, then reached into his attaché and, very slowly, withdrew the sheaf of papers bound in a red vinyl cover he had shown to Rebecca the day before.

"Counsel is conveniently forgetting one or two provisions of this Act, Your Honor," Steinholz said as Zuckerman paled. "For example, Section Six provides that the court should grant the government the ability to introduce this kind of statement only if doing so would still allow the defendant to make his defense just as well as if he had all the secret stuff."

Steinholz turned to face Zuckerman, opened the folder and read the exact language. " 'Substantially the same ability to make his defense.' " He let that sink in for a moment, Zuckerman not returning his gaze. "Now I hardly think that the introduction of a statement crafted by the prosecution affords my client the same ability to defend himself as if we cross-examined the person making the statement."

Goldin turned to Zuckerman but didn't say anything. It was clearly his turn to respond.

"It doesn't have to be a statement, Judge. We can hold a hearing instead, outside the presence of the jury, and we can object to any line of questioning that might reveal classified information."

"In which case, you can't use it," Steinholz responded. "And, by the way, if the government reveals classified information to the defendant, and the court prevents the defendant from disclosing any of it"—he turned back to the bench—"then Your Honor must dismiss the indictment."

"Uh, not quite," Zuckerman threw back with contempt. "Your Honor doesn't have to do that if she determines that the interests of justice would not be served." He looked up at Steinholz. "According to Section Six."

"But Section Six also states," Steinholz said to Zuckerman, "that if the court decides not to dismiss the entire indictment, it has to dismiss relevant portions, or throw out all that secret testimony altogether."

Before Zuckerman could respond, Steinholz, taking no prisoners, pushed ahead. "Your Honor, it is *unthinkable* that this court would allow into evidence a statement from some nameless State Department bureaucrat without an offer of proof that it is legitimate. Otherwise, the prosecution might as well conduct its whole case based on a stack of letters. And might I point out to the court that this is not an unreasonable interpretation of events thus far, since this is exactly how the prosecution is handling its case regarding the chip itself: we haven't even *seen* the thing, and all we get is pieces of paper telling us only what the prosecution wants us to know!"

The defense team had been assuming all along that the government would rather drop the case than expose its intelligence assets, and it was the strongest lever they had to keep the most damning evidence out of the trial. Zuckerman was equally determined to get the evidence in, and he and Steinholz continued to argue forcefully, citing competing provisions of the federal rules and the Classification Act: the defendant had a right to face his accusers; on the other hand, the government had a duty to protect national security. Goldin thought such debates were the very glory of trial law, and would let it go on so long as the debaters kept on track and didn't start repeating themselves.

"Without a more substantive statement," Steinholz said, "subject to defense cross, there's no case left because a reasonable jury would never convict."

"Why don't we let the jury decide that?" Zuckerman suggested.

"Those kinds of decisions aren't left to juries," Steinholz fired back. "They're left to judges."

"I'm not getting any closer to being able to rule on this," Goldin interrupted brusquely. "Obviously, there is a built-in conflict here that isn't going to be resolved by partisan arguments." She took a moment to enjoy the blissful sound of two lawyers not speaking while she tried to figure out what to do. She decided to give the lawyers a chance to try to solve the dilemma. "Any suggestions as to how the court should deal with obviously conflicting laws?"

Zuckerman tried first. "I believe that, in the absence of any authority to do otherwise, the court should follow the letter of the most recent law, since the legislators can be assumed to have taken into account prior law and precedent when they drafted it."

Steinholz took an opposite stand. "We believe that, in the absence of authoritative guidelines for the resolution of diametrically opposed laws, the court should do what's fair. And that includes adhering to constitutional principles two centuries old rather than to a sloppily written, ill-considered and untested law less than two *decades* old."

"Well, that was a terrific help." Goldin looked away for a few moments, then turned back. "Do either of you know how baseball salaries are arbitrated?"

The sudden non sequitur threw both of them equally, as Goldin had intended, and she went on to explain. "The player and the owner each put a sealed figure in an envelope and submit it to the arbitration board. The board then picks the figure they believe is most fair, and that's the end of it. So if the player throws in a number that's way too big, and the owner puts one in that's perhaps on the low side but not unreasonable, the owner's figure wins. And vice versa. So each side is motivated to try to be reasonable because if they're not, the other side's bid is going to win. And, interestingly, the two bids are often surprisingly close."

Steinholz and Zuckerman nodded respectfully, but neither of them had any idea why she was talking about baseball salaries.

"Here's what we're going to do," Goldin said. "I'm going to let the jury go for today, and then I want you both to go off for the rest of the afternoon and separately work out proposals on how best to solve the dilemma and continue the trial. You must take into account all the elements argued: the defendant's rights, the government's rights and obligations, and the letter of the applicable laws. I don't expect you to resolve all the obvious conflicts. What I expect is that you will be creative in advising this court on how to proceed in a manner that maximizes fairness to both sides. And before you return with strongly partisan briefs that do nothing but expand on the arguments heard today, here's the catch: the court will select one of the two proposals in its entirety, based on which one solves most of the problems and is fairest to both sides."

It was an ingenious tactic, displaying the kind of creativity Goldin was legendary for. Rather than fight unilaterally for their own ideal positions, Rebecca's and Zuckerman's teams now had a tricky balancing act: how to get the best possible position for their side without going so overboard that their proposal would be rejected.

Steinholz tried one last gambit. "I understand, Your Honor, but there's one small problem. Section Fourteen of the Classified Information Procedures Act prohibits the attorney general from designating anyone other than the associate or assistant AG from carrying out his duties under this Act. Therefore, it would appear that Mr. Zuckerman has no authority to do anything."

"Not quite," Zuckerman responded. "Whatever I agree to will be approved or rejected by the AG's office within ten minutes, and therefore won't interfere in any way with the continuity of the trial."

Goldin nodded. "Gentlemen," she said, looking at her watch and gathering her papers, "start your pencils."

C h a p t e r   1 6

"Ten minutes?"

"Ten minutes what?" Justin Ehrenright asked Rebecca. The two of them and Arno Steinholz were back in the office trying to deal with Judge Goldin's latest feat of legal imagineering.

"Zuckerman said he can get anything okayed in ten minutes. Which can only mean he must have a direct line to the higher-ups in the DoJ."

"And that means the full force of the AG's office is behind this case," Ehrenright added.

"What the hell ever," Steinholz said, looking at his watch and then dumping the contents of his attaché on the conference room table. "What I suggest, Becky, you let me and Justin figure out a proposal, and you go away and think about what we're gonna do when we lose."

"How do you know we're gonna lose?"

"Doesn't make any difference; we gotta be prepared. And the two of us know this Classification Act bullshit better'n you."

Rebecca nodded, but didn't make a move to leave just yet. "You were great in there, Arno." Ehrenright rapped his knuckles on the table, indicating agreement. "Like you wrote the damned laws yourself."

"Thing is," Steinholz said, embarrassed and delighted at the same time, "I believed what I was saying. Law's a crock; musta been written by the same kinda people dreamed up ballot propositions."

"Nothing like believing in your argument," Rebecca agreed. "Although the true test of a good defense attorney is *not* believing it and sounding like you do."

Her colleagues laughed as Rebecca rose to go. "Hint for you

two," she said as she headed for the door. "You don't have the basic gist of the thing down in an hour, you're never going to get it. One hour to craft the concept, two to anticipate schmecklehead's objections." She glanced at her watch and opened the door. "Good night's sleep is more important than anything else you're likely to come up with."

Back in her office, Rebecca began making notes on how to deal with whatever proposal Zuckerman could come up with that the judge might accept over their own. She was well aware that this completely unexpected turn of events could affect their entire trial strategy, but tried not to dwell on it.

"Hey!"

She snapped her head around to see Ehrenright standing in her doorway, cup of coffee in hand. He hadn't walked up but had simply appeared, wraithlike, as though he'd materialized out of thin air.

He was smiling. "Boy, when you get lost in thought, you don't kid around."

Rebecca wondered how long he'd been standing there as he walked in and took a seat in front of her desk. "You're gonna do something, do it all the way, that's my motto."

Ehrenright nodded and took a sip of the coffee, the lack of any wincing indicating that it had gone cold. "You're thinking how this could change everything."

She leaned her head back on the soft leather of her chair and returned her stare to the blank wall next to the window. "Amazing how one small, totally unanticipated defining moment can change your case forever."

"Or your life."

"That too. What was yours?"

"Day I decided to become a lawyer. Yours?"

"The day I stopped living my life as Wendy Verona's older sister, what's-her-name."

It had shot out before she'd had a chance to recognize what was coming so she could stop it, and she froze, waiting for Ehrenright to sit bolt upright and slosh his coffee over his pants in surprise. *Hey: Rebecca Verona doesn't* do *true confessions!*

He didn't move. "What was it like?" he asked casually.

"What was what like?"

"When Wendy got hurt. I mean, I know all the facts, everybody does. But what was it like?"

Nobody knows all the facts. And how did Ehrenright know that was the day I was talking about? "Hard to describe."

"How'd you find out?"

Leave it to Ehrenright not to ask if she wanted to talk about it, the most surefire conversation destroyer in the lexicon. "I was at the skating rink. All pissed off because Wendy was late for practice." *She got away with a lot at home, temper tantrums and flashes of inconsiderateness rationalized as the typical eccentricities of the unusually gifted. As long as she practiced and worked hard, as long as she came home from competitions lugging some shiny new hardware for the mantel, she could probably set the house on fire and get away with it.*

"I called home and my mother was crying, hysterical, couldn't even tell me what was wrong." *But I could hear Uncle Charlie in the background telling her to get off the goddamned phone so he could call the Coca-Cola marketing VP. Then the line went dead, and I stood there like a worthless slug holding the receiver in my hand.* "So I got off the phone and found out from someone at the rink that something'd happened to Wendy. My coach drove me to the hospital, and I had to wrestle with some officious warden of a nurse to get into my sister's room." *It smelled of antiseptic sheets, alcohol and disaster. Wendy was lying in the bed, one arm thrown across her forehead, a doctor standing nearby looking at the charts with a frown.*

"You were the first one there?"

She nodded. "The rink was pretty close. But my uncle got there a minute or so later, just in time for both of us to hear the bad news from the doc." *Charlie blew in and brushed past me, barely glanced at Wendy, and demanded that the doc tell him what was going on.*

"A broken knee," Ehrenright said. "From falling on a marble floor."

"Yeah. A nondisplaced tibial plateau fracture, to be exact. Painful as hell, but fixable, over time. Few weeks on crutches, some physical therapy . . ."

"Championships were coming up, weren't they?" Ehrenright asked.

"Two days. So much for that." *Dr. Janos said every step would be like a jab with a knife. Uncle Charlie wanted to know if they could shoot the knee full of painkillers so she could skate in the Worlds, and the doc explained that it might be possible, but one wrong move, or a fall, and the nondisplaced fracture becomes dis-*

placed, and then they have to operate, and never mind skating again, she might not ever even walk normally. "But it might work, right?" Uncle Charlie insisted. "Let her compete?"

Which is when Dr. Janos threatened to throw him out of the room if he didn't leave on his own. Charlie'd never said a word to Wendy the whole time, never consulted her, even as he considered the trade-offs of risking her being a cripple for life.

Ehrenright shook his head. "Damn," he breathed, then sat quietly for a few seconds, fingering the rim of his coffee cup. "So that was your defining moment, huh?"

"Yep."

Nope. That came a few minutes later, when Dr. Janos leaned over Wendy, pushed a lock of hair back from her forehead and whispered, "Congratulations, kid," which I wasn't supposed to hear. Nor was I supposed to notice Wendy grabbing his hand and hugging it tightly to her chest as she earnestly breathed back, "Thank you, Doctor. Thank you!" and Janos answered, "Don't mention it."

Now, there's a goddamned defining moment for you.

"So, you gonna play Freud or go help Arno?"

Ehrenright looked at his watch and stood up quickly, but said as he walked toward the door, "You miss it? Skating?"

"I still skate. You mean competing."

"Right."

"No. I don't even watch it."

"How come?"

How come? Because I couldn't bear it, knowing the truth behind many of the faerie queens, media anointed with the kind of uncritical coverage normally reserved for saints and fading movie stars. Could there be a more irrelevant sentiment for a fourteen-year-old figure-skating hopeful than deciding this just isn't fun anymore? What does fun have to do with it when your childhood has been transformed into a Dickensian existence of indentured servitude, and every missed practice carries with it the potential to throw your entire family into ruin?

"Just got bored, I guess."

Ehrenright grunted, looked at her, and grunted again, sensing something else behind her words but missing the real enormity of it, and then was gone.

On her way to the conference room two hours later, Rebecca spotted Wysocki too late to duck away and avoid him.

"So?" he asked. "How're things going?"

As she had resolved to do, Rebecca started off civilly. There was no percentage in antagonizing The Man unless there was a damned good reason, or even if there *were* a damned good reason. Everything else aside, they were two human beings who had to work in close proximity, and who needed any more tension than the amount normally attendant to the job?

She leaned against the wall and scratched her head. "Some of the things Terescu's coming up with give me a little cause for concern."

"You following all the techie talk okay?"

She shook her head. "Yeah, but it isn't that. I got him thinking right. Just seems . . . I don't know . . . like our sole expert ain't quite as committed to the cause as he should be."

"So you're worried, can he perform on the stand."

"Exactly. But we have no choice." She braced for the inevitable criticism regarding her choice of this expert witness in the first place.

"If you got him set up right, you need to believe that he won't get up there and willingly make himself look like an asshole. Best thing, put it out of your mind so you can concentrate on getting prepared for trial. There aren't any other options, so spend your time worrying about what you can control, not what you can't. Okay?"

It was good advice. "I'll do that."

"Good. If everything was exactly the way you'd like it, they would have dropped the charges months ago. Now, I need to know when I can schedule you to meet with Ricky."

The media consultant under retainer to the firm. "What for?"

"Get you prepared for dealing with the press. Yeah, yeah, I know, what's the big deal, right? Everybody thinks that talking to reporters is a no-brainer, that all you have to do is—"

"I'm not talking to any reporters."

The last time she had, it almost put a damper on what should have been a perfect, no-loose-ends victory. Silverlight Electronics, a university-centered consortium of smaller companies fully subsidized by the Taiwanese government, had developed a unique testing device with the potential to drastically reduce the rejection rate of integrated circuit chips. The company, after investing nearly $35 million in startup costs, had just begun marketing the machine in the U.S. when it found itself bitterly opposed by an American firm that manufactured a competing, albeit much less capable, device.

The firm, Bonwitt-Baker, after obtaining a temporary restraining order forbidding sale of the device in the U.S., sued Silverlight for patent infringement, then mounted a public relations campaign within the industry claiming that, if this testing machine were to be allowed into the country, it would represent a major threat to every American manufacturer who depended on patents to protect them from the insidious encroachment of overseas pirates who had no respect for U.S. laws. As regulatory authorities struggled to come to a decision, the campaign began to take on racist overtones, with caricatures of the Taiwanese coming close to those employed in the propaganda posters of World War II that whipped up hatred and fear of the "Yellow Peril" from Japan.

To combat Bonwitt's diatribes against her client, Rebecca told reporters that Bonwitt was misleading the American public by claiming that Silverlight was using one of its key patents when, in fact, their far superior machine did no such thing. After shooting her mouth off, and even arguing with one or two surprisingly knowledgeable reporters, her expert witness on the case reported back to her that, well, it really kind of did.

Horrified, Rebecca dove into the case documents with a vengeance, reading everything herself over a period of three largely sleepless days and nights. Then she called for an administrative hearing to settle things once and for all.

The only witness she was interested in was the Bonwitt scientist, Josef Candell, who had developed the central process in the first place, and in whose name the patent had been issued.

"How long has the patent been in effect?" she asked him.

"Since 1982," Candell announced proudly. "Twelve years."

"I see. And when had you actually developed the process?"

"Oh, I'd say within a year or so before that."

"You sure?"

"Fairly certain."

Rebecca pulled a yellowing, soft-bound book out of her attaché. "Do you recognize this book?"

"Of course. I wrote it."

"So you did." She opened to a page and handed it to Candell. "Mind reading the sentences I've underlined?"

"Not at all." He took the book from her and read aloud. "This special variation of the Fast Fourier transform has been proven in real-world situations countless times over the past three years. Bonwitt-Baker test-site customers have successfully been employing it during the manufacture of some of their most complicated circuits, and have slashed rejection rates by as much as twenty-seven percent."

"Thank you. And that variation you developed forms the basis of the patented process, is that correct?"

"It most certainly does."

"Okay. Mr. Candell, would you please check the publication date at the front of the book?"

He turned to the relevant page and announced, "First printing, October, 1982."

"When did you finish the draft of the manuscript?"

"The previous, uh, winter or thereabouts."

Candell, a very smart scientist, knew very little about patent law. Specifically, he hadn't been aware that there was a limit of a year from the time a process was "reduced to practice" to when a patent could be applied for. Reading from his own book, he had just shown that his development had been in use, at the latest, in February of 1979. Rebecca was able to get the patent overturned because it never should have been issued in the first place.

Silverlight Electronics and the Taiwanese government were overjoyed, as was Rebecca, but she had still been left with the problem of explaining why she had denied the company's use of the Bonwitt process in the first place. She'd just been shooting from the hip, thinking she had an obligation to take her client's side no matter what. When it turned out that the client had misled her, she was sorry she'd ever spoken to the press in the first place, recalling one of the few truly valuable pieces of insight Uncle Charlie had ever imparted to her. *Never pick a fight with someone who buys his ink by the gallon.*

Wysocki didn't answer right away, although he did fail to hide his surprise.

"No reporters," Rebecca said with added firmness. "Not once, not ever."

"You have to."

"Why?"

"Because the government's going to get cozy with the press, and they're going to slay you and your client in public."

"Fine, then you talk to them."

"It has to be you."

She shook her head. "It's nonnegotiable, Allen."

"You're telling me what's negotiable and what isn't?"

"In this case, I am. You want to fire me, go ahead."

Obviously, he couldn't do that. But Rebecca knew that this minor victory was truly a Pyrrhic one, because once this case was over, Wysocki wouldn't hesitate to demonstrate definitively who the boss of this outfit was.

Rebecca continued on to the conference room to check in on the associates, and found them struggling without much success. "There's really very little middle ground," Steinholz said, running a hand through long, disorderly hair that looked as though he'd been tearing at it in frustration for hours. "You kind of have to pick one side or the other, or nothing will make much sense."

"There's another thing, Becky," Ehrenright added. "What if she picks our proposal? Then we're on the record with a suggestion which was accepted in its entirety by the court. What will that do to our appeal if we lose the case?"

Steinholz shrugged helplessly as he agreed with Ehrenright. "It *is* kind of a tacit agreement with the judge's procedure."

Rebecca thought it a nonissue. "She ordered us to do it. Wasn't our idea."

"But if we present a proposal as our best thinking, that it's what we really want . . . ?"

Rebecca began to shake her head. "So what do *you* think?" Ehrenright asked timidly, knowing that Rebecca had a rule against being presented with problems without well-considered alternatives to discuss.

"I think you both should knock off," she said. "Go home."

The two looked at each other in confusion. Rebecca, thinking back to her sister lying in the hospital, considered how silly it was to always play it careful when, at any given moment, something can come along out of the blue and change your whole life in spite of all your planning.

"I mean it. Go home." She made a motion with her hands, and they began to gather up their papers as ordered.

Chapter 17

Friday, November 6

Rebecca nodded a perfunctory hello to Steinholz and Ehrenright as they took their places at the defense table, then resumed reviewing her notes. The two lawyers exchanged troubled glances at her uncharacteristic aloofness.

They had no way to know that she was protecting them, and she couldn't tell them without compromising the shield she was trying to maintain for their own good. She had sent them home early the night before so nobody could later accuse them of complicity in what she had decided to do, should it fail. She also hadn't informed Philip Mastilir; let him add a claim of malpractice to his appeal of a conviction if it came to that.

But she'd sure as hell told James Perrein. By phone, because he was back up in northern California. She made certain he didn't understand her when she explained it, but there was a note in her case file showing the date and the time of the call, with "Client concurs—all aspects" written next to them. She hoped he hadn't noticed that she had spared him her now-standard harangue that he make certain to appear in court.

Zuckerman and his team looked haggard. They were fingering sheets of paper scattered over their table, pulling some into a pile, then taking them apart again and rearranging them in new ways. They hadn't made a final determination of how to proceed. Zuckerman looked over to see Rebecca sitting calmly, checking her nails, her attaché not even opened yet.

Court came to order and Goldin was seated. The jury was not present. All the attorneys knew that this judge would not be in the best disposition since she considered any time spent without the jury to be an affront to her sense of protocol.

With no preliminaries, Goldin pointed her gavel at the defense table and said, "I'll hear your response to the court's order now."

Rebecca rose and stepped to the podium. "Your Honor, I've examined this situation carefully." It was not lost on her team that she was taking whatever credit or blame might accrue from what was to follow. Knowing Rebecca as well as they did, Steinholz and Ehrenright knew she was anticipating blame. "In my judgment, there is no conceivable procedure by which my client's rights can be protected without the ability to challenge the evidence counsel proposes to introduce, and therefore anything short of full cross-examination in court is unconstitutional. Our proposal is that this court follow the federal rules of evidence."

Goldin, clearly disappointed, said, "Do I take it you renew your arguments from yesterday?"

"Yes, Your Honor. And I'd like to make certain the court understands that I mean no disrespect. I just believe that this is the proper course of action."

"And you understand the nature of the risk, should your actions result in the court's acceptance of the prosecution's proposal?"

"Fully, Your Honor." *And we both understand I'm laying the groundwork for an appeal.*

The judge shrugged and turned to Zuckerman. "Counselor? I trust you were slightly more creative . . ."

Zuckerman stared at the papers on the table for another half second, quickly pulled several into a pile and carried them to the podium. One of his colleagues smiled, the other frowned and shook his head.

"I should hope so, Your Honor." He set the papers down and leafed through them quickly, then stood back and looked up. "The United States proposes that Your Honor examine our evidence regarding the source of the chip in private, outside the presence of the jury. Following that, the court would instruct the jury as to what evidence to accept, based on your own judgment."

The judge listened respectfully, then asked Zuckerman, "How does this proposal solve the issues raised by the defense?"

Zuckerman took a deep, weary-sounding breath. "I find it difficult to believe that the Act hasn't survived similar challenges during the twenty years of its existence. The prosecution is satisfied that the course of action we've outlined will stand up to appellate scrutiny." He paused and turned to Rebecca.

"I find it difficult to believe it *has* survived such challenges, but I also don't think we should be arguing based on groundless supposition." Rebecca exhaled loudly and let some irritation creep into her voice. "Your Honor, have we really gotten so wrapped up in

arcane technicalities that we're forgetting the most basic founda-
tions of the law? Every element of the alleged offense must be presented to the jury in order that they might consider it in
determining whether the standard of reasonable doubt has been
met. Handing them a piece of evidence that they are to accept as
proven violates more canons than I can even begin to enumerate!"

"The law is not a series of concrete pronouncements," Zuckerman countered. "It is always flexible when it needs to be in the interests of fairness and justice."

"No, it isn't!" Rebecca nearly shouted. "How many people get
the shaft because of technicalities used in absurd ways that were
never intended?"

Before Rebecca could continue, Zuckerman took a step forward
to get Goldin's attention and said loudly, "May I remind Your
Honor that it was the court's own order that one of our two proposals be accepted in its entirety, and since the prosecution is the
only side that has put one forth—"

"That's a gross misstatement!" Rebecca interrupted back, irate
now. "We most certainly did come up with a proposal, that the
court direct a dismissal of the case, and it's the only fair and constitutional decision. It isn't at all unusual for seemingly strong cases
to be dismissed on constitutional grounds, even if it appears that
justice is being denied. How many vicious murderers have been released because they weren't read their rights? How many drug dealers have been let go because of illegal search and seizure? All my
client is accused of is export violations, for heaven's sake, so
where's the great miscarriage of justice if this case is dismissed to
preserve his constitutional rights!" She turned to face Zuckerman.
"What is he, Charles Manson?"

It was a powerful point, well presented, and Rebecca decided to
stop and not risk diluting it by further argument.

"Response, Counselor?" Goldin said to Zuckerman.

Rebecca knew she had him. She tried to keep her face neutral
and not let the judge see even a trace of smugness as she waited to
hear Zuckerman's rejoinder, which seemed to be taking him a long
time to formulate.

"I believed Your Honor has already ruled," Zuckerman finally
said, "so I see no need to respond."

"I don't get you."

"The court committed to selecting one of our two proposals in
its entirety," he explained. "The defense has put forth no proposal

as per Your Honor's specifications, whereas *our* proposal is completely consistent with both the law and the wishes of the court. Therefore, I believe it fair to say that the court has already ruled on this issue and the prosecution respectfully requests that further argument cease and the court's order be executed."

Rebecca started to say something again, but Goldin, who had begun nodding in agreement halfway through Zuckerman's statement, waved her down without even looking at her. "If I were to rule in your favor, how soon could you have the State Department employee ready to give a deposition?"

Rebecca and Steinholz wilted visibly upon hearing this, Steinholz sensing their case going out the window, Rebecca visualizing her career going down the toilet.

"Immediately, Your Honor, but it won't be somebody from the State Department."

"Oh? And who would it be?"

"We'd prefer not to state that in open session, if it please the court."

"Whatever. We'll recess for fifteen minutes and I'll return with my ruling."

"You made a big mistake in there, lady," Zuckerman said to Rebecca on the way out.

"And that is?"

"You blew an opportunity to get this handled your way. There's no way in hell she's gonna dismiss the case. So she's going to do things my way." He shook his head and gave her a pitying look. "Good thing your terribly concerned client isn't in court today."

"So you think I blew it."

"Yes, and so do you. I mean, she practically told you that several times."

"Doesn't make any difference," Rebecca said casually as they began walking down the hall together. "One way or the other, a statement from the spooks is going before the jury. We both knew that. What I did was just pave the way for the appeal. Because once the statement is on the record, it'll be a piece of cake for me to show later it shouldn't have been, and that's the end of your conviction."

Zuckerman smiled in amusement. "So you know you're going to lose?"

"I'm just hedging against the possibility. Even if I were dead certain I was going to win, I would've done the same thing."

"Interesting."

"Speaking of interesting: how does it feel not to have control over your own case?"

He stopped as they approached a pitted marble column. "What are you talking about?"

"C'mon, David, we're off the record." She stepped closer to him and kept her voice low. "Are you trying to tell me you didn't get pressure from above to get this case to trial before you were ready?"

"I call the shots on my cases."

"Lame, Zuckerman." Rebecca shook her head in sympathy. "You have about as much control of this case as you do of the tides."

"What makes you—"

"Why didn't the FBI simply get a court order to search Tera-Tech's premises and find some real evidence?"

Zuckerman shrugged. "It might have tipped them off and allowed them to hide evidence."

Rebecca made a gagging sound in her throat. "That's a good one! You guys could have had a hundred agents halfway through the front door before tipping anybody off. You know what I bet?" She poked a finger into his chest. It felt as firm as a barely thawed steak, momentarily disconcerting her. "You tried to get a court order, but some smart judge realized you didn't have shit and turned it down. Of course, I'll never know, because there wouldn't be a record, this being a matter of national security and all."

Zuckerman stayed silent, fiddling with the buckle on his attaché.

"Or maybe it was because they were afraid of the publicity storm if you'd'a shut down one of the most respected businesses in Silicon Valley and come up empty-handed?"

Zuckerman put the attaché on the floor and folded his arms across his chest. "You're off your rocker. Too many falls on all that hard ice you grew up on."

She pretended not to hear. "Or maybe, since a place like Tera-Tech is built on deep secrets, maybe the pile of grief that would have come down on the DoJ for invading the premises, romping through all their labs and research records, and finding nothing . . . well, man oh man, that would look like a high-tech version of Waco, wouldn't it?"

"Rebecca, what the *hell* are you talking about?"

She grew suddenly serious. "Why'd they bring the case, David?"

She stepped in still closer, nailing him with her eyes. "Did they think they could spring something damaging loose from one of my witnesses? Something that might give them the ammo they didn't have when the trial started? Was that it?"

"You keep saying *they* all the time. This is *my* case!" He couldn't keep a note of sophomoric petulance out of his voice.

"Oh, is it? See, I was pretty impressed when you told the judge you could get any deal approved by the attorney general within minutes. I thought, wow, the man is truly wired right into the *capo di tutti capi.*" She turned her head slightly and looked at him from the corners of her eyes. "But the wire is more like a leash, isn't it. They're telling you what to do, and you're putting the best face on it, but you know for good and damned certain this case never should have been brought to trial!"

Zuckerman's breathing had quickened, but he kept his composure. "This from a lawyer can't even get her own client to come to court." He bent down and picked up his case. "I'm bored now, Counselor. Think I'll go watch some grass grow instead."

"Yo!" They both turned at the sound of the gruff voice and saw the bailiff poking his head out from behind one of the swinging doors leading to the courtroom. "Judge is back, folks."

"On our way," Zuckerman replied, then turned toward the courtroom.

"David, wait!" Rebecca hurried to catch up with him. He stopped and turned, but his tightly pressed lips signaled to her his impatience.

"Lemme ask you something," she said as she pulled up next to him. "Even if you can prove Tera-Tech made the chip, how are you going to prove they sold it to China?"

"I won't have to."

"What the hell are you talking about?"

"Are you going to put Perrein on the stand?"

"You know I have to."

"Is he going to testify that Tera-Tech didn't make the chip?"

"Absolutely. Are you kidding?"

"Then I'll indict him for perjury."

"On what basis?"

"If he testifies that Tera-Tech didn't make the chip, and we can prove they did, then he was lying on the stand."

"And if he didn't make it?"

"Then you've got nothing to worry about, do you?"

"Nothing except the government manufacturing evidence."

Zuckerman wouldn't let himself be drawn in to getting insulted. He cocked his head to one side and gave her a condescending half grin. "Little life lesson for you, Beck: If you're going to fling accusations like that, be prepared to back them up."

"I don't have to make the accusation. All I have to do is show it's possible. Reasonable doubt, remember?"

"I do, as a matter of fact."

The bailiff poked his head out of the courtroom again and spread his hands: *You guys coming, or what?*

"And speaking of proving the chip came from China," Zuckerman said as he turned toward the courtroom, "let's go hear the judge's decision on our motions."

He stopped to hold the door open for Rebecca. As she passed him, he said, "Gee, I wonder what it'll be: allow me to get a statement in? Or throw the whole case out?"

As the door swung shut behind them and they walked together up the aisle toward the attorneys' tables, he whispered sarcastically, "Suspense is just killing me."

Chapter 18

UNITED STATES DISTRICT COURT
FOR THE CENTRAL DISTRICT OF CALIFORNIA

Honorable Catherine M. Goldin, Judge, Presiding

The People of the UNITED	)	
STATES OF AMERICA	)	
	)	
vs.	)	No. CR 98-10322-JGD
	)	(KX)
TERA-TECH INTEGRATED, INC.;	)	
JAMES M. PERREIN, a human	)	
being; and Does 1 through 25,	)	
inclusive,	)	
Defendants.	)	

Deposition of WILLIAM CHANG, taken on behalf of the People, at 255 E. Temple Street, Los Angeles, California, commencing at 9:50 a.m., on Monday, November 9, before KEVIN CHEVIER, CSR-RMR, Certified Shorthand Reporter No. 2737, pursuant to Notice.

APPEARANCES:

For the People:

UNITED STATES DEPARTMENT OF JUSTICE
BY: DAVID ZUCKERMAN

For Defendants:

WELCH, TOBIAS & WYSOCKI
Attorneys at Law
BY: REBECCA VERONA

Also Present:

HONORABLE CATHERINE M. GOLDIN, JUDGE

Los Angeles, California, Monday, November 9
9:50 a.m.

WILLIAM CHANG,
produced as a witness by and on behalf of the Plaintiff, and having been first duly sworn, was examined and testified as follows:

EXAMINATION

JUDGE CATHERINE M. GOLDIN
Let the record reflect that present in the room are David Zuckerman, Rebecca Verona, William Chang and myself. Reporter is Kevin Chevier. Formal security oaths have been signed by Mr. Zuckerman, Ms. Verona and me. Mr. Chevier is an employee of the Central Intelligence Agency, which will retain the original of this transcript. Mr. Zuckerman, please proceed.

DAVID ZUCKERMAN

Thank you. Mr. Chang, are you—

REBECCA VERONA

Excuse me a second, Your Honor. I'd like the record to reflect my objection to this testimony and this procedure.

GOLDIN

Your objection is already noted in the trial record, Ms. Verona, but if it makes you feel better, so noted. Mr. Zuckerman.

ZUCKERMAN

Thank you. Mr. Chang, you are an agent with the Central Intelligence Agency?

WILLIAM CHANG

Not exactly. Our own people are called officers. Agents are the other side's guys who work for us. I'm an intelligence officer.

ZUCKERMAN

Didn't know that. Thanks. Which department do you work for?

CHANG

Covert Action Staff, under the Deputy Director for Operations.

ZUCKERMAN

Can you tell us when you first became aware of the existence of high-speed, enhanced encryption chips in the People's Republic of China?

VERONA

Objection. Leading, stating facts not in evidence.

GOLDIN

Ms. Verona, are you serious? This is a deposition, not a trial.

VERONA

Sorry.

ZUCKERMAN

You may answer the question, Mr. Chang.

CHANG

Approximately eighteen months ago, the National Security Agency, this was during routine surveillance of data transmissions from the People's Republic, the NSA began picking up coded transmissions that they couldn't decode. They can pretty much crack anything, but these transmits were giving them a hard time. The patterns looked an awful lot like the kind you find when a public key encryption system is used, except they know how to break those now, and these they couldn't. And that got them a little upset.

ZUCKERMAN

That's when they realized the Chinese were using American chips?

VERONA

Your Honor, this is hearsay. Mr. Chang doesn't work for the NSA.

GOLDIN

Ms. Verona—

CHANG

I did on this deal, ma'am. We often cooperate and I was assigned to the team trying to puzzle this out.

ZUCKERMAN

Okay. So was this when they realized the Chinese were using American chips?

CHANG

No, not yet. They dug in some more, and discovered that the only times they couldn't decode these transmissions were when they were being sent back and forth within the People's Republic. When they were communicating outside the country, say, with Moscow or South Africa, they were using more standard encoding and the NSA didn't have any trouble with that. Only inside China, that's what was giving them fits.

                    ZUCKERMAN
Okay. Then what?

                    CHANG
Um, one of the NSA mathematicians, real bright guy, reads all the latest literature and everything, he thinks it looks a lot like the enhanced key system, which everyone tells him is impossible. So this guy, on his own, he programmed up a simulation of the enhanced key encryption system and ran some plaintext through it. Took a helluva long time, even on their own supercomputers, but when he compared the encoded text to the Chinese transmission, he saw a lot of similarity in the output patterns, and that's when they started thinking that, somehow, the Chinese maybe had access to the technology.

                    ZUCKERMAN
Why only for transmission inside China?

                    CHANG
The only country that has the technology, or is supposed to, is the U.S. So who were they going to communicate with, since no one else could handle the coding scheme? Outside the country, they had to go standard.

                    ZUCKERMAN
Who in China was using the enhanced key system?

                    CHANG
We confirmed seven locations sending and receiving transmissions using the system. Four of them were known intelligence centers, the other three were banks. One in Beijing, another in Nanjing, the third in Szechwan.

                    ZUCKERMAN
Okay. Now, the actual formulas for the system aren't se-

cret, isn't that true? They've been published in scholarly journals, even sent around the Internet?

CHANG

That's true.

ZUCKERMAN

So why did you think they were using microchips to do the encoding?

CHANG

Because there was too much data flying around to have been coded using just software. Like I said, it took our computers forever just to encode a couple of paragraphs. These guys were flinging millions of characters around every day. The encoding had to have been done with microchips, and damned fast ones—

ZUCKERMAN

You mean like signal processors?

CHANG

Exactly. Signal processors. Only kind of chips fast enough to do the job. And there was no way the Chinese could have built them. They had to be American made. And that could only mean that some sonofa—uh, sorry—somebody in this country violated national security and sold them to the PRC.

ZUCKERMAN

A lot of supposition there, lot of indirect evidence. Not enough to convict.

CHANG

Right. Tera-Tech could always argue that the Chinese must have developed it on their own, starting with the journal articles. See, that's why we believe all those guys should be clearing their stuff with us before being allowed to publish any of it.

VERONA

Oh, is that so? Any of you guys ever hear of the First—

ZUCKERMAN

Mr. Chang, let's stick to the facts here. Your people felt that the evidence thus far was too circumstantial—

CHANG

Yes. Not enough to go after Tera-Tech. That's when we decided we had to go get one of these chips as proof. And that wasn't going to be easy.

ZUCKERMAN

Of course not. You couldn't just ask for one, right?

CHANG

Right, but that wasn't the real concern. See, we couldn't let the Chinese know how much we knew about their intelligence operations, or even what we knew about how their banks work. If they caught on that we knew about the chips, well, that'd blow the lid off half our intelligence ops in the PRC. So the trick was to get proof that they had the chips without tipping our hand. Better yet would be to actually retrieve one of them without giving ourselves away. And we also needed to be able to go back to them, confront them about having the chips, without revealing how we found out.

ZUCKERMAN

Sounds impossible.

CHANG

Impossible just means it takes a little longer.

VERONA

Oh, how precious. What is that, like the Company motto or something? Sorry, Your Honor.

ZUCKERMAN

So what'd you do?

CHANG

We decided to break into the bank in Beijing and steal their chip.

ZUCKERMAN

Break in? But you said you didn't want to reveal—

CHANG

Wait, I'll tell you how it worked. I went into the PRC under cover. At this point, because it was a covert op, control of the operation was transferred from the NSA to the Company. Like I said, I back-channeled into China using the name Li Xiaoxiang.

REPORTER

Spell that for the record, please?

CHANG

Sure. Li, l-i, then x-i-a-o-x-i-a-n-g. Anyway, I made contact with some criminal elements, and eventually picked out three veteran thieves who were not only wild and crazy but who somehow managed to never have gotten caught, don't ask me how. Far as they were concerned, the deal was to break into the bank from underneath, through an old water tunnel, and rip off an illegal currency trading operation. Once we were inside, I snuck off and broke into the main computer room, located the transmission equipment and yanked the box containing the chip. Then I got the other guys in, and they know what American computer parts are worth on the black market, and we proceeded to grab as many boards as we could. When the others were out of sight, I trashed the place.

ZUCKERMAN

Why'd you do that?

CHANG

What, trash it?

ZUCKERMAN

Yeah.

CHANG

So it'd look like it was a bunch of amateurs rather than pros. It had to look like grabbing the chip was dumb luck, just part of stealing whatever they could. And, see, they couldn't report the rip-off in the trading room, because that was an illegal operation and shouldn't have been there in the first place. So we got a double goodie out of it: not only do we make off with the chip without the Chinese catching on, but they can publicize the heist because something other than the currency room was hit. The news stories lent credibility to the rest of the mission.

ZUCKERMAN

Now I still don't see how the CIA could let the Chinese know it was in possession of the chips without revealing our ops in China.

CHANG

That was the best part. See, these other three guys, they dumped the computer parts on the black market, scattered them all over the place. And you already know that the Chinese are notorious for pirating hardware, software, all kinds of stuff. So we went to the Chinese and said, look, one of our guys, he was investigating computer pirating, stolen parts, stuff like that, and he bought some hot parts on the black market as part of making his case, and what do you know, he comes across one of these encryption chips, you want to tell us where you got it?

ZUCKERMAN

And what was their response?

CHANG

They said, don't look at us, it didn't come out of any of our gear. So we said, the hell it didn't. Newspapers are full of the heist, we know it was an Amdahl computer, we pulled this thing out of an Amdahl box that appeared on the market three weeks later, so who you kidding? But they wouldn't budge. Said there were hot Amdahls all over the place, so where was our proof? And, of course, there's no paper trail in a black market transaction.

ZUCKERMAN

So then what did you do?

CHANG

Nothing we could do. Except wait for you to squeeze Tera-Tech. Once they admit what they did, or get convicted if they keep denying it, we go back to the PRC and say, here, now what do you have to say? And demand all of them back.

ZUCKERMAN

Got it. And do I understand that this operation was carried out at great personal risk to yourself?

VERONA

Okay, come on now. Very touching, but what's it got to do with anything?

GOLDIN

Let's can the editorializing, Zuckerman. And Ms. Verona, I'm the only one that's going to be privy to this, so why get so excited?

VERONA

If we appeal, a lot of other people are going to see it.

GOLDIN

That remains to be seen. Zuckerman, you got anything else that's relevant?

ZUCKERMAN

I think that'll about do it for me. Thank you very much, Mr. Chang.

CHANG

No problem.

GOLDIN

Ms. Verona?

VERONA

Thank you. Mr. Chang, I represent Tera-Tech in this matter—

CHANG

Yeah, I know.

                         VERONA
You got a problem with that?

                         CHANG
Nope. It's a free country.

                         VERONA
So I've heard. Mr. Chang, you said the main reason for
this grand deception was so that you could confront the
Chinese with these chips without them catching on to your
intelligence gathering operations in the PRC. Is that right?

                         CHANG
That's right.

                         VERONA
Any other reason?

                         CHANG
I don't get you.

                         VERONA
It's a simple question. Was there any other reason for this
elaborate cover story other than concealing CIA activities?

                         CHANG
Could have been.

                         VERONA
Care to share one with us?

                         CHANG
Not sure what you're driving at here.

                         VERONA
Okay, let me run a possibility by you and see if it flies. Another reason for the cover story on how you got the chip
was because it was the only way to hold a public trial in
this country, right? Without the chip as evidence, there
couldn't be a trial, because you'd have no physical proof
that the PRC ever really had one. Isn't that correct?

CHANG

I suppose so.

VERONA

You suppose so? Are you telling me this never came up in conversation when the CIA and the NSA got together for one of their cooperative little chats?

CHANG

I can't reveal the contents of—

VERONA

Your Honor—

GOLDIN

Okay, okay. Mr. Chang. Don't sit there and tell us you can spill every detail of a major covert operation but not the contents of conversations that led up to it. You were instructed on how to handle this deposition and I know what those instructions were. So please answer the question.

CHANG

Could you repeat it please?

VERONA

Certainly. I'm asking about the reasons you decided to retrieve the chip, and conceal how you got it. Wasn't one big reason to make it possible to bring charges against my client and have a public trial?

CHANG

It was discussed.

VERONA

Really. And what led you to believe that Tera-Tech was guilty of this?

ZUCKERMAN

Objection. Your Honor already ruled on this question.

GOLDIN

I'll allow it in this new context. Please answer the question, Mr. Chang.

> CHANG

Okay. There were several things. There were numbers printed on the chip enclosure. The fonts and the ink color used match those commonly used by Tera-Tech. Further—

> VERONA

Wait a minute. You could only have known that once you had the chip in hand. What I'm asking, and listen carefully here, what led you to suspect Tera-Tech before you retrieved the chip, when you didn't know diddly about fonts and ink colors?

> CHANG

I guess I'm not sure.

> VERONA

Is that so. Were you aware that my client was locked in a bitter dispute with the intelligence community over whether or not this kind of technology should be cleared for sale to foreign countries?

> CHANG

Heard something about it.

> VERONA

Did you. And James Perrein stirred up quite a little fuss, didn't he, made life difficult for your fellow spooks?

> ZUCKERMAN

Hey, wait a minute—

> VERONA

So what you guys were really doing was trying to nail his ass to a wall, right? Pay him back for all the trouble he caused?

> ZUCKERMAN

Objection!

VERONA

Goes to motivation, Your Honor.

ZUCKERMAN

Motivation isn't relevant here! All we care about is where the chip came from!

GOLDIN

Afraid he's right, Ms. Verona, much as I'd like to pursue this myself. Anything else?

VERONA

Yes. I want to go off the record. Outside this room.

GOLDIN

Very well.

WHEREUPON A CONVERSATION WAS HELD OFF THE RECORD.

Rebecca, jaw firmly set, was first out of the room, leaving the court reporter and the bewildered Officer Chang behind, Judge Goldin and Zuckerman hard on her heels.

When she heard the conference room door click shut behind her, she whirled around and got right up into Goldin's face: "What the—what *is* this, Judge?"

"Take it easy, Verona. What're you talking about?"

"What I'm talking about is just how much of a railroad job this is! Am I to understand that we're simply taking this spook's word for everything, that what he says, goes?"

"Who you callin' a *spook*, paleface?"

Rebecca said, "You know what I mean, Judge," but without smiling. She wasn't about to be dissuaded by charm. "Since when does a witness get promoted to the ranks of the unimpeachable?"

"You know better than that. But you're getting far afield of what—"

"Hah!" Rebecca spat back, then thought better of it. "With all due respect," she said with a smile this time, hoping it would disarm Goldin.

"What's your point here?"

"My point is simple." Rebecca dropped her arms and rested one hand on a chair top, pointing with the other. "What if he's lying?

What if he's putting spin on this cute little story, blowing smoke up our collective whatevers?"

"Now why would he want to do that?" Zuckerman asked.

"Why don't you let me cross-examine him," Rebecca shot back, "and maybe I can answer that for you!"

"What do you mean, cross-examine? This is a deposition, not trial testimony!"

Rebecca turned her attention back to Goldin. "That's my whole point, Your Honor. This guy gets to sing his little hymn and I have no opportunity to see if he's off-key. That means my client has no chance to cross-examine an accuser, and that's unconstitutional." *A major travesty, at least when it happens to my side.*

Zuckerman watched as Goldin seemed to consider the argument, and sought to head her off. "We're here for a limited purpose, Your Honor. The only point is to—"

Goldin waved him off impatiently. "I know, I know. But she has a point. Am I to just accept him at his word?" She shook her head. "What do you propose, Verona?"

"Let me ask him a few questions that go to his possible bias. Look, you know I'm going to appeal this whole thing anyway. If we're going to play it out for the time being, let's at least give my side a fair shot."

"What makes you think he's biased?" Zuckerman asked.

"What're you afraid of, David?"

"Not a damned thing. Just wasting time, is all."

"Think ten minutes is going to hold up the cause of justice, do you?"

"All right, all right," Goldin said. "Okay, look: I'll give you a little leeway here, see if you can make a case for some bias. But the minute you go on a fishing expedition, I'm calling it off. Now let's get back in there and finish this up. For Pete's sake, I'm already on shaky ground, I don't want to invent any more new law."

WHEREUPON THE DEPOSITION RESUMED

GOLDIN

Okay. We're back on the record. Ms. Verona, you may proceed.

VERONA

One last question. Mr. Chang, you testified that the Chinese deny that the chip came out of one of their machines, right?

CHANG

Correct.

VERONA

A categorical denial? They are absolutely adamant that this chip we have in evidence did not come from a Chinese-based computer?

CHANG

Yes, but of course we know—

VERONA

Never mind what you know. I'm just asking if high officials of the People's Republic, all the way up to the Ministry of Foreign Affairs, if those officials are formally on the record, in writing to our State Department, as denying that the chip came from one of their computers. Is that in fact the case?

CHANG

They are denying it, yes.

VERONA

At the highest levels.

CHANG

Yes.

VERONA

Thank you. No further questions, Your Honor, except to renew my earlier objections.

GOLDIN

So noted. Mr. Chang, thank you for your cooperation. You're excused.

CHANG

Okay.

WHEREUPON DEPONENT WILLIAM CHANG LEFT THE ROOM

GOLDIN

Mr. Chevier, could we impose upon you to stick around for a few more minutes, so we can get some case matters transcribed for the trial record?

REPORTER

Sure. Glad to help.

VERONA

Your Honor, a minute, please?

GOLDIN

Okay.

VERONA

Let's get a cup of coffee. David?

WHEREUPON A CONVERSATION WAS HELD OFF THE RECORD.

"Your Honor, this reporter is an employee of the CIA!"

"I know that, Verona. What's your—"

"I'd rather not discuss case matters in front of him."

Zuckerman chuckled as he poured a cup of inky black coffee. "Isn't that a little paranoid, Counselor?"

"Not after what I heard in here today, it's not."

Judge Goldin took a sip of her coffee and made a face, then reached for the powdered cream and two packets of sugar. "Well, we need a reporter if we're to have a discussion, and I'd rather do this right now than later."

"Me too, so I'll get one over from my office."

"And how long is that going to take?" Zuckerman asked, looking at his watch.

"About eight seconds," Rebecca replied, dipping a tea bag into the cup of hot water she'd drawn from the side of the coffeemaker. Goldin looked at the tea, then at her own cup, and dumped the coffee into the sink before reaching for a tea bag. "I've had one sitting outside since we got here."

"Don't miss a trick, do you?" Goldin said.

"Try not to." *And thank you, Justin Ehrenright.*

The trio made their way back to the table, trying to make it look to the reporter like they didn't just have a discussion about him behind his back.

"Well, you're off the hook, Mr. Chevier," Goldin said with a smile as she took her seat. "We're not going to need you after all."

Chevier blinked and hesitated. "Perfectly happy to stay, Your Honor. No problem."

"And we appreciate it. But why don't you go on ahead and get started on that transcript. We're going to need it tomorrow morning, first thing."

Chevier looked at Rebecca, who stared back at him, causing him to return his gaze to the judge. "You sure? Because I don't—"

Goldin was bringing the cup of tea to her lips but stopped it halfway up and held it there. "Quite sure, Mr. Chevier. Please end your transcription where it sits now."

The reporter sat still for another moment, as though not entirely convinced he was now obligated to leave. Goldin and Rebecca stared at him, and Zuckerman looked down at his lap in some discomfort.

Chevier tapped the side of his recording transcriber several times, then shrugged. "Okay. Gimme just a second."

The other three sat silently while he packed up his equipment and left without any further pleasantries.

DEPOSITION CONCLUDES.

Certified: _____
          Kevin Chevier, Reporter

Sealed by order of the U.S. District Court, Central District, Western Division, the Honorable Catherine M. Goldin, Judge, Presiding.

Rebecca stood and walked back to the coffee bar, picked up the phone, and punched two digits. "Janine? Yeah, right now. The judge is waiting."

They made small talk until Osterreich arrived, then reentered the fray.

"Okay, here's how this is going to play out." Goldin set her cup down and wiped her fingers on a napkin. "What I'm going to do, assuming Mr. Chevier finishes his transcription before he reports everything to CIA Covert Ops—take it easy, Zuckerman, just kidding—I'm going to have it couriered down to the director of Central Intelligence and ask him to certify it as true. If he does, what are your suggestions as to how I instruct the jury?"

"I recommend instructing the jury that it is stipulated that the chip came from a computer in the PRC," Zuckerman said. "Then—"

"Your Honor, if you do that, I'm going to file an emergency appeal." Rebecca was looking at Zuckerman as she said this to the judge, then turned to her. "You'd essentially be telling the jury that the defense agreed that the chip came out of the People's Republic and that's a patent . . ."

"Yes? A patent what?"

"Well, it's disingenuous. If you want to allow the introduction of evidence to which the defense strongly objects, that's one thing, and we can argue about it, as we already have. But to tell this jury that the defense has agreed that the testimony is true? As politely as I can put it, Your Honor, you'd—"

"I'd be an officer of the court lying to the jury."

Zuckerman tried to head off any unproductive soul searching on the judge's part. "I think it's within the spirit of the Classified Information Protection Act that a judge—"

"You're not about to argue that the Act authorizes a federal judge to lie to a jury, are you, Counselor?"

"There are all kinds of necessary subterfuges in order to protect national security."

"I agree with him," Rebecca said.

"You do?"

"Absolutely. That's why I think it quite likely that they'd lie about where they got the chip. If they felt it was in the interests of national security."

"She's got you there, Counselor. If you ask me to lie to the jury, you might as well go all the way and just have me dismiss them and declare the defendant guilty."

"That would be unconstitutional, Your Honor."

"And lying to the jury wouldn't be good for *my* constitution. What wording do you suggest, Ms. Verona?"

"I suggest that you tell the jury that a representative of the CIA has testified that this chip came out of a Chinese computer. That happens to be true."

"Sounds reasonable. Mr. Zuckerman?"

"Well, as long as we're so interested in telling the truth, I would like it entered that the director of Central Intelligence signed a sworn affidavit that the representative's statement is true."

"In that case," Rebecca said, trying to maintain a conversational tone of voice, "I want the opportunity during our defense to demonstrate that the CIA has lied before under similar circumstances, that they regularly and routinely operate outside the law."

"Are you serious?" Zuckerman said, smiling.

"Your Honor, counsel wants to underscore the credibility of Chang's testimony by telling the jury that the big deal head spy himself says it's true. So why shouldn't I be allowed to demonstrate that the head spy, as the prosecutor has already admitted, regularly engages in . . . what did he call it . . . necessary subterfuge?"

"But only in the interests of national security!" Zuckerman retorted.

"What if the director of Central Intelligence believes it's in the interests of national security to throw my client into prison, and therefore feels justified in lying to the court!"

"Hold it, hold it. When in doubt, just tell the truth. So here it is: I will instruct the jury that the DCI has signed a sworn affidavit that the chip in evidence was recovered from a computer in the PRC, but that this doesn't mean that the jury has to accept it as fact. The statement is being entered into the record for the limited purpose of hearing what the agency alleges about its investigation, not for the truth of what Agent Chang said. I will also point out that the defense is not being allowed to cross-examine the DCI, for reasons of national security, and they need to factor that in. Nothing more than that. Yeah, yeah, I know, Verona; it's still an appealable issue. Fine. I'll live with it. And Zuckerman, I know it isn't as strong as you'd like, but that's all you get because it's the only thing that's true. And don't either of you dare to bring this issue up in open court until your closing statements. Anything else?"

"No, Your Honor."

"No, Your Honor, except to put on the record that none of the preceding negates any of my earlier objections."

"Fine. Reporter, that concludes this session."

Chapter 19

"Well, that didn't take long," Philip Mastilir said as Rebecca walked into the case conference room at Welch, Tobias & Wysocki. Sandwiches, salads in transparent plastic cups, bags of various kinds of chips, cookies, cans of soda, napkins and paper plates were gathered in the center of the table. "Now we can eat." He reached for an overstuffed roast beef on rye, a bag of corn chips and a full-strength Coca-Cola.

"See you got all four major food groups represented there, Phil," Steinholz observed as he himself went after a chicken and pasta salad.

"You betcha. So . . . ?" Mastilir queried Rebecca, without taking his eyes off the sandwich as he wrestled with the stubborn cellophane wrapper.

"I'd tell you, but—"

"You'd have to kill me, yeah, yeah. The jury gets the statement?" He motioned for Ehrenright to slide a napkin over to him.

James Perrein made no move to pick up anything on the table. He just watched, knowing that it made people nervous and self-conscious when somebody important declined to eat. Client-oriented people such as lawyers were used to those kinds of petty power plays, and the lawyers attacked the lunch with an extra measure of gusto.

Perrein hadn't wanted to be here in the first place, but Rebecca had prevailed upon Mastilir to get him down. She told him that Perrein would be on the stand himself in less than a week, and if he wasn't familiar with every last detail of Radovan Terescu's testimony, Zuckerman would fry him on cross.

"Yeah, but don't worry," Rebecca said as she dropped her attaché and leaned over to grab a fruit juice. She wouldn't touch a Coca-Cola or anything even remotely connected with the company that made it. "She's going to tell them they don't have to believe the signed statement."

Mastilir laughed heartily and slapped his hand on the table. "The jury will disregard that it was sworn to by the director of Central Intelligence."

"Something like that." Rebecca twisted off the top as Ehrenright handed her a bag of jalapeño-flavored potato chips.

"Make you fat," Mastilir said, taking a bite the size of a hot plate out of his sandwich.

"Good. Winter's coming." Rebecca tore open the bag of chips. "They're gonna rest tomorrow."

"Zuckerman say that?" Steinholz asked.

Rebecca shook her head. "No more witnesses on their list."

"Seems to me," Perrein said stiffly, as though he disapproved of the lighthearted picnic atmosphere, "that the government has failed to prove its case." It was a fairly accurate observation. Under Rebecca's cross, every single prosecution witness had left room for reasonable doubt.

Mastilir, nodding his agreement, swallowed and said to Rebecca, "Was wondering what your thoughts are on not mounting an affirmative defense."

"What does that mean?" Perrein asked.

"As the defendant, you're not required to prove anything," Steinholz said as he worked loose the top of the plastic salad container, trying not to splatter anything. "You're innocent until proven guilty. That means that if the prosecution fails to make its case against you beyond a reasonable doubt, we can just rest without calling witnesses, because there's no basis for convicting you."

"So what's the problem?"

"The problem is the jury." Rebecca looked over the food on the table. She knew it was exasperating Perrein that nobody seemed to be paying him the proper deference. "They're the ones who get to decide what's reasonable. If we let the judge decide the case, I believe she'd throw it out in a heartbeat, because she knows the law and respects it. But the jury, well, that's another matter."

She settled on a fruit salad. "Juries don't like technical defenses; if there's a statute of limitations dispute, or illegal search and seizure or lack of proper notice or somebody didn't get read his rights, a judge is likely to throw the case out. But juries want to believe they're doing justice, and they don't get hung up on something as minor as the defendant's rights. Judge will say to himself, I've got to follow the law. Juries?" She looked up from the unopened salad to Perrein. "They vote with their bellies, not their heads." *And their bellies don't like the fact that you're not in court full-time.*

She considered telling him about the breast implant case as an example, but shuddered and thought better of it, especially in front of two associate attorneys of Allen Wysocki's firm. "What the prosecution has done is built up a preponderance of circumstantial evidence—"

"That standard doesn't apply in a criminal case!" Mastilir objected forcefully.

"You and I both know that, Phil, and so does the judge. But the jury . . ." She pulled off the top of the container and licked it before setting it down, then turned to Perrein. "See, here's the thing: the jury doesn't have to follow the law. They have complete freedom to do any damned thing they want. If they believe in their gut that you sold out your country, they'll nail you without hesitation, proof or no proof."

"But the judge can still reverse the jury's decision," Mastilir said. "Or we could win on appeal."

Rebecca shook her head and picked up a plastic fork. "Mighty damned rare for a judge to reverse a jury's decision. We might have a good shot on appeal. But maybe not. And besides, if Jim is convicted, no appellate reversal is going to clear his name to the public."

"So what do you suggest?" Perrein asked impatiently. Rebecca half expected him to start complaining about how much money all this lawyerly byplay was costing him per minute.

"We mount an affirmative defense," Mastilir answered for her, as understanding dawned. "Instead of simply denying the charges, we offer new evidence on your behalf."

Rebecca bowed her head in acknowledgment of his having made the connection, hoping such small bits of behavior might compensate for her harsh treatment of him after he'd tried to voice a small criticism outside court the first day of trial. "Technically," she explained to Perrein, "what we'd be doing is calling our own witnesses to demonstrate that the government failed to prove your guilt. In actuality, it means we do what we're not supposed to have to do: we prove your innocence."

"So what's the problem with that?"

"Couple of things," Ehrenright said, taking up the thread. "First, we're admitting to the jury that the government has a good case: Instead of just resting, we feel we have to fight. Second, it effectively shifts the burden of proof to us. And, maybe most important, it means we have to put our own witnesses on the stand. We only have two, you and Terescu."

"And that means that Zuckerman gets to cross-examine the living hell out of both of you," Steinholz said ominously. "Which means he's going to get one helluva lot more information than he had before presenting his case in chief."

Perrein shrugged, the perfect innocent. "We've got nothing to hide."

"Everyone's got something to hide," Rebecca threw back at him. "First rule of litigation. And I've seen Zuckerman in action, and I promise you, time he's through, you'll feel like you've been run over by a steamroller."

"But you think we should do it anyway."

"Don't see much of a choice."

Mastilir seemed uncomfortable with the idea of Perrein taking the stand. "What if we put the case in front of the judge and forget about the jury?"

"Uh-uh." Rebecca had already thought of that. "Forget about a bench trial. After the deposition this morning, it's clear that she firmly believes the chip came out of China."

"You think so?" Ehrenright asked.

"I know so. Besides, we need our own opportunity to go to work on that jury."

"You'll make a motion to dismiss anyway, won't you?" Mastilir asked.

"Of course. Can never hurt, and it's out of earshot of the jury." *And a total waste of time.* "Not gonna make an opening, either."

"Good idea," Mastilir said, and let it go. Rebecca was surprised that he saw the wisdom in this, since he wasn't a litigator.

In order to make an opening statement, Rebecca would have to remind the jury of all the evidence that the prosecution had brought forth against Perrein so she could tell them how she was going to refute it. Essentially, she'd be summarizing Zuckerman's case, which is something he himself would love to do mid-trial rather than have to wait for the end, so why do it for him? Worse, the jury wouldn't remember much about the refutation part because, without having had any defense evidence presented yet, they'd have nothing to relate it to, no context within which to store the information. An opening statement would therefore do more harm than good for their side, so they might as well just get started with their witnesses.

Tuesday, November 10

"Ladies and gentlemen, I have some instructions for you."

Goldin waited until she had their full attention. "Normally, a judge's instructions to the jury come just before you begin your deliberations, but the attorneys and I held a meeting yesterday, and I feel it makes more sense to deal with it now."

The judge put on her reading glasses and looked over the notes she had arrayed before her. "The director of Central Intelligence of the United States has signed a sworn affidavit"—she held up a single sheet of paper—"that the chip in evidence in this trial was recovered from a computer in the People's Republic of China."

She set the sheet down and took off her glasses, then folded her hands and looked back at the jury. "Now, we have to be very careful here, so you understand exactly what this means. It doesn't mean that you have to accept it as fact that the chip came out of China. The only fact is that the director signed this piece of paper. I'm allowing it to be entered into the record for the limited use of hearing what the intelligence community alleges about its investigation, not for the truth of what they say. Not to muddy the waters, but that's an important distinction and I want to make sure you understand it. It is definitely true that they're *saying* the chip was recovered from China. It is not definitely true that it *did* come out of China. Am I being clear?"

She got answering nods and murmured "Yes, ma'ams" from the jurors before continuing. "I will also point out that the defense is not being allowed to cross-examine the director or any intelligence community staff, for reasons of national security, and you need to factor that in however you see fit."

As agreed, Goldin allowed Rebecca to make a motion in front of the jury opposing the introduction of the deposition evidence.

"Defense objects to the introduction of this statement, Your Honor, in the strongest possible terms. Under the dubious rationale of protecting national security, my client has been deprived of a right that goes back directly to the founding fathers, the right to confront his accusers and cross-examine them. For all we know, the government made up a story about finding this chip in China. They could be lying through their teeth and we'd have no way of knowing. And if they deliberately set my client up, framed him for something he didn't do, well, he has no opportunity to try to demonstrate that. We therefore move that this statement be stricken from the record and the jury be instructed to disregard it."

Goldin overruled her objection, as expected.

Zuckerman rose to speak. "Your Honor, the United States rests."

Then Rebecca stood up. "Defense wishes to make a motion outside the presence of the jury."

Goldin excused the jury for a break, and Rebecca made the defense's motion for judgment of acquittal under Rule 29.

"Your Honor, the criterion for granting a dismissal is simply whether the prosecution has made enough of a case against the defendant to justify allowing the jury to make a decision. In this case, it is clear that no such *prima facie* case for guilt has been established.

"There has not been one among all the government's witnesses whose testimony would lead any reasonable person to conclude that my client might be guilty." Rebecca began to pace as she clicked off one purported absurdity after another. "We heard from Dr. Melanie Fuster, whose big contribution to the evidence was that the chip in question uses an encryption technique that was published in a public journal. We heard Anthony Frazier, a supposed industry expert, who basically testified that he'd heard unsubstantiated and unattributed rumors and took them as gospel truth. Lawrence Krazny thinks that Tera-Tech Integrated is the only place on the face of the planet earth that uses the type of magnetic ink found on the chip."

Rebecca could feel that the audience was hanging on her every word, and only wished the jury could hear her as well. They would, when Goldin denied her motion and she could repeat everything in her closing statement at the end of the trial. "In addition to all of that, my expert wasn't even allowed to touch the chip, much less test it for himself. And to top it all off, we've got a piece of paper from an intelligence director whose job is to lie on behalf of the government, and we can't even cross-examine him!"

She stopped pacing and came to a stop a few feet away from the podium. "In short, Your Honor, this is starting to feel more like Salem than Los Angeles. It is inconceivable that any rational jury would convict my client on the basis of this rattletrap agglomeration of innuendo, rumors and legal trickery. We move that the court terminate this proceeding and dismiss all the charges against my client, with prejudice." Meaning that, once dismissed, the charges could never be refiled.

"Response, Mr. Zuckerman?"

Rebecca sat down. Zuckerman scratched at his ear before rising to speak. "Judge, counsel is asking for the case to be thrown out because, among other things, she doesn't believe the jury ought to put any stock in the DCI's statement. She doesn't believe that, in our desire to protect intelligence sources, we have put enough out on the table to prove our case."

"I already know that. So how do you respond?"

"I wouldn't try to defend the proposition that a conviction is feasible based on any one witness. But I feel that the sum total of all the testimony is compelling. Way too compelling to warrant a dismissal of all the charges. Counsel spoke of how a rational jury might behave. I believe that no rational jury in the world would dismiss the charges at this point."

Zuckerman was keeping his voice so casual it bordered on insolent, as though he had difficulty believing that anyone could fail to grasp concepts so simple and obvious. "So what do we do when two sides in a lawsuit disagree?" He held out his hands and let them drop to his sides. "Well, we let the jury decide. After all, that's why we have trials." He turned and walked back to his seat, dropping onto it and slouching backward with his hands folded across his middle.

"That's a little too glib, Your Honor," Rebecca said. "This jury is in no position to make decisions like that. What are they going to base it on, their vast knowledge of the law? Their fears of being harassed by the CIA if they acquit?" She could match Zuckerman's sarcastic and condescending tone any day of the week, but now was the time to get serious again. "There are prejudices floating around that make a sham out of any proposition that a lay jury can do what's right in a case like this!"

"Okay." Goldin, not unaware of Rebecca's implied criticism of how she had handled matters thus far, took off her glasses and rubbed her eyes. "Why not waive the jury and let me decide the case?"

The simple-sounding question zinged in from some distant corner of the outfield, too late for Rebecca to duck, so she stood there startled and flummoxed. There was no way she wanted the judge to decide this case.

They had a much better shot with the jury. Rebecca knew quite well that Zuckerman had made more of a case than she was willing to admit openly, especially if one were to accept the DCI's statement concerning the chip's Chinese origin. If it came to that, Rebecca had a better chance of bamboozling the jury than trying to slip something past a judge like Goldin. In a difficult and complex case, especially one involving sophisticated technologies, you could sow the seeds of reasonable doubt not just based on the evidence but on your ability to confuse the jury *about* the evidence. If the prosecution built a case that was bullet-proof but only an expert in the relevant science could see that, you asked the witnesses a lot of crazy, irrelevant questions in a sarcastic tone of voice, snorting your derision left and right, and the jury would start to wonder what was wrong with the prosecution's case. They would *doubt*, and they would feel those doubts were reasonable, and therefore would not bring a conviction because, after all, if they had doubts about the evidence, weren't they duty-bound to acquit? This fundamental misunderstanding of the law had led to many wrong-headed criminal acquittals and civil judgments.

So depending on how the defense case went, dismissing the jury and leaving a verdict to Judge Goldin was a potential disaster. It had to be averted at all costs.

"Fine by me, Your Honor," Rebecca said. She turned to resume her seat, trying to ignore Steinholz, Ehrenright, Perrein and Mastilir, whom she could clearly hear gasping in astonishment and shock somewhere behind her. She sat down slowly, her insides in so much turmoil she could hardly move her legs. If prayers were visible, she would have been hidden beneath a fountain of them shooting up through the ceiling.

The holy reply came an instant later. "Your Honor," Zuckerman said, rising. "The United States would prefer to let this jury continue hearing the case and render a verdict." He was under no obligation to offer an explanation, and he didn't.

Goldin replaced her glasses as Rebecca's tightly knotted stomach relaxed and threatened to exit through her throat. Goldin nodded her head slightly, lost in thought. "Your argument was very well presented, Ms. Verona," she said after a long interval. "Cogent and articulate."

"Thank you, Your Honor." Rebecca couldn't help smiling, knowing exactly what was coming.

"Your motion for dismissal is denied. Please call your first witness."

Rebecca shook her head at the old trick. She had already known that there was zero chance of Goldin dismissing the case at this point, but the motion needed to be made for use in appeal in case they lost the trial. She turned to see Ehrenright and Steinholz, disappointed and crestfallen, even though still slightly dazed by her bold maneuver. Rebecca would have to explain to them later about the oldest trick in a judge's book.

She stood up and started toward the podium, winking at the shaken Philip Mastilir to make sure he understood that her risky gambit was done on purpose to get the prosecutor to be the one to reject a bench trial. Had Zuckerman not done so, Rebecca would have used some pretext to change her mind.

She turned and dropped a file folder on the podium. "Defense calls Professor Radovan Terescu."

Even though she had known in advance that the judge would not grant a dismissal, Rebecca sensed that the prevailing atmosphere in the room was that she had lost something important. She couldn't care less about the general audience, but she was getting that feeling from her associates, as well as Perrein and his corporate attorney.

Rebecca glanced at her watch. A few hours of direct examination coming up to make sure she ended this day a hero in their eyes again.

Rebecca watched with satisfaction as Terescu stood up and began walking toward the witness box. He was calm and dignified, as much at ease as if he were entering a familiar classroom to begin a lecture. He didn't look around nervously or cast his eyes anxiously at courtroom personnel to see if he was heading in the right direction. He stepped up to the witness box and remained standing to take his oath, then tugged at his pants legs, sat down and stated his name and address for the record.

Rebecca waited for a nod from Judge Goldin and began her direct examination in a conversational tone. "Doctor, where are you employed?"

"I'm professor of electrical engineering at the California Institute of Technology. Cal Tech, if you will."

"And how long have you been in that position?"

"I started as an instructor eleven years ago; I'm currently a tenured professor."

"Isn't that an unusually fast career progression?"

"That's a fair statement." No embarrassed smile indicating forced immodesty, just a straightforward recitation of the facts.

"What is your specialty?"

"I concentrate on research involving the fabrication of semiconductor microprocessors." He turned to the jury, addressing them as though this were a family gathering in a living room somewhere. "I study better ways to make computer chips." Nothing condescending in his manner, just a learned scientist explaining jargon to intelligent lay people. He was rewarded with vigorous nods, not just of understanding but of appreciation. Rebecca found herself beginning to relax.

She asked a number of questions to establish that he was not only highly respected but generally considered one of the best in the field, and also brought out that he was not a professional expert witness. Their exchange sounded natural, and much less rehearsed than it actually was. Terescu was charming and modest, and was clearly having an effect on the jury.

They got into Terescu's responsibilities with regard to technology transfer, a Cal Tech policy of promoting commercialization of its scientists' discoveries in order to help fund further research.

Then Rebecca suddenly switched gears. "Doctor, is it true you were under consideration for the Nobel prize?"

Terescu looked embarrassed for the first time, reddening slightly, stealing a small look at the jurors that said, *Gee, this is really uncomfortable.* He cleared his throat. "Well, Ms. Verona, we don't really have a way of knowing what was on the committee's mind. I'd, uh . . . I'd prefer to answer that I simply don't know." Which the jury read as, *You bet I was.*

"I understand." Rebecca then delved into his traumatic childhood, trying to bring forth a description of the suffering his family endured under a totalitarian regime in Romania and their harrowing escape to the United States. . . .

"Your Honor." Zuckerman rose to object, his lips pulled into a sneer to indicate that he had been as patient as possible, but enough was enough already. "The people will stipulate to this witness's unflagging patriotism, so can we dispense with the hearts and flowers?"

"Counselor, you know better than to editorialize in my court. If you want to make a stipulation, just say so."

Rebecca, hand on her hip, suppressed any display of emotion that might give the jury the impression that her annoyance stemmed from the interruption of a well-planned script. Instead, she sounded personally offended. "Your Honor, we're entitled to establish through testimony a witness's orientation and state of mind. This isn't a matter of ink content, it goes directly to this witness's credibility."

Goldin rocked her head skeptically, but said, "I'll overrule the objection, but please stay on track."

Rebecca got through it quickly, forgoing some detail in order to get the gist down without further interruptions, and moved on to the nature of his work.

"Doctor, let's talk about the work that got you the Nobel nomination."

Zuckerman snorted and stood up. "Stating facts not in evidence. At the very least."

Rebecca smiled amiably. "I'll withdraw it. Doctor, can you tell the jury about the work you've been doing for the past several years? Simply, so even I can understand it?"

"It's not that difficult to understand. In theory, at least. Actually *doing* it is a different story. There are two different technologies involved."

Rebecca didn't like his use of the passive voice, probably a habit so he wouldn't look like he was drawing attention to himself. "These are technologies you developed?"

"I am largely responsible for them, yes." Terescu turned to the jury and began his explanation, not as a lecturer in front of a class of graduate students, but as he might have to curious neighbors gathered around the pickle barrel in the general store, with respect for their intelligence and appreciation for their interest.

"The challenge in making these computer chips is to get them to work as fast as possible. One of the ways you do that is to make them smaller and smaller. Now a computer chip is about the size of your thumbnail, but it contains many millions of transistors. The only way to get more transistors on the chip is to make each transistor smaller."

He leaned back and shook his head slightly, taking a deep breath at the same time. Slowly, carefully, he described the standard process by which conventional microchips were made, then revealed how he was able to use an X-ray laser to carve out vastly smaller components. As Rebecca had expected, he had the jurors enthralled.

When he had finished, she asked, "And how small can the components be? In terms we nonscientists can understand."

Terescu looked up at the ceiling and chewed the inside of his cheek for a few seconds. Then he exhaled slowly and turned to the jury again. "We could build a very simple computer and fit the whole thing inside a human hair."

The jurors' shocked faces were immensely gratifying to Rebecca as she stole a look at them. She waited for the enormity of his statement to fully sink in before continuing. "Have you built a chip like that?"

"Don't I wish!" Terescu laughed, and shook his head. "No, we've only managed to make a handful of transistors that small in the lab, and only on a very limited basis. We're still a long way from figuring out how to scale the process up to make a complete device."

Since his last, ill-received interruption, Zuckerman had been staying quiet. He was dying to object, but his observation of the jury told him that to do so, to break the rapport that they had obviously developed with the witness, would do him more harm than good. Better to let it go until something else broke the spell, and then do it gently.

Like now. Zuckerman rose. "Your Honor, I'm as fascinated as everybody else, but I do feel this is largely irrelevant. Can we move on?"

"No problem, Your Honor, and I apologize to the court." Rebecca looked at the jury and smiled conspiratorially. "I got caught up in that explanation, too." She returned her attention to Terescu. "Doctor, you said that you were responsible for two new technologies. What is the second one?"

"As I said before, every time you solve one problem, you find another. As it happens, now that we've gotten the individual transistors so small, we have to figure out a way to connect them all together."

"Is that a big problem?"

"Oh, yes. The transistors are connected by wires, usually aluminum, because they're easy to make and they don't rust. The problem is, the amount of electricity a wire can carry depends on how big it is. As the chips get smaller and smaller, the wires must shrink as well, only that makes them less able to carry electrical current. If we tried to connect our little transistors with conventional aluminum wires, they couldn't carry the load, and they would burn up."

"How do you solve that one?"

"There are several possibilities. One is to use something better than aluminum, something which can carry more current."

"Such as . . . ?"

"Copper or silver can do a much better job. The problem is, silver tarnishes and copper rusts. Instant disaster inside a chip. Which leaves us with gold."

"Gold carries more electricity than aluminum?"

"Much more. And it doesn't oxidize. Doesn't rust, I mean. The problem is how to make a small enough wire, and then figure out how to cram it in close to other wires without electricity leaking from one to the next. And gold has its own share of problems, starting with the fact that it doesn't like to stick to anything. It's not just a noble element, it's positively arrogant"—he waited for the appreciative laughter to die down—"which makes it hard to keep it in one place even if we were able to shape it in the first place."

"Can you tell us, briefly, how you're solving that problem?"

"Of course. We developed something called the ovalauricle wire, which actually takes *advantage* of gold's reluctance to adhere to surfaces. Basically what we do is use the X-ray laser to dig a channel in the surface of the chip. Think of it as a trench, like when workers put down a water pipe? They dig a trench, put in the pipe, and then cover it over.

"But what we have to do is actually build the pipe in the trench. We heat up some gold until it becomes a very fine vapor, then we let gold atoms from the vapor drop down into the trench, almost one by one. Using a small electrical charge, we can help those gold atoms avoid the walls of the trench, but it's very delicate: surface tension wants to pull the gold atoms into the trench, and the electrical charge wants to shove them out, and if we balance things just right, they kind of float around just above the bottom.

"The atoms clump together as more of them fall into the trench. Since they're all trying to stay away from the walls and floor, they begin to form a round shape, just like a pipe, except slightly oval because the channel is higher than it is wide. When enough atoms have joined together, we're left with a perfect, solid wire that can carry enough current between the transistors. We zap it with a laser to get it well settled into the trench, then we cover it over with some stuff to keep it there."

"What do you call this process?"

"Charged vapor deposition."

"And is the oval shape important?"

"Oh, yes. I should have mentioned. The oval shape keeps each wire just a bit farther away from its neighbors than if it was perfectly round. That makes it less likely to leak electricity to other wires."

"And these are called *ovalauricle* wires?"

"Yes. *Oval* is obvious, and *auricle* comes from the Greek word for gold." Terescu turned to the jury again. "Remember the movie *Goldfinger*? You may not remember that Goldfinger's first name was Auric. Greek for gold, see?"

Rebecca nodded while the jurors laughed. She was through with this particular line of questioning. She now wanted to jump right into the substance of her expert's testimony. "Professor, what is the highest number of transistors on one chip you're personally familiar with?"

"About eighty million."

"And do you have an estimate for how many are on the chip in evidence in this case?"

"I would estimate 256 million."

He and Rebecca were both pleased at the audible inhalations from the jurors, who clearly grasped that this was a huge number. Rebecca let it settle in before she asked her next question, which was just a point of clarity that wouldn't distract the jury from their surprise at the density of the government's chip. "Seems a strange number. Why not 250 or so?"

Terescu smiled. "Computer scientists deal only in numbers that are powers of two. Two, four, eight . . . like that." He turned to the jury again and smiled with self-deprecating sheepishness. "Strange bunch."

Rebecca laughed along with the jurors, who she hoped saw that Zuckerman was the only one frowning. "Do you know of anybody, anywhere, who can produce that kind of density?"

"No," Terescu answered without hesitation. "Only two companies have claimed to have hit even half that density, the most prominent being Dallas Digital, but most of us doubt they really did it."

"What about Tera-Tech Integrated?"

Terescu waved his hand. "Not even close."

"How do you know that?"

"I'm very familiar with their equipment and their personnel. They simply don't have the capability. Years from it."

"So who else might have done it?"

Terescu frowned in thought. "Hard to say. A limited number of highly advanced university laboratories might have made some strides in this direction, but . . ."

"Couldn't it be done using an X-ray laser and those ovalauricle wires?"

Terescu smiled. "Maybe in four or five years." He admitted he'd achieved very high densities in an extremely limited way, but further progress was fiendishly difficult. "And besides, at the time this chip was made, or was alleged to have been made, I hadn't even publicly announced the ovalauricle wire yet."

"Now, Professor, your lab is on the very cutting edge of this kind of miniaturization, isn't that true?"

"That would be a fair statement."

"And you're not anywhere close to the density that's inside this chip, correct?"

"Definitely not."

With that, Rebecca had now brought the subject full circle. While ostensibly presenting Terescu's credentials by having him describe his work in some detail, what she had really done was establish that Terescu was the world's leader in component density. Then she had worked things around to demonstrate that, whatever was inside the government's chip, it had to be light-years ahead of even Terescu's creations, which wouldn't be seen inside a working chip for years. In this way she was making it impossible for any rational person to believe that the chip worked as the government claimed it did.

Even if this was lost on the jury now, she'd highlight the connection during her closing. Right now there was more work to be done with this witness.

She got Terescu to disdainfully wave off the encryption technology embedded in the chip as not indicative of anything: Tera-Tech scientists had published several scholarly papers prior to the State Department's ban, so any number of researchers might have had access to them.

Rebecca gave the jury a meaningful look, driving home that Terescu had just validated the point she'd made in prior cross-examinations, then asked him, almost as an afterthought, "Doctor, have you actually seen this chip yourself?"

"Just through a plastic bag, in court last week."

Rebecca acted surprised. "You didn't even touch it?"

"No."

"Did you weigh it?"

"No."

"Test its heat output?"

"No."

"Did you hook up any probes?"

"No."

"Hmm." Rebecca bit her lip, puzzlement all over her face. Then she looked up, helpless to ask any but the most obvious question: "So how did you reach your conclusions?"

"I based it on reports supplied to me."

"By . . . ?"

"The prosecution."

"You mean everything you know about this chip came to you from reports supplied by the prosecution, is that correct?"

"Correct."

"You had no way at all to verify what they were telling you?"

"None."

"Did this cause you any concern?"

"Oh, a great deal."

"And why is that?"

"Several reasons. I have no way of telling if they were being truthful, and, more importantly, I have no way of telling if they did the tests correctly."

With a long, piercing look at the jury that told them there was probably nothing but milk chocolate inside the chip, Rebecca ended her direct examination. "Thank you, Professor. No more questions."

Rebecca returned to her seat. Steinholz leaned over to whisper effusive praise regarding her performance, but she didn't appear to have heard him. "What's with you?" he asked. "You practically won the whole case just now!"

"Dallas Digital?" she said, mostly to herself, then she turned to Steinholz, confusion in her voice. "Do you remember him talking about Dallas Digital during prep?"

"Now you mention it, no. Why?"

She shrugged. "No reason, I guess. Just seems like it would have been worth mentioning."

She brushed away the minor concern as a delighted Philip Mastilir walked up to pump her hand and congratulate her on a sparkling performance.

Goldin adjourned court for the day, and Mastilir took the defense attorneys and Radovan Terescu out for an expensive celebratory dinner. On James Perrein's tab, of course, even though he declined to attend.

Chapter 20

Zuckerman walked to the podium while leafing through some papers. When he arrived, he shot Terescu the same kind of smile an Olympic gymnast flashes before a vault: a perfunctory raising of the corners of the mouth while the eyes are focused elsewhere, fading as quickly and insincerely as it had started. Rebecca thought Terescu looked a little tense, but otherwise in control, and she tried to put aside any misgivings she had about his ability to withstand cross-examination so she could stay alert for opportunities to derail the prosecutor.

"No matter what," she said to Perrein *sotto voce*, "your face is stone."

"But—"

"I don't care if he says your mother's a communist spy; twitch one cheek muscle, you get a pencil in your eye."

Zuckerman laid the papers down and wouldn't look at them again for the duration of his examination. "Professor Terescu, you submitted some test data you asked us to have encrypted by the chip in evidence, right?"

"Yes."

"And I assume that you also ran the data through your own computer version of the technique to compare the two, right?"

"Objection." No free rides for the prosecution. Rebecca rose halfway out of her chair, and then started down again as she said, "Assumes facts not in evidence."

Zuckerman was unfazed. "I'll rephrase: *Did* you run the text through your own version of the technique to compare it with the output of the chip?"

"Yes."

"And your results?"

"They matched."

"Perfectly?"

"I was not able to detect any discrepancies."

Rebecca nudged Steinholz: great answer—maybe Terescu's performance would be better than they'd hoped.

Zuckerman wasn't going to settle for hired-witness spin. "So we can conclude that the method in the chip was the precise method described in Tera-Tech's published papers, right?"

"It would appear so."

"And therefore, you are in complete agreement with the testimony of our encryption expert, Dr. Fuster?"

"I don't recall all of her testimony."

"The part about the two results being identical."

"Objection, irrelevant." Rebecca tried to sound bored. "He already said they were identical."

"Just trying to show that whatever biases Dr. Fuster may have had about the export issue didn't enter into her analysis."

"The jury can draw that conclusion for themselves," Goldin pointed out, "as I'm sure you'll point out in your closing statement. Let's move on."

"Okay. Let's talk about how many transistors can be built into a chip. You say that, as far as you know, Tera-Tech has not achieved the densities that would be required to make a chip capable of the performance of the chip in evidence, is that right?"

"That is correct."

"And you don't know of any other company that has achieved it either, right?"

"Correct."

"How about you, Professor? Have you achieved this density?"

"No, of course not." Terescu was getting more comfortable with each question. Rebecca had warned him about this, the desperate fishing expedition to uncover something, anything, that might be damaging. So he recognized it for what it was and settled in to ride it out.

"Are you sure?"

"Objection. Asked and answered."

"Just want to make sure I heard it correctly," Zuckerman said politely.

"Then let's have the transcript read back," Rebecca volleyed back, less politely.

"Ms. Verona . . ." Goldin warned sternly, then to Zuckerman: "Let's move on, Counselor."

"Professor, you stated under direct examination that there have been laboratory demonstrations of advanced fabrication techniques, did you not?"

"Yes, I did."

"Now, this ovalauricle wire you invented. What's the smallest one you've managed to make in your own lab?"

"It's difficult to be specific."

"I'm just looking for a rough idea. For instance, have you gotten below, oh, say, half a micron wide?"

"Yes."

"How about even smaller, say, a twenty-fifth of a micron?" Terescu sat still and didn't answer. "Professor?"

The scientist folded and refolded his hands. "Yes, I have. But on an extremely limited scale."

Steinholz leaned over to Rebecca and whispered hoarsely, "How in the flaming hell did Zuckerman find that out!"

"He's fishing," Rebecca answered.

"Fishing!" Steinholz shook his head forcefully. "You fish with half of something, or a quarter. But a *twenty-fifth*? The hell kind of fishing is an oddball number like that!"

Rebecca didn't answer.

"What does that mean?" Zuckerman was asking the witness.

"I—" Terescu paused to cough into his fist. "I constructed a tiny device containing only eight wires of that size. A production chip would require many, many millions."

"I understand. But the density you achieved, in that tiny fragment of a chip, that density is about the same that would be used to make a full-scale chip, right?"

"Well, in some sense, perhaps, but the techniques—"

"Just a simple yes or no, thank you."

"He's entitled to explain his answer," Goldin interrupted to say. Then she turned to Terescu and said soothingly, "Go ahead, Professor."

"Thank you. Well, that would be like saying that, uh, because a child's rocket toy can lift a mosquito up to treetop level, what's the big deal about sending a bunch of people to Mars?" He shook his head. "But the difficulties of scaling up are immense."

"I understand. But the point is, you achieved the required density on a small scale using one technique, and so somebody else might have done so on a larger scale using a different technique, correct?"

"Inconceivable."

"Inconceivable?" Zuckerman drew back, startled. "Doctor Terescu, we seem to be forgetting something here: *somebody* has already done it. *Somebody* built this chip."

"Ob-*jec*-tion," Rebecca spat with annoyance. "Counsel's making a speech."

"Mr. Zuckerman?" Goldin inquired. "I assume there's a question here?"

"There is. Professor, somebody built this chip. Therefore, it's been done. Do you disagree?"

Terescu was ready for this one, even welcomed it. "Sir, I haven't been able to examine the chip, so I don't know."

"Assuming it was, don't the results of your analysis show what kind of density was required?"

"Using conventional techniques, probably. But what if somebody discovered a shortcut, a way to do the encryption calculations without so much brute computer power?"

"Good point. That would have to be somebody awfully smart about the enhanced key system, wouldn't it?"

"Probably."

"Probably?"

"Certainly."

"Because something like Dr. Fuster's program needs only a detailed recipe, which the programmer doesn't even really have to understand, right?"

"Yes."

"But somebody who wanted to use some kind of shortcut, he'd have to understand the technique intimately, so thoroughly that he doesn't have to blindly follow the recipe, but can be creative in how to get the same result with different ingredients, wouldn't you agree with that?"

"Yes, I suppose so."

"Okay. So is there anybody in the world who knows more about the enhanced key system than Tera-Tech?"

"Objection!" Rebecca kicked back her chair as she stood up. "Speculation. Counsel hasn't established that the witness knows everybody in the world. Also outside the witness's area of expertise."

"Sustained. But only on the speculation part of your objection."

"What about his expertise?"

"He's already answered at least four questions about it. Overruled."

Zuckerman knew he'd hit an open nerve. "Let me rephrase it as a hypothetical: If the chip in question uses some shortcut methods rather than brute force computing, isn't it likely that Tera-Tech developed the technique?"

"Objection!" Rebecca said, still standing. "Your Honor, this is the worst kind of deception. Counsel is deliberately attempting to confuse the jury by posing hypotheticals that are completely irrelevant!"

Goldin motioned both attorneys up to the bench for a sidebar, a practice she normally forbade. She leaned over the top of the bench, turned her face away from the jury and whispered, "Mr. Zuckerman, are you going somewhere with this?"

"I'm just trying to show that, no matter what's inside that chip, Tera-Tech had something to do with it."

"That's absurd, Your Honor," Rebecca said. "If all counsel is doing is demonstrating likelihood and probability, then he's conceding reasonable doubt and we might as well dismiss the case right now! He needs proof, not speculation, and therefore this is all a waste of the court's time."

"She's right, Mr. Zuckerman, however stridently she may have stated it. Let's drop this avenue and try another street." Goldin waved them back without allowing further conversation.

"Professor, what technique did you use to create those tiny ovalauricle wires?"

"X-ray laser etching and charged vapor deposition. As I described previously."

"And you've published your results, isn't that correct?"

"I've published *some* results, mostly of a theoretical nature."

It was all irrelevant, Zuckerman hunting around for something to latch on to, but Rebecca decided it was better to give him plenty of rope than to object and cut it off. If she did that, it might appear to the jury as though she were trying to forestall some potentially fruitful testimony. By just letting Zuckerman peter out, it would be clear that he had no way to trip Terescu up.

"So you haven't yet told anybody exactly how you fabricated those wires," Zuckerman said. Rebecca almost felt sorry for him.

"That is correct. Well, not outside of my laboratory."

"So the encryption chip in evidence could not have been built using your techniques."

"I have no idea if that's true."

"But you just said—"

"Sir, I have never seen the inside of that chip. I don't know for certain that it even works, or if there is anything inside at all. All I have to go on is reports that you people gave me!"

Zuckerman seemed unfazed by Terescu's outburst. That made Rebecca decide to pay closer attention as Zuckerman continued. "Okay, let me rephrase it as a hypothetical. If everything our experts have been saying is true, then would you agree that the chip could not have been built using your X-ray technique and gold wires?"

"Under those conditions, I don't see how it would have been possible."

"So it had to have been built some other way."

"If it was built at all."

"Fair enough, Doctor. Again, assuming my experts aren't lying, how else could those densities have been achieved?"

"They weren't necessarily lying, they might simply have made errors."

"All right. Assuming their reports were completely accurate, how else other than by X-ray laser and ovalauricle wires could those densities have been achieved?"

"Probably using a much more refined variation of a method called ion beam lithography, in its conventional form."

"Simply, what is that?"

"It's what I described before. I didn't want to unnecessarily confuse things, but the beam used to print a circuit image on the chip surface doesn't have to be light. It could be an ion beam."

"That would allow for smaller components than regular light, right?"

"Yes."

"But the rest of it is the same, correct? Washing off the photo surface . . ."

"Only the printing of the image differs, yes."

"So pretty much everybody out there who's trying to get more density is using this technique?"

"Yes, only with much more precision and power. Sometimes they use X rays, but not to write directly on the chip. They still use a slide to print a picture."

"Got it. So, would you be fairly certain that anybody who built the chip in evidence did so using pretty conventional photolithography?"

Where could this be going? Time to find out. . . . "Objection, calls for speculation."

"It's within his area of expertise, Your Honor," Zuckerman countered politely. "Speculation is perfectly permissible."

"But it doesn't prove how the chip was built!" Rebecca said.

Zuckerman remained unperturbed. "No problem, Your Honor. I'll rephrase. Professor, in your expert, professional opinion, was the chip in evidence built using ion beam or related lithography?"

"I have no idea."

"Assume that all the test results we provided to you are truthful and accurate."

"But I don't know if that's true!"

Rebecca marveled at the prosecutor's unruffled demeanor as he patiently said, "Professor, do you know what a hypothetical question is?"

"Of course I do," Terescu sniffed huffily.

"Good. This is a hypothetical question. It doesn't mean the facts are true. It means you are to *assume* they are true for the sake of argument. Now I ask you again." Standard technique: convince the witness that he will look like an idiot if he pretends not to understand the question. "Assuming that all the test results we provided to you are truthful and accurate, would it be your expert, professional opinion that the chip in evidence was built using standard photolithography?"

Terescu no longer had any alternatives available to dodge the question. "Then I would have to say that, in my opinion, it was *probably* built using ion beam or X-ray lithography. And that's a very big *probably*."

"Thank you. Professor, in your opinion, which semiconductor manufacturer is the world leader in advanced ion beam lithography?"

Now Rebecca saw it. "Objection! Irrelevant!"

"Irrelevant?" Zuckerman whirled on her. "Are you serious?"

"It doesn't prove anything!" Rebecca addressed Judge Goldin. "Its prejudicial impact outweighs any probative value and will only confuse the jury!"

Goldin, clearly irritated, called them up to another sidebar. "Mr. Zuckerman," she said, "are you going to back up this connection somehow?"

"Your Honor, we have a purely circumstantial case here. There are no fingerprints, no confessions, no dead bodies with the suspect's hair on them. It's all indirect, and no individual element proves the case. But what we're going to do is show that the sum total of all the circumstantial evidence is so overwhelming and compelling that nobody else could *possibly* have built that chip other than Tera-Tech!"

Rebecca rolled her eyes ostentatiously. "Hardly proof beyond a reasonable doubt."

Zuckerman spoke to her without turning away from the judge. "Why don't we both do our jobs, Counselor, and then let the jury decide that, since that's *their* job!"

"Okay, I'll allow it," Goldin said. "But at some point, Mr. Zuckerman, I may ask you into chambers to show me where all of this is heading." She turned to the court reporter. "Objection is overruled."

Zuckerman went back to the podium without looking at Rebecca. "Professor," he began before he even turned around, "I'm going to repeat the question. In your opinion, which semiconductor manufacturer is the world leader in advanced ion beam lithography?"

"Tera-Tech Integrated."

"And your understanding is that Tera-Tech has built transistors how small?"

"One tenth of a micron. But only in the lab, and still a whole lot bigger than what would be required to make that chip."

"I wasn't referring to that chip. Tell me, how do you know what size Tera-Tech has achieved?"

"They published their results."

"And when was that?"

"About two years ago."

"Two years ago. And what have they announced since then?" Zuckerman waited, and got no response. He looked as though he hadn't expected any. "Professor? What have they announced since that time?"

"Nothing."

"Nothing? I don't understand." Zuckerman looked down and scratched the back of his head, then seemed to have a sudden thought and looked back at the witness box. "Did you stop reading the journals?"

"No."

"Then what happened?"

"They stopped publishing results."

"Seems strange. Do you know why?"

"Only rumors."

"Well, we don't want rumors. I'll return to the topic later. Okay, even though they stopped publishing, do you believe Tera-Tech stopped doing research in component fabrication?"

"No."

"And why is that?"

"Because the company has told me its research was continuing."

"This was during your preparation for trial? During your analysis?"

"Yes."

"So, since the time Tera-Tech achieved half-micron-sized components, which was two years ago, their research has continued?"

"Yes."

"And they're the best in the world?"

"I believe so."

Rebecca groaned inwardly, having seen it coming too late, and cringed as Zuckerman slammed all this seemingly extraneous information together into one great big bottom line: "Then isn't it a virtual certainty that they have gone much further in reducing component size in the two years since they stopped telling the world about it?"

"Calls for speculation!" Rebecca nearly shouted as she leaped up.

"Overruled."

"Professor?" Zuckerman urged casually.

"Maybe."

"Maybe." Zuckerman looked at the jury: *Maybe, my foot.* "Professor, given the typical strides made in this field, isn't it almost a certainty that Tera-Tech has already achieved the densities necessary to build this chip?"

"Objection!" Rebecca said, still standing. "Why not ask him if he thinks somebody's grown a three-ton pumpkin!"

"I'll rephrase." Rebecca gritted her teeth at Zuckerman's maddening refusal to get flustered. "Professor, microprocessor component densities have been doubling about every two to four years, right?"

"Roughly."

"So isn't it only natural to assume that, right about now, somebody would have figured out how to get another doubling?"

"No." Terescu seemed to sigh in relief. "First of all, you're not dealing with a doubling, it's at least a quadrupling. A two-generation leap over existing technology, maybe even three. And secondly, that process of doubling cannot go on ad infinitum. I don't want to get too technical, but as the components get smaller and smaller, funny things start to happen, things you didn't have to worry about when everything was larger."

This did appear to surprise Zuckerman. "Such as?"

"As things get smaller, they also get closer together. And that means that electricity can leak from one wire to another. Like when you wire up spark plugs in a car? You're not supposed to bundle the wires together in a nice straight bunch, because the current in one can leak over to another and make the wrong plugs fire. So imagine when you have wires so tightly packed that a million of them would fit across a dime. How do you keep the signals separated? It's a terrible problem, and there is an ultimate limit to how small you can get. And I haven't even touched on quantum effects, which are even worse, because things get so uncertain you have to invent a whole new technology to handle them."

"I understand." The prosecutor looked crestfallen, the wind taken from his sails. "So what you're telling us is that the densities in this chip are very likely not the result of natural technological evolution; they could only have resulted from a radical breakthrough in research. An entirely brand new way of fabricating microprocessors, right?"

"I would have to say that this is very likely."

Rebecca was well aware that Zuckerman had worked things around so that the subject of whether or not the chip actually existed was no longer coming up. She decided to stay silent for the time being.

"And they'd probably want to keep that a secret until they worked out the details and got a patent, wouldn't you agree?"

"Objection, calls for speculation." Something about this was worrying Rebecca.

"Witness may answer. Professor?"

"They may want to keep it a secret. But you can patent interim processes until you figure the whole thing out."

"But if you do that, somebody else might read your patent and figure it out before you do, isn't that so?" Rebecca's exact argument to Anthony Frazier, come back to haunt her. How could her own expert refute what she demonstrated just days before?

"As you said, that *might* be so."

"Dr. Terescu, would it surprise you if you learned that Tera-Tech had achieved the required densities?"

"Yes, it would."

"Are you aware that in the last two years James Perrein, owner of Tera-Tech, has hired some of the top scientists from Dallas Digital, Extel and DigiLogic into Tera-Tech's Fabrication Research Group?"

"I knew that, yes."

Zuckerman stepped aside to make certain that Perrein and Terescu had an unobstructed line of sight between them. "And isn't it a fact that, two years ago, James Perrein hired away one of your very best graduate students, an expert in signal processing technology?"

"Yes." Terescu barely got it out through lips that had suddenly clenched tightly.

Everybody in the room who had been paying close attention to the prosecutor's vocal timbre and body posture was aware that he was building momentum. They began to doubt their earlier perception that he was blindly thrashing about, and to suspect instead that he hadn't wasted a single question on his way to wherever he was going. His obliviousness to their presence only strengthened that perception.

"Two years ago, Tera-Tech announced they had achieved half-micron component size. In your professional experience, given that this company has pursued a vigorous course of research in all that intervening time, with some of the top scientists in the business, do you think it likely that they have made no progress whatsoever in making transistors even smaller, despite the fact that they may have chosen not to publish those results? *No progress whatsoever?*"

"No, that is not very likely." Terescu looked helplessly at Rebecca: *What else could I have answered?*

"Thank you very much. In your opinion, what kind of an application would be ideally suited for this kind of chip technology?"

The non sequitur unnerved Rebecca even more.

"Oh, there are too many to count. Miniaturized television cameras, picture phones, voice recognition . . . but software and other support technologies don't yet exist to exploit those kinds of uses."

"What I'm asking is, given those techniques that do exist today, and are only awaiting chips powerful enough to make them practical, what would be the ideal use for such a chip, that could be implemented virtually the same day as the chip became available?"

Terescu could only shrug, having no idea what Zuckerman was after. Zuckerman, on a roll, didn't bother to take the time to remind the witness that shrugs couldn't be taken down by the court reporter. "Okay, let me give you a possibility." He paused for effect. "How about enhanced public key encryption?"

"Objection! Leading the witness!" Rebecca almost came across the table.

"It's a simple hypothetical, Your Honor," Zuckerman explained.

"I'll allow it."

"Professor?"

"Encryption would be a suitable application."

"*Suitable?*" Zuckerman dragged the word out through a wide smile, looking from the jury back to the witness. "Isn't that a little bit of an understatement? In fact, isn't it the case that a blindingly fast digital signal processor is *tailor made* for this kind of encryption?"

"I suppose so."

"And wouldn't the market for these chips be enormous?"

"Objection! Outside the witness's area of expertise."

"Overruled. He's already stated during direct that he's involved in technology transfer. You may answer, Professor."

"It would be a sizable market."

"Sizable, right." Zuckerman mulled this over for a second, then said, "Like every bank, every brokerage firm, every stock exchange, government and large corporation on the face of the planet, is that what you mean by *sizable?*"

"I suppose so."

"And then there are smart-cards. The size of a credit card, everybody could carry one around that contained all their bank balances, their complete medical history . . . even electronic cash. Are you familiar with the concept?"

"Yes."

"Is it technically feasible right now?"

"Yes."

"Well, then!" Zuckerman's eyes grew large. "Why don't we have them?"

Terescu rubbed his knee. "The data would be very sensitive. Without a means of keeping it secret, no one would dare allow such private information to be put on a card."

"And how might it be kept secret?"

Terescu seemed to perk up. "The card would actually have a small computer built into it that encoded the data."

"It would take a pretty powerful computer, wouldn't it? In a very small space?"

"Yes."

"So a chip like the one we're talking about would be ideal. And there'd have to be one in every smart-card in the world."

Terescu agreed.

Rebecca thought she sensed a mounting anxiety in her star witness. She'd warned him that it wouldn't be all milk and cookies, but he had gotten complacent, which is precisely what Zuckerman wanted him to be while he set him up for the kill.

"Indeed. Professor, in your proposal for grant money to fund your research, what was your estimate for the size of the market for such a chip?"

Steinholz leaned in to Rebecca. "Where does he come up with this shit! What the hell is going on here?" She couldn't answer, because she didn't know and was too rattled to form a coherent reply anyway.

"I don't remember exactly."

"Let me refresh your memory: how does a hundred billion dollars over seven years sound to you?"

"I think I may have said something like that."

"And what percentage of that would be for encryption applications? And in case you don't remember exactly, does fifteen percent ring a bell?"

"Yes."

"So that's a fifteen-billion-dollar market. Isn't that the same market James Perrein was panting after when he started his campaign to have export restrictions on encryption devices lifted?"

"Objection!" Rebecca shook herself loose, knowing it was critical that she disrupt Zuckerman's momentum. "The witness has no way of knowing—"

"Withdrawn," Zuckerman said contemptuously, as though it made little difference because there was nothing Rebecca could do to stop him. "Professor, is there a company anywhere on earth that stands to gain more from the marriage of encryption and high-speed microprocessors than Tera-Tech?"

"Objection!" Rebecca was angry now.

"Sustained." Rebecca's ire seemed to have jarred the judge loose as well. "Mr. Zuckerman, that's getting into some speculation that this witness has not been certified to answer."

"Sorry, Your Honor. Let me get right to my point." He stepped back from the podium and put his hands in his pockets. He didn't say anything, but only looked at Rebecca, who didn't get it until she looked toward the front of the room and saw Goldin motioning her back into her seat.

Zuckerman then turned back to Terescu, hands still in his pockets. "I'll start with another hypothetical, sir. Would you agree that the perfect test of a high-speed encryption device would be inside a foreign country, one that had a vested interest in keeping it all a secret while giving the device a thorough, real-world workout?"

Zuckerman turned toward Rebecca for no apparent reason, only to find her already half out of her seat. "I said it was hypothetical," he snarled. Rebecca looked at Goldin, who nodded, and she sat back down slowly. "Professor?" Zuckerman prodded.

"It would be a good test, yes."

Zuckerman didn't nod or in any other way convey appreciation for Terescu's honesty. "And if the export restrictions on these kinds of devices are ever lifted, Tera-Tech would be in a position to dominate the market because of their head start, wouldn't they?"

Terescu admitted that this would likely be the case.

"It's also a way," Zuckerman continued, totally in control of things now, "of getting 'black' funds, off the books, for continued development, without the government catching on by examining the company's financial records. True?"

Terescu wasn't keen on allowing himself to be led by the nose like this. "I can't imagine that they would sell out their country for money!"

Zuckerman seemed only too happy to move to a different topic. He already had heavy ammunition that he could recall for the jury in his closing statement, so there was no need to continue pressing Terescu just to underline the points. Besides, as you learned in Cross-Exam 101: no sense killing a witness who was already in the process of committing suicide. "Well, then, since you seem to have such a handle on the defendant's character, let's talk a little about your relationship with James Perrein."

Rebecca tried to object, but Zuckerman countered easily. "Her own witness brought it up, Your Honor. They opened the door when he put forth an opinion about the character of the defendant. There's no way to get that bullet back in the gun once the jury's heard it, and I must be allowed to try to impeach the statement."

"Despite your mixed metaphors, I'll let you proceed, but within limits."

"It will only take a few minutes, Your Honor, if the witness will let us get right to the heart of the matter." This time Zuckerman redirected his seemingly random pacing to be sure Terescu couldn't see the defendant. "Professor, you had somewhat of an altercation with James Perrein once, didn't you?"

"An altercation?"

"A run-in," Zuckerman said as he started pacing impatiently. "Some bad blood. A dispute." He stopped moving and bore in on

Terescu. "You want me to dig up a few dozen more metaphors until I find one that suits you?"

"Objection. He's badgering the witness."

Goldin agreed, but also understood his irritation. "Ease off, Mr. Zuckerman. And Professor, please just answer the question."

"Yes, there was a bit of unpleasantness."

"About what?" Zuckerman prompted.

"As you brought up before, Mr. Perrein hired one of my graduate students."

"Did he do it illegally?"

"No."

"Then why the unpleasantness?"

"I took the boy in, trained him, taught him more than anyone could have."

"And then the defendant hired him away from your lab?"

"Yes."

"And that's it?"

"Pretty much."

"Do you want to leave it like that, Professor? Is that your sworn testimony to this court?"

"Not entirely."

"What's the rest?"

"I was doing highly advanced work on chip design. The graduate student knew a great deal about what I was doing. I believed at the time that Mr. Perrein wasn't just stealing some raw talent, he was stealing my work."

"So the graduate student, in your opinion, would take your ideas and lay them at Tera-Tech's feet."

"Something like that."

"Did you have reason to believe that the defense wanted to capitalize on your animosity with the defendant to sway the jury?"

"Yes, I had reason."

"And why was that?"

"Um . . ."

"Because they told you so, isn't that true?"

"Objection, leading the witness!" Rebecca said loudly.

"Permission to treat this witness as hostile, Your Honor!" Zuckerman fired back.

"Granted." Goldin was probably wondering what had taken him so long. Her permission to treat Terescu as hostile meant Zuckerman was now free to ask leading questions.

"Professor, defense counsel told you that she wanted to capitalize on your ill will toward the defendant to sway the jury, isn't that correct?"

"Yes, she told me so. But what difference would that make to my analysis, which was completely objective?"

"We'll get to that in a minute. Are you being paid for your participation in this trial?"

Another transparent trap. Terescu answered as Rebecca had told him to. "Of course. Just as you are."

Zuckerman smiled graciously. "Quite so. Please tell the court how much you're being paid."

"Four hundred dollars an hour."

Zuckerman raised his eyebrows, and looked like he might have given a low whistle if he thought he could get away with it. "Is that a typical rate?"

"Objection," Rebecca said. "How should he know that?"

"Do you know if that is typical?" Goldin asked Terescu, solving the problem simply.

"I don't believe it is typical."

"And how do you know that?" Zuckerman asked.

"Because Ms. Verona told me so."

"It's roughly double the going rate, isn't it?"

"So she said."

"Zuckerman knew it before he asked!" Steinholz gripped the front edge of the table, his knuckles reddening. "How does he *know* this stuff!" he whispered to Rebecca, who could only shake her head by way of reply.

"And," Zuckerman went on, "if your opinions early on weren't coming out in favor of the defendant, you would have been dropped from the case, and that would have been the end of your four-hundred-dollar-an-hour gravy train, right?"

"Objection!" Rebecca was genuinely angry now, and the differences between feigned and real emotions were always clear to experienced courtroom observers. "Argumentative, calls for speculation, it's insulting and he's baiting the witness!"

"I'll withdraw it. Now—"

"Mr. Zuckerman." Goldin's voice stopped him in his tracks. "The court is not amused by these little grenades tossed in from left field and then withdrawn. Confine yourself to proper lines of inquiry."

"Understood. Doctor, why do you figure you rate so high an hourly rate?"

"I assume it's because I am—because I'm believed to be a leading expert."

"And one who is willing to testify even though you hate the defendant."

"Objection! Where are we going with this, Your Honor?" Rebecca asked.

"I believe that's self-evident, Your Honor." Zuckerman sounded like the relevance of this line of inquiry should have been obvious to an eight-year-old.

"I assume it will become crystal clear?" Goldin asked.

"I guarantee it."

"Are we getting close to wrapping up?"

"I don't think so, Your Honor. But let me go for a little longer and we'll get to a good breaking point for today."

He waited for the judge's nod and continued. "Professor, am I correct in saying that most of the findings you told us about under direct examination related to the fact that other companies besides Tera-Tech could have made this chip?"

"I believe that's fair, for the most part."

"But, at the same time, you also went a bit further, stating that, in your opinion, Tera-Tech *could not have made* the chip themselves, right?"

"I don't believe they could have."

"Because they lack the capability."

"Yes."

"They have no devices capable of achieving ion beams of sufficient strength and resolution to craft components small enough?"

"Right."

"That, of course, assumes that the technique that was used *is* ion beam lithography."

"I know of no other technique that is even remotely close to being ready to do the job."

"But didn't you also state that you don't believe even ion beam lithography is ready to do the job?"

Terescu didn't answer. How could he, when Zuckerman had put his finger on a major contradiction in his testimony?

Zuckerman pressed the point to make sure the jury understood what was going on. "In one breath you tell us Tera-Tech didn't make the chip because they don't have the right ion beam machines. In the next breath you tell us that even *those* machines couldn't have made the chips."

"My belief may have been mistaken."

"Is that because the chip in fact exists?"

"Because you *say* it exists. I still haven't had a chance to examine it for myself."

"Is it fair to say that you have doubts about whether the chip does what my experts say it does?"

"Great doubts."

"But even if it does do it, you still don't believe Tera-Tech could have built it."

"No, sir."

"Again, because they don't have the equipment."

"Because the equipment doesn't exist."

"But I said, *if* it does exist. It was a hypothetical."

"That makes no difference. If you told me that, hypothetically, the moon is made of green cheese, I wouldn't change my entire conception of physics just to deal with your question. *The equipment doesn't exist!*"

"Doesn't exist." Rebecca shuddered as Zuckerman repeated Terescu's words. He was getting what he wanted, that was obvious, even though she couldn't figure out exactly what that was. Something told her she was close to finding out.

"Speaking hypothetically," Zuckerman said, "are there any machines that exist which could conceivably be modified to do the job? Assuming the technology was available?"

"That's an absurd question! You're asking my opinion about modifying a machine to accommodate a nonexistent technology? How on earth should I know!"

"Good point. But we do know we're talking about extremely high-energy, high-resolution ion beams, right?"

"Most likely."

"So what kinds of devices would be the logical choices to evolve into the required capabilities?"

"Obviously, the highest-energy, highest-resolution ion beam machines which exist today."

"Who has the most powerful such machines? Dallas Digital? Extel?"

"Possibly."

"And Tera-Tech? Did they have one on the inventory list you were given?"

"No. And the president of the company told me they didn't have one after I asked him directly."

"Objection!" Rebecca said without conviction. "Calls for hearsay testimony."

"I didn't call for anything!" Zuckerman said, smiling incredulously. "The witness volunteered the information. And, besides, he's an expert. He can use anything he relied on in forming his opinion."

"Objection is overruled."

"So the president—the defendant, James Perrein—the president of Tera-Tech told you they didn't have a high-energy, high-resolution ion beam machine."

"He was quite definitive."

"So it wasn't just a clerical error on the list. Because he told you himself that they didn't have one."

"Precisely."

"I think we're all getting a bit tired." Zuckerman watched for signs of relief on Terescu's face as he said this, and was amply rewarded, especially at Terescu's startled reaction as he said, "Last couple of questions." Terescu wilted and seemed to shrink even smaller upon hearing this. "Have you personally visited Tera-Tech's facilities during the course of your analysis?"

"No."

"Really? How did you analyze their capabilities without a visit?"

"The exact same way I analyzed your chip, Mr. Zuckerman: I was given written information."

"Touché." It was a good answer. "But you would have examined the chip directly if you were allowed to, right?"

"Of course."

"Then why didn't you visit the Tera-Tech premises? Weren't you allowed to?"

"Mr. Perrein preferred I didn't."

"And why was that?"

"I don't know what was in his mind, and he didn't say. Why don't you ask him?"

"I will. Was it perhaps because there was something there he didn't want you to see?"

"Possibly."

"Some evidence that might implicate him for the crimes charged here?" It was a good shot, and he winced at the expected burst of outrage from Rebecca. He was stunned when none was forthcoming.

"I don't think so."

"Why, then?"

"I think it was because he thought I might steal some of their technical secrets. The same way I believed he stole mine."

Zuckerman seemed not to care. "Your Honor, I think this might be a good breaking point."

"Okay," Goldin announced wearily as she sat up straight. "I've got several matters from a previous case tomorrow. Don't know how long it might take, so we'll hold off continuation of this trial for a day. Court is recessed until Friday morning, and let's start at eight."

Steinholz shook his head as he stood and began packing up his papers. He waited until Perrein had passed through the rear courtroom doors before speaking. "All of that juggernaut cross-examination and Zuckerman didn't establish a damned thing!"

"Except bringing up a half dozen reasons why it would have benefited Mr. Wonderful to sell the chips to China." Rebecca remained silent for a few moments, staring at the doors in the back, making no move to gather up her notes and get going, lost in thought and biting on a fingernail. "I think we're in trouble," she finally said, facing forward and letting her hand fall onto the arm of her chair.

Steinholz halted his packing and looked at her in surprise as Ehrenright came up to the table. "Why?"

"He may not have come to any conclusions, but he's only partway through his cross." Rebecca stood up and slowly began pulling her papers together and jogging them into place. "I think I know where he's going, and he's hurting us."

"I agree," Ehrenright said, laying his briefcase down on the table and putting his hands in his pockets. "The encryption technique in the chip is the same as Tera-Tech's. We might have shown that Melanie Fuster was biased when she did her analysis, but our own expert just backed her up."

"But so what?" Steinholz said. "It was a published technique. Any programmer could have done it."

"Yeah, but that's not the bad part," Ehrenright said. "Zuckerman got Terescu to pretty much admit that there are only two possibilities: either the chip is extremely fast, or it uses a novel method of implementing Tera-Tech's technique, which only someone intimately familiar with it could have done."

"And this tells you what?"

"That, either way, it looks like Tera-Tech probably made the thing," Rebecca answered. "It was their guy invented the technique in the first place."

"Zuckerman also got him to say that the chip was likely made using an ion beam method," Ehrenright added, "and that Tera-Tech is the world leader in that technology." He jiggled his hands in his pockets. "Not conclusive, but it looks bad."

"Not bad enough to overcome reasonable doubt," Steinholz argued.

Rebecca knew that Steinholz had the raw cerebral horsepower in this group, but she also knew that Ehrenright had a better feel for the human side of things, and let him respond. "A jury's deciding this case, Arno, not Felix Frankfurter. Emotions over brains. And there's still more stuff coming up. Zuckerman also brought out that Tera-Tech hit the half-micron mark two years ago, and got Terescu to admit that they've probably gone well beyond that by now."

Steinholz answered quickly, "But what everybody seems to be forgetting is that the chip is probably a year or two old. What happened since then is irrelevant."

Ehrenright continued to play devil's advocate. "That's what Tera-Tech *published* two years ago; who knows what they were really able to do back then? Remember, this is an outfit that stopped publishing results altogether. Maybe they weren't so forthcoming even when they were still hitting the journals."

"Sure would have been nice if Perrein had warned us about this publishing freeze. I need to remember to ask him about that." Rebecca stared straight ahead for a second, then turned just as Terescu was walking out the courtroom doors and into the corridor beyond. She banged her fist angrily on her attaché. "I *told* him specifically not to get into this business of denying the chip is real!"

Steinholz nodded, but said, "He couldn't help it, Becky. There was no way for him to worm out of the direction Zuckerman was taking him. Does it matter?"

She turned back, knuckles reddening as her hands gripped the case. "I can't say for sure how, but I've got a really bad feeling about it. Zuckerman didn't come to any bottom lines today, but for damned sure he's got something in mind."

She looked down for a moment, then shook her head. "Shit, just look at everything he's creating! What could have been more perfect for Perrein than a deal with China? And that thing you came up with in the very beginning, Justin: Perrein a traitor? Hell, he'd think he was doing the country a *favor* by making those chips and selling them overseas!"

Steinholz waited a decent interval, then said, "Did we get anything at all?"

"Yeah, we did," Ehrenright answered. "There's still the question of capability. Tera-Tech just plain hasn't got the equipment, a high-powered ion-whooziwhatsis or whatever." Emboldened by this thought, he said to Rebecca, "They can spin all the happy horseshit they want about motivation, expertise, what the hell ever, but if the accused didn't have a damned gun, then he didn't pull the damned trigger."

Rebecca thought about that, then nodded slowly. "Right. So let's not get too morose just yet. We can still rehabilitate Terescu on redirect."

"But we've got a bigger immediate problem," Steinholz said tentatively, not wishing to leave things on a down note.

"Like where is Zuckerman getting his information?" Rebecca asked, resuming her packing.

Ehrenright nodded. "Which I'm finding mildly terrifying." He put a hand over Rebecca's to stop her from focusing on getting her notes put away. "You gotta confront him, you know," he said.

Rebecca closed her eyes and exhaled. "I know."

"Today."

She held up her hand to silence him. "I said, I know."

Although stunned by the things Zuckerman dug up, she had tried to put them out of her mind so she could concentrate on his cross-examination of Terescu. But there was no way to avoid dealing with it now.

As she made her way across the street toward the offices of the U.S. attorney, she reluctantly allowed the real reason for her reticence to crawl out of its hiding place and grip her heart: someone was leaking information to the prosecution, and it had to be someone on her own team, or close to it, someone with access to their documents and conversations. And not only was the prosecutor getting raw information, he seemed to be getting guidance on how it all fit together.

In the elevator on the way up, Rebecca tried to put aside whatever personal distress such a realization was causing her and get ready to deal with it as a lawyer.

Zuckerman was standing next to a file cabinet in his office, one drawer open, a folder laid out on top of it. He was reading it with his back to the open door. Rebecca knocked on the jamb. As Zuckerman turned, his first expression was one of pleasant surprise, which he tried fleetingly to suppress, but it would have been too obvious so he just left it there. "Well, hey there."

"Hey yourself." She tried her best to return his easy smile but failed in the attempt, which, of course, Zuckerman saw.

He turned and closed the file folder, then laid it on top of the cabinet and slid the drawer shut before motioning her to a seat. "Take it this isn't a social call."

"No." Rebecca sat, dropping her purse and attaché on the floor beside her. Zuckerman sat behind his desk and waited.

She knew that the best way to deal with him was in the most straightforward manner possible. He could thrust and parry obliquely with the best of them, but in the end, he always had you just coming out with it anyway, so there was no sense wasting time. "You got friends in low places, Zuck," she said. "You know stuff you ain't a'posed to know."

He sat, expression neutral, and raised two fingers in inquiry: *Tell me what you got before I say anything.*

"Like Radovan Terescu hitting a twenty-fifth of a micron in his lab, like the contents of his grant proposal . . ." She watched his face for clues to his reaction, but got nothing, which told her everything. "That he's getting double pay for his time as an expert witness. That Tera-Tech's been hiring top scientists in the field. You knew about Perrein hiring away Terescu's grad student and the bad blood that resulted . . . and you know, or think you know, how all of that might fit together." She stopped. "Your turn."

Zuckerman stared at her a few moments longer, then swiveled his chair toward his window, folded his hands and tapped his thumbs together. After a while, he shrugged and turned back toward her. "Not as big a deal as you think. Plain old legwork, really."

He sniffled and scratched the side of his nose. "The component density Terescu got in his lab was a stab in the dark. We knew he was working in the area, which is kind of obvious, and we figured he must have achieved something on a small scale, so I asked."

This time it was Rebecca's turn to give nothing away as Zuckerman spoke.

"As to his grant proposal," he went on, "that's public knowledge. It's on file at Cal Tech. And the high billing rate, well, hell, that was just dumb luck." He lifted his hands into the air and grinned. "Even a blind pig finds a truffle once in a while."

She kept still, making sure he was finished, then spoke. "Truffles." She squeezed her lips together and nodded. "Pigs hunt truffles by smell, Zuckerman, so it doesn't make a difference if they're blind." Any lingering trace of pleasantness left her face once she realized that her straightforwardness wasn't being met halfway. "Dumb luck, my sweet ass."

Zuckerman tried to maintain his smile under Rebecca's piercing, humorless glare, but the strain of doing so showed through, and he let it fade.

"I don't buy any of it," she said. "I don't believe you formulated the follow-up questions about density right on the spot. I don't believe you would have gone after a grant proposal unless you already knew it existed. Lucking into Terescu's double billing rate is obvious bullshit, and we both know it."

"So what are you—"

"Someone on my team is feeding you information. You know the details of unrecorded conversations between Terescu and me."

She waited to see if that would shut him up, and it did. "Your source might be guilty of criminal malfeasance. You have no choice but to tell us who it is. You should have come forth sooner, but I'm willing to let that go if you do the right thing now."

"Very generous of you."

"Cut it out, David."

Zuckerman bit the inside of his cheek, then leaned back on his chair, which reclined slightly under his weight. "We're being fed the odd tidbit here and there."

Despite her firm suspicion that this was the case, Rebecca couldn't suppress the icy feeling that crept up her back at hearing it confirmed that there was a traitor in her midst. "Who is it?" she said, trying hard to keep any wavering out of her voice.

"We call him 'Deep Silicon' around the office."

Rebecca ignored the joke. "I asked you who it is."

"That's all you get."

Rebecca knew she needed to stay on reasonably good terms with Zuckerman, in case there was ever a need to negotiate a plea bargain with him. If she irked him into a testosterone war now, his recalcitrance might work against her client later, and she couldn't let that happen. She was the one who had to break the standoff, even though it meant losing face, since she was the one who had come to him and she was the one who needed information. Dropping the subject now meant a victory for Zuckerman.

So be it. At least she had gotten him to admit there was an informant. She sat back on her seat and tried to convey the impression that she was willing to let this go for now, but that it was by no means over. It was obvious to both of them that she was backing off, but Zuckerman was too smart to gloat.

He sat up straight and made a show of nervously looking at his watch. "Listen, Becky. Probably some stuff we ought to discuss." She nodded, returning her attention to him. "You want to meet before court tomorrow, or, uh, maybe we could—"

Rebecca looked at her own watch, then reached down for her things. "What about we get together for dinner later," she said before she even realized that words were coming out of her mouth. She fought the impulse to look around and see who could have uttered such nonsense, but instead decided to be ready to let Zuckerman off the hook easily rather than watch him squirm for an excuse.

"Sure," he said, nodding as casually as he could, like the invitation was the most natural thing in the world. They'd had dinner together dozens of times in the past two years, but now the circumstances were completely changed. They were adversaries, certainly, but that wasn't really it. James Perrein was suddenly back in the picture, and his was a name that had gone unuttered between them since the first time he'd appeared. Each thought the other had a notion of what the protocol was for handling the topic, when in fact neither of them had a clue. "Where?"

Rebecca looked around, as though a good place might be right on his bookshelves, but she was only looking away from him. "I dunno. Probably wouldn't do being seen together. . . ."

"Right. Absolutely right. Something out of the way, then. Maybe that—"

Out of the way. Rebecca didn't hear the rest as she snapped her head around to look at him, to see if he intended some subtle reproach by using that phrase. But his eyes were guileless, their only expression one of being startled at her reaction. *How much does he know!*

"Beck, you okay?"

"Yeah. Just remembered something I forgot to do. How about— what was that place up in Malibu, it overlooks a little valley?"

"Spyro's, right!" Zuckerman nodded enthusiastically, then spoke without thinking. "Haven't been back there since, ah . . ."

Out of the way.

"Seven okay?"

Zuckerman nodded, mostly out of relief. "I'll be there."

Chapter 21

Charles Malacore was Rebecca's mother's brother. Her father, Vincenzo, died when she was six and Wendy two. Undoubtedly she had, over the years, idolized Vincenzo into near sainthood, but that was the way it was when you lost a parent at that age. He had read to her, sung lustily at the slightest provocation, even taught her some Italian. She'd resisted the language instruction at first, but Vincenzo had made a game of it, seeing which of the two of them could roll those delicious syllables off the tongue with greater exaggeration, trilling their *r*'s like hack opera singers and drawing the vowels out as long as they could.

He'd taught her important lessons as well, not so much to indoctrinate her to his way of thinking but to prepare her to consider her own. Not a great believer in religion, he nevertheless was strongly bound to tradition, and once or twice each month took his daughter to a small church in the Catskill foothills, less than an hour outside of New York City. It wasn't a fancy cathedral, just a plain wooden building barely more substantial than a log cabin, about all its parishioners could afford. Vincenzo and Rebecca were always made to feel welcome, and were never overtly solicited for contributions other than by the routine passing of the plate.

Shortly after she had turned five, they made their way to the church one Sunday only to discover that it had burned to the ground the previous day. They came upon several dozen of the congregants standing around a deep depression in the earth that had once been the foundation but now contained only blackened timbers and still-smoldering rubble.

"Daddy!" Rebecca had cried in dismay. "Where's the church?"

Vincenzo put his hand on his daughter's shoulder. "It's standing around looking at this hole, Rebecca."

He had also taken her ice-skating at Prospect Park in Brooklyn and seen the latent talent in his daughter, and then paid for skating lessons. So it had originally been Rebecca who was the skating star in the clan, still in the family spotlight at the age of six despite the birth of her sister four years before.

Her mother, Angela, whom Rebecca saw as a traditional European wife, hadn't always been that way. A first-generation American born to Florentine immigrants, Angela had attended Hunter College where, much to her parents' chagrin, she had adopted many of the fashionable philosophical affectations popular among postwar college students in New York. Among these was a religious outlook that, while not quite atheistic, ascribed to God not the generally comprehensible motivations of humans but rather the hopelessly obscure ones of deities.

So when Angela contracted a particularly virulent form of cancer at the age of twenty-three, even at the nadir of her despair when she was tempted to appeal to God, she stood firmly by her conviction that prayers went unheard and that God acted with complete irrationality, at least as far as a human's mind could perceive. She successfully fought the temptation to pray, went into complete remission, and thanked God (figuratively) that she hadn't succumbed and compromised her beliefs during the toughest test.

Only it turned out to be the second toughest; the first came eight years later, when Vincenzo lay dying of a previously undiagnosed congenital cardiac defect. This time, unwilling to bet her husband's life on her beliefs, Angela prayed—fervently—making reckless promises to the Almighty that she'd never be able to keep, in exchange for the restoration of Vincenzo's life. He died despite her entreaties, and her bitterness was cast in cold steel forever.

With Vincenzo gone, Angela appealed to her brother, Charles, who took them in, but not without constantly impressing upon the three of them his enormous personal sacrifice in providing for them. He softened only slightly after becoming aware of Rebecca's talent on the ice, but hardened in other ways, pushing her to extremes unsuitable for a first-grader newly fatherless. Rebecca got all of the attention, and all of the stress, until a canny coach teaching private students at the rink noticed Wendy, skating on her own, imitating her older sister's moves. The coach urged Charlie to start investing in the little kid, and right now, Vincenzo apparently having been too dense to have seen Rebecca's talent early on, when they could have done something about it. But with Wendy, well, they had plenty of time.

So Charlie, with cold calculation, switched things around, never even bothering to explain to Rebecca why, at the age of eight, she was being tossed onto the slag heap in favor of her sister.

Wendy tried to quit the rink many times, but Charlie wouldn't let her. *What else have you got?* he would say. *You're not smart and you're not pretty, except for all those clothes and that sparkly crap I pay to put on your face.* But she was beautiful, and she was very bright, although it's hard to get good grades on tests when you spend four hours a day on the ice and your college-educated mother does all your homework.

So Rebecca idolized her real father, and her idealization of him expanded in direct proportion to her experience of her uncle. Lord only knew what Vincenzo might have turned out to be had he lived. But in the absence of any evidence to the contrary, in her mind she had built him up into the perfect friend, protector and provider. With only Charles Malacore as a baseline comparator, it wasn't a difficult image to conjure.

Wendy was only two when Vincenzo died; she'd never really known him, or what a father was supposed to be like, and although Uncle Charles made her life miserable, she wasn't in a position to realize that this was an unnatural state of affairs.

But Rebecca had been six when Vincenzo died. She had known a real father, a loving one, and naturally expected that her new guardian would slip easily into the same role. While she could never honestly claim to have successfully surmounted that futile yearning, over time it was largely replaced by generous dollops of furious resentment that didn't disappear but accumulated, layer by layer, like cooling magma. Occasionally, and always inadvertently, when Charles did something that, if liberally interpreted, hinted faintly at some kind of affection toward Rebecca, it triggered her against her better judgment to reflexively and eagerly lap it up and beg for more. Her pain, when he subsequently made damned sure to correct her misimpressions, was blinding and paralyzing.

No matter what conscious decisions Rebecca might have made about how to stand up to Charlie in the face of his frequent cruelties, in his actual presence it was an almost physical impossibility for her to do so. Instead, the pressure in her just kept growing, and even sobbing out her searing frustration at night, with her head buried deep into her pillow so nobody could hear, couldn't come close to relieving it. It was being bottled up tight. And like most such things, the bottling was a delaying, not an erasing.

College, paid for partly by Vincenzo's parents, was for Rebecca much like the Waldorf would be to a newly released inmate of a maximum security facility. Her finely tuned athletic discipline generalized well to an academic environment, and her grades, coupled with stellar scores on the LSATs, landed her in law school with several modest, private scholarships that combined with her grandparents' contribution to pretty much subsidize her entire legal education. The required year of postgraduation public service work conditioned by her sponsors turned out to be a blessing rather than a burden, and she even signed on for a second year, which was abruptly cut short following an unanticipated and unfortunate appearance before the U.S. Supreme Court in which the truth, as she saw it, proved to be an unacceptable substitute for deference.

But that passed quickly. Rebecca, like most driven people who thought they were striving toward a goal but in reality were being chased by demons, pretty much excelled at everything she tried. She thought she'd pretty much managed to rid herself of Uncle Charlie, and her career advanced steadily, although not as quickly as she might have were it not for this odd habit of periodically shooting herself in the foot.

The original plan had been for her to work until about six, an early day for her, then head for Malibu. It was pretty standard procedure for a business dinner not to start until nearly eight so she could attend to all the things a lawyer needed to get done before court the next day. People unknowledgeable in the actual day-to-day logistics of trial work tended to look askance at all this high-priced talent leaving court at three in the afternoon, but for most of them, judges and lawyers included, the day was only half over when the formal session ended.

That was especially true in Catherine Goldin's court. She met with the lawyers in chambers every day after the trial session, going over the next day's testimony in order to preclude sidebars. These meetings began to get longer as the number of sidebars in *United States* v. *Tera-Tech Integrated, et al.*, increased well beyond Goldin's tolerance threshold, which was roughly zero. She understood well enough the complex and, to some extent, unprecedented issues arising in the case that made it difficult to anticipate problems, but she kept that to herself, communicating only displeasure to Rebecca and Zuckerman in order to motivate them to plan better. Every time a sidebar was held, Goldin felt compelled to apologize to the jury. This was not only a matter of civility and politeness, but also telegraphed a warning to the lawyers: judges didn't like to have to apologize to anybody, especially when it wasn't their fault.

The lawyers usually didn't get out of chambers until sometime after four, and then it was back to their respective offices for several hours in order to frantically rewire the carefully planned examinations that were no longer applicable owing to what had transpired in court that day. Trial work is like a space mission laid out in advance in the most excruciating detail imaginable, except that every day a different piece of critical machinery goes on the fritz, and every once in a while, even the planet you were supposed to be visiting is changed without warning. Planning is a useful skill, but revising the plan while the ship is traveling ten miles each second is the more vitally important talent.

So what was Rebecca doing home at just after five, sitting in front of her vanity in her underwear, combing her hair and fixing her makeup to make certain it didn't look like she was wearing any?

> *Losing love is like a window in your heart*
> *Everybody sees you're blown apart*
> *Everybody sees the wind blow. . . .*

She shivered, quickly picked up the remote control and flipped the stereo to another station.

> *My Mercury is up on blocks*
> *My fishin' pole is broke*
> *She hid the kids at Grandma's house*
> *My life's gone up in smoke.*

Much better. She put down the remote and began combing her hair again, then stopped, dropped her hands in her lap and let her shoulders slump. Images, unbidden and unwanted, started to form in her mind as she abandoned the effort to suppress them.

Her thoughts were interrupted by the music, which seemed actually to have played a few seconds before but was only now hitting her consciousness as something impish in her mind replayed it back to her.

> *Hang me up there with you, Jesus*
> *For the world is cross with me*

She exhaled audibly in exasperation and grabbed for the remote again, hitting a key to no effect, then stabbing at it repeatedly until the stereo shut off. She closed her eyes and rubbed her forehead, elbows resting on the small tabletop.

What the hell am I doing?

She took a damp towel and began rubbing all the makeup off, hard at first, then softly so as not to redden her skin. Everything went: mascara, lipstick, eyeliner . . .

Rebecca looked in the mirror once again. This time she approved of what she saw: a strong, pretty face. *Her* face, not Estee Lauder's idea of a makeover "before" shot. She liked it this way.

So did he.

Why was she so depressed?

Only a few minutes left before she had to leave. She was sure she would have no problem once dinner started and there was important business to be conducted, but right now she didn't feel so good.

She stood up and put her favorite CD on the stereo, a modern opera about Christmas and nightmares and the Pumpkin King, then turned to the full-length mirror mounted on the closet door.

Regarding herself critically, she had no cause to complain about anything. Hips were slim, legs strong but not overly muscular, lightly discernible abs rising to breasts to make any cheerleader envious. Her posture was erect but relaxed, and even when she stood still it was easy to tell that, when she moved, it would be a smooth and effortless glide. And she was much too smart to waste time hunting down the kind of barely discernible, usually nonexistent flaws that drove other women to anorexia or bulimia. All those years of intense practice on the ice may not have yielded a great number of medals, but they did leave other beneficial legacies, not just the body but a knack for critical and accurate self-appraisal.

The ice. She inhaled deeply and exhaled slowly, sensing the volumetric uptake capacity left over from her skating days that expanded not only her chest but her abdomen as well. Breath control was as important to a trial lawyer needing to sustain momentum during an extended harangue as it was to a soprano during a difficult aria. Rebecca remembered how she learned exactly when to take a deep breath in her routine, making sure she had sufficient air to get her through an exacting series of combination jumps during which drawing breath would be awkward.

Rebecca closed her eyes and leaned forward, lifted her left leg off

the floor and raised both arms languorously into the air. Not ana-
lyzing, not consciously executing, just letting the muscle memory
take over while the rational part of herself stood off to the side and
marveled at the ease of it, just as she had the last time she had com-
peted. There was no hope of winning the thing: unknowns never
won anything in sports scored by judges. But the simple joy of
knowing she was as good as her sister, maybe even better, infused
her with a sublime joy. Mother and Uncle Charlie would know it,
too, would know she was capable, and much less schizophrenic,
than Wendy.

Skating backward in preparation for a fiendishly difficult triple
loop, she had a moment to look into the stands, just in time to see
her mother in animated conversation with the Coca-Cola rep on
her right, an empty seat to her left. Sensing movement at the scor-
ing table, Rebecca looked in that direction to see her uncle huddled
with three of the judges, gesticulating wildly, no doubt vehemently
protesting whatever egregious error of judgment they had committed against Wendy in their numerical assessments of her.

While Rebecca had a great deal of physical skill, she didn't have
Wendy's practiced single-mindedness to ignore distractions. The
images she saw cut into her immediately, all the implications exploding in her mind in the time it took to put one skate behind the
other. Her acceleration faltered, even as the dreamy ecstasy written
on her face disappeared and was replaced by the warring forces of
anger, humiliation and, almost immediately, protective numbness.

Rebecca came dangerously close to the end of the rink before
turning, carrying insufficient speed to whip around properly for the
upcoming move, which disintegrated from an inspired triple sal-
chow into an insipid double lutz, a maneuver even a novice ob-
server could see hadn't been planned but was just a fallback.

In addition to the other emotions fighting for dominance within
her, there was also confusion: she failed to comprehend how her
own mother and uncle could be so heartless. Did they have any
idea at all of what they were doing to her, or were they really that
oblivious? And which of those would be worse? She tried to remember not to let the audience see her tears, but all she could concentrate on was how she could get back at the two cruel people
disguised as lawful guardians. At him, mostly. Because Mother was
trying to turn her head to watch the ice, but the Coca-Cola guy insisted on her attention, and Mother was too weak and submissive
to resist.

*   *   *

Spyro's was distinctly unyuppified. Blue-and-white checked tablecloths, travel posters from Athens and Mykonos, signed photographs of Telly Savalas and Anthony Quinn, the latter actually Mexican, but what the hell.

Spyro Kazantzakis remembered them well, bringing out a steaming plate of *spanakopetes* without waiting to be asked. "On the house," he announced happily, gutturalizing the initial *h* so that "house" sounded more like the throat-clearing of a chronic smoker than a word. He stood beaming at the two of them, ignoring their embarrassed half smiles and awkward glances at each other. "So, what you gonna have, some *moussaka*? Nice eggplant, thin slices, some chopped-up lamb, plenty tomatoes, onions, a little cinnamon. . . ? Okay, maybe a nice *yalantzi dolmathes*, ah? I make tonight wit' rezzins, from grepps we grow right here. You see in back, growing on what . . . a *trellis*?" He put two fingers to his mouth and kissed them as he pulled them away. "Pearls from Olympus, belliv me: you gonna like."

"Pearls from a mountain, Spyro?" Rebecca looked up at him. "Where's the lamb come from, the Aegean?"

He shook his head sadly. "Two years away, you lose your soul. I gotta teach you to dance again?" He didn't wait for an answer, but turned and yelled, "Katerina! *Hupa. . . !*"

"Hold it!" Rebecca grabbed his arm before his wife could put on some *bouzouki* from his treasured collection of Hiotis and Nikolopoulos records and pipe it into the tiny dining room.

He turned to her, eyebrows raised in surprise. "Listen, Zorba," she said, smiling so his feelings wouldn't be hurt. "Last time you gave me dancing lessons, I had a headache for two days."

"Wasn't the dancing, was the *retsina*."

"Yeah, but you don't teach dancing without *retsina*. So how about two glasses"—she looked at Zuckerman and waited for his assenting nod—"*small* glasses, and you let me stay conscious for court tomorrow."

He blinked at her a few times, then shrugged. "Sure. But is big mistake." He turned and walked back toward the kitchen, waving for his wife to stand down his last order.

He returned seconds later with two large glasses of the potent Greek wine made from tree resin, and Rebecca could almost feel her head start to pound as the pungent smell bit at her nostrils.

"Couple minutes, Spyro," Zuckerman said to him. "I hardly remember the menu."

"Hell with the menu," Spyro replied. "I fix what you want." He looked at Rebecca once more, shook his head in wonderment at her refusal of his invitation, and wandered off.

"You mean you haven't taken a single one of your conquests to this place?" Rebecca asked.

"Took 'em all. But Spyro's too wise to rat anybody out. Bad for his business." Zuckerman picked up his glass and held it out. Rebecca took her own and touched it to his. Smell is the most powerful sense for summoning up old memories, and *retsina* had a powerful smell. Rebecca wasted no more than half a second trying to analyze the transmissions that were flashing between Zuckerman and her. She took a sip, and he did the same, closing his eyes in satisfaction as the fiery liquid coursed its way to the back of his mouth and down his throat.

"The hell you know about my conquests anyway?" he said lightly after he'd swallowed, setting down his glass.

"Oh, we all keep track of the personal lives of prosecutors. Helps us maintain our log of blackmail possibilities, you get too nasty."

"Ah, I get it. And in my file . . . ?"

"Fear of commitment," Rebecca answered briskly. "Bad rep for that among the females in your office."

Zuckerman dropped his head and shook it. "God, I hate that phrase."

"Too close to home?" She hoped he wasn't seeing through her pathetic attempts to get some idea of what his personal life had been like. In all their quasi-business dinners during the past two years, by unspoken, mutual consent they'd never ventured into those treacherous waters.

"Too much crapola," Zuckerman said as he looked up at some point on the far wall behind her. "Christ, I'm dying to get committed. Just not to any of *them*."

"Sounds like a cop-out."

"Who am I copping out *to*?" he replied quickly, an edge to his voice indicating that, while this might be idle chitchat and harmless jabbing between friends to her, it wasn't to him.

"Lemme ask you something, you've got so much penetrating insight." Zuckerman put his elbows on the table and leaned in toward her. "How come it never seems to occur to a woman that what she sees as fear of commitment is just fear of committing to *her*?"

"Never?" Rebecca answered. "Some generalization."

Zuckerman seemed not to have heard her. "What, she can't admit that to herself—What could possibly be wrong with *her*, after all!—so she chalks it off to a damaged commitment gene on her boyfriend's part? And if she comes across ten men in a row who won't commit to her, you think she starts to catch on, like, Gee, maybe it's something about *me*?" He sat up straight, slapped a palm on the table. "Hell, no! She just concludes that this is a terrible failing shared by all men, and writes a cover article for *Cosmo*."

"My, my, aren't we touchy!" Rebecca said, genuinely amused. "What the hell's been going on, you're all heated up . . . you getting marriage proposals?"

"You brought it up," he answered sullenly. "Somebody doesn't want me, I chalk it off to bad chemistry, or she doesn't like the way I hold a fork, not some alien virus eating away at her brain."

Rebecca laughed, at both his colorful mode of expression and the childish scowl that furrowed his brows as he fidgeted with his hands, but mostly in order not to dwell on the message that flashed across her brain: *Whom had he wanted to commit to?*

She sat back and picked up a fork, then let one end drop back onto the table. "So what is it, David?" She bent forward and speared one of the small triangles of baked filo dough surrounding a core of aromatic spinach leaves and bit off one corner, the heady taste of onions, scallions and garlic threatening to derail her train of thought. "You still nursing a grudge because I bruised your precious ego?" she mumbled around the delicate morsel, trying to move some air through her mouth to keep the *spanakopetes* from burning her tongue. She set the rest of the piece down on the small plate off to her side.

Zuckerman's hands became still. "What are you talking about?"

Rebecca stopped chewing for a second, looked at him and then resumed, cutting off another piece of the delicacy with the side of her fork. "Oh, come off it, David. We been friends the past two years, why don't we just have it out, clear the air? Aren't you gonna eat some of this? Better than I remembered."

Zuckerman made no move toward the appetizer plate sitting on the table midway between them. "Okay. I'm game. How does my precious ego enter into it?"

"Simple." Rebecca forked up the newly cut piece and put it in her mouth, trying to convey the impression that, while this seemed to be difficult and appetite robbing for him, she was as sanguine as could be and totally at ease. "We had a nice thing going for a while"—she looked at him as she realized the extent of her presumption, adding—"or so I thought. Then Jim Perrein comes along, sweeps me off my feet. . . . I made a great, big goddamned mistake and you've never forgiven me." She finished chewing and swallowed. "And that's how I see it."

Zuckerman hadn't yet moved. "That's how you see it."

"Yeah. You see it differently?"

"First of all, there's nothing to forgive." Zuckerman sniffled and picked up the glass of *retsina*. "You didn't do anything to me," he said, then took a sip with his eyes still on her.

"Dumping you for Mr. Wonderful wasn't doing anything to you?"

Zuckerman shook his head and set the wineglass back down. "You acted the way you felt. Who can fault you for that? I'm not saying I wasn't surprised, but I wasn't angry with you." He did a fairly good job of forcing his voice to remain casual, but it was the kind of hammy act that did more to call attention to the performer's skill than make you forget that acting was taking place.

Now it was Rebecca's turn to get irked. "Then what the hell *is* it, David?"

"Not sure what you're talking about."

Her knuckles whitened slightly as she gripped the fork. "We were good together, that's what! How come, after that sorry business with Perrein ended, how come you never gave it another shot? Never forgave me, tried to put it behind you?" He was still trying to fully integrate the full breadth of her question when she added, "Why are you trying to kill me in court?"

That broke the spell. "Ah. I see! And you think it was because of my easily damaged male ego."

"What else?"

Zuckerman sighed deeply and shook his head, as a parent might when his child still failed to grasp a homework problem after the fifth try. "You never understood any of that, Rebecca. And that's part of the problem. Why I never *gave it another shot*, as you put it, like it was some kind of racquetball contest."

His condescension was irritating but beside the point. "Okay," Rebecca said, no longer willing to play riddles. "I said my piece. Now you tell me what I don't understand." She folded her arms across her chest and slumped back in her chair, not an attitude of studious inquiry but a challenge.

"I wasn't angry with you, Rebecca. I was just terribly disappointed." He hesitated, as if coming to a decision. "I wasn't just in—"

What? Rebecca wanted to shout out as he came to a stop. *Wasn't just in what!*

"I admired you," he said instead of finishing his original thought. "You were bright, ambitious, self-possessed. You may think men look for women who are stupid and weak and have nice tits, but that's not me." Rebecca raised her eyebrows and allowed a hint of a smile, despite her seconds-old resolve to remain annoyed with him for the time being.

Zuckerman returned the smile with a mischievous one of his own. "Okay, I'll admit to the nice tits part." Rebecca's smile widened even as Zuckerman's faded and his voice grew serious. "But the point is, what rings my chimes are smart broads who can hold their own. And that's what I thought you were."

"And I'm not?"

"I don't know." He scratched at the tablecloth for a few seconds before looking back up at her. "I can only tell you my illusions were shattered when that overprimped, self-centered asshole dazzled you so easily. Man like that, he uses women like I use Kleenex. He expects them to fall in love with his face and his money and his power, because something deep inside him knows that there's little of emotional substance once you get past the suntan and the flashy teeth." He caught himself and stopped, not having really intended to deliver what sounded like a rehearsed monologue.

"Nice speech. But how do you figure all that out about someone until you get to know him?"

"You use your brains, Becky," he answered earnestly, tapping two fingers on the tabletop. "You take it slow. You keep your sunglasses on till the light dies down, when the novelty wears off and the person inside comes through. You think about all the crapped-out marriages that got started because he saw her ass in a dimly lit bar and she thought he danced real good, then they woke up one morning and realized you don't live your life in a bar. It happens a thousand times a day but, dammit, I never thought it would happen to you. And when it did, well . . ." He looked away, trying to find the right words, then gave up. "Like I said, there was nothing to forgive, and I didn't hate you. I just saw a part of you that I hadn't seen before, and I didn't like it. All of a sudden, where I once saw healthy ambition and self-assurance"—he looked directly into her eyes, not wanting to cop out on the hard part—"I saw thoughtless grasping."

Rebecca closed her mouth as soon as she discovered her jaw hanging open. "Goodness, all of that. And because you thought I liked the way he danced?"

Zuckerman knew she understood perfectly well. "A more elevated version of that. You saw a trophy with power and a public presence. I always liked your ambition, Becky; it's not that different from my own. But there are limits to what you ought to do to feed it."

Her eyes hardened. "Now you're calling me a whore."

Zuckerman didn't take her perception of an insult seriously. "Of course not. Or, maybe so, in the sense that we're all whores to some degree, the only open issue being price. But whore or not, you did start sleeping with a married man. What should I have thought about that?"

Why play games when he was entitled to an explanation? "I didn't know that. I mean, he told me they were separated, that a divorce proceeding was in full swing. Only a matter of time, and his making sure she didn't take everything he had."

"And you believed him?" He blurted it out without thinking and instantly regretted it. "No, wait. I'm sorry. No reason you shouldn't have, I guess."

He grew quiet, and Rebecca was grateful for the interlude. She didn't see any need to tell him all the details, how Perrein had taken her to "out of the way" little spots, special romantic places where he wouldn't be bothered in public, not wanting to "share her with the world." Two days after he stopped calling, his Taiwanese import license in hand, she saw him on the evening news, him and his charming socialite wife, who also turned out to be the human resources director of Tera-Tech, smiling and dancing at a black tie New York charity function, looking as happy as two rich little clams. She checked with the clerk of the court to get hold of the divorce filings but, of course, there weren't any. And then she understood the why of all those little romantic spots, those quaint little *out of the way* places: his wife had no idea, and still didn't. Rebecca had actually phoned her up once. Mrs. Perrein recognized her name—"Oh, you're the attorney who helped us get that import license. Excellent work, Ms. Verona!"—and Rebecca decided to just let it go, to just write it off to a learning experience.

"You just should have given it a little thought." Zuckerman's voice jarred her out of the self-flagellant reverie.

"What you're really saying is I should have thought about you."

Zuckerman didn't rise to the bait. "No, you should have thought about *you*. About what it said, that you were willing to turn your back on a good thing and jump into the arms of a conniving sleazeball—"

"I didn't know he was a conniving sleazeball!"

"Bullshit!" The outburst was involuntary, and Zuckerman looked around quickly to see if he'd disturbed any of the other customers. As if somebody uttering a profanity in an L.A. restaurant could turn any heads. "You knew and you didn't care," he said angrily, but with his voice subdued. "Maybe you thought you'd be the superwoman to finally turn him around."

"Maybe I could have." It was a dumb remark, a kind of last refuge for the dialectically unarmed.

"But you didn't even know the guy, for chrissake! Why take on the challenge if it might turn out you despised him?" It sounded to her like more than simply a rhetorical question, like he wanted to know the answer, and had wanted to for a long time prior to this conversation. "Doesn't love enter into the picture at all here? Or at least some affection, some *connection*?"

Zuckerman's sincerity, and the hint at an ache long suppressed, sobered Rebecca into not wanting to blurt out any more ill-considered remarks. She sat silent for a few moments, and he let her have the time. "I think it hurts more," she said finally, very quietly, "that you're disappointed in me than because we're not, you know, like that anymore. Together, I mean."

Zuckerman nodded, his anger apparently spent. "It was hard staying away. But I didn't want to spend the rest of my life worrying about the next time you decided to ignore your good sense."

"So if you're not mad at me, why are you busting my chops so hard about this case? You really expect me to believe that Perrein has nothing to do with it?"

"He has everything to do with it, but not because of you. Unlike you, I remember why I decided to practice law—"

"And I don't?"

"Doesn't seem like it. All this playing fast and loose with the rules, what's the point of that?"

Rebecca felt cheated: she thought they'd reached some kind of a diplomatic understanding to go easy on each other, but here he was on the attack again. "The point is to represent my client."

"And where does justice come into play?"

Rebecca fluttered her eyelids and looked up at the ceiling. "Jeez, you were always such a damned romantic about the law."

"Weren't you, when you started?"

"Weren't we all?" She tilted her head back down and looked across the table. "Don't you feel like a bit of an idiot prosecuting a guy who's been fighting to make real privacy possible?"

Zuckerman also seemed relieved to hop onto a more comfortable and clearly defined set of tracks. "You didn't let Petorsky finish telling the court the other side of the story so all you know is what your client told you."

"So you tell me instead."

"Child pornographers," Zuckerman answered. "Using encryption to transmit pictures over the Internet." The look on her face told him she was hearing this for the first time, and hadn't contemplated the issue from any point of view besides Perrein's before. "Drug kingpins using portable voice-encoding devices, making it impossible for federal agents to figure out what they're doing. Militia groups, foreign terrorists, embezzlers . . ." Without realizing it, Rebecca had leaned forward, focusing on Zuckerman as he continued. ". . . kidnappers. It's going to get harder to save lives, and it could become damned near impossible to gather enough evidence to make a criminal case stick even if the suspects are caught."

Rebecca was lost in his words: this wasn't exactly how Perrein had put it. But she was still Perrein's lawyer. "I understand all of that, but doesn't it bother you a little to know the government can poke its nose into any private business it wants to?"

"But they can do it right now anyway! Why aren't you bothered by phone taps and hidden videocameras and undercover agents infiltrating terrorist organizations?"

"Who say I'm not?" she replied.

"Becky," Zuckerman said, not smiling back at her lighthearted ribbing. "I'm not afraid of my government."

"Of course not; you *are* the government."

"I'm just an employee."

"They're *all* just employees! Do you really believe," Rebecca asked, going along with his serious tone, "that the CIA and the defense intelligence community aren't going after Perrein because of all the trouble he's caused with his crypto bandwagon?"

"I'd be a schmuck if I didn't believe that." He took a sip of wine, waiting for that to sink in, pleased at the surprised look on her face. "These people are human, they get pissed off, there may even be some glee in this prosecution, but I'll tell you one thing, Becky, and don't bother to argue with me on it." He set the glass down. "They really and truly believe that Perrein is behind those devices falling into foreign hands. We can argue all day, did he strike a proud blow for free enterprise or a low blow against his country, but he's guilty. And we're going after him."

"You don't have enough to convict him."

"The jury will make that decision."

"And you're comfortable with that?"

"Why shouldn't I be? We're using lawful means and due process to go after him legally."

"Gee, how nice," Rebecca said sarcastically. "As opposed to what?"

"As opposed to taking him out and shooting him."

Rebecca let loose a laugh, then cut it off because Zuckerman wasn't laughing along with her. "Christ, you can be such an asshole." Rebecca made sure his reaction to that was to smile before she went on. "What about this glee they have in pummeling Perrein?"

"Well, Becky, I imagine it's the same kind of glee you experience when you get a client acquitted and you know for damned sure he's guilty."

"Never happens." She smiled as Zuckerman snickered.

Spyro, having waited patiently for some levity to make itself evident at this heretofore morose table, approached quickly before it could evaporate. "Time to eat, my friends! What, you don't like the *retsina*?" He pointed to their nearly empty glasses, disappointed that they weren't on their third or fourth after all this time. "Katerina!" he yelled, turning around and sticking out the thumb and little finger of his right hand and making a waggling motion.

He pulled out a little pad, licked the end of a pencil stub and held it above the paper. "What's gonna be? Maybe you like start with some *feta*, ah? Maybe sprinkle a little—"

"Spyro," Zuckerman interrupted gently but with authority. "I got an idea."

Spyro's eyes lit up. "Ah, good! Whatever you want, we fix up right—"

Zuckerman shook his head. "Listen. You got two hungry people, we never ate anything here we didn't like. . . ."

Spyro pushed his head forward and lifted his shoulders. *So . . . ?*

Zuckerman folded his menu and handed it to Spyro. "Fix us up something special. Whatever you think."

Spyro looked at Rebecca, who promptly folded up her own menu and handed it to him. His whole face seemed suddenly to become one giant smile, and he spread his arms out wide, yelled *"Hupa!"* then danced backward away from them, fingers snapping at the ends of his outstretched arms, remarkably light and nimble for a man his size.

Rebecca, anxious to resume the conversation, spoke as soon as Spyro was safely back in the kitchen. "So are you claiming some kind of moral high ground here?"

"I do have the moral high ground," Zuckerman answered. "You already know that. Your job is to get your client off, even if he's guilty. My job is to see that justice is done, even if it wrecks my case."

"I have a legal obligation to represent my clients to the very best of my ability, and to exploit every possible avenue in doing so." It came out more like a sound bite than she had intended.

"Nice speech yourself. But you forget that it was every *legal* avenue."

"That's obvious."

"Is it?"

Rebecca stiffened. "You got a problem with how I'm defending Tera-Tech?"

"Don't know yet." He shrugged. "Possibly." And shrugged again. "Probably."

"Why?"

He fidgeted awkwardly for a few seconds, then dove in. "I don't think you liked what Terescu was coming up with in his analysis. I think you twisted his words and confused him during preparation for his testimony."

Rebecca felt a tremor start to play itself along her spine. "And why would you believe that?"

"Because every time I ask him a question, he starts off authoritative and confident." He was looking directly at her now, almost accusingly. "But when I try to dig underneath his answers, he comes up lame."

Rebecca sat perfectly still. "So the guy's not very articulate."

"Yeah." Zuckerman nodded, as though he were giving this some serious thought. "He gives fifty public lectures a year to standing-room-only audiences and now he's tongue-tied." He shook his head. "The reason is that he's spouting off conclusions he doesn't believe, because they're not his conclusions, *you* put them in his mouth. He has no analytical backup so he can't defend them under cross."

"And you think I was able to do that to a guy smart enough to be considered for the Nobel prize."

An indecipherable look came over Zuckerman. "Well, that was the challenge, wasn't it." He could see her stiffen, but she wasn't going to otherwise react. "A stubborn, older male authority figure whom none could even hope to deflect from his beliefs. You saw that, must've been like a fat, juicy worm to a trout."

Barely breathing now, Rebecca said, "I don't think I like the way this conversation is going."

"It was your idea. And I'm warning you in advance, professional courtesy, I'm going to discredit the hell out of this witness, and if that means you get jammed up while I nail his ass to a wall . . ."

It's my ass, too, she read into the unexpected threat. Rebecca felt a tightening in her chest that made it difficult to speak. She stayed quiet to let her breathing slow, and Zuckerman dropped back against his chair, glaring at her.

"And by the way, Counselor," he added, "there *is* no Nobel prize for engineering."

Rebecca kept her trembling hands under the table. "When'd you get to be so hard, David?"

"What are you talking about?" he practically snarled.

But Rebecca wouldn't let herself be drawn into the hostility he seemed to be trying to create. "I've kicked myself in the butt every day for two years over what happened with Perrein. It was embarrassing and painful." She heard the pleading in her voice but was powerless to do anything about it. "Don't I get to screw up once in a while and learn from it? Isn't that what being human is all about?"

"Why are you defending him?"

"He has the right to be defended!" Just exactly how long did he expect her to stay apologetic, on the defensive? "You're gonna mouth off about the glory of the law, you ought to remember that!"

Zuckerman closed his eyes and shook his head, his pursed lips telling her, *You're not getting it.* "I'm asking why *you're* defending him."

"He asked for me specifically."

"Why do you suppose he did that?"

"I don't know."

"Sure you do."

Of course I do: it was because you were the prosecutor.

But enough of this, already. "Hey, I got a good idea: why don't you climb down off your high fucking horse and just tell me."

He pointedly ignored her anger, which only made her feel childish and even angrier. "Because he knows that you'll fight like hell for him if you believe he didn't do it. Because he knows I'm the prosecutor." He tapped his forefinger on the tablecloth. "Because everybody knows you're pissed off at him for the way he used you, so if you're still willing to take his side, that must mean he's innocent!"

"Wait a minute, wait a minute!" Her eyes grew wide. "What do you mean, the way he used me? What the hell is *that* all about?"

Zuckerman sniffed contemptuously and looked around, as if to say, *Is anybody else hearing this nonsense?* "For chrissake, Becky, just how stupid do you think our little fraternity is? You really think the Department of Justice doesn't know how Tera-Tech Integrated got its Taiwanese import license?"

Rebecca could only stare at him, horrified, her mouth hanging open and no smart comeback immediately available or even possible. He returned the stare, a hint of smug victory in his expression, which faded rapidly as he sensed her distress, and then Rebecca closed her eyes slowly, put her arms on the table and dropped her head onto them. "Oh, God . . ."

Zuckerman, taken aback by her wilting reaction and lack of return fire, mumbled, "Sorry," and waited for her to recover. When she'd lifted her head back up and leaned against the chair, looking everywhere but at him, he said gently, "I've got to ask you something, Beck. Been bothering me for a long time."

Rebecca rolled her head around to face him, all the fight gone as she listened.

"When Perrein asked you to help him get the license, what did you think?"

"I don't understand. . . ."

"In that moment." Zuckerman's voice was intense now, probing, the question clearly important to him. "Did you think it was a remarkable coincidence? Or did you realize what his game had been all along? It couldn't have been that, I'm guessing, because you went along and helped him, and you wouldn't have if you'd known in advance what he was up to. So you must have thought it was all a coincidence. Is that it?"

Rebecca could tell from his eagerness and the rush of words that this really wasn't an idle question he'd suddenly thought of. How long had he been stewing over it? When did he find out? Had he always known?

What the hell difference did it make? "We were on his boat. A Sunday. Just the two of us, which was unusual, because he was normally surrounded by a handful of adoring sycophants, the kind who wouldn't rat him out to his wife." Her voice was flat, neutral; she might have been reading aloud from the phone book. It was better than trying to imbue her voice with emotion when half a dozen different feelings were tugging at her simultaneously.

"He gets this cellular call, somebody from overseas, and he's all upset. I tried to ask him about it, but he said no, didn't want business to intrude on a nice day. I insisted, and he finally told me that they had run into some major roadblocks getting permission from the Taiwanese to bring computer parts into the country. His people had given it one last try, and failed. They'd already geared up production in anticipation of getting the license, hundreds of millions were at risk . . ."

Zuckerman had been listening intently, and he'd spent too many months thinking about it not to know where it was going. "At which point, you give him the good news, the great surprise, that the Taiwanese owed you a big one, on account of you winning their patent case." She answered with a nod. "And you called in that favor on his behalf."

She nodded again. "Should have been worth a seven-figure fee," she said, sighing.

"When did you find out that Perrein had known about your connection all along?"

She wrapped her arms around herself and seemed to shrink back into her chair. "As soon as the deal was signed, he stopped calling. Wouldn't take my calls, either. One day I managed to get hold of one of his assistants. I tell him my name, and he says, 'Oh, of course. Becky.' " *I perked up at that; even the staff knew who I was. Maybe Jim had just been busy, or out of the country.* " 'You're the lawyer Jim hired to help with the Taiwanese deal.' "

"But he hadn't hired you, had he?"

"No."

"Did he pay for the service anyway? Give you a transaction fee of any kind?"

"You know he didn't."

"I wasn't sure. So I ask you again: why are you defending him?"

"Because he didn't do anything wrong."

"How do you know that?"

"He told me."

"He told you?" Zuckerman's carefully planned interrogation promptly went off the tracks.

"And I believe him."

He stared at her, incredulous. "After what he did to you, you believe him?"

"That's *why* I believe him." Finally, an opportunity to try to go back on the offensive. "As much of a scumbucket as he is, can you imagine what it must have taken for him to come to me and ask for my help?" *Of course, that was all before I knew you were on the case. By then it was too late.*

"But it's such transparent bullshit!" Zuckerman said, the anger returning. "Becky, the man is guilty as hell. We've got evidence up the wazoo . . ."

"Yeah, go on . . . ?"

He caught himself and replied awkwardly, "It's not all fully developed yet."

Rebecca's radar lit up. "Are you holding out on us, David? You got stuff we should know about?" Blips all over the screen as Zuckerman didn't answer. "Don't you give me shit about playing fast and loose with the rules if you're withholding relevant information!"

"Like I said, it's not fully developed, and it's nothing we have to show to you yet. But I'm telling you, Tera-Tech made those chips and Perrein sold them to the Chinese."

"I don't think so."

"Because Perrein told you so."

"Something like that."

"Yeah, well," he said, sitting back and flicking some imaginary lint off his jacket, "you're a helluva judge of human character."

"You know, for somebody who used to admire me, you sure don't give me a lot of credit."

"Credit for what? Thinking with your crotch?"

Even though the abrupt shifts in topic and line of thought were impossible to clearly decipher, even if it wasn't clear moment to moment whether they were talking about the case or themselves, Rebecca was acutely aware of the emotional tone of this conversation. The individual sentences were unimportant; they were just heavily encrypted emotions, scrambled by some complex code into words bearing only a fleeting resemblance to the feelings boiling beneath them. And neither of them possessed the correct key to decode all the fury, embarrassment and regret.

Zuckerman sat quietly. *Did he regret his last remark?* she wondered. Was he struggling to find a way to apologize? Or was he simply hanging back while it sank in?

Rebecca, suddenly dizzy and short of breath, watched as faces floated up at her from her wineglass, morphing from one into the other until their features coagulated into a single presence her mind couldn't resolve. Hovering above was David, not his body but the naked and confused jumble of his rage and crushing sense of loss.

Then she saw that the presence was the Pumpkin King and soon he, too, was gone, and she could see only herself, sailing on a flat white sea, back arched to its limit, head looking almost backward as she raised one leg into the air and held her hands gracefully above her. She glided backward, holding that position, slight shifts in her center of gravity resulting in a curving path toward the far corner of the rink.

As she turned, the Pumpkin King came into view, sitting in the second row of the empty arena, leaning over the back of the seat in front of him and watching her intently. She worked each leg over the other to increase her backward velocity. As the opposite end of the rink approached, she leaned into the turn and whipped herself around the end zone, coming out onto the straightaway with plenty of speed. Still she dug her skates in, powering her legs into the ice and accelerating rapidly, almost dangerously, except that what used to be fear was now replaced with exhilaration.

At the halfway point of the rink, she suddenly turned around so she was skating forward, and she knew that Charles, along with anybody else who might be watching, must have drawn in his breath and held it, because there was only one jump in all of skating that started facing forward.

She bent into a final shove for one last burst of speed, then lifted her right foot off the ice and held her hands in front of her, prayerlike, standing upright and motionless, waiting for her spot to come into view.

With one last dip of her head and shoulders, she gritted her teeth, swung her arms way back and then poured every available drop of stored energy down into her thigh and calf and sprang into the air off her left outside edge. The sideways pressure threw her body violently to the left, and as she rose up off the ice, the angular momentum translated into a pure spinning motion that turned her into a tornado. . . .

"You've become a crude and supercilious bastard, David," she said to Zuckerman matter-of-factly without looking up from the wineglass, "but I'm not falling for it. At least I learned something from the whole sorry mess: once bitten, twice shy, right? What have *you* done other than feel sorry for yourself and nurse a grudge toward me?"

"I told you, I don't hold any—"

"Oh, come off it!" she spat, eyes flashing as she looked up and paralyzed him with her intensity. "Your whole manner drips with it! You think I'm buying this hyper-analytical, above-it-all crap you're feeding me here?"

She felt it, the train. "You hate Perrein because of me, you think I'm compromising my ethics because I want him back, you're already convinced he's guilty and you're gong to 'nail his ass to a wall' for cheap, petty revenge!"

Zuckerman could only stare at her, totally unprepared for her counterattack. This wasn't the way it was supposed to have gone. *Clear the air,* she'd said. But in preparation for what? Obviously something different than he had originally suspected. And had hoped for.

"What did you think, I was gonna sit here and choke down this morality play you've been rehearsing for two years?" She could feel the momentum building even as the brakes groaned and began to fail from the effort of holding the willful locomotive back, steam from the boiler hissing through cracks as the pressure rose to the bursting point.

"I told you—"

"What you told me and what I heard are two different things, bucko. You thought I'd sit back and wallow in my guilt and remorse while you worked your hurt out on me, well, you can fucking well forget it."

"Rebecca—"

She didn't hear him, felt it coming, the whole roiling boiler full of it, powering its way forward from the back of her throat, knowing it would be a lance through his heart, a blow to the chest so great he wouldn't be able to speak. The best part of her knew that such cruelty was not only vicious but unnecessary, just another notch on her garter belt, but the vengeful litigator in her was determined to shoot it out before she could stop it, and no apology could ever bring it back.

She held his eyes with her own. "Go ahead and tell me you never wondered if he was better in bed than you were!"

It was all there in his guileless, gentle brown eyes. She knew the moment would play itself out on an endless loop of film in her mind for the rest of her life, a low point in her existence, maybe the lowest of all.

And now that the boiler had blown all its steam, it grew empty and cold, its sides already collapsing in on their hollow center. Rebecca watched from a distant cliff, wondering what light breeze it would take to push her over the edge to speak what she yearned to say to him.

David, if you only knew. Better than you? Inconceivable. I never even climaxed with him, not once, and with you it was so easy and so often. With him it was a performance, a circus act demanding my applause at the end. Athletic, yes, and skillful, in the way that all world-class, pussy-chasing misogynists pick up tricks along the way, but soulless and mechanical. I blamed myself. I assumed that my notions of love and caring were anachronistic and unrealistically romantic, the stuff of dime novels and old movies, and that his were so sophisticated, the way the world-weary rich and famous did it, as Olympic events rather than the meeting of minds, and maybe I would catch on in time.

Why did I do it, fall victim to a predator, with such callous disregard for you? For us. . . ?

They'd started out as friends, Rebecca and Zuckerman, mutually respectful adversaries perfectly comfortable beating the crap out of each other in court all day, then getting together for dinner the same evening and laughing about it. They gravitated naturally toward each other, spending time together not as the result of overt planning but because no such formality was necessary. They fell inexorably into a relaxed and satisfying affinity, proceeding to each successive level effortlessly, without the awkward, obligatory, spoken pronouncements so prized by ordinary people in an ordinary world. Even their sexual relationship had an aura of inevitable default about it, two close friends sleeping together because each was too busy to seek the more usual kind of relationship requiring formal professions of never-ending love and traditional covenants.

So when James Perrein came along, it didn't really occur to Rebecca that her behavior constituted betrayal. Betrayal of what: two friends behaving as lovers out of mutual convenience? Because of the very seamlessness of her relationship with Zuckerman, the lack of official declarations or promises, Rebecca had somehow failed to recognize that she had inadvertently fallen hopelessly and profoundly in love with him.

Not until it was too late. Which was the point at which she realized that he had felt the same way about her, except that he was wiser and more perceptive and had known it all along. So his pain had been instantaneous and searing, paralytic in its severity. He hadn't had the opportunity to consider things, to come to a slowly dawning epiphany over an interval of time that might have eased his suffering. Instead, the safe had simply fallen on his head, and the breathtaking shock of it had snapped shut pieces of himself it had taken months for her to expose in the first place.

A dish clattered noisily somewhere in the kitchen.

But enough of that; there was business at hand. The melded faces in the wineglass grinned at her maliciously, daring her, and the lawyer in Rebecca was once again a runaway train helpless against the wrenching mindlessness of gravity.

"And one last thing: You'd better not let your balls get in the way of your conduct in court. One shred of evidence you're putting the screws to my client to get your personal rocks off, I'll nail *your* ass to a wall!"

She reached down for her purse, trying not to look at the shattered remnant of a man sitting opposite her. "See you in court, Counselor," she said as she rose, turned, and began walking away before he could see the tears forming in her eyes.

Her brisk steps faltered, threatening to ruin the drama of her exit. She stopped, tried to discreetly wipe her eyes, then turned and walked back toward the table. From the corner of her eye she spotted Spyro, grinning with delight and looking from one to the other of the two huge platters he was hoisting proudly as he strode from the kitchen. When he saw her standing, purse in hand, the smile faded and was replaced with a questioning incomprehension.

Rebecca ignored him and looked at Zuckerman, and it was easy to see the steel walls that had slammed shut behind his eyes, evolution's defensive tricks coming on-line to save him.

"You need to tell me who your informant is," she said, grabbing the back of the chair to steady her hand. "You don't, I'll press charges against you in the morning."

Zuckerman became distracted, not having expected her to come at him once again, barely trusting his voice. "I don't know who it is."

"Bullshit."

Spyro had stopped halfway across the room, some sixth sense unique to restaurateurs and bomb disarmers warning him that coming any closer was probably inadvisable.

"I'll swear to it in an affidavit." Zuckerman was all business now. "Just a voice on the phone, electronically disguised." He was back in control of himself, pushing all else aside before his obligations as a professional. "And I don't have to disclose anything to anybody, because he's not giving us any hard information or evidence, just suggestions for where to take the cross-examination. All I know, it could be from some completely uninvolved third party sitting in the audience who happens to be very smart."

"You don't believe that."

"Prove it." He waited for a response but got none. "It's plausible enough, so there's not a goddamned thing you can do about it, *Counselor*."

"Why didn't you tell me that the first time I asked you, instead of letting me believe you knew his identity?"

Zuckerman took an unhurried sip of his wine. "Didn't like your attitude."

Rebecca took a deep breath, and tried to sound dispassionately businesslike. "It would seem to me that it's in our mutual best interests not to file formal charges against each other. You for failing to disclose a source of evidence, me for, uh . . ."

"Manipulating a witness." He nodded his agreement without waiting for her to argue with his terminology. "But I *am* going after Terescu. No holds barred."

"I assumed you would."

"Good. Then we understand each other."

Rebecca's stomach felt like lead. The crippling ache beneath Zuckerman's words was as palpable as the chair she was holding onto. There was no way she could leave it like this, Zuckerman struggling gamely to look composed and professional, his hands wrapped around his glass so as not to betray their trembling. Simple human decency demanded that she stay and make it right.

She turned and left without another word or a backward glance.

Chapter 22

Thursday, November 12

She'd lain awake the first half of the night because of what she had done to David Zuckerman, and the second half because of what she needed to do to Arno Steinholz and Justin Ehrenright.

With Zuckerman, it wasn't just about her vicious behavior at dinner, it was about a whole raft of behaviors going back two years. Dinner was just the capper, like going back to toss a live grenade at a car you'd just broadsided on the freeway, but having no idea why.

Every avenue she explored as she twisted around in bed made the whole thing only more inexplicable. A good part of the reason she had tried to become friends with Zuckerman again was that she needed to be reassured that he was all right, that he was getting on with his life. Even when she knew he was seeing other women, even when it looked serious and the ache she felt made her cry herself to sleep at night, some part of her was happy, because it reduced the awful feelings of guilt that had haunted her relentlessly following the realization that she'd broken his heart.

And then she had made a small stab in his direction, seduced him to an old haunt, bravely dived into the conversational forbidden zone and softened him up, only to once again smash through the already enfeebled defenses he was trying desperately to maintain, crushing his soul in her hand.

Torturing herself with those thoughts was only good for a few hours, until she had to turn to the issue of asking her two colleagues and friends whether one or both of them was selling her out. So she sat in her office, third cup of coffee in hand, until a secretary buzzed to tell her they were in the conference room. Then she rose on shaky legs and walked down the hall.

"Yo," Ehrenright said, barely looking up from notes he was making for Rebecca's eventual redirect of Terescu. "Hope you either plan on sharing that coffee or have more on the way."

"Jeez, you look like shit," Steinholz said. "You okay?"

At that, Ehrenright did look up, confirming the diagnosis. Rebecca closed the door behind her, and the two associates exchanged glances at the complete lack of humor in the boss's normally amiable face. They both put down their pens as she took a seat and studiously avoided their eyes.

"What the hell, Becky," Ehrenright pushed. "Our client go and kill somebody?"

"Had a conversation with Zuckerman last—yesterday," Rebecca said, adding, "and on into the evening," because it had already slipped out anyway. "Someone on our side is leaking information to the prosecution." She looked at them for the first time since she'd arrived.

"He admitted it?" Steinholz asked.

Rebecca shrugged. "I didn't leave him much choice."

"Well, that's something," he said. "I'm not sure he was required to—"

"And you think it might be one of us," Ehrenright said, as though Steinholz hadn't been speaking. Steinholz halted in midsentence, incomprehension registering on his face, only to be replaced by something that looked like shock.

"Or both of us," Ehrenright added.

Rebecca didn't answer, but carefully and succinctly repeated the parts of their post-court conversation the day before dealing with the specifics of the information Zuckerman had that could only have come from someone inside. "So unless you think this place is bugged, we've got a mole, and it isn't me."

Steinholz sank back in his seat, face growing pale, and Rebecca felt her stomach begin a slow roll, which quickly turned to out-and-out vertigo as Ehrenright looked down at the table and began tapping his fingers on the tabletop.

She tried not to move, having no idea what movement might have been appropriate under the circumstances. She heard Ehrenright inhale.

"This is the part where I'm supposed to get all indignant," he began carefully, "tell you I'm insulted you'd even suspect me of such a thing."

He picked his head up, and looked into her eyes. "But I won't. You got a perfect right to ask, and I don't blame you a bit. But I'm telling you—" He slapped a hand on the table. "There's no way in hell I'd ever do something like that. And certainly not to you."

Jolted out of his temporary insensibility, Steinholz added, "Same here. Jeez, Becky, me and Justin, we've hitched our wagon to your star. Why the hell would we want to bollix up your case? We want to win it bad as you do."

She looked from Steinholz's confused and uncertain expression to Ehrenright's confident and forthright gaze, and knew beyond certainty that they were being truthful. Waves of relief began to dissolve the anxiety and depression that had haunted her since the night before. She exhaled loudly and closed her eyes, slumping in her seat.

"On second thought," Ehrenright said, "you're a flaming shithead."

"Goes double for me," Steinholz threw in.

"Maybe," Rebecca responded, taking a deep sip of her coffee, then passing it along to Ehrenright. "But it still leaves us with a spy in our midst. Zuckerman swore to me he doesn't know who it is."

"You believe him?" Ehrenright asked as he brought the cup to his lips.

"I think so. The prosecutor's office has been calling him Deep Silicon."

Ehrenright laughed just as he was starting to drink and almost coughed up the still steaming coffee. "Deep Silicon?"

He offered the cup to Steinholz, who waved it off, saying, "Maybe Perrein's been speaking to someone inside Tera-Tech, and that someone has been passing the information on."

"Why?" Ehrenright asked as he handed the cup back to Rebecca.

"How the hell should I know? Just listing possibilities."

It made sense to Rebecca, but only because no other alternatives did. "I'll ask our client if he's been yakking things up at the company."

"Ask his lawyer, too," Steinholz said. "And Wysocki."

Rebecca laughed, for the first time that day. "Sure, you bet. 'Hey Allen, you been opening up your yap and ruining my case?' Bet he'll crumble and 'fess up right on the spot." *If we can find him. When the going gets tough, managing partners get gone . . .*

"Speaking of 'fessing up," Ehrenright said, "what else happened with Zuckerman last night? I mean, yesterday. I mean, that you care to tell us about."

"You're a real comedian, Justin." She took a sip of coffee. As little as she wanted to start thinking about it again—*What was he doing this very minute?*—she at least owed them a précis of the business portion.

What *did* happen? "On the Richter scale of unpleasantness, it was about an eight point five."

"Did you hit him?" Ehrenright asked eagerly.

Would've been better if I had, and nothing else. "I'm gonna pop *you* one in a second. He said that I had manipulated our expert witness and programmed him against his will, but only after our client had manipulated me against mine."

"All true," Steinholz observed. "And you responded . . . ?"

"Basically, I told him that he was defending an idiotic law, that he wasn't in control of his own case because somebody else was pulling the strings, that he was withholding evidence and I might file against him for sanctions, that he's a total jerkoff because he really believes our client is guilty, and that I'd nail his ass to a wall if I could prove that his case against Perrein was just a thinly disguised personal vendetta."

Ehrenright stared at her, open-mouthed, then turned to the equally aghast Steinholz and said, nodding, "This is good. This is a good thing."

"Oh, yeah," Steinholz responded. "Rubbing salt in the bull's eyes." He pursed his lips. "I like it."

Rebecca shrugged, then sighed. "Picking me as lead counsel was about the dumbest damned thing Jim Perrein ever did in his life." The only thing that kept her spirits from collapsing completely was the thought that any plans Perrein might have had about Zuckerman going easy on an old flame were backfiring in a major way.

"When you're through feeling sorry for yourself," Ehrenright said, "we got a bigger problem."

"I'm not through feeling sorry for myself yet."

"Then get over it and listen up."

"Terescu had been working on component density in his lab," Steinholz explained. "And it's likely that's one of the secrets his grad student took with him when he went to work for Perrein." Rebecca looked up as he finished, already knowing what he was going to say. "Is it conceivable that the exported chips really were built at Tera-Tech?"

It was not a new thought to her, not by a long shot, but she wasn't ready to give in to it. "The great Radovan Terescu hadn't been able to do anything like it in his lab," she argued.

"But he was only one man with some green students," Steinholz countered easily. "Tera-Tech had dozens of the best scientists in the world, all working as a team. Well funded and highly motivated."

She thought about that for a long time, then said, "I don't want to talk about this anymore." She gave both of them piercing looks.

"Talk about what?" Ehrenright asked.

Friday, November 13

As soon as Terescu was seated in the witness box and reminded that he was still under oath, Zuckerman, despite the one-day delay in the resumption of the trial, wasted no time on idle conversation or recaps of where they had left off two days ago. "Professor, did you participate in defense counsel's case strategy?"

Terescu barely had time to compose himself in his seat, and wasn't quite prepared for an immediate dive into substantive matters. "I don't understand."

"Were you actively involved in discussions of how to get the defendant acquitted?"

"No. As I told you yesterday, I performed objective scientific analyses."

"Yes, you did tell me that." Zuckerman waited for a moment until the hum and buzz of people settling in around the courtroom had come to a halt. "Professor, every time I asked you about the chip, you made certain to keep reminding the jury that your analysis was based not on what you believe about the chip, but on what you would believe *if* the test results we reported to you were true."

Terescu nodded in agreement. "Because I have no direct knowledge of the chip. I've not examined it myself."

"I understand. And yet you don't have any direct knowledge of Tera-Tech's capabilities either, since you never visited the company, isn't that right?"

"That is true. . . ."

"So tell me: how come you don't feel it necessary to keep reminding the court of *that* fact every time you express an opinion about their lack of capability?"

Terescu swallowed, but was smart enough not to try to fabricate an answer on the spot. He seemed to Rebecca to be growing fearful of Zuckerman and probably thought it better to just plead ignorance. "I don't know. I haven't given it much thought."

"Is it because your job is to do your best to try to get the defendant acquitted?"

"No, I told you: my analysis was scientific and objective!"

"Ah, yes, you did say that. And you stated categorically, under Ms. Verona's direct examination, that you don't believe that Tera-Tech made the chips."

"Correct."

"Because they don't have the capability, right?"

"Exactly."

"But you don't know that for sure, do you."

Terescu rocked his head back and forth, a pained expression on his face, like he was being forced to say something he didn't really believe. "Not for dead certain, no."

"Because your knowledge of their capabilities isn't direct."

"Yes."

"Now I wonder how you can prove a negative. I mean, I can understand why you might believe that it's possible that others might have made the chip, but how on earth can you go so far as to tell us, definitively, that Tera-Tech didn't?"

"Well, I'm not sure I agree with you that I stated it *definitively*. As you said, one can't be absolutely certain."

"Then why express that opinion?"

"It seems reasonable given the information supplied to me by the company."

"But you didn't explain it to the jury as a *reasonable* assumption. You simply said, they didn't do it."

"Perhaps I did say something roughly along those lines," Terescu said, offhandedly, as though it was of minor significance.

But Zuckerman obviously didn't think so. "Shall I have the transcript read back?"

Terescu looked away and cleared his throat. "That won't be necessary."

Zuckerman looked over at the jury to make sure they were following the foundation he was building for claiming that this witness sympathized with the defense. "Professor, another hypothetical. And I'm looking for a reasonable opinion here, not certainty, okay?"

"All right."

"Suppose I said to you that a super-high-speed encryption chip with over two hundred million transistors on it does exist."

Terescu lifted a hand and let it drop back onto his lap, then rocked his head back and forth again, conveying his skepticism at such a premise, but eventually said, "All right, suppose."

"And since it exists, somebody somewhere made it, agreed?"

"Yes." Terescu leaned forward and pointed a finger at Zucker-man. "Hypothetically, of course," he said amiably, smiling.

"Of course." Zuckerman spread his hands and returned the smile, playing the good sport. Terescu sat back and relaxed, but Rebecca straightened up and went to DefCon 4 as the smile left the prosecutor's face and he stepped to the side of the podium, away from his notes. With one more quick look at the jury—*Pay attention, folks: this is where it gets good*—he turned his full attention to the witness.

"Now I tell you also, sir, *hypothetically,* that there exists a company that is in the forefront of high component density, in the forefront of high-speed digital signal processors and in the forefront of very advanced encryption technology. I tell you this company has hired some of the best researchers in the world in these fields." Zuckerman's voice was slowly increasing in volume, pitch and speed as he went on. "I tell you that the president of this company has fought long and hard against export restrictions on chips that marry up exactly these three technologies. I tell you that the en-cryption methodology in the recovered chip is precisely the same one as that developed by this company, and even the ink used in printing markings on it is the same ink this company uses on its own chips. I tell you all of this"—his voice finished its crescendo and peaked—"and then I ask you if it's possible, just a *possibility,* that this company made that chip, and you tell me *no?*" He banged his fist on the podium, nearly shouting. *"It isn't possible?"*

The courtroom reverberated with the echoes of Zuckerman's voice in the sudden silence that followed. The attentions of every-body present seemed to merge and then streak, laserlike, toward Terescu, slack-jawed and squirming in the witness box as he strug-gled to frame an answer to what had sounded like a purely rhetorical question.

Perrein grabbed Rebecca's arm. "What the hell is that sonof-abitch doing to us!" he whispered hoarsely.

Rebecca yanked her arm out of his grasp, then quickly turned her head to see if any of the jurors had noticed. Probably not, but Judge Goldin was giving her a stern look. She leaned in toward Per-rein and put her mouth near his ear. "Why don't you look a little more guilty and frantic, Jim. Tomorrow I'll bring in some rope and you can start weaving a noose in front of the jury, save us all a little time later, okay?"

"But Terescu's—"

"Shut up!" she hissed as forcefully as she dared.

"I—I don't believe they have the capability," Terescu was saying.

Zuckerman let the painful inadequacy of that answer sink in among the jurors. He knew that they were hanging on to his words, like playgoers on opening night, hoping that the lines to come would fulfill the dramatic promise that had been building. But Terescu, even though not a lawyer, was nevertheless smart enough to realize that, had he responded in the affirmative, all Zuckerman would have to do is prove that each of those hypothetical conditions was in fact true, and Terescu would effectively be admitting that Tera-Tech could have built the chip.

Zuckerman spoke softly, making the jurors strain to hear him. "Who does, Professor Terescu?"

"Who does?"

"Yes. Who has the wherewithal to have made this chip?"

Terescu spoke into the expectant hush that blanketed the room. "Well, nobody that I know of . . ."

Zuckerman threw his head back and looked at the ceiling. "Exactly," he breathed meaningfully, as though deep secrets had been revealed and it was only left for him to interpret and explain them.

He brought his gaze back down and slowly focused in on the witness. "Because the fact is, Dr. Terescu, you don't believe *anybody* out there has the capability, do you?" He didn't wait for an answer. "As far as you're concerned, *nobody* could have made it because *nobody* has the necessary technology. Isn't that right?" It sounded more like a dare than a question designed to elicit testimony.

Suddenly, the whole complex structure Zuckerman had been constructing for the past two days appeared before Rebecca's eyes, an entire cathedral supported not by the grace of a capricious deity but by stone buttresses and steel girders. She fast-forwarded through all of his cross-examination of Terescu and realized that Zuckerman hadn't been on a fishing expedition at all, hadn't asked a single, solitary extraneous question. What he had done was simply scramble the sequence so he had all the facts he wanted without the defense team or the witness being able to discern the outline of the edifice as it rose.

Sweat appeared on Terescu's upper lip, and his breathing speeded up, a direct reflection of Rebecca's own incipient panic. "I believe . . . I . . . that would seem to be the case, yes." He winced noticeably in anticipation of the inevitable counterattack.

Zuckerman took three quick steps toward the prosecution table, grabbed a flat plastic bag and thrust it high into the air, shouting, "But here it is, Professor!" He gave the bag a single shake, his voice thundering now. "Here's the chip that cannot exist! *Somebody* made it! And the only reason you testified before this jury that Tera-Tech couldn't have been responsible"—he brought his arm down and pointed at Terescu, the bag hanging below his hand—"is because you don't believe *anybody* could have been responsible, isn't that correct!"

"Objection!" Rebecca bounced to her feet, kicking her chair back forcefully as she rose. "Argumentative, compound, and he's badgering the witness!"

"Overruled," Goldin said, then turned to Zuckerman. "But calm down a little, Counselor."

Zuckerman clenched his jaw so tightly that a vein in his cheek became visible. "Professor," he said quietly, then paused and looked at Rebecca as he waited for her to resume her seat. Her face grew hot at the prospect of following the unspoken orders of this bully in front of the whole courtroom, but she had no choice and sat down.

Zuckerman stared at her for another moment, as though in rebuke for some childish indiscretion, then turned back to Terescu and said, very slowly, "Professor, your entire testimony on behalf of Tera-Tech is based on the fact that you don't believe this chip is real, isn't that right?"

Terescu was supposed to have tried to compose himself in the few seconds Rebecca had bought him, but his agitation hadn't abated in the slightest. "I, um, I never thought of it that way. I suppose . . . maybe . . ." He frowned and shook his head, looking downward. "I was confused. . . ."

Zuckerman spared him nothing. "Bottom-line this for us, Doctor." He squared his shoulders and clasped his hands behind his back. When he was certain that every eye in the courtroom was on him, he tilted his head back and announced, rather than asked, "If this chip is real, then all your testimony is completely irrelevant, isn't it."

Rebecca felt the oxygen *whoosh* out of her brain. Zuckerman could forget that whole diversionary list of hypotheticals he'd trotted out moments before and rely solely on the single premise he'd just stated. Rebecca thought it likely that she was witnessing the single most brilliant cross-examination in her memory. She might be able to rock the cars a little, but this train was planted firmly on the tracks. Was it better to just let it finish and be done with, or try to toss some mudballs at it and risk prolonging the devastation?

Steinholz, sitting next to her and stunned into near catatonia, now saw clearly how prescient Rebecca was when she told Terescu early on not to bring up the fact that he didn't know of anybody else who could have made the chip: that notion could negate his entire testimony. But Zuckerman had dragged it out of him anyway, and set things up so that if the prosecution could prove that the chip worked the way the government investigators said it did, then the testimony of the defense's only expert would be completely neutralized.

Terescu sat quietly, looking at the hands resting in his lap.

"Point is made, Mr. Zuckerman," Judge Goldin said, admiration evident underneath the gentle admonition. "Let's move on."

Zuckerman took his time, shuffling his notes and dragging out the moment. While it was possible the jury hadn't followed everything, they did know that something significant had occurred, and he would have ample opportunity to explain it to them in his closing.

"Professor," he said, "when you first presented your analysis to defense counsel, had you independently come to the conclusion that Tera-Tech couldn't have made the chip?"

"Well, it's difficult to recall. . . ."

"Take your time."

"I don't—"

"Let me put it this way: What did you come to the meeting with, an overall conclusion, or a list of the results of your analyses?"

"I believe it was a list of results." Terescu's voice was throaty and tentative, that of a blindfolded prisoner deathly fearful of taking even a small step as ordered, somehow knowing that, whether it was just five more or five hundred, eventually he would wind up in front of a firing squad.

"And what was the general gist of those results?"

"I'm not sure I follow."

Zuckerman clarified patiently and without sarcasm. He didn't want to appear to be browbeating the witness unnecessarily. "When you came to the meeting, did you generally feel that the defense wasn't going to like your results, or that they would be happy?"

"Objection," Rebecca said calmly. "Vague and calls for a legal conclusion."

"I'll rephrase. Did you think your results weighed in favor of implicating the defendant or exonerating him?"

"Objection!" Rebecca said again, louder this time. "Calls for a legal conclusion!"

"No it doesn't," Zuckerman countered, annoyed. "You don't have to be a lawyer to know whether a key piece of evidence is good news or bad for a defendant."

"I'll allow it," Goldin announced.

"I, uh, I believe there might have been one or two points that would be harmful to his case, uh, potentially, yes."

"And those might be . . . ?"

"I don't remember specifically."

"Let me see if I can refresh your memory." *May I assist you in getting this noose around your neck?* "There was the fact that the encryption method in the chip is the same as that invented by Tera-Tech, right?"

"That was one."

"Then there was the high speed of the chip and its enormous component density, which you knew to be a prime goal of the company."

"Yes, I believe so."

"And then there were all those scientists the company had hired into their advanced research lab."

"Yes."

"All those things pointing to a problem or two for the defendant."

"I thought so initially."

"What changed your mind?"

"Difficult to recall." As Rebecca had put it to him, *He can't hurt you if you don't remember, but remember that you forgot!*

"Was it further analysis on your part?" Zuckerman asked, unperturbed, still being helpful. "More tests on the chip, more research?"

"Mmm . . ."

Zuckerman smiled, telling the jury that he was on to Terescu's game but could play it just as well, so there was no need to get tough. "Professor, from the time you walked into that meeting with defense counsel, how much time elapsed before you found yourself drawn to a different set of conclusions than the one you started with?"

Terescu didn't answer.

"Months? Weeks?"

"Not sure. I . . ."

"Well, let me throw something wild out here." Zuckerman crossed his arms, then lifted a hand and began stroking his chin, pacing at the same time, a scholar at the front of the lecture hall.

"By the time that same meeting ended, had you pretty much come to the conclusions you've been testifying to here at trial?"

"Possibly."

"And how did that happen?"

"I'm not sure. Things were a bit confusing. A bit fast . . ."

"Think about it. Take your time." Zuckerman kept pacing, looking at the floor, a seeker of truth who wouldn't dare hurry things along for the sake of expediency.

Terescu knew he couldn't just sit there. "Well, I had formed some general impressions. Nothing concrete, mind you. Just some preliminary notions. And then we went through them one by one. I realized as we were talking that each individual point of my analysis didn't actually prove anything because, in each case, there was a possible alternative explanation."

Zuckerman stopped dead in his tracks, frozen, only his blinking eyes betraying that gears in his head were spinning at top speed. When he stirred again, Rebecca understood every twitch, every seemingly meaningless motion in his body, and knew with certainty that a golden feather had just dropped from the heavens and landed in front of him. Everything he'd accomplished so far had been planned, but this was pure serendipity.

Zuckerman turned to the witness box, slowly, as if moving too fast might disturb some delicate balance he needed to maintain, and nodded his approval comfortingly. *See? That didn't hurt a bit.* "And what did that mean to you?"

"Well, if there was an alternative possibility, then it had to be considered."

"Okay, let's hold up there and talk about that for just a moment." He had probably not forgotten the line of questioning he had been on, but was willing to abandon it for the moment. "You come across possible alternatives all the time in your own work, don't you?"

"Certainly. Always."

"And yet you don't feel compelled to explore every one of those possibilities, do you?" Rebecca heard his voice strengthening, and knew that it meant his confidence in his spontaneous change of direction was growing by the second. Now that he had it nailed in his mind, he could take his time and do it right.

"No. It's often easy to tell when such branches would be fruitless."

"Of course! You're a skilled scientist and you can usually tell when alternatives aren't worth pursuing, but can be dismissed out of hand."

"Exactly."

Exactly? Rebecca shot Terescu what she hoped he would see as a stern rebuke: *Not exactly, you idiot: just* yes! *What the fuck do you think this is, a faculty tea?*

"Well, then, you must have felt the same way about some of the alternative possibilities in your analysis in this case."

"I did at first. But I wasn't aware of how different law was from science."

"Oh?" Surprise showed on Zuckerman's face, as though this was news to him. Rebecca read it more as the kind of rapture a lawyer gets when he himself couldn't have scripted the witness's answers any better. "And how is that?"

"Well—I feel a little silly telling this to a lawyer. . . ."

Zuckerman laughed agreeably. "No problem at all, Doctor! I've been talking about technology for weeks and I'm no scientist. Let's hear it!" he invited with a friendly shake of his fist.

Rebecca would have preferred to simply shoot Terescu on the spot, the only thing stopping her being lack of a gun, and did the next best thing instead. "Objection, Your Honor. What is this, a bar exam class?"

"Counselor?"

"Her own witness brought it up, Your Honor. I'm simply trying to determine the degree to which his understanding of the law is reflected in his testimony."

Rebecca knew that what he was really saying was something along the lines of let's see how defense counsel tricked the witness into altering his testimony by confusing him on points of law, but Zuckerman's diplomatic doublespeak prevented the subtext from reaching Terescu. Rebecca hoped *her* subtext would reach him, having told him repeatedly: *When I object, it's as much a message to you as to the judge.* Goldin, of course, overruled the objection.

"So as you were saying, Professor," Zuckerman prompted. "The difference between law and science . . . ?"

"Okay. In science, we dismiss certain alternatives based on our experience and intuition. But in the law, as I understand it, if there are other explanations possible that would mean the defendant was innocent, then you have to assume that that's the way it happened."

"That's well stated. Do you know what that concept is called?"

"Reasonable doubt, I believe . . . ?"

"Very good! And how did you learn about the concept of reasonable doubt?"

"From Ms. Verona."

"Defense counsel herself. Sounds to me like you were coming to legal conclusions all over the place."

"Is there a question here, Your Honor?" Rebecca asked with imaginary weariness.

"No," Zuckerman answered, looking at Terescu and shaking his head. Then his face grew serious as he looked from Rebecca to the judge. "But I am hopeful that the court will entertain no further objections from counsel as to this witness's ability to come to a legal conclusion, Your Honor."

Goldin, as appreciative as she might be of a skillful and absorbing cross-examination, was not about to become part of the prosecution's cast of supporting players. "Why don't we wait until defense counsel makes an objection before you ask me to rule on it," she said sternly. "Please proceed."

"Certainly," Zuckerman agreed, unfazed. "Okay, Professor, to see if I got this straight: you went through each of your analytical points one by one."

"Right."

"And for each one, if there was a possible alternative explanation—in other words, if there was *reasonable doubt* about your point—then you felt you had an obligation not to consider it in your overall conclusions, is that about right?"

"Yes, that's exactly correct!" Terescu seemed pleased that Zuckerman understood. Rebecca seriously considered getting a high-powered pistol during the next break, but wasn't sure whom she'd use it on, Terescu or herself. Black clouds began to swirl up from inside her head and fog her vision.

Zuckerman maintained his amiable voice as he calmly and unambiguously skewered Terescu. "And so this totally objective, one hundred percent purely scientific analysis that you said you performed was basically turned completely on its head because of reasonable doubt on each individual point."

"Well . . ."

Rebecca stood up. "Objection. Argumentative, mischaracterizes previous testimony, and it's vague."

"I'll withdraw it. Doctor, when you sat down at that meeting, you believed in your heart that Tera-Tech could have made the chip, didn't you."

"No, no, it wasn't that definitive. . . ."

"And by the time Ms. Verona got finished with you, you believed exactly the opposite."

"Objection!"

"On what grounds?" Goldin asked Rebecca.

"Argumentative and badgering!"

"Overruled. Witness may answer the question."

Terescu was like a prison escapee recaptured before he even made it to the fence, his joy at his brief reprieve so quickly extinguished that the return to his cell was far worse than if he'd simply stayed put in the first place. "It is possible—I'm a little confused, I'm not sure—but it is perhaps possible that, uh, in my eagerness to be, um, supportive? Yes, supportive—that I might have . . . well, I might have maybe overlooked a point or two."

"Because when you testified that Tera-Tech couldn't have made the chip, which looked good for the defendant, you didn't allow for any *reasonable doubt* about that, did you, the way you came to allow for such doubt about the parts of your analysis that looked bad for the defendant."

"But my understanding was that reasonable doubt works only in the defendant's favor!" Terescu whined.

"That's true. But that's something for a jury to decide, not an expert witness supposedly performing objective, scientific analysis. And *your* analysis was completely distorted by legal concepts as explained to you by Ms. Verona, isn't that true? Professor?" Zuckerman prompted when Terescu hesitated.

"I—I don't know. I'm a bit overwhelmed. . . ."

"I'm sorry. I'm sure it's a blow to learn how cleverly you were manipulated."

"Your Honor . . . !" Rebecca cried, still on her feet. Her expert was crumbling, and was now worse than useless. Her only hope was to forget about him and go after Zuckerman, maybe even exploit his growing cockiness and push him into going too far.

"Mr. Zuckerman . . ."

"Sorry, Your Honor. Withdrawn. One last question. Professor Terescu, isn't it in fact the case that you really believe that it's quite possible that Tera-Tech produced this chip?"

Rebecca tried again. "Objection! Asked and answered, leading, argumentative!"

"Overruled. Witness may answer. And please sit down, Ms. Verona!"

Terescu's agitation was fully in the open now. "No. No, I don't see how . . ."

"Let me remind you that the chip does exist, Professor," Zuckerman pressed. "*Somebody* built it. In your expert opinion, as a scientist and not as a lawyer, *could Tera-Tech have manufactured this chip!*"

"I—I . . . please! I don't know! I'm too—please, I don't know. . . ."

Zuckerman saw Rebecca start to get to her feet, undoubtedly to request a recess for the benefit of the distraught witness, and he headed it off. "No further questions at this time, Your Honor, but the people reserve the right to recall this witness at a future date."

They sat, Rebecca and her collaborators, in a private room off the attorneys' lounge on the third floor of the federal courthouse. Were Chopin's *Funeral March* being piped in over the PA system, their mood couldn't have been any darker.

It wasn't a time for detailed analysis. That would come later, like taking a medical history only after the crash victim was carted off to the ICU. Right now the objective was one of recovery, not for the case but for themselves, so they would be able to think clearly about how to resuscitate their defense in court. They spoke in low tones, touching only on the major categories of damage that had been done, until they could think of no further ways to torture themselves and lapsed into silence.

Ehrenright stretched his shoulders back against the small couch, then craned his neck first to the left, then the right, producing audible cracks that made Rebecca wince. "Gotta hand it to Zuckerman, though," he said. "Absolutely incredible performance."

"Yeah, definitely amazing." Steinholz sat opposite Rebecca at a square table. "The way he—"

"Hey! Fuck *him* and fuck the both of *you!*" Rebecca said, her loud, angry voice startling them as much as the invectives she'd hurled. She jumped out of her seat and walked toward the door, whirling on them as she pushed it shut and leaned against it with her arms folded. "He wouldn't have looked so goddamned terrific if some sonofabitch hadn't leaked his whole script to him!"

Ehrenright drew back subconsciously at the fury streaming out of her. "Jeez, Rebecca, you don't have to—"

"For chrissake, Justin, what the hell do you think your hero is, clairvoyant?" She unfolded her arms and waved her hands as she spoke. "I mean, a brain-damaged parakeet could've torn Terescu apart armed with all the information Zuckerman had!"

They'd worked with her long enough to know not to take offense when she got crazy, that it was never personal. But there was usually an element of self-deprecating humor in her tirades. It wasn't there now, which didn't make it easy for them to remain calm and hang in until she chilled out, but they tried anyway.

And it passed quickly. "Even one a'you two bozos might have been able to do it without tripping over your own *schvanz.*"

"You're taking this very personal." Ehrenright turned to Steinholz. "She's taking this very, very personal."

Rebecca took a deep breath and exhaled slowly, then went back to the table and sat down heavily. "You know what bothers me the most?"

"That we had to learn through a spy how truly shitty our case really is?" Steinholz volunteered.

Rebecca looked up to meet his level stare. "You scare me sometimes, Arno. You really do."

Ehrenright looked from one to the other and sniffled. "Well, when this episode of the Psychic Network is concluded, I say we talk some more about who Deep Silicon might be. Arno started to mumble something this morning before we—"

"Yeah, I had a thought. A good one." He stopped speaking.

"You want a goddamned drum roll?" Rebecca said.

"A court reporter. One of our internal ones, who transcribes privileged notes from meetings."

Rebecca didn't say anything, but Steinholz knew he'd gotten to her with that one and went on. "Example: I remember that Janine Osterreich was in that meeting with Terescu, the first one. Where he presented his preliminary results?"

Rebecca nodded slowly. "Component densities. He told us about what he'd been doing in the lab."

"Come to think of it," Ehrenright added, "she was also there when his billing rate was discussed."

"What we gotta do," Steinholz suggested, picking up a pencil, "we gotta sort through the notes and see if there's a pattern. When did we discuss the stuff that Zuckerman found out about, and was she in those meetings."

"Don't bother," Rebecca said. "She was in every one."

"I think we oughta do the work and make sure," Steinholz said.

"I'm telling you, it was Osterreich."

"What have you got against that woman, Becky?" Steinholz slapped the pencil on the table in annoyance. "Everybody else seems to think she's okay. What, you don't like her teeth?"

As Ehrenright began to laugh, Rebecca said, "That's part of it. Spends too much damned time at the dentist."

"You're serious?" Steinholz asked. "She can't help it!"

"Oh yeah?" Rebecca leaned forward. She had wanted to have this conversation with someone for a long time. "You think she was born with bad dental genes? It's her own goddamned fault!"

"The hell're you talking about, Becky?" Ehrenright asked skeptically.

"I'll tell you what I'm talking about, Justin. She stuffs herself silly with doughnuts all the time. I saw her once; it was disgusting. She takes a bite, walks away, comes back and takes another one . . . she does it a whole damned morning!"

Steinholz stared at her for a few moments, then said quietly, "You don't like her because she sneaks doughnuts?"

"No, I don't like her because she's got no self-control. *I* don't eat doughnuts."

"You don't *like* doughnuts!"

"That's besides the point."

"No, it *is* the point."

Rebecca dismissed it with a wave of her hand. "All that sugar," she said, turning away and ignoring Steinholz's last comment, "damned miracle she's even *got* any teeth."

Steinholz, incredulous, kept looking at her and said, "Jeez, give her a break, Becky. She's *bulimic*, f'chrissake!"

Rebecca snapped her head back toward him, eyes wide. "She eats and then pukes?" At Steinholz's affirmative nod, she said derisively, "That's bloody ridiculous! Doesn't she know she's rotting her teeth away with all that sugar?"

"It's not the sugar," Steinholz explained. "It's all the gastric juices she upchucks. It's so corrosive it eats away at the backs of her teeth—common problem in bulimics."

Rebecca eyed him suspiciously. "How do you know all this?"

"Everybody knows."

"Well, why the hell does she do it? Why doesn't she stop?"

"Who knows why anybody has compulsions?" Steinholz responded, a little surprised at Rebecca's naïveté. "Maybe she didn't get enough affection as a child. Mommy stuffed pastries in her mouth instead of picking her up and hugging her, now she gets love from double-death eclairs . . . who the hell knows?" He shrugged. "Point is, she can't help it."

Rebecca sneered at him. "What do you mean, she can't help it? You just don't do it!"

"You know, you really oughta start reading some women's magazines instead of *Muscle Madness*," Ehrenright said.

"What, you read women's magazines?"

"Course. Makes me sensitive so I can get laid."

"I told you, it's a compulsion," Steinholz tried to explain again. "No matter how hard she tries to stay away, it keeps building, like air in a balloon. It has to pop every once in a while or the stress gets to be too much."

"Give it a rest, Arno," Rebecca said scornfully. "It's lack of willpower, is all it is. She knows those things are bad for her but she's too weak to do something about it."

"And this is why you don't like her," Steinholz said. "Because you think she's weak?"

Rebecca shrugged and thought about it for a few seconds, recalling the feelings of revulsion that had risen up in her as she watched Osterreich in the coffee room. "Well, maybe it is."

"Why're you getting so wrenched over Osterreich eating doughnuts?" Ehrenright demanded. "Nobody else seems to have a problem with her. Least she doesn't go out and commit murder every full moon."

But Rebecca was puzzled and interested. Why would someone deliberately and regularly engage in clearly self-destructive behaviors when they knew better?

"You just don't get it, Becky," Steinholz said.

"I don't get it," Rebecca echoed. "She *knows* she shouldn't do it. You can see it as she dances around the box. She eats them anyway, knowing she's gonna regret it, which she does as soon as she swallows the thing, then she pukes it up and starts all over again and *I* don't get it?"

"What *I* don't get is why it bothers you so much."

"How can it *not* bother you, somebody doing that to herself on purpose!"

Steinholz took a deep breath, tiring of the topic and getting irritated with Rebecca's refusal to drop it. "Everybody does self-destructive stuff once in a while, some just more than others."

"Well, I don't."

"Oh yeah?" And now Steinholz was interested again. "Whaddaya call those temper tantrums when you rip some poor unsuspecting slob's head off? Want me to read back the transcript of you putting Lawrence Krazny's testicles in a Cuisinart?"

"That was business. I was trying to impress the jury."

"Really. Who you kidding, yourself or me? You didn't need to reduce him to rubble to impress the jury. And, by the way"—he was starting to enjoy himself—"it's one thing if you do it to a witness on cross, but your boss? A federal prosecutor?" He paused, clearly not finished. "A client?"

"What client?" she asked him disbelievingly.

"Perrein." Ehrenright nodded his agreement. "First meeting with him?"

She shot him a look. Perrein couldn't possibly have told him about their few minutes alone. "What do you know about that?"

"What do I know?" Ehrenright asked as Steinholz chuckled. "We were three offices away and thought it was the Northridge quake all over again!"

"I still say it's bullshit."

Steinholz stood up to get some coffee, laughing. "Five minutes ago you couldn't even recognize an obvious case, now all of a sudden you're an expert?"

"It's bullshit. And you want to psychoanalyze me some more or talk about the goddamned case?"

Having received firm confirmation that his words had struck home from the fact that she was now finally willing to let it drop, Steinholz was happy to get off it himself and get back to business. But he also knew that Rebecca had been correct in recalling that Osterreich had probably been in every important meeting. "Question is, why would Janine violate confidences in this case?"

"Maybe she's bucking for a job with the prosecutor," Ehrenright offered, but Rebecca started shaking her head immediately.

"If I believed that David Zuckerman knew the source and didn't tell us, I'd quit the profession."

Steinholz looked at his watch and gave a sudden start. "We got a more immediate problem, campers. What about Terescu?" He addressed himself to Rebecca. "How're you going to rehabilitate him in redirect?"

"I'm not."

"You're not? What are you talking about?"

"Perry Mason couldn't rehabilitate that fucking toad," Rebecca said with finality. "Every time he opens his mouth he hurts our client." *And me.* "I want him gone and forgotten. And I want to wait until Monday to get started again, without the jury seeing him anymore. Maybe they didn't follow everything that just happened, so why take a chance on talking about it some more?"

Ehrenright rubbed his lip and looked at the ceiling. "You're right," he said, looking back down at her. "There's nothing that can be done with him."

"And then what?" Steinholz asked. "On Monday."

Rebecca rapped her knuckles once on the table. "Might as well jump right to the last act." She took a deep breath and shuddered. "And God help us all if *he* screws it up."

Chapter 23

Monday, November 16

"Defense calls Mr. James Perrein."

The courtroom was packed. There was little doubt in Rebecca's mind that Perrein, in defiance of Goldin's gag order, had leaked word that he was to testify today. He stood up quickly and smartly shot his cuffs as he strode purposefully to the witness box. Every gesture was meant to convey that he wasn't the least bit worried, and was in fact anxious to finally tell his side of the story. Rebecca didn't have a problem with that.

As soon as he was sworn in, Perrein dropped into his seat and folded his hands in his lap. He looked around the courtroom, then at the jury box, giving a slight nod before turning to Rebecca and giving her his full attention.

Rebecca asked him to state his name and occupation for the record.

"I'm James Perrein"—

An interesting way of phrasing it, she thought. Not *My name is*, but *I am*, like *I am the Pope* instead of *My name is Joe Blow*. Like *somebody* had to be James Perrein, because everybody knows who that is, and it happens to be me, folks. Sonofabitch couldn't even state his own name without—

Cut it out! Rebecca shouted to herself.

—"owner and president of Tera-Tech Integrated."

"Mr. Perrein, reminding you that you are under oath, did you manufacture government exhibit three, the alleged encryption chip?"

"No, I did not."

"Was it manufactured at Tera-Tech?"

"No."

"Have you ever sold such a chip?"

"No."

"Do you have any personal knowledge of anyone, anywhere, having manufactured or sold such a chip?"

"No, I do not."

Rebecca nodded and looked down at her notes, stalling for a few seconds so the jury could absorb the rapid-fire questions and answers they'd just heard.

"Mr. Perrein, I can understand your certainty that you yourself didn't have anything to do with this device, but why are you so certain that someone in your company didn't make it?"

Perrein frowned slightly, not in concern but concentration, showing that he wished to think about the question carefully and answer it to the best of his ability. "How can I put this?" he said, half to himself. "Ms. Verona, the scientists in my company have dreamed about constructing a processor like this for years. We've spent many millions in pursuit of that goal. The simple truth is, we don't know how yet." He sighed and shook his head. "Believe me, I wish we did."

"I see." Rebecca leafed through some sheets of paper she'd laid on the podium. "Now, it has been stated by prosecution witnesses that you have been on a sort of, well, a crusade, to get the government to allow the export of encryption devices. Is this in fact true?"

"It most certainly is," Perrein stated emphatically. "I make no secret of that. I'll even tell you that I think that U.S. policy in that area is controlled by idiots, and that they're badly harming the American business community. I plan to continue my efforts to get those restrictions lifted."

"Well, then . . ." Rebecca pursed her lips and seemed to think about that. "Sounds to me like you might be motivated to sell some encryption chips overseas."

Perrein smiled, a thousand-watter that radiated charmingly from his face. "I own a Lamborghini Countach and I'm motivated to do a hundred and fifty on the freeway, too. But I don't."

Rebecca shrugged. "Why not?"

Perrein let the smile fade, to be replaced by a more serious expression. "Because it's against the law, Ms. Verona. Why do you think I spent so much time and effort going through legitimate channels?"

"So you had absolutely nothing to do with the chip in evidence, is that right?"

"I never even heard of it until Mr. Zuckerman jumped to a conclusion and indicted me because I expressed my point of view on this issue."

"Objection." Zuckerman stood up. "Speculative, states facts not in evidence."

"Sustained. Jury will disregard the witness's answer."

Rebecca piled the sheets of paper on the podium into a stack. "I have no further—oh, wait. Sorry, Your Honor. Mr. Perrein, is it true that scientists in your company stopped publishing scholarly papers about two years ago?"

"Yes, it's true. I ordered it."

"Why?"

"To stop other people from stealing our work. Our scientists publish for their own recognition in the field, and I've always encouraged that, even though there's little benefit to the company other than prestige. But when you're the leader, it's all give and no take."

"So you admit that Tera-Tech is a leader in this field?"

"You bet I do. And I'm damned proud of it."

"Have there been any instances of others taking your ideas?"

"Yes."

"Can you give us one, please?"

Perrein nodded. "A couple of years ago, one of our best encryption specialists, Dr. Whitman Helfie, published the details of the encryption scheme he'd invented. It appeared in a respected international journal."

"Was that the enhanced key system?"

"Yes. Inside of six weeks it began popping up all over the world. Some unethical son of . . . an unethical mathematician even published it on the Internet."

"So it's essentially available to anybody who wants it."

"I'm afraid so. And that's what led to my ban on further publishing of our trade secrets."

Rebecca stayed still, only a slight crease on her brow indicating that she was thinking about something. "Mr. Perrein, there's one thing I still don't understand." She stepped away from the podium, folded her arms and put a finger to her chin, looking terribly confused. "If it's against the law to export these powerful encryption systems, and one of your people published it in a journal available all over the world, then aren't you guilty of violating the law?"

The jurors, amazed that an attorney would purposely implicate her own client, were on high alert, leaning forward visibly. Rebecca tried not to smile.

Perrein gritted his teeth, made a fist and banged it lightly onto the arm of his seat several times. "No, I'm not," he said, appearing to be fighting to keep his temper in check. "It isn't against the law to publish the system, only to program it into a computer and export it."

Rebecca tried to look even more confused. "But if you publish it, then can't anybody in the world program it into his own computer?"

"Well, of course."

"But that doesn't make any sense!"

"That's what I've been saying for years!" Perrein nearly shouted. "It doesn't make any—"

"Objection!" Zuckerman shouted himself. "Irrelevant, Your Honor! This defendant isn't on trial for *not* breaking the law, and the law itself isn't on trial at all!"

"Withdrawn," Rebecca said, puzzlement still etched deeply into her face. She shook her head, opening her eyes wide and blinking, as if to clear her mind of nonsense that had no business invading it in the first place. "No more questions, Your Honor."

Her direct examination of Perrein had lasted less than fifteen minutes. All she wanted to do was have him proclaim his innocence, and then hold his own against Zuckerman's cross. If he could do that, maybe the jury would forget about the Terescu disaster and acquit for lack of hard evidence.

"Do you wish to cross-examine, Mr. Zuckerman?" Goldin asked, for form's sake.

"Yes, Your Honor." Zuckerman got up, and Rebecca was bewildered to see that he wasn't carrying any notes to the podium. He didn't have even a single scrap of paper in his hands as he walked away from the prosecution table.

Zuckerman stepped up to the podium. There were no polite preliminaries. "Mr. Perrein, does Tera-Tech have a machine called a CyberDesign XT-5055?"

Until this precise moment James Perrein had looked like a man who owned a remote control for the whole world. Now, in barely the time it took for Rebecca to notice, he seemed to have been transformed into a fish that suddenly found itself lying helpless on a dock, a hook still hanging out of its mouth. His lips froze for a second, then began working themselves soundlessly, terror dancing around his eyes.

"Mr. Perrein? Did you understand my question?"

"Yes." It came out as a croak, and Perrein cleared his throat noisily. Just as quickly, the unfamiliar creature he had become disappeared. "Yes. Sorry. I, uh, was thinking of something else. We have no such machine, the one you mentioned, we have no such machine on the production floor."

Rebecca perked up at this, forgetting for the moment Perrein's fleeting metamorphosis. *Production floor?* That was the same phrase Perrein used when Terescu had asked him a similar question way back in their first meeting, although she didn't recall the scientist having asked about a specific machine.

Zuckerman didn't seem at all perturbed by Perrein's strange reaction. Rebecca wondered if he'd even noticed.

Stupid wondering. "Sir, I didn't ask you if there was one on the production floor," Zuckerman said evenly. "I simply asked if Tera-Tech has one."

Perrein, most of his composure regained, licked his lips. "I'm not really sure."

Rebecca felt dizzy, and subconsciously gripped the edge of the table to steady herself. Steinholz was too absorbed to notice. Neither of them knew what kind of machine Zuckerman was referring to, but they knew it was not good.

"I understand." Zuckerman nodded sympathetically. "Your Honor, might we take a break to allow the witness the opportunity to call back to his company and find out for sure?"

"Can you do that, Mr. Perrein?" Goldin asked.

Perrein nodded absently, then remembered where he was. "Yes. Yes, Your Honor." He looked about distractedly at nothing in particular.

Goldin banged her gavel, and said as she stood up, "Court is recessed for fifteen minutes. Witness is ordered to comply with counsel's request."

Rebecca rose unsteadily and moved to the front of the defense table just as Zuckerman stepped away from the podium. As their eyes met, Rebecca expected an intensely reproachful look filled with gloating and triumph. What she got instead was anger, and she knew that it wasn't directed at her behavior as a lawyer in this case but at her gullibility. The opening act of Zuckerman's cross-examination of James Perrein may have been a legitimate prosecutorial impeachment of Perrein's testimony, but it was also a demonstration for Rebecca: *He told you he was innocent and you believed him.*

If she had any doubt about her perception of what was transpiring between them, Zuckerman dispelled it by inclining his head toward the witness box and raising his eyebrows: *What do you think now, Counselor?*

It ended as quickly as it had begun, Zuckerman growing embarrassed as his co-counsels grasped his hand and slapped his back. Perrein, still seated in the witness box, took a sip of water and began to rise.

At the defense table, Steinholz had taken a large bundle of papers from his trial bag and had them laid out on the table. He was leafing quickly through the top portion, and Rebecca saw him stop and go stiff at what appeared to be a typed transcript.

"What?" she asked as she sat down next to him.

"Something about the production floor," Steinholz said haltingly, without looking away from the papers. He was holding about twenty clipped sheets up and away from the one he was fixated on.

"I caught that, too. He said that when Terescu—"

Steinholz slammed his hand down on the sheet he was reading. "When Terescu asked him about high-resolution ion beam machines. The kind you need to etch extremely small components onto chips."

"Jim said they didn't have one."

Steinholz opened his fingers slowly and let the pages he'd been holding fall back over the transcript. "He said they didn't have one on the production floor."

"So what's that mean?"

"It probably means," he said, turning toward her, "and I'd bet a year's income on it, that the XT-5055 is an extremely high-resolution lithography device, and Tera-Tech has one in their lab."

* * *

By silent, mutual assent, neither Rebecca nor Perrein said a single word as she led him to the third floor attorneys' lounge. By the time she'd closed the door behind them in a private room, she was trembling with anger.

"It's an ion beam machine, isn't it?" she said, her teeth clenched tightly as Perrein sat down. "The XT-what-the-fuck-ever?"

His silence told her all she needed to know. She closed her eyes and leaned against the door. "You stupid bastard," she said wearily, barely knowing how to begin to tell him what he'd done. "Why didn't you tell us?"

"I didn't see any need to confuse things by bringing it up."

She opened her eyes. "Confuse things? You didn't want to confuse things?" She took a step toward the chair opposite his, put her hands on the back of it and leaned forward. "You hid a key piece of evidence from your own lawyer. I don't know about it, I can't deal with it. I don't have time to think, to plan. Now the prosecutor springs it on us and we stand there with our thumbs up our asses . . . ?" She smacked the chair back. "Why the hell didn't you tell me!"

"I thought it would look bad. It's a very high—"

"Look bad to whom, Jim! What difference does it make how it looks to me? I'm your goddamned lawyer!"

"But if it came up—"

"Well, sure as shit *I* wasn't going to bring it up! What in God's name were you thinking!"

It dawned on her just then exactly what he'd been thinking. "You didn't want *me* to know. That's it, isn't it? Because it would make you look guilty in my eyes, and you needed me completely on your side."

She laughed bitterly and shook her head. "You arrogant sonofabitch. You don't even trust your own lawyer to handle your case. Gonna do it your own way, because nobody's smart as you."

"Listen to me, Rebecca. You can't make a chip like that even with a 5055. It just can't be done."

"The prosecutor seems to think it can."

"It can't! Just ask your own expert. And by the way, that was some great play on your part, *lawyer*. You expecting a bonus for recruiting that piece of shit to the case?"

"Don't change the subject on me, Jim! The point is, you misled us and now—"

Perrein slammed his fist down on the small table that separated them. "My company didn't make those chips, Rebecca! These idiotic temper tantrums aren't about ion beam machines or Terescu or that fucking student of his, they're about *me* and you damned well know it! So get over it and start behaving like a lawyer!"

His egotistical presumption that her fixation on him was compromising her legal abilities floored her. "You lied to my team and now you want me to fix it?"

"I didn't lie, I was just being accurate. I told you that device was not on the—"

"Don't bullshit a professional bullshitter, Jim! You expect me to pull your sorry ass out of the fire when you've effectively nuked your own defense by trying to hide some evidence from your own attorney. Now I've got about eight minutes to figure out how to handle something I should have been thinking about for months."

"Well, it *is* my ass, and I made a decision, and I'll live with the consequences, so there's no need for you to get all indignant."

"Oh no? Listen, pal: all I care, you and your precious company can rot in hell for all eternity, but now you're taking me down with you. Prosecution surprises make me look stupid and incompetent, and when my own client withholds things that even the other side knows about, it makes me look like a fucking idiot! And you'd better understand something else." She waited until he looked directly at her. "There is no way on God's green earth I'm letting you take me down with you."

The implications of that pronouncement were not lost on him. His lawyer was establishing a line she would not cross, telling him that, if it came down to it, she wouldn't risk her reputation to save his case. If it wasn't clear to him before, it was now: he was in terrible trouble and his captain had no intention of sinking with his ship.

"Nobody needs to go down, Rebecca. Maybe I made a couple mistakes, but I swear on my mother's grave, I have no knowledge of any wrongdoing within my company."

Rebecca caught the change in nuance. Before, he always swore that his company hadn't done it. Now he was saying only that he had no knowledge of it.

An opportunity presented itself, and Rebecca took a moment to calm herself down and get back in lawyer mode. "Is it possible that somebody at Tera-Tech did it without your knowledge?"

He considered it. "It's logistically possible. I mean, in the sense that I don't know everything that's going on in the lab and wouldn't understand most of it anyway. But technically?" He shook his head. "I was telling you the truth. The XT-5055 is the best there is, but it couldn't do what was necessary to produce that thing."

As Rebecca mulled that over, he added, "Terescu was right, you know. I don't see how it's possible for *anyone* to have made that thing."

"But there it is," Rebecca said.

"If it really is."

"Don't fall for our own crapola, Jim. You know damned well that chip is for real."

He looked down at the table, spent and in real distress. This was where she was supposed to feel sorry for him and lighten up. "What about your wife?"

"What about her?"

"The divorce. Was it messy?"

Perrein grunted, but showed no real emotion over the breakup of his marriage. "If you call an obscene financial settlement messy, yeah, it was. She was our human resources director and I paid through the nose for that little management misjudgment."

"What I want to know, could she have had anything to do with it?"

He looked up suspiciously. "With what?"

"With anything that somebody in the company might have done that got you into this position."

"That stupid bitch?" He smiled with disdain. "She had money, she had connections, she cleaned up nice for the customers . . . she was dumb as a goddamned walnut. Day I dumped her?" He looked up at the ceiling. "Happiest day in the last two years."

She watched him for a few moments, dumbstruck, unable to find words at first. But what would be the point, anyway? He wouldn't understand if she tried to explain to him how he sounded. "Jim," she said softly. "About that first meeting . . ."

"What?"

"You know, when we were discussing whether I'd take the case?" She smiled sheepishly. "I sent everybody else away and I said some things to you . . . some harsh things?"

The beginning of a smirk appeared on Perrein's face. "What about it?"

She kept smiling. "I meant every damned word of it. I'm making you a solemn vow: lie to me again or do anything else to make me look like a fool, and I'm off this case."

"You can't get off this case," he sneered. "You think I don't know the law? Only way you can get off is if you know I'm going to lie on the stand."

"Or if I know you already did lie."

"But I didn't."

"Well, have fun proving it after I quit the case. I'm prevented by law from disclosing how you lied, but the implication would be as clear as if I tattooed it on my chin."

He shook his head emphatically. "You can't do that."

"No sense arguing about this, Jim. It's nonnegotiable. Cross me one more time and I'm in Goldin's chambers quitting."

Perrein laughed, but nervously. "Allen'd never let you do that."

Rebecca's voice was easy and businesslike. "Allen Wysocki can go fuck himself. Matter of fact, you can go fuck each other in Macy's window, for all I care."

The smile left Perrein's face.

"Seen him around much lately, Jim? Your old buddy, my managing partner? You think he wants his name associated with this noble cause of yours anymore?"

Perrein stayed quiet; assessing, calculating . . .

Rebecca pulled at a stray lock of hair near her ear. "I've already told him I'm quitting after this case is resolved—"

"Horseshit."

"Ask him." She waited, gauging his reaction. "There's nothing either of you flaming assholes can do to me anymore." There was a loud knock at the door. "And this conversation is over," she said as she got up.

"Rebecca, you leave this case and I'll see to it you never practice law again." His delivery was quiet, unhurried, dripping with barely disguised, malignant resolve.

She paused, hand on the doorknob. The insistent knocking was repeated, but she ignored it and turned around.

He still didn't get it, so blinded by his self-interest he didn't even realize when it was being threatened by somebody who was an equal match for him.

She floated up off the ground, the dizzying speed of her rotation making it impossible to focus on anything until she touched down. From the corner of her eye, the teenaged Rebecca could see the Pumpkin King sit bolt upright in amazement as she landed the dead perfect triple-axel, the king of jumps, three and a half revolutions and the finest she'd ever done, maybe the finest anyone had ever done, because what improvement was possible? Before she

*turned away, she could see him waving her over, his gestures grow-
ing more emphatic as she at first pretended not to see.*

As she approached, Charlie made his way down to the front
row and stood before the barrier. *Rebecca twisted to her left and
dug the sides of her skates into the ice, bringing herself to a stop in
front of him. She put her hands on top of the barrier, and hoped he
would notice that her breathing was normal following the strenu-
ous maneuver.*

You realize you're our only hope now, Rebecca, the only hope
for this family.

*Family? Rebecca stayed silent. Charlie pulled a can of Coca-
Cola out of his pocket, popped the top and set it atop the low wall
between them.*

You won't let us down, will you? You'll work hard, make
sacrifices?

She frowned, as though insulted he even needed to ask. Of
course I will.

Good. *Charlie reached out with one hand, hesitated, then patted
her on the shoulder several times.* Very good. *Rebecca half expected a doggie treat to appear next.*

Don't you worry, Charlie. I won't let you down.

*She dropped her arms, picked up the Coke and skated backward
away from him.* No sirree, *she said loudly, continuing to distance
herself as the coach pulled up next to her uncle. Charlie nodded at
him, and relief washed over both their faces.*

*As she approached the entryway on the other side of the rink,
she tossed the can of Coke on the ice, spilling the brown liquid in a
long streak that pointed to the two men watching her. She waited
for it to register on their faces, then shouted,* I'm gonna be the best
goddamned lawyer in the world, Unc . . . you can count on me!
*and continued skating away from the last man in the world she
would ever let manipulate her.*

*Or so she had believed, with the untutored, arrogant and irra-
tional confidence of youth.*

"If I leave this case," Rebecca said to Perrein calmly, as though
reading from an instruction manual for assembling a child's toy,
"the prosecution can get a mistrial. That means they can try you
again, but the second time around, they avoid all the mistakes they
made in this trial, the ones I exposed. You won't be able to discredit the ink expert because he'll cover his bases this time, and we
both know he was right in the first place. Fuster, Frazier . . . they'll

all polish their testimony so your new lawyer can't touch them. You won't have any experts to testify for you, either, because the whole world will think you committed perjury—and my answering every reporter's question with 'No comment' will pretty much seal it, and you'll become what we call a toxic client: to touch you is professional death, for lawyers as well as experts."

The knocking again, louder and more frantic.

She shook her head. "If I quit this case, you're going to spend the rest of your life in prison."

Perrein opened his mouth to speak and Rebecca said, "I'm sorry: were you going to say something?"

They stared at each other. Perrein blinked and looked away, and Rebecca opened the door to find Justin Ehrenright standing there with his fist poised high to start knocking again.

He waited for Rebecca to pull the door shut behind her, then leaned in and whispered loudly, "Terescu's throwing a shit-fit." His hair looked to Rebecca as close to being disheveled as the short, low-maintenance cut would allow, and he had his non-knocking hand balled into a fist at his side to keep his fidgeting fingers from betraying his anxiety to onlookers.

"Where is he?"

"Office just outside the courtroom. You done in there?"

Rebecca turned and opened the door, reaching in for her purse as she said to Perrein, "Got a problem. We're through here."

She could practically see the steam boiling off Radovan Terescu as he paced about the office, running his hands through his hair and alternating rapidly between rage and despondency. Steinholz and Ehrenright had figured out his path and stayed well to the sides of it.

"He told me they didn't have that machine!" Terescu shouted, eyes blazing, as Rebecca entered the office.

"What if he does?" Rebecca asked as calmly as she could, laying her purse down on a couch and hoping that her show of composure might have a calming influence on him.

"What if he—what do you mean, what if he does! He might have used it to make those chips!"

"C'mon, Rado. You've been saying all along that the technology doesn't exist!"

"But if it does?"

"But it *doesn't*!"

Terescu stopped pacing and shook a fist in the air. "Then why did your client hide this machine from me!"

She tried, but there was no mollifying him. Beneath his blustering Rebecca saw that he was terrified that his egocentric overconfidence may have led to the public ruin of his heretofore sheltered reputation. She tried to keep him talking, looking for an opening to win him back, but his despair at his humiliation rapidly deteriorated into bitter condemnation of how these three attorneys had taken advantage of him, and once he'd managed to channel his all-consuming rage in that direction, he saw little point in continuing this conversation with those who'd deceived him.

Badly rattled and shaking with swirling emotions, he bolted out of the room.

First to speak after a painful silence was Steinholz. "I think we just figured out the real reason Perrein was so insistent Terescu not be allowed anywhere near the company."

"Shit." Rebecca looked at her watch and tried to think. "Justin, go get him back. We're already late and he needs to be in that courtroom."

"The state he's in? And what if he won't come back?"

"Act pissed yourself. Explain to him that we all got bamboozled, not just him. I'm gonna try to stall for time, hope he cools off. Arno, call Goldin's assistant in chambers, tell her we're asking the judge to hold off on bringing the jury in. Tell her we're gonna make a motion or something."

Steinholz nodded and headed for the door. "I'd better tell Zuckerman, though, so he won't think it's *ex parte*."

"You do that. But after you call chambers."

As Goldin gaveled court back into session, Rebecca was relieved to see Terescu sitting in the audience with Ehrenright. His arms were folded tight across his chest, and he was scowling, but at least he was here.

"Ms. Verona, I understand you have a matter to bring before the court?"

"Yes, Your Honor." Rebecca stood up. "And I apologize to the court for not having anticipated it earlier, but it was unavoidable."

Goldin wouldn't let her off the hook. She just waved a hand for her to continue.

"In light of certain developments in testimony, the defense wishes to renew its demand to be allowed to examine government exhibit three, the microchip, including an option to disassemble it if we deem it necessary."

When he was sure she'd finished speaking, Zuckerman stood. "The government renews its earlier objections, Your Honor. I'm not sure why this topic should even be reopened for discussion."

"Counsel opened the door himself," Rebecca responded. "His cross of the defendant carries the implication that he is going to try to show that Tera-Tech possessed the equipment to produce the chip. To defend him properly, we must be allowed the opportunity to demonstrate that his equipment couldn't have done it."

Zuckerman smiled patronizingly. "Is defense counsel making motions based on what she thinks I *intend* to do?"

"I'll withdraw the motion," Rebecca threw back, "if the prosecutor agrees not to pursue that line of questioning. Otherwise, let's deal with it now before the jury hears him try and it's too late."

"She's got a point, Counselor," Goldin said. "If you're going to try to match up the defendant's equipment with what's inside that chip, well . . ." She flipped up a hand and let it drop.

"Approach, Your Honor?" Zuckerman said. Goldin, surprised at the request since there was no jury present, waved them up.

As the court reporter came up ready to record the sidebar, Zuckerman asked, "May we keep this off the record, Judge?"

Goldin looked at Rebecca, who said, "Sure," and then waved the reporter back.

"Sorry," Zuckerman said. "But I shouldn't even be telling Ms. Verona this."

"What?"

"Even when this trial is over, there's a good chance the Chinese will continue to refuse to return their remaining stock. If that's the case, this one chip we're holding might be used to scramble Chinese intelligence transmissions and completely neutralize the damage of the remaining Chinese chips."

"I don't get it," Goldin said. "How?"

"Our side could transmit disinformation at the same high speed they're using, so they can't tell what's real from what we're planting. But without this one chip we have, we can't do it."

"And the alternative would be . . . ?"

Zuckerman took a deep breath. "Our people would have to find the exact locations of all the other chips and destroy them. Probably buildings and all."

Goldin and Rebecca both blinked and drew back slightly. "Good God," the judge whispered.

"Way it is, Your Honor," Zuckerman said offhandedly. She shuddered and turned to Rebecca. "Ms. Verona?"

Rebecca was still looking at Zuckerman. "Uh, this is all kind of news to me, Judge. I wasn't expecting a whole new line of objections, and I don't feel qualified to respond on the spot. May I confer with my team?"

"Certainly. But let's not drag this out, folks."

"Understood," Rebecca said. "But I don't feel counsel's cross can continue till we get this straightened out."

She walked quickly away from the bench. Zuckerman took his time. Still moving, Rebecca motioned to Ehrenright and Terescu to join her and Steinholz at the defense table. She filled them in quickly as they huddled, finishing by saying, "They say they can use the one remaining chip to scramble up Chinese intelligence transmissions."

"No!" Terescu said loudly. Ehrenright patted him on the back to remind him to keep his voice down. "No!" he repeated quietly, but without any loss of emphasis. "He's wrong! The coding keys are built right into the chip, and they can't be changed to match up with any Chinese transmissions, because each chip has different keys. So that argument is nonsense!" He seemed to have momentarily forgotten his earlier ire in the excitement of having fathomed so important a logical error.

Rebecca looked at him, then slowly broke into a smile. "Really . . ." she said.

Terescu nodded. "Now that I think about it, if they agree to open up the chip, they might be able to figure out how to change the keys, and then really go to work scrambling up Chinese intelligence data!"

Steinholz agreed. "That would render all the chips still in China completely useless, and that's what they want, right?"

Rebecca stood up from the huddle and walked back to the bench, Zuckerman trailing closely behind. Goldin leaned forward to listen.

"Seems counsel has things a little backward, Your Honor. No way they're gonna change the codes in those chips to match the Chinese transmissions. They're fixed in place and can't be changed!" It was a powerful counterargument to the stand Zuckerman had taken, and Rebecca tried not to look too smug as Goldin turned to Zuckerman for a response.

The prosecutor looked down at his shoes and fiddled with his belt buckle. "Hate to break this to counsel," he said somewhat timidly, "but the keys are not fixed in place." He looked up again. "The chip is programmable."

Rebecca had no idea what to do with that bit of news. "I'll file a writ of *habeus corpus* if I have to."

"For a microchip?"

"Far as I'm concerned, that's the dead body in this case."

She argued mechanically for a few more moments, but since she hadn't expected to win the motion anyway and Terescu seemed to have regained some control of himself, she didn't drag it out very long.

She shrugged at her team as she walked back to the table, and Goldin asked the bailiff to fetch the jury.

"Good try, Rado." Rebecca passed a puzzled Terescu as she came around to her chair, grabbed hold of it and pulled it away from the table. "But the thing's programmable."

"Damn!" Steinholz shook his head and grunted. "Thought we had him there."

"Programmable?" The confusion on Terescu's face increased even as his limbs grew rigid, and he made no move to return to the audience. "Programmable?"

Rebecca dropped onto her seat and jerked her body forward to move the chair closer to the table. "So what's the big deal?"

"What's the big deal?" Terescu seemed to fight for control of his voice as shock replaced confusion on his face. Rebecca, sensing another explosion, turned to look at him. "I'll tell you what the big deal is: There are only two people on the whole planet who have even a theoretical notion of how to make a chip like that programmable!"

"Okay, you're one. Who's the other?"

Terescu seemed not to have heard her, but was staring off at someplace distant. "Bao Tranh," he hissed, mostly to himself, struggling against something Rebecca couldn't quite make out.

"Tranh," she repeated, worried by his increasing agitation. "Vietnamese?"

Seemingly unaware of her, or of anything else around him, Terescu turned and began walking away. Ehrenright put a hand on his shoulder, but the scientist jerked his torso spasmodically, shaking it off. Rather than resume his seat in the audience, Terescu kept going until he reached the courtroom door, walked through, and was gone.

Rebecca, hearing a rustling as the jurors took their seats,

frowned and looked at her co-counsels. "Who the hell is Bao Tranh?"

Steinholz, still looking at the door through which Terescu had exited, answered, "I got a really bad feeling it's his old graduate student."

He turned to Rebecca. "The one who left his lab to go to work for our client."

Rebecca stared at him, aghast, then jumped up out of her chair. "Your Honor, defense requests a meeting in chambers."

Judge Goldin tore off her glasses and pointed them to her left. "May I remind you we just had the jury brought in?"

"It's an emergency!"

Goldin looked at her for a few seconds, then angrily threw the glasses down onto the benchtop in front of her. "Court is adjourned for the remainder of the day. Jury is excused." She shot Rebecca a furious look and added, "With the apologies of the court!"

She stood abruptly, then stormed out through the door behind the bench that led to her chambers.

Chapter 24

Judge Goldin didn't bother to ask Rebecca why they were in chambers instead of court. The look on her face was inquiry enough.

"Mr. Zuckerman has been withholding vital information from the defense, Judge. This was the first we heard their chip can be reprogrammed. The codes aren't built into it; they can be changed."

"I just discovered it myself, Your Honor," Zuckerman said. "Besides, it's a matter of national security."

Rebecca clenched her jaw and said as she took a breath, "I am getting mighty damned sick and tired of that phrase."

Goldin, by not chastising her, hinted that she was beginning to agree. "Why, Mr. Zuckerman?"

"Terescu was correct. If we can't reprogram the codes, we can't use our chip to scramble up Chinese intelligence transmissions. So we don't want the Chinese to know we've figured out how to change the keys by revealing it in open court. Otherwise, they'll go to great pains to conceal those transmissions, whereas right now they think they're safe."

"Wait a minute," Rebecca said. "Are you trying to tell me that if you keep this feature a secret and scramble up their most important data, they're, like, not gonna notice?"

"Not at first," Zuckerman replied, ignoring her sarcasm. "It might buy us time to figure out a less risky way to get the rest back. But if the chip's programmability is revealed, we're dead in the water. Our only choice would be to mount some very dangerous covert operations to go into China and physically get the rest of the chips back."

"Sounds a little fishy to me, Counselor." Rebecca, sensing sympathy from Goldin, tried to exploit it before it faded away. "Your Honor, the government had no right to withhold that information from us and now it's way too late to rectify the situation. Defense requests a mistrial."

It was airtight. How could Zuckerman possibly counter it? But it worried her that Zuckerman didn't look at all worried.

"Your Honor, Ms. Verona is missing something rather vital here. The fact is, had we chosen to introduce this feature of the chip, it would have been one of our best arguments to prove the defendant guilty. If she were to bring it up in court, it would nail her client's coffin shut!"

"And why is that?" Rebecca demanded.

Zuckerman looked down at the carpet and patted his leg. "You'd better ask your client what the graduate student was working on when he was still in Terescu's lab."

He gave that a moment to register before looking up at Goldin. "And by the way, Your Honor, had we allowed the defense to destructively examine the chip, we never would have found out about this feature. And that might have caused the country great damage."

Rebecca, looking for an opportunity to regain ground, tried to sound appalled as she said, "You mean you're still working on the chip? You withheld that from the defense and this court?"

But Zuckerman would not be fazed. "They are working on it, but not for this case. They're just doing the kinds of analysis that intelligence people do when they get their hands on something like this. Your Honor, this country desperately needs to get those chips back. What we're hoping is, once Perrein is found guilty, or he knows that it's inevitable, he'll tell us to whom he sold the chips in exchange for a reduced sentence."

The judge asked him if he still thought he had enough of a case to sway a jury.

"Definitely. We have a mountain of indirect evidence. And while defense counsel tried to get her expert witness to ignore the big picture, I don't think he can do that anymore. I believe we can convince this jury to bring in a verdict of guilty."

Rebecca felt it slipping away. "And even if you convince them that Tera-Tech built the chip, how are you going to implicate Perrein specifically?"

"I don't have to. *Respondeat superior.* If the company did it, then the president is responsible."

"Ms. Verona," Goldin said, "what would your side have done differently had they known about the chip's programmability earlier?"

Despite its being what seemed to her such an obvious question, Rebecca found herself at a complete loss. "I don't think it's fair to put me on the spot like that, Your Honor. It's kind of a shock, and I haven't had time to think about it or confer with my expert."

It was a transparent ruse to buy time, and Goldin saw through it. "Withholding of the programmability feature in the interests of national security doesn't seem to have had a material effect on your case, Ms. Verona. The prosecution may even have done you a favor by keeping it out." She turned to Zuckerman. "I assume you're going to show that Professor Terescu's graduate student was working in that area when he went to Tera-Tech?"

Zuckerman said, "There isn't going to be any doubt about it."

"So the implication is that he brought that knowledge to the defendant. Do you plan to dispute this, Ms. Verona?"

How could she? Terescu had revealed that to her in their very first meeting. "I don't know yet. It's still new news."

"Then for the time being, your motion for a mistrial is denied. And Mr. Zuckerman, I'm giving you fair warning: if you can't make a *prima facie* case using only the evidence available to the jury, I'll dismiss the charges before the jury ever gets to deliberate. And on the topic of what's available to the jury, I'm ordering the both of you not to mention this programmability business in open court. And make sure your witnesses don't, either. Anything else?"

"Yes." Rebecca paused, wanting to make this sound objective and professional, and only their reactions would reveal her degree of success. "I'd be real appreciative if neither counsel nor the court did me any more favors. I'd prefer to simply have all the information to which I'm entitled, and then try *my* case *my* way."

Zuckerman looked as if he were trying to liquefy and drip down through the seams on his chair. Goldin was unreadable.

"And," Rebecca went on, "I'd like the record to reflect that the prosecutor and Your Honor agreed on what was best for the defense, and then the court imposed it against my objections."

She could tell that Zuckerman had stopped breathing and was leaning away from the judge, steeling himself against an impending detonation.

Goldin splayed her hands out on the desk blotter in front of her. "I'll have it noted in the record, Counselor."

As Rebecca and Zuckerman turned to leave, Goldin said, "And, Ms. Verona, also off the record?"

Rebecca turned around.

"Ease up on these witnesses a little, will you? You can impeach them without tearing their heads off."

The two attorneys didn't speak as they left chambers, Zuckerman hanging back for a second to watch which way Rebecca turned, then going down the opposite corridor.

On her way to the attorneys' lounge, Rebecca felt so weary and beaten that she briefly entertained the notion of resting her case, taking the conviction, and getting an appeal started based on the pile of legal atrocities being committed against her client in the name of national security. It was more of a fantasy than a real plan, the thought of being able to walk away from this for a while presenting an ice cream cake full of temptation. If Zuckerman kept succeeding at getting the court to stymie her defense at every turn, Perrein didn't have a prayer of getting out of this one.

Things didn't improve in the little gathering that followed.

"Terescu is harboring some pretty serious doubts about our client's innocence," Ehrenright reported.

"Dammit to hell!" Rebecca retorted, still smarting from the chambers conference and her strained interaction with Zuckerman. "I really wish that prick would stop worrying about who's guilty or innocent and just worry about what we *hired* him to worry about!"

Steinholz rubbed his chin. "So let me make sure I understand," he said after a few seconds. "You're not okay with that?"

Rebecca tried to smile at his attempt to cheer her up, but it would have looked too forced, so she rolled her eyes instead, then threw her attaché onto the table and popped open the snaps. "I decided in chambers to back off our demand to take apart the chip."

"You're kidding," Ehrenright said.

Rebecca rested her hands on the lid of the case. "All of a sudden I'm afraid of what they might find." She expected amazed looks, and got them. "If the government loses the case without the chip being opened, because of double jeopardy they can't come after Perrein again, even if they subsequently discover something incriminating. But if they take it apart now and they *do* find something . . ."

It was not lost on her colleagues that Rebecca seemed to believe that opening the chip would implicate Perrein, but it went unspoken. The way Rebecca had been careful to phrase it, she was dealing only in probabilities, not suspicions. But if they talked about it some more, they might end up revealing things concerning how they felt about their client that were better left unsaid.

"You'd better call Jim and let him know," Ehrenright said. He pointed to a row of private pay phone booths just off the lounge.

She went to one, closed the door behind her and dialed, got put through, and told her client that she was no longer pressing to get the chip opened. She settled in to handle the answering tirade.

"I agree."

"You do?" She sat up straight. "Why?"

"Because I don't want Terescu to get his hands on the chip." When she didn't respond, he explained. "If he figures out how it was built, he's going to steal it and jump our efforts by at least three years. I'd rather *nobody* saw it, including us, if it means keeping it out of his hands."

"But it could get you off the hook, Jim!"

"I'm already off the hook. You're doing a terrific job and the government is screwing up all over the place. Don't forget, I got a business to worry about here after I'm cleared."

He made some logical sense, a pool player worrying not just about sinking the ball but also making sure he was well positioned for the next shot. But Rebecca was badly troubled as she hung up the phone. If Perrein truly wasn't guilty, opening the chip was his best tactic for ensuring an acquittal. And how did he figure the prosecution was screwing up?

Back with Ehrenright and Steinholz, sitting glumly, Rebecca asked, "Do you guys believe our client is innocent?"

Neither answered. "Arno?"

"Gee, that's a helluva thing to ask."

"*Do* you?"

"Listen, what difference does it make if I do or not? It's irrelevant, you know that."

"I *know* it's irrelevant, goddammit! I want to know anyway: *Do you think he's innocent!*"

"I'm not sure anymore."

"Anymore. Does that mean at one point you were?"

"When I first met him. He seemed sincere, believable. . . ." Steinholz looked out the window. "Now . . . ?"

Ehrenright indicated a similar feeling. Then Rebecca told them about Perrein's reaction to her telling him that they'd stopped the fight to get the chip opened. "It didn't give me the warm and fuzzies."

But Ehrenright put another possible spin on it. "Well, wait a minute. He didn't have a problem earlier when we tried to get it opened."

"So what's that mean?"

"It might mean that he was confident at the beginning, but now he's starting to have his own doubts."

"Why?" Rebecca pushed.

"I see where Justin's going," Steinholz said. "Let's say the grad student did bring over some secrets from Terescu's lab. And let's say Perrein really didn't know anything about it. So early on, he was dead convinced Tera-Tech wasn't guilty, and he was willing to open the chip to prove it."

He stood up and began to pace the small room. "But now the evidence is starting to point to Tera-Tech. And maybe Perrein is thinking, oh boy, what if my company really did do it?" Steinholz paused to see if the others were tracking.

They were. "And that would leave only one open question," he finished. "Did Perrein know about it and participate in the deal?"

"It's a possibility," Ehrenright opined. "But let's not forget that Zuckerman doesn't even know about the student's expertise in programmability, so maybe Perrein's right in keeping the chip buttoned up."

"Except Zuckerman does know," Rebecca said, evoking a startled reaction from both of them. "He told me in chambers, as if *I* didn't know."

"Yikes." Ehrenright thought about it for less than a second before he saw a potential problem for the team. "Does that mean we're going to get more shit for not telling *him*? Did we have some kind of an obligation there?"

"No," Rebecca said without hesitation, having had plenty of time to think about it on the way over. "It's up to the prosecution to discover such things on their own. We're not obligated to present them with damning evidence. And besides"—it was a mildly bright spark in the midst of all the darkness—"the judge specifically excluded the issue of programmability from even being mentioned, so all we're doing is following the court's order, right?"

Despite her being so upset, Rebecca needed to make sure her team didn't get down in the dumps as well. The clever bit of turnabout she'd just constructed seemed to have done nothing to lift their spirits, and they continued to bewail the state of their case.

She tried to think of something positive and uplifting about the situation with which to bolster them, but the only thing that sprang immediately to mind was that Allen Wysocki had disappeared like a vampire at dawn as soon as things had started going south. But that probably wasn't a very appropriate sentiment to share with young associates the firm had placed under her wing.

"Don't you guys go fading on me now," she said sternly. "Life in court isn't a matter of always holding good cards, but of playing a poor hand well. You don't get to be a brilliant and respected lawyer by trying only the sure things." Which was really easy to believe when you had a good hand and it was the *other* guy who had to play the poor one well.

"So what's our next move?" Steinholz asked.

Rebecca reclosed her attaché and stood it up on end. "As long as we're on card metaphors, I'm reminded of what Hoyle used to say."

"Hoyle, as in 'according to Hoyle'?"

She leaned on the case and stood up briskly. "When in doubt, win the trick."

As she opened the door to leave, Steinholz said, "Hey, wait a minute: win *what* trick?"

Rebecca gave him a look of utter contempt, communicating to him that he was too thick-headed to see the obvious. Steinholz creased his brow in concentration but couldn't grasp what she was thinking. Finally, he picked up his hands and shrugged.

"Actually," Rebecca said, turning to go, "I was kinda hoping you weren't going to ask me that."

Their laughter as she walked away was a good sign. She'd have to remember to be careful not to let them think that each setback during a trial was a total disaster.

Even when it was.

* * *

Allen Wysocki stayed quiet until Rebecca had finished, then said, "Are you looking to prosecute Osterreich, or just get rid of her?"

The bluntness of the question startled her. "I'm, uh, not really sure, to tell you the truth. I thought the first thing was to bring it to your attention."

Wysocki sat stiffly, in stark contrast to the normal relaxed posture that was supposed to communicate his unflappability under fire. He picked up a hand and let it drop. "So now you've done that. What do you want to do?"

"Maybe we've got grounds for a mistrial, if we can show that she passed confidential information to the prosecution."

"Hold it, hold it," Wysocki said quickly. "Do that, it means getting the assistant U.S. attorney disbarred."

"Only if he knew who it was. But if we get a mistrial, we start with a clean slate. All his cards are on the table."

Wysocki, betraying some agitation now, ran a hand through his hair. "Because one of this firm's employees betrayed a client confidence?" He shook his head. "No, ma'am. Uh-uh."

She was starting to understand his take on the matter. It had nothing to do with justice, ethics or the good of the client, but with the reputation of the firm and its ability to attract and retain other clients. "At the least, shouldn't we fire her?"

"On mere speculation? You have no proof!"

"Well, we're not going to hold a full-scale investigation and trial, Allen." Was this a new side of Allen Wysocki, the managing partner actually concerned about a nonbillable employee?

"You ever fire anybody in the state of California, Verona? It's pure hell. You practically have to prove they committed murder and catch them in the act. Otherwise they come after you with guns blazing and sue your ass off."

That was more like it. "Look, we've got some problems with our case. I don't know how much you—"

Wysocki glanced at his watch. "Listen, I'm already late for an appointment. We'll pick this up another time, okay? Come up with a plan for what you want to do about Osterreich and, uh, go over it with Personnel. Yeah, they know the ropes down there. . . ."

That solved the immediate problem of handling the secretary-reporter, but what about the ongoing conduct of the trial? Wysocki stood up and buttoned his suit jacket, fidgeting until she got the message and stood up herself.

She was alone on this case. Probably wouldn't see Wysocki again until James Perrein's first parole board hearing.

Chapter 25

Tuesday, November 17

Zuckerman pulled Rebecca aside as they neared the courtroom. "You'd better make sure you warn Terescu not to mention that the chip is programmable."

"Why would he do that?"

"That's my business," Zuckerman answered gruffly. "I'm just telling you there are pieces of my cross-examination that might lead in that direction, and he's not to mention it."

Terescu turned a far corner, and Rebecca pointed to him. "So tell him yourself."

"I can't, and you know it. He's your witness, you've had privileged conversations with him, and I can't talk to him."

"What makes you think I can control him?"

"Start with you controlling everything he said in your direct examination."

Rebecca iced up and spun away. "Get the judge to issue an order," she said as she walked away.

"She already has, Becky," he called after her, trying to keep his voice low so Terescu wouldn't hear him, and she stopped. "It'll only waste time to get her to do something about Terescu specifically, and the end result will be the same anyway."

She turned to face him. "You got someplace else you have to be?"

He gave her an exasperated look. *Why are you behaving like a child!*

The bailiff motioned them into chambers, where the judge asked Rebecca if she had repeated to Terescu the same admonition she had given to the two lawyers.

"Haven't had a chance, Your Honor. He just came in."

Goldin grew angry at this waste of the jury's time. "Couldn't this have been handled yesterday, or between the two of you?"

To Rebecca's surprise, Zuckerman didn't say a word about her petulant noncooperation, but took half the blame without protest.

She found Terescu in the audience section and explained to him that Zuckerman was going to recall him to the stand, and that the judge had issued an order that he was not to mention anything to do with the programmability feature of the chip, or even to say anything about the topic in general.

"But that may not be possible," he argued. "After all, what if—"

"Listen, Rado," Rebecca said. "This isn't a negotiation. I told you what I had to tell you. Do whatever the hell you want, but I won't defend you against a contempt charge, understand?"

He was surprised into silence by her harsh tone. She started to walk away, but suddenly turned and came back, leaning down to whisper in his ear, "And let's do each other a favor: I don't play scientist, you don't play lawyer." She gave him a humorless smile and clapped him on the shoulder. "Okay?"

Zuckerman and Rebecca both knew that even if the whole first floor of the courthouse were on fire, neither of them had better call for a sidebar to tell Goldin about it. Zuckerman called Terescu to the stand as soon as court was in session. It looked to Rebecca like the scientist had already fully recovered from whatever scare she had thrown into him.

"Professor," Zuckerman began, "do you recall your testimony concerning the meeting you had with Ms. Verona after your preliminary analysis?"

"I believe I do."

"During that testimony you were unsure as to the sequence of events regarding your conclusions, is that correct?"

"Yes."

"And have you had a chance to review that sequence?"

"Yes, and I've consulted with my notes as well. I hadn't done that prior to my testimony because I didn't know it was going to be asked of me."

Rebecca had her hands on the defense table, palms down, as if poised to leap, drinking in Terescu's every word.

Notes?

Without even looking at him, she could sense the tension in Steinholz as well.

"And what was your preliminary opinion going into that first meeting?"

"I had some great misgivings about our client's position regarding the manufacture of the chip in evidence."

"And can you tell us briefly what some of those were?"

"I believe so." Terescu glanced at Rebecca again, not with worry or hesitancy, but steadily, as if she were the one who ought to have been concerned and intimidated. "The fact that the encoding technique in the chip was the same as Tera-Tech's system. The number of transistors that had to be crammed inside, an area in which Tera-Tech has a great deal of emphasis and expertise ..." He essentially produced a succinct list of every bit of damning evidence the prosecution had against Tera-Tech. It was the kind of all-encompassing summarization that the prosecution normally wouldn't have an opportunity to present to the jury until closing, and here they were not only bringing it out in the middle of the trial but eliciting it from a defense witness during the defense's presentation of its case.

When Terescu was finished, Zuckerman asked, "Sir, have any of those opinions changed since you first presented them to defense counsel?"

"Well, I'm not sure what you mean. Uh"—he cleared his throat, trying to clear his discomfort—"my earlier testimony, well ..."

Zuckerman shook his head. "Let's not worry just yet about what you said, Doctor. What I'm really interested in for the moment is what you think. Have those opinions changed appreciably?"

Terescu nodded his understanding of what Zuckerman was driving at. "Those opinions have not really changed."

"And yet, meaning no disrespect, you weren't as clear about that under my last cross-examination, is that a fair statement?"

Terescu sighed. Remorsefully, it seemed to Rebecca. "I'm afraid that is the case, yes."

"And why is that?"

"I believe I may have confused the line between objective science and legal considerations."

"How did that come about?" Zuckerman asked forgivingly.

Terescu looked down and inclined his head to one side, as though reluctant to talk about it. "Things got, ah, a little confused for me during the subsequent conversation with Mr. Perrein's attorneys."

"Confused how?"

Terescu looked up. "We went through my preliminary analysis

point by point, and in each case, they showed me how other explanations were possible. And they also explained that the law required those alternatives to be considered."

"And that's when they explained the concept of reasonable doubt."

"Objection, leading," Rebecca said, but it was perfunctory and useless. She only did it to show Philip Mastilir, who was in the audience, that she was paying attention. So she added something more substantive. "Your Honor, didn't we already go through all of this?"

"I'll withdraw it." Zuckerman had just been eliciting a recap to ensure continuity in the jury's understanding of the significance of this testimony. "Doctor, is it fair to say that your testimony under Ms. Verona's direct examination was not an accurate representation of your opinion?"

Terescu lifted his chin, looked Zuckerman square in the eye, then turned toward the jury box. "Yes. And I apologize to the court and to the jurors. Furthermore—"

"Objection!" Rebecca shouted, coming to her feet. "Irrelevant, extraneous—"

"Sustained. Jury will disregard the witness's statement after he answered 'yes.' And Professor, please restrict your answers only to the questions put to you."

Goldin said it gently, clearly sympathizing with Terescu's predicament and impressed with his willingness to own up to his errors in open court. Rebecca could see the jurors' estimation of him shoot up the meter, the judge having stamped her judicial imprimatur on everything he would say from now on. Rebecca had discussed with Steinholz and Ehrenright the impossibility of rehabilitating Terescu as a credible expert for their side, deciding to seek only to neutralize him as much as possible, and here he was, more trustworthy, noble and downright believable than if the Pope himself had blessed his testimony.

And he was on the government's side. Rebecca recognized the examination style Zuckerman was using today: it was the same as when questioning one of his own witnesses.

"Doctor, did you know that Tera-Tech Integrated owned an XT-5055 machine?"

"Do you mean now, or . . . ?"

"No, prior to the defendant's testimony yesterday."

Terescu looked at the defense table grimly. "I had no idea."

"Had you asked the defendant to give you a list of all of their equipment?"

"Objection," Rebecca said. "It's a leading question."

"He's been declared a hostile witness, Your Honor," Zuckerman replied.

Rebecca shook her head disdainfully. "Yeah, well, under the circumstances, I'd say that no longer applies, wouldn't you?"

Goldin called them up to the bench. "She's right, Counselor: for all practical purposes, he's become a witness for the prosecution."

Before Goldin could wave them back, Rebecca said, "To save time later, Your Honor, I'll tell you now that I intend to ask permission to treat him as hostile in my redirect."

Zuckerman whipped his head around toward her. "He's your own witness!"

Rebecca shrugged and said, "So what?" While having Terescu declared hostile would allow her to ask leading questions, there was another, more important implication: it sent a signal to the jury that the witness was not necessarily being truthful.

"It doesn't really much matter whose witness it is, Mr. Zuckerman," Goldin said. "The only criterion is whether his testimony may be prejudiced against whoever happens to be examining him. Now am I just tripping or are you and this witness bosom buddies all of a sudden?"

Back at the podium, Zuckerman had to rephrase his question to elicit the information he needed from Terescu without overtly leading him to it. "During the course of your analysis, had you occasion to ask the defendant for certain items of information?"

"Yes."

"And among these, did you ask about the company's equipment?"

"Yes, the very first time we met."

"And did he supply you with a list of their equipment?"

"I thought he had."

"But . . . ?"

"It turned out only to have the devices used in the factory, not in the laboratory."

Rebecca rose to object. "Assumes facts not in evidence, Your Honor." Zuckerman had not put Perrein back on the stand after the break yesterday, electing to reexamine Terescu instead. There had been no formal testimony regarding what Perrein had told Terescu.

"Sustained. Jury will disregard."

Zuckerman bit the inside of his lip and took a moment to craft an admissible question. "Following Mr. Perrein's testimony yesterday, did you have an opportunity to speak with members of the defense team?"

"Yes."

"And during the course of those conversations, did you come to learn whether or not Tera-Tech had an XT-5055?"

"I did. They have one in the lab."

"But no one told you of its existence."

"Definitely not."

"Had you asked?"

"Not specifically by name. I did ask whether they had an ion beam machine of higher resolution than the one on the list Mr. Perrein gave me."

"And his answer?"

"He said no."

"And do you now view this as the defendant having lied to you?"

"Objection. No foundation, speculative and calls for a legal conclusion."

"I'll withdraw it. Doctor, what was the purpose of requesting a list of Tera-Tech's equipment?"

"To help me see if they possessed the capability to make a chip such as the one you have in evidence."

Steinholz leaned in toward Rebecca. "Didn't it used to be an *alleged* chip?" he whispered.

"Yes," she answered. "Back when he used to be *our* witness."

"And would it have made a difference to you where inside the company that equipment was located?"

"Of course not."

"So it was the defendant's decision to limit his answers to only the machines in the production division of his company?"

"Objection," Rebecca said. "How's he supposed to know who made the decision?"

"I'll rephrase. Who handed you the piece of paper?"

"Mr. Perrein."

"Thank you."

"This a good time for a recess, Counselor?" Goldin asked, sensing restlessness among some of the jurors. Mornings required more breaks owing to the endless supply of free coffee in the jury room at the beginning of each day.

Rebecca stopped Terescu as he tried to walk past the defense table to the back of the room. "Professor?"

"Yes?" he said warily, looking around, as if to make sure protection was close at hand.

"You're fired," Rebecca said. "You'll be paid for your time through the end of prosecution's cross, and then you're off the case."

It didn't surprise him, and Rebecca turned slightly to see that Zuckerman had been listening to their interchange. He stopped what he was doing.

"I'll testify as requested without compensation," Terescu said to Zuckerman, who nodded his acknowledgment, looked at Rebecca, and turned back to his own table.

Thinking she was alone at the defense table, Rebecca put her hands down and leaned forward, head bowed. She felt something grip her shoulder, hard, and turned to see Ehrenright standing next to her.

"What was that about playing a poor hand well?" he asked with a smile.

"I didn't mean *me*, dummy."

Following the short break, Terescu resumed the stand. Zuckerman took only a few minutes to confirm that Terescu's graduate student likely took important research secrets to Tera-Tech when Perrein stole him away, then turned the witness over to Rebecca for redirect.

The defense had taken a serious nosedive following Zuckerman's devastating cross of Terescu and his subsequent resurrection of the scientist as a near-Messianic believer in James Perrein's guilt. Now it was up to Rebecca to try to discredit the same man whose credentials she had so painstakingly established before beginning her direct examination of him exactly one week ago, when she presented him to the jury as an unimpeachable Nobel nominee.

She felt like the guy who'd killed both his parents, then pleaded for leniency in court because he was an orphan.

"You stated during Mr. Zuckerman's examination that you asked my client whether he had a high-resolution lithography machine in his company, did you not?"

"That's correct."

Rebecca stood with her arms folded, consulting no notes. "And he answered, 'No'?"

"I believe so," Terescu said.

Rebecca abandoned any pretext of civility or ordinary politeness. Regardless of how well the jury had taken to him, she had to convey her displeasure, then make sure the jury sympathized with the basis for it. "You didn't tell the prosecutor you believe so. You said my client answered, 'No.' Isn't that right?"

"What I meant was, he responded in the negative. Those may not have been his exact words. He also said he knew every machine they had and couldn't be mistaken."

"What were his exact words?"

"I can't recall."

She'd taught him well: *They can't hurt you if you just don't remember.* "During Mr. Zuckerman's questioning, it seemed to me that you were suddenly remembering just about everything with perfect recall."

"Objection! She's—"

"Withdrawn. Doctor, let me offer a possibility. Might he have said something like, 'We don't have one on the production floor'?"

"Could have been something like that." Terescu was doing a good job of keeping his cool.

"Would you like me to show you the transcript of that meeting?"

It was the first time today that Terescu looked unsure of himself. "No, that won't be necessary. I believe those were his words, yes." He had no way of knowing that Rebecca didn't have a transcript.

Rebecca nodded, underscoring that he had lost the point, and that she was getting to one. "And do you recall Mr. Perrein's testimony before this court as to where the machine actually was?"

"I believe he said it was in the lab."

"The lab. Is that the same as the production floor?"

"Of course not."

"So he was telling you the truth, wasn't he?"

"Objection," Zuckerman said. "Calls for a conclusion."

"Withdrawn. Professor"—Rebecca looked at the jury, bidding them to pay close attention—"was it your intention during Mr. Zuckerman's questioning to convey the impression to this jury that my client lied to you?"

"Objection! Argumentative, and she's badgering the witness!"

"I'll allow it. Witness may answer."

"Professor?" Rebecca pushed him.

"My intention was to reply truthfully to the questions."

"Ah, I understand. No problem. So when Mr. Zuckerman was

questioning you, your best recollection was that Mr. Perrein simply answered 'No' when you asked him about this machine, is that right?"

"That's right."

"But now you remember a little more detail."

"Maybe. But you supplied the words, not I."

Rebecca reached for her attaché, and Terescu could practically see a transcript of that meeting through the leather sides. "But that is how it happened, yes," he said quickly.

"And the difference is, now it appears that my client had been telling you the absolute truth, whereas before, under Mr. Zuckerman's questioning, it appeared that he had been lying."

"Objection, calls for speculation," Zuckerman said quickly, before Terescu could answer.

"Overruled."

"Object again, Your Honor. Calls for a legal conclusion."

"Sustained."

Rebecca could care less. The jury knew by now that Terescu was spinning heavily for whichever side he happened to be on at the moment.

Time to move on. "Now, you testified earlier that this machine, what was it . . . the XT-5055? You testified that this machine is incapable of making the chip in evidence, isn't that right?"

It was a straightforward establishing question, not meant to bring forth new information but simply to summarize and reintroduce a prior topic. *Previously, on* NYPD Blue . . . So Rebecca needed a moment to figure out what was going on and gather herself when Terescu said, "It might be modified to do it."

In real, not feigned, annoyance and wonder, Rebecca said, "How on earth could you possibly speculate about that since you still have no idea how the chip could even have been made!"

Terescu seemed to have given this some thought. "No matter how it was done, they'd still need a high-powered lithography machine to lay down a dense enough mask for the components."

"But there is still nothing you know of that could actually fabricate components small enough, even if you had such a mask in place, isn't that true?"

"Yes, well . . ." Terescu cupped his hand over his mouth and cleared his throat, looking away from both Rebecca and the jury as he answered, "but somebody built the chip, so somebody figured out how to do it, didn't they?"

Rebecca heard a stirring to her left and looked over to see Steinholz shaking his head. They were both thinking the same thing: Terescu had gone so far over to the other side he was even using the same arguments Zuckerman had used against *him* during cross-examination.

She knew enough to get off this topic immediately; in that direction lay only ruin. One good shot before she switched tracks, though. "During your prior testimony, you continually doubted that the chip in evidence could do anything remotely like what the government said it could, and now you're telling us that for sure, somebody built it. Do you want to explain to the jury how you came to change your—"

Rebecca froze. Had she completely lost her mind? The answer Terescu would give to this question was obvious: *It was because of you, Ms. Verona. You manipulated me into altering my original opinion!*

Rebecca sneered, and waved her hand dismissively, saying with great exasperation, "Never mind. Withdrawn." Telling the jury, *This guy is so pathetic I doubt I have to do anything else to prove it to you.* She was probably moving too fast for them to grasp most of the other nuances anyway, but she was operating according to old rink wisdom: *When you're skating on thin ice, speed is your only friend.*

"Doctor, let's talk about a project in your lab. The details aren't important; we'll just call it Project X." It was the programmability research, the forbidden topic. "How much work did you yourself do on this project versus how much your graduate student did?"

Zuckerman's head had jerked up as he heard Rebecca's oblique reference to that research area. Terescu mumbled something innocuous, and Rebecca realized she'd lucked out on her fishing expedition. "Sorry, what was that?"

"My student was the primary investigator."

"So he did most of the work."

"Well, no, not necessarily. Depends on how you define work. Do you mean the number of hours put in, or the intellectual contribution to the endeavor? Without the latter, there is no spark, no inspiration. No direction, if you will."

"I understand. So let me phrase it another way: if a panel of experts were to read all the lab notes, to whom would they ascribe most of the credit for the success of Project X?"

Terescu scratched his head, pulled at his lip, drummed his fingers on the arm of his chair. "Hard to say."

"Is it reasonable for us to assume that your graduate student did most of the sleeves-up as well as the brain work?"

"I suppose that would be fairly accurate."

"And, therefore, he didn't really 'steal' anything from the lab, did he? From you?"

Zuckerman, still trying to integrate this bit of news, objected on grounds of relevance, which was overruled, and then on the grounds that it called for a legal conclusion, which was sustained. As Rebecca turned to go back to work on Terescu, Steinholz caught her eye. She asked the judge for a moment.

When she got back to her seat, Steinholz was beside himself with anxiety: "Do you know what you just did? You just admitted that the student was an expert in programmability. You just verified that Tera-Tech had that technology all along!"

"Zuckerman already knew."

"No. I very much doubt it. He was fishing. And now he's pulled up a prize trout."

"So what?" Rebecca said, surprised at his concern. "Zuckerman will never put the programmability issue before the jury because it would be a security violation. They have no idea where 'Project X' fits in, and even—"

"*Fuck* the jury!" Steinholz responded impatiently. "You just told the FBI! Zuckerman could get a postponement, go into Tera-Tech's labs and get all the evidence he needs!"

"Based on what? The only link is the programmability issue, and he can't use it! If he tries to, I'll get the whole case thrown out because he sabotaged us, claiming it was a national security secret and then changing his mind so he could get a court order to search."

Steinholz wasn't buying it, but saw no point in arguing any further. "Why'd you even bother with those last questions to Terescu? About who should really get credit for Project X?"

"I was trying to damage his credibility, make him look bitter and irrational over his hatred of an old student who never really stole anything from him at all."

Steinholz pointed toward the jury. "They're so confused it's pathetic. And Terescu's killing us. There's nothing you can do with him anymore except let him hurt us further." He leaned in closer and drilled his eyes into hers. "End this, Becky."

She found his intensity disturbing. And she was having trouble trying to keep things sorted out in her own head. Every time she thought she'd defused one land mine, she found herself inadvertently stepping on another, and she felt herself getting lost. *Who wouldn't get confused?* she thought, dealing with a witness who used to be yours and whom you were now trying your best to discredit, attempting to make him look like a liar and a scoundrel but not in those instances when he said something that might exonerate your client, except that in many of those instances, the prosecutor was successfully showing that it really damned the client in the first place.

Somehow, Steinholz seemed to have a better handle on what was going on, and what effect it was having on the jury. Rebecca chanced a look at them now, and saw that Steinholz was dead right; there was confusion, discomfort . . . even fear, of not being able to track along with what was going on during testimony. They had every right to feel that way, and Rebecca realized that the spoils of this case would very likely go to whichever side eased that confusion, not the one that added to it. The management of those doubts and anxieties that were plaguing the jury might even be more important than the technical details of the matter at hand.

"No further questions, Your Honor," she announced to the judge. Zuckerman declined to recross Terescu, and Goldin adjourned court for the day.

Staying seated at the table, Steinholz said, "I'm a little worried." As Rebecca started to gear up a big *No shit!* look, he said, "Not just about the case. I'm worried about whether we did anything improper in not disclosing the student's work on the programmability project to Zuckerman earlier."

"Why the hell should we have told him?" On this point, Rebecca had no qualms. "It wasn't relevant until we found out that the government's chip is programmable, and Zuckerman withheld that from *us!*" Rebecca slapped Steinholz on the shoulder and stood up. "Listen, don't work yourself up over it. We got bigger troubles."

I got bigger troubles. Whatever minor, inconsequential points Rebecca might have scored against Terescu on the stand, it was quite clear that his confessional honesty could be a death knell not only for Tera-Tech but, more than likely, for her, too.

It was her idea to hire Terescu as an expert despite his open enmity toward Perrein. She might be able to argue that she had been justified in believing that Terescu had a well-developed sense of right and wrong, but she'd have to mention in that same argument that neither Arno Steinholz nor Justin Ehrenright had agreed with her, and both of them had voiced their objections clearly.

But that was a simple judgment call, an innocently motivated mistake that could be passed off easily as the kind of either-or decision that might have been handled with a coin toss. Much less innocent was how she had bullied Terescu into spinning his analytical conclusions toward the defense, apparently against his own better judgment and professional inclinations. It would not be difficult for someone less than charitable to make a persuasive case that she was guilty of malfeasance for browbeating an expert witness unschooled in the law into—when you got right down to it—misleading a jury while under oath.

Before they left the courtroom, Rebecca blew Judge Goldin a silent kiss for not allowing cameras in the courtroom.

Chapter 26

Wednesday, November 18

One thing about smog: it made for the damnedest sunrises.

Rebecca leaned back on her chair, feet up on the desk and sipping decaf as she watched the first morning rays refracting through a hundred known carcinogens that broke the light up into a shower of glowing reds and oranges. As the minutes passed, the light show faded depressingly, the deep, far spectrum colors disappearing behind the pale and washed-out blues and grays that overpowered them. The shimmering city lights that had sparkled out of the darkness were likewise extinguished under the increasing glare, slowly revealing the surrounding bleakness that only night could hide.

Rebecca sighed and glanced at the elegant gold clock face that hung suspended in a block of crystal on her desk, a gift from the government of Taiwan. She had about fifteen minutes before her meeting with Steinholz and Ehrenright at seven, an hour before James Perrein was due to show up. Plenty of time to continue working herself into a sucking morass of self-pity and then snap herself out of it.

Everything that the born-again Radovan Terescu testified against Tera-Tech was proving to be as substantiated and as devastating as the prosecution could possibly want. Zuckerman couldn't have scripted it better if he had made it all up. Had Terescu started out as a government witness, Rebecca could have deployed the usual arsenal of weapons to try to impeach his testimony. But he was a defense witness and, like a reformed smoker or a religious convert, he was becoming a proselytizer against that which he once embraced.

The hopelessness of the situation and its implied consequences dragged Rebecca down into consideration of her long and often lonely struggle to build a life for herself. It had not been a naturally progressing sequence of routine milestones but a series of battles in a larger war. There had been no one on the home front rooting for her, no familial safe haven as a contingency in the event of setbacks. At each step of the way, the prospect of failure did not portend a romantic opportunity for reflection and character building but a terrifying plunge into a black hole of hopelessness. Failure was, NASA-like, simply not an option.

And now Rebecca felt like her painstakingly constructed world was disintegrating. It wasn't that she was defending a guilty client. She didn't feel bad about that, nor was anybody condemning her for it; that was her job, and it was the client's right to be vigorously defended.

The problem lay in the question of whether she might have pushed the envelope a little too far in her determination to win the case. Her old affair with Perrein could come out in court, and Zuckerman might even imply that her zeal to defend him stemmed not from her conviction that he was innocent or from her sense of duty according to her place in the system, but from some poorly hidden desire to be a hero in rescuing his company in the hopes of getting him back. Wouldn't the passion that arose from such an unhealthy and conflicted state of affairs tempt even the strongest and most ethical advocate to step outside the bounds of judicial propriety?

Rebecca's anger at Perrein was nearly out of control. In the heat of trying a difficult but interesting and visible case, she had almost managed to suppress her outrage at his having used her for the second time. But since discovering that he had lied to her, risking not only his case but her hard-won reputation, fury swirled in her gut and threatened at times to overwhelm her. That she was constrained by the attorney-client privilege from doing anything about it only added to her frustration and feelings of helplessness.

It also dawned on her that she'd been taking it all out on Zuckerman. Well, why not? He was the enemy, and she was a licensed warrior, a *Kagemusha*. She owed it to her client and the system demanded it.

She set the coffee cup down, closed her eyes and rubbed her temples. That wasn't it at all. It was because letting it all out and venting on Zuckerman was safe.

"Tell you what I think," Ehrenright said. "Terescu is so frazzled and pissed off, he's actually trying to frame the company."

The thought, in various forms, had already occurred to the other two, although not necessarily in terms as harsh as Ehrenright's. "What if it's not a frame-up?" Steinholz threw in. "What if they're really guilty?"

Rebecca could tell from their faces that both of them had gotten about as much sleep the night before as she had. "Terescu couldn't possibly know that with certainty. He's just doing his best to implicate Tera-Tech, and I think maybe he doesn't give a damn if they're guilty or not."

"Which would make him an even bigger shit than I thought," Ehrenright responded.

"And a potentially felonious one, too." Steinholz was convinced that Zuckerman's central theory was that Terescu's old grad student gave Tera-Tech the tools to build the chip, and that the prosecution had the evidence to back it up but couldn't use it all. "Zuckerman knows everything we know, and then some. He's probably bouncing off the walls because the higher-ups won't let him use the programmability evidence on account of national security. If he could use it"—Steinholz looked from Ehrenright to Rebecca—"he'd win the case."

"As Samuel Goldwyn might have put it," Rebecca said to him, "never be definitive. Especially where juries are concerned. Besides, we'll never know, because Zuckerman can't bring it up to the jury. His biggest problem is how to nail Tera-Tech without revealing a national security secret."

"Face it, Becky," Steinholz said, swirling a last bit of coffee around in his cup, "he's already done it. And he's gonna be relentless because he's dead convinced the company is guilty."

"At least he is now," Ehrenright added, "even if he wasn't so sure in the beginning, and that's gonna make him twice as determined."

Great, Rebecca thought. *Two newly revivified crusaders: my expert and the prosecutor.* "What I'd like to know, what does he think about Perrein personally?"

"Good question," Steinholz said. "Been wondering about that myself. I think we may be able to show that Jim probably didn't have any idea what was going on."

"Because . . . ?"

"He was all for cracking open the chip. Shows he wasn't afraid of what was inside."

"Until recently," Ehrenright countered.

"But Zuckerman doesn't know that," Rebecca replied. "That was a privileged conversation."

A thought occurred to her. "And while we're at it," she said, giving both of them meaningful looks, "let's not fall into the trap of trying to figure out if he really knew or not. We don't care, remember? All that counts is what the government can prove."

"All right," Steinholz said. "I think the government is going to prove that Tera-Tech made the chip. If we think we have a good case for Jim not knowing what went on"—he hesitated, well aware of the implications of his impending suggestion—"can we get him a deal?" Meaning, throw Tera-Tech to the dogs and keep Perrein out of prison.

Ehrenright wasn't surprised, but had a different concern. "*Somebody* inside that company is a felon, maybe a couple of somebodies, and the FBI is going to track them down. Do we have an obligation to protect *them* in this deal?"

"No," Rebecca said with certainty. "We only have two clients, and one of them is a corporate entity. Individual employees are not our concern, and Perrein is the owner. If he wants to give up the company, that's his call."

"So are we now conceding Tera-Tech's guilt?" Steinholz asked.

"Not necessarily." Rebecca was glad he'd brought that up. "We're just playing with possibilities. Perrein's gonna be here soon and we have to give him an assessment. Decisions are all his." With most clients, the lawyers' recommendation would be followed almost all the time. With Perrein, there was no way to know.

"Then let's play with another possibility," Steinholz said, looking at his watch and realizing they were running out of time. He clasped his hands and leaned forward. "And this relates to why Perrein was willing to have the chip examined. What if he not only knew about it being made in his company, what if it was made under his orders?"

Ehrenright frowned. "Then why would he agree to have the chip examined?"

"Because he believed that there was nothing in that chip that could be traced back to Tera-Tech," Steinholz explained. "Who would have the expertise? The world's greatest expert was on *our* side. So Perrein looks innocent as hell, demanding that it be opened, totally confident that there is nothing that would point specifically to Tera-Tech."

Rebecca saw the logic. "Now the same world's greatest expert is out to nail him. Now he's not so sure he's safe anymore."

"And he also discovers that the prosecution knows a helluva lot more than he ever thought they would," Ehrenright offered. "Now he's worried that opening the chip really could give him away."

"Which would explain why he changed his mind," Steinholz finished.

It all fit, and it was so obvious Rebecca was surprised she hadn't seen it herself. But were they giving up too easily?

"Wish we had a good way to test some of these theories," Ehrenright mused out loud.

Rebecca looked at her watch. "Good way's arriving in about three minutes."

Rebecca let Arno Steinholz lay it out for Perrein. Among the three attorneys, Steinholz was the best at keeping complexities organized in his mind and explaining them coherently. Without any attempt at this point to imply a preferred course of action, he tried to present a balanced assessment of the strengths and weaknesses of the prosecution's case and the defense's ability to refute it.

It was a delicate tightrope walk of diplomacy, necessitating constant reference to evidence, provability and witness credibility but never a single mention of whether any of those things actually bore any relation to the objective truth of the situation in the real world. It was about who held what cards, not about what really *was*.

"The prosecutor's making a very strong case for Tera-Tech being the manufacturer of that chip," Steinholz explained, "mostly by default, nobody else being much of a candidate for having done the job. We kept pressing to get hold of the chip and have it disassembled, which shows that you weren't afraid of the government discovering what was inside." Whether Perrein really had any knowledge of the chip's genesis was beside the point. To the trier of fact, his behavior implied innocence, and reasonable doubt would work in his favor.

"But that was all out of the jury's earshot," Perrein observed. "How would they know that even happened?"

"We can bring it up," Rebecca assured him. "Just not the details. We wanted it opened, at your request, and were denied for reasons of national security."

It went on, the lawyers slowly and gently but firmly helping Perrein to understand that they'd already thought of everything he was likely to, and none of it came up good. They had known that this was probably the trial's darkest hour, and now Perrein knew it, too. He didn't look well. Paler than usual, almost sallow, even his basal surliness rate seemed to have dropped a notch or two.

"Is it possible to work out a settlement with the government?" he asked. "Maybe a no-contest plea?"

Her co-workers looked surprised at this too easy laydown, but Rebecca saw it only as a hard-core businessman's objective cut to the heart of the matter. "Remember that this is a criminal case. Money might not get you out of this one. You could be facing serious prison time, even if you go *nolo contendere*."

"What's the harm in feeling Zuckerman out?"

"The usual. Shows him we think our hand is weak, things like that. But I think you may be on to something." *Especially since this was the point we were trying to get you to in the first place.* "So if you want me to make the approach, I'll do it."

And thus it was Perrein's decision, without even a recommendation from his lawyers on the record.

Rebecca liked tweaking him, but didn't want to let it interfere with her responsibilities as his lawyer. "Your call, Jim."

"So let me see if I got this straight," Zuckerman said, sitting forward on his desk chair, pen poised over the yellow legal pad in front of him. "You're asking me to let James Perrein plead *nolo*, and in exchange he gives up control of his company but does no time?"

Rebecca looked around at Zuckerman's roomy office, as if to ask the walls if he could have been serious about needing a restatement of the proffered deal. "That's the deal."

Zuckerman laughed, once, mirthlessly. "Explain to me why

someone who broke national security laws should get off so lightly." He put his hands behind his neck and leaned way back.

"Lightly?" She started to shake her head and grunt a sarcastic riposte, then remembered that a negotiation like this had more to do with personal interaction than the letter of the law, especially since the law really didn't enter into a plea bargain. She tried to sound soft and reasonable.

"Incarceration isn't the only legitimate form of punishment, David. You have to take into account the punishment's effect on the defendant. If a person is poor, the only thing you can deprive him of is his personal freedom, so your only option is imprisonment. But if someone is well off, there are all kinds of painful things you can do to him."

Despite his look of skepticism, he was listening, so she went on. "The net effect of punishment is not the condition in which you leave the convicted person, but how much you've taken away from him. Who suffers more, a CEO shamefully thrown out of his company, or an indigent doing six months in minimum security? The indigent gets his life back after he walks the walk; the CEO is done forever. So don't be too quick to think this guy gets off easy. He'd jump at the chance to go away for a while and pick up where he left off." She put an elbow on the armrest of her chair and rested her chin in her hand, awaiting his comeback.

"But what kind of message would that send to those indigent citizens, Rebecca? A guy has money, he doesn't have to go to jail? You think a dishwasher is going to have a lot of sympathy for someone who pays his way out of prison time?"

"I'm not sure a dishwasher's sympathy is the first thing I'd worry about in determining the appropriateness of a punishment. Jeez, David, dishwashers I know, they'd castrate neighborhood drug dealers without a trial, and you're going to solicit their advice?"

"It was a just metaphor. *Reductio ad absurdum.* When the hell'd you get so literal, anyway?"

She was not about to let herself get distracted, and she was also not going to allow herself to get drawn into a philosophical argument and lose her cool. "Take that same CEO, maybe one with a big reputation for integrity and fair dealing. He speaks at Rotary clubs and business conventions. People stand around for hours hoping to shake his hand. Then you brand him a criminal, deprive him of his job, send him home in disgrace and effectively destroy everything he holds dear. Is it necessary after all of that to deprive him of his physical freedom as well?"

"But inequitable punishment isn't constitutional."

"The Constitution." Rebecca clenched her jaw and tried to get past it. Then she slammed her hand down on her armrest and looked away, hissing, "I *hate* the goddamned Constitution," thereby losing all the decorum she had been trying to maintain.

Zuckerman stretched his arms. "Done pretty well with it so far."

Rebecca looked at him in disbelief, then jumped out of the chair and stalked over to the window. "Everything's changing at the speed of light. We change car models every twelve months but that tectonic plate of a charter averages five new sentences a decade!"

Zuckerman laughed despite himself, which encouraged Rebecca to continue. "We're supposed to be a democracy," she said as she reversed direction and headed for the other wall, "but instead we pay nine crusty old farts *we the people* didn't get to vote for to sit in Washington and do any damned thing they please!"

"C'mon, Becky. That's a little harsh. You really have that little regard for the Founding Fathers?"

He was back to "Becky." *Good sign.* "You mean the ones who owned slaves, or the other ones? I'll tell you what the problem is, Zuck. Those guys believed the country would look the same in 1987 as it did in 1787, so they locked the Constitution in concrete. Just as soon as they got rid of the British, they replaced them with a piece of paper that was stricter than George the Third!"

"Good Lord!" Zuckerman stared at her, frowning and smiling at the same time. "What the hell got into you?"

Her loss of respect for the Constitution began during her representation of a group of abortion activists before the Supreme Court. Standing before the bench for the first time, she'd said to the Justices, *I did a strange thing last week: I read the Constitution. All of it, cover to cover, including the amendments. And you know what I discovered? Abortion isn't in there. Not anywhere. And trying to pretend it is by referring to privacy rights and other unrelated clauses doesn't make a lick of sense. The issue simply doesn't belong before Your Honors. Send it back to the states and let the people decide for themselves!*

The justices were so indignant they could barely speak. Imagine the temerity of this overgrown law student to tell *them*, the Justices of the U.S. Supreme Court, that there was an issue in this country they shouldn't be deciding!

The group that had hired Rebecca fired her before they even made it out of the main chamber, and she knew that the only way she'd ever appear in front of this court again was if every one of them died and got replaced before she retired. Which was roughly when Allen Wysocki got hold of her and taught her how law was really practiced.

"Hey," Zuckerman said, snapping his fingers. "You still here?"

"Yeah. As if I could even give a shit what the founders would have thought, anyway."

"Nice speech, Becky." Zuckerman said amiably. "That supposed to convince me to go easy on Perrein?"

"No, it's supposed to make you less smug about falling back on some brittle piece of parchment glaciating its way across the ages when you know I'm right." So much for self-control. "What are you worried about, how it's going to play out in the press?"

"Course I am. Are you telling me you're not?"

"So what's it to be, Zuckerman? You want to deal or do we go back to court?"

Rebecca knew those were really the only two options he had, and that he was smart enough not to be put off by her having phrased it as an ultimatum. He would put personal differences aside and try to salvage something out of this case, because his boss wasn't going to care if he saved face, only if he got the job done. So maybe it wouldn't be such a friendly negotiation but at least their mutual self-interest would stop them from getting too emotional and missing an opportunity. Rebecca opened up her writing pad and settled in for a protracted debate.

"See you in court, Counselor," Zuckerman said, standing up and pointing toward the door.

She was so deeply absorbed in planning how to make this sound like it was all Zuckerman's fault that she let out a little yelp when Arno Steinholz opened her office door from the inside.

"The hell are you doing here?" she said as she blinked away her surprise and walked in. Justin Ehrenright was seated behind her desk, swiveling back and forth in her chair, fingertips below his chin in an attitude of prayer.

"You'd better hear this, Becky," Steinholz said, motioning her to a visitor's chair in front of her own desk.

"I take it there's no deal," Ehrenright said.

Rebecca tilted her head to one side and shrugged. "This is what I'd better hear?"

Ehrenright closed his eyes. "Uh-uh."

Steinholz took the seat next to Rebecca and leaned in toward her, saying in a loud stage whisper, "Justin's had a revelation."

"Oh!" she whispered back equally loudly, nodding her understanding, as Ehrenright spread his hands apart and gazed heavenward, swami-like. "But this isn't funny, is it?" she asked him.

Ehrenright dropped his hands into his lap and shook his head. "No. I've been thinking."

"That's what you're good at, Butch. And . . . ?"

"There are an awful lot of pieces of this case that don't fit. I'm not talking about the usual testimony bullshit and spinning."

Rebecca dropped her attaché on the floor next to her chair and crossed her legs, indicating she was ready to listen.

"Why did Terescu really agree to be on the defense team?" Ehrenright asked rhetorically, holding up his thumb. "Why was it so easy to get him to see things our way during trial preparation?" He stuck out his index finger. "And how come he discovered the true faith and flipped so zealously to the prosecution's side?" He put up his third finger and dropped his hand to the desktop, palm up.

"What's the big mystery?" Rebecca asked. "He probably thinks we believed from the beginning that Tera-Tech was guilty, and that we tried to set him up to testify for them anyway, making him look like a bought-and-paid-for hired gun."

"That only answers the last question," Steinholz responded. Clearly, they'd thought this all out while she was at Zuckerman's office. "As to why he agreed to help us in the first place, well, Justin and me, we just figured you'd offered him sexual favors when you two were alone."

"Okay, that answers the first question," Rebecca said with a straight face. "As to why he was so easy to twist, well, hey"—she held out her hands—"it's why they pay me the big bucks, boys."

"That's not it, Becky," Ehrenright said, his expression sober once again.

"Then why don't we skip to Act Three and you can tell me whodunit."

Ehrenright sniffled and sat back on the chair. "The real reason Terescu agreed to be on the defense team in the first place was so he could get his hands on the chip."

He waited until it penetrated, which he knew it had when he saw Rebecca stiffen. "Why?" she asked.

"So he could examine it, find out how it works, and steal the underlying technology," Steinholz answered.

Rebecca didn't move at first, her eyes focusing on some distant point even though she was still facing Ehrenright. After a few seconds, she lifted her head slowly and turned toward Steinholz.

"It occurred to Justin right after you left that this chip couldn't have been patented, since nobody even knew it existed until recently. That means it's open season for whoever wanted to try to duplicate it and put it on the market."

Ehrenright stood up and walked to the window, seating himself on the sill with one leg dangling. "But nobody on our side was allowed near the chip. Once Terescu was denied the opportunity to open it up, he just figured he might as well turn around and screw Tera-Tech, and Perrein, *and* his old grad student, as badly as he could by siding with the prosecution."

"Would have been easy for him, too," Rebecca said as the sense of it became obvious, "since I talked him out of all his doubts in the beginning. All he had to do was just dredge them up again."

"Well." Steinholz cleared his throat nervously, and Ehrenright turned away to stifle a laugh. "I hate to break this to you, but it had nothing to do with your innate genius for preparing expert witnesses. If Terescu hadn't played ball during trial preparation, he wouldn't have been allowed to continue on the team and wouldn't have had a chance to get at the chip. That's the only reason he was so cooperative."

Rebecca felt a tremor run through her belly. "*He* was manipulating *me?*"

"Starting to look that way," Ehrenright said. "If he didn't come around to our way of thinking, he was out of the picture."

Rebecca dropped her head and massaged the sides of her face with her fingertips. It was a devastating and irrefutable insight, and everything they'd done was now coming back to haunt them in the worst possible way. And what could they do, cry foul because their expert was more guilty of playing their own game than they were? It would be like a drug suspect complaining to the judge that he only had two grams on him instead of the four the cops were claiming.

She wasn't ready to concede it entirely just yet. There were still some loose ends. "How come Terescu was so reluctant to give the student credit for the work he did on programmability? If he wanted to implicate Perrein, he should have brought that out himself, to make him look bad."

Steinholz had begun smiling halfway through the question: another issue he and Ehrenright had dealt with. "Simple. It was much more dramatic to let you beat it out of him."

"But how'd he know I was going to do that? It was a last-minute decision!"

"He didn't," Ehrenright answered. "He probably thought that Zuckerman would. But then you started in on trying to get him to look like an irrational old man for calling his grad student a thief . . ."

". . . and I stood there pummeling him into admitting that the grad student had done most of the work."

"He lapped it all up. You were trying to get him to look like an idiot, while *he* was trying to prove that the student supplied Tera-Tech with the expertise it needed to make the chip."

"Kind of like shooting the ball at the wrong basket," Steinholz observed.

"I think I got the point already, okay?" Rebecca frowned and tried to think. "He tricked me and nailed Perrein at the same time." She took a few more seconds, then said, "How is it possible that he could really have been that venal? Or that smart? I mean, I understand what you're saying, but for heaven's sake, step back a bit. Isn't this a little intricate?"

"It's a theory," Steinholz said offhandedly. "A good one, but we need to confirm it or refute it."

"What we were thinking, why not call Dr. Muller?" Ehrenright suggested. "Ask her about that conversation she had with Terescu, the one in which he agreed to speak to us."

"Ask her what?"

"Who placed the call that led to that lunch they had together? If Terescu was the one who initiated that conversation, that would pretty much seal it, wouldn't it?"

"Because it would mean he actually took steps to get on this case." Rebecca saw it now, and stood up, reaching across her desk toward the speakerphone. She turned it on and punched a speed dial code, then picked up the handset.

"Jessica?—Rebecca Verona.—Good, and you?—Don't be crazy. Trial's practically over, what do I need you for? Listen, I want to ask you a question, all right?—Lemme put you on the speaker so a couple of my guys can listen in."

She turned the speakerphone on again and dropped the handset into the cradle. "You there?"

"Yep." Muller's voice, clipped of texture by the telephone circuitry, sounded even more tinny and flat when amplified by the speakerphone.

Steinholz and Ehrenright moved in closer to the desk.

"Jessica, remember back when you got Dr. Terescu to agree to speak with us?"

"Sure. Helluva nice lunch."

"Right. What we're curious about, who called whom when you set that up?"

"Uh, lessee . . . oh, yeah. I called Rado."

The three of them exchanged puzzled glances. It had all seemed to fit, but how could it if Terescu hadn't initiated the call to Muller? He *had* to have wanted on the team, or nothing else of Ehrenright's theory made any sense. Were they all just reinforcing each other's paranoia?

"Anybody still there?" the speaker crackled.

"Yeah, sorry. You're sure about that, are you?"

"Uh-huh. Why, that not good?"

"No, no," Rebecca responded quickly, trying to keep the dejection out of her voice and at the same time not give Muller cause to worry or suspect anything. "No big deal."

Ehrenright and Steinholz began standing up from their huddle around the speakerphone and sullenly turning away.

"Yeah, I remember it real well," Muller was saying, "because I phoned him right after you told me the other side had gotten hold of an actual chip."

The desk shook as the three of them scrambled to get back in position, causing some pencils and a glass to rattle around. "What was that?" Muller asked.

Rebecca held up a hand to silence everybody. "Nothing," she said as calmly as she possibly could. "Knocked my purse over. Listen, did you tell Terescu that, about the chip? On the phone, I mean."

"Oh, sure. That's why I bothered to call him at all. I think it piqued his interest a little."

Ehrenright dropped his jaw. "A little?" he mouthed with as much exaggeration as he could muster. Steinholz pressed his lips together and nodded slowly.

"That's kind of what I figured," Rebecca said, anxious now to end this conversation as quickly as possible. "Listen, thanks, Jessica. I appreciate it, and sorry for the intrusion."

"Anytime. Sisterhood thing, you know?"

Rebecca laughed so Muller could hear it, then rang off.

"Well, I'll be dipped in shit," Ehrenright said slowly as he stood up straight.

Rebecca tried gamely to smile as her two friends indulged in a few minutes of self-congratulatory banter reminiscent of the about-to-be-executed engineering student who managed to fix a problem with the guillotine. In their excitement over having decrypted the difficult code of Radovan Terescu's behavior, they forgot not only that it could mean the end of the case, but the end of their friend Rebecca as well, the overconfident genius who'd engineered Terescu's presence despite the protests of everybody else associated with the defense.

She made it a point not to sound critical as she said, "Well, what happens to our case now?"

Steinholz had a ready answer. "Expose the bastard and get a mistrial."

"Expose him how?" Rebecca asked.

"What do you mean how?" Steinholz said. "We just tell the judge what he did. You have any doubt she'll grant a mistrial?"

"What are you going to tell Goldin?" Rebecca persisted.

"That Terescu agreed to join our defense team in order to peek inside the chip," Ehrenright said impatiently, as though explaining the obvious to a child. "That he started out on our side, then jumped ship when his plan failed. That he was essentially lying on the stand, that he—"

"Prove it."

Ehrenright stared at her, then looked to Steinholz for some support. It didn't take much more discussion for them to realize that there was not a shred of evidence that would allow them to back up their theory about Terescu. Intent was a difficult thing to demonstrate definitively, and without evidence of their expert's intentions, there was nothing to compel the judge to accept their version of events.

Worse yet, Rebecca realized, despite their conviction that Terescu purposely sabotaged their case, nobody on the team believed in Tera-Tech's innocence anymore. But she didn't want to get into that just yet. For reasons she would probably have difficulty articulating, Rebecca still didn't believe Perrein had been aware of it. Knowing how silly that would sound, she kept it to herself.

"So what's Plan B?" Ehrenright asked.

"I think that trying to prove Jim's innocence is a dead end," Steinholz said after a few moments, standing up to stretch. "We need to explain that to him, because he still thinks he's not supposed to have to prove anything, being the defendant."

Rebecca could just see that explanation: *Fact is, Jimmy, they've already proven you guilty, which is how it'll stand if we just sit back.* "What are we suggesting to him?"

"I think there's only one possible way out of this," Ehrenright ventured.

Rebecca knew that whatever Ehrenright came up with wouldn't be based on irrefutable logic or brilliantly incisive legal argument. That would be more Steinholz-like, and this situation was beyond resurrection by the standard protestations of demonstrable proof. It always was, when you had a guilty client.

"Jim has to go on a hunt for a perpetrator within his ranks," Ehrenright said. "If he can ferret out somebody who sold out the corporation, or even a small group who did it"—he turned up a questioning palm—"maybe we can persuade the government to go after the real perps, and let the company off with something along the lines of a stiff fine for, uh, I don't know, lax security procedures or something."

"And lay off Perrein completely." Steinholz put his hands on his hips. "I like it."

The idea was compelling, especially since they all considered the case otherwise lost. Ehrenright questioned whether Perrein would agree to it, as opposed to continuing the fight in court.

"I can guarantee it," Rebecca said with surprising assurance. Steinholz asked her why she was so certain.

"Why?" She stood up and walked to the window, staring down at passersby hundreds of feet below, people who were worrying about car payments and crabgrass and their rotten, snotty kids. Those worries sounded pretty attractive to her right now. "Because he knows Tera-Tech made the chip."

She turned from the window. "Even if he wasn't involved at the time, he knows now. Just like we know. And since he believes he's now got a problem, he really has no choice except to try to put the best face on it. He may be a galaxy-class asshole, but he ain't stupid."

For no reason she could imagine, Uncle Charlie's face popped

int her mind, so real and three-dimensional it startled her. She re-
called how, as she grew older, her perception of his personality had
changed. He had started out as a nasty and self-centered sonofabitch, not much different from a million others, an unthinking
automaton hitched to his id with steel straps. But as years passed,
she saw something different: he wasn't simply insensitive and un-
feeling. His gratification sprang at least partially from the knowledge that others hadn't fared so well, and he made the parents of
other skaters feel twice as miserable as they already did whenever
their progeny were bested by his Wendy. *Second place is the first
loser, Sylvia,* he'd once remarked to a rival's mother. He had a hundred hurtful phrases like that. Charles Malacore couldn't enjoy a
meal unless he knew someone else was starving.

"Holy shit . . ." she muttered.

"Hey, you okay?" Ehrenright asked her, real concern on his face.

She had no idea how long she'd been standing there. She'd even
forgotten where she was, and it took her a moment to reorient as
she looked at her fellow attorneys.

"Terescu didn't stumble into anything," she said. "He planned
the whole thing, right from the beginning."

"What are you talking about?" Steinholz said it quietly, not as a
challenge but as an invitation. There was something hanging out in
space that he could sense but not see, and he had a strong feeling
Rebecca was about to tell him what it was.

"He knew how dramatic it would be if he started off as a defense witness and then jumped to the other side mid-trial." Deep
lines creased her forehead as the ineffable truth of it became even
clearer. "He knew it in advance. Wait a minute . . . !"

She grabbed the side of her head, and couldn't help smiling at
the brilliant audacity of it. "Terescu triple-whammied us," she
said, almost admiringly. "He not only had an opportunity to get at
the chip, he had the chance to finally get his revenge on Perrein,
and maybe even his grad student as well. If things had gone a little
differently, I'd bet anything he would have examined the inside of
that chip, gotten everything he needed, and *then* stood up and announced that his examination proved that Tera-Tech had built it
with his old student's help!"

Ehrenright was dumbfounded. "You're telling us he had this all
worked out before . . ."

"Before he even came to the office for lunch. Shit, he had it figured as soon as Jessica Muller hung up the phone before *their* lunch!"

"What makes you so sure?" Steinholz asked skeptically.

Rebecca laughed. How to explain a type she knew so well? "Here's a guy who doesn't know who he hates more, Jim Perrein or his traitorous student, and he agrees to defend the company that one owns and the other works for. Smartest engineer in the world and all of a sudden somebody plunks down a quarter-inch chunk of metal that stares up at him and says, 'Hey, big shot. You want to see some *real* science?' And yet he's willing to get on a stand in full public view so the world can find out he got trumped by some anonymous nobody that makes his lab look like they're still playing with Tinker Toys?"

"But *you* hate Perrein," Ehrenright said, "and you were willing to defend him."

"But I had something to gain!" Rebecca said forcefully. "I had a *reason* to keep it in my pants and play the game. What the hell did Terescu have, other than to make himself look like an idiot?"

"That chip staring up at him."

"Exactly. With the added bonus that he might be able to get inside it and fuck over his enemies at the same time. How could he resist?"

"And all he had to do," Steinholz ventured, "was play long enough to open it up, then he was free to turn around and throw Perrein to the wolves."

"But he never got to open it up," Rebecca said. "So he just busted Perrein a little early. Either way, he accomplishes quite a bit of very satisfying damage."

Now she caught herself displaying the same kind of self-congratulatory excitement as they had just a short while ago. It was inappropriate, and it didn't take long for her to find a reason to dampen it.

"But it's all irrelevant," she said, evoking startled reactions in the other two. "What I mean, maybe Terescu did do that, maybe he did trick us, but that's not what's important right now."

She walked around behind her desk and sat down in the chair Ehrenright had vacated. "What's important is that not only does he truly believe Tera-Tech built the chip"—she looked up—"he believed it before he ever even came on the case."

Ehrenright's eyes widened. "Why would he have believed that?" He asked it like he'd rather not hear the answer.

Rebecca swiveled her chair to the side, closed her eyes and

leaned her head back. "Because he's smarter than all of us, and he doesn't have a client he's paid to believe in."

"So our client is guilty?"

"How could it be otherwise."

"Hold it just a second." Ehrenright's voice was stern. "We have two clients, Tera-Tech and Jim Perrein. Which one are you talking about?"

"Tera-Tech for sure," Rebecca answered without moving. "I'm going to have to think real hard about whether I believe Perrein knew about it."

"Well, don't think about it too hard, Becky," Ehrenright admonished. "Let's not forget we're still obligated to defend him."

Rebecca nodded. "True." She sat up straight and turned back to them. "But we're also obligated to tell Perrein he's going to lose the case, and tell him in enough time for him to try to do something about it."

Rebecca was now in even deeper trouble than she'd thought she was. Her strategy to get Terescu on the defense team not only failed to support their case, it had probably doomed it from day one.

Steinholz looked around, seemingly annoyed at the atmosphere of surrender that appeared to have taken hold in the room. "Are we really going to let Terescu get away with this?" he said angrily. "It's unthinkable that someone could cause this much damage and walk away scot-free! Hell, there's fraud, perjury, breach of contract . . ." He banged a fist on Rebecca's desk. "There's got to be a way to prove it!"

Rebecca felt a frightening sensation, a desire to choke the life out of Terescu with her bare hands, and she had to consciously fight it down, not daring to speak until it had begun to subside. But seething anger remained. "There's no way in hell we're going to let him get away with it," she said quietly, but with venom. "I promise you that. If we have to, when this case is finally over, I'll go to Zuckerman and file a formal complaint and demand that the Department of Justice investigate it. But for right now, we need to worry about our client."

Steinholz thought of something. "Terescu's the one who suggested that we be allowed to open the chip because the encryption was hardwired and wouldn't interfere with national security requirements. But all along he knew the chips were really programmable. Isn't that perjury?"

Rebecca shook her head. "How do we prove he knew they were programmable? Look, let's not worry about this now. . . ."

"Fine, but that's the key right there," Steinholz insisted, "and I don't want to forget it. If there's a way to show that he *knew* that chip was programmable, then he's dead meat."

"Okay. We got about half an hour to figure out how to handle Perrein when he gets here, so let's start worrying about that."

It was easy enough to say to the others, but one thought persisted and she couldn't shake it: all along, she'd assumed it was her brilliant persuasiveness that got Terescu to sign on. Now she knew that it had been a done deal from the beginning, and that *she* was the one who had been manipulated. Terescu'd had her panting for him, and must have been inwardly laughing his head off at her impassioned, quasi-sexual entreaty to join the case.

Perrein had said barely a word as the three of them laid it out for him.

"So the way we figure it," Ehrenright finished up, "your only chance is if a lone perp is found within your ranks. If you fully co-operate and make it possible for the DoJ to find the guy, Zuckerman might be willing to go easy on you if we can convince him you didn't know about it."

Ehrenright sat back, looking at Perrein, who remained motionless. The lawyers exchanged glances, not having gotten any feedback from him during the whole explanation.

"I thought the burden of proof was on the government," Perrein said finally. "I'm not supposed to have to defend myself if they can't prove their case." It was accusatory, a message to them that he felt they were not looking out for his best interests.

"That's true." Rebecca needed a way to explain this without telling him that he now looked so guilty he might as well get fitted up for striped overalls. "But according to the law, if it happened in your company, you're automatically guilty, especially since you own the place lock, stock and barrel. So the burden shifts to you, and we have to take the offensive, show them that, in reality, you were an innocent dupe."

Perrein closed his eyes, then opened them and exhaled slowly. He knew they had thought this all out thoroughly, but he was still having trouble making up his mind.

Steinholz decided to try to push him. "Remember in our first meeting, when you explained how you had no earthly reason to do something that stupid for no return? You said the money was peanuts."

Perrein flicked his eyes toward him. "You going to tell me that all those bullshit reasons Zuckerman wormed out of Terescu are really—"

Steinholz shook his head. "There's gotta be a helluva lot more direct motivation than some ethereal hands-across-the-water marketplace advantage, which is pure crap in the first place." Perrein apparently liked Steinholz's spirited partisanship, and nodded his encouragement to continue.

"The Chinese aren't stupid. They'll go for the best stuff at the best price no matter who thinks they're great friends, and their old fart hard-liners still don't like cozying up to running dog imperialists."

"Bet your ass on that one," Perrein agreed. "Asshole lawyers locked away in the Justice Department don't know squat about real business."

"Right. But now go down lower in the food chain at Tera-Tech." Steinholz tilted his head and bore in on Perrein. "How much are you paying your research scientists? Forget the ones at the top, but maybe the second tier, those fresh young Ph.D.'s who don't know diddly about the commercial worth of their work yet. You figure a couple million tax-free might motivate one or two of those guys?"

Perrein was wilting under this logical assault, and wanted to change the subject for at least a few minutes while he let it marinate. "How could Terescu do all this just to get back at me for stealing a lousy graduate student?"

"Towering egotists do strange things sometimes," Rebecca answered, looking Perrein straight in the eye. She hoped that this jab might jar him into seeing that their way was the only way right now, but he didn't get it.

"Maybe his life under Ceauşescu," Ehrenright said. "Back in Romania."

Perrein didn't buy it. "Still doesn't fit."

"It doesn't matter," Rebecca said. "There's always some kind of explanation no matter what anybody does. Serial killers and bank robbers always have good reasons. Personally, I'd like to shoot anybody using a leaf blower. And that's why we have laws."

"She's right, Jim. It doesn't really matter." Steinholz picked up that he was having the most sway on Perrein right now, and took advantage of it. "We gotta figure out our next move. They're killing us in court, so it's time to move out of there and into an arena where we have a better chance."

They spent some time going over the details of how to frame another proposal. With each sign that Perrein was growing more convinced, Rebecca grew increasingly mortified at the prospect of slinking back to Zuckerman for the second time that day. But as she'd said to her associates on many occasions, if you want to catch a hat in the wind, run past it, not after it.

Chapter 27

Zuckerman hadn't said a word in nearly half an hour. Except once, about twenty minutes ago, when his secretary rang in and he told her he didn't want any interruptions, no matter what.

But now Rebecca had finished, and it was his turn to speak, which he was having some trouble getting around to. She'd just told Zuckerman everything, right down to the last detail, spending most of her time describing her team's suspicions about Terescu. She waited patiently.

"You just handed me the whole case. You know that."

She shrugged. "You were gonna win it anyway."

"So why don't I go back into court and put it to the jury?"

"You can if you want to. But you know, and so does Judge Goldin, that it can't possibly stand up to an appeal. We'll be back in court having a new trial, only this time we'll be ready for you."

"I might be willing to take that chance."

"Shall I leave?"

He took his time thinking about it. "No." He stood up and went to the door. "Cup of tea?"

As she stood up, Rebecca felt her panty hose snag momentarily on some unseen splinter on the chair leg. She walked behind Zuckerman so she could sneak a quick glance; sure enough, there was a tear toward the side of her left knee. In short order it would begin to run.

They walked down the hall together, keeping their voices low as lawyers and various other DoJ personnel walked past them, Rebecca keeping to Zuckerman's left side so he couldn't see the gaping hole at her knee that was actually barely visible at this point.

"I've got my own suspicions about Terescu," Zuckerman said. "I'm a good lawyer, but I ain't that good." They came to the door of the coffee room, and he stepped aside to let her in first. "When I was cross-examining him? He practically read my mind for the answers I wanted. Way too easy."

Having an informant probably didn't hurt you much either, Rebecca wanted to say but didn't. She needed him now, and there was no sense bringing up volatile issues. Crab-walking sideways into the room, she took a tea bag from a teak box containing a dozen varieties and began unwrapping it, noticing that Zuckerman was making no move to get something for himself. "So what do you think of my proposal?"

"Might be workable. You can sit down over there," he said, pointing to several comfortable-looking chairs arrayed on the other side of the room. "I'm going to go back and make a few phone calls."

She didn't needle him about who was in control of his case. No prosecutor in his right mind would make this kind of decision without conferring with a handful of other people among whom blame could be peanut-buttered should things go sour. She dawdled over the tea so he'd leave before she had to walk to the chairs with her knee exposed.

It took less than twenty minutes for his secretary to enter the coffee room to escort her back to Zuckerman's office. Rebecca grabbed her arm. "Lily, you got any nail polish?"

Lily Botero immediately glanced down at Rebecca's legs, first the right, then the left, and nodded. "No problem. You sit here so it doesn't run."

She was back in less than a minute, and Rebecca dabbed the polish over the tear. They sat together chatting for a minute while it dried, then got up and left the coffee room.

"Here's the deal," Zuckerman said when Rebecca was seated and the secretary had pulled the door closed behind her as she left. "The investigation will be carried out by the FBI and CIA, with complete access to every nook and cranny of Tera-Tech, including all its research facilities and records. The company will be shut down, and all the personnel sent home."

"Agreed," Rebecca said.

Zuckerman put up his hand. "There's more. . . ."

"Sure hope you know what you're doing." Zuckerman paused before the glass doors and craned his head up, using one hand to shield his eyes from the sun's glare bouncing off the aluminized window coatings. "Lord, what a freaking monstrosity," he said as his eyes ran up and down the sleek sides of her office building.

Rebecca tried to follow his gaze. All she saw was story after story of steel and glass, the entire edifice unsullied by any shapes other than perfect right angles clear to the top, which itself was nothing more than a straight, unadorned line separating the building from the sky. "S'matter with it?"

"Nothing." Zuckerman dropped his hand and pulled open a door. "Brilliant piece of design. Really."

Inside the building, Rebecca walked past the security station, then heard Zuckerman's voice behind her.

"Hey, Frankie, whaddaya say?"

"Mr. Z, how y'doin'?"

She turned to see him speaking with one of the guards as he walked toward the station.

"Can't complain. Thought you'd be running this building by now."

"Fools wun't recanize talent, it bit 'em in the ass."

They shook hands, and then Zuckerman turned and caught up with her. At the questioning look on her face, he said, "You're not the only defense firm in this building. I'm here a lot."

"How do you know that guard?"

"Like I said, I'm here a lot."

I'm here every day, and I don't even know his name. She looked at her watch. "Why don't you wait here for a couple minutes, then come up."

"Got it." So her client wouldn't think she was getting too cozy with the prosecutor. He went back to hang around with Frankie.

As she walked through the firm's reception area, she spotted Perrein sitting with Ehrenright in the glass-walled main conference room. She held up her hand as they both looked up, mouthed "Two minutes" at them, then walked to her office.

When the receptionist rang her that Zuckerman had arrived, she went out to greet him, making sure Perrein could see, and they walked into the conference room together, Arno Steinholz right behind them.

"I take it you two worked something out," Perrein said, looking from one to the other.

"Still your call, whether you want to go along with it, Mr. Perrein." Zuckerman opened the thin folder he was carrying and drew out several sheets of paper stapled together. "Deal is, you sign this agreement right now, first thing before anything else happens. You agree to be under surveillance for the next couple of hours, and—"

"Surveillance? What the hell for?"

Rebecca tried to warn him with her eyes to back off; this was no time to get into a testosterone war, which Zuckerman would probably welcome. But the prosecutor looked unperturbed, and didn't soften his answer, either. "So you can't make any warning phone calls to Tera-Tech during the time it will take for my inspection team to get inside the company."

Perrein stayed quiet, but Zuckerman knew what he was probably thinking. "Also, since it's obvious you all must have discussed a proposal amongst yourselves previously, it's possible you've already done something like that."

"I did nothing of the sort."

Zuckerman went on as though Perrein hadn't said a word. "Which is why the agreement includes a sworn statement for you to sign, swearing that you gave no such warning to your company, and never took any steps to hide evidence."

"I just told you, I didn't do anything of the sort."

"I believe you a hundred percent, Mr. Perrein, which is why I assume you'll have no problem signing this agreement. It says that any evidence we uncover later that you *did* warn somebody will constitute an admission of guilt on your part."

Perrein motioned for the paper and Zuckerman slid it across to him. He picked it up and began to read.

"You yourself won't be allowed on the premises during the investigation without supervision."

Perrein looked up suddenly and started to open his mouth. "If it turns out," Zuckerman said before Perrein could get any words out, "that someone in your company did this without your knowledge, we'll work something out."

Perrein turned back to the agreement. "If not," Zuckerman continued, "I'm going to put you away for the rest of your life, with perjury and obstruction of justice charges piled on top of the ITAR offenses."

He was finished, and Perrein waited to see if anybody else had anything to say. When no one spoke, he motioned to Ehrenright for something to write with. "You know, Zuckerman," he said as he accepted a fountain pen. Ehrenright had pulled off the cap before handing it to him, his way of making sure the pen came back. "You got a big mouth. But . . ." He flipped through the document and scrawled his signature in bold characters at the bottom of the last page, then shoved the agreement back across the table so the pages fluttered and Zuckerman had to lurch forward to catch them. ". . . I didn't do anything wrong."

He stood up and walked over to the end of the room where coffee and a carafe of water sat on an electric serving plate. "Makes you happy, tear the whole damned place apart."

Zuckerman gathered the agreement together, betraying no emotion. "Can you suggest a place for us to begin?" He stood up as he slipped the document back into its folder.

"Yeah." Perrein picked up the pot of coffee and gestured with it. "Start with that snot-ass graduate student I hired away from Terescu."

Zuckerman nodded politely; it was an obvious answer. He started to walk toward the door to begin making the preparations when Perrein's voice stopped him. He turned, watching as Perrein slowly placed the pot back on the burner, not having poured any coffee out of it.

"And I might as well tell you," Perrein was saying. "He's in charge of the XT-5055."

Hard as they tried, Rebecca and her two associates were unable to hide their shock, not something they wished to share with Zuckerman. "Either he's the one," Perrein added, "or Terescu's trying make it look like he is."

Rebecca turned slightly so she could see Zuckerman's face. There was no sign of surprise at all on it as he listened to Perrein. She realized he must have known it all along. "Okay," he said calmly. "We'll do that."

He turned and motioned to a uniformed special agent who'd materialized in the reception area. The agent waved back. "That's your baby-sitter, Mr. Perrein," Zuckerman said. "You go to the bathroom, he goes with you."

Rebecca walked Zuckerman out of the conference room, then

pulled him off to the side. "How quickly can you get on the grad student?"

"Screw the grad student. First thing we're gonna look for is whether anybody mucked around with that XT-5055."

"Whoever might have 'mucked' with it, they've had plenty of time to unmuck it."

"I doubt they could hide every last detail from my guys. And I need physical evidence before I go after suspects this time." A tacit admission that the present case had come to trial too quickly? "And I don't normally follow the defendant's advice during an investigation."

She smiled. "But you were *so* polite in there."

He smiled back. "Well, I'm just that kinda guy."

"How long will this take?" she asked. "I want to let him know how long he's gonna be here, and should I order dinner. Is Goldin on call?"

Zuckerman nodded. "We should be in and out of chambers within the hour. I'll have my investigators on their way to Tera-Tech in two minutes"—he reached into his jacket and pulled out a cellular phone—"and ready to move in as soon as they receive my call from Goldin's chambers. Then figure a half hour to clear the place out. . . ." He looked toward the conference room. "Two hours is a good bet."

Rebecca went back to let Perrein know while Zuckerman placed his call. A few minutes later, the lawyers were on their way to court.

"Fine."

Zuckerman and Rebecca looked at each other.

"Fine?" Zuckerman said to Judge Goldin. "That's it?"

She'd been listening to him lay out the tentative agreement for about fifteen minutes. "What else you want me to say?"

"I want you to say, 'I'm issuing a court order for the inspection.' "

"What for?"

"To make it all legal and court ordered. How am I supposed to go evacuate a major corporation and ransack its records without a court order?"

Goldin shook her head. "You struck a private deal with the defendant. He's given you permission. You don't need a court order."

"But—"

"Listen, Counselor, I've already got my whatsis in a wringer in this case. I'm lucky if I'm doing small claims in Van Nuys by the time this is all over and you want me to officially authorize a corporate Waco?"

"You want me to do it without authorization?"

"Doesn't Perrein own the place?"

"Yes . . ."

"So it's authorized." Goldin picked up the copy of the agreement Zuckerman had given her. "Which, by the way, is the only way you'd get to do this little invasion, because there's no way I'd issue such a sweeping investigative order toward the end of a trial anyway."

"And also by the way," she continued, "off the record, given just the evidence I've heard so far?" She set the papers down, that part of the discussion now over. "Had the jury come back with a verdict of guilty, I would have overturned it."

Rebecca snapped her head toward the judge. "You think my client is innocent?" was all she managed to get out while thinking about spending the rest of her life having picked Door Number Two when the grand prize had been behind Number One the whole time.

"Hell no!" Goldin answered. "I think he's guilty. But the fact is, the government has so far failed to prove its case beyond a reasonable doubt. And it would take the District Court a good thirty seconds to toss the conviction out on appeal, so I might as well do it for them and save myself a reversal."

Rebecca tried to process this information quickly. "Well, in that case—"

"Forget it, Verona. You've worked out a deal to get at the truth, which, let's face it, you don't know yourself, so get on with it. But as long as we're just talking off the record here . . . I've got a suspicion—well, a couple of suspicions."

She turned to Zuckerman. "At first I figured maybe the only reason you brought this to trial in the first place was that you thought you might luck onto more damaging evidence during the trial, probably from a defense witness. Then I thought some more, and now I think maybe bringing this case wasn't your call at all. My bet is that maybe the CIA or the NSA or the State Department brought heat down on the attorney general, who pushed it down to the U.S. attorney, and he dumped it on you."

She peered at him intently, as though trying to read his mind. "You've been in my court plenty of times, Counselor: you're a damned good lawyer." She shrugged and closed her eyes. "For a Jew, anyway . . ."

Zuckerman rolled his eyes heavenward and shook his head, thankful that he was still well enough planted in the judge's good graces for her to crack a volatile joke at his expense.

". . . and your heart hasn't been in this from day one. Don't get me wrong, I think you really believed the defendant was guilty. I just think you're too smart not to have known you basically had no case."

Zuckerman appeared to shrink in his seat. Rebecca felt terrible for him, but had no lifeline to throw him as he had done for her in the pretrial meeting. She felt bad for him not because of what Goldin was telling him, which he probably already knew, but because the judge was echoing the exact sentiments Rebecca herself had expressed to him only days before. Any further protestations on his part that Rebecca was manufacturing fantasies about his control of his case would be acutely embarrassing.

Goldin sensed a reaction out of proportion to her little scolding, and changed the subject. "How're you going to go about this investigation?"

Zuckerman cleared his throat. "We're going to guess at what the method to build the chips ought to look like, kind of a hypothetical manufacturing process. The investigators will draw up a list of things that might constitute evidence of that process having taken place. Then we'll hunt for them at Tera-Tech."

"How long will it take?"

"Couple days . . . ?"

Goldin reached for a pad of paper. "I'm going to postpone the trial for one week, and keep the jury on hold. At the end of that time, there's either a plea agreement, a dismissal, or we resume."

And that was that.

On their way out of chambers, Rebecca said to Zuckerman, "You already have that list all made up, don't you."

"Off the record?"

"Of course."

"I'm not telling you."

She giggled, and Zuckerman said, "But what makes you think I already have a list made up?"

"Just a wild stab," she replied amiably. "I'm guessing you had it made up back when you originally wanted to search Tera-Tech." *You know, before your bosses made you start the trial?*

Zuckerman sped up his walk to a pace beyond Rebecca's ability to match, then said over his shoulder, "That's getting real tedious, Rebecca."

She smiled as he walked away, then turned to go.

His voice calling her name stopped her. He had done an about-face and was walking in her direction.

"There's one thing I think you should know, Rebecca," he said as he walked up to her, looking around to make sure no one else was in earshot.

"What's that?"

"That whole business with Terescu? Your theory, how he deliberately sabotaged your case?"

"What about it?"

He patted her lightly on the arm. "It's the biggest crock of shit I ever heard." He reached into his jacket pocket and pulled out his cell phone.

It took her a moment to find her tongue. How could he possibly think that, after all the evidence she'd laid out for him? She was flustered, not knowing whether to argue the point or ask the obvious question. "But . . . then why did you agree to all of this?"

"What have I got to lose?" He speed-dialed a number and put the phone to his ear. "We find something, I got another perp. We don't, I burn Perrein."

He waited for her to say something else, but she didn't. "Like you said, Becky: your job is defense, mine is justice." He held up a finger. "Shep? Zuckerman."

He listened for a few seconds, nodded, then said, "Do it."

Chapter 28

Saturday, November 20

None of the employees had ever heard the fire alarms go off before, except for individual units in single locations for testing purposes. The blaring klaxons at full tilt scared hell out of a good number of people, and several injuries resulted from the mad stampede to get out of the line of fire of whatever menace those ear-shattering wails implied.

Any notions that it might be a false alarm were dispelled by the sight of dozens of uniformed, oxygen-bottled firefighters running through the corridors, self-importantly warning the sluggish to move their asses or risk being carted out later in trash bags. Their demeanor was so fierce and convincing that few in their path spent much time wondering how they had managed to arrive less than thirty seconds after the sirens went off. The frightened employees also had no way of knowing that the firefighters had first cleared out the laboratory areas, executive suite and computer room before proceeding to the production building and accounting department, despite that sequence having necessitated a circuitous and inefficient route through the campus.

Things didn't go as smoothly in the actual factory, known as *fabrication* in the business. There, Tera-Tech employees barely looked up when the alarms went off.

Fab employees generally only worried about three major imperatives, and didn't allow irrelevant concerns to distract them. The first, and the one that demanded by far the most attention, was cleanliness.

Because the raw components of the devices they were building were less than half a micron across, even a microscopic particle of dust could ruin an integrated circuit under construction. So the fabrication area, in this case Tera-Tech's Fab 1, was protected by three layers of air locks, each one progressively cleaner. The outermost layer, which connected directly to the outside world, was where the gowning room was located. Fab employees spent about ten percent of their working day just getting cleaned and dressed prior to entering the second level, wearing special gowns, caps, shoes and face masks that allowed no contaminants from the employee to leave his body, and which gave off no dust themselves. The shoes were off-the-shelf Reeboks, but once they first entered the gowning room and were decontaminated, they never saw the outside world again.

In the innermost level, designed to Class I standards, ceilings consisted entirely of air vents blowing purified air straight down. Even the housings of the fluorescent lights were shaped like airfoils so as not to disrupt the smooth, laminar flow. Every worktable was perforated with large holes, and every rack and shelf was made of widely spaced wires, to minimize blockage and turbulence as the air dropped down until it was sucked off to the sides at floor level, returned to micropore filters up on the roof, and recirculated. The air was changed six times each minute, and the goal was no more than one offending particle in each cubic foot of air. By contrast, a typical office environment would have a million such particles in the same cubic foot.

The second fear was earthquakes. Not the Big One, but micro-tremors that couldn't be felt but could ruin a wafer in the process of being etched. Whenever there were an unusual amount of rejects in a lot, the tendency was to start investigating to find out what went wrong, which could entail considerable time and expense. But at Tera-Tech, the exact time that each individual fabrication process started and stopped was logged; if the reject rate was high, the first step was to call the University of California Seismology Center, to which the company was a significant contributor, and see if any temblors had been recorded. If there were, they didn't waste time on expensive diagnoses and instead assumed it was the quake's fault.

Finally, and largely in the backs of most people's minds, was the issue of the terribly toxic and corrosive chemicals that were used in the chip-making process. The chemicals themselves were stored in blockhouses behind the plant, doled out in small quantities by process control computers only as needed. The blockhouse walls were constructed of thick concrete, but the ceilings were thin plywood. In the event of an accident, the poisonous explosion would be directed upward instead of blowing out the walls and sending heavy chunks of concrete rocketing around the neighborhood.

Every enclosed area, and every major piece of equipment, had at least one plastic tube connected to it that ran through ceilings, walls and floors until it reached a bank of specialized monitors that continuously sampled for the presence of any one of a dozen dangerous gases. Upon detection, alarms would sound, and a highly trained Emergency Response Team would spring into action. The ERT specialists were among the most highly regarded—and highly paid—employees in the company, who underwent months of intense training before assuming their roles. Thus far, they'd never been deployed at Tera-Tech except during practice drills. The number one cause of death among semiconductor workers in Silicon Valley wasn't poisoning by toxic gas, it was electrocution caused by discharges from high-voltage fabrication devices.

At first, it was only with mild interest that the Fab 1 employees noticed unusual activity outside the production area. All of the walls separating the various cleanliness levels were made of glass in order to minimize the claustrophobic effects of continuous isolation, and the workers couldn't help but notice a large number of people running around out in the halls.

The interest turned to concern as the outer door to the gowning area opened and half a dozen very large men and two equally formidable women ran into it. Two people working at an ion implantation device exchanged anxious glances as they realized that they could actually feel the vibrations caused by the running, and they quickly began shutting down the delicate process they had just started.

Real shock set in as the second set of airlock doors opened. The intruders were not gowned, and the experienced workers could almost see the dust and dirt raining down from their street clothes. For people whose working day consisted largely of ensuring a sterile production environment, the fab denizens could barely comprehend what they were witnessing. When the inner set of doors was finally breached, they could only stare in horror at the unprecedented violation of their pristine world.

But true panic didn't set in until they finally noticed that the invaders were wearing oxygen bottles, goggles and protective hoods, bright yellow and stamped "ERT" with large block letters. Nobody had ever actually seen that equipment other than hanging on their pegs. Nobody had ever seen an emergency response guy inside the fab, even during announced drills. That, coupled with their cavalier violation of anticontamination protocols and the damaging vibrations they were setting up, finally translated in the workers' minds that this wasn't a drill. This was real. Roughly $135,000 in partially constructed microchip wafers was abandoned as the workers scrambled past the ERT specialists to get out of the fab area. They had no way of knowing that the real ERT staff had been taken out of the building five minutes earlier.

As employees from every department began streaming out the doors and into the parking lots surrounding the company buildings, they noticed the distinct lack of any pumpers, ladder trucks or ambulances, and assumed that they must be on the other side of the complex, which, they also noticed, didn't seem to be burning. Shortly thereafter, the crowd trying to get away from the building slowed down, congealing into milling knots of puzzled technoids accustomed to indulging their curiosity, which at the moment had been heightened by the presence of approximately two dozen men and women in blue windbreakers carrying thirteen-round-per-second MP-5 machine guns, urging the groups of people to continue moving away from the building. Initial thoughts that maybe they were being taken hostage were eased by the presence of the letters "FBI" stenciled on the backs of the windbreakers in bright yellow. Realizing that the weapon toters were friendlies, the naturally inquisitive employees slowed down even further.

It was at just about that point that someone yelled, "It's a bomb!" The incipient hysteria behind the voice galvanized the people standing close by, who began running at top speed out of the parking lot. Word flashed around the complex at warp speed, and in short order the immediate perimeter was clear of all but official personnel. Less than two minutes after that, the few independent-minded stragglers who insisted on remaining in the building, the interloping thugs having no moral authority to evict them, were marched out by very large men and women adept at convincingly demonstrating their authority, and were loaded into vans that would take them away for processing on obstruction of justice charges, just as soon as their bruises were attended to.

The entire evacuation had taken less than twelve minutes, starting from the time the lead investigator had walked into the Human Resources Director's office and explained to her what was going to happen, and why she was going to cooperate. Then smaller men and women began emerging from the thirty or so nondescript automobiles, all of American manufacture, that had been parked outside the parking lot fence line. Rather than guns, these people carried briefcases, laptop computers, scrambling devices, portable fax machines and large metal-sided boxes betraying nothing of their contents.

That was three nights ago. Since then various teams of investigators had swarmed, virus-like, throughout the premises. Twelve accountants from the GAO ensconced themselves in the administrative wing of the central building, poring over every purchase order, shipping receipt, receivables notice and any other document in the trail of paper left behind whenever parts and supplies went in and out of the company. Each of them carried a small booklet containing several hundred words, which, if they appeared on a document, would cause that piece of paper to be pulled and placed in a special cardboard box.

Sixteen computer specialists on loan from Lawrence Livermore overtook the data processing facility, and used a sophisticated search program to root through the entire collection of Tera-Tech's digitized files. The search program was loaded with the same set of words and phrases the accountants carried with them. When one of these words was encountered, a copy of the offending file was transferred into a small computer the team had brought with it. A slightly different program was loaded into a stand-alone Tera-Tech machine that was dedicated to the processing of electronic messages that flowed within the company as well as between the company and the outside world. Audit trails were generated of every message that contained one of the key words or phrases, along with the entire path that message had taken since its inception: who generated the original, who received it, who forwarded it on to others and who were those others and what had *they* done with it.

Seven border patrol agents descended on the human resources department, pulling personnel records and running preliminary cross checks on every employee, using the same national database that tracked who was coming into or going out of the country at various border crossings, airports and shipping sites. Names sent up by the computer specialists cracking the mail system over at the data center were cross-correlated using a different set of databases, but those were handled in a separate room by the five CIA officers assigned to that task, using scrambling devices to communicate with computers at Langley, Virginia, all of which had the curious property of being, as far as anyone could tell, nonexistent.

Down in the laboratory area, four National Security Agency people, whose regular job it was to build the NSA's computers because the agency didn't trust any outside entity to do it for them, were busy turning on and operating selected pieces of Tera-Tech equipment to verify that they did what they were supposed to do, and nothing else. After each such test, the device under scrutiny was disassembled, down to its last screw, and each part examined for anomalies. A second team of seventeen people was doing essentially the same thing out on the production floor.

A group of FBI special agents from the organized crime division had Terescu's old graduate student under covert surveillance, in case he decided to flee. Nobody had said a word to him, not wanting to arouse his suspicions, but there were never less than three agents on his tail at a time, around the clock.

As of now, nearly three full days later, none of the ninety-two investigators assigned to the case full-time had turned up anything even remotely incriminating.

"He was thinking of going after the automotive world," Rebecca was saying, "the same way he went after airplanes and breast implants."

Steinholz looked down at his submarine sandwich: papery roast beef, wilted lettuce, plastic tomato slices on a loaf of sickeningly bland institutional bread. He shoved it away, wondering if it was worth getting in the rental car to go get something decent after three days of this stuff.

"Not the people making the cars, necessarily," Rebecca was saying. "The out front guys, sales and rentals, leasing agents, that sort of thing." Steinholz wondered where she'd gotten that delicious-looking salad. Ehrenright was happily munching away at his own particle-board sandwich, and Zuckerman had nothing in front of him at all. Steinholz figured he must be eating out of the company's executive dining room with the FBI and the other DoJ guys. The hell'd they do, bring their own chef?

"So me being new on board, I get one of the early cases, kind of a test run, right? Let the new kid do it, see if this is worth pursuing." Rebecca smiled and shook her head at a mixture of memories of one of the first cases she'd handled for Allen Wysocki.

They were sitting around a large table that had been moved into one of the employee cafeterias. After two days of trying to look busy, Rebecca and her two co-counsels, along with Zuckerman, finally resigned themselves to the fact that they were largely useless here, and the best they could do was stay out of everybody's way unless something came up that required their involvement.

"New immigrant from Belarus, you know the type: thinks the whole United States is one giant Disneyland and he needs to sample it all before somebody closes the gates on him. So he goes to this auto dealership out in El Monte, takes a new car out for a test ride. But he doesn't come back." Rebecca dug her fork into the salad, spearing a perfect piece of lettuce, half a string bean, a cauliflower bud and a chunk of deep red tomato that looked to Steinholz like it was garden grown.

"About eight hours later the cops finally catch up with him. Guy's tooling down the Ten with the top down, a Big Mac in one hand, his wife next to him and three kids in the back snarfing down Baskin-Robbins. And they haul him in on grand theft auto."

Steinholz finally looked away from the salad, wondering where this was going. Ehrenright sat expectantly, so bored that any story right now sounded like Dickens, and Zuckerman, who was smiling skeptically, turned up a hand: *So?*

The sound of someone moving quickly down the hall echoed faintly off the walls. "Wysocki tells me to go handle it, on account of the dealership was for one of the companies he was thinking of taking on. So I interview this guy in lockup, and he's about as much of a car thief as your Aunt Thelma—"

"Selma," Zuckerman said.

"Whatever. Then I go down to this dealership, I find the same salesman and I tell him I'm interested in buying a car, but gosh-darn it, I can't make up my mind. Say, that Gran Turismo Whoozits over there sure does look good. . . ."

She took another bite of the salad, but this time Steinholz, listening raptly, didn't notice; nor did he notice the sound of someone else running out in the corridor. "And he says, Oh, yeah, that's one of our best sellers. He kind of looks me up and down and I'm thinking, here it comes, but then he says, Y'know, you'd look mighty fine driving this car. Made for you, now that I think about it.

"Then he walks over to this little rack and pulls off a set of keys. Tosses 'em to me, says, Lady, take her for a spin! And I say, Really, just like that? Yep, just hop on in there, go have some fun, take all the time you want. Get comfortable, see how it fits, make sure you like it. He goes on and on: Hate to sell you a car unless I know you're gonna be happy. Go on, get out of here, have fun!

"Just to nail this thing, I look at my watch, like I'm not sure I have the time, and he says, Lady!" Rebecca put down the fork and waved her hands around in the air. "This is a big decision, don't be worrying about where else you have to be! Take your time, take all the time you need!"

Steinholz started nodding and shaking his head, knowing exactly how this was going to end up. "So you go before the judge," he said, "and you tell him that this aggressive salesman, trying to sell a car to a brand new immigrant, gave him reason to believe that there wasn't any time limit on the test drive."

She nodded. "Fresh off the boat, has no idea how it's done, this guy throws a set of keys at him, tells him to take his time . . . what's he supposed to think?"

"And you got him off?" Ehrenright asked admiringly. More people were moving along the corridor outside the cafeteria.

"Got him off?" Rebecca laughed and dug into the salad again. "Dealership knocked five grand off the car so he wouldn't sue their asses for having him arrested!"

Zuckerman laughed along with the rest of them, then said, "What the hell's going on out there?" and got up to walk toward the cafeteria entrance.

Just as he reached the doorless entryway, he nearly collided with a short, mousy, bespectacled man with a bow tie who looked up at him. "You Zuckerman?" he asked breathlessly.

"Yeah . . . ?"

The man pointed down the hall. "They said to come get you. I think maybe they found something. And, uh, also—"

"Verona?"

"Yeah, that was it. Her, too. In the lab . . ."

The three defense attorneys scrambled up from the table, leaving behind the remains of their lunches and following Zuckerman down the corridor. At the heavily secured entrance to the laboratories, a uniformed guard waved them in without formality.

Filling one corner of the main lab area was the massive XT-5055 ion beam lithography machine. It was partially disassembled, standing almost obscenely exposed. Wires sprouted from openings where access panels had been removed, and subassemblies were visible on their swing-out bases, thin pipes hanging in space where they had been disconnected from matching tubes protruding from still other assemblies.

There was nobody near the machine, but about ten people were standing around a workbench a few yards away, indistinct murmurs rising from the group as people on the fringe strained to see what was resting on the benchtop beneath a lamp.

Someone noticed the lawyers, and tapped someone else on the shoulder, and soon the group began standing aside to make room. Zuckerman asked Steinholz and Ehrenright to hang back for the time being, and he and Rebecca moved forward.

Lying on the bench was a curved section of some blue-gray substance that might have been porcelain. It was roughly rectangular, approximately the shape that might be expected if you cut a foot-square section out of a sphere the size of a beach ball. Its outer surface shone dully beneath the strong worklight.

"From the 5055?" Zuckerman asked.

The man sitting on a stool before the bench nodded. "From stage seven. Place where the finishing touches happen before the chip's ready to be wired up."

Rebecca bent down to peer more closely at the part. "And what's the problem?"

"Somebody monkeyed around with it," the investigator said. He reached out with gloved hands and grabbed the short ends, flipped it over and set it back down. Resting on its convex outer surface, it rocked back and forth several times before settling down. "The machine, I mean, not this shell specifically."

Zuckerman stepped in closer. "What's your name?" he asked, putting his hand on the man's shoulder.

"Oh, sorry. Jude Weller." Zuckerman noticed that Weller didn't seem to notice Rebecca, which meant he was either blind or truly absorbed.

"What am I looking at?" Rebecca bent down closer over the bench. "I don't even know what it's supposed to look like normally."

Weller picked up a slender screwdriver and pointed it toward one end of the concave surface facing upward. "See these fractures here?"

"The little hairlines?"

Weller nodded. "They're from stress. Heat stress. Repeated cycles of heating and cooling."

"What is this part supposed to be?" Zuckerman asked from behind them.

"It's an oven wall," Weller answered.

"An oven?" Rebecca twisted her head to the side to look at him. "Then isn't it supposed to—"

"No. I mean, yes, this is a ceramic compound, and it's supposed to be heated, but"—he jerked his thumb over toward the XT-5055—"the finishing station on that machine has a max temp of about six hundred degrees Celsius. This here"—he tapped the shell with the screwdriver—"designed for at least two hundred degrees more than that. But these fractures?" He shook his head. "Rough calculation, I'd say at least seven, eight hundred degrees above that."

"Heating element in that machine?" a voice from the group said. "Couldn't get up that high."

"Which means . . . ?" Rebecca prompted.

"Either this shell came from some other device," Weller answered, "or else there was a different heating element in the 5055 at one time."

"No," yet another voice said. "The heating was done on this machine."

"How do you know?" someone asked.

"Because the gold trace patterns on the shell match the ones on the mounting brackets."

Weller smiled sheepishly. "A little early for us to have gotten coordinated. This is, like, twenty-minute-old news."

"No problem," Zuckerman said amiably. "We're not holding

you to anything yet." He turned toward the people standing nearby. "What was that about gold?"

A thin, dark-haired young man with wild eyes and an unkempt beard stepped forward. "Used all the time. Connectors, leads, stuff like that. But . . ." He held out his hand and Weller gave him the screwdriver. "It doesn't belong here," he said, pointing to a spot near the hairline fractures.

"Yellowish stuff?" Rebecca asked, focusing on where he was pointing.

He nodded. "We'll check, but I'm sure it's gold. See this pattern here, near the edge?"

"Yeah?"

He waved Zuckerman and Rebecca away from the bench and over to the ion beam lithography machine, pointing to a subassembly still inside the machine but visible through an access panel. "This is where the shell was mounted," he said, pointing to two large metallic brackets bolted just above the assembly.

He pulled a small flashlight from his shirt pocket and shone it into the opening. As they looked at it, Rebecca said, "There's a bit of that yellowish stuff, the gold." She reached a hand in.

"Don't . . . !"

"I won't touch it," she said, pointing with her forefinger. "Right here."

"Right. And if you put the shell back in, you'll see that the pattern matches perfectly. Which means that the gold got onto the brackets and the shell at the same time."

"Couldn't the brackets have been together with the shell in some other place?" Zuckerman asked.

The man shrugged. "Possible, but not very—"

"That's not the point anyway, Max," Weller said from the bench.

"What is?" Rebecca asked, turning toward him. Steinholz and Ehrenright were bent over the table behind him, looking at the shell.

"There isn't supposed to be any gold in there at all."

"You mentioned that before," Rebecca said. "I don't get it."

Weller stood up and pointed to the machine as he walked over. "This is a finishing station. It's just supposed to bake the chips in. By the time the chip wafer gets here, everything's already been done and there isn't any spare stuff floating around. Only thing you should find on the oven walls is maybe a little bit of carbon once in a while."

Zuckerman turned back to the machine, thinking. "So what's it all mean?"

"Can't tell you specifically," Weller said, sitting back down on the stool. "But for damned sure, somebody modified this machine at one time, then returned it to normal operation."

"No doubt about that?" Rebecca asked. "Any other possible explanations?"

Half the people milling around shook their heads. "None," Weller said on their behalf.

She stood there, not knowing what else to do or say. She was no technologist, but she was smart enough not to ask if the modified machine could have made the encryption chip: nobody knew how the chip was made in the first place, and so there was no way to know if the changes to the 5055 played a part.

But one thing was obvious: somebody modified it to do something, and none of the assembled wizards had any idea what that might be.

"So what's next?" Zuckerman asked.

Weller took a deep breath, and let it out slowly. The rest of the team seemed to defer to him. "We already know there's nothing in any of the lab records or notes that refers to the mod. Only thing, I guess, get the rubber-hose boys to question all the lab personnel."

There were some nervous giggles at Weller's little joke, but Zuckerman smiled and put them all at ease. "Okay. Let us know right away if anything else crops up, all right?"

"Isn't gonna turn up shit," Rebecca said as they walked back toward the cafeteria, leaving Steinholz and Ehrenright behind in the lab.

"I know that. But we gotta go through the motions."

She said it before he could. "Doesn't look so good for my client, does it."

"Uh-uh." His voice was free of any gloating overtones. "Whatever the hell it was, though, somebody covered it up."

"But it's hardly definitive."

"I know that. But it's enough to convince me to resume the trial if we don't get something harder one way or the other."

They sat down. Rebecca began a desultory attempt to pick at her salad, then pushed it to the side. "I think it's time to bring that grad student in and go to work on him."

"You mean the rubber-hose boys?"

She smiled, but it faded quickly. "If that charred chunk of

Wedgwood in there is the best you've got so far, I don't think much more is gonna turn up."

Zuckerman had to agree. The plan was to do as much physical examination as possible prior to beginning any interrogations, to preclude suspects from wriggling out of full disclosure when confronted with clearly incriminating evidence. But in the absence of such proof, there was no reason not to begin questioning the employees right away, starting with the grad student.

Steinholz and Ehrenright came through the entryway and up to the table. "Becky, can we get a few minutes with you?" Steinholz asked.

"No offense, Zuck," Ehrenright said apologetically.

Zuckerman put up his hands. "Do what you gotta do," he consented, then stood up and left.

Rebecca raised her eyebrows in inquiry but said nothing as the two associates sat down and pulled their chairs in closer to her.

"Who told Zuckerman about the XT-5055?" Steinholz asked without preamble.

Rebecca shrugged. "Deep Silicon, whoever that is."

Steinholz nodded, as if he'd expected her to say that. "Thing is, Deep Silicon has to be from the defense team. On account of all that privileged shit he's telling Zuckerman."

"Or *she's* telling him. But okay . . . so?"

"So nobody on the defense team knew about the 5055," Ehrenright said. "And that includes Janine Osterreich."

He stopped, watching realization settle on Rebecca's features. "Holy shit," she finally said quietly.

"It had to have been someone from inside Tera-Tech," Steinholz proposed, "maybe someone who was trying to blow the whistle but was afraid to go public."

"Which means that someone inside Tera-Tech was doing the work," Rebecca realized. "Making the chip."

"On the 5055," Ehrenright added, "which we already know was modified at some point and then unmodified."

"And who was in charge of the machine?" Steinholz asked rhetorically.

Rebecca closed her eyes. "The student."

"So how much longer are we going to hold off on having Zuckerman haul the kid's ass in, considering that we've suspected this about him for how long now?"

Ehrenright pressed the point. "What are we waiting for? There isn't going to be any more physical evidence. All we know, the little prick might crumble in the first ten seconds, save us all a lot of time."

"Or he might clam up, knowing we have shit, and we'll never worm it out of him."

"Becky, what's gonna happen that might get you to change your mind?" Before she could answer, Ehrenright said, "Not a damned thing. It's now or never."

Steinholz, assuming she would agree, had a suggestion for where to start. "First thing, we find out who was working for him in the lab. Maybe someone really hated him, enough to blow the whistle."

There was little room to argue. They were right: she'd been holding back, hoping that the investigators would find some great smoking gun so definitively incriminating that the guilty Tera-Tech employee would emerge, confess to his Lone Ranger crime, and get Perrein off the hook.

But that was not going to happen. "It's still Zuckerman's call," she said. "I can only suggest."

Ehrenright looked at Steinholz, then sat back. *When you've made the sale, stop selling.*

They saved the student himself for last. The hope was that one or more of his fellow scientists would point a finger at him, but during the interviews that lasted all afternoon, not one of them had so much as hinted that anything untoward had occurred in the lab, much less that the student had anything to do with it.

From a distance, that ought not to have seemed too surprising: anybody who indicated that he or she had any knowledge of illegal events was, by implication, somehow involved. On paper, this seemed a reasonable assumption.

But the experienced interrogators of the FBI and CIA had shifted uneasily on their seats as they filled Zuckerman in on their results. Rebecca wasn't allowed in any of these meetings, of course, but Zuckerman saw no harm in reporting back to her. He wouldn't have done so had he come across anything that might have bolstered his case against James Perrein, and Rebecca already knew about the modifications to the ion beam machine.

"So what was making them uncomfortable?" she asked him.

"Well, the student denied everything, of course. He—"

"What's his name again?"

"Bao Tranh."

It sounded familiar. "Oh, sure, Terescu told me that in court once. So he denied everything. . . ."

"Which is not all that big a surprise. But my guys . . ." He referred to all the investigators as his guys, even though only the FBI agents really were, being part of the Justice Department.

"Your guys believe him, don't they."

They'd summoned Tranh with a phone call, asking him to come in on his own, to which he agreed without hesitation. He had no way of knowing he was being followed the whole time, nor was he aware that had he tried to leave, he would have been apprehended on the spot.

"For the time being," Zuckerman answered, "which doesn't mean they're letting up on him."

They were sitting in the office of the public relations director, a room that had already been thoroughly vetted by the spooks and cleared for use by ordinary citizens. Zuckerman pulled a videotape out of his attaché and inserted it into the VCR mounted on a wood-paneled wall, then powered up the television set just above it.

The door to the office opened, and a tall man somewhere in his early fifties walked in. Everything about him—suit, tie, shoes, shirt, wristwatch—was colorless and undistinguished, except his face. His gray eyes were calm but watchful, the kind that seemed to take everything in but did so naturally, without his expending any extra effort.

Rebecca could tell that he was a serious man when it was called for, but one who smiled easily, as he was doing now.

"Becky, say hello to Special Agent Frank Shepherd. He's head of the whole investigation."

Shepherd had his hand extended before Zuckerman finished the introduction. "So you're the pain in the neck causing all the trouble."

"So's your old man," Rebecca replied, taking his hand as his smile widened.

"That the Tranh interview?" Shepherd asked Zuckerman as he let go and sat down next to Rebecca on a large couch.

"Yeah. Part about why he left Terescu."

A bright blue field on the television indicated that no signal was coming in, and Zuckerman pressed the Play button on the VCR. Zigzagged lines shot across the screen, then resolved themselves into a picture Rebecca recognized as one in a row of identical offices in the accounting department. Bao Tranh appeared face-on, with Shepherd's profile off to one side. Shepherd was speaking but no sound emerged. Zuckerman hunted around until he found the volume control and turned it up.

". . . again why you left Professor Terescu's laboratory at Cal Tech."

Bao Tranh sighed and let his shoulders slump. Rebecca guessed that he had been asked this many times before Shepherd had gotten around to asking it yet again.

It was hard to tell his height when he was sitting down, but Rebecca estimated that he was probably a good six inches shorter than Shepherd's six two or so. He was slightly built, with distinctly wide and pronounced shoulders and an erect bearing, even when seated. Several locks of his jet black hair fell across a high forehead, but he seemed not to notice. There was a calmness about his face, an almost serene expression despite the fact that the time markings on the tape indicated that he had already been interrogated for over two hours.

"It was for the money, I'm almost ashamed to say." His English was excellent, the enunciation almost musical.

"No problems in Terescu's lab?" Shepherd asked.

"No. The professor and I got along very well." He hesitated, then added, "Which is not to say we always agreed on everything." He smiled, as if in fond reminiscence. "Sometimes I thought he was too slow and methodical; in turn, he thought I was headstrong, and at risk of missing important things. But between the two of us, we made progress."

"Nevertheless, you left the lab."

Tranh's smile faded slightly, and he nodded, looking down at his hands, which were folded on the table and didn't fidget. "My family is still in Vietnam. They used their last money to send me here. I'm saving as much as possible so I can bring them to America, but one won't leave until they all can."

"Large family?"

"Typical Asian clan," Tranh answered, laughing with self-deprecating good humor. "Aunts, uncles, grandparents . . . I'd have as much luck sending for just one of them as I would for just an arm or a leg."

"But *you* came."

"I was the best prospect. I had an invitation from Cal Tech, from the professor. . . ."

After some more of such questions and answers, Shepherd said, "But you left him for more money."

Tranh dropped his head again. "The offer from Tera-Tech . . .

how could I resist? It might speed up by two years the time at which I could bring my family over."

"Some heavy-duty motivation right there," the live, not-on-tape Shepherd said. Zuckerman turned down the volume.

Rebecca tried to put the brakes on such speculation. "You find out where his family is right now?"

"Course. They're all still in Vietnam, and there don't seem to be any accounts anywhere with large sums of money in them."

"Doesn't mean he didn't squirrel it away somewhere, waiting for all of this to blow over."

"Except why would he even have thought there was gonna *be* 'all this'?"

"I don't get you."

"If Tranh had sold those chips to the Chinese," Shepherd explained patiently, "that would have taken place long enough ago for him to have gotten his family over, quit Tera-Tech and begun living a different lifestyle. And he wouldn't have expected the *merde* to have hit the fan, for it to be discovered, traced back to Tera-Tech, an indictment handed down, a trial . . . none of it. And that means there was no reason for him to hide the money waiting for something to blow over."

"If Tranh's the guy," Zuckerman explained further, "why's he still here, his family still in Vietnam, and he isn't rich?"

But Rebecca had understood it perfectly in the first place, and was only trying to buy time to think. Tranh was her last hope, the last real possibility that someone other than James Perrein had been behind all of this.

She blinked at Zuckerman, then sat back on the couch, not even having realized that she'd slowly inched up until she was sitting on the edge. She was acutely aware of the contrast between her anxiety and the relaxed posture of the veteran FBI agent, who had crossed his legs and thrown one arm over the back of the couch.

"Thing is," Shepherd said, "I like this kid. We all do. He doesn't seem to be hiding anything, he uses different words and phrases on each go-around of the same questions. . . . There's—I don't know— an integrity about him, somehow."

He stood up and put his hands in his pocket, walking over to the window and looking out. The lab building was directly opposite, and he seemed to be trying to see through the walls. "And he's cooperating. Already told our guys more than they could have dreamed about that XT-what-the-hell-ever."

"Can I talk to him?"

Shepherd turned and looked at her, then at Zuckerman, who shrugged. "Sure, what the hell. What can it hurt?"

"I know you think I'm guilty of this, Ms. Verona."

"Well, uh, I'm not really, you know, saying that you—" She was flustered and disarmed by Tranh's candor, and gave up trying to weasel out of his accusation.

"It's okay. These men have explained to me what's going on with Mr. Perrein. In more detail than I was able to get from the newspapers. I understand that you wanted me to be guilty, so Mr. Perrein wouldn't be. But I didn't make those chips."

"Do you know who did?"

Tranh shook his head. "If I knew who it was, I'd be working for him right now. For no salary."

"Why?"

He thought about it for a few seconds. "Imagine it's the year nineteen ten, your life's work is improving the radio, and one day, out of nowhere, somebody suddenly shows you a television set."

The disappointment she felt must have been evident on her face. "Ms. Verona," Tranh said, "I'm a refugee from a terrible place. My family was loyal to the Americans, who even tried to take them out during the fall of Saigon. You can check the military records. My parents were afraid to leave the only home they ever knew, and hoped that there would be reconciliation after the war. But the people from the North were not kind to them. Our lives were in danger constantly.

"In America, I can take a breath in the morning without worrying if it will be my last. This country is the last hope for my family."

He leaned forward and peered at her intently, forcing her to return his gaze. "Do you truly think I would betray heaven itself? And if you don't believe my gratitude to my adoptive home, then do you think I would risk my presence here for something as stupid as money?"

"But you need money to bring the rest of your family over," Rebecca responded weakly.

Tranh smiled indulgently. "You still don't understand. If I was the one who made that chip, the money from the Nobel prize alone would be enough to bring them all over!"

She caught Shepherd's eye as he grinned at Tranh's mild rebuke, and he looked away in embarrassment.

"There isn't any Nobel prize for engineering," Rebecca said confidently.

"Engineering?" Tranh shook his head. "For *physics*, Ms. Verona. You still don't grasp the magnitude of this breakthrough."

"You said that you left Cal Tech for more money," she said, changing the subject abruptly.

"Yes. Mr. Perrein offered to nearly double my salary. I still felt bad, though, and didn't think it was right for me to, ah, as they say, jump ship."

Rebecca realized she was getting caught up in Tranh's story, even though her case might depend on discrediting him. She couldn't let that happen.

"You were reverse-engineering U.S. computer chips in Vietnam, weren't you?" she asked suddenly, hoping to throw him off guard. "Cracking them open to discover how they worked and then selling the secrets to Asian companies?"

"You're just joking, yes?" He looked around to see if Shepherd or any of the others in the room thought Rebecca's question was a serious one, but was unable to read any reactions. "You think I was pirating American technology?" he asked incredulously.

"Weren't you?"

He stared at her for another second, then his features relaxed into a smile as he shook his head and comprehension dawned on his face. "Professor Terescu told you that." He sighed as he met Rebecca's eyes once again. "I was taking apart Asian chips to see whether they violated U.S. patents." Sensing her skepticism, he added, "Call Motorola, National Semi, Texas Instruments . . . they were all my clients."

Rebecca, face turning red, saw Shepherd turn away with a hand over his mouth, his eyes crinkling up under the strain of suppressing a laugh.

"What finally convinced you to leave Terescu's lab?" As she finished the question, she sensed a slight stir in the room. Had nobody asked this question yet? Maybe not: wasn't more money a sufficient reason unto itself? She noticed that Shepherd had turned back and cocked an ear, interested in what Tranh had to say.

"Actually, it was Terescu's wife who finally persuaded me." Shepherd was behind him, and Tranh didn't notice that he was now sitting up straight. "We had become close since I joined the lab. She's a very nice lady. She felt that I didn't owe Terescu my whole life, and besides, she explained that in America people changed jobs all the time. She said I needed to do what was right for me, for my family."

He had begun speaking faster without realizing it, and took a moment to slow himself down. "I was very moved that she would put my interests ahead of those of her husband's lab, and . . . well, I took her advice. Excuse me . . ." His voice was on the verge of cracking, and he rose to step over to a folding table holding a bottle of water and some paper cups.

Ehrenright leaned toward Rebecca and whispered, "So much for the mystery of Terescu's divorce!"

No shit. "I'm curious about something, Tranh." She waited until he turned to look at her. "Are you sorry now you left the lab?"

He paused, the pitcher in one hand, a paper cup in the other. Then he started to put the pitcher down. "If not for my family, I would have stayed."

"Because . . . ?"

"Radovan Terescu is a genius," Tranh said with conviction.

"I know that, but—"

"No, you don't!" Tranh set the pitcher down with a loud thump, then blinked and looked around. "Sorry!" he said, laughing.

Rebecca laughed as well. "It's okay."

Tranh looked down in mild embarrassment. "None of you know how smart he truly is. No offense, but you would have to be in the field to understand." He looked at Rebecca. "You already know that I'm the one responsible for figuring out how to program a superchip with barely any loss of speed."

Rebecca looked quickly at Shepherd. "We told him we knew about that," he assured her. "Project X, and all."

"The thing is," Tranh continued, "it took me six solid months of work to do it. Terescu assigned me the task and he gave me free rein, and I solved the puzzle." His gaze turned inward and he chuckled, but sadly. "What I didn't learn until later was that the professor had already worked the whole thing out in his head. But he wanted me to understand the process, to come to it myself so I would learn. And he wanted me to have the credit." He looked away and swallowed. "But I only came to discover what he already knew."

With Tranh turned away from her, Rebecca looked at Shepherd and raised her chin. The special agent nodded back, and Rebecca suddenly said, "Are you willing to take a polygraph test?"

Tranh turned in surprise. "A polygraph?"

"A lie detector. It's—"

"I know what it is." He turned back and began pouring water into a cup. "No problem. When?"

"Right now, if you're willing."

"No problem," Tranh said again. "Here?"

"Two rooms down. You ready?"

Not a crack showed in Tranh's demeanor as he followed Shepherd down the hall, sipping his water as calmly as if they were going out for a beer.

Less than half an hour later, Shepherd came back accompanied by a man carrying a long strip of paper folded several times, accordion-style, and covered with machine-made squiggles and hand-drawn notations in dark black ink. Shepherd pointed toward Rebecca and nodded his okay at the man.

"How'd he do?" she asked, already knowing the answer.

"How'd he do?" The polygraph examiner held up the strip and waggled it at her. "My own sainted mother wouldn't come out this clean."

She sat with Zuckerman in an isolated corner of the cafeteria, staring morosely out the window as the last bits of daylight receded into the distance. The issue of Tranh as a suspect was dead, the law enforcement and intelligence personnel working the premises so convinced of his innocence that they even acceded to his request that he be allowed to stick around and try to be helpful. As a precaution, though, he wasn't allowed to actually touch anything or be in the lab area without supervision.

"Couple things I don't understand," Rebecca said, turning a paper cup of tea in her hands.

"Just a couple?"

"I mean, things that really don't fit."

"Ah." He looked at her, and seemed to be trying to make some kind of decision. "Like, how did Deep Silicon know about the XT-5055?"

She looked up at him, startled. "What made you say that? You been talking to Arno?"

He shook his head. "It's been bothering me, too." Zuckerman looked down at the table, then out the window.

"Who is he, David? Or she?"

"I don't know," he answered without turning from the window. "You should have known that." He turned to look at her. "If I knew, I'd have to tell you." When she didn't answer, he added, "You were thinking that I did know, and was withholding it from you."

"The thought had occurred to me." In fact, she had believed all along that he was holding out on her. It was only at this very moment that she realized what an absurd notion that was. This was David Zuckerman they were talking about.

He wisely let the transparent understatement go. "But that's not what you were talking about anyway, was it."

Rebecca propped an elbow on the table and rested her chin in her hand. She ran her finger idly around the rim of the paper cup. No more vapor rose from it as the untouched tea grew colder. Zuckerman looked toward the entryway to make sure no one else had come in, then put his hand on her arm. "What's troubling you, Becky?"

Right now it was the feel of his hand, making her lose focus as she found herself wishing he would leave it there for about a year. "Terescu," she said.

"Gee, what a surprise."

"Not that." What should she be doing? Putting her other hand over his? But that would seem too eager. Look at him, look out the window, take a sip of tea, pretend he wasn't touching her? "Setting out to destroy Tera-Tech. It seemed a bit of an overreaction to just losing his student."

Zuckerman started to say something, but she cut him off. "I know, you don't believe it, okay, but . . ."

He kept quiet, giving her the chance to say whatever she felt like. "It made me wonder, could he really have concocted this whole mess. But after talking to Tranh myself, I checked with the clerk of the court, his divorce papers, and he filed right after his wife helped Tranh leave the lab."

"So you're thinking . . ."

She took her other hand away from the cup, tapped her palm on the table several times. She still didn't dare move her other arm. "I'm starting to think, does this brilliant scientist have a pattern of exacting revenge out of all proportion to the perceived transgressions? Losing Tranh may have been a blow, but come on, why frame an entire company for it?"

Zuckerman bit the inside of his cheek, thinking seriously about it. "Assuming, for the moment . . . and this is a big damned assumption on my part . . ."

He took his hand away as he leaned back on his chair and folded his arms across his chest, his typical posture when he was thinking hard. Rebecca felt as though a bright light had been turned off somewhere, the buzzing circuit formed by the touch of skin suddenly broken. An ache, surprising in its depth for so minor a cause, took hold of her. Was he at all aware of what had just transpired, or was it all just a mental fabrication borne of the longing she was becoming progressively worse at trying to suppress?

"But let's say you're right about Terescu conspiring with himself in this insidious plot." He was looking at her to make sure she was taking his jibe in good humor, which she indicated by showing him the middle finger of her left hand.

He grinned and unfolded his arms, laying them on the table and leaning forward. His closer proximity warmed her.

"So why are you surprised by what you perceive to be an over-reaction from an egocentric genius?"

That comment threw her. She'd thought he was about to be sympathetic to her bewilderment.

"After all, isn't genius just a couple inches from insanity?" he continued. "Why is he such a surprise?"

"Somebody that smart, that acclaimed . . . why the need?"

"You really surprise me, Becky," Zuckerman said gently. "After all the time you've spent trying to figure a rational motive for this guy's malice and vengefulness, maybe he's simply just a few fries short of a Happy Meal, you ever think of that?"

"No. And I'm not thinking about it now. People don't have one pocket of craziness while they're normal in every other respect."

"Is that so."

She was so absorbed she didn't even notice the intense way he was looking at her when he said this, but was thinking to herself, *Or maybe you're right, and he didn't just dream this up at all . . . ?*

"Bottom line, Becky, it's kind of irrelevant at this point. Just because Terescu tried to screw him doesn't make your client innocent."

They heard footsteps, and turned toward the entryway. Bao Tranh walked in but didn't stop at any of the vending machines, instead heading straight for their table.

"Mr. Ehrenright said I might find you both here. Please . . . ?" he said, pointing to an empty chair.

"Oh, sure," Rebecca replied, and Zuckerman stood to pull the chair closer and position it so that Tranh could sit at the unoccupied side of the table between Rebecca and him.

"Mr. Shepherd explained to me some of the details of what you're trying to do here," Tranh said. "His people are extremely frustrated because they can't find out who within Tera-Tech made the illegal chips."

"And you're gonna tell us that nobody here could have done it, right?" Zuckerman said with friendly sarcasm.

Tranh rocked his head back and forth a few times. "Some weeks ago, I would have said that it was impossible for the chip even to exist."

Rebecca looked sharply at Zuckerman: those were practically Terescu's own words.

"But I am a scientist," Tranh went on, "and an empiricist. In the face of hard proof, I am inclined to change my hypothesis, not deny the evidence."

"So now you believe it," Rebecca said.

"No." He seemed pleased at the confusion his inconsistency was causing. "Not until I see the device for myself. It's too fantastic to take at face value. But let us assume its existence as a hypothetical."

"Okay . . ." Zuckerman said tentatively.

"Then it is not too far a leap to suspect that it was done here." Rebecca and Zuckerman stayed quiet. "After all, that was basically the premise for your indictment, correct?"

It was not a bad summary, although it left out the matter of James Perrein's zealotry in trying to get the export laws overturned, and the implied motivation for his willingness to break the law. "Where is this going, Tranh?"

The scientist's face lost all traces of its earlier good humor. "I'm telling you this, Mr. Zuckerman: it would have been impossible for anyone to have done it on the XT-5055 behind my back. I have practically lived with that machine since it arrived here. First, it isn't capable. Second, it's inconceivable that anybody here could have done that kind of work on it without my knowledge."

"What about the heat damage in the oven section?" Zuckerman asked. "Did you know about that?"

"No," Tranh admitted. "But that must have been there when we first got the machine. And the heating chamber is a very basic, unsophisticated element of the device, not the kind of thing we would even bother spending much time with."

Rebecca had a thought, a question so obvious that she was surprised no one else had come up with it before. "Had that machine been with another company before it arrived here?"

Zuckerman raised his eyebrows and looked at Tranh for the answer.

"No. We got it straight from the manufacturer, Cyber-Design."

Rebecca slumped backward, unable to hide her disappointment. For a moment, she was sure she had stumbled onto a whole boulevard full of new possibilities.

"Well, Tranh," Zuckerman said. "You've told us what wasn't possible. You got any bright ideas about what is?"

"Probably not, but I do have one question for you both."

"And that is?"

Tranh spread his hands and looked from Zuckerman to Rebecca and back again. "Why not just open up the gosh-damned thing and look inside?"

Chapter 29

Monday, November 22

James Perrein couldn't stop staring out the window. Not two miles down the road from this diner in Sunnyvale, his company was besieged by hostile forces out to destroy him, and he wasn't allowed anywhere near the place. Rebecca wondered how he now felt about his decision to fight back with her as his *Kagemusha*, his shadow warrior, because his incredible cleverness in engineering that bit of legal sleight-of-hand in order to impress a jury sure didn't look so damned clever now that, for all practical purposes, there was no jury left in the picture.

She dipped the food service tea bag in the cup of hot water several times, then pushed the whole thing aside. "What I'm telling you, Jim, is that you're going to lose if you continue with this trial."

He seemed at first not to have heard her, but then he turned his head away from the window. "When did we go from *we* to *you?*"

When you sabotaged my *case by lying to me.* "Just trying to get you to understand that *you* might go to jail."

"You said they didn't turn up anything at my company."

"Right. Which puts us back to square one." She hadn't told him that Judge Goldin had been prepared to overturn a verdict of guilty. In any case, that was before the events of the past week, and she couldn't tell how those would affect the judge's inclination. "It's not like you came out ahead."

"Even though they turned up nothing incriminating?"

"Finding a key machine that was modified and then restored to its original condition isn't exactly nothing."

"It doesn't prove anything!"

"It adds to the suspicion. And we both know your people had months to clean out whatever else might have been there. From the time you got indicted up until last week."

"Then why'd they bother with this search?"

"Maybe they figured nobody could hide everything. And they were right, by the way, as the residue in the 5055 demonstrated. But what the hell difference does it make? The only chance you have left is to bet the entire case on opening up that chip and praying there's nothing incriminating inside."

"Yeah, like trying on the gloves, right?" Perrein snorted with derision. "Look how *that* turned out for the lawyer who dreamed it up."

"I don't understand you, Jim! What have you got to lose? You expected it to turn out that Tranh built it, you were prepared for that. Well, he didn't do it. So maybe *nobody* in your company did it."

What in heaven's name was going on here? Was her client actually admitting his guilt? She held her breath as Perrein considered her argument.

"Is Zuckerman even willing to have it opened?"

"Haven't mentioned it to him lately. My guess, he'll fight like hell."

"So what makes you think we can get around that?"

"Well, how the hell am I supposed to know!" She glanced around to see if anyone had heard her outburst, then lowered her voice and leaned across the table. "You want to come up with three thousand other reasons why it might not work or just let me try to get it done!"

"Okay," he said at last, wrapping his hands around his cup of coffee. "But I got a couple of conditions."

"Conditions?" She straightened back up.

"Unless they're met, I'm not going along with this."

"You're giving *me* ultimatums?" Rebecca stared at him in astonishment. "Like you're doing me some kind of a favor here?" She laughed and shook her head. "Swear to God, I don't believe this."

"Yes, well, I'm sure you couldn't care either way if you win or lose this case, Counselor," he said sarcastically, and it sobered her up a bit. "But we do it my way or it doesn't get done at all."

"Forget it."

Rebecca had barely gotten half a sentence out before Zuckerman stomped on the proposal.

"Ah," Justin Ehrenright said, "you want some time to think about it, is that it?" Zuckerman tried to laugh but it emerged awkwardly.

"At least listen to the rest of it," Arno Steinholz said. "You got something better to do?"

Zuckerman folded his hands in his lap and twitched his shoulders, adopting a comical attitude of eager readiness. "Okay, I'm listening."

Rebecca ignored the sarcasm. "Perrein will sign an agreement that states that if we lose the chip or destroy evidence, Tera-Tech will automatically plead guilty."

"I understand," Zuckerman said, nodding agreeably. "No."

"I think we're making progress," Ehrenright said to Steinholz. "You think we're making progress?"

"Definitely. Got him right on the edge."

"I'm going to file a motion with Goldin," Rebecca said.

"Fine by me," Zuckerman responded. "I was starting to feel guilty hanging around here and doing nothing anyway."

"I was beginning to miss you guys," Judge Goldin said. "Thanks for flying all the way to L.A. to cheer me up."

"I still can't believe you have a fax machine with an encryption chip in it," Rebecca said, looking at the judge's copy of her motion. "No wonder you knew so much about the technology."

"Other way around, Ms. Verona. First I knew, then I got the machine. Anyway . . ." She adjusted herself on the wingback chair. "I'm ready to hear argument."

"It's real simple, Your Honor. The DoJ's investigation has turned up nothing. There's some evidence that one of Tera-Tech's machines may have been modified at one time, but nobody in the company or the DoJ seems to know how, why or by whom, and there isn't a scrap of evidence that would link it to the government's chip. The prosecutor's own investigators aren't even ready to contend that there's a link."

To preclude a protracted and convoluted debate later on, Rebecca stopped and held a hand out toward Zuckerman, an invitation to respond to what she'd said so far. "Basically, I agree, Judge, except that this business of the machine having been modified isn't as easily excused as counsel would have you believe. Tera-Tech is the only owner that machine's ever had, somebody did something to it, and nobody can explain why."

"But you don't know exactly what it means," Goldin said.

"Not yet. But considering the mod was found less than forty-eight hours ago, that's not too surprising."

"Gimme the net on this, Ms. Verona."

"Sure. The answer's inside the chip. And that's the only place it is. To deny us the opportunity to open it up is to invite an egregious violation of the most basic tenets upon which the law is constructed."

Rebecca thought she saw the beginnings of a smile on the judge's face. "I'm not kidding, Your Honor," she said with deep seriousness, "and I'm not trying to be literary, either. I'm betting that you're no longer willing to overturn a jury verdict of guilty—"

"Why do you think that?"

"Because you wouldn't have mentioned it unless it were no longer an option. You didn't tell us about it until we brought the proposal to you that the DoJ investigate Tera-Tech's premises. It was at that point you decided to let it play itself out according to procedure, otherwise you wouldn't have brought it up."

Judge Goldin stared at her appraisingly for a few moments, then nodded slightly. "And the relevance is . . . ?"

"If we go back into court and that jury convicts my client, you'll let it stand. Oh, sure, we'll appeal, might even win a reversal, who knows. But the damage to James Perrein will have been done, and that's an unconscionable result."

Rebecca saw that she was making great headway, and dove in for the final assault without waiting to be invited. "Your Honor, my client was willing to bet his reputation and his freedom when he gave Mr. Zuckerman and nearly a hundred investigators from seven different governmental agencies free access to tear his company apart. They came up with nothing, but counsel still wants to pursue the case."

She looked at Zuckerman, to make sure he wasn't taking this personally, but she got nothing from his neutral expression and turned back to Goldin. "Now my client's willing to risk it all again, by asking that this chip be taken apart so the truth can finally be determined. How can that possibly be denied him and the system still call itself just?"

Goldin readjusted herself again. "Mr. Zuckerman . . ."

"First of all, Your Honor," Zuckerman said, casually scratching the back of his head to emphasize that he wasn't concerned about how this would wind up once the judge understood his point of view, "there seems to be an underlying assumption here that there's a genie inside that device that's going to emerge and tell us everything we want to know. I have no way of knowing if that's the case, and neither does counsel."

"But maybe it is," Goldin responded. "In which case, isn't the defendant entitled to find out?"

"Depends on the risk, Judge. Let me remind you, if the chip is destroyed, and the Chinese refuse to return the other six, U.S. intelligence operatives might be forced into some destructive acts to neutralize them."

"So drop the case," Goldin said offhandedly.

Rebecca thought Zuckerman was going to pass out from the sudden relocation of all the blood in his head, but he somehow managed to recompose himself fairly rapidly. "I won't do that." His voice was tenuous, as though he felt his statement represented overt disobedience to the judge.

"Fine," Goldin said, still just as indifferently as before. "Then blow up all the damned buildings you want. Ain't my job to front for CIA covert ops."

This time Zuckerman only managed to blink a few times, probably thinking he'd walked onto the wrong set and the script he was holding no longer applied.

But Goldin hadn't yet ruled, and he realized she was still willing to listen to argument. He switched to a different tack. "What if they destroy incriminating evidence in the process?" he said.

Rebecca came back immediately. "We'll agree that nobody from Tera-Tech ever handles the chip directly. It'll all be done under the supervision of your investigators. They do all the work, with someone from our side directing."

"And just who would that be?" Zuckerman challenged.

"Bao Tranh."

Zuckerman burst into genuine laughter. "Are you nuts?" he exclaimed, then looked over at Goldin and apologized before addressing Rebecca again. "Don't you think the guy's just a touch biased toward Tera-Tech's side?"

Rebecca smiled goodnaturedly. "He's no more biased toward Tera-Tech than your people are against them."

He looked at the judge for some support, but all her face seemed to say back was, *Sounds reasonable to me; what else?*

All traces of merriment disappeared from Zuckerman as he realized that the judge wasn't sharing his sense of absurdity. He knew he had to get serious and put forth some cogent points, or he might actually lose this one. "Once the chip is ruined in the destructive testing process, the defense might argue that, evidence having been lost or destroyed, the government has no case. After all, they weren't allowed to do any of their own testing, and relied only on our own reports. What if they appeal a conviction and a higher court says they had the right to test the chip's performance, except it's been wrecked?"

He threw Rebecca a defiant look: *Handle that one, lady!* But it troubled him that she didn't look at all troubled.

Rebecca addressed Goldin directly. "My client will stipulate that all the evidence put forth so far by the government based on their testing of the chip is true and accurate."

Goldin frowned at her. "That's a pretty enormous concession."

"Of course it's enormous. That's the whole point."

"But are you sure you know what you're saying, all that it implies?"

Are you kidding me? "Well, let's see, Judge. Before, I was basing a great part of my defense on the possibility that the government's test reports on the chip were a sham. Now my client is willing to tell the jury that they can believe all of it as gospel. That pretty much describe the implications?"

Goldin showed some chagrin for the first time in this meeting as she nodded.

"And if Mr. Zuckerman's job is supposed to be a search for the truth," Rebecca continued, "and not just the blind prosecution of suspected evildoers, then how could he be opposed, given all the conditions to which the defense is willing to be subjected?"

Goldin, having satisfied herself that Rebecca was going into this eyes open, said to Zuckerman, "Seems awfully generous on the defense's part, Counselor."

"Well, of *course* it's generous," Zuckerman said with some irritation. "She knows their case is lost, why shouldn't they try something desperate?"

"Desperation is the whole point, Counselor," Rebecca said without rancor. "That's why the prosecution can hardly refuse. We're betting the entire case on the truth, based on what's inside that chip."

But Zuckerman wouldn't surrender, and continued to argue vociferously that the loss of the chip could be devastating.

Finally, Rebecca thought she'd heard enough, and interrupted him to nearly shout, "Well, if it's so damned devastating, dismiss the charges and keep your precious chip! You think the republic's gonna fall if Perrein doesn't go to jail?"

Goldin shot Zuckerman a threatening look, the implication being that if he didn't start playing ball, she might consider a dismissal despite her earlier pronouncement that she'd abandoned that notion. As long as she was staying quiet, he had the opportunity to appear reasonable, to give in to the basic demand to open the chip but at least still have some bargaining power to negotiate the exact terms. Once she ruled, though, if he forced it to that by remaining recalcitrant, he would suffer for it.

Zuckerman, cornered, correctly perceived the signal. "Okay, hold it a second and let me think about this." He eyed Goldin surreptitiously and saw that she had backed off, ready now to let the two attorneys hash this out.

"If I agree to this—and I'm speaking hypothetically now, Your Honor—I'd ask counsel, in turn, to agree to the condition that the prosecution receives the right to reopen its case."

Unbidden, he went on to explain his reasoning. "Rebuttal alone is not enough, since we'd only be allowed to address points made by the defense during their part of the case. But if they introduce brand new evidence based on their examination of the chip, then we must be permitted—"

"Agreed."

Zuckerman, flustered, snapped his head toward Rebecca. "Uh, what?"

"I said, the defense agrees." She turned to Goldin. "Will the court approve it?"

"Yep."

And it was over, just like that, Zuckerman looking like he'd just been teleported down from another planet. Not willing to suffer the silence that seemed to be gloating at him, he shook himself loose and said, "Probably we ought to have Professor Terescu involved, too."

But Rebecca wouldn't hear of it, and shook her head forcefully. "The guy is so crazy angry at me, at Tera-Tech, at Bao Tranh . . . I wouldn't put it past him to deliberately sabotage the integrity of the investigation and falsely implicate Tera-Tech."

Goldin, not having been privy to Rebecca's suspicions before, was taken aback by this bold assertion. "Pretty strong, Counselor!"

"With all respect, Your Honor doesn't know the half of it."

"There's nothing to know!" Zuckerman countered.

Rebecca sensed that petulance was beginning to overtake Zuckerman's normally acute good judgment. "Your Honor, you mind if I step outside with counsel for a couple minutes?"

"Stay here," the judge replied as she quickly stood up. It was like a redwood suddenly springing full blown from the earth, and the intimidating effect wasn't lost on either of the two attorneys: *Don't screw this up while I'm gone.* "I gotta go talk to one of my externs anyway." She started to walk away but stopped. "Figure it out without any more decisions from me, will you?" She resumed her walk toward the doorway to her assistant's office. "You two agree," she said over her shoulder, "consider it approved by the court."

It wasn't a request, it was an order.

"I think she's bluffing," Rebecca said, but it didn't get even the glimmer of a smile from Zuckerman.

"David," she said, losing the clown act, "let me ask you something, okay?"

He was still scowling, and she knew that he was smarting from what he perceived to be a stinging defeat. She'd have to take that into account in dealing with him. Her goal wasn't to win, to be the king of the hill, it was just to make sure the right things happened.

"I know you think I'm way off base with Terescu," she said, imploring rather than lecturing. "But are you really willing to let such a volatile and unpredictable loose cannon stick his hands in this case any more than he already has?"

Zuckerman continued to pout for a few moments, then looked down at the coffee table separating them and began tapping the side of it with his shoe.

"You know," Rebecca went on, "we're both betting the trial on the outcome of this examination, and you were dead right before: it may not even be conclusive. I know that."

Her conciliatory tone made him look up as she went on. "So why complicate things by taking a chance with Terescu? I'm not saying you have to believe my theory, but will you at least acknowledge that the guy's an unknown, and neither of us can afford the gamble?"

Zuckerman eyed her carefully. "You know, I just freakin' hate it when you're right."

She flashed him a wide smile. "And it's so often, too!"

He sighed and dropped back onto the couch, closing his eyes. She hadn't noticed before how worn out he looked. "Okay. But as a courtesy, I gotta at least tell him what's going on."

"A courtesy, well. Is he *your* expert now?"

It was just a joke, but Zuckerman saw seriousness beneath it. "Who the hell knows anymore?" he responded wearily.

"And have we learned to play well with our neighbors?"

Zuckerman jerked himself upright at the sound of Goldin's

voice behind him, and gave Rebecca a dirty look for not warning him. "Think we got it worked out, Judge," he said as he rearranged himself.

"Good. Everybody gets a petal on their good manners clover."

"But I'll need an hour or two to get agreement from the powers that be."

Goldin halted just as she was about to resume her seat. "May I remind you that you said you could do that within minutes?"

"Normally, yes. But I had no idea it would come down to something like this."

Given that the two attorneys had worked out an agreement, Goldin saw no need to make waves. "No matter. I'll need the rest of the day to put together the paperwork anyway. We'll reconvene in the morning, in chambers again, and get things rolling."

She ushered them out quickly, before either of them had any opportunity to throw sawdust on the delicate machinery they'd just constructed.

"Cuppa joe?" Rebecca asked once they'd reemerged into the late afternoon sun. She pointed to a tiny coffee bar just across the street.

"You really do believe he's innocent, don't you," Zuckerman asked once they were seated opposite each other across a giant spool that used to hold telephone cable.

"Yes."

"Tell me why."

First things first. And quickly, before I change my mind . . . "Is he still a sore spot with us?

"No." *Yes.*

An intellect maybe, but still an open book to her. "You have to believe this, David: I hold nothing for him. I never loved him, I never cared for him . . . I'm not sure I even liked him. I was just fascinated, that's all . . ." It was a blubbering eruption, and she saw it as clearly as if she were standing off to the side watching herself, but she couldn't stop. ". . . like a schoolboy is fascinated by, I don't know, by a cigarette. It's forbidden, it's dangerous, there's a mystique, it glows brightly and has a certain attraction. But if the kid has half a brain, he discovers after a couple of puffs that there's nothing sexy or alluring about it. All it does is burn up and become a pile of ashes. That's what Perrein is to me, a stupid thing I had to try once. Everybody found him compelling, so I did, too, but they didn't really know him, and I came to."

Zuckerman was staring at her with undisguised amazement, not even knowing what he was supposed to make of it. She noticed it only fleetingly, because something suddenly occurred to her, and she frowned, as though confused, but her words were clear. "And you know what?" She looked up at him, eyes wide with revelation as her brow unfurrowed. "I don't even hate him anymore. How can you hate someone you don't even respect? I just feel"—she tried to put a word to the emotion even as she dug around to understand it—"nothing."

The frown returned momentarily, and then relaxed into a quizzical look, Rebecca staring at something unseen on the floor. "I just realized that, you know? I think of him, and try to conjure up some anger"—she looked up at Zuckerman, blinking—"and nothing comes up." She shrugged. "Except maybe pity."

It was the most perfect thing she could have said to him, that this intruder on their small corner of the world didn't have the power anymore to evoke an emotion within her. Hatred could have been thinly sublimated desire, but indifference was the grandest refutation, the ultimate declaration of finality.

And Zuckerman could see in her eyes that it was true, and that she really had just realized it at the moment she said it. *I believe you,* his eyes told her, revealing to Rebecca the first glimmering of some serenity condensing out of the clouds of his poorly disguised despair.

He let the moment pass, reluctantly, but saved its residue for later reflection. "So tell me why you think he's innocent."

It took Rebecca a moment longer than it had taken him to reorient herself. "I see into his pathology," she said. *We despise most in other that which . . .* She shook that thought off. "He's selfish. And egotistical. Supremely so, to such an extent that those words don't quite convey the depth of it. He's self-absorbed to the point of obsession." She stopped to consider where she was going with this.

"Okay," Zuckerman said, mistaking her deliberation for hesitation. "And therefore . . . ?"

"Therefore, the only way he would ever place his precious hide in any kind of high-risk situation was if the payback was enormous." Perrein's own explanation. Was she parroting her client or finally seeing what he'd meant? She stared off past Zuckerman as she spoke. "Almost incalculable."

"And you don't think there was enough return in this deal?"

She snapped back into focus and looked at him. "I'll tell you what I think, David. I think you and your people sat around in a room one day dreaming up a menu of possible motives for what you say—sorry, what you believe—Perrein did, and all you could come up with to put into testimony was that nonsense you rehearsed with Frazier."

She said it without malice or implied accusation, and Zuckerman took no offense. "They were all reasonable possibilities."

"Maybe," she admitted. "For some other defendant. But for this particular guy, for James L-for-Bigshot Perrein?" She shook her head definitively. "Unthinkable. It would be like me risking a climb up Everest for a nice pair of earrings."

"But a guy like Perrein," Zuckerman argued, "he'd climb Everest to show off to the rest of the world that he could do it."

"David!" Rebecca said loudly, reaching forward to rap her knuckles on the top of his head. "Don'tcha get it?" She dropped back onto her seat. "Perrein doesn't give a rat's ass about the rest of the world!"

Zuckerman smiled at Rebecca's effort to get something through his thick skull. "Are you kidding? He's going through all this stuff, not leaning on technicalities, so he can clear his name, preserve his reputation . . . isn't that for the rest of the world?"

"Yeah, but not for the masses! Not for shoeshine boys and waiters and unwed welfare mothers." She leaned forward again. "It's for *business*. Hell, ninety percent of his customers have government contracts; you think those people are gonna get involved with a guy's been branded a traitor, proven or not?" She brought the fingertips of her right hand together and whipped them apart. "It's *business*!"

Zuckerman thought about it, but his look remained skeptical.

"Okay, think about this," Rebecca said. "Why the hell would a guy, he's opened his mouth in public to lambaste these laws, why would that guy risk *breaking* them when he knows the DoJ is on his tail every second of the day and he'd be their first suspect?" She bent lower and looked up at Zuckerman. "It doesn't make a lick of sense."

She waited a second longer and then said, "And if there's no good reason to justify a risk, well, you can bet your ass James Perrein won't be in that game."

It was hard to refute. "My assumption was that he's enough of a shit to have tried to pull it off."

"It's *because* he's such a shit that I know he didn't. Because of the *kind* of shit he is."

Zuckerman looked away, mulling it over.

"The usual bet?" Rebecca said, by way of a challenge.

"Bet like that, stakes should be higher than just dinner."

Rebecca sat up straight—*The bet nobody loses?*—then slouched again, hoping it was before he noticed. *Couldn't have meant that anyway.* "You're on." Time to take a risk herself, and only time would tell what the stakes really were.

Zuckerman nodded nonchalantly. Too nonchalantly, it seemed to her. He stood up, eyes averted. "Gotta go tell Terescu the news." He signaled for the check. "I don't think he's gonna be amused."

As per their standing agreement, Rebecca pulled a five out of her purse to cover her end and dropped it on the table, then stood up as well. "Yeah, like the captain of the *Titanic* wasn't amused by an iceberg. Breakfast before court tomorrow?" It slipped out before she could stop it. Facing away from him as they walked toward the door, she winced, gritting her teeth.

"Sure. See you then."

Neither of them had to ask where, or what time.

C h a p t e r   3 0

Tuesday, November 24

They'd managed not to mention the case even once during breakfast. The first time the relaxed conversation showed a hint of stalling, Zuckerman had looked at his watch and suggested they walk back to Spring Street and wait in the courtroom until it was time for their meeting with the judge.

Rebecca was first through the door, and Zuckerman almost bumped into her as she stopped abruptly once inside the courtroom.

"What the hell is *he* doing here!" she whispered, not taking her eyes off the third row of the audience section.

Zuckerman followed her gaze to find Professor Radovan Terescu occupying one of the benches, two well-dressed men flanking him.

"Who're the other two?" Zuckerman asked by way of a reply.

Rebecca took in the imported, custom-tailored suits, the layered haircuts with several locks perfectly out of place, a Ferragamo shoe poking out from beneath the wooden bench, and the kind of relaxed patience that could only come from the practiced visualization of hundred-dollar bills raining out of a bottomless horn of plenty. "They're lawyers."

"Really, really expensive ones," Zuckerman agreed. "How can he afford those guys?"

Rebecca turned and ushered Zuckerman out the door ahead of her. "Let's wait outside chambers."

Judge Goldin was speaking with her secretary in the outer office and waved them in as soon as she noticed them.

"Looks like we're going to be in open court," she said as she led the way into her office.

"But this is a settlement discussion," Rebecca said. "Sort of, anyway."

"Yes, but this isn't about that." Goldin stepped behind her desk and motioned them to the two chairs in front of it. "Seems the good professor blew a gasket after your little chat with him yesterday, Mr. Zuckerman. He got himself his own attorneys. Pair of heavy hitters from Trepany, August and Diener."

"What for?" Zuckerman asked apprehensively.

"For this." Goldin picked up a stapled set of papers and slid them across the desk. Zuckerman picked it up and Rebecca moved her chair closer to read along with him, spotting "Temporary Restraining Order" in bold letters across the top.

"TRO to prevent examination of the chip," Goldin said.

"Pending . . . ?" Rebecca asked automatically, running her eyes down the page to try to find the answer while fighting down panic.

"His formal application to the court to act as *amicus curiae* in the examination."

Rebecca and Zuckerman both whipped their heads away from the paper and toward the judge. They started to speak simultaneously, but Goldin held up her hand. "Afraid we can't talk about this in here," she said. "Might be considered *ex parte*, since the petitioner isn't present."

She shrugged helplessly, obviously not pleased herself with this development. "Finish reading and then we're back in court."

"I've given the attorneys in the case an opportunity to read your motion, Professor," Goldin announced from the bench. "The court assures you no other discussions took place related to your matter outside your presence. Who's representing?"

The men on either side of Terescu stood up and identified themselves.

"Alec Rousselot, Your Honor."

"Gerald Wynan."

Goldin nodded and waved them back down. "Your motion seemed self-explanatory. Do you need an oral presentation?"

"Only if there's an objection," Rousselot said. "Otherwise, we're happy to have the court rule."

"Defense objects to this motion, Your Honor," Rebecca said, standing up. She walked to the podium without awaiting formal permission from Goldin.

"An *amicus* is a 'friend of the court,' " she began, casting an unfriendly glance at Terescu and his two attorneys, "nonpartisan and not prejudiced for or against either side of the case. An *amicus* has to be an uninvolved party. And if Your Honor will recall Professor Terescu's testimony in this case—*all* of his testimony—you will see that he is involved up to his eyebrows." She explained briefly, then sat down.

Alec Rousselot rose, buttoning his jacket with one hand, evincing a kind of bored, heavy-lidded, swaggering insouciance that could only come from many years of courtroom experience. He looked to be about twenty-four.

"Your Honor," he practically slurred as he reached the podium, as though this were already so obvious it was an imposition even to have to explain it. "My client's reputation is at stake here. He was hoodwinked by the defense team, and took it upon himself to risk looking foolish by coming forth and recanting certain opinions. Had he been allowed to complete his testimony, there is little doubt he would have restored his reputation as a result of his unflinching honesty."

Rousselot stopped and pointed to the defense table without looking at it, then to the prosecution table, then back and forth several times as he continued. "But now these two attorneys are seeking to resolve the matter out of open court, in secret session. Well, that's fine and dandy for the purposes of this case"—he stopped pointing, made a fist, and banged it on the podium—"but where does it leave my client, Professor Terescu! He must be given an opportunity to clear his name, and we therefore maintain . . ."

As he went on, Zuckerman, puzzled by Terescu's extreme reaction, turned to Rebecca, caught her eye and shook his head slightly: *You were right. We need to keep him out of it.*

When Rousselot was finished, chin high and righteously defiant, Zuckerman rose to speak. To Rebecca's surprise, and contrary to his earlier reaction, Zuckerman affirmed that the prosecution was satisfied that Bao Tranh, working with the government's people, would be honest, objective and capable. "The government is fully confident that, if there is something of substance to be learned from the disassembly of this device, the investigative team as currently configured will find it."

Aware of some disturbance back in the audience, Zuckerman turned to see Terescu jabbering away at Gerald Wynan and gesturing frantically. Wynan, clearly taken aback, looked around in embarrassment as he tried to wave Terescu down, but the scientist began poking him in the chest in order to get his full attention.

Meanwhile, Rousselot continued his vehement insistence that his client be allowed to clear his reputation before the incompetent investigators destroyed the only piece of physical evidence. "My client knows Bao Tranh's work, and he is fearful that, with his former student working as part of this team, nobody will ever learn anything, and may irretrievably damage future efforts to do so."

He stayed at the podium, and Rebecca stood up, speaking from behind the defense table. "May I point out to the court that the defense and the prosecution are in total agreement on this point, and wouldn't it be unusual for the court to appoint an *amicus* neither side wants and to whom *both sides are opposed*!"

"Okay, anything else?" Goldin asked. "Anything new, I mean, not a rehashing."

Terescu was waving Rousselot back with expansive gestures. The attorney raised his eyebrows at the judge, silently asking for a moment, and Goldin waggled a finger at him to go back and confer with his client.

There was some excited conversation, then Wynan stood up and said, pompously, "Your Honor, inadvertent destruction of the chip could irreparably harm my client."

Goldin just stared at him. Within a few seconds some of the smugness had left his face.

"That's it?" Goldin asked. "This is new?" She shrugged with obvious derision, then looked from Rebecca to Zuckerman. "Someone want to respond?"

She hadn't been expecting either of them to take her up on it, but Zuckerman rose, thought for a moment, and said, "Your Honor, does the court need any further evidence of Professor Terescu's bias in this matter?" He pointed back into the audience. "His own attorneys are basing their argument solely on their client's self-interest, and haven't once even mentioned the interests of the court or this case!"

Goldin put out her hand and pumped it downward until Zuckerman resumed his seat. She folded her hands on the benchtop and addressed herself to Rousselot and Wynan. "If Professor Terescu was so concerned about his reputation, he might have given that some thought prior to his testimony."

Rebecca and Zuckerman both started to relax, until they heard the judge say, "That aside, the court agrees that the petitioner has the right to protect his reputation," and then they tensed up again.

". . . but acting as *amicus* is not the proper way to exercise that right," Goldin finished up. "Motion is denied."

Terescu became so agitated that Rousselot and Wynan both put a hand on his shoulders as if to hold him down. Judging by his intense reaction, not only Rebecca and Zuckerman, but now Goldin as well, were relieved that he had been excluded.

"You believe me now?" Rebecca said to Zuckerman as she stepped over to his table.

"Yeah, he is an unguided missile. No telling what kind of disruption he—"

"Not that," she interrupted, watching Terescu becoming progressively more unglued. "Reason he's acting so crazy, he's now got no chance of ever getting to examine that chip himself to figure out how it was built." She turned to Zuckerman. "Which is the only reason he wanted on this case in the first place, bucko. I'm telling you . . ."

But Zuckerman was watching the scientist continue to gesticulate wildly even as his attorneys tried to explain to him that they'd lost and that's all there was to it. When Terescu happened to turn in his direction, Zuckerman quickly averted his eyes. "So tell me this," he asked Rebecca. "How come he didn't get this bonkers earlier in the trial, when we kept getting the judge to agree not to let you have the chip examined?"

"You really are getting thick in your old age," Rebecca answered. "As long as *nobody* was going to be allowed inside, Terescu may have been disappointed, but he wasn't going to lose out to a potential competitor, either. Now that the chip is going to be opened, it's gotta be killing him to be left out."

Zuckerman shook his head pityingly. "He hadn't've been such a freaking yutz, he might have gotten the chance."

Rebecca didn't say a word in response. If Zuckerman was starting to entertain the possibility that she and her team were correct in their assessment of Terescu, best to just let those thoughts ferment for a while without throwing in his face that she'd been right once again.

"Your Honor . . . ?"

Zuckerman and Rebecca turned at the sound of Rousselot's voice. Goldin looked up from some papers she'd been looking at. "What is it, Counselor?" she asked, an unmistakable edge to her voice.

"Um, sorry. . . . My client is still upset because he doesn't feel his interests are being protected. In his expert opinion, this Bao Tranh is not capable of performing a proper examination, and all you've got on the team is antagonists from both sides of the case."

Goldin stared at him without moving for a few seconds, then waggled her finger, beckoning him forward. Rousselot did as ordered, placing his hands over the top of the bench when he'd arrived.

"Get your client out of the room," Goldin said, loud enough for Zuckerman and Rebecca to overhear.

"If it please the court, Your Honor, he has a right to be here to see that his interests are served!"

"No, he doesn't. He's not a party to this matter since I denied his motion. He's just a spectator and he's disrupting my court."

Rousselot began to argue again, but stopped instantly as Goldin barked, "Bailiff!" without taking her eyes off him. He threw up his hands quickly, backed up a few steps, then turned and strode back toward the audience section, jerking a thumb toward the door so that Wynan would begin ushering Terescu out.

When they were finally gone, Goldin motioned Zuckerman and Rebecca to the bench. "Hate to tell you this, kiddies, but the man had a good point."

"That being . . . ?" Zuckerman asked her.

"I'm a little worried myself, you only got antagonists on the team that's going to take the chip apart. They get in each other's faces, might lead to charges and countercharges so complicated that neither the jury nor I will be able to unravel them."

Goldin made sure they understood, then said, "So what I'm going—"

"A suggestion, Judge?" It was never a good idea to interrupt a federal judge when she was speaking, especially if she was about to issue an order, but Rebecca risked it because she needed to forestall Goldin from doing something that could undermine the process it had been so difficult to set up in the first place.

"Okay . . ."

"Thank you. Why not let counsel and I go off and agree on an independent third party to lead the team? That way it's our mutual decision." Meaning, *Nobody can fault you personally for it afterward, Judge.*

Goldin had understood the implication before Rebecca had finished speaking. "Fine by me. Fifteen minutes all right?"

Rebecca tugged at Zuckerman's arm and began leading him back to the attorney tables.

"I take it you have someone in mind?" he asked needlessly.

"Dr. Muller speaking."

"Jessica? Rebecca Verona." She closed the folding door of the phone booth. "Got a question for you. You ever done anything like tearing apart a microchip, see what makes it tick?"

"Reverse engineering? You kidding? One time, some fishing trawler off the coast of San Diego picked up a Soviet sonobuoy. It had a microprocessor inside, and some other guys and I peeled it back layer by layer. It was an exact copy of the old Intel 8086 chip, and I mean *exact.* They even reprinted the initials of some Intel designer who'd signed the original."

"Signed it? How?"

"With a *show-off.* Chip designers like to put little pictures and things on bare spots on the chips. Usually they're corporate logos, but you'll find pictures of Mickey Mouse or Yoda, even some porn once in a while, or a designer's name or initials. You can only see show-offs with a strong microscope, and only if you take the chip apart. Anyway, the Russians couldn't figure out what these initials were doing inside the original but they were afraid to leave it off, so they duplicated it. We called the chip the '8086-ski.' "

Rebecca laughed at the story, then said, "I need some help."

"Becky, Becky, I told you, I'm not—"

"It's completely off the record. No depositions, no testimony, a lot of hard work and I'm not going to pay you a damned thing."

Rebecca held her breath during the silence at the other end.

"*Now* I'm interested . . ."

A few minutes later, she and Zuckerman were back in front of Judge Goldin. A few minutes after that, Tranh, Muller and the rest of the investigators had their go-ahead to try to coax the chip into revealing its secrets. They could start as soon as Jessica Muller walked into the lab.

PART III

CLOSING

Chapter 31

Wednesday, November 25

DAY ONE

Special Agent Frank Shepherd was normally a specialist in securities scams and other types of business frauds. His particular expertise lay in the examination of written and computerized records, but he was also unusually adept at organizing and leading large teams of mixed types of talent. While he had thus far spent some of his personal time during the Tera-Tech investigation helping to hunt through company files, he was now charged solely with making sure that the almost deliriously happy technical people working on the encryption chip stayed on course and didn't get sidetracked, as curious scientists were wont to do.

Some of the components inside the chip were so small that visible light waves were too thick to reveal them, making an ordinary microscope useless. Instead, the primary tools employed by the investigators were powerful electron microscopes, devices that used electrons rather than light to peer deep into minute substructures. The most sophisticated of these was an atomic force microscope, a recent development that relied on a needle with a point so sharp it was only a few atoms wide. As the needle was moved across the chip, an intricate system of extraordinarily precise devices automatically moved it up and down in order to keep its distance from the surface constant. As a result, the up-and-down movement of the needle made a perfect trace of the chip's various components. This information was fed into a computer that drew a breathtakingly clear picture of the surface, revealing in stark detail features barely larger than a few atoms.

But it was a slow process, and the AFM would be used only to zero in on features of interest hinted at by the other, more "conventional," electron microscopes. Jessica Muller also pointed out that the atomic force machine could actually be used to *move* atoms around on the surface, and so extra supervision was required to ensure that the evidence was not being changed even as it was being observed. Bao Tranh was the best of the bunch at operating the device, and, while the investigators had come to trust him, Shepherd and the attorneys well knew that any solo work he did could cast suspicion on any subsequent court proceeding.

As anxious as the technicians were to get started, Shepherd had insisted that the work not commence until a detailed plan of attack had been drawn up. He organized teams in overlapping shifts so that the examination could continue around the clock, with a minimum of time wasted in handing off results from one team to the next. While no individual could work more than twelve hours at a stretch, at any given time each team contained people from both the incoming and outgoing shifts. Each person coming on spent roughly an hour just getting up to speed on where things stood, but did so largely by just reading the most recent notes, studying the latest photographs and simply watching the others work until reasonably sure he was caught up. It was basically the same method by which air traffic controllers came on and off duty.

The chip would consist of many discrete layers, but the team would work on only one at a time; there was little sense getting started on a new layer until mapping of the previous one had been largely completed and the nature of the interlayer connections was at least preliminarily understood. For each layer, hundreds of photographs would be taken and the sliced sections carefully cataloged before being passed off to subgroups that conducted electrical tests. Each testing group had at least one reporter whose function it was to take down the spoken words of researchers and transcribe them into a database so they were accessible across teams.

Shepherd had some other ideas, but he began to get the uneasy feeling that he risked being taken outside and beaten if he didn't let the work begin, so he dispatched the first shift to get started.

The initial task was to remove the plastic casing enclosing the chip. This involved a series of chemical baths and delicate planing operations that took about two hours. Once the case was removed, a thin, metallic cover over the actual working guts of the chip was peeled off and set aside, exposing the topmost layer of the circuits themselves.

The now naked chip was placed in the scanning electron microscope and thirty yammering people tried to cram into the small space in front of the screen as the first image began to form. Rebecca and Zuckerman hovered in the background, since they wouldn't have any idea what they were looking at anyway.

"Here it comes!" an excited voice rang out. Between the jammed bodies, Rebecca caught glimpses of light flickering from what looked like a black-and-white television screen mounted above the microscope's control panel. After about thirty seconds, the flickering ceased, the image stabilized and the crowd grew quiet.

Nobody said a word. Rebecca and Zuckerman exchanged curious glances.

Then a voice, high pitched with surprise and puzzlement, said, "Now, what the holy hell is this!"

As Rebecca and Zuckerman watched, heads bending in toward the screen began to rise as people stood up straight.

"I'll be goddamned if I know," another voice said.

"This isn't possible."

"Somebody kidding us here, or what?"

People in front stepped sideways to give others a closer look at the screen. Comments of equal sentiment began to issue forth.

Finally, Zuckerman called out, "Somebody want to fill us in here?"

A white-coated scientist turned to him. "You the lawyer?"

"Prosecutor, yeah."

The man beckoned with a finger, and Rebecca and Zuckerman both walked through the slowly parting throng, stopping before the control panel. On the screen they saw an incomprehensible but neatly laid out array of alternating gray and white stripes. They ran in several directions, some of the stripes crisscrossing one another. Atop some of the crisscrosses were roundish blobs. The edges of the stripes were very rough, the surfaces badly pitted, and the blobs were also irregular in appearance.

"What are we looking at?" Zuckerman asked.

"What you're looking at," the man who had beckoned them forward said, "is a piece of shit."

"Meaning . . . ?"

"Meaning, if this thing is your friggin' superduper computer, then my Oldsmobile is the goddamned Concorde."

"What's that mean in English?" Rebecca asked impatiently, irritation shading her voice.

Someone on her right answered, "It means that this thing is a basic, ordinary, vanilla prototype chip, the kind you make one at a time in a development lab before committing to production."

Rebecca continued to stare at the image. "You mean it isn't capable of high-speed encryption?"

"Lady," another man said as he turned in disgust and began walking away, "this pile a crap couldn't run your damned wristwatch." Murmured assent from others in the group accompanied his departure.

Rebecca could tell that Zuckerman was in a state of shock. He couldn't stop staring at the screen, and his eyes were darting back and forth as though trying to see something that everybody else was missing.

Anticipating what Rebecca was about to say, he jumped in first. "Becky, I'm telling you, honest to God: this chip did everything my people said it did. Everything!"

"Apparently, that isn't possible."

"It has to be!" He leaned in closer so nobody could hear his next sentences. "Besides, you already stipulated to it in front of Goldin. Far as the court's concerned, the chip's performance is a matter of proven fact."

Rebecca turned to him in astonishment. "You wouldn't *dare* hold me to that if this thing—"

"What's all the excitement?" a female voice said from the back. Rebecca recognized it as Jessica Muller's and waved her up.

The first man who had spoken started to fill Muller in as she studied the screen, but she quickly cut him off. "Yeah, yeah . . . I see it. So what's the big deal?"

"What's the big deal?" Zuckerman asked, incredulous.

"They're saying this chip couldn't do high-speed encryption," Rebecca said. "It's too crude, and the components are too big."

Muller frowned in confusion, then turned to look at the assembled investigators. "What the hell are you talking about?"

Now it was their turn to be bewildered. *This* was a professor of electrical engineering at Cal Tech?

"Look at the size of those things," somebody finally said. "They couldn't possibly be connected to components small enough."

"I'd be surprised if this thing had even a million transistors on it," someone else said.

Muller continued to look around, perplexed. "Why would it need more than that?"

Rebecca spoke out in the ensuing silence. "Terescu said something that powerful would need about a quarter of a billion transistors."

Muller blinked a few times, then seemed to relax. "No, no, no.

It wouldn't need anywhere near that many." She looked around at the investigators. "He was talking about *density*, not the actual number of components in this particular chip." She was pointing to the screen as she finished, and exclamations of understanding began to sound in the group.

"I don't get it," Rebecca said.

"What he meant," Muller explained, "was that whatever part of the chip was doing the actual encryption would have to be that dense, not the whole chip."

She could tell that it wasn't sinking in. "If this chip does what he says it does"—she lifted her chin toward Zuckerman—"then somewhere inside is a special processor that must be extremely small. Dense, okay? A lot of transistors and other stuff crammed into a very small space."

"Okay . . ." Rebecca said hesitantly.

"And if you had a whole chip that dense," Muller continued, "it would probably contain a couple hundred million components, just like Radovan said."

She turned to address the majority of the investigation group that hadn't caught on yet. "But the whole chip doesn't have to be that sophisticated. Look, this thing is taking data from a computer, putting it into code, then giving it back to the computer, right?"

Impatient nods. *Obviously. Get on with it!*

"Well, those pieces of the chip that do the giving and the taking, they can't run any faster than the computer this chip is connected to. What would be the point? It'd be like dumping six tons of bananas on a monkey who could only eat one a minute."

She turned back to Rebecca. "It's called a hybrid chip. Completely different technologies for different functions. The only part of this chip that needs to be superfast is the part that does all that complicated coding work. The rest of it?" She waved her hand at the screen. "Just the basics. No need to get fancy."

Muller turned back to the investigation group. "Somewhere inside this thing is an embedded processor. That's what you're looking for."

She turned and walked back toward the lab door, pausing with one hand on the knob. "It's gonna be very small," she said, then opened the door and left.

For the first several hours following Muller's reorientation of the investigation, Frank Shepherd had his hands full trying to stop the technicians from spending time attempting to figure out how the chip worked. All they were supposed to be interested in at the moment was evidence regarding who might have made the thing. Each time he thought he'd driven that point home, he would return to find his people heatedly debating the purpose of various components, why they were here instead of there, did this thing over here really have any purpose or did the maker just throw it in to confuse whoever might want to take the chip apart, and so forth. Finally, Shepherd had to assign a person to each shift to do nothing else but make sure everybody stayed on track. To prevent mutiny he promised that once the main event was over, they would all have the opportunity to go back and play with the thing to their heart's content.

Toward the end of the first day, things were humming along pretty much as Shepherd had tried to set them up, and he went off to eat something and try to get some sleep.

As per Shepherd's ironclad rule, Bao Tranh was yanked from his post as soon as his hours were up. He sat with Rebecca in the employee cafeteria, smoking a cigarette and nursing a cup of tea he'd prepared using his own blend that he kept in a jar in his desk. He had just finished telling Rebecca that they hadn't yet found anything unusual in the chip.

"But so far we have only gone through all the interconnect layers," he said, fatigue evident in his voice. He rubbed his eyes and yawned, then quickly covered his mouth and apologized, smiling sheepishly.

Underneath his weariness Rebecca was still able to sense great excitement and anticipation. "So where's the important stuff?"

"Bottom layer," he answered. "The part that does the real work. But we have no way to know where on that layer it is, although probably in the middle, so it's not too far from any other part. That's where we'll start."

"Damned thing's only the size of my thumbnail," Rebecca said, "and distance still counts."

"It's critical," Tranh said, nodding and flicking the ashes off his cigarette. "When you're doing many millions of operations each second and sending the results of each on to different parts of the chip, those distances can add up quickly."

"I still don't see how, with electricity moving at the speed of light."

"It travels that fast only in a vacuum," he explained. "In a wire, the electrons bounce into atoms on their journey and get deflected all over the place. That slows them down, and it's one of the main reasons that chips have to be so small in order to be so fast."

Rebecca grimaced in self-reproach. "I should have known that. Terescu explained it to us once."

"Terescu." Tranh shook his head and smiled grimly to himself, turning his cup idly in his hand. He looked up at Rebecca. "Still can't believe he agreed to testify on behalf of Tera-Tech."

"Me neither," Rebecca agreed; no need to fill Tranh in on the truth just yet. "After he lost you, he hated James Perrein."

Tranh waved his cigarette dismissively. "Small potatoes compared to sleeping with his wife." He lifted his cup to take a sip of tea, barely noticing that Rebecca had suddenly gone rock rigid.

She stayed still for a few seconds, struggling mightily not to outwardly betray her shock but not daring to move anything just yet. "Who was sleeping with whose wife?" she managed to ask calmly, hoping Tranh didn't notice the effort it was taking.

The cup paused halfway to Tranh's lips. "You didn't know?" he asked, a smile beginning to form. "Mr. Perrein was having an affair with Mrs. Terescu."

As he started to drink, Tranh had the faint suspicion that most of his companion's vital functions were threatening to cease operating, and he set the cup back down on the table, uncertain as to the cause or what ought to be done about it.

Rebecca gulped, trying to make sure at least her larynx was still operational. "Did Terescu know?"

Tranh shrugged. "Everybody else did, why not him?" He took a deep drag on the cigarette. "Americans," he said, shaking his head as he blew out a thick cloud of smoke. "That's how Mr. Perrein found out about me. From Mrs. Terescu. And he eventually hired me away from the professor's lab."

Rebecca tried to remain calm while all her synapses were firing at maximum capacity trying to integrate this new data into what she already knew. One thing, at least, jumped to the fore as self-evident: if there had been any lingering skepticism at all up to now about Terescu's scheme to sabotage her client, this little tidbit had just put it to rest.

Rebecca didn't bother to point out to Tranh what had just occurred to her, that Perrein's "discovery" of him was no accident. She had not a shred of doubt that the only reason Perrein took up with Terescu's wife in the first place was to get his hands on Tranh.

It wouldn't be the first time he'd cruelly exploited a woman to get what he wanted.

Further revelations assaulted her. It probably wasn't because of Tranh's brilliance, either, but because he had intimate knowledge of Terescu's research discoveries that could be worth a fortune to Tera-Tech.

And it provided a more reasonable explanation for Terescu's plan for revenge, his wife's infidelity making more sense as a catalyst for broad-scale vengefulness than if it had been only about the loss of a prized grad student.

"Ms. Verona?"

"Ah." She tried to look casual as she turned to him. "Well, you look pretty tired." She slapped her hands down on the table and leaned on them. "Why don't you go get some sleep, okay?"

She pushed down on the table and stood up, trying to make it look like it took an effort, so he would see that she was tired as well and not try to keep her there.

She preferred the open cubicle to a closed office because it was possible to see people coming a long way off. Sometimes the best way to ensure privacy was to sit right out in plain view.

None of the other three made any attempt to indicate they weren't surprised. The news had thrown them all, and there was no pretending that, well, they'd kind of had a feeling about that all along. In addition to Steinholz and Ehrenright, Rebecca had asked Zuckerman to sit in. Since they were working amicably on an out-of-court agreement, it wouldn't do to withhold such vital information. For one thing, this might wind up going back to trial and she still had to play by the rules. For another, now was not the time to make displays of bad faith.

"One thing I don't get," Steinholz said, "is why Perrein would let Terescu in on the case, knowing that Terescu knew about him and his wife."

Ehrenright seemed untroubled by the issue. "What choice did he have? What was he gonna say to us, don't get the world's leading expert because, uh, one thing I forgot to mention, I diddled his wife?"

"Maybe Perrein wasn't aware that Terescu knew about the affair," Zuckerman offered. "It had probably been all business for your client."

Rebecca looked, but didn't get a hint of anything directed

obliquely toward her in that remark. "What did it being *just business* have to do with it?" she asked.

"If it was purely business, Perrein wouldn't have seen any need to humiliate Terescu in the process. So maybe your expert never knew."

"You know," Ehrenright threw in, "if Terescu did know, it might explain why Perrein didn't want him anywhere near Tera-Tech premises. God only knows what kind of damage he might have caused, including stealing trade secrets."

The conversation petered out much faster than Rebecca had expected. Tranh's news, however interesting and revelatory it might have been, really added nothing except some additional rationale for Terescu's behavior, lending credence to their theory of how he had deliberately tried to sabotage their case but contributing nothing toward the matter's resolution.

As that became clear, Steinholz and Ehrenright drifted off, leaving Rebecca and Zuckerman alone in the depressingly colorless cubicle lit only by overhead fluorescents.

Zuckerman looked at his watch. "Dinner?"

"The government buying?"

He snorted. "You lost your mind completely? How's that gonna look on my expense report, I took the defense lawyer to dinner."

"So *my* client's buying."

"Same problem."

"So who pays for this one?" Rebecca asked, frowning in genuine confusion.

Zuckerman smiled pityingly. "Swear to God, Becky, you private shysters are all alike." He stood up and stretched, reaching for his suit jacket. "Well, brace yourself: *I'm* buying."

Rebecca widened her eyes to their limit and let her mouth drop open in amazement. "With your own money?" she asked incredulously.

Thursday, November 26
DAY TWO

There were about two dozen people scattered around the employee cafeteria, so Rebecca and Zuckerman occupied a small table in a windowless corner where they wouldn't be overheard. Zuckerman appreciatively sipped the coffee

Rebecca had brewed herself after a visit to a gourmet shop on her way in.

"Justin wanted me to ask you something, David."

"Damn, this is good," he said, setting the cup down. "What?"

"Remember when we found out the chip was programmable? That the codes weren't fixed, but could be changed?"

"Course I remember. What about it?"

Rebecca stirred her own coffee slowly, even though she'd added no cream or sugar. "You said in chambers that you hadn't told us because you'd just discovered it yourself." He nodded. "Well, what Justin wanted me to ask you, how were you able to test the chip without knowing the code?"

Zuckerman stared at her, but didn't answer. Then she realized he wasn't looking *at* her, only in her direction. His mind was elsewhere. "Before you realized the chip could be changed," she went on, "you had to know what the secret key was in order to test it and prove it used Tera-Tech's encryption method. Because you needed to program the exact same key into your computers and see if you got a match."

Seeing that he was concentrating hard, she finished it off. "And there's no way to know what that code was if it was wired right in by the manufacturer. So you *had* to know from the very beginning that it was programmable, that you could change the codes at will. The people testing the chip had to be able to program it right from day one."

Zuckerman continued to stare for a while, then said, "They knew. I didn't."

"Who?"

"My investigators. The people who were running the tests so we could make our case."

"And they didn't tell you?"

"I didn't even know it was an issue at the time. Maybe they didn't, either." He waited for her to jump out of her chair, threaten to file for sanctions, run off to ask Goldin for a mistrial. . . .

But she sat quietly, lost in her own thoughts. "You know what that means?" Zuckerman didn't answer. "It means Terescu knew from the beginning as well."

Zuckerman understood. "Because he requested all the tests and examined the results. He couldn't have done that unless he knew the chip could be programmed."

"That sonofabitch . . ."

"Yeah, but now you have some of that hard proof you were looking for. Now maybe you can make a solid case against him."

"How?"

"When we had our sidebar with Goldin about opening the chip? Isn't Terescu the one who sent you back up to the bench with an argument based on the assumption that it *wasn't* programmable?"

As Rebecca stared at him, openmouthed, he glanced at his watch and looked over at one of the windows facing the lab building. "What the hell are those guys *doing* in there!" he said irritably.

"Let's go see," she said.

Sitting on a well-worn, castered office chair at the control panel of the scanning electron microscope, Bao Tranh, seemingly oblivious to whatever was going on around him, peered intently at the display screen as he carefully manipulated various controls, using both hands simultaneously. From where they were standing, Rebecca and Zuckerman thought they heard him muttering to himself, but they couldn't make out the words. They moved in closer, and several agents stepped aside.

The display screen was a jumble of blurry images, jumping constantly as Tranh worked the controls. Each time it seemed that it was about to come into focus, it would abruptly shift back into incoherence, and Tranh would angrily start talking to himself again.

Shepherd came up from behind and put his hand on Tranh's shoulder. To everyone's shock, he reached forward and flicked a switch labeled "Dspl-Pwr." The screen went dark, and Tranh shot up straight in alarm.

"Take a break, son," Shepherd said gently. As Tranh glanced anxiously at his watch, Shepherd added, "Don't worry about the time. Nobody's gonna pull you off at this stage."

With that, Tranh slumped back on the chair and closed his eyes. As the others began drifting away, Rebecca said to Shepherd, "What's going on?"

"I think we're finally zeroing in the doodad, but our boy here is working himself into a head case trying to get the protective coating off without wrecking the thing. Gonna drug him and tie him down, he don't ease up a little."

Tranh seemed not to hear, but then he smiled. Opening his eyes and looking up at Rebecca, he said wearily, "We couldn't find it." He sat up straight and turned in his seat to look at Zuckerman as well. "At first. It wasn't anywhere on the main layer."

"Where was it?"

Tranh rose slowly from the chair. His labored movements betrayed his long stretch in front of the panel without a break.

Rebecca and Zuckerman followed as he walked over to a worktable piled high with photographs. He pulled one off the stack and held it up for them to see.

The image was blank except for the Tera-Tech corporate logo, three *T*'s radiating out from a common center, like spokes from a wheel hub. It was about an inch long on the photo. "This was on the metal cover of the chip," Tranh said. "It's very small, maybe a ten-thousandth of a meter across."

"A show-off," Rebecca said.

Tranh blinked in surprise. "How did you know that?"

"Jessica Muller told me about them. Just a joke, right?"

Zuckerman looked at the picture and shrugged his shoulders. "So . . . ?"

Tranh put the picture down and picked up another one. It showed the same logo, but much enlarged, filling the entire photograph. He held it next to yet another photo, this time showing one of the *T*'s blown up to full size.

He pointed to the top bar of the *T*. "See this little smudge?"

Zuckerman reached for the picture and held it so that he and Rebecca could look at it together. The top bar of the *T* was blurry, making it appear twice as thick as it should have been. "What about it?" Rebecca asked.

Tranh rubbed his bloodshot eyes and turned back toward the electron microscope, yawning with deep fatigue. "It was in there," he said as he began walking. Someone handed him a cup of coffee, someone else turned the display back on, and he dropped down onto the chair once again.

Friday, November 27

DAY THREE

They sat together in one of a long row of functionally integrated work group modules, which they'd learned were no longer referred to as cubicles, on the floor above the lab area. Inhabitants of the uniformly sterile-looking enclosures did their best to try to cheer them up, adorning the steel desks and gray fabric walls with family pictures, posters of places they'd rather be than here, cartoons clipped from newspapers and bits of cleverness rendered in their word processors. The wag who usually occupied this particular warren had brazenly pinned up a parody of his CEO's favorite platitude: *When cryptography is outlawed, bayl bhgynif jvyy unir cevinpl.*

Looking over the low partition, they had a clear view of the only unlocked door, some seventy feet down the hall. Should anyone decide to come and look for them, they'd have a good ten-second warning so Rebecca could sit up, get her foot off Zuckerman's knee and into her shoe, and he could pick up a phone and pretend to be productive.

"Forgot how good that felt," Rebecca murmured lazily.

"Makes two of us."

"Could look an awful lot like collusion, though, defense counsel and the prosecutor cozying up in a secret hiding place."

"What collusion?" Zuckerman said, pressing his thumb into the soft part behind the ball of her foot, eliciting a grateful moan. "You and I, we're out of the picture."

"We are?"

"Yup. They find something, your man goes down; they don't, he walks. Everything's in writing, it's all automatic. . . ." He stopped rubbing for a second and tapped her big toe. "How's it feel to be superfluous?"

"Wonderful." She wiggled back, a signal for him to resume the massage. "But do us both a favor and don't refer to Perrein as 'your man.'"

"Sorry. Is it really true that figure skaters often have broken bones in their feet?"

She nodded without opening her eyes. "Like ballet dancers. They once X-rayed Edward Villela's foot, just to see, and he had seven broken bones. Danced that same night."

"Get out!"

"Wendy, she had this funny pain in her heel once and they X-rayed her. Three hairline fractures. And they had nothing to do with her heel."

"Sounds cruel."

Rebecca fought the urge to laugh out loud—to her younger sister, a few broken bones were the very least of cruelties—but just settled deeper into the chair instead. "I like this colluding." She waited for some answer from him, some sign he felt the same. She knew he did, but some reassurance would have been nice.

He stayed quiet, though, and she could feel the sudden tension in his fingers. And he knew that she could feel it. "What's gonna change, Rebecca? Why would anything be different?"

Under the influence of Zuckerman's digital expertise and the general warming trend of the past few days, her normal defenses had become complacent and she had relaxed into vulnerability. Now, newly alert, she opened one eye halfway. "*I'm* different."

He shook his head. "Use the same recipe, you get the same bread."

"I love it when you talk like a bumper sticker. And I'm not the same recipe. Haven't we been through that?"

"Yes. And no. What I'm saying, you've got to do something, Beck. You can't just declare victory." He dug into her arch with renewed vigor. "You gotta *do* something."

"And I also love it when you talk in riddles."

"You can't keep fighting the same battle over and over again. You win, then you fight it some more. It never ends."

"What are you talking about?"

"This habit you have of blowing smoking craters in people, only to regret it later. Every time you win, you really lose."

"What people?"

"All my witnesses, for example."

She checked to see if he was smiling. He was, but it was a *Gotcha*, not a joking smile. "You can't be serious. It was cross-examination, it was my job."

"No. Your job was to discredit them, not cut their balls off."

"But that's how—"

"Becky!" He stopped rubbing and wrapped his hand around her foot. "There wasn't a person in that courtroom who didn't cringe when you incinerated Melanie Fuster, Anthony Frazier, Krazny. . . . I'm surprised they didn't just go home and stick their heads in the oven by the time you got through with them."

"So I was a little overzealous. Makes for good theater."

"Theater? You and I almost had a deal last week, first time you came to me. Then you lost it when you backed me up against a wall."

"Your fault. You took it personal."

"Was it good theater when you tried to pummel your boss?"

"When?"

"When you found out I was the prosecutor."

She opened both eyes this time, wide. "Are you psychic, or isn't anything sacred anymore?"

"Not when your rampage scores a seven-nine on the Richter scale." Now that he'd gotten her to address the subject, he unwrapped his hand and continued working her arch. "Arno Steinholz couldn't stop laughing when he told me about it."

"I'll fire his ass."

"He adores you, Becky. Arno, Justin Ehrenright . . . every associate who ever worked for you loves you. Make up your mind that somebody's a good guy, there isn't a better mentor alive. They'd all follow you anywhere."

"Very flattering."

"Up yours. So what did that little tête-à-tête with Wysocki buy you?"

"Nothing much. But it didn't hurt, either. I really did agree to take the case because it was a career maker, very visible, interesting stuff"—she felt Zuckerman stop again—"and, oh yeah, forgot to mention: Wysocki said he'd chuck my ass into the street if I didn't take it."

"Really." Zuckerman tapped the top of her foot again. "Now, why do you suppose he'd act against his own self-interest and threaten to get rid of his best litigator?"

Why? It hadn't started out that way. He was pressuring me, sure, but he wasn't threatening much other than the standard bullshit. I still had a choice about the case. My professional life wouldn't have been very joyous for a while had I turned it down, but I could have gotten past that.

Then I decided to give in to the urge to rip his heart out through his throat, and backing Allen Wysocki up against a wall is generally not a good career move. By the time I slinked out of his office, my options were either to take the case or find another job . . . and probably in another state.

"Who knows?"

Zuckerman grunted. He may not have known the details, but he knew she'd brought it down on herself. "Funny I didn't see this side of you when we were hanging out together."

It wasn't there when we were together.

"Who you been fighting since . . . me? Perrein?"

"I'm not fighting anybody!"

"Just everybody." He sensed that he may have been pushing the boundary of her tolerance a bit, and concentrated on her foot for a few minutes before daring one last nudge. "You gotta do something, Beck."

"You keep saying that. What?"

"Don't know." He sensed tension in her foot again, and worked on it silently until he felt it starting to relax. "When I was a kid," he said as casually as possible, "grade school, I used to pick on kids littler than me, make their lives miserable."

"Doesn't sound like you," Rebecca said in surprise.

"It wasn't. Way out of character, but I couldn't help myself. Meanwhile, there was this other kid, I'll never forget him. Isaac. A real bully, and he picked on *me* all the time. Twice my size and there was nothing I could do about it except try to stay out of his way."

"Doesn't sound like you either."

"Anyway, the more he pushed me around, the more I pushed the littler kids around. I thought, well, that's the natural way of the world, right? Like a food chain."

Zuckerman shifted around in his chair to better align himself with the outside of her foot. "One day I couldn't take it anymore. Isaac was in a good mood, which means he tortured me even more. He grabbed me in a headlock, and finally let go when I wouldn't stop yelling, and when he stood back, I jumped at him without thinking and hit him as hard as I could. Caught him on the ear, that real stinging pain, kind that pisses you off? You could see every other kid in that schoolyard stop breathing."

He knew that he had Rebecca's full attention, and paused before continuing. "Isaac got crazy and came back after me. I got him another one in the nose, blood all over the place, and then we both just started flailing away, like kids do. *I* was so crazy I didn't even feel any pain, had no idea if he was landing good punches or what." He went silent.

"What happened?" She expected that the athletic Zuckerman had broken a few of Isaac's bones and put him in the hospital.

"He kicked the shit out of me, that's what happened." Although Rebecca's eyes were still closed, she could tell he was grinning as he said it. "I was a mess, but so was he. We didn't get into trouble, though. A very wise principal, Talmudic scholar, he sent us home to get cleaned up and never said another word about it. And after that Isaac never went near me again."

"He figure you were off your rocker?"

"No, I think he just figured it wasn't worth the trouble. Why risk picking on someone who might fight back?

"But that's not the point. I didn't realize it back then, but I never picked on a littler kid again. Ever. I wasn't being mature, I just didn't feel like it anymore. Because every time I pushed one of them around, it was because I couldn't push back at Isaac. And it wasn't going to end because there was no way to win. How could I win against Isaac if I was fighting everybody else *but* Isaac?"

She couldn't keep the sarcasm out of her voice. "Which is what I'm doing?"

"Maybe."

We despise most in others that which we despise in ourselves.

Without warning, Janine Osterreich flashed into her mind. Staring at a box of doughnuts, aware they were poison, trying desperately to resist, knowing full well it was impossible. Stuffing herself with them, experiencing the blissful but momentary glow and then regretting it, paying dearly and then doing it all over again. Rebecca remembered the loathing she felt for Janine, her amazement that somebody could have so little willpower and self-respect.

But what had it felt like to Janine herself? For Rebecca, the momentary, transcendent rush of pounding somebody into oatmeal was so powerful that to deny it would be like refusing a breath if you were suffocating. Succumbing meant feeling that warm adrenaline, that fountain of endorphins washing over her brain. Is that what a binge felt like to Janine Osterreich?

And what about the aftermath? Janine was lucky: one good upchuck and she was back to ground zero, with only rotting teeth left as a reminder. But the consequences of grinding another person's sense of self into fine dust were a little more significant, and took longer to fix. Rebecca had to spend days, weeks sometimes, repairing the damage she'd done, soothing feelings and making amends, dispensing endless apologies, hoping the consequences were reversible. But even if it was made okay with the other guy, there was no caulking up the fissures it was leaving in herself.

"So what are you telling me?"

"You've got to find your own Isaac, Rebecca. Otherwise you'll spend the rest of your life fighting the same useless battles over and over."

It sounded like an ultimatum. A condition. *The rest of your life, but not mine along with it . . . ?*

"But I don't even know what the hell you're talking about!"

She knew exactly what he was talking about, but she had no way of knowing that she knew. Somewhere, just beyond the reach of her conscious mind, like Tantalus' grapes, was the dim awareness that the moments of runaway maliciousness she had always blamed on "the lawyer inside of her" or her difficult periods or the random intransigencies of people she was forced to deal with in her work had nothing whatsoever to do with any of those things. They were certainly handy and convenient rationalizations, and maybe they acted as catalyzing agents to trigger her episodic volatility.

But at some point, that distant piece of her knew, she was going to have to figure out how to stop the obsessive cycle of self-destructive attempts to exact from the rest of the world some futile and hopelessly belated revenge for the injustices suffered elsewhere in her life. She knew it but didn't know it, suppressing it so effectively that denial was not only easy but technically truthful, at least as far as her conscious mind was concerned. That was the same mind that was convinced it had effectively dispatched Uncle Charlie the day she told him to stuff his dreams because she was becoming a lawyer instead of Wendy II.

"I don't know if it's a who or a what," Zuckerman was saying, "but it's a something. Somebody as smart as you doesn't go around sticking her finger in a socket all the time for no reason."

Rebecca's foot stiffened up and Zuckerman stopped rubbing. Her eyes were fully open again. "You saying I need professional help?"

The far door opened. With no sudden betraying movements, Rebecca and Zuckerman smoothly recomposed themselves, she scratching notes on a legal pad, he speaking on the phone. Both looked up in well-rehearsed earnest surprise as Justin Ehrenright came around the partition. "They've found something," he said between panting breaths. "They're going nuts down there."

He was too worked up to notice that Zuckerman had hung up the phone without saying good-bye to anybody at the other end.

Chapter 32

As they came out of the stairwell on the first floor, the first thing they noticed was the eerie quiet. For the past three days the area outside the lab had been active and noisy, agents carrying files or milling about or talking constantly on cell phones. Now there wasn't a human in sight.

Rebecca and Zuckerman slowed as they entered the lab itself, instinctively assessing the room's gestalt before risking an intrusion. A good number of the investigators were huddled near the atomic-force microscope, a massive machine the size of two very large refrigerators stacked one atop the other. They were watching the display screen from a respectful distance even though most of them had no idea what they were looking at.

"What's he got on?" Zuckerman asked Ehrenright, who was just catching his breath.

"I can't tell exactly. It's like they're speaking Sanskrit or something. But I think it may be the encryption processor."

"He get the coating off okay?"

Ehrenright nodded, and Zuckerman looked around. "Where's Muller?"

"On the production floor," Ehrenright said. "Somebody went to get her."

FBI Special Agent Shepherd walked up. "Guy won't say a word to anybody. Few minutes ago he's looking at the screen, suddenly he yells and starts talking to himself."

"The hell's he saying, Shep?"

"Beats the shit out of me."

Shepherd turned and started to yell out across the room, then thought better of it and walked over toward a group talking quietly nearby. "Hey, Willy," he said to one in particular. "You were in 'Nam . . . you speak any?"

"Just enough to get drunk and laid."

Shepherd beckoned with a finger, and William Feeney followed him over to the microscope. Feeney was the man who had shouted something about a bomb in the parking lot several nights ago when the herds of evacuated Tera-Tech employees weren't dispersing fast enough to suit him.

Tranh was still in his own world, but quiet now, the images on the screen clearing, blurring, shifting as he delicately moved a trackball with his right hand and a slide control with his left. Shepherd pointed to Tranh and gave Feeney a questioning look.

Feeney watched for a few seconds, waiting until Tranh's fingers stopped moving and the screen image stabilized, then put a hand on Tranh's shoulders and gave a squeeze. *"Có gì không?"* he said gently in Vietnamese. *What's going on?*

"Có lẽ nao!" the young scientist answered without taking his eyes off the screen.

"Whud he say?" Shepherd whispered.

"He says, 'It can't be.' "

"What can't be?" Shepherd asked impatiently, and Feeney pressed Tranh for details.

Tranh looked up at him, wild-eyed—*"Không thê!"*—then returned to his fiddling with the controls, causing the screen image to waver and blur again.

" 'Impossible,' he says." Feeney shrugged. "S'all I can get out of him."

Shepherd pursed his lips and exhaled loudly through his nose in frustration. Surprisingly, Tranh held up his left hand, as if for quiet, and said, *"Xin cho tôi thêm vài phút nöã tôi gân xong rôi."*

"He says, uh, wait a minute," Feeney said, "or give him another minute or something like that. Says he's almost finished."

Jessica Muller burst through the lab door, but slowed instantly as she caught the atmosphere in the room and stopped halfway to the microscope. The people standing behind Tranh didn't turn at the noise of her entry.

After about another three minutes, as Tranh's deft manipulation of the controls slowed to barely perceptible movements, the watery and jerky image on the screen began very gradually to resolve itself and stabilize. Tranh breathed out slowly, as if finally releasing a long-held breath. He watched the screen for another few seconds, then lifted his hands off the controls, careful not to jar them, and sat back as others crowded in and jostled for the best viewing positions.

Rebecca leaned forward and peered at the display. She couldn't interpret the image that had been generated by a computer based on the signals received from the microscope's electronic probe, but it fascinated her nonetheless.

A patchwork of thousands of barely discernible, whiskery lines, it looked like an unlabeled map of a vast and intricate subway system. The lines ran in groups, as many as ten or fifteen in tightly packed parallel bunches, traveling along in harmony until reaching some junction where they split off in different directions, often rejoining other groups, which then splintered again. There were stations, too, rectangular blocks from which lines radiated outward, as well as larger terminals that seemed to command whole sections of the terrain. Rebecca noticed that there was not a single curved line anywhere on the screen. When lines needed to change direction, they did so at an angle.

In the upper left of the screen, filling about an eighth of the whole image, she saw a grid consisting of dozens of exact copies of a single small design, a square filigree, laid out in row after perfect row.

"That's memory," Shepherd said, seeing where she was looking. "Copies of the same circuit repeated over and over again."

Zuckerman bent in closer and held his finger up to the screen without actually touching it, running his hand first across, then sideways. "Sixteen by sixteen," he announced, straightening up.

Shepherd nodded knowingly, and said, "Two fifty-six. Exact number of bits in the Tera-Tech coding system."

Zuckerman turned to Rebecca and pointed to the screen. "It's the encryption processor."

Tranh suddenly whirled in his chair, startling Rebecca, and looked around. Spotting Muller, he waved her over with one hand, while pointing on the screen with the other. As she walked toward the microscope, one of the FBI scientists took advantage of the sanctioned interruption to quickly step forward and join her.

Muller came up behind Tranh and looked over his shoulder, examining the image as Tranh began explaining it to her, but he'd forgotten himself and was still speaking Vietnamese. Rebecca noticed that Muller seemed to have no trouble following him, then realized that it was because she understood not Vietnamese but the image on the screen itself.

Shepherd leaned in and pointed to an area containing a thick pack of the subway lines that were relatively isolated from most of the blocklike elements. "What're these?"

Tranh, in English this time, his voice barely a whisper, answered, "Wires."

The FBI scientist, who had been listening to the interchange, tapped Shepherd on the shoulder and stepped in to take his place before the display panel. He looked at the image, then punched a panel button that brought up the scaling factor along the side of the screen that indicated the magnification strength, and straightened up.

"No way," he said authoritatively, shaking his head. "Not that small. Can't be done."

Tranh said quietly, "Yes, it can."

Muller looked first at Rebecca, then Zuckerman, and nodded her agreement.

PART IV

VERDICT

Chapter 33

It had nothing to do with Zuckerman. Not with Wysocki, either, or opposition witnesses, or judges, or the guy who cut her off on the freeway or jostled her in line at the theater.

It wasn't about Perrein, either, not really. Not unless she tried to pretend that her self-destructive flashes of temper had begun only after her dismal fling with him, and there were any number of prosecutors, witnesses and even a couple of U.S. Supreme Court Justices who could attest to the contrary. Besides, Perrein hadn't been the cause of anything; he had simply been the worst symptom.

She'd been pleasant to Janine Osterreich the last few weeks, surprising several other lawyers, and the secretary-reporter now looked at her gratefully each time she passed her desk.

Rebecca started wondering if people talked about her behind her back. Did they make inferences about her childhood, as Steinholz had made about Osterreich's? Did they interpret her behavioral quirks as a kind of mental bulimia, gorging herself on periodic binges of displaced vengeance followed by purges of apology and restitution?

The thought of what people might be thinking unnerved her. Maybe she should tell them about the one, all-too-brief period in her life when those irresistible urges had dissipated, so quietly over the course of a few months she had barely noticed. But that ended two years ago, and they had since returned in full force, Lord only knew why. Like her delayed period, they sure made up for lost time, all right: just ask Jim Perrein or David Zuckerman or Allen Wysocki or any one of a number of people whose dicks she'd shrunk by the force of her anger.

Dicks? Why did a picture of emasculation pop into her head? What about all the women she'd treated with abruptly uncorked venom?

She tried to think of some. Any. Even one.

She could easily spend the rest of her life gorging herself on Janine Osterreich's doughnuts, beating up everybody in the world.

But in the end, her Isaac would still be left standing, so what was the point?

"She had it all," Charles Malacore said to his niece. "Everything. Then threw it away by getting careless, not taking care of herself. Tripping on a smooth floor, for Chrissakes." He looked down, shaking his head at the stupidity of it all. "Everything we worked for, gone, just like that."

"And you're still stewing over it, all these years later?"

Charles looked at her for a second, then turned his head elsewhere. "You were always mad, Rebecca. Spent your whole life being pissed off, since you were a kid."

It might have seemed, were it read in a transcript, that Charlie Malacore was engaging in a meaningful conversation with his niece, being insightful, even concerned, and somehow trying to connect with her despite the harsh things that were being said.

But the illusion of his words was broken by the reality of his manner. To the Pumpkin King, ruler of the patch, Rebecca's presence was just a coincidence. It could have been a dinner roll he was talking to, because he wasn't having a conversation with another human being, he was just talking, and it was convenient to have someone there upon whom to spray his endless supply of self-pity.

Rebecca felt it coming, way in the distance, that hundred-ton steam locomotive hurtling down the tracks. Except this time, rather than fearing it, she was standing at the tender shoveling great heaps of coal into the roaring fire under the boiler.

"I was always pissed off?"

Charles waved a hand at her, as though any petty and self-indulgent concerns she might have about herself were puny in comparison to his far deeper sea of legitimate woes. That casually dismissive, toweringly egocentric gesture plucked sharply at a harpful of her most susceptible strings.

"So damned sensitive all the time," he said with irritation. He screwed up his face in exaggerated imitation of a bratty kid and said, in a childishly whining voice, "Oh, Uncle Charlie, my belly hurts, how come I can't get new skates, how come I have to take the bus and she gets to fly . . ." He grunted sarcastically as he let his face muscles relax back into their usual malicious scowl, then sneered at her and turned away again. . . .

* * *

"Ladies and gentlemen, in preparation for landing, would you kindly . . ."

The jarring voice blaring out of the speaker directly above her head made Rebecca jerk her body as though rudely awakened from a long and involving dream. As she blinked in an effort to orient herself, a voice beside her said, "You okay, miss?"

She twisted her head so fast it made the elderly gentleman sitting next to her draw back. She smiled and put her hand on his arm. "Yes, I'm fine. Sorry if I scared you. Must've been dreaming."

The man smiled back. "You always dream with your eyes open?"

"Daydreaming, then. Are we landing?"

"Soon."

Rebecca was fairly certain that she had never felt this much raw fury since the day she'd been born. She had to consciously remind herself that there would likely be dire consequences should she reach across the table and plunge a fork into her uncle's chest. The train, powered by the momentum of years of stored anger, hurt, and humiliation, was rocketing down the steep mountainside so fast that nothing in the known universe could stop it, and the only way to relieve the pressure threatening to destroy her was to dump it all on him, on Charlie, in one great, heaving landslide.

But hadn't he been hurt enough? Weren't his years of suffering already sufficient punishment? What good could this possibly do? Rebecca restrained herself even as red lightning bolts zigzagged behind her closed eyes.

"Tell you what your trouble was, miss: your trouble was you never forgave that weak, pathetic father of yours for dying on you."

Rebecca opened her eyes, slowly, and saw Charles nodding his head self-admiringly at this epiphany.

"Yeah, that's it! And you took it out on me, see? You're still taking it out on me! I'm the one who really suffered in that cockamamie arrangement my idiot sister came up with, not you kids, nosirree. You two had it all! Think old Vin-chen-zo coulda given you that if he hadna croaked?"

In the time it took for Rebecca's heart to complete its next beat, the world went still. Even the smoke rising from the serving dishes at the buffet across the room seemed to halt its upward motion.

The only thing that moved was Uncle Charlie, and he was nodding his head even more vigorously now, having determined that his revelation was so self-evidently valid that no further discussion about it was necessary, or invited.

The man in the seat next to her pointed out the window and Rebecca turned, only to wince as impossibly brilliant sunshine lanced her eyes. She grabbed for her sunglasses in the seat pocket as the plane banked gently to starboard. The sun gradually made its way aft, and as the plane began to level, she looked down to see a virginal white beach reaching out to water so thickly blue it looked almost gelatinous. The plane continued its bank, and soon palm trees and a mangrove forest came into view. Farther inland she was able to make out thatched roofs, a few low concrete industrial buildings and, finally, a small city center. Beyond the northwest corner of the island, she spotted small, thready wakes that dissolved quickly behind the sailboats creating them. As the plane descended, she could make out people standing on larger boats, fishing poles poised and waiting over the gunwales, straw hats shielding them from the midday sun.

Quiet. A desert just before a thermonuclear device is detonated by remote control.
What good would it do . . .
"Tripped, for God's sake," Charlie said. "Jesus H. Christ . . ."
She thought her heart was in danger of exploding out of her chest.
But what good would it do!
For him, nothing. For Rebecca, everything. Besides, she couldn't stop it now even if she wanted to.
"Wendy didn't trip on anything."
Charlie blinked, nothing else, but she knew he was listening even though he was facing away from her.
What could be better than to be alive in a moment you'd die for?
"She cracked the knee herself, Charlie. On purpose."
Nothing. Then, very slowly, he turned his head toward her. His vacant eyes told her that it hadn't quite sunk in, some primordial defense mechanism in his brain trapping her words and holding them in temporary storage, leaking them into his consciousness slowly in order to protect him from getting hit with it all at once.
Rebecca watched, rapturously, as the four stages of dying began to work their way through him in an orderly fashion.

Stage 1, denial. "Bullshit," Charlie said, *voice barely above a whisper.* "You made that up just to get back at me."

"A Coke bottle, Charlie. Unopened. It's all she had to drink because that's all you packed in her lunch. She took it by the neck and whacked it into her knee as hard as she could." *She feigned the motion with her hand, ending with a light slap on her knee and a* Whaddya think about that? *expression on her face.*

"No, sir." *He shook his head very slowly.* "I don't believe it."

Rebecca just stared at him, drinking in his blossoming astonishment.

He stopped shaking his head. "She did that to me?"

Rebecca rolled her eyes heavenward and tried to keep from laughing.

Next, anger. "I'll kill her," *he said softly, but with feeling.* "Swear to God I'll strangle her with my bare hands."

"You don't even know where she lives." *Rebecca said it calmly. Who needed theatrical histrionics when this kind of ammunition was available?*

Now, depression. "My God." *He hung his head in his hands, fingers rubbing his temples, as if trying to massage out the toxins within.* "She ruined my life. On purpose! Why would she do that to me!"

"She didn't do it to you!" *Goddammit, what was the point of this if the dumb fuck didn't even get it! Rebecca caught the startled glances at other tables, and lowered her voice.* "Why does everything always have to revolve around you! She didn't do it to you, she did it for herself!"

"But why?" *He was practically whining now, this time for real.*

"Whhhyy!" *Rebecca whined back, aping his earlier brat imitation, only more obnoxiously, before resuming with her own voice.* "To get her life back, that's why!"

"Her life back? What the hell are you talking about? She had it all in the palm of her hand!"

"She didn't have anything, Charlie; you had it all. She was miserable, in more kinds of pain than you could imagine. She was adored by millions of people she didn't know, and felt unloved by the one person who mattered."

He blinked his confusion.

"You, Charlie. She wanted to be loved by you." *Almost as much as I did.*

"But I did love her!"

"*Really.*" Better now—he was starting to catch on. *Rebecca folded her arms across her chest and relaxed against the back of her chair.* "And just how was she supposed to have figured that out?"

"How? I hugged her all the time, laughed with her, shouted encouragement. You can't deny it." *His eyes grew accusatory, and momentarily hopeful.* "It's all on film!"

"That's just the thing, Charlie. It was only when it was on film. Every time the cameras started up you were Jimmy Stewart and Grandpa Walton rolled into one. But as soon as the lights dimmed, she was just the prime pork belly in your portfolio."

The hopefulness died. "I spent all my money on her, lavished my time, sacrificed everything!"

"Sounds more like an investment. What did she get out of it?"

"How can you ask such a question! People everywhere were crazy about her. Little girls just wanted to touch her for a second. She could have made millions, could have been the best in the world, the little bitch!"

"Is that what she wanted?"

"Of course she did! Who the hell wouldn't?"

"You ever ask her?"

"I didn't have to ask her! I knew!"

"Guess you got that one wrong."

Charles turned away from her again, slumping sullenly on his chair, arms folded across his chest. "You don't know what the hell you're talking about."

"Maybe. Probably. But why do you figure she ruined her own knee?"

"Simple. Couldn't take the pressure." *He waved his hand.* "Didn't have the right stuff."

"The right stuff? She was a fourteen-year-old kid, not a goddamned fighter pilot!"

And here we are, talking about Wendy again. What about me, Charlie! Fifteen years since the ungrateful little squirt ruined all your plans, and all you can talk about is her!

And, finally, acceptance. "Ah, what the hell. Water under the bridge, right? We had our shot in the sun. How many people can say that?"

Easy for you to say, Charlie. You're still famous. You hired all the public relations goons, built up your story so you looked like the most self-sacrificing relative since the earth cooled. You had your picture taken consoling Wendy in the hospital, and only Doctor Janos and I knew that less than an hour before you considered letting him cripple her for life so she could win the world championship. People still stop you in the street to shake your hand. And what do you tell them when they ask how Wendy's doing? You tell them she wants her privacy, that you respect that, so no comment, but you don't tell them you've only seen her twice in the last ten years and don't even have any idea what continent she's living on. . . .

Rebecca had expected waves of ecstasy to wash over her, for the pressure to disappear in a thunderous detonation, and she was not disappointed. But when it was all done, there was none of it left, just the perception of something dark and loathsome skittering away forever, leaving behind only a slate gray ache with a hollow core.

She didn't even hate Uncle Charlie anymore.

Chapter 34

Tuesday, December 22

Rebecca walked casually along a beach on the newly independent island-state of Santa Rosalia. She paused in front of a recently restored resort hotel, then turned and walked toward it, to a spot near the pool where well-heeled guests were lying on lounge chairs sipping tropical drinks. She looked around, then signaled the beach boy for a light folding chair, giving him a U.S. dollar when he set it up for her.

She picked it up, carried it a few feet and set it down next to a man wearing a straw hat and thick sunglasses. His face was turned up to the sun and he appeared to be sleeping, but as soon as Rebecca unfolded the chair and sat down, he said, "I was wondering how long it would take someone to get here."

She looked at him directly for the first time. "Hello, Rado."

He took off the sunglasses and turned his head toward her. "Justice Department paying for this trip?"

She smiled. "No, but I suspect they will when I get back, now that I've found you."

He turned his face back toward the sun and put his glasses back on. "I doubt it. Not when you go back alone. Santa Rosalia doesn't have an extradition treaty with the U.S. Of course, you know that already."

She was unfazed. "Guess I wasted my time."

"Not really. White sand, blue water, perfect weather . . . a nice boondoggle, I'd say."

He glanced at the lounge chair on the other side of his own. A middle-aged but clearly still fit and smelling-of-money woman lay peacefully, the slightly parted lips indicating that she was probably asleep. Terescu watched for a moment, as though to ascertain whether there was any chance of being overheard, then turned back to Rebecca. "Must rub some lotion on her before she fries."

Rebecca continued to stare at her. Something awfully familiar about that face . . .

Terescu grinned lasciviously and picked up a tall glass containing a pinkish liquid topped with a paper umbrella. He took a sip, licked his lips, and said, "It wasn't important to fool you forever, you know. Just . . ."

"I know," she interrupted. "Just long enough for you to wreck Tera-Tech and get out of the country."

Terescu wiped a hand across his chin. "Something like that. Although I hadn't originally planned on leaving the country. I suppose Perrein was overcome with gratitude to you for clearing his name?"

She pursed her lips but didn't answer, wanting to keep the memory of that delicious moment all to herself. *Rebecca, what can I ever do to repay you? And she had answered, Well, I'll tell you, Jim: you can make sure all our invoices are paid by the end of the week, and then stay the hell out of my life forever. Yep, I think that'll about do it.*

Rebecca pulled a bottle of sunscreen out of her bag, dribbled a bit onto a finger and began rubbing it on her face. Terescu waited, and when she didn't say anything, he took another sip of his drink and said, "Not that it matters a whole lot, but tell me about the chip. Tranh find something unusual in there, did he?"

She was in no hurry, wiping the lotion away from her mouth before speaking. "That was part of it, but there were other things." She could tell without looking that she had his attention, and took her time dabbing some lotion first on one shoulder, then the other. "You did know Perrein was fucking your wife, didn't you?" she asked as casually as possible. The involuntary jerk in his arm gave her some indication of his chagrin, which she was surprised to discover gave her little satisfaction.

"Of course I did," he said after regaining some measure of control.

But you're still not over it, she thought, embarrassed at his pain. "Wasn't too great a leap to figure out that's how he got to Tranh. Musta been awful, that sonofabitch using your wife to steal your—"

"Does this have a point, Rebecca?" Terescu asked with his teeth clenched, turning his head toward her and leaning in so the woman on the other lounge chair wouldn't wake up and overhear.

She turned to look at him in surprise. "You asked. I'm just telling you. None of this is news, is it? I mean, *you* know how you did it, you're just asking how we figured it out, right?"

"Seems to me you can't prove anything, anyway."

"Oh, I don't know. Jessica Muller and Bao Tranh think they can."

"I doubt it."

"Then what are you doing in Santa Rosalia instead of Pasadena?"

"Just playing it safe. Who knows what the Department of Justice is liable to do if they get a notion." He lay back in the chair. "Look what they tried to do to Perrein."

"What kind of notion you figure they might come up with?"

"Now you're toying with me, Rebecca. What did Tranh find in the chip?"

Rebecca readjusted herself on the chair, closed her eyes and tilted her face upward toward the sun. "We all thought you wanted a peek inside of it, but we were wrong, weren't we? The reason you wanted to get your hands on it and open it up, at least at first, was so you could make sure nobody else found out what was inside."

"Now, why would I want to do that?"

"What Tranh spotted in the chip was wires, Rado. Really thin ones. Made out of pure gold. They were fabricated with vapor depa-, depo-what?"

"Deposition."

"Right. Charged vapor deposition." She twisted her head around to try and get a look at a spot she might have missed on her shoulder. As she dabbed a bit more lotion on, she said casually, "Which is why you've been formally indicted on a perjury charge—among others."

"Perjury! Hah! Tell me one time I lied on the stand!"

Rebecca rubbed her fingers together to get some small bits of sand off. "When you testified that you didn't believe that the chip could be built. Because the technology to do it didn't exist yet."

"And how do you know I lied?"

"Because you knew that the technology did exist. And you knew those chips could be built."

"How do you know that?"

"Because you built them."

Terescu swallowed, trying not to make it obvious.

"And you sold them to the Chinese."

He took another sip, waiting until the liquid coated his dry throat before speaking. "And you figured this out how?"

"Just told you. Tranh found tiny gold wires made using the charged vapor deposition process. Name me one other person in the world who could have done it. There's nobody. So you did it."

"Did I?"

"Why play coy, Rado? Like you said, you're safe here, indictment or no indictment. You put me through a lot of grief, almost ruined my life. Least you could do, I came all this way, is give me the details."

"If I'm so safe, why was I indicted?"

"In case you ever decide you want to step foot back in the States, or any other country on planet Earth with a mutual extradition treaty. But mostly because it helped clear Perrein's name. That was a whole lot easier to do when we could identify the person who was really guilty."

"What do you want to know?"

"How much did you get for them?"

"About seven million. In U.S. dollars."

"Didn't bother you to sell out your country?"

Terescu laughed for the first time. "Typical self-righteous lawyer bullshit. Your own client's been screaming for years to get those silly regulations lifted. You were ready to defend him even when you thought he was guilty, and *I'm* a traitor for jumping the gun on the inevitable?"

"Good point." Rebecca pursed her lips. "Gotta give you that one." She threw him a sly smile. "Not above a little hanky-panky myself now and again."

Terescu sniffled and stirred his drink. "That include Perrein fucking you to get a Taiwanese import license, then dumping you like a sack of rotting turnips?"

Touché. She felt it best not to risk speaking just yet.

"Why'd you defend him, Rebecca?"

"He was paying us a lot of money," she answered, her voice now subdued. "And I thought he was innocent."

"Thought you could get him back?"

"Don't be silly. That was over and done a long time ago."

"Really."

"Really. And I didn't see any need to try to destroy him, like you tried to do. How did you know the chips would be discovered, that there would even be a trial?"

"If the NSA hadn't figured it out, I would have tipped them off. Being your expert witness was just an extra added bonus."

"You knew that if you started out on our side and got born again in the middle of the trial, you could make it look as bad for Tera-Tech as possible."

"Didn't take a whole lot of brainpower to come up with that. Although that idiot prosecutor sure took his time coming around to asking the right questions."

"Ah, but you were right there helping him. Deep Silicon himself."

Terescu responded with a lopsided grin. "Way things were going, I was close to winning the damned case for you, which would have ruined everything. So I phoned in a few hints to the good guys."

Rebecca rubbed her temples and squeezed her eyes shut, murmuring, "Jesus, you practically *choreographed* the whole thing."

"Almost pulled it off, too, until you got permission to dismantle the chip without me there. But no matter." He waved a hand at the beach and the palm trees. "This isn't such a bad place to spend one's twilight years."

"But you hadn't planned on it, right, Rado?"

He stayed silent.

"We couldn't figure out why, at the beginning of the trial when you wanted to examine the inside of that chip, you didn't make that big a deal of it. Then, all of a sudden, way late in the game, you go ballistic, screaming and yelling, hiring lawyers. . . . What the hell is this, we were thinking? And it was only after all of that ruckus that you decided to hightail it out of the U.S."

"And you know why, I suppose."

"That's an easy one." She set the drink down and clasped her hands around her knees. "As long as Zuckerman kept winning his arguments to prevent dismantling the chip, you had nothing to worry about. Even when the judge finally agreed to let us get inside, well, you didn't think anybody would really be able to dig down deep enough to discover your creation, much less recognize it. But then Zuckerman told you your old grad student was the one going to be doing the looking."

She dipped her head to look up into Terescu's eyes, which were fixated on the blank sand at his feet. "Bao Tranh, Rado. You know, the one you wanted us to believe built the chip? During your testimony you let us think that he'd done all the work on programmability, but he didn't. You did. All Tranh did was come up with just what you guided him to; then he tested your theories by building actual devices. It was actually a pretty enlightened way for a professor to behave toward a bright student. But by publicly crediting him with your discoveries during the trial, you pointed the finger straight at him as the one who fabricated the chips."

Terescu didn't move or acknowledge in any other way that he was listening. But Rebecca knew he was, and went on. "And then, just when you thought you had him nailed to a wall, you found out he was the one who was going to be looking inside the chip. Bao Tranh, who you knew was the one man in the world who could spot your handiwork and blow the whistle. So you had to get your hands on it first, and make sure nobody saw the incriminating layer. That's when you panicked, hired a lawyer and filed a motion to let you be the one to look inside the chip." Rebecca raised a hand in the air. "Judge denies the motion"—she dropped her hand back onto her knee with a loud slap—"Terescu takes off for the sunny Caribbean."

Terescu rocked his head back and forth. "You're some smart cookie, Becky. Now you answer one: how'd you find me here?"

"From the computer on your desk at school. Zuckerman got a search warrant. You made your reservations through the Internet, but I guess you forgot that your Web browser keeps track of the last several hundred sites you visited."

"Clever."

"Yeah. You're a helluva a scientist but you make a lousy fugitive. Oh, incidentally, there was a message on your phone machine."

"From?"

"CyberDesign Industries. Another interesting thing, that. See, we couldn't figure out how you knew that Tera-Tech had an XT-5055. Then we lifted this phone message from your machine. They said they have a new machine ready to ship and they need for you to check it out first. Which is how we found out you had a consulting contract with them. You were the one who calibrated every 5055 before it got shipped to the customer. So you knew long ago that Tera-Tech had one. Nice bit of acting, all that fussing and fuming about Perrein not telling you about it."

"It's even better than that." Terescu craned his head back and scratched his neck where a bead of sweat had formed.

"How can it be better than that?"

Terescu reached to the side and patted the sleeping woman on the thigh. "I used it to build the chips. Every time I checked out a 5055, I built another layer. I figured, nothing's harder to fabricate than those little buggers, so if the machine could do it, out the door it went, hundred percent certified."

He yawned and stretched. "Of course, CyberDesign had no idea. Had I told them, they'd want to share in the profits from the chips, since I used their machines to build them. So I didn't tell them. I never told *anybody*, not even Bao Tranh. And when Perrein seduced my wife so he could lure Tranh away? What do you know, there was a 5055 waiting to be shipped to Tera-Tech, and I simply couldn't resist." He grinned smugly.

Jigsaw puzzle pieces swirling around in Rebecca's brain suddenly fell to earth and snapped into place. "*You're* the one who modified Tera-Tech's machine!" She closed her eyes. "All that heat damage, the gold residue . . . and you left some evidence of the modifications inside, just in case anyone ever got around to examining it later."

The woman on the other lounge chair stirred, rubbed her eyes and sat up. Seeing Rebecca, she smiled brightly and said, "You must be Ms. Verona. I'm Allison. I believe we spoke by phone once?"

Oh, Jesus Christ! Rebecca's jaw dropped as she finally recognized the face.

Allison Perrein giggled and kissed Terescu on the shoulder.

Rebecca felt lightheaded. After a moment she said to Allison, "He told me you two were separated, that a divorce was already under way."

Allison's smile faded, and some long-nurtured pain flitted across her even features. "I'm sure he did, but don't worry about it. Believe me, I bear the innocent pawns in this little drama no ill will."

Rebecca frowned. "You were Tera-Tech's human resources director. How come you stayed on after? I mean, after you knew what was going on?"

"It was only for another few months," Terescu explained. "Couldn't have done it without her. She had access everywhere."

"Including the company's supply of specialized ink." Rebecca shook her head to try to clear it.

Terescu smiled and lifted his hands, then let them drop. "Although you certainly did surprise me when you were cross-examining, what was his name, Krazny? Government's ink expert? I didn't know the stuff was so common. What'd you have in that paper bag that scared the hell out of him?"

"My lunch."

Terescu stared at her incredulously, then laughed loudly, shaking an admonishing finger at her. "You see?" he said as his laughter subsided. "We have a lot in common, you and I!"

"No, we don't. If Krazny had done his job properly, I wouldn't have had to pull that stunt. But he was just another whore expert, Radovan." *We're all whores,* as David had put it, *the only open question being price.* She sat up and swung her legs over the side of the lounge. "Excuse me for a minute, would you?"

Terescu set his drink down and patted Rebecca's hand with exaggerated concern. "There, there now. You take all the time you need."

She picked up her purse and started to head back toward the main bar, getting only a few steps before hearing Terescu and Allison's self-satisfied laughter behind her. She stopped and turned. "Oh, one thing: CyberDesign wouldn't have had any rights to your work just because you used their machine. It's called the work-made-for-hire rule. Look it up sometime."

The laughter didn't resume as she walked away. Entering the bar, she spotted a man with distinctly Asian features sitting by himself, about thirty-five years old, his clothes nicely complementing his trim and clearly fit physique, nursing a soft drink and intently reading his newspaper. She discreetly tried to catch his eye but failed, then made her way toward a uniformed and heavily be-medaled man seated at one of the back tables. He wore a Police Special .38 service revolver at his hip.

"Is that your man?" he asked her without preamble, nodding toward the beach.

"Men."

The police officer raised an eyebrow. "The woman as well?"

She nodded. "Both of them."

Santa Rosalia Chief of Police Enrique Olivera signaled the waiter to bring a drink for Rebecca, who said, "So, how do we go about this?"

Olivera took a cigarette out of a gold holder, tapped it against his wrist and put it between his lips. The waiter appeared with Rebecca's drink, but lit the chief's cigarette with a hastily retrieved lighter before setting it down in front of her. Olivera mumbled his thanks and waited until the waiter was out of earshot.

"We are a small country, Miss Verona, and grateful to the United States for the aid it has provided us. We are also a new democracy, and still feeling our way around the laws and regulations, which are, shall we say . . ." He made a waving motion with his hand.

"Fluid?" she offered.

"Ah!" He slapped the table top with the palm of his hand. "Fluid! Exactly so. Tell me, have they been indicted yet? Formally?"

Rebecca reached for her purse and, after switching off the tape machine that had been running while she was out on the beach, withdrew several sheets of paper stapled together. Looking up, she said, "One of them has," and handed the sheaf of papers to Olivera. "Why?"

He smiled. "And the other one? The woman?"

"I'll have it faxed to you by this afternoon. But why?"

"Because he has applied for citizenship here. Mr. Terescu. The other I do not know because I wasn't aware she was part of all of this."

"Neither was I, but I suspect she has applied as well. What has citizenship got to do with it?"

Olivera folded the papers neatly and put them in his satchel. "While we as yet have no formal extradition treaty with the United States, we strongly desire one and will get around to it before too long. However, we are not receptive to new citizens who are under indictment for felony offenses in their home countries. It is our preference that they come to us unburdened with such overhanging problems."

"But they could stay as visitors," Rebecca protested, visibly upset at this turn.

Olivera held up his hands and closed his eyes. "It is also the policy of this country that visits by foreigners be strictly limited in duration."

"I see." She looked hopeful again. "I see. And what is the limit on a visit?"

"Thirty-eight days."

What the hell kind of a number was thirty-eight days? "And how long has Terescu been in the country?" she asked, catching on in mid-sentence and answering with him simultaneously:

"Thirty-eight days!"

She laughed, but Olivera kept a perfectly straight face as he continued. "And there is only one flight out today, as luck would have it. It seems"—he groped for words—"that our poor and underfunded air traffic control system has broken down again, severely limiting our ability to maintain safety standards if it is overloaded."

"And this flight is going to . . . ?"

"Miami." He inhaled on his cigarette and blew a gray cloud towards the ceiling. "If memory serves."

Rebecca looked at him admiringly. "What about the money?"

"Ah, yes. Well, it seems as though the bulk of it, some six point six million, has been deposited in the National Bank of Santa Rosalia and, as you know, we also have no formal agreements that govern adjudication of property disputes. Generally, this is viewed as a 'safe harbor' for funds of dubious origin." He waited for her look of disappointment before continuing. "However . . ."

She cocked her head to one side. "This is going to be good, isn't it."

He went on, as though not having heard her. "However, in the event that a formal complaint is filed by a contentious party, it would be our duty to restrain the withdrawal of such funds. Not out of any notion of bias against one side or the other, you understand, but purely to limit the liability of our own meager bank should we err in the disposition of those funds. We would merely say to those parties, there are competing claims for this money, which we are powerless to judge. Go, settle your differences, and let a court of competent jurisdiction advise us according to the principles of international law and fair play." He spread his hands before him and straightened up, a questioning look on his face.

"I think your little democracy is off to a splendid start, Captain

Olivera. A fax from the State Department will be on your desk within the hour. Now, what can I do to repay your cooperation?"

"Stay here and make little police babies with me."

She dipped a finger in her drink and flicked it toward him. "What would be your second choice?"

Olivera sighed in resignation. "You and your useless, misbegotten boyfriend, who doesn't properly appreciate you—what was his name again?" He pulled the sheaf of indictment forms out of his satchel, flipped to the last page and ran his finger to the bottom line. "Yes. Zuckerman. Both of you must come back and spend a week as guests of my government. Perhaps you would honor us by spending some time with our police force and prosecutors and passing along any useful observations?"

Rebecca smiled. Olivera might have thought it was in appreciation, but her mind had suddenly jumped back to a week she and David had spent in Hawaii. Staring in awe at Mauna Kea, he had said, *All those ancient secrets.*

What secrets? had been Rebecca's reply.

You know; all those secrets shrouded in mist and mystery.

Gimme an example.

Well, if I knew, they wouldn't be secrets, would they?

Then how do you know there are any?

Gotta have some secrets. Been around for a million years.

So's my grandmother; only secret she's got is how something that small can spew out as much gas as that volcano.

Jeez, you're a real romantic.

If your idea of romantic is spouting meaningless literary clichés, knock yourself out.

She put a hand over her mouth to keep from laughing, and said to Olivera, "It's a deal." Why not? She wasn't currently employed anyway. Allen Wysocki had tried to pressure her into attending a news conference to announce details of how the case was cracked, and she'd replied that, if he made her attend, it would be the same conference at which she announced her resignation from the firm. Taken aback, Wysocki inquired as to whether that meant she'd stay if she didn't have to do the conference, to which Rebecca had replied: "Oh, hell no: I'm quitting. It's just a question of how loud I'm going to be about it."

"Are your men in position?" she asked.

"Yes. Don't bother to look around. You won't see them."

Rebecca stared out the open windows, a distracted look on her face.

"Are you going on the same plane as they?"

"No," she answered idly. "New York. Christmas with my sister."

"Ah." Olivera took a deep drag on his cigarette and nodded knowingly. "Family is important." He was crushing the cigarette out in the clamshell ashtray and didn't notice Rebecca shiver as she turned her face farther away from him. "Are you ready?" he asked.

She hesitated before answering. "Give me a few minutes, will you? I'll give you a signal."

He leaned back and reached for another cigarette. "As you wish. There is no hurry."

She turned back to him and put out her hand. As he clasped it, he said, "What we are doing is good, yes?"

"Trust me, Captain. You will have my government's gratitude."

She rose as casually as possible, turning her eyes but not her head as she walked in order to see what the Asian sitting alone was doing. As before, he was reading the paper, seemingly oblivious to whatever was going on around him.

Rebecca put two fingers to her head and resignedly gave his back a purely symbolic half salute. To her surprise and amusement, CIA Officer William Chang saluted back, without taking his eyes off the newspaper. It had taken him less than half a day to track Terescu to Santa Rosalia. It had taken him nearly three more days after that to find the travel reservations on Terescu's computer so Rebecca would have a way to explain how she found him without revealing the CIA's involvement.

She walked back out to the beach, content and at peace. She'd anticipated no joy in what she was about to do, and was experiencing none. It just had to be done, and that was all.

"Need a fresh drink?" asked Terescu, noticing that she had not brought her briefcase back out but not thinking anything of it.

"No. Would you mind if we walked for a few minutes?"

"Not at all." He set his drink back down and stood up, then watched Rebecca as she did the same. "Aren't you going to bring that silly tape recorder along with you?"

Rebecca froze, but Terescu said, "Don't worry about it. I couldn't give a damn. Let him know the details of what I did to him."

Allison watched them curiously as they walked down toward the water.

"There's something you should know, Rebecca."

"And that is?"

"The enhanced key system can be broken."

Rebecca stopped suddenly. Terescu took a few more steps, then turned to face her. "I don't believe you!" she said.

"It's true."

"But they said it was a mathematical impossibility!"

"In a sense, that's true. If you have only the original message and the encoded versions, it cannot be broken."

Rebecca could only stare at him, so he continued. "But remember that business about the smart-card? The one everybody is going to carry, with all their deepest secrets in code so no one can discover them?"

She nodded.

"Well, in that example you have something additional. You have the computer itself, inside the card."

"So?"

Terescu grasped his hands behind his back and stretched them upward, grimacing with the effort, then let go and swung his arms back and forth. "As it turns out, you can introduce a fault into the computer. Cause it to make mistakes as it codes the data."

"So you can screw it up. But you still can't get the data."

"Yes, you can. Because, you see, if you introduce a known flaw, and then put in new data and see how the computer puts it into code, you can begin to learn how it behaves. You begin to understand what it was doing when it was working correctly. And by comparing the flawed coding with the correct coding . . . well, the mathematics is kind of complicated, but after running about fifty or so messages through it, you have everything you need to discover the key and read all the secret data."

"You're making this up."

"As you wish. Makes no difference to me. Except you should understand that, whenever you hear that something can't be done, there's a whole bunch of people out in the world who take that as a personal insult." He turned to look up at the sun, his eyes closed. "They said wires could never be made small enough to match the smallest possible transistors without burning up. That was an insult to me, so? I proved them wrong."

"Jesus . . ." Rebecca whispered, mostly to herself, trying to fathom the implications. "So this was all for nothing?"

Terescu only shrugged in response, still sunning his face.

"God, wait'll Perrein finds out." She looked down at the sand, shaking her head.

"He knows."

She jerked her head toward him. "How do you know that?"

"His man who invented the system—Whitman Helfie?—he'd have heard about it five minutes after it was discovered. The code *breakers* live only to thrust their work in the face of the code *makers*. Perrein knows, all right, and is probably hard at work getting his PR people to spin some tripe about how, even if it's theoretically possible to break the code, as a practical matter, it's still impossible."

"And it isn't?"

"Trust me."

For some reason, she did.

"Would you explain something to me, Radovan?"

They had resumed walking again. "Sure. You got caught in the middle, no fault of your own . . . you've got something coming."

They reached the water and waded in ankle deep. Rebecca looked out at the sailboats backdropped by the late afternoon sun, then turned toward Terescu.

"You were the most gifted computer scientist in the country. Hell, you were even nominated for the Nobel." She looked directly at him. "Why give all of that up?"

The smirk was gone and his face had gone sober. "Why'd you set this whole thing up?" Rebecca pressed. "I can't believe it was the money, because the technologies you were creating might have made you a billionaire. And you weren't sure it would ever come around to point to Perrein, so revenge certainly wasn't a sure thing. What made you come unglued like that?"

He shrugged, reluctant to answer.

"Okay, let me put it a different way," Rebecca said, unwilling to drop it. "It turns out that you didn't do Perrein much damage at all. It cost him a few dollars and some tense moments, but he walked away clean. So explain to me why you seem so satisfied when, at the end of the day, nothing you did worked."

"Well, I got seven million—"

"Forget it. We both know it's not the money."

"Don't be so cavalier about seven million dollars." But Rebecca wasn't buying it, and Terescu looked away, breathing in the sea air, rubbing his shoulders and running his eyes over the sand. "Frankly, I just sort of feel better about the whole thing. And besides—"

"Yeah, I know, you've got his wife. But when the novelty and excitement wear off, and you wake up one morning, you're making coffee, and suddenly realize you're in for life, how are you going to feel about being wed to a trophy you don't really love?"

He looked at her in surprise. "But I *do* love her. I had no idea I was going to, but I truly do. To *Perrein* she was a trophy. He seduced her for her family connections, and her looks and poise and social charm." He paused and looked at Rebecca meaningfully. "Sound familiar?"

He could see the momentary pain behind her eyes, and softened immediately, seeing no point in adding to her humiliation. "Just be thankful you didn't marry him. Look, rescuing Allison made the whole escapade worthwhile for me. Think of it as an extra bonus, the prize in the Cracker Jack box. You know, it's enough for me already; I'm satisfied. You may think I didn't do Perrein much damage, but the press reported it all and the whole world now knows that he's the worst kind of scum. He may not have broken national security laws, but if he ever even gets so much as a date again, I'll be surprised. What woman would go near him?"

About 3 or so million I could think of. Rebecca chose not to voice that out loud.

"Well, anyway. I'm not one to go all sloppy and sentimental, but falling in love with Allison, having someone to care so deeply about, seemed to put the whole world into a kind of perspective I had been unaware of. Things that seemed important before, don't now. It made the pain of what happened with my wife seem to recede into meaninglessness. It was more about a blow to my ego than losing her, especially now that I can see because of what happened that she wasn't worth loving."

It was a nice speech, very romantic, very tidy. But Rebecca wasn't surprised to see anxiety and hesitancy in his face. He bit his lip, then caught himself and stopped.

Rebecca looked into his eyes with as much sincerity and *simpatico* as she could muster. "It's nice it ended up like that for you, Rado. But you didn't know that would happen when you started out. Like you said, it was the surprise in the Cracker Jack box. So tell me: why'd you do it in the first place?"

He stared at her for a moment, then turned and walked slowly along the water, Rebecca keeping step at his side.

"I had to."

"Why?"

"As near as I can figure, I had to in order to keep from going crazy."

She stopped, and he did, too. "What are you talking about?"

Whatever he had to say, it was going to be difficult, so he looked right into her eyes and dove in. "All my life, I was the reliable one, the rock. Colorless, flat. I was expected to be that way. It's how I kept the family together when my parents died and we fled to America as children. I couldn't be human, couldn't mess up occasionally. Couldn't let anybody see any weakness."

He took a step closer to her. "I had a pretty good idea that Marion was sleeping with Perrein—hell, I'm an observant scientist, what would you expect?—and I couldn't deal with the pain of it, the awful betrayal. It would have been different if she'd just left me, but this way? It was pure contempt, of who I am, of how much my feelings were worth. And Perrein, luring Tranh away from my lab, after all I'd invested in that boy, and ruining my marriage to do it . . . I started to feel my mind slip."

Rebecca looked at him quizzically. "So you went after revenge, okay . . ."

Terescu smiled bitterly. "It had nothing to do with revenge, or very little, anyway. It had to do with preserving my sanity, quite literally."

She shook her head and looked away. "You're talking in riddles."

"Rebecca, have you ever read *Hamlet*?"

Brought up short, she answered, "Sometime back in high school or college, I guess. Why?"

"What do you remember of it?"

"What has this got to do with—"

"Indulge me. What do you remember?"

Rebecca screwed up her face in concentration. "Hamlet's dead father appears to him in a dream, and tells him he was murdered by his own brother and must be avenged. Hamlet delays, trying to figure out a way to see if the accusations are real. If I remember, he seems to go mad from all the betrayals and the—"

"Mad, yes. Crazy, as you would say."

"What's that got to do with you? You never seemed over the edge, and you were just saying—"

"That's just it, you see. I don't believe Hamlet really was crazy, only pretending to be."

"Of course. It's how he was able to uncover the plot."

Terescu smiled. "Not exactly. Not the way I look at it. I think he pretended to be crazy in order to stop himself from going really insane."

This only puzzled Rebecca further, and it showed.

"It's not straightforward, Rebecca, I'll admit. But if Hamlet hadn't pretended to be seriously unbalanced, he would have lost his mind for real. Acting like a lunatic was his safety valve, the only way to release the pressure."

"But doesn't that mean he was in fact mentally ill?"

Terescu laughed and started back up the beach the way they'd come. "It's an interesting conundrum, don't you think? In fact, there are many who think the very definition of mental illness is aberrant behavior as a means of survival."

"But Hamlet was just pretending."

"And who's to say precisely what the nature of such pretending is? If I act crazy, and I can't help it because otherwise I'd go insane, am I not truly crazy?"

Rebecca's exasperation was beginning to show. "What's this got to do with you, Radovan? Is this some psycho-babble bullshit excuse for what you did?"

"Not so much an excuse as an explanation, maybe. If I hadn't done something, anything, to try to recapture my sense of self and worth, I would have disappeared inside my own soul. It wasn't revenge, it was self-preservation. They got everything, while I lost my wife, a good student, the potential income from discoveries I made that Tranh brought to Tera-Tech. . . . I had to get something back. Anything. If it was just the money, that would do it for me. Anything beyond that would be gravy."

Rebecca stopped walking again, prompting him to do the same. "It's complete bullshit, Terescu. You can dress it up and deck it out in academic finery, but it isn't any different from anybody else's motive for getting even."

"It was not revenge!" he protested vehemently. "It was more than that, it was—"

"Bullshit again! What do you think revenge is? It's inflicting a hurt back on somebody else in order to give you the last word, to make you one up on the other guy because it's too painful to let it stand the way it is. Only you can't deal with that. You had to construct some high-falutin' rationale to prove to yourself that you're not subject to the same base motivations and primal desires as ordinary people."

Terescu smiled condescendingly and shook his head. "I knew you wouldn't be able to understand."

"There's nothing to understand. Your wife cheated on you and the thought of it angered you out of all proportion to her transgression. That she fell for Perrein's slick line of crap only made it worse. Your little scheme was all you had to get back at her, back at Perrein, because you couldn't live with the shame. If you hadn't pulled this off, you . . ."

She trailed off, letting it hang in the air, and stared dumbly at Terescu.

"I what, Counselor? What were you going to say?"

Her shoulders slumped in resignation, and she turned her eyes toward the sea. "You would have gone out of your mind."

Terescu felt no need to respond.

"All this technology," she said softly, gazing at the waves that cared not a whit for any of this, or of anything at all, "and it still comes down to the human heart." She hitched herself up and looked at him once more, then continued walking. "Fine, but it doesn't excuse anything. Plenty of people feel the same way but their respect for the law keeps them in check."

They had arrived back at the lounge chairs. "Quite right. Although you mean fear of the law, don't you?"

"You two have a nice walk?" asked Allison.

Rebecca ignored her. "But it didn't work, Rado. Perrein is completely exonerated. So why do you treat it as such a victory?"

"Like I said, I was never really sure how soon, or even if, it would come back to Perrein anyway. It was enough for me to wait, knowing that the day *might* come. Besides"—he took Allison's hand in his—"I still got seven million bucks out of the deal while my bitch of a wife runs around courtrooms all day trying to wangle alimony out of me!" He turned to hug Allison and they laughed in unison.

Rebecca, to their surprise, joined in with them.

When Terescu had regained his breath from the laughing jag, he wiped away a few tears. "I must say, Counselor, you're taking this like a good sport."

"That's what I am, all right. A good sport."

Rebecca stood, nodded to someone or something behind them, then looked back at Terescu, who craned his head around to see just what was so interesting going on over at the bar. . . .

AUTHOR'S NOTES

In June of 1991, a cryptography specialist transmitted a powerful new piece of encryption software around the world via the Internet. He became the subject of a grand jury investigation initiated by the San Jose, California, office of U.S. Customs, which declared that his software was a "munition" as per 22 CFR 120.1 *et seq.* of the Code of Federal Regulations. In January of 1996, after three years of investigation and harassment, and following a worldwide outcry of protest, the U.S. Attorney's Office in the Northern District of California "declined to prosecute." No explanation was given.

On October 3, 1996, the Clinton administration announced a plan to allow for the export of encryption techniques using up to 56-bit keys, an increase from the previous maximum of 40 bits. This would be tolerated for only two years, after which exporters would have to complete their promised development of escrow recovery keys that would allow the government access to encoded data. As of the date of the announcement, it was not yet known how to provide that kind of a key.

Within weeks of the administration's conditional approval for a 56-bit key to be the strongest that was legally exportable, a graduate student at the University of California at Berkeley attempted to crack a message encoded with this technique. Using "spare" computer time on the campus network of workstations, it took him less than four hours.

On December 19 of the same year, a federal judge ruled that U.S. laws limiting the export of encryption software and devices, including the ITARs, violate the First Amendment. He stopped short of ordering implementation of his decision pending the outcome of related actions.

The smart-card flaw described by Radovan Terescu in the final chapter is real; it was discovered by a team at Bellcore in Morristown, New Jersey. Researchers at the University of Cambridge in England and Purdue University in Indiana have already demonstrated that it could be used against smart-cards now in use. Within weeks of the Bellcore announcement, scientists at the Israeli Institute of Technology (Technion) discovered a way to use the method to attack shared-key encryption systems, one of which, called DES, is the most popular system currently in use to protect electronic financial transactions around the world.

On March 6, 1997, the Computer Security Institute disclosed that fully three quarters of the 563 U.S. corporations, government agencies, financial institutions and universities it surveyed reported suffering financial losses as the result of computer security breaches. It is generally believed that only a small fraction of organizations victimized by computer crimes report such incidents owing to fear of negative publicity.

On December 2, 1996, following the collapse of a settlement two years earlier, Dow-Corning proposed a new arrangement in the breast implant case in which $1.4 billion would be withheld unless a court ruled that the implants actually made people sick. This more stringent offer partially reflected mounting scientific evidence that the implants, contrary to the testimony of expert witnesses, may not have been responsible for the wide range of ills claimed by thousands of women.

ACKNOWLEDGMENTS

Many people were helpful during the writing of this book, even though they had only the scantiest knowledge of what it was to be about.

The author is indebted to Tony Denboer, senior vice president of Laboratory Services, Integrated Circuits Engineering (ICE), Scottsdale, Arizona—co-inventor, with the author, of the ovalauricle wire and the charged vapor deposition process; Nick Ellison—whatever merit this book may possess is due in no small measure to his efforts on several fronts; The Honorable Consuelo B. Marshall—United States District Judge, Central District of California; Morgan Chu—Attorney at Law, Irell & Manella, Los Angeles, California.

Gracious assistance was also provided by Dr. Marcia Angell, executive editor, *New England Journal of Medicine*; orthopedic surgeon Kevin Michael Ehrhart, M.D., president, Medical Staff of St. John's Health Center in Santa Monica, California; Lewis Lapham, editor of *Harper's* magazine; and Joe Pittman, my editor at Dutton, who maintained his equanimity and professionalism when to do otherwise would have been legally excusable.

Thanks also to Dick Bernacchi and Brian Hennigan of Irell & Manella, Los Angeles, California; David M. Brenner; David Chamlee; Paula Daniels of Kudo & Daniels, LLP; Bob Dolen of Gaglione & Dolan; Stephen J. Hillman, United States Magistrate Judge; Theresa Lopez, assistant to Judge Marshall; Terry Pogue; and Michael Starnes, Ph.D., vice president of Process Technology Development, Cypress Semiconductor, San Jose, California.

A special debt is owed to Professor David Emmerich of the State University of New York at Stony Brook, who years ago helped me to see the scientific method not as a stuffy laboratory concept but as a way of life, even if he didn't warn me about the difficulty of keeping the faith in a world slowly going mad.

And, as always, Cherie, for reasons that grow too numerous to list.

The typeface used in this book is a version of Sabon, originally designed in the 1960s by Jan Tschichold (1902–1974) at the behest of a consortium of manufacturers of metal type. As one who began as an outspoken design revolutionary—calling for the elimination of serifs, scorning revivals of historic typefaces—Tschichold seemed an odd choice, but he met the challenge brilliantly: The typeface was to be based on the fonts of the sixteenth-century French typefounder Claude Garamond but five percent narrower; it had to be identical for three different processes, working around the quirks of each, such as linotype's inability to "kern" (allow one character into the space of another, the way the top of a lowercase *f* overhangs other letters). Aside from Sabon, named for a sixteenth-century French punchcutter to avoid problems of attribution to Garamond, Tschichold is best remembered as the designer of the Penguin paperbacks of the late 1940s.